THE EPIC OF THE MAGUIRES

It begins tragically more than a century ago, during the great potato famine in County Clare, Ireland, and ends dazzlingly in our own day on the lush California coast. It is a saga of ancient poverty and sudden wealth, agonizing grief and unexpected ecstasy, the love between man and God, and the passion between men and women.

It is a story of our time you will remember for a lifetime.

A Coward for Them All

❧ ❧ ❧

James Kavanaugh

A COWARD FOR THEM ALL
A Bantam Book / September 1979

ISBN 0-553-12794-2

Published simultaneously in the United States and Canada

Bantam Books are published by Bantam Books, Inc. Its trademark, consisting of the words "Bantam Books" and the portrayal of a bantam, is Registered in U.S. Patent and Trademark Office and in other countries. Marca Registrada. Bantam Books, Inc., 666 Fifth Avenue, New York, New York 10019.

PRINTED IN THE UNITED STATES OF AMERICA

To my father and mother,
and my Irish Catholic
rite of passage.

Contents

Acknowledgments

To Peter Gethers of Bantam Books for energetic and gifted editorial assistance.

In my research of Irish history I am particularly indebted to *The Great Hunger* by Cecil Woodham-Smith (Harper & Row, New York, 1962) and to *The Passing of The Gael* by Rev. John Whalen McGee (Wolverine Printing, Grand Rapids, 1975).

I

☙ ☙ ☙

The Maguires from Kirkwood

My blood flows from some ancient spring
In a silent country graveyard,
Nestled among green hills,
Covered with mist in the morning,
Where the fog drenches the grass
And gives ghostly shapes to the trees.

My blood flows from angry peasants
Now reduced to bitter gray ashes,
With too many children to fight the inner wars,
With too little time to tell an untold story.

These are not my scars you see;
Mine are simple enough.
These are not my wounds you tend;
Mine are normal enough.
My blood is the piled-up pain of peasants
Who laughed away their hurt in rollicking stories,
Who sang away their sadness in melancholy songs,
Who walked to church in winter to honor the God
Who had no time for cowards.

Now I will be the coward for them all . . .

1

Nestled Among Green Hills

Memories that are carried in blood and bone disappear slowly, like glacial scars or ancient riverbeds, defying logic and experience. The memory of an indignity, forgotten in survival's slime, can erupt without warning to wreak strange and excessive vengeance. A secret anxiety, buried for generations, can return to erode a child's only chance at life. And so the sins of a previous age are said to be visited on helpless and unsuspecting offspring.

Man's law has little tolerance for such bizarre testaments, murderers are locked away or executed and fierce and angry men suppressed or reformed as if their actions were forever free. War heroes and canonized saints, pioneers and explorers are praised for deeds that may be as compulsive as any suicide, yet to dissect such behavior is not to mock freedom or to disdain virtue; rather it is to marvel at a strong and independent personal will. It is to try to understand history.

Thus, the story of the five children of John Patrick Maguire and Margaret Ann Muller, newly arrived in southwestern Michigan at the start of the Depression, actually begins in Ireland. Our tale concerns particularly their three eldest sons—Jack, Jim, and Thom—whose diverse and passionate struggles to survive reflect the wounds and triumphs of an Irish Catholic history.

In County Clare, in 1835, Michael O'Brien, great-grandfather of Margaret Ann, married Anna Conway, a quiet, witty, sometimes sharp-tongued country girl from the wild isolation of County Sligo. They settled on a small farm near Ennis, the ancient Irish town that guards the river Fergus on its winding westward way to the sea. Despite the poverty of their mud hut and their potato diet, Michael and Anna were a proud couple in a land grown apathetic after two centuries of English enslavement. Michael was a powerful man with the broad shoulders, muscular forearms, and lean legs of an outstanding hurler. A skilled horseman and brave fighter, he was slow to wrath although, by the 1840s, he and his compatriots had every right to be seething with anger.

Before Cromwell and the seventeenth-century penal laws, the O'Brien family had owned vast acreage from Ennis to the pale blue cliffs of the sea. And despite the British larceny of their land, his own father, bitter tears streaming down his face, had willed the lost estates to his son in solemn testament.

He had spoken in lilting Gaelic: "All of this is yours to feed the poor and honor God. When it is ours again, you must rip down every stone of every high wall built with Irish sweat and blood."

For two centuries the O'Brien family had fought the English although they did not harbor the vigilante hatred of the Irish White Shirts and Ribbonmen who burned landlords' houses, roasted their animals in barns, drove their fat cattle over steep western cliffs into the sea, and beat their wolfhounds to death with clubs.

In the 1830s, a *shoneen*—or Irish sycophant—who betrayed his people was buried to his neck in a peat bog by laughing tormentors. "Now do we have your undivided attention . . ." Then his ears were sliced off.

Michael O'Brien's anger was more creative. He taught his children to read and write in hedge schools, transcribed family history, committed to memory the epic stories of the *seanachies,* and most of all fought to preserve the Catholic faith, which had been outlawed by the English. Even as a boy Michael brought food to priests in hiding in mountain caves and arranged the sacred mass stone in a secret glen where frightened worshipers knelt on straw. He later defended the restored clergy, who took the side of the landlords, saying, "A good Catholic must pay his rent," even when paying the rent meant starving one's children. And he loved his people, especially in the quiet months from November to April when there were no potatoes to tend or harvest. He gathered with Anna and the children around turf fires in the smoking mud cabins, sucking his pipe and sipping illicit poteen, listening to the fiddler, and laughing and exchanging stories in the traditional Irish way.

There was no land in all the world like this, with its hedges of pink roses against lush green hills and blue harebells blossoming along sparkling streams. White rocks and clean lusty air; ancient castles and circular towers; fat sheep like mounds of snow. Cattle winding their way in warm rain and brown trout and fat salmon flashing in silver water. The smell of seaweed and white potato blossoms, the pungence of manure heaps, and the bite of ancient squares of turf. Rugged solitude, lonely isolation, secret caves, and circling ducks; and the angry, churning, devouring sea of the west that became tamer and gentler in the south.

A land of laughter and contemplation, of ancient culture and mellifluous harps, of medieval poetry and silversmiths and fearless missionaries. A land of conversation and stories and faith. But now a land no longer its own.

Once the O'Briens had drunk mead from beakers of gold. Michael's children knew the stories well. Their ancestors had feasted on quail and fat oysters, tasted *usquebaugh,* the golden whiskey they had invented, and listened reverently to epics immortalized by skilled harpists. Now even the harps were gone, smashed by Cromwell's brutal psalm-singing fanatics who ravaged wheat fields and slaughtered the country's cattle, destroying huts, burning fields, transporting terrified girls as slaves to Barbados or the Americas, conscripting thousands of brave young Irishmen to fight the greedy British wars.

For generations, the Irish could not vote or attend school, have pastors or churches. However, more than any of these English crimes, it was the loss of their land that drove the Ribbonmen to murder and pillage, that filled Michael O'Brien with a silent, burning hate.

At times he spoke out, as when a sick old widow couldn't pay the tithe and an oily *shoneen* auctioned off her cracked wooden plates, her three-legged stool and hearth tongs, a few chickens, and a frayed baby's pilch. Michael forbade his neighbors to bid and the same evening replaced the widow's furniture and chickens, but when the Ribbonmen butchered the proctor's cattle and burned his barn, Michael refused to participate.

In spite of everything, no tragedy, in a land of tragedy, matched the great potato famine of 1845–49, for the potato was their primary food, frequently all they had. A million and a half people died; another million left the land they loved. Parents ate their own dead children. In one instance, a group of God-fearing women waited behind the hedges for an English nobleman who summered in east Clare, knocked him from his mount, murdered him in a swarm of rocks and ash clubs and a rusty pitchfork, and devoured his horse before the flesh was cold. Proud, angry men cursed helplessly as British barges carried off barley and oats in payment for rented land.

Michael and Anna O'Brien lined up with the rest of the people for doles of harsh Indian meal and, later, for watery soup given out from giant makeshift kitchens. In 1846, there were no potatoes at all and few if any seeds. It was Ireland's darkest day. Most of the area's clergy, restored to their positions by England in 1829 and well fed, preached forbearance and told of another happier world. Suddenly the countryside of Clare became a scabrous horror. Ragged women with naked children roamed the fields for rotten turnips and cabbage leaves, eagerly devouring nettles and grass. Mud huts sheltered parents who had died in their beds, sunken-eyed children too weak to get off the floor, and silent babies half eaten by rats. Carts and wagons departed laden with sacks and jars as neighbors headed for the ports to take any ship to Liverpool or North America. The gravel roadside was strewn with familiar bodies, and, frequently, bloated corpses rolled onto the beaches, hapless victims of fragile ships in a raging sea.

At first England made a serious effort, but the government never anticipated the magnitude and duration of the horror. Most people were not concerned. The Public Works was organized to provide specious jobs and thus preserve the "wealth of nations"—to build unneeded roads and pointless bridges. No one built houses or churches. Landlords and middlemen competed for billets that guaranteed work; prosperous farmers and relatives were admitted to the rolls; and even when the poor got jobs, the money was slow in coming. Michael's lifelong friend, the fun-loving John O'Dea, dropped dead while working on a road project: he had not eaten for seven days or been paid for a fortnight. Nor had he stopped working.

Somehow, the O'Brien family survived. Anna continued to deny herself food in order to feed the children, and she grew weaker. The last of the seed oats was boiled for porridge. Michael had to walk five miles to the soup kitchen, even when he worked on the roads, for his mare had been slaughtered, salted, and divided among the poorest. Anna had wept bitter tears over the mare. Her proudest moments had been seeing her husband riding across the hedgerows and over the rocky mounds like a nobleman. "God's ways are not our own," said Michael gently.

Crowds of unemployed gathered in Ennis, demanding work, but there was no more to be had. In December 1846, a Public Works overseer named Hennessey, accompanied by five soldiers, was shot on a country lane at point-blank range with a blunderbuss. When the assailant explained that he had no intention of harming anyone but Hennessey, who had denied work to the poor, the five soldiers permitted him to walk away.

Although Hennessey did not die, the British retaliation was outrageous. The entire Public Works in Clare were shut down. There were no jobs at all until Hennessey's assailant was found, and England increased the troop buildup in the area. It was early in December of 1846, and a rare snowfall ushered in the harshest winter in memory. The temperate west wind was silent, and bitter gusts roared from Russia across the Irish Sea and the English Channel to build giant snowdrifts. For three weeks twenty-five thousand people were denied work, but they would not reveal Hennessey's assailant. Children vainly screamed for food; mothers in rags and bare feet sifted through the deep snow searching for weeds to feed them. Corpses were frozen in the fields, the population too weak to bury them, and still Clare refused to give in. Finally a British official reported to his superior: "Although I am a man not easily moved, I confess myself unmanned by the intensity and extent of the suffering. . . . When may we expect to resume the works?"

Clare Abbey reopened on December 28 and Hennessey's assailant was never recorded. But the Cusack family had died. And the Magraths. The O'Dea children and their mother were frozen outside their hut. So were Ada Lynch and Patrick Creagh. Genevieve MacBrodin had died in her bed holding two bloated babies. Michael O'Brien's oldest child, Julia, had also died, and Anna's leaden eyes somehow blamed her husband for their daughter's death.

In 1847, the British Parliament became concerned that the Irish had grown too dependent on the doles and the Public Works. The sacred principles of laissez-faire must perdure. England demanded money from the landlords, who squeezed the middlemen, who in turn pressured the tenants, creating a golden chain that would choke Ireland to death.

Hardly had the decision been made when the fever hit. The Irish called it the famine fever because it always accompanied the famine. Or black fever because of the discoloration of the victims' skin. Actually it was typhoid, and it raced across the land without mercy. The O'Briens' favorite clergyman, a crusader for the poor, died during the second week, and so did Michael and Anna's only son, Robert, black and gangrenous. Anna did not speak for days after the shriveled corpse was thrown into a mass grave at the quarry. Or look at her husband.

England pushed on, and the Irish fought back. A high official at the Board of Public Works was pursued by a screaming mob for four miles, and even the well-fed British troops were hard pressed to keep order. Yet there could be no real rebellion among a starving people. Meanwhile, in the comfort of Dublin, life went on as usual. British balls and parties, Chinese lanterns, fowl and roasted almonds, petits fours and sweet oranges, music and dancing.

West Clare was a sprawling mortuary. The workhouses were turned into hospitals, and corpses rotted in their beds until they could be piled onto wagons.

The peasants couldn't pay their rent. But laissez-faire had decreed they must; and so had the local pastors. Rent strikes were denounced from the pulpits. Finally, the "drivers" came and dragged the starving, feverish people from their huts, destroying the feeble dwellings with crowbars and mallets. Naked children and women clung to the ground, weakened men fought back but were felled with little effort. Still they would not leave the land. They gathered in ditches, in caves, made shelters on the sides of hills or against rocks. The drivers pursued them, demanding the rent, tearing down their paltry gardens now stripped bare.

Michael and Anna fought through the spring of 1847, when even the dying rivers moved slowly, as if God had forgotten His own. Anna contracted the fever but preferred to remain at home since the workhouse hospital customarily meant death. She cared for a skinny three-year-old Mary and a five-year-old Maggie who had pale blue sunken eyes that had forgotten how to smile. Michael struggled to find food. Finally, he took home-spun sacks and walked weakly to the sea to find dillisk and raw limpets, perhaps a fish. He spent the whole day and part of another gathering food for a week, and he picked up a few strings of seaweed bladder beads to amuse his little girls. Then he made his way back across the rocky land, his worn brogues hardly protecting his feet against the sharp gravel, his famine-ravaged body dizzy from the journey. As he walked, he decided he would make it. The rent would be paid. They would move to the sea on alternate weeks, Anna would recover from the fever, and Mary would get gifts on Saint Stephen's Day. Maggie would smile again and sing about the wren and the blackbird. He was almost happy as he returned home.

Then he saw it.

Like a vision of hell, even for eyes that had seen the horror of the last two years, even for Irish eyes that had witnessed every degradation for centuries. The drivers had come to his mud hut, his three-roomed home with its generous hearth and a place for Anna to spin! As Michael passed the blossoming hawthorn hedge and drying turf and climbed the stile in a neighbor's field, he expected to see the smoke coming from the wicker chimney. But there was no chimney. Only a pile of thatch with a dark brown smoke spot where the chimney had been when the gable still stood. He began to run, ignoring the weight of the sack of food, while one of the drivers, a man he recognized, was pulling at Anna's arm and dragging her from the land. She tried to cling to a large rock by the road. The children were clutching their mother's skirts and screaming. The other driver, a younger, unfamiliar face, was still destroying Michael's house, smashing a luster jar and scattering the straw bed where Anna had conceived his children.

In a single motion Michael dropped the food and picked up a rock. Patience and endurance and God's ways now abandoned, resignation be damned! The hurler's forearms swelled, the weariness of the journey from the sea was forgotten, and with a fury of blows he smashed one man's forehead. The other man heard his friend's brief cry and ran toward Michael with a piece of splintered rafter, but the weakened Michael scarcely felt the blow on his shoulder; he felled the younger man with a crushing blow of his fist. Michael hit him twice more and then quietly choked the air from his lungs until his own thumbs were covered with blood. It had taken but a few minutes.

Anna was breathing heavily against the rocks. Michael stroked her damp hair and spoke lovingly to the sobbing little girls. When he opened the bag and offered them food, Mary took it hungrily, but a feverish Maggie refused.

During the night he tended his brood, built a rough shelter over a drainage ditch, and struggled frantically to nurse and pray them to health. In the morning Anna and the once-laughing Maggie were dead. Anna's final look had been a painful reproach. Michael wrapped Mary in his coat and dug the graves without a tear.

Later, he took little Mary to a neighbor's shack, gave them the food, and asked if they would care for her for a few days. Then he walked three miles to the stone mansion of his landlord's agent, a man named Edward Hamilton.

The house was set back from the road on a small hill, surrounded by a beech hedge, some larger chestnut trees, and a six-foot stone wall that Michael had helped build. He walked past the property, noticing the two "peelers"—British soldiers with long muskets—who stood near the forged iron gate. When he had circled past them he crouched low and worked his way through a stretch of scattered hawthorn bushes and the beech hedgerow. He slid around a small grove of oaks and approached the wall on the side opposite the soldiers. He heard them laughing. The sun had already set when he grasped the top of the wall, pulled his body up and over, then slid softly onto the flagged stones of the courtyard. He could hear sounds of loud conversation inside the mansion, and he saw the reflection of a small lantern in the carriage room. Sudden footsteps pinned him against the wall behind a large oak tree as a groom walked from the carriage house out through the thick wooden gates and headed toward the soldiers at the main entrance. The crunch of boots on gravel grew more distant, and the horses in the courtyard whinnied. He leaned against the protected corner of the house and listened cautiously. Three men were talking and drinking near the hearth fire in the main dining room. Hamilton's gravelly voice was the easiest to detect.

"I need a thousand pounds for my daughter's wedding. We'll have boiled potatoes if you bowsies don't start collecting rents."

The women had already retired to the drawing room to talk of wedding plans, and Michael could hear their soft chatter and high-pitched giggles on the floor above. He grasped his grandfather's shillelagh and moved along the edge of the house toward the kitchen. The festive conversation became louder as he let himself in the thick wooden door, slid softly across the oak plank floor, and stood next to the giant stove on the dining room side of the dark room. He waited for several minutes until he heard the lanky, big-jawed Hamilton move toward the cool box in the kitchen for a jar of water. The other two men remained by the open hearth and continued jesting boisterously. Hamilton saw Michael only for an instant in the semidarkness, and he dropped his candle.

Michael sprang forward. "Murderers must die!" he whispered hoarsely as he crushed Hamilton's skull and, with a second blow, split his nose. The others heard the commotion and came quickly to see what had happened. He killed one with a series of brutal chops and he bludgeoned the side of the other man's face. While the voices in the drawing room upstairs continued to babble, Michael rubbed his worn brogues in the dead men's blood. Neither had uttered a prayer.

Michael stole a horse, made his way out the side gate, and circled back along the road to Tipperary. There he abandoned the horse and slept for several hours in the back of a tinker's gig being pulled by a bony jennet to Dublin.

Reginald Davies, his authentic landlord, lived in a Georgian mansion on Dublin's Saint Stephen's Green with his wife and two ruddy-faced teen-aged sons. Michael watched the house carefully for two days and two nights. On the evening of the third day, he saw the wife, dressed in a fur-trimmed red velvet mantle and pale silk gown, leave the house with her sons. A coachman assisted them into a carriage while two gray horses waited at restless attention and then moved out as directed. Michael was faint with hunger and, though the evening was not quite cold, he shivered.

He rang the bell, and a servant admitted him cautiously. When he asked to see Mr. Davies, the servant hesitated, but Michael's studied diffidence and gentle charm put him at ease.

"Only for a moment." Michael said it humbly. "Mr. Davies has done me a great service."

He was ushered unceremoniously into the study, and he was not asked to sit. Michael studied the mahogany paneling and the leather-topped desk. The lambskin hearth rug seemed to glow in front of the blazing fire, and rows of books lined the side wall. Apparently Reginald Davies was a man of broad culture.

Davies entered the room briskly, almost impatiently, with a glass of claret in one hand and a long cigar in the other. He had just finished a good dinner and was anxious to relax for the evening. Yet he had a reputation for a democratic interest in the peasants, so he stood in front of the desk and motioned Michael to state his business.

A shy, peasant's smile. "I'm worried about Clare."

"Frightful! Are you all the way from Clare?" He drew back almost reflexively in fear of the fever.

"You're my landlord."

Davies still did not sense danger. "You Irish are a strong people. Somehow you'll survive." He puffed his cigar reflectively.

"My wife and three children didn't."

"I'm very sorry. I'd like to help." He reached for his purse.

Michael bowed graciously as if in gratitude, pulled his shillelagh from under his wool coat, and, remembering Anna's hollow eyes, crushed the right side of Davies's face. He dipped his weapon in Davies's blood, traced a rough Celtic cross on the leather-topped desk, then muttered a prayer for his soul. "God's holy will be done!" he said as he took the purse and let himself out past the carved mahogany door. A wolfhound growled in the side yard and the air seemed warmer. Almost balmy.

Somehow Michael and little Mary survived, living like nomadic exiles along the sea west of Ennis. They lived—on dillisk and shellfish and occasional oat cakes—until the fever was gone and potato leaves were green against the rocky slopes. Then they returned to the land near Ennis, sharecropping their conacre until Mary, seventeen by now, was wed to James Mulqueen. A simple, unimaginative man, he worked hard, bore Mary's frequent complaints without a word, and endured Michael's increasing religiosity, as well as his ancient tales of rich, powerful O'Briens.

The murders he had committed and the memory of Anna's angry eyes tormented Michael to near madness over the years, and he could find only brief forgiveness in prayer and carnal mortification. He fasted for days, walked barefoot over rough stones, frequently troubled by sordid visions and tortuous dreams. He confessed as often as the priest would permit, walked to daily mass, received communion only at Easter time, and a dozen times sought permission to be a Cistercian monk. And yet he remained, at intervals, an O'Brien.

Among Mary and James Mulqueen's children, only the second daughter, Kate, seemed exceptional, and Michael determined that she would go to America.

He filled Kate with family lore, drowned her in superstition, and even as he damned the clergy for betraying the poor, he honed her faith to near fanaticism. Only her native wit and inherited common sense provided balance. Finally he produced money saved for her passage, and the day before her departure he stood with her on a hill west of Ennis and willed to her all of the O'Brien lands. She shared his pride, honestly believing that one day she would return as a queen to take possession of her property.

He stooped and handed her a sackful of soil from the base of a small oak tree. Across the sedges and fern grass she could see the trembling waters of the Fergus and in the far west a few palm trees and the blue angular cliffs. Two fat cows were munching grass, and a Connemara pony walked along the gravel road carrying two small children. Peasants were still planting and spading potatoes, hawthorn bloomed, and wisteria climbed cautiously over an English wall.

"It's all yours. It won't be long now," he told her.

It was 1884, and Kate was fourteen. Her last night in Ireland she dreamed of a real bed with sheets and a white silk dress. She also dreamed of mice, the sign of approaching tragedy. The next day Michael splashed her with holy water to dispel the evil omen.

A week later Michael's body was found floating face-down in the Fergus River. Jimmy Hallinan had seen him the same morning, kneeling along the bank with his arms outstretched crosslike in the traditional *crosfigill* of Irish monks. There were deep mysterious gouges in the palms of his hands and a bruise on the left side of his chest, as if he had been beaten with a rock. It was reported in Ennis that he had suffered a heart seizure and slipped into the swollen stream. In a brief homily the priest said that he was an example for the whole community. Then he was buried next to Anna and Maggie.

Only Jimmy Hallinan knew that Michael had taken his own life.

2

Kirkwood

It was in 1884, three years after the great fire, when Kate O'Brien Mulqueen arrived in Chicago to live with relatives, Tim and Meg Conway and two mordant maiden aunts. Her dream of a silk dress was soon waylaid in a crowded brick flat amidst shabby furniture and the Murphy bed she shared with one snoring old aunt. Her sack of soil was hidden in a back closet, and even as the rasping women mocked her straight hair and country brogue, she dreamed of being rich. Chicago was bursting with life: wagons and puffing trains, new houses and expanding stockyards, and bicycles rushing in every direction.

Her uncle Tim, a self-effacing bookkeeper, wanted her to go to school, but the matriarchy had other plans.

"School indeed! She'll find a job! There's little enough money on a bookkeeper's income."

Their own dreams had long since died and, increasingly, they despised the men who struggled to make a living in a Yankee America.

"You should have married the butcher, Meg. At least he had enough to buy you a diamond."

"As big as my thumbnail."

"Remember when Tim blew out the gaslight thinking it was kerosine?"

Tim silently looked away, escaping into his newspaper.

"The open window saved his life."

"Too dumb to smell the gas."

"He thought it was his own from the cabbage."

It was their favorite joke. They roared and wheezed and sipped their tea and bourbon. Meg slipped out her teeth, her sister scratched the inside of a fat thigh, and Tim excused himself and went to bed.

A week later, the shy Kate, with cream complexion and auburn hair, went to work.

First as an envelope stuffer, then as a domestic for a wealthy bachelor, scrubbing his floors and serving his meals; and she turned over every cent of her pay to Meg.

"We've made sacrifices enough. If it weren't for us, you'd still be cutting turf in your bare feet!"

When Kate was seventeen, she took a job as a telegrapher with a brokerage house, and her country charm and quick mind brought rapid advancement. Even then the matriarchy attacked when she spent her meager allowance for a new dress.

"Quite a lady now with her fancy styles."

"Too bad her teeth are crooked."

Still she was not defeated, even when they mocked each Irish beau that came her way. She clung to her dreams of linen sheets, her own bedroom, and a husband who would buy her a white silk dress. She also clung to her faith, as her most important connection with Ireland, and the brick and buttresses of Saint Brigid's Church reminded her of County Clare. She was thrilled when the pastor stopped to chat with the matriarchy in the vestibule after mass.

"Ah, the saints are gathered at the door."

"Pigeons you mean, father." But Meg, overjoyed, rushed home to celebrate the attention with fresh tea and warm soda bread and even a kind word for Tim and for Kate.

There were no kind words when Kate began to date Johnny Muller, an ambitious and prosperous young baker. When he sold her fresh rye bread with caraway seeds, gently mocking her brogue, she knew his strong hands and stocky German energy would buy a dozen silk dresses, and his laughing blue eyes and soft chuckle would rescue her from the bitterness of life with her aunts.

The Mullers were skilled craftsmen and prosperous farmers who had emigrated from Darmstadt in the late 1840s. Unlike the starving and feverish Irish herded on Staten Island, they were successful and healthy and eager to pioneer. Johnny had moved to Chicago to help an uncle in a shining new bakery, and in two years had mastered his trade. Yet he was only a "stupid kraut" to the Irish matriarchy as they sat drinking and smoking endless cigarettes.

"Does he have the cyclist's crouch, or is it the heavy dough he lifts?" They teased relentlessly.

Despite their harsh salvos, Kate married him in Saint Brigid's Church in 1894, and Margaret Ann, their oldest daughter, was born at the turn of the century after Kate gave birth to a boy, Vincent, and suffered two miscarriages. Kate's youthful dreams of being rich had vanished by the time Johnny Muller bought his own bakery. It was not enough that she was the first of her Irish relatives to own an apartment, even though it was above the bakery, and that she supplied every distant cousin with fresh soda bread and warm apple turnovers. Her cream complexion had faded with the difficult pregnancies, and the pert Irish smile had grown as dry and sarcastic as the faces of Meg and the aunts. Gradually, Johnny became remote, and he usually excused himself from their Sunday-evening gossip to salvage enough sleep to rise at three and prepare his dough. Even as he settled into bed he heard the biting voices of the chorus.

"Not too loud," Meg would caution. "The baker's sleeping."

"Don't worry," said Kate. "He only wakes once a week."

They roared drunkenly as Johnny's sad eyes grew moist with the memory of a shy country girl who had made him laugh until he loved her. He had lost her to the mordant matriarchy, who ate his tarts and whined helplessly while he fixed their faucets and repaired their window sashes.

Despite Kate's bitterness, Johnny could still chuckle at a bright and energetic Margaret Ann who, like his own relatives, found deep joy in fragrant cherry blossoms or in the serenity of a summer's lingering twilight. She had her father's soft blue eyes, his shy glance, and stubby hands that could grow roses and fat tomatoes in the backyard garden.

Yet, she was an O'Brien, too, with the firm mouth, russet brown hair, and strong chin of her mother, and a smoldering bitterness that could, when suitably provoked, transform blue eyes into shiny black agates. And she had the O'Brien voice—too weak to be resonant, as if some forgotten anger had knotted the strands of the vocal cords, releasing them only at rare moments of sudden passion. Like her mother, she seldom smiled, lost in a hundred trifling anxieties, and when she finally laughed, she giggled helplessly to the point of tears and gasped for breath. She had the Irish faith of Michael O'Brien that refused God no sacrifice or secret discipline.

When Kate forced her out of school at fourteen, despite the nuns' protests that she was a brilliant student, she obediently rose before dawn with her father without a murmur. She fell to her knees to recite the Morning Offering "of every word and deed" to God; she helped Johnny with the bread and rolls, punching down the stiff dough, cutting the assorted shapes, sprinkling the streusel and cinnamon, washing the pans, and cleaning the glass showcases; then she took off his white baker's apron and rode the streetcar to work ten hours as a stenographer at Larkin's Jewelers. At her lunch hour she would sneak to Saint Peter's Church, often in a raw Chicago wind, to say her rosary and beg God to let her enter the convent. It had been her childhood dream since she left the Ursuline Academy.

The coifed nuns rustling crisply from prayers to class seemed gentle and joyful in comparison with Kate and the coterie of cynical aunts and rasping Irish neighbor women who gathered after mass or novenas to smoke or drink away their Sundays. Margaret Ann prayed she would one day escape them in the service of her God, but when she fearfully approached Kate about the convent after a Sunday mass, her dream was rudely dismissed. If Kate could not have her silk dresses, Margaret Ann would never be a nun.

"But mother, maybe God is calling!" Margaret remembered the dark shadow on the Sorrowful Mother's face at a novena service—the very same day she had smiled at a handsome dark-haired boy in the bakery.

"I've denied myself long enough. Leave the convent to the rich ones."

So Margaret Ann went to work, a tiny figure lost in the roar of the Loop; she turned over her pay envelope to Kate for a small allowance, and she endured the complaints of her mother and the matriarchy if she bought a new dress or saw a Mary Pickford movie.

"Quite a lady now. Too bad she's got such a pug nose."

Yet Margaret never complained, even when her work extended beyond a tedious day at Larkin's Jewelers. Since Kate was an impossible cook in the Irish tradition, Margaret helped her father with the thick stews and soups and lean pork roasts. Her older brother, Vinnie, Kate's favorite even though he had flunked out of school and was working as a carpenter, was exempted from any of the household chores.

"It's not work for a boy."

It did not bother Kate that Johnny cooked most of the meals—until Margaret was old enough to do it all herself.

For eight years Margaret worked without protest despite the shattered dreams of a life that seemed over before it began, despite the bitter matriarchy that mocked every accomplishment and made fun of each of her few friends. Even a vacation she took at Lake Winnebago would never have happened if her employer, Morris Larkin, had not given her extra money without Kate's knowledge.

It was on this first vacation in Wisconsin, in the summer of 1924, that she met John Patrick Maguire.

She was almost twenty-three. A sudden rainstorm had driven assorted picnickers into a boathouse, and Margaret looked away too late from the bold stare and broad smile of the handsome Irishman. He strode to her side, hip flask in hand, and a picnic and a dance later she forgot about the convent for the first time in her life. Before she returned to her job at Larkin's Jewelers he had stood with her on the shore of the lake and kissed her firm mouth until she softened and trembled and shyly asked him to stop. He knew from the gentleness of her request that she already loved him. He did not know it was the first time she had ever been kissed.

Four weeks later they were engaged. Johnny liked him; Kate, who had recently suffered a stroke, thought he had a lazy country look, but she admired the two-carat diamond he bought for Margaret after selling his beloved Metz two-seater. His own mother, Ellen, knew he was serious when he began attending mass.

Although his mother was a devout Catholic, and her

people, the O'Dwyers from Tipperary, had risked their lives to steal food from the English to feed the starving poor, John Patrick had little of her religious fervor. But he had her beguiling blue eyes and the smoldering blood that remembered the bitter crossing of the sea in 1847 when a third of the four hundred passengers died of typhoid. Only an impossible religious faith had brought the O'Dwyers to Chicago after they had shoveled New York's garbage to earn their fare. John Patrick was Ellen's second and final child, and she feared he was his father's son.

The Maguires were from Fermanagh in the north of Ireland, and they were active Ribbonmen during the 1830s, butchering landlords' cattle and burning their homes, until a brawling forebear escaped to Batavia, New York. They were hard-drinking, loud-laughing bricklayers and charming ladies' men. John Patrick's father, Daniel Maguire, was no exception. He had the Maguires' great thirst and bragged that he had converted more Yankee girls in the back of his lumber wagon than any missionary. The summer that two of his "converts" got pregnant, he was sent to Chicago to live with cousins, and there he married Ellen O'Dwyer, who managed to keep him sober long enough to survive as a mason and to perform occasional free services for the Church. She did not manage to keep him from the Knights of Columbus or Grady's Tavern. Neither could she really manage his son, John Patrick, nor dare to dream that the boy would marry a devout Catholic girl.

John Patrick had avoided Irish girls with caustic tongues and virginal morals. Sex had been taught to him by cheap whores at the Great Lakes during his stint in the navy at the end of World War I. After the war, when a good job at the Illinois Audit Bureau made him prosperous enough to buy his Metz, assorted working girls found it hard to resist his Celtic charm and his powerful lust for life. But Margaret Ann upset his bachelor pleasures. Hers was a beauty he had not seen in his thirty years of freedom: fragile and athletic all at once, she still possessed a country shyness and a lively Irish mind with none of the biting defenses he had anticipated.

They were married in Resurrection Church. At the

reception, Daniel Maguire did a rousing drunken jig, much to Ellen's embarrassment, while Kate sipped bourbon, smiling in a rocker her new son-in-law had graciously provided. Margaret was serenely radiant in Kate's own wedding dress, and John Patrick smiled his proud smile in a dark suit. Kate said his cuffs were too short; Ellen overheard and was deeply offended. The families would not be close, but Johnny Muller matched Daniel Maguire beer for whiskey until they both fell asleep.

Margaret Ann was too frightened to sleep on their nuptial night, and John Patrick made no sudden moves to disturb his timid bride in her long flannel nightgown. She lay next to him blushing furiously and trembled like a sparrow when he put his arm around her and drew her close. His fingers, too slender and gentle for his large frame, played with her reddish-brown hair and stroked her child's face. He complained of being a little warm and removed his black silk pajama top. She shuddered at the touch of his bare shoulders. Cautiously he brought her small fingers to touch the curled red hair on his thick Irish chest. Again she trembled helplessly and sighed softly. She looked for the crucifix on the wall, then remembered the luxurious suite they were in at Chicago's Edgewater Beach Hotel and worried that he had spent too much money. She glanced at her rosary on the night table and saw a shadow on the red brocade drapes. Someone laughed in an outside corridor, and then she heard John Patrick breathing heavily. She felt his fingers move under her gown, and her pale legs froze at his touch.

His hands explored gently and moved up her legs as she felt a strange new excitement that had to be sinful. He sensed her fear and reassured her of his love. Over and over he called her his darling, and she prayed fervently that it was not wrong to enjoy him. She could not stop shaking. When finally his fingers touched her moistening hair and she felt his strong legs hard against her, she would have cried out had he not kissed her more passionately than before. There was no going back.

She heard him call her name as he caressed her small round breasts for the first time, and she bleated like a tiny helpless animal. He had never known such arousal and it was almost impossible not to hurry. His groin ached as he slipped off his pajama pants and leaned over her, the huge frame almost comically trying to be gentle. His swollen penis frightened her. She dared not look, and she prayed fervently, afraid he would hear her. She felt the pain and offered it to Mary beneath the cross. Then she lay on the ground with Jesus in Gethsemane, begging forgiveness, hoping she would have a child to justify this new pleasure she felt. The brief spasms of agony somehow calmed her.

She reached for her rosary and tried to pray away the shadow that still clung to the red drapes. Then she finished her beads and snuggled close to the snoring man who would fearlessly protect her for the rest of her life. She recalled the morning's vows to love, honor, and obey her husband. It would never be a problem, even when he wanted sex. She only hoped God would forgive her, and she renewed the more important vows made at her own baptism—"to renounce Satan and all his works and pomps."

John Patrick, Jr., called Jack, was born in Chicago in 1926 and Grandma Kate was happier than anyone had seen her in years. Three days before his delivery she had dreamed of mice running over an empty cake pan, but despite the fearful omen, Jack's broad shoulders and almost orange hair on a large Irish head reassured her. John Patrick bragged of a triple-threat quarterback at Notre Dame, and Margaret thanked God and Saint Anthony, but she was further distressed the night before Jack's baptism when she herself dreamed of an old man in a long coat standing on a highway in the moonlight. However, she dismissed the disturbing portent when the priest washed Jack's soul clean of sin. John Patrick Maguire could not stop smiling.

Margaret recalled the awesome signs a few months later when a bloated Kate dropped dead of a second stroke.

Over the protests of the Irish matriarchy, Johnny Muller draped his wife in a white silk dress and placed in her hands, along with her rosary, the sack of soil Michael O'Brien had given her the day before she sailed from Ireland. More than forty years had passed since Michael had made his promise: "The land is all yours. It won't be long now."

John Patrick received notice of a promotion to manage a new office of the Audit Bureau in Kirkwood, Michigan. His superiors agreed that marriage and a young son had settled the wild, gifted Irishman into a new maturity. It was a rare compliment to a Maguire, and Daniel, his father, stayed drunk for three days in celebration.

Margaret was delighted to leave Chicago. A smiling John Patrick bought drinks at a South Side speakeasy and promised to return only when he could pay cash for all of Marshall Fields. They left late in 1927 with their Tin Lizzie and a stocky year-old Jack, who had his father's red hair and Margaret's light blue eyes.

Kirkwood, a prosperous town of forty thousand in southwestern Michigan, was a strange, angry setting for Margaret Ann, daughter of Kate and great-grandchild of Michael O'Brien. Neither she nor John Patrick had ever known the sordid religious bigotry of a small midwestern town.

Kirkwood was a Dutch Protestant stronghold, and the young Maguires arrived there when Alfred E. Smith, "the Happy Warrior," was running for president, the first Catholic ever to do so. Assuredly, Kirkwood was no extension of Chicago's South Side. There were no First Ward politics or illegal hooch at the Knights of Columbus, no boisterous White Sox games and Irish camaraderie that battled niggers and insulted Polacks. Almost overnight, the Maguires were the "niggers," and the pride of John Patrick's promotion was turned to bitterness. Three times they were unceremoniously refused access to Dutch neighborhoods. They finally rented a small frame house, purchased simple oak furniture, and unloaded Jack's crib. Margaret sprinkled the rooms with holy water as John Patrick struggled with boxes. They were crushed to see anti-Catholic cartoons splashed in the *Kirkwood Gazette*, depicting Al Smith welcoming an owl-eyed, salami-nosed pope to the White House. Crosses were burned in front of Saint Raphael's gabled brick rectory, and crude jokes about lusty nuns conceiving priests' fat babies in drunken orgies—Smith favored the repeal of Prohibition—drew lunchtime laughs in the Victory Cafe and in John Patrick's office. It was a rude awakening for a proud Irishman and his shy wife who had known only the security of a giant city where twenty percent of its three million inhabitants were Irish Catholic.

John Patrick had come to Kirkwood with the dreams of a young businessman on the way up, and his dreams were magnified when he surveyed the dozen young women who seemed delighted by the handsome charm of their new manager. Although the fierce bigotry against Catholics outraged him, he tried to ignore the snide attacks, only snarling back when the remarks were too crude to tolerate.

A white-shoed salesman in the Victory Cafe joked about the Blessed Mother's virginity, unaware of the red-faced Irishman in a spotless gray suit who studied a menu at the same counter.

There were two or three loud laughs until John Patrick threw down his menu, knocked over a water glass, and stood up with fists clenched, his face as red as his tousled curly hair. The silence was sudden and total, and no one moved to pick up the shattered glass.

"You've got a filthy mouth!" he bellowed fiercely. "Another word and I'll break your face!"

There was not a sound, nor were there any challenges. He lowered his fists, still lusting to fight, then picked his own smoldering cigarette out of the ashtray and ground it into the man's roast beef sandwich. Still no one made a move; and even the counterman remained frozen, a plate of toast in his hand, until the hulking John Patrick sat down and again surveyed the menu.

Although a few hundred Irish had settled in Kirkwood almost a century before, the Dutch had come in greater numbers with much more money and the finer skills of successful artisans and experienced farmers. They also possessed a historic hatred of Catholics that was born of Europe's religious wars and the fury of the bloody Spanish Inquisitions. These same Dutch Reformed had emigrated to Kirkwood, bought its rich black land, built it up to its present prosperity, and even named it in honor of God as a "church in the woods."

It was no wooded church to John Patrick Maguire, but a concrete coliseum where he was daily fed to mocking lions who soon learned to circle him at a safe distance. The Dutch believed Tammany Hall to be a papal plot, and they despised Franklin Roosevelt as a turncoat for supporting Smith against Herbert Hoover.

But even when Hoover won the 1928 election and the Dutch of Kirkwood rejoiced, John Patrick knew that his own Irish victory was only a matter of time. He knew it especially when he watched his fearless infant son gleefully raise his fat fists to battle his own father. John Patrick lovingly buried Jack in awkward arms and told the boy's favorite story of a giant, grizzly bear. Then told it again until he kissed his beautiful son good night.

Margaret was apparently content to bathe her infant with hymns to Mary and the baby Jesus, and she nursed him for over a year until he bit her breast fiercely a third time. She knew little of angry politics, yet she shared John Patrick's bitter pain, especially when neighbors shunned her or suddenly talked in Dutch and laughed together in the grocery store at her pregnant belly when Jack was not yet a year and a half old. Remarkably, she reported none of this humiliation to her husband, sharing it only with God in whispered aspirations all day long and during the daily six o'clock mass she attended at Saint Raphael's. She begged heaven's forgiveness for not entering the convent, not convinced that an ambitious, handsome husband and a healthy son had released her from God's wrath.

Early in 1928, a great shame came to Saint Raphael's parish in Kirkwood. The soft-spoken and kindly Irish pastor, an uncomplicated farmer from rural Sligo, was shot to death at the dinner table by a crazed monk from Europe. The *Chicago Tribune* reported it as an unspeakable tragedy, but the *Kirkwood Gazette* kept the scandal alive with a disgusting prurience that delighted the Calvinist bigots.

Was it a love triangle with a nun? An illegitimate baby in the rectory basement? A Vatican assassination? All the historic crimes of Rome and its infamous popes were recalled, and wild-eyed ex-priests appeared in Dutch Reformed pulpits to recount in sordid detail the horrors of Roman Catholicism.

The Irish community was numb and embarrassed, and the Saint Raphael parish became divided: hostile cliques wanted vengeance, and passive groups prayed to ignore the new persecution. School attendance dropped, Catholics were denied jobs and publicly ridiculed, students left the seminary. Margaret cried for an entire week and she was terrified to go to the grocery store. John Patrick read the *Kirkwood Gazette* to shreds and swore bitterly at each new accusation. When his regional supervisor at the Audit Bureau, J. R. Harris, a tight-jawed WASP with thin lips and rimless glasses, hinted at a drunken orgy, John Patrick felt the blood rush to his head and had to leave Harris's office lest he break his jaw.

The scandal could have destroyed Saint Raphael's parish had not the bishop of Detroit, the archdiocesan seat for Kirkwood, appointed James Michael Doyle as pastor six weeks after the tragedy. A stocky Irish American with a booming voice and dark brown eyes glaring under bushy black hair, Doyle whipped the parish back into shape within two months. The parish council was fired, the ushers disbanded, the ladies guild terminated; James Michael Doyle was to be consulted about everything from altar boys to the menu at the Saint Patrick's Day banquet. Pockets of resistance were confronted with excommunication and wiped out; the editor of the local paper was threatened with legal action as well as receiving anonymous phone calls in a thick Irish brogue predicting a long stay in the hospital. James Doyle himself invaded a luncheon meeting of Dutch Reformed ministers and promised an all-out war if "God's more peaceful ways are not observed." His muscular body rippled defiance and commanded such respect that he was finally applauded when he quoted Jeremiah.

Almost overnight, the parish had its pride back. The high school football team got new emerald green uniforms and were informed that any missed blocks or "gutless" tackles would be dealt with in the rectory office. Sports, always significant, now became a religious crusade. James Michael Doyle conducted pep rallies personally. During the half time of a game Saint Raphael's was losing to Bay Harbor Central 6–0, he slapped a star halfback, knocked two powerful tackles over a locker room bench, and watched his lads win 27–6. The team was undefeated the very first year, and schools twice the size were not only defeated but humiliated. John Patrick roared his approval from the sidelines with Jack on his lap. Even Margaret, on the brim of delivery, cheered her support. The *Kirkwood Gazette* called the team the Fighting Irish, after Notre Dame, and gave the games more space than was given to a mediocre Kirkwood Central, three times the size. When the Fighting Irish humbled Central 42–7 and four Dutchmen were carried from the field, a special mass of thanksgiving was offered by James Doyle. John Patrick smiled proudly at J. R. Harris and thereafter ignored his pompous initials, calling him "Jimmy boy" in front of the office staff.

Nor did it end with the football team. Ushers began dressing in tuxedos. A new statue of Saint Patrick with bishop's miter and green robes was placed in a special grotto, and evergreens were planted around the church. School attendance shot up. James Doyle preached eloquently that his parishioners were engaged in a holy war to save civilization, just as the Irish monks had done ten centuries before. The pastor soon became a legendary hero—even among the men.

Irish men traditionally were not fond of priests. Too many men remembered the stories of the famine when the priests had upheld England's right to tax the peasants to death. In the eighteenth century, priests had been persecuted heroes who defied English law to say their masses in caves and secret glens, protected by thick Irish shoulders bearing clubs, but when the clergy were reprieved in 1829 and permitted to conduct their services, a fearful new conservatism scarred their ranks. Most, as in Clare, supported landlords' rights from the very pulpits, and the brooding Irishmen would never forget. Even as they tipped their hats, begged a blessing, or permitted their own sons to enter the seminary, they cursed under their breath.

The women were more tolerant, almost obsequious, not because they truly loved the clergy, but because they recognized them as the only real defense against the total chauvinism of their oppressed and angry husbands. The women knew instinctively that the Holy Mother Church was a matriarchy as fierce and domineering as their own real control of the family. They well understood the clerical arrogance, and they also knew that the priests ate and drank better than most parishioners. They saw the expensive clothes and vestments, the lavish episcopal dinners, the extravagant rectories and cars, the vanity and selfishness. But they also saw the true shepherd who would give his life for the flock, who cared about the poor and gave his every waking hour to console the sick and lonely. They knew his devotion came from God himself, and they kissed his hand or the hem of his cassock in genuine love. They felt his tenderness and understanding in the confessional, his compassion at times of tragedy and death. He was the same priest who had defied the landlords, blessed the people's defiance, and died with his flock in the Great Famine of 1845. There probably was no finer or nobler love among the Irish than that lavished on such a priest.

James Michael Doyle did not know that kind of love. His was the respect given to a leader in war. Even the men knew they could not survive without him, and his powerful word became law. No one was to date a non-Catholic; every child was to attend a parochial school; and a boy who didn't go out for football needed a doctor's exemption or congenital blindness. Anyone who hadn't voted for Al Smith was in serious danger of excommunication.

There were twelve babies christened James Michael that very first year, and to have a vocation to the priesthood, always an honor, was suddenly a mark of divine preeminence. Even to be appointed an usher was an invitation into a sacred oligarchy controlled personally by James Doyle. In such an environment, John Patrick became an exemplary Catholic and a bellowing threat to every careless referee who officiated at a Saint Raphael game. He was James Doyle's kind of man, and at the baptism of his second son, James Michael Maguire, John Patrick was asked to be an usher. Of course he accepted, and he doubled his weekly donations. Only Margaret knew that he had never actively practiced his faith before he met her.

James Michael Maguire was born at the end of 1928 at the edge of the Depression, and he was the opposite of Jack. A small baby with no Maguire traits, he had light brown hair and serious, almost frightened eyes that gradually became hazel. He seemed docile and unprotesting from birth. He seldom cried. A week before his delivery, Margaret felt a shadow fall across her face, and a strange black bird stared at her from a cherry tree close to the house. Nor did it move when she emptied the garbage. She was afraid to mention it to John Patrick, and she rejoiced when the delivery was an easy one and the new baby seemed reasonably healthy. But James Michael Maguire was an anomaly, and even a two-year-old Jack, freckled and boisterous, twice slapped him in his crib and had to be restrained from tormenting Jim when he first began to crawl.

John Patrick made light of it. "It's the Maguire blood. Jimmy will learn to defend himself."

Actually John Patrick was thrilled with both sons, wrestling for hours with the feisty, oversized Jack and patiently teaching a tentative Jimmy to fight back. Jack was the powerful exemplar of what it meant to be a Maguire, and James Michael was expected to measure up. There were subtle signs even in infancy that he would withdraw from the impossible contest, but John Patrick was too happy to notice. Margaret, too, was never happier, fussing endlessly over the children and preparing her husband's favorite roasts with mashed potatoes and thick, rich gravy the way Johnny Muller had instructed her. Baking bread and Parker House rolls and apple slices with white frosting, and trying as best she could to satisfy her husband's strong sexual appetite although she didn't understand it and was embarrassed when he fondled her enlarged breasts while she was nursing Jimmy.

Curiously, in the early years, when success at work absorbed him and the joy of children was a novelty, her very shyness about sex excited him. He was satisfied to be the aggressor, charming her little girl's fears, and well pleased to feel some minimal compliance. She gazed at the bleeding crucifix on the wall or the serenely cold china madonna on the dresser, but she never refused him, for she knew that his salvation depended on her service and prayers, and that her own sanctity, like the Blessed Virgin's, was measured by the performance of God's will. God's will was of far greater concern than even John Patrick.

Thus she left her husband's bed every morning at five to attend the early mass with the nuns; her closest friend, "old maid" Mary O'Meara; a scattered two dozen other devout women; and two or three effeminate men she did not admire. At first John Patrick had protested her daily departure, not admitting his need to feel her warmth next to him, but insisting protectively that she required more sleep.

"I can sleep for all eternity," she said softly.

She would have honored any other request, but God came first, and there was no way on heaven or earth to dissuade her. At times he held her tightly and feigned heavy sleep, but she fought her way free. Occasionally he pretended sickness, and then she would attend to his needs quickly and go off to mass in the new Oldsmobile he had taught her to drive. Finally, he gave up and accepted her going to mass as he did his own job.

She was transformed when she entered the old brick church. With its vaulted arches and huge plaster pillars, the smell of incense and the creaking of oiled wooden floors, it gave her a few moments of peace, without interruptions or babies to attend or coffee to make. Her face became like that of a child. Her lips, normally thin and drawn tight to hide an overbite that had always embarrassed her, relaxed with the fullness of a passion John Patrick would never know. The blue eyes glowed and stared rapturously at the giant crucifix suspended behind the altar. She readied her missal like a teacher preparing for class, read the special prayers on holy cards gathered since childhood in Chicago. Then came the organ and the ancient Gregorian melodies of the Kyrie and the Gloria and the triumphant preface chant that had startled Mozart, the solemn Pater Noster that brought her close to tears. There was no greater joy. She made her way to communion, calling out in her heart *Domine, non sum dignus* and thrilling to the soft strum of the organ's *Adoro Te.*

With tangible redemption, the morning became suddenly brighter, and Margaret chatted briefly with the round-faced Mary O'Meara, then sang her favorite hymns on the drive home. She drove into the garage carefully, put her missal away, took off her brown cloth coat, and was once again a wife and mother, ready to do anything that did not interfere with her primary allegiance to God.

"Will you have a nice fried egg?" she always asked, and he always said no.

"Just a piece of toast and some coffee." He didn't look up from the *Chicago Tribune.*

She always made two eggs and he always left one.

"It's a cold morning. I could make a little oatmeal. It'll stick to your ribs."

He didn't answer. A second cup of coffee and a second Camel cigarette smoked to the ash, and he was ready to face the day. He lifted Jack over his shoulders a few times, stroked Jim's hair, and made his way to the Michigan Audit Bureau after a perfunctory good-bye to Margaret and a kiss on the cheek. Still silently wounded because she had left his bed.

The office transformed him as the church did her. His booming good-morning and always new Irish palaver about "so much beauty in a single room" or "how lucky can a man get" reduced the female office staff to giggles. Even his firmness, when reports were late or quarterly rating charts incorrect, made him attractive. He had an incredible mind for figures, could multiply or divide complicated problems in his head, and stored endless statistics of insurance rates and projected costs almost effortlessly.

His private secretary, Doris, was secretly in love with him and found his dramatic dictations of letters an eloquent delight. Although forced out of school in seventh grade to help support his family, John Patrick had an impressive vocabulary and perfect grammar. He was exceptionally clean, had manicures with his twice-monthly haircut, and dressed handsomely. Always a fresh white shirt and appropriate tie, shoes shined, rusty hair flattened as much as the stubborn curls would allow. He held his head proudly, tilted almost arrogantly, and usually opened his mouth when he smiled. He liked his own looks, especially the proud, prominent nose that gave immense character to his face and justified a touch of swagger when he walked.

He was often a father figure to many of the young women in the office. He showed concern about a parent's illness, always remembered birthdays with small gifts, and teased about boyfriends or new marriages. He talked with his hand on a girl's arm or shoulder, patted rumps or stroked hair, and hugged anyone for the smallest reason.

When he left the office to visit insurance offices or banks, he spoke to everyone he knew, smiled at women, and stopped to talk at frequent intervals. Even the WASPs and bigoted Dutch found it hard to resist his charm. Waitresses received his special compliments and suggestive pats, cooks were applauded, business associates were kidded boisterously, and names were always remembered. No one would ever have believed that he was a shy, sensitive man beneath the bravado.

If, on rare occasions, an employee or acquaintance resisted his gentle advances, he turned away and never approached them again, as bruised by rejection as he was playful and charming. He was singularly hurt when his lack of education was discovered. A literary reference he did not understand, a play or a musical composition he knew nothing about, an intellectual reference to religion that eluded him, and John Patrick retreated. Although he devoured the newspaper every day, he had no knowledge of books or authors. His favorite song was the Notre Dame fight song, which he always requested, even from strolling violinists at fine restaurants. He knew nothing of art or architecture, music, philosophy, or even theology. When J. R. Harris questioned the divinity of Christ at lunch one day and announced that Jesus had brothers and sisters—"even the Gospels admit it"—John Patrick was outraged almost to tears.

He hated J. R. Harris more than anyone in the world. A graduate of the "Godless" University of Michigan (as Father Doyle had called it), a snob who made much of his elegant tastes in food and his knowledge of literature and music, Harris looked upon John Patrick as a bright peasant who covered his crude background with expensive clothes. Yet he was jealous of the Irishman's looks and charm and terrified of his temper. He sent in good reports about his manager because he knew that John Patrick kept the office together. He also knew that John Patrick would have killed him with his bare hands if he had threatened his job. J. R. Harris was forced to content himself with biting subtleties that angered John Patrick without really putting him down, using pompous words, making historical comparisons John Patrick had barely heard of. It was an unusual day when John Patrick did not want to slap the haughty face or choke away the priggish aristocratic inflection.

John Patrick kept himself going with the persistent dream of having his own business. His two boys brought him endless joy, and he took them to parish football games and proudly displayed them at mass and occasionally at his office. Only when the boys were in bed did he give in to the pain of his daily humiliations, surrendering to the black moods that were to be a lifelong curse. Brooding over Margaret's increasing devotion to the Church and her absorption in the children, hating the prominent citizens of Kirkwood who ignored him on the streets, seething over the indignities of working for J. R. Harris. And longing for the day when his boys would avenge his wounds against all of Kirkwood.

His own religion was more identity than faith. His father had kept them in poverty most of their lives, living in cheap boardinghouses and moving frequently when they couldn't pay the rent. John Patrick had known nothing but poverty and shame until he joined the navy and then took the job at the Illinois Audit Bureau. His marriage to Margaret and the move to Kirkwood had finally given him the focus he needed. He would be an incredible success; his children would be recognized and applauded; he would finally get even, and his Catholicism was only a convenient vehicle to make it all possible. No matter the personal cost.

Despite his booming voice and his charm, despite his fine mind and brave energy to succeed, John Patrick was, finally, a rawboned rural kind of man who should have been chopping peat in country bogs or laughing like a bellows in an unthreatening Irish village pub. His hands told a separate story: they were the hands of a scholar or poet, too small and sensitive for the rangy body that was always too awkward to be really athletic. His eyes gave credence to the hands, gentle and sadly blue, deep set and far away when they were not trying to charm.

The city somehow wearied him, as if he had never lost his Irish longing for the land. "Maybe one of these days when the boys get older, we'll leave the city and get some acres up north."

"I'd like that, John, but I'm grateful to God for what we have."

The religious remark angered him, but he recovered. "A real place with our own pond and some big oak trees where the crows could hide out." His face was soft and beautiful, but she did not know how to tell him that.

He put his arm around her and she blushed like a schoolgirl. She glanced at Jack who was watching them. "Not now, John—"

He ignored her. "We could raise a few sheep or maybe a cow or two. Hell, we could build our own place!" He knew nothing of animals or of building; he could not even repair a toaster.

"I'm happy here, John, but you work so hard—"

"Not like you'd be there," he said wistfully. "The land clears your head. We'll have it all when I get my own business."

Then he was suddenly sad, and he drifted away, and Margaret left him to his dreams. And pain.

A month later he bought a house despite the alarmist talk of troubled economic conditions and an end to prosperity. He surprised Margaret one evening after work by inviting her and the children out for a ride.

"Dinner's in the oven—"

"It'll keep," he said. "I feel like taking a ride on such an evening."

She feared he had been drinking with his new friend, Mike McNulty, a short, stocky ex-middleweight he had met at a football game.

They drove to a Dutch neighborhood in the south end of Kirkwood, hardly two blocks from where J. R. Harris lived, at the fringe of Protestant affluence.

"Beautiful houses here," he mused aloud.

"That's not important," she said. "We have everything we need." She didn't admit that she wanted a refrigerator to replace the dripping old icebox that was rotting the linoleum.

He stopped the car in front of a corner house that had brick wainscoting and an enclosed front porch. There was a front and side yard and a separate garage. A neat hedge surrounded the entire property and a peach and a cherry tree bloomed gracefully in separate yards. Small evergreens flanked the front porch and contrasted elegantly with the fresh white paint. It was two stories with an attic and basement and half again as big as the house they were renting.

"That's a fine house," he said. "Let's take a look."

"My God in heaven, John. You might get shot just wandering around." Now she was certain he had been drinking.

He picked up Jack and walked to the front entrance. Margaret did not move from the car, and little Jim was crying. She prayed aloud when John Patrick walked up on the porch.

He shouted to her. "It's empty, Margaret, let's take a look." He disappeared inside with Jack.

Still she did not understand, and she feared for his welfare. She slid out of the car with the baby and walked nervously up the front steps, reassuring herself that the children afforded protection. Her heart almost stopped when she saw the open door and realized he had stepped inside.

"For God's sake, John," she hissed. "What on earth has happened to you?"

Then he came to the front door with the beaming smile that had won her love at Lake Winnebago.

"How do you like it? It's empty. I think I'll buy it."

"Don't talk foolish, John, we never could afford it." She walked inside cautiously, as if she were robbing a bank.

"Dear God, it's beautiful," she whispered.

There were refinished hardwood floors and a living room fireplace with an ivory painted mantel. A formal dining room with double windows and wide window seats, a bright kitchen, and three bedrooms upstairs. The basement was large, though unfinished, with a fruit cellar and a coal bin.

Margaret was speechless, giggling like a little girl now, delighted by the daring escapade that reminded her of their courtship, still not realizing that the house was hers.

When he used the toilet upstairs she was frantic. He put his arms around her and smiled that proud smile again, and then she burst into tears of joy.

"O John, John, but so expensive!"

"It's too late now," he said. "We'll move in next week. And I've ordered a refrigerator."

There was no brooding that night as he ate seconds of pot roast and peas, gravy and apple pie. After a third cup of coffee and another cigarette, he helped her bathe the children and they talked till almost midnight about the business he would have, all his own, and the place in the country besides.

For once she only listened, delighted that they had room for all the children God might send and worrying if her lust for a refrigerator had been sinful.

"I only wish my mother had lived to see it." It was one of the rare times she made such a request.

Then they went to bed and he made love to her. With special gentleness and as much pleasure as she had ever allowed herself. When he was finally asleep, she slipped from bed to ask God's forgiveness for her enjoyment and thanked Him for the new house. Then she cuddled next to her husband and set the alarm for early mass.

She prayed more fervently when the Depression came crashing down in October 1929. Although Kirkwood, with its furniture factories, paper mills, and chemical plants, its apple orchards, dairy farms, and celery marshlands, was not nearly as scarred as the larger Michigan cities that depended on the automobile, the impact was, nevertheless, dramatic. The Audit Bureau cut back employees and with them John Patrick's salary. Still he did not admit his concern as he brooded in the new leather recliner he had bought along with Margaret's refrigerator. "A chair worthy of Doyle himself," he had joked.

Now he was not joking. It was a tense struggle to survive from day to day. Gene Tunney's retirement from boxing and a vacant heavyweight throne seemed inconsequential although Notre Dame's continuing dominance of college football under Knute Rockne gave John Patrick consistent energy to hold up his head in Kirkwood. No Depression could change that, nor could it ever force his fierce pride to admit aloud that he was frightened. He even permitted himself to gloat over the bungling "medicine ball" administration of pudgy Herbert Hoover with his Quaker background. Al Smith would have handled it all.

Somehow, with the money they had saved and Margaret's fierce management, they were able to endure and keep the new house. But there could be no thought of starting a new business or buying an old one. Or of having more children. Margaret did not agree with his decision about children as he uttered it one brooding evening from his brown leather recliner. To have a dozen children was, for her, a small enough sacrifice for ignoring the convent. Yet, to her credit, she would never have disputed her husband's judgment if he had not introduced a condom into their bedroom the week after Jim was weaned. Although she had never seen one, she instinctively knew it was evil, and she blessed herself nervously.

"My God in heaven, John Patrick!"

"It's a way of not having children for a while."

He was embarrassed, but it had never occurred to him that it was really wrong.

There had been no discussions in Saint Raphael's pulpit about birth control. Informed Catholics may have known the law, but Margaret was too naïve to have wondered, and John Patrick believed he only had to be a faithful husband and a good father. He had never heard the pope's opinion, nor did he care about it. Thus when Margaret turned from him, as much perhaps from fear as from any spiritual rejection, he became furious. The condom shriveled and fell on the sheets and Margaret grasped her rosary.

"For God's sake, Margaret, I'm a man!"

"We can deny ourselves and be grateful for what we have."

"Damn it. I am grateful, but we're entitled!"

"If Father Doyle says it's—"

He shouted, ripping the condom to shreds, "Doyle doesn't run my bedroom! You're my wife!"

She was trembling, then crying, and the two boys were crying besides. "What's it all worth if we go to hell?"

He charged from the bedroom and slammed the door. The crucifix fell to the floor and Margaret gasped in horror. As she arose to replace the crucifix and sprinkle holy water from the small ivory font by the door, John Patrick poured himself some bourbon, smuggled from Canada by McNulty's brother, and sat for several hours in his recliner. The sadness engulfed him until even the beautiful new house had lost its luster. Tears formed in his eyes but would not fall. Then he heard Jim crying and brought him in and held him tenderly, rocking him in the chair until he gurgled softly in his father's arms. He put his son back in the crib and fell asleep on the couch.

That night, something changed in their marriage.

On the surface he seemed to conform. He did not approach Margaret sexually for more than a year, and he never lost his temper or fought with her. Instead he began to sit silently and drink more and to spend longer hours away from home. She secretly thanked God for his conversion, naïvely unaware of how repressive her decision was to a man such as John Patrick Maguire.

Margaret Ann felt no repression. She had never really liked her body. She was almost unaware of it, had never looked at her own nakedness, and would have considered it grievously sinful to touch her breast or merely to stroke her own skin. Even John Patrick had never really seen her naked; sex had meant slipping up her nightgown until he could do what he had to do. She enjoyed his embrace and his man's smell far more than any sex. Even her own face was not appealing to her on the few occasions when she really looked. There had been too many criticisms from Kate and the matriarchy about her buck teeth and straight country hair. Her nose had been deemed too round, her mouth like a chicken's rear end, and her eyes too small to be noticed. Margaret had believed it all.

Gradually, from the power of their criticism, she had learned to bow her head until it became almost a customary position. She rarely looked directly at anyone when she spoke. Even her posture was crouched to conceal her breasts in self-effacement, With makeup and attention she would have been a pixielike beauty, and even with none, her alive, child's blue eyes gave her a kind of glow. She moved quickly and gracefully like an alert teen-ager, conversed intelligently when she was comfortable, and was most beautiful of all with her children. Jack and Jim helped her make oatmeal cookies, and Jim worked with her in the garden when she planted tulip bulbs or fertilized her roses. She taught him to feed the birds and squirrels, to scold blue jays and talk to robins, to bring flowers to Mary's altar in a corner of the window seat, and to fill the holy water font at the top of the stairs. She patiently taught both of them to make the sign of the cross every time they passed up or down, and she was especially beautiful when she took them to the silent church on Saturday mornings to talk to God.

She told them of the good thief at Jesus's side and of the fierce Roman soldiers. A dozen times she reminded Jack not to talk aloud or belch and not to pick up the sheep or wise men in the crib. Jim was always silent and staring in some private wonder. She showed them Mary and Joseph and a marvelous Saint Patrick casting the snakes from Ireland.

Her whole complexion became transformed, her blue eyes danced, and she smiled more frequently than ever as she worked among her roses and daffodils in the backyard. John Patrick had not seen her that way for many years, and never in his bedroom. But even as he approved of her almost perfect mothering, he resented the attention she lavished on the children.

As he continued to worry about the Depression and lose himself in work, he drank more. At home he was even more subdued and melancholic, content to work his crossword puzzle and bury himself in the newspaper or to drink white lightning with McNulty, who had become his only real confidant. Margaret did not like McNulty's flushed cheeks and slicked-down hair even though he treated her with almost too much respect, but she was grateful that he lived in the Irish district on the north side. It was a lower-middle-class area almost three miles away, so it restricted his visits to once a week. Although John Patrick and Margaret were certainly not wealthy, their house was the nicest McNulty had ever been in, and in his eyes John Patrick's middle-class income was real affluence. McNulty was a construction worker John Patrick's age and was as trim as the day of his last fight some six years ago. He had never married and he lived with his whining mother. It was during one of his visits, when John Patrick was showing off Jack's quick right hand, that Margaret embarrassed her husband in the presence of his friend. She abruptly called the boys into the small parlor off the dining room to say the family rosary, suggesting bitterly, loud enough to be heard, that the two men would be far better off joining in the rosary than drinking. McNulty got up to leave. John Patrick continued to drink silently and most likely would have ignored her remark had she not attacked again after the prayers.

"A fine example to your sons. Maybe we should say the rosary at the Shamrock." It was his favorite speakeasy.

"A fine idea. I'll invite Doyle."

"*Monsignor* Doyle." She emphasized his recent promotion.

"Oh, the banty rooster." He had detected Doyle's vanity as the priest preened in the new red cassock at an ushers' meeting despite his disclaimer: "Christ was never a monsignor."

"You've an angry tongue, John Patrick."

"It's the example you give."

There were tears in her eyes as she heard the children's prayers. She put them to bed, then tidied up the kitchen in silence. He poured himself another drink noisily, as stubborn as she in refusing to admit his pain, and as angry at the Church as she was dependent on it for nourishment.

By midnight, under the mist of alcohol, he was repentant, recalling her washings and ironings, the bountiful stews and roasts, and the care she took of his children. He also remembered the shy girl at Lake Winnebago and the moment when he had first touched her breast. He was on the verge of Irish tears when he stumbled into bed. He reached out clumsily to touch her, but she clung to her rosary and moved away. It crushed him, and he battled tears as well as fierce anger. He touched her again and felt her body freeze. His pain was unbearable, and he wanted to punch Monsignor Doyle or smash a crucifix as he fought not to scream out.

He spoke softly, his words slurred, and she knew he was drunk. "I'm sorry, my darling, I'm really sorry."

He began making love while she clung to her rosary, felt the sting of the Roman scourges on Jesus's back, and made no further protest. Still he was not through, and she endured another crucifixion as he struggled for the second release that alcohol made difficult. She begged God to forgive her for ever ignoring a vocation, she promised extra prayers and a self-denial of all candy and sweets, and she swore never to lie in bed a second longer than was absolutely necessary. Then he was snoring and she finished the rosary at rigid attention on her knees. After a few hours of restless sleep, she arose for mass. Hating him. Two months later, at the end of March—on the day Knute Rockne was killed in a Kansas plane crash—John Patrick learned she was pregnant.

Their third son, Thomas Aloysius, was born on the Feast of the Holy Rosary in October 1931. The fair hair and white skin, the light blue eyes and perfect body assured her that he was an O'Brien. She remembered the night of conception and thanked God for His generosities. "Behold the handmaid of the Lord." As if in response, at the very first nursing, a great light shone above the baby's head. As his lips touched her nipple, "an almost sinful pleasure"—as she described it to Mary O'Meara—enveloped her body, a hundred times greater than any she had permitted herself in John Patrick's bed.

She would always remember Thom's birth as a private Bethlehem.

John Patrick remembered it too and wondered if Knute Rockne's death was a sign that this son would play for Notre Dame.

By late 1933, as the Depression feebly responded to Franklin Roosevelt's New Deal, life with Margaret and the family had improved. Banks were reopened with cautious new confidence and federal guarantees (although John Patrick would never trust them again). Congress had completed a ninety-nine-day emergency session, and Roosevelt had given the first of his fireside chats. His only serious mistake, according to John Patrick and McNulty, was to appoint a woman as secretary of labor. More important, Notre Dame had three men on the all-American team, the Chicago Bears beat the New York Giants to win the national football title, and Jack Sharkey had succeeded the hated Max Schmeling as heavyweight champion of the world.

It seemed as if Margaret and John Patrick had weathered some crisis and finally decided to make the best of a life that offered no alternative. She found her peace at mass and amid her flowers, and he was absorbed in business and future dreams for his boys.

Although each of them was a good parent, Jack, at seven, became more difficult to control, and Margaret was obliged to threaten him frequently with an ominous, "Wait till your father gets home!" John Patrick did not hesitate to spank him with brief, firm strokes, but neither Jack nor his father held a grudge. Secretly John Patrick was proud of Jack's rebellious spirit, and it pleased him when he rounded the corner of Maple Street to see his son throttling a young Dutchman, Jack's red hair damp, his freckled face ready to take on the world. John Patrick always broke up a fight as soon as he was convinced that Jack had done enough damage, then chided him briefly and carried him like a sack of potatoes into the house.

Jim was still as pale and serious at five as he had been at birth, gentle and patient with little Thom, and lost in the brawling shadow of Jack. He was apparently happiest exploring gopher holes in the backyard or rising early to startle the rabbits that were munching on

Margaret's lilies. There was a distant wisdom in the solemn eyes that were not really as shy as they were absorbed in private thoughts. He was delighted when his father picked him up and threw him in the air, but he was content to hold the sleeve of his father's coat while John Patrick pummeled the irrepressible Jack or the affectionate, cherubic Thom.

Thom was a truly beautiful child. Even Dutch neighbors in the grocery store could not restrain themselves from stroking the silken blond hair. At two, he was a talker, speaking often in full sentences, asking questions about pictures in magazines, learning the names of people in the neighborhood, shaking hands with anyone, and chattering endlessly until John Patrick told him to "Pipe down!" Margaret always answered him, especially when they visited the church and he whispered his questions about every saint and angel. She never forgot his very first visit, when he wanted to see God in the tabernacle, and another time, when she returned from communion, when he requested innocently to see God on her tongue. Jim never showed the same interest, and Jack had to be restrained from chewing the Host when he made his first communion.

Despite the Depression, it was during this period of relative peace that John Patrick was able to save and borrow enough to buy his own business, an ailing general insurance company that had suffered during the crash and was improperly managed by its aging founder. The final five hundred dollars came from Margaret's father, who still rose at four o'clock every day to bake his bread. The decision was made the night Prohibition was repealed, over a bottle of Old Grand Dad shared with McNulty in the Shamrock Lounge. It was December 1933.

"If you don't buy it now, you may never have another chance." McNulty goaded his hero on.

"I don't really trust that damn Roosevelt." John Patrick had voted for him, but had begun to have suspicions about increased federal spending.

"I don't like the bastard either, but he wants the vote. If he don't get us out of this, he'll be as dead as Hoover."

Three drinks later, it was settled, and John Patrick Maguire, expatriate from Chicago's First Ward, founded Maguire's Insurance Company. With every penny he had.

The business did well. He curtailed his drinking and devoted all his time to making it succeed. He sold to the ushers and the parish council, to McNulty and his relatives, to the girls at the Audit Bureau and Monsignor Doyle, and to Greeks, Jews, Poles, even a few Dutchmen who ignored his heritage in the face of such eloquence and humor. At home he was, of course, far less expansive. Lost in the melancholy of the brown leather chair, he was exhausted from what gradually proved to be a daily charade that rubbed raw his underlying sensitivity. Then he would receive a customer's phone call and he was all palaver again, ready to resolve any problem. He hand delivered his fire and auto policies, explained new rates with great detail, worked far into the evening on beer bonds, and silently ate a nine or ten o'clock supper that Margaret had kept warm in the oven.

The business was far more important than the Church, and Margaret feigned resentment at his refusal to say the family rosary or attend Sunday-night benediction. In truth, she did not expect it of him and was secretly delighted to remain forever the better Catholic. It was his straying affection that she really wanted, but she was forever powerless to tell him. Even when he began making a hundred dollars more a month than he had at the Audit Bureau, it meant nothing to her, and only when he complimented a meal or played with the children was she really happy with him. If he demanded that she buy a new dress for a Saint Patrick's Day banquet, she always brought three home on trial, chose the one he liked, then blushed and giggled helplessly when he hugged her and forced her to sit on his lap in the presence of the boys.

It was during one of his more expansive periods, when he had sold an expensive blanket policy to a lumber company, that he decided they should have another child. Thom was past three, and Roosevelt had convinced most of the country that the Depression was almost over.

John Patrick was jubilant when their first daughter was born, and he insisted on calling her Anne Margaret. It was 1935. She was the image of her mother, only bigger boned and sturdier. John Patrick fussed over her with clumsy affection and delighted in showing off his four children on Sunday walks through the neighborhood, tenderly holding his grinning baby girl. He knew his vengeance was at hand.

Jack was already the scourge of the hostile neighborhood. Jim could be frightened home—once with a butcher knife when he tried to retrieve an errant tennis ball that Thom had accidentally thrown too far. On Halloween, Jim's Maguire face had been recognized under a clown's mask, and several doors had been closed to him and his smaller brother. Meanwhile, Jack was off knocking over garbage cans and tying tin cans on Dutch cars. Jim dried the tears in Thom's sad blue eyes when they were ridiculed or chased away, and Jack planned revenge.

His flaming red hair frequently swooped down to snatch a Hollander's bike as he laughed hoarsely at a Dutch housewife's screaming threats. He briefly confiscated a new Flexible Flyer sled, whizzing precariously down an icy, much-traveled street, daring, then double-daring Jim to try the same stunt. Yet he was not at all a bully, challenging skinny "potlickers" half again his size, tackling twelve or fourteen year olds in brutal sandlot football when he was only ten.

When a peculiar Dutch neighbor woman called Crazy Nellie washed Thom's five-year-old face with snow for falling against her on an icy sidewalk, Jim struggled vainly to stop her. Jack came belly flopping by on someone's sled, noticed the attack, then tackled the woman and proceeded to wash her face in the same snow, calling her a dirty son of a bitch. It took two sixteen year olds to drag him away.

Curiously, Jack seemed afraid of Jim, as if Jim's pale composure threatened his own bravado, and he was jealous of the warm relationship Jim had with Thom. Certainly Jack had no physical fear of his quiet brother who was content to wander off by himself to search for field mice. Rather, it troubled Jack that Jim refused to compete and did not seem impressed by his strength, his daring leaps from trees, and his candy thefts from the grocery store. Jim did not permit Jack any power to hurt him. When Margaret insisted that Jack include Jim in after-school games or snowball fights, Jack agreed reluctantly, but once out of Margaret's sight he raced away and cursed his younger brother as a sissy until Jim walked off by himself, without any sadness. Jim never reported Jack to Margaret although Jack would have been much more satisfied if he had.

Jim was instinctively more patient with the younger Thom. He pointed out birds' nests, picked wild crab apples in a vacant lot, and tried to teach Thom to climb trees without breaking the branches. Only with Thom did Jim feel free enough to talk. He answered Thom's questions, permitted him to chatter endlessly, and loved him more than anyone—except John Patrick. But if Jack saw them together, he usually lured Thom away, permitting the little boy to play on his team and never inviting Jim. Often Thom left Jim reluctantly, but it was next to impossible for anyone to refuse the exuberant, fun-loving Jack. Margaret had given up trying to control him, and he seemed afraid of nothing but his father's wrath. One stern word from John Patrick was all it ever took.

Despite John Patrick's firm discipline, he loved his boys and they him. When he rounded the corner on Maple Street after work, he signaled them with a triumphant melody on his horn, alerting the whole neighborhood and bringing his sons from every direction to jump on him with hugs and kisses. Unlike Margaret, he was an openly affectionate man, mussing their hair and grabbing them frequently in rough gestures of love. Jack, especially, was his legacy, and John Patrick overlooked the older boy's abuse of Jim unless it got out of hand.

At ten, only two years older than Jim, Jack was more than a head taller. He loved to mock his brother's attempts to please Margaret by fixing a leaky faucet or a faulty toaster. Margaret was always quick to encourage Jim, and her praise angered Jack.

"Jimmy's the only one around here who can fix anything," she'd say.

One warm spring afternoon after school, Jim was tinkering with a leaking lawn sprinkler while Jack was teaching Thom how to catch a bullet pass. Twice he sent passes out and purposely hit Jim in the head with the football.

"Sorry, mother's little helper, it slipped."

When Jim ignored a third slip as he hunted for a washer, Jack grabbed the sprinkler and danced around the yard in a sissified manner. Jim tried to take it back, and Jack flattened him with a vicious ankle tackle. Even Thom, who quarreled with no one and usually defended Jim, snickered.

"You dirty son of a bitch!" Jim screamed, and Margaret overheard from the kitchen window.

"Get right in here!"

Tears of anger flowed down the boy's cheeks. "But mother, he grabbed the sprinkler. I was only trying—"

"I still won't have that kind of talk! You stay right in here till your father gets home." When she turned to reprimand Jack, he was over the hedge and gone.

Margaret remained concerned about Jim, and it was at her nagging insistence that John Patrick bought his second son a dog on his eighth birthday, something he had vowed he would never do.

"If you don't take care of him, he goes right back. Your mother's got enough to do!"

Sandy was his, a mongrel from the dog pound: part collie, with a friendly disposition and long wheat hair, and part chow, with its size and squat strength. And a coyote's fluorescent, intelligent eyes. It was the eyes that set Sandy apart from a hundred yelping dogs begging for a home.

Sandy stared at Jim, mouth slightly parted and panting too excitedly to bark, legs dancing impatiently to follow him. It was as happy a moment as Jim had ever known when John Patrick paid the two dollars and Jim carried Sandy to the car. He arranged old blankets for a warm bed in the garage, commandeered one of Margaret's discarded cake pans for food and another for water, and shouted to the whole neighborhood when Sandy fetched a stick on the very first try.

"Maybe he's a bird dog!" Jim's cheeks were flushed excitedly.

Jack laughed. "He's a stupid mutt; you should have got an Irish setter." He faked throwing the stick and hid it under his shirt. Sandy jerked his head and danced in confused circles. Then Jack produced the stick, rapped Sandy on the head, and ran off. Jim put his arms around Sandy's neck, rubbed his head gently, and fought back tears. From that moment they were inseparable. Occasionally Jack tormented Sandy, and the gentle Thom petted him affectionately, but Jim loved him, talked to him in the silent woods, watered him at the secret spring, and embraced him after school or Sunday mass.

Every afternoon Sandy waited on the sidewalk in front of the house for half an hour before Jim was due from school. When he saw the white and gold city bus, he barked and danced until Jim came charging across the street to wrestle the pup playfully to the ground. Margaret reminded him to change his clothes, and he shared fresh cookies or homemade bread and jelly with Sandy. When there were thunderstorms, Jim snuck out in the rain to comfort Sandy in the garage, and if they wandered through the woods, Jim lovingly pulled the cockleburs from his matted hair. All through his childhood Jim seemed to have no consistent friend but Sandy. When he played ball, Sandy waited patiently until the game ended, and on Halloween Sandy followed him from house to house and shared his candy. Most neighbors never saw James Maguire without his dog.

From the day of Sandy's arrival, Jim was no longer dependent on his brothers or on unfriendly neighbors for company, and he spent more and more of his time with Sandy exploring the woods near Walker School.

"I don't understand that boy," said John Patrick.

Margaret's reply went unheard. "Jack torments him so."

But Jack didn't torment his brother when Irish loyalty erupted. On a crisp Saturday in October, Jack excluded Jim from a routine football game in the backyard, even though six-year-old Thom was awarded the signal honor of centering for both teams of twelve year olds. Jim's dismissal was abrupt: "You're too little, twerp. Go chase your hound."

Jim wandered off with Sandy, wrestled with him in the leaves, then stood on the curb watching a dozen neighborhood children begin an elaborate game of hide-and-seek in which signals were written on the sidewalk as vague clues. Jim excelled at the game and noisily kicked a tin can against a stump, hoping someone might choose him. He edged closer to the group, most of whom were older than he was.

"I'd like to play if the sides aren't even."

"You better get home, the pope might be calling." It was Lois Bonner, a chubby twelve-year-old girl with uneven teeth and sweat marks under the fat arms of a black sweater. "Tell your mother to have another baby."

Others surrounded him and increased the taunts.

Jim struggled not to swear or give a bad example to Protestants, but he made a fist as they closed in.

Lois jeered, "Maybe you're one of the nuns' babies."

"You look like you're ready to have a toad yourself." Jim couldn't help retaliating.

Her taller brother shoved Jim down on the pavement, badly bruising his knee. Jim lunged and drove his nine-year-old fist into the boy's nose. Blood spurted and he ran screaming. A bigger boy tackled Jim from behind and someone else pounded his head. He fought to get up, but it was hard to breathe, and he wanted to cry. With a free finger he gouged someone's eye and savagely bit Lois on the arm. Someone bounced his head against the curb. Sandy was barking furiously, and Jim could feel the blood trickling from his lip and down his hand.

Sandy snarled helplessly, but Jack had heard the noise and sent Thom to investigate. When Thom came running back with the news, Jack turned almost insane with fury. Size and age were of no consequence, nor was sex.

Someone yelled. "Here comes his brother!"

It was almost comical. The whole mob turned tail, but it was too late. Jack caught two of them, bloodied their mouths, and cracked Lois Bonner fiercely across the back of the head, knocking her to the sidewalk. Jim jumped back into the fight and slammed insanely in every direction. Thom had picked up a large stick, and Sandy ran in circles growling ferociously. In three minutes the battle was over, and Jack stood triumphantly in the middle of Maple Street, his arm around Jim, challenging the whole neighborhood.

"No one lays a hand on a Maguire!"

Then he spat fiercely and resumed the football game, inviting Jim to play and even praising him for two good catches and a clean tackle.

Tomorrow Jack could begin tormenting him again, but the day of a religious war was different. Stones, bats, fists—it didn't matter to history's children. It only mattered that they won.

Margaret would have been deeply disappointed to have a weakling for a son; however, her primary concern was the religious formation of her children. Monsignor Doyle reminded from the pulpit that faith was created in the home long before a child went to the Catholic school, and it was the example of parents that shaped it.

Jack, of course, had always been a problem. Even as

an altar boy he resisted learning his Latin. More than once he was publicly rebuked by the assistant pastor for making faces at a companion while pouring wine in the chalice or for smiling at girls in the congregation. During the family rosary he slouched over a chair or made his brothers laugh, and he constantly had to be reminded to say his night prayers. On such occasions he leaped from bed, said the words "night prayers" jokingly, and jumped back in. Margaret had to be content that he made the nine first Fridays, gave up movies and some candy during Lent and Advent, and did not swear in her presence. She knew he had a good heart.

So did John Patrick, but it still worried him when a neighboring parent reported that the twelve-year-old Jack had taken off the panties of his teen-aged daughter in a wrestling match at Walker playground and tied them to the top of a flagpole. Once the police came to the Maguire house to report that Bonner's woodshed had been set afire shortly after Jack was seen hovering on the premises; and a seventh-grade nun sent home obscene pictures Jack had drawn of the only girl in his class who had developed tits. Margaret was too mortified to say anything, but she secretly sewed a green scapular inside the lining of Jack's brown winter coat. John Patrick hoped that the excitement of contact sports in high school would straighten out his brawling rebel who feared no one—apparently, not even God.

At times, Jack provided his own scriptural commentaries that would even have upset John Patrick.

"Hey, Jesus, what's up?" he would bellow in a falsetto. Then he would answer in a deep baritone, "Nothing much. Fishing at the fork in the Jordan." "How come you always get fish?" "Lucky, I guess."

Jim and Thom were always afraid to laugh.

Jim had filled out, but he was still too thin and pale. His straight brown hair had an impossible cowlick; his mouth was small, but strong; and he had the firm jaw and prominent nose of all John Patrick's sons. Like Margaret, he slouched slightly and had to be reminded frequently to take his hands out of his pockets. He did not fight his mother over religious obligations, but neither was he enthusiastic. When he first served mass in fourth grade, Margaret dreamed that he might want to be a priest, but when she mentioned it to him, Jim did not even reply. She wondered if he were ever really happy.

Only Thom did not confuse her.

Thom was her son from the moment of the mysterious light and the strange pleasure at his first nursing. Even in the hospital the saintly Sister Caritas had told Margaret, "This one will be your priest." When she had first taken him to Saint Raphael's to visit the Christmas crib, he had been compelled to caress the infant Jesus with his tiny fingers. He was barely seven when, at her suggestion, he said a thousand Hail Marys on Christmas Eve. Thom would be her priest. Mary O'Meara and the nuns were certain of it. So was Monsignor Doyle.

Thom, with his clear blue innocent eyes that softened a strong face and his broad athlete's shoulders, was the pastor's favorite. Of all the Maguires, only Thom was free to approach the pastor in a crowded Sunday vestibule. Monsignor Doyle had forgotten that the reserved Jim had been named in his honor.

"Going to the game today, monsignor? Jack's playing against Caldwell." There was no fear in Thom's voice.

"I wouldn't miss it for the world."

Monsignor Doyle tucked his breviary inside the red sash that supported his full belly. The black cassock was smudged with ashes and the book disappeared in its folds. He rubbed Thom's golden hair with stubby fingers and his jowls shook as he laughed his wheezing giggle. He seemed old in his early forties, but his voice was still the booming baritone that had reformed Saint Raphael's a dozen years ago. Thom was as unabashed in his presence as Margaret and Jim were intimidated. Jack had not been interested enough to hang around and was challenging another boy to leapfrog a drinking fountain.

"Caldwell's not much of a contest for the Irish," Doyle said. "I'll plan on leaving at the half." He winked at the blushing Margaret, wheezed again, then adjusted his sash and rubbed his belly as if to cherish it.

Jim remembered the time monsignor had called him a stupid ass when the mass was held up because Jim couldn't find a linen corporal in the sacristy. Margaret had prayed breathlessly until Thom rushed out to locate it.

"Caldwell's undefeated—and they're real big."

"But they're not made of the same cowhide."

While Thom continued to chatter, Jim felt a strange jealousy he would have shared with no one, even the priest in confession. Margaret beamed, delighted by her vicarious admission into the sanctuary. She knew Thom would be her priest, but she was afraid to mention it to John Patrick, who had recently discovered how far his young Thom could hit a baseball. He already had plans for a White Sox contract.

Even the Dutch neighbors continued to approve Thom's beauty and boyish charm. He was the first Maguire ever to be invited to a neighborhood birthday party, and he was even permitted to join an occasional baseball game. Although he was shy around girls, Thom rarely teased or attacked, as Jack did, or withdrew silently like Jim. At eight, he was especially fond of a dark-haired teen-ager who loved to mother him. She combed his hair and even kissed him twice—until Margaret found out.

Thom's religious faith was somehow not offensive to his brothers. He delighted in Jack's elaborate vengeance on feisty neighbors; he never tattled or abused his mother's obvious preference of him over his brothers; and he made light of his own Lenten sacrifices and frequent prayers.

He was the youngest altar boy in the history of Saint Raphael's, struggling to move the giant mass missal when his freckled nose barely touched the altar. When most first graders were stumbling with the Hail Mary and the tongue-twisting "Suffered under Pontius Pilate" of the Apostles' Creed, Thom already knew his mass Latin. The complex *"Suscipiat Dominus sacrificum de manibus tuis . . ."* was the last phrase to fall to his fierce energy. Few adults could memorize it. Neither of his older brothers had learned it until fourth grade.

Spelldowns, reading tests, arithmetic, geography—his mind and memory were made for school, and he had the ease and endurance of the gifted. He was asked to read for Father Doyle, to make presentations of spiritual bouquets on feast days, to provide the various mysteries of the rosary at family prayer. Even John Patrick didn't know them although he was never pressed to admit it.

Most astonishing of all was Thom's rare ability at sports. The grace of the natural athlete was obvious at an early age. Legs at full speed in an instant, the rhythm of catching and throwing, instinctive shifting of weight and feinting, and a body strong and sinewy enough to dispense the poised energies. Broad shoulders and thick chest in the traditional Irish mold, trim waist and solid legs, strong hands and healthy bones, he could have excelled at any sport—tennis, golf, even hurling, like his forebear, Michael O'Brien. His face almost made the athletic prowess ludicrous: soft, rosy cheeks; fine straight hair and a shy smile and charming lisp through separated front teeth. A distant, serious look in repose. Sometimes sad, often intense, but otherwise smiling. Forever smiling. The kind of smile that made adults regret they had ever lied, inflicted pain, or lost innocence.

Thom's warm religious faith pleased Margaret as much as his athletic prowess ignited John Patrick's dreams. Although John Patrick already feared Thom's priestly aspirations, he reassured himself silently that the Maguire blood would assert itself in puberty.

John Patrick had a different kind of religious faith, and as he grew more successful in business he expressed himself more confidently. Although he had voted for Roosevelt in 1936, it was only because Alf Landon seemed to be a "horse's ass." Roosevelt had lost his trust, not only because of Al Smith and excessive spending, but for "religious" reasons. The 1935 Works Progress Administration had been the final straw, paying "shiftless, unemployed no-accounts" to be lazier by building unnecessary roads and parks. He had the same scorn for the Townsend Plan, which proposed two hundred dollars a month for everyone over sixty. When McNulty, out of work for three months, praised Townsend and talked about taking a WPA job, John Patrick exploded and found him work helping with an addition on the house. For John Patrick, hard work was a matter of real religion. As was generosity.

Thus he considered his donations to the Church, the fruit of his own labors, to be the true mark of faith and loyalty. It was far more impressive to him than any daily mass. And, as much as he despised any "welfare" programs, he hated even more the Catholic Church's preferential treatment of the rich. Especially those who donated scantily to the parish. He studied the elaborate annual financial statement published by Monsignor Doyle that listed everyone's contributions down to the penny. John Patrick Maguire was always among the leaders. When a wealthy automobile dealer had taken over one of the ushers meetings, John Patrick stormed home, poured himself a drink, and scanned the offender's contributions for the previous year.

"What the hell has Daniels given? Now he's running the ushers meetings." He knew the Gospels had it wrong; the rich were passing through the eyes of needles every day.

Margaret liked his anger when it was not directed at her. She sent the two-year-old Anne to play in another room.

"Maybe he'll leave all his money when he goes. Monsignor likes the rich ones. He hardly sees me lately."

"I was giving before he knew his ass from the twelfth station." Daniels was a convert of only twenty years.

"John, not in front of the boys—" He knew she didn't really care.

"I'll call Doyle and increase my donations another two hundred dollars and a German fart."

Jack laughed loudly and Thom blushed.

"For the love of God, John. Not when you're drinking."

He knew she was almost amused. "Why the hell not? He takes a drink. At Quinlan's wake the Hail Marys sounded like *Smile Harry*." He laughed loudly at his own joke, and Jack fell on the floor with glee. Even Jim smiled, and Thom continued to blush more painfully and looked apprehensively at Margaret.

"God will strike you dead for talking about a priest. He has spells, you know. Mary O'Meara says it's his heart."

"Spells, my ass. He likes his bourbon." He got up and poured himself another drink, unable to talk about his anger.

It was not only the Church that upset him. Jimmy Braddock had just lost the world heavyweight championship to a nigger from Detroit, named Joe Louis, who couldn't read or write. John Patrick had been ignored when he made a bid on a big policy for a local paper mill. And Monsignor James Michael Doyle had made him share the commission on Saint Raphael's Church and school with a new convert insurance agent and another man who had just moved in from Akron even though John Patrick had written the policy and showed the pastor how to save almost four hundred dollars.

John Patrick slipped again into the melancholy of his recliner and escaped with his newspaper. He was not really strong enough to challenge Margaret's Church, only to mock it.

Although he was seldom home early enough from work to interfere, his presence was strong enough to prevent the world of God and Margaret from completely devouring his children.

He was almost too gentle with Anne, but only rarely did he relate to his growing sons without humor or sarcasm. In a strange way he loved all of them more than he dared say, but conversations always ended abruptly. "You better get your homework done," or "Help your mother in the kitchen." It was a signal that they had talked enough, and he returned to his crossword or his bourbon, sometimes with Anne on his lap.

He anticipated tragedy, expected it, and knew at the very moment of his greatest pride that some news would cast him again into suffering and darkness. He knew tragedy was the curse of his blood. It was built into his people and the life they led. As far as he was concerned, all Catholics were immeasurably superior to WASPs, but he instinctively knew that the Irish were not like the screaming Italians or stupid, sentimental Poles. Irish had no stomach for elaborate religious feasts or sloppy, extravagant rituals. They were legionnaires somehow, fierce soldiers who could tolerate immense pain and force themselves forward to escape the melancholic curse that could destroy them. Thus he respected the American Legion and attended monthly meetings and Memorial Day services to honor suffering and loyalty and death, certainly not a WASP America. But if any of his sons had joined the Boy Scouts, John Patrick would have been furious. Not only were Scouts a Protestant substitute for religion, they were a pack of sissies who learned how to light a campfire rather than kick someone's ass on a football field. Irish Catholicism had taught him that life was hard and that the strong alone survived. Only endurance was admired, and John Patrick's own capacity to suffer was extraordinary.

In 1939, he learned of his older brother's death just as

Margaret was rushing an evening meal so that she could drag the children to a special benediction to honor Pope Pius XII's elevation. All the children were dressed in their Sunday best. Even Jack had not been able to escape, and John Patrick had to reprimand him for snarling about "just another dago in a skullcap."

The sudden tragic news of the death brought them all into the living room. John Patrick had made no outburst when he received the phone call. He simply made the announcement. Margaret burst into prayers and laments, but he ignored her.

"A train crushed him on the way from work. Never knew what hit him." He felt the tears but refused to release them. "He was a good lad. I'll miss him."

He read the paper as always, poured himself a single drink, and sat silently for a long time.

"He was a good lad," he said again. Then he went to bed. The tragedy only confirmed what he already knew of life.

John Patrick was hardly over his brother Tom's death when his father was shot outside of a Chicago bar, a case of mistaken identity. John Patrick took it in stride, making no reference to his father's drinking or his neglect of the family.

"I'm only sorry he had to endure Tom's funeral. But it would have been a hundred times worse if mother had gone first. He was a helpless old bastard." He smiled slightly. "Like his son."

Margaret looked up tearfully from her rosary. "I always liked your father, John. He was a gentle man." She had never seen Daniel Maguire sober, and she secretly blamed his wife.

"You knew him too late, Margaret. He was a brawler like they'll never see again on the South Side. When the niggers were moving in he used to take them on two at a time and crack their nappy skulls. Gentle indeed! He was only getting tired when you met him!" He did not weep at his father's death but he sat quietly the first evening and refused Margaret's rare offer of a drink.

At the wake, he was expansive. "They had to shoot the old fart to take him out! He'd have outlived us all! And dug the holes to throw us in. Remember the night he threw McGeorge out the front door without his shirt?

It must have been ten below." Even the widow was laughing. Death was a release from pain, and it deserved a celebration.

"He could drink," Rafferty added.

"And he paid for his own—which is more than I can say for you, James Rafferty."

"I'd like to have a dime for every bottle you've murdered in my kitchen! It seems your memory's not too good when you're drinking, John Patrick."

"The mouth works well enough," McNulty added.

"Like father, like son," the widow whispered, and they all roared.

It was a shock when a dark-haired young Irish curate appeared to lead the rosary. A thin man with rimless glasses, he approached the widow nervously.

"Your husband was a fine and decent man. There are no words to describe the sorrow of the parish and my own."

The room was suddenly electric with ancient anger. The worth of a corpse was decided by the importance of the ecclesiastical representation. To send a nameless curate had been a fatal and unpardonable mistake. John Patrick was suddenly flushed and furious, and Ellen O'Dwyer Maguire stiffened in some archaic dignity.

As the young priest felt the cold silence and looked awkwardly away, the tears formed in Ellen's eyes, and John Patrick reached out to hold her.

"We're grateful you could be with us at this time of sadness, father. We're only sorry the monsignor could not be here, too. My Dan thought so much of him," Ellen said.

The young curate made a fatal mistake. "Monsignor was called to the bishop's for dinner. He sends deepest regrets."

"No need at all," she said. "The recreation will do him good. God knows he gets little enough with all his holy labors." She had always hated his arrogance.

"Indeed," said John Patrick. "I know it must be important business. He well appreciates the bricks in his church that carry scars of my father's trowel. Not to mention the widow's faith."

He spoke with a greenhorn's brogue to conceal an impossible burst of fury.

No one moved as Ellen continued to stare, certain

that the monsignor's absence was an angry rebuke of Dan's drinking.

The young priest fidgeted nervously and the tension mounted. Then John Patrick led his mother by the arm and, like a proud usher, directed Margaret and his children, then the entire group, to his father's coffin. Solemnly they knelt to pray. The room was full of mounting anger.

Ellen broke the silence. "The same oil anointed your own hands, father. Please lead us in the holy rosary."

With obvious relief, the priest left when the lugubrious prayers were finished.

"So the good monsignor is dining with the bishop these days? I suppose the pope will feed him when my own mother is waked."

"Perhaps it was God's will he didn't come."

"God's will be damned!" John Patrick snarled. Margaret gasped. "He knows where to come when he wants bingo callers!"

"Don't take it too hard, John. We saved ourselves some bourbon." It was McNulty.

Soon they were back drinking again. Margaret's brother Vinnie was resplendent in the blue serge that replaced his carpenter's overalls two or three times a year. His own wife had died of blood poisoning the previous summer, and now he lured John Patrick into a jig.

"Your knees have lost a little spring, John Patrick."

"Your own sound like walnut shells."

"Maybe the widow has a little life left." They pulled Ellen to her feet and she put her drink down carefully on the edge of the Victrola.

"I'll be dancing on Vinnie's headstone."

The party continued far into the night. Fourteen-year-old Jack snuck beer into the kitchen and a tattling little Anne told her mother.

"A final toast to the old man," someone said. They rose solemnly and held their glasses aloft.

John Patrick spoke devoutly in a soft slur: "He was a good husband and a decent father. He didn't pray as much as some, but when he did he meant it. He took a drink, but who wouldn't if he had to make a hard living all his life without an education? May he rest in peace."

"Amen!" they all answered. The widow was already asleep in her rocker, finally freed for a few hours from the monsignor's insult. She would not forget. Nor would John Patrick.

On the night of his father's funeral, in the spring of 1941, an intoxicated John Patrick carelessly slept with his wife. Margaret had no heart to resist his pawing attentions, and secretly she had been longing for another child. Already nearing forty, she feared it would be her last. In another year Anne would be in school and her own life would be too lonely without a final baby to attend.

Nine months later, three days before Japan assaulted Pearl Harbor, Timothy Joseph Maguire was born without incident. The excitement of his arrival was almost lost in the horror of a devastating war that lulled the nation from sleep and brought a final end to the shadows of the Depression.

John Patrick had known it was coming. His favorite commentator, Father Charles Coughlin, had predicted it, publicly calling Franklin Roosevelt a liar, then was silenced by his Church. For the first time in his life, John Patrick, almost forty-eight years old, voted for a Republican. John Patrick and McNulty hated Roosevelt and the Japanese almost as much as they hated WASPs and the English. Margaret understood none of it, but she was delighted to have a healthy, outrageously happy baby. And just as grateful that Jack, barely fifteen, was too young to enlist.

3

Saint Raphael's

Throughout World War II, Kirkwood was still owned and operated by Protestants. The few Jews were mocked and laughed at; the increasing number of blacks were frightened and kept in their place near the old Irish neighborhoods on the north side; Greeks and Italians and Poles were still greasy and their accents a mark of scorn. Irish Catholics were growing more abrasive, and they continued to have large families.

On the surface, however, the Dutch were more tolerant, owing to increasing Catholic affluence, as well as to a fear of Hitler and Hirohito. Neighbors complimented John Patrick on his fine children. Women in the grocery store, now troubled by meat and grocery rationing, recognized a "Maguire" and nodded at Margaret. The Maguires went to mass and sacrificed, played more sports, and practiced telling funny stories to camouflage their rage.

When the Irish Catholics enlisted, it was more out of a sense of courage than any devotion to America. America was still Protestant and they themselves would have to run America before they could ever love it. They knew that Roosevelt had forced Japan's hand to drag America into the war and save England's "bloody neck." The fall of Poland was painful, and Paris a tragedy, yet it would not really have troubled the Irish had the British died at Dunkerque or London burned to ashes. Of course they despised Hitler—he was only a maniacal flowering of what Germany had always been—but still, England was the very symbol of their lifelong oppression.

As were the American WASPs. John Patrick's generation lived with hostile prejudice toward countless enemies even as they accepted a historic religion as a normality of life.

The Church remained his inevitable support, not the country that had driven his father to drink and made his mother an indentured domestic. Even as John Patrick despised the arrogance of the clergy, the priest was his leader, not a Kirkwood mayor who had watched crosses burn or a Roosevelt who sold out to Churchill and the Russians. Like most Irishmen of his generation, John Patrick did not know how to forgive, and he would never forget the America that abused his grandparents and mocked simple faith as popery and witchcraft.

Whenever possible, the Irish created their own politicians—as deceitful as the rest, but often kind and considerate of their own. Otherwise, sons became policemen until they could be priests and doctors, salesmen until they could run companies, laborers until they could own big houses. They would not be farmers again because the rotting land had killed too many of their skinny children. Even as they talked of heaven, they wanted wealth and power. Like his peers, John Patrick laughed easily at parish picnics, pitching horseshoes and playing softball with a beer in his hand, but his charm and buffoonery masked an unyielding melancholy that time might easily turn to madness. Only the same discipline that made light of tragedy could control his rage, but he knew his enemies and bided his time impatiently to destroy them.

Under the pressure of such anger, an explosion could erupt at any moment. When Jack first began to play varsity football, John Patrick was waiting in line to buy a ticket for the Saint Stanislaus game. A huge Pole barged ahead of him in the line, and John Patrick's smile disappeared. He flushed fiercely. "Hey, you Jap Polack, wait your turn!"

"You and what army's gonna make me?"

"I am!" He stepped out of line.

Margaret screamed. Anne began to cry.

"For the love of God, John!"

He didn't hear.

The Polack saw his sudden impossible rage and thought better of the battle. John Patrick might not have won, but he would unquestionably have fought. He would have been fighting every educated snob or arrogant WASP who put him down, every priest who mocked his lust and stole his wife, every current and ancient insult. God, he would have fought! Not the giant Pole, but life itself, even if he died beaten and breathless in a ticket line.

In a less obvious way, Margaret was filled with the same rage. She fought for a final victory that extended even beyond death, where hell would eternally burn her foes. Like an ancient prophet, she would survive long enough to watch her enemies crushed under her feet, and her loyalty to the Church was the only apparent measure of her anger. Although she had gained weight, she was still a small woman with a weak and unresonant voice, almost timid; however, the self-effacing posture belied her incredible power. She was as strong as the Church itself, as resistant to change and novelty, as unyielding in her contempt for sin and weakness, and as unafraid of pain or self-sacrifice. Prayer was always on her lips, as fierce as any crusader's battle chant, but the God she worshiped was still not satisfied. Even her increased suffering with five children was only another proof of divine love. "God loves those he chastises," she said, in her personal paraphrase of King Solomon, and she attacked weakness unmercifully wherever it appeared.

"The Bertelsons are getting divorced."

John Patrick remained silent behind his paper, counting the totals of destroyed Messerschmitts and Zeros versus the Mustangs.

Her tone was bitter, some fountain of unexpressed anger gathered in her throat and grew rank, poisoning her words.

"Always so highfalutin! He with the camel hair overcoat and she with the fancy furs. As if God cares," she snarled bitterly. "They'll be excommunicated, won't they?" She was testing her own marital security, and he knew it. They had not had sex in the year since Tim's birth.

"Maybe they'll burn them at the homecoming." Jack laughed.

"Don't make a mockery of it, John. They've given up their souls. I suppose he has a tart somewhere lighting his spark. Well, he'll get his sparks where the water won't put them out!"

"Where might that be, Margaret? Up his asshole?"

Thom was angry and wanted to come to his mother's aid. Jim looked away so as not to grin.

"Don't be crude, John! Hell's fire is nothing to joke of."

"Maybe he's had his hell. She seems no prize to me." He offered the bait and Margaret snatched it.

"She has a mouth on her; she could blow out candles from the front pew where she always sits. So educated and proper! 'How nice to see you, my dear. How are the children? How many are there now? I don't see how you do it.' Indeed she doesn't—with her one. She'll have her pleasure. It passes soon enough!"

Pleasure meant sex, but it was never mentioned. The whole conversation was her justification of their finally silent bed. Although she knew he would never get a divorce, she remained troubled about their sexual dilemma. Still, she expressed her concern only in self-justifying condemnations of someone else's sin. Five children was almost enough of a family to satisfy Monsignor Doyle and to appease God for not entering the convent. She reassured herself that sexual abstinence was no sin. Even if John Patrick increased his drinking.

It had never occurred to Margaret that John Patrick would be unfaithful. No matter how late he came home, no matter his state of intoxication, she would have bet her life that a woman was never a reason for his straying. She was almost right. Only once did he ever get dangerously involved. With Doris, the young woman who had been his private secretary at the Audit Bureau.

Doris was not particularly attractive, yet her dark brown eyes always sparkled in his presence and her total affection for him made her appealing. Especially to a sexually starved John Patrick with a few drinks in him.

At first they had lunch together when they happened to meet in the Victory Cafe. It was pleasant to gossip about the Audit Bureau and to vent their mutual hatred for J. R. Harris. She was delighted to hear about the success of his business and she commented on his new blue suit. Occasionally he stopped by at her house when her automobile policy came up for renewal, and once, when her husband was out, she offered him a drink. It was the first time he kissed her and she responded passionately. He gently pulled himself away, and at his next confession he mentioned the indiscretion to Monsignor Doyle. Doyle made no comment and gave him the usual penance of five Our Fathers. After that, John Patrick dropped off her policy only at the Audit Bureau, but a few months after Tim's birth, Doris's husband took a commission in the air force.

John Patrick arrived at her house about seven o'clock, accepted some pea soup she knew he loved, and had a bourbon and water. He had two more drinks as he talked about Admiral Nimitz's victory at Midway Island and the tragedy of the *Yorktown,* then about his three oldest sons, especially the athletic ability of Jack and Thom. She said she'd like to attend a game. There was no mention of Margaret.

He did not really know how it started. They shared another bourbon and then she was lying half-undressed on the living room couch and moving pillows to make more room. He kissed her fiercely and began kneading her breasts. He stripped off her skirt and loosened the belt to slide down his pants, kissing her at the same time. She had already surrendered and begged him, her words slurred, to take her into the bedroom.

The sound of her voice ended it as quickly as it had begun. Even the drink and a fierce hard-on were not enough. Whatever he was, John Patrick Maguire was a man of honor, and he withdrew gently, expressing his sorrow and assuring her that the whole thing had been his fault. They put themselves back together, shared two cups of coffee, and he kissed her gently on the cheek as he left, promising always to be her friend and apologizing for his outburst. He was never alone with her again.

It was an embarrassing confession, but Monsignor Doyle provided no lecture, asking only a private rosary. And Margaret, totally unsuspecting, was delighted when he joined the family rosary devoutly in the parlor, even demanding that Jack kneel up straight. The same evening he agreed to hear Anne's first communion prayers, helped Jim with some algebra problems, and sang the Notre Dame fight song to Tim. It was an evening Margaret would not forget.

Margaret had grown more beautiful with the years; her life of faith had proved effective in an impossible struggle to survive. John Patrick's periodic binges, more frequent after Tim's birth, were her constant cross, and shame was the one thing that could reduce her to tears. She could handle sickness and most death without much display of grief, but to be shamed in the community was more than she could tolerate. Increasingly the children found her weeping inconsolably in her chair by the fireplace.

"Mother!" Seeing her, Thom was on the verge of tears.

"Your father will be the death of me. Drinking again." Her mood forecast two or three days of unrelenting gloom and loud arguments.

"He called from work. His words were slurred! He knows the Ryans are coming for cards tonight—and God only knows when he'll get home."

Jack disappeared silently out the back door.

The others hated their father and the familiar binges that always ended with John Patrick spending a day in bed. There would be silence among them all for days, as well as mounting bills that worried the whole family, but for Margaret the worst of it was the shame.

At these times Jim and Thom could put their arms around her, wanting desperately to take away her pain and make things right. Such intimacy, however, was short-lived, and soon they all retreated again into the nontouching relationship that characterized the melancholic shadows of house and church.

As her grief and shame diminished, her anger and outrage grew. She was ready when he arrived home, her thin lips snarling, her blue eyes cold and strong, her small body rigid and ready to strike. Tim was crying; Anne, now almost eight, with Kate's blue eyes and dark curly hair, stood defiantly next to her mother.

"It's nice you could get here! I'm sick with worry! We could all be dead. Scrimping and saving so you can throw money away on almighty booze! A sorry sight you are—your clothes all rumpled and your hair all over your head. Maybe you should go and sit in the front pew so the whole world can see! A fine usher you'd make at this point, preening in front of the congregation." She was seldom so eloquent. "I've worn the same brown coat and I'm cutting down on expenses to buy galoshes for the children! Some example you are with all your palaver and fine intentions. Now the Ryans know! I can't invite anyone to the house without worrying! Well, I won't put up with it! The Church has no law against separation. You can get out and stay out. It's easier to take than worrying half the night—every time I hear a car." She began to weep again.

The tears pushed at Jim's cheeks and reluctantly flooded his eyes. Thom wanted to murder his father with his own hands, and Jack returned to console Tim. Margaret did not speak to John Patrick for three days. After he had slept, he helped with dishes and carried out garbage—things he never did in normal times. She would not have permitted it, for it was not a man's place to work around the house, but now she accepted his servitude in silence. He bought candy on his way home from work, heard Tim's prayers, ignored Anne's refusal to kiss him good-night, and even went with Margaret to evening services. He finally went down to the rectory to ask Monsignor Doyle to let him take the pledge, a solemn promise to God not to drink. He took it for thirty days and always kept it.

"You should take it for thirty years." They were speaking again. The forgiveness came in cycles—from anger and silence to a gentle sarcasm that successfully fought to suppress a smile.

"I suppose you'll be home in time for pot roast and gravy."

He put his arms around her expansively.

"Now I'm your darling, is it? And how long will that last?" She was embarrassed by his affection in front of the family, and she squirmed like a child. Anne was still repulsed, but Thom and Jim were delighted at the new happiness. Jack hadn't even been troubled.

"We could have a few of your canned tomatoes?" He loved her cooked tomatoes with stale bread.

"If I'm strong enough—you'll have your tomatoes." She tried not to smile.

"Maybe I'll be able to find a little caramel ice cream in my travels." He said it with an impish lilt which made Jack laugh.

The shadows were gone, and John Patrick was humorous and charming. He didn't bury himself in the leather recliner to read the paper after dinner or to brood in silence about the war. During the repentance periods, he forsook his chair to join the family rosary, and his devotion was matchless. He prayed more slowly than was customary, dragging the words. After the rosary, Margaret would finally laugh, and a time of great happiness for everyone followed for several days. Even for Anne.

"I had a cup of coffee with Rooney today." He settled into his chair. Margaret asked if Rooney still drank from the saucer. He opened a pack of Camels and lit one, sucking it noisily. She waited like an excited child. It was one of their favorite discussions, and she loved his caricature.

"Indeed," he said, imitating Rooney's thin face and prominent lips. "Now he's taken to dunking the doughnut and slurping the coffee through the hole." She began to laugh uncontrollably. The cycle had turned. A few weeks of relative peace, then the emergence of the quiet despair and boredom, and finally the explosion came again and the repentance scenario was repeated. She would retreat into her hard work and self-effacing martyrdom, attempting to please the God who was in every moment of her day—hoping against hope that He would one day forgive her sins and reward her for lifelong service. She knew that hell was the reward for the complacent, thus she asked more of herself than anyone else, even refusing to spend more money or buy new clothes when John Patrick offered.

Margaret did not choose her sexless, mothering, martyred role. There was a historic pattern that fashioned the women as inexorably and compulsively as the men. Women were to suffer beneath the cross like the Sorrowful Mother, Mary.

A few men, like Mr. Foley, were devout, and they followed their wives to church like chickens, but they were not admired—even by the women. Nor was John Patrick ever really sanctioned. He was feared, appeased, excused for his lack of devotion, catered to, and isolated by the very authority he was given in the home. The celibate priest was the children's model, and the docile, virginal Saint Joseph, or the too gentle John who leaned on Jesus's breast. Their father was a deviate paradigm for sons to grow up and not be like, even though their mother would serve him faithfully until the end.

"Why don't you sit down, Margaret, and eat your dinner?"

"I just want to see that everyone has enough. Are the potatoes lumpy? Lately they always turn dark."

"Everything's fine. Sit down and eat."

"Well, I'll just nibble. I'm not really hungry after cooking all afternoon."

"The meat's tough, Margaret. Tell that jabbering butcher he's charging enough to give a good cut. It's like leather." He loved his meat and gravy and had accumulated black market ration stamps from a friend of McNulty's.

"Maybe I didn't cook it enough?" She was back on her feet. "There's probably a tender piece around the bone. See if that's any better."

"God, I hate tough meat." He cut fiercely.

"Don't swear, John."

"What's for dessert?" He shoved his plate aside.

"Apple upside-down cake." Anne had made it.

"Just bring me coffee." He had not eaten cake in years.

"You used to eat cake." Silently she remembered their courtship.

"I used to stand on my head." And he drifted off into his own melancholy again, unable to admit that he had lost an important account.

The children were silent. Thom stared at the red and white squares on the tablecloth and scraped some dried gravy from a spot next to the potato bowl. Jim could see his face in the mirror on the walnut buffet across the room. The blessed candles were flanking a blue glass crucifix he had won in a school raffle, and a fragment of palm was tucked behind it. There was a handle missing from one of the buffet drawers. The folded ironing board was still standing in the corner of the pantry and a pile of clothes waited to be dampened near the broken mangle. The sudden tension was unbearable.

"What happened in school today?" Margaret asked quietly to dispel the mood. Jack knew she was talking to him. It was time for a Ben Whalen story about eating salamanders on lettuce and releasing snakes in science class.

Margaret was laughing nervously, one eye on John Patrick, uncertain if his mood were too deep for the distraction.

"Didn't Ben get sick?" She put her hand over her mouth when Jack said that raw salamander improves the eyesight, and Anne began to giggle. Tim gurgled and spit his potatoes. Since John Patrick continued silently sucking on his cigarette and drinking coffee, Jack was comfortable with the performance.

"All right, clown! Finish your meal." John Patrick turned to Margaret. "I'll have some gravy bread." She jumped up and went to the kitchen to heat the gravy. "Some hot coffee, too." Soon they were all smiling.

They never really knew him. They knew he was proud to be Irish. They knew he read the paper to shreds, worked the crossword puzzle every day and never consulted a dictionary. They knew he worked long hours, never had a missing button, and said his night prayers alone in the parlor, his hands resting on the lace covering of the gateleg table where the statue of the Sacred Heart surveyed the room. They also knew that he was not ever to be trifled with. There were moments he crept from shadows, handsome, smiling, proud and alive, but soon again he was tired and overworked, laconic and distant. Lost in a world they didn't really understand.

In 1942, the wartime prosperity enabled John Patrick to buy a summer cottage at Lake Watseka, some fifteen miles northwest of Kirkwood. He showed it to Margaret only after he had decided.

"It's beautiful, John. And so good for the children." She was beginning to be worried about Jack's friends and the lipstick she had seen on his collars.

Jim was delighted with the prospect of the solitude and the exciting swampland at the north end of the lake. Sandy would go wild over the mud turtles and bullfrogs.

The same year, John Patrick purchased a 1936 Oldsmobile that had only twelve thousand miles on it, confident that it would get them through the war. The move to Lake Watseka required it, for Margaret would not forsake her daily mass with Thom and Anne, and since there was only a small mission church at the lake, served on Sundays by Saint Raphael, they would need a second car. Besides, Jack had a summer job and Thom was hoping to play baseball. John Patrick even permitted Jack to get his driver's license to relieve his own and Margaret's chauffeuring duties.

John Patrick looked forward to the cool lake breeze

after a stifling Michigan day selling insurance. The business had grown, necessitating a new young agent and an additional secretary, and John Patrick expected to have more time for leisure. He dreamed eagerly of the day when Jack would join him in business.

"That wild redhead will sell the hell out of these Dutchmen," McNulty agreed. "Moerdyke won't turn him down!"

"Especially if he plays for Notre Dame."

Notre Dame was the ultimate for John Patrick Maguire. A losing season in South Bend would have made him question the divinity of Christ. He was finally able to afford tickets to their games, and South Bend was only some sixty miles from Kirkwood. He always took McNulty and one of the boys, and it never crossed his mind that Margaret would enjoy going. To the boys, of course, it was nirvana. Notre Dame had never been stronger. Jack and Thom mimicked the fake stutter of the famed quarterback, Angelo Bertelli, and Jim was always excited about spending a whole day with his father.

Actually, John Patrick made a sincere effort to share himself with each of his sons. He and Jack and Thom always listened to the radio broadcasts of football games and boxing matches. Joe Louis was now a hero, and the three of them fought blow by blow when Louis whipped Tony Galento. They only let their allegiance to the Brown Bomber wane when he fought Billy Conn, a dark-haired Irishman, and won a close decision that left John Patrick and his sons screaming and exhausted. Jim was not a boxing enthusiast, but he laughed with John Patrick every Sunday evening over the groans of Jack Benny and the meanderings of Fred Allen down his famed alley. John Patrick exempted himself from the "Catholic Hour" when Fulton J. Sheen attacked Marx and Freud and tried to tell people how to live. It was a command performance for everyone else in the family, even Jack—when he was not out challenging Kirkwood.

Of course there were fights. Anne complained continually, out of the hearing of John Patrick, because she was expected to help with all the housework while the boys did nothing but clean the basement and garage. Jack tormented Jim, his childhood roommate, ordering

Jim to shine his shoes and hiding Jim's homework assignments. John Patrick was forced to move Thom in with Jack, letting Jim share a room with Tim. Anne had her own room, filled with madonnas and assorted holy cards for good behavior and spelldown victories. In general, the Maguires survived without serious incident.

Although Jim wished he could share the room with Thom, he wasn't able to tell him so. It was not the Maguire way.

Margaret loved her children through a tireless service that cooked and sewed, typed compositions and said prayers from morning till night. John Patrick loved them by rising up every morning to take on Kirkwood and the world.

In the spring of 1942—Jack's sophomore year—John Patrick was still riding the crest of his son's football prowess that had sparked an undefeated season. Even a warning from the principal that Jack had skipped school on successive afternoons warranted only a mild rebuke from his father.

"He'll never be a scholar," he told McNulty.

"He'd be a great fighter!" McNulty still had hopes of training a champion.

John Patrick sucked his cigarette angrily. "Nowadays that's for niggers and dumb dagos! Jack'll be my salesman—after Notre Dame."

"Margaret and Doyle might make him a priest."

"Margaret would have me a priest. Hell, he's too much man for the priesthood." He smiled proudly. "Besides, the ladies like him. This one will be my football player."

There was a reverence for gridiron greats even at the high school level. It did not matter that they never went on to college or how they spent the next thirty years. When they attended a parish dinner or walked from Sunday mass there was always someone who remembered the time Saint Raphael's beat Springfield in the rain. Two concussions, a broken leg, and a recovered fumble in the last seven seconds! When Jack was in grade school, the hero of the high school team was an all-state fullback named Charlie Davenport. He was six foot four, 225 pounds, and he could run the hundred in eleven seconds. A young Jack never dared more than a nervous

"Hi," but when Jack was in high school, he and John Patrick ran into Davenport one day after Sunday mass. He had been exempted from the army because of bad knees.

"How's it going, Charlie?" John Patrick was thrilled to see him.

"Same old shit, man. Three kinds!" He looked at young Jack. His eyes seemed sad, almost frightened. "You're doing okay, I hear." Jack grinned. He knew Charlie had seen every game.

John Patrick instinctively tried to encourage him. "Still hauling sinks and toilets, eh?" He was a plumber's assistant. "Get your own license one of these days."

"Yeh, that's what I'll do." His speech was slow, his posture hunched and mooselike, and he had gained forty pounds. There was a scar above his right eye, and John Patrick remembered the Davis Tech game. He had come back in the second half with nine stitches to score three times. It hurt to see the brown curly hair thinning and one front tooth chipped and partially discolored.

"I'll never forget the Tech game. No one could stop you that night." John Patrick's eyes shone and he grazed Charlie's shoulder with an affectionate punch.

"I had a real great line." Just like the interviews with the *Gazette* in the old days. "A real great line—a truck coulda gone through. A lotta desire, that's what it takes, a lotta desire." He slouched against a car in the parking lot and John Patrick chuckled and feinted another pair of awkward punches.

"You made holes that weren't there, Bronk."

"Hey, you remember the old nickname." His smile revealed another decayed tooth.

"See you around."

There was a poetry to football when it worked. In one game, Jack scored a touchdown on a kickoff. He didn't know how it happened, but suddenly the field opened and there was no one in front of him. The crowd began to rise and roar, and for the last thirty yards he was fast and alone. Teammates surrounded him, their hands beating tattoos of congratulations.

He had died and gone to heaven. So had John Patrick.

Nor did he ever forget walking through the crowd after

the game, his father's face flushed with excitement, the booming voice finally hoarse. McNulty called it a "hell of a run," and even Bronk Davenport walked up and slapped him on the shoulder. Grade school kids stared when he walked up to take communion before a game or waited at the bus stop. Monsignor Doyle went out of his way to say hello, and the nuns beamed respect. He neglected schoolwork for a week and rehashed the game with John Patrick and McNulty a dozen times.

Football was a way out, and Jack understood this almost as clearly as his father. He did not belong to himself, nor did he have the freedom to fail. He had to get even with Kirkwood and America, to play for Notre Dame, to earn the respect his father never got and thus to take away the pain. Most of all, he had to become a success. To be a teacher or plumber was to be a failure. A Bronk Davenport could fail, not a Maguire.

It was an edict. Make money, but beware of the rich. Get educated, but shun intellectuals. Work hard, but go to school so you won't have to. It all made sense in the paradoxical way the Irish understood America. It was praising the priest even as they hated him. Loving the country even as they despised its injustice, and laughing at endless jokes, even as they lived with a quiet despair.

Margaret, however, seldom understood jokes except slapstick and giddy ones, then she laughed to tears as if some sealed faucet had burst. She had more reason to be serious, since the salvation of the family rested in her disciplined body—as in a fragile vessel. Every baby was both a blessing and a challenge from God, and the moral character of the child was determined by the personal devotion of a mother to her faith. Each new birth was carefully noted and remembered, and most devout women could recall the time span between brothers and sisters in any active family in the parish. The men were not so attentive, John Patrick least of all. He had his own family's success to preoccupy him, and when things went well he was indifferent to anyone else's triumphs or failures. In times of deep disappointment, petty gossip was of no comfort to him. Increasingly, only alcohol seemed capable of alleviating his despair.

In the early stages of his drinking, he smiled expansively, gave Margaret rumpled money from his pockets, rubbed Jim's head, and kidded Jack with special warmth. And embraced his giggling, protesting wife. They liked his soft hands and the smell of his body. He gave them money for a movie and told Thom how handsome he was and even charmed Anne while Tim sat contentedly in his lap. Only gradually did he become bitter and angry, finally attacking Margaret and the Church. A few times during the war years, he even invaded the family in the parlor and made silly remarks during the Hail Marys or mimicked Monsignor Doyle's brogue. He fabricated ridiculous mysteries of the rosary: "The fifth sorrowful mystery: Mary and Joseph get caught in a terrible snowstorm." He laughed uproariously.

Margaret was filled with hate and hurt. He disgusted her at such times, and all the children but Jack were afraid of him. Somehow, Jack understood that whiskey was John Patrick's therapy, his avenging angel and lover all at once. After such intrusions, John Patrick would laugh and stumble from the parlor, staggering on the oval loop rug in the doorway and settling in his recliner. The drone of the prayers continued; there was no way to win such a solemn contest and soon he would fall asleep and begin snoring. Loudly.

In spite of himself, Jack giggled.

Margaret and the others never did.

When he seemed tired and graying as he neared fifty, she had him and she knew it. Yet when she saw the distant look in his eyes, she knew she had lost him and clung to her God. What else was there? She could only love John Patrick with a furtive glance or in his absence. She was hardly a wife, but his long-suffering multi-mother. He lived alone. Even the children belonged to her. They were always hers and would be until they died. He was separate, stubborn and difficult, and Jack was his only son.

In 1942, the athletic awards banquet was held on Saint Patrick's Day in the parish gym. Green and white crepe paper, leprechauns on the long wooden tables, bowls of green mints, lime Jell-O with shredded carrots, corned beef and cabbage, hot rolls and cold beer. A special exemption from Lent. John Patrick accepted the plaudits for his oldest son who had brought Saint Raphael's a football trophy. Monsignor Doyle was thrilled, and the war and private troubles were forgotten for a day.

"Give the tyke seconds. He's got a stomach like a flour barrel."

"A tapeworm he has."

The men were frolicking. Dancing a jig. The ladies in aprons were laughing and Margaret was unusually beautiful. The little boys threw each other's hats through the baskets, and no one complained. Loud singing—"Oh, my name is McNamara"—and the sound of dishes. The Notre Dame song with John Patrick leading—way off-key.

The Maguires were proud of their father on such days. He was at home among his own and seemed strong and unafraid; the brooding melancholy was gone and Margaret did not carp at him. He put his arm around everyone, and the children giggled as shyly as she did. He was as loud and boorish as he wanted to be, as profane and brash as the parish hall allowed. He held his chin high and circled the crowd, basking in the glory he had dreamed of all his life.

John Patrick, with his arm draped around Jack, circled the hall a dozen times, pausing to joke with each group. Then he accused Monsignor Doyle of getting fat, and they shared a private snort in the kitchen. It was the ultimate respectability.

The summer of 1942 at Lake Watseka was everything John Patrick had hoped, especially when Jack's shouts and unbridled laughter erupted across the water, roaring along with the firecrackers on the Fourth of July, bellowing with Thom and Jim in water fights, patiently teaching Tim to dive and swim, tormenting Anne with ice cubes dripping down her back in roasting sunshine, prodding his brothers to new and dangerous feats. As their swimming improved, it was Jack who initiated exciting turtle hunts around the lake.

Gradually the brothers learned the turtles' habits and captured dozens of them in open water, diving beneath webbed feet and squat legs that struggled to get away. Jim or Thom emerged to Jack's triumphant shouts, turtle in hand, and tossed the clawing victim into a large corrugated tub on the Maguires' dock. Then Jack dived in the water to catch the biggest snapping turtle of all as John Patrick sipped his beer and grinned proudly on the shore.

To Jack it was only an adventure, but Jim and Thom were more curious about the exciting varieties of strange, ancient life. Jim fed his turtles ant eggs and flies or bits of fish and whole minnows, studying their habits with passionate interest, then releasing them. Thom was only interested in the challenge of the catch, but Jack liked to tease and torment the turtles, and on the Fourth of July he held out a zebra cartridge to an angry rubber back who snatched it in a locked overbite. Jack lit the fuse, and the turtle's head flew off, the once-proud body twitching convulsively on the gravel near a WPA drainage ditch. A crowd of Jack's young admirers cheered over Jim's protests, and Thom got sick to his stomach. When Jack threatened to repeat the horror on Jim's camelbacks in the garage, Jim released them from the dock just before Jack threw him in the water.

During the following fall in his junior year, Jack's life changed dramatically. A fight in the locker room with Mickey Crotty started it.

"Put my towel back, Crotty. You didn't ask—"

"Adams took my towel."

"That's between you and Adams." Jack ripped the towel from his hands and began drying himself. Crotty snatched it back, and Jack knocked him over a wooden bench against the green metal locker. Cutting the back of his head.

Coach Art Doolan, once a great halfback and now a successful dentist, heard the commotion. "What the hell's going on?" He saw the blood from Crotty's head and glowered at Jack.

"Save that shit for the game, Maguire. Get dressed and get your ass out of here."

"Not till I get my towel."

"I said *now.*"

Jack's face was beet red, and his eyes narrowed. "And I said not till I get my towel."

Doolan moved quickly toward him, grabbed his clothes, and threw them out the door; then he spun Jack around and pushed him across the room.

It seemed to happen in an instant. Jack charged Doolan

with a fierce tackle and splattered him back over a bench and into the lockers. The coach pulled himself up and struck Jack a glancing blow on the forehead. Jack countered with two fierce blows to the face, blackening Doolan's left eye and knocking him momentarily unconscious; then he dressed slowly, picked up his towel, and moved toward the door.

Doolan sat up groggily on the bench and rubbed his eye. "Take your gear, Maguire, you're all through." There were still three games left if they were to have an unbeaten season.

"Give it to the nuns." Then he walked out the door.

John Patrick was furious, and Margaret was "mortified to death." A meeting with Monsignor Doyle unraveled the facts, and Jack agreed to apologize publicly to the football team and privately to Coach Doolan. He was permitted to remain in school.

"Only because of your parents," said Monsignor Doyle.

Privately, John Patrick admitted to McNulty, "He's too damn much like me."

"He can still play for Notre Dame. They got lots of boys who never did shit in high school." McNulty paused. "He'd make a hell of a fighter—"

They both laughed and sipped more Old Grand Dad. And were secretly pleased when Saint Raphael's lost its last two games.

Jack had a special relationship with the eleven-year-old Thom. There was enough difference in their ages to prevent the fierce competitiveness, somehow instilled by John Patrick and Margaret, that had marred Jack's friendship with Jim. Thom was the only natural athlete in the family and did easily what Jim struggled with and Jack accomplished with brute power. Jack encouraged Thom's vocation for the priesthood and was generous with his assistance and affection. Thom was crushed when Jack was dismissed from the team.

"You should learn something from it," Jack said.

"What?" Thom asked.

"Control your temper. That's what!"

"But Coach Doolan hit you first."

"Hey! You're gonna be the priest. Turn the other cheek—" He laughed. "Doolan did and I belted him."

Thom giggled. Jim overheard their intimacy and felt a familiar jealousy. He was also upset that all the fuss over Jack had made his own achievement on the junior varsity team seem inconsequential. As if Jack's failures were more exciting than Jim's success.

For the remainder of his junior year, Jack was far more docile and subdued. When he was forbidden by Coach Doolan to play varsity basketball, he spent more time romancing sexy Maria Anselmo and drinking beer with Steve Danaher at the Maguire cottage on Lake Watseka—even though John Patrick had sternly forbidden it. He admitted the secret drinking bouts to Thom but said nothing about the time spent with Maria. Thom was aware, however, that he avoided the family rosary and seldom received communion. One night when Jack came in late, Thom was still awake.

"You want to go to confession with me?" It was as direct as Thom could be.

"Sure, why not?"

The following day Thom noted that Jack was in the confessional for several minutes. He was delighted when Jack received communion at Sunday mass and joined in the family rosary. Once Thom stopped Jack in the driveway when Steve Danaher was standing there waiting impatiently.

Thom was almost in tears. "Won't you say the family rosary first?"

"C'mon, Jack, the beer's getting warm!" called his friend.

"How about tomorrow night instead?" Jack said to Thom.

"It'll only take ten minutes."

Jack grinned, mussed Thom's hair gently, and motioned Danaher into the house. "Get your beads out, Steve. The little padre's gonna save your soul."

Of course Margaret was pleased. John Patrick read the paper in his leather chair, lost in his unspoken sadness.

The following year Jack was expelled from school for drawing a caricature of a nun with bare breasts and a cluster of pubic hair. John Patrick slapped him across the face and then got drunk. Again, Monsignor Doyle readmitted him since it was close to graduation, but his marks had slipped badly and with them any serious hope of going to college. Two months later at baccalaureate, Jack wore his tennis shoes, muttered "Thanks, pop" to Monsignor Doyle for his diploma, then went to the cottage with the lusty Maria and stayed drunk for two days. When John Patrick finally found him, Maria hid naked in the bathroom and Jack greeted his father with a drunken grin.

John Patrick blackened his eye, angrily delivered Maria to her mother, along with some eloquent advice, then joined McNulty at the Shamrock. He lectured about "dago bitches with no morals" until he was drunk, then admitted that he wouldn't mind a "taste of that sweet little ass" himself. When he arrived home after midnight, Margaret screamed that his example was responsible for all Jack's problems. Even Thom's vocation to the priesthood was in jeopardy.

"Monsignor Doyle may forbid it." She was heartbroken, and she demanded that he stop drinking. Jack and the oblivious young Tim slept through it all. Thom and Jim chatted nervously in the kitchen.

"It won't hurt your priesthood. It's not your fault," Jim told him.

"It doesn't matter. I won't leave mother in this mess!"

"Staying home won't make dad quit drinking, but high school might be fun." Jim had just begun to notice a busty Connie Hackett.

"I don't want to lose my vocation." Thom, now almost thirteen, had grown more serious, and his intense young spirit felt Margaret's pain personally.

Jim sensed his distress. "I can take care of things at home. Don't worry about it! Sometimes Dad just needs to drink."

Thom was at the point of tears, but he appreciated Jim's strength. "I just don't understand why he does it!"

Jim's eyes were suddenly soft and distant. "Maybe he's lonely."

Thom, not sure what Jim meant, made no comment. Then he joined a weeping Margaret in the rosary, knowing that only the priesthood could bring him the peace that seemed to elude his parents.

A week after the Allied invasion of Normandy in 1944, John Patrick instructed Jack to enlist.

McNulty agreed. "It'll settle him down. Notre Dame will take him as an ex-GI."

When Margaret overruled, John Patrick was glad to have Jack at home. They bet on baseball games and sat up late drinking beer on the porch at Lake Watseka, and John Patrick revealed more of his life to Jack than Margaret ever knew.

John Patrick seemed alive again, and Margaret made little comment about their drinking. She knew it was useless to complain, and, besides, his business continued to prosper with the war.

Jack, however, still too young to join his father's business, was having difficulty holding a job. He worked for a week as a carpenter's helper, got angry at an arrogant boss, and boarded him up in a closet overnight. He then lost two more positions. The first was as a grinder's assistant in a sausage factory, and he was fired when he spat into a fresh batch "for flavor." The second was as a Fuller Brush salesman, and he held the job successfully for four weeks, breaking all sales records, until a husband came home early one day to find Jack in bed with his young wife.

"I don't know where I went wrong," said Margaret.

In August 1944, when the Allied troops were already in southern France and John Patrick insisted the war would soon be over, Margaret agreed to permit Jack to enlist to avoid the draft. Her other children were still a source of great satisfaction, and after a novena for peace to our Lady of Fatima, she dreamed of Jack in a dark uniform. It was a heavenly sign. She was also especially pleased when Monsignor Doyle agreed that Thom could enter Saint Robert's Seminary in Grandville after he finished eighth grade the following year. Jim, halfway through high school, was a very good student and a decent athlete, and he looked like a solid college prospect. Anne was still a precise all-A student, and John Patrick nicknamed her Mother Superior after she refused to sit on his lap because he "smelled like beer bottles." Timothy, just short of three, a plump replica of John Patrick, remained a content, friendly child who liked to sit on his father's lap and, much to John Patrick's delight, refused to learn the prayers that nine-year-old Anne struggled to teach him. Even when she threatened him with purgatory.

A week before Jack was to leave for the navy, Margaret was crestfallen.

John Patrick reassured her. "It's not like there's a war. He can use the discipline."

McNulty gave him a month.

John Patrick laughed. "The navy's had Maguires before."

The Sunday before Jack's departure, Margaret had planned that the family would all attend rosary and evening benediction at Saint Raphael's to pray for lasting peace and her son's welfare.

Jack refused.

"It wouldn't hurt you to join the family." She wanted John Patrick to intervene, but he said nothing.

As Margaret and the others drove off from the cottage, Steve Danaher appeared. They shared a beer with John Patrick and then left for a dance at the Crooked Lake Pavilion.

At benediction, Margaret crossed herself before the upraised monstrance and prayed for her errant son. In the afternoon she had seen a strange shadow near the dogwood tree in front of the cottage, and she was again troubled when a faceless old man in a long black coat briefly blocked their exit from the church parking lot. She was very relieved to arrive safely back at the cottage.

Late that same night, when John Patrick was snoring the guttural rhythms of alcohol and deep sleep, she heard the wind moaning in the twisted willow at the lake shore. She moved to the bedroom window and saw another strange shadow drift across the placid water in the moonlight. She knelt and crossed herself devoutly, said three Hail Marys and soon fell asleep.

At two o'clock the same morning, Margaret's 1936 Olds rolled off the lake road at the end of an S curve and ricocheted off three large oak trees near Kelly's bait house. Jack Maguire and Steve Danaher were killed instantly.

Kelly called the sheriff who recognized the car and notified John Patrick for positive identification. The sight of Jack's red hair crushed against the shattered windshield almost destroyed him. It took an hour to remove the bodies.

Deathly pale and silent, John Patrick drove with the ambulance to Mulaley's Funeral Home in Kirkwood. The coffin would be closed.

When he returned, his eyes were red and almost raw, his face drained. The broad shoulders finally drooped, the firm jaw slackened; he had aged ten years in two hours. Margaret, Thom, and Anne were sobbing helplessly and Jim was ghostly white, staring at the willow tree near the edge of the lake. Tim did not really understand any of it but hugged his father and tenderly stroked the hair on his hands.

John Patrick tried to comfort his family. "The lad was likely headed for trouble. There was no talking to him—" Moisture formed in his eyes and he walked out to the screened-in front porch and burst into tears. He stayed for almost an hour, and no one disturbed him. Then he walked back into the living room and sat in a rocker near the fireplace.

"He was a good boy," he said softly, and then he led the family in prayer, not knowing what else to do.

Margaret could not stop crying. Even the thought of Thom's seminary could not comfort her. An irreplaceable life was gone. Jack had been a beloved failure she could not satisfactorily explain. Three crowded rosaries at Mulaley's and the packed church for the solemn requiem comforted her briefly. Especially when Monsignor Doyle was the celebrant. He talked about God "writing straight with crooked lines," then extolled a young man who loved life and lived long enough to make a family and a parish proud. There was no mention of Art Doolan, or the caricatured nun.

"The whole parish is saddened, and no explanation apart from our holy faith can wipe away the tears."

John Patrick did not hear a word he said, nor was he satisfied with faith's explanation. His beautiful, stubborn, angry Jack was dead. His future salesman and alter ego. There were no words as he struggled with the impossible tragedy, helpless and alone. He sat slumped and motionless in his pew, hating God and refusing to pray, unable to forget the raised fists of a one-year-old redhead.

Margaret continued to weep through the rest of the summer.

John Patrick gave her the time he felt she needed.

Then one day he interrupted her tears at dinner. His voice was firm, and the family stopped eating instantly.

"That's enough grief, Margaret. Do you understand?"

She nodded. No one saw her cry about Jack again.

Only Jim really understood his father's broken heart, and from that moment on he longed to replace Jack.

4

No One's Son

While the long-range B-29 bombers were beating Japan and Taiwan into subjection in the late summer of 1944, James Michael Maguire fought his own private war on the football field to win a silently grieving John Patrick's admiration. Jim was quick and shifty, although only 140 pounds and barely five foot nine, with strong shoulders and thin muscular legs. He just didn't look like a football player, still pale and seemingly fragile, and his misty hazel eyes focused on some unspoken internal struggle. His Margaret-like slouch only really disappeared when he canvassed the woods with Sandy, but he was determined to be a good ballplayer.

The September practice sessions were among the most hated experiences of his life. The horror of calisthenics after the gentle laziness of summer—even though, until Jack's death, he had worked every day on a Lake Watseka milk route—caused grueling anguish. He dived on mythical fumbles, jogged in place and circled the cinder track in the still oppressive Michigan heat, duck waddled and did sit-ups until sadistic coaches released him to the showers where the water was always cold, the towels mildewed, and the conversation usually about the biggest tits or the easiest twat in high school. It also meant pointless time away from Sandy.

He learned to "submarine" linemen on the worn turf behind the goalposts. No certified expert in oriental torture could have been more imaginative than the hostile little assistant coach in the green and white imitation-leather jacket with the frayed *R* on it. Every afternoon as the leaves were changing colors in the woods and the cooler days were inviting new beginnings, his tight mouth and beady eyes prodded boys like cattle in a march to slaughter bins. Jim hated him and his yellow leering teeth.

"Keep your ass down!" He kicked Jim's arms out from under him and sent him sprawling. "What the hell do you think this is, Maguire? A square dance?" Jim wondered why a potential halfback was groveling in a lineman's chores, but questioning was forbidden.

He was told to lunge under two opposing tackles who outweighed him fifty pounds apiece. His throat was dry and rasping, but he made his move on the three count, and a ton of cartilage and bone drove his head into the dirt, snapping his neck.

He lay on the ground for several seconds, afraid to move. He thought of the weekend, when he would be free to wander with Sandy in the woods, to rest in the splendor of Lemmert's Grove and watch the leaves change into all shades of red and gold. There would be no bruised bones or cursing coaches, only the chattering of squirrels as they rushed to store up their treasures for the long Michigan winter. And Sandy's ringing bark of joy accompanied by lapping kisses for his beloved master.

The coach's scream interrupted his reverie. "Jesus Christ, Maguire, they made a monkey of you."

He climbed to his feet, Sandy and his private paradise forgotten. He rearranged his shoulder pads, adjusted the oversized helmet, and lined up again to await the impossible charge.

Again they drove him to the ground like stampeding cattle, and he struggled to his feet.

"Christ, you're stupid. At least you oughta learn some guts! Do it again." He kicked him savagely in the rump. "Try cheerleading!" He goaded the opposition.

Jim tried it again and they fell on him like drowning men thrashing for life. He felt the bite of teeth against his upper lip and blood spurted down his filthy jersey. He walked a few feet away, fighting tears. Wishing he could quit.

"Get back here, asshole! Ain't you never seen blood before?"

Jim wiped the blood and knelt before Moloch and his monsters.

"Get up! We'll try a little three point."

It was a raw test of masculine guts. Three of them formed a triangle of defense with Jim at the vulnerable front. The coach called to a pair of beefy tackles and tossed the first one a ball. He tucked it under his left arm and ran directly at Jim full speed. Jim waited until the last second, threw his body at the charging cleats, and the tackle fell in a heap five yards beyond him. He couldn't get up. Two players helped him off the field, and he heard the shrill voice in the distance: "It's about time I saw some guts around here." Jim had broken his nose and a rib.

Of course Margaret was upset. She forced a gallon of milk on him every day to heal his bones, and she was delighted when he was taped and well enough to practice with the team again. "An idle mind is the devil's workshop," and a healthy young man not playing football could only be smothered in immoral thoughts. A couple of broken bones was a paltry price to pay for salvation.

He was never able to impress his father as Jack had done although he became a swift, gutsy halfback who got his letter near the end of his junior year. No matter what he accomplished, he was compared to the bigger and stronger Jack, whose memory was magnified in death.

"They don't give you the ball much."

"Burns is faster than I am."

"A Maguire doesn't take second place."

Jim disappeared out the side door and wandered alone in the woods with Sandy. When he returned for dinner, John Patrick was still talking about the game.

"McNulty says you start too slow." John Patrick stood up from his chair. "Find the hole and cut to the sidelines. Thom does it naturally." Thom was the triple-threat star of the eighth-grade team and already was almost Jim's size.

Margaret felt Jim's hurt. "Just do the best you can. That's all God expects." She didn't really believe it and was humiliated when he fumbled during the next week's game.

Jim finally scored near the end of the season on a three-yard sweep against Saint Mary's of Sheffield, but it reminded a tearful John Patrick of the night Jack had dragged the left side of Saint Mary's line into the end zone.

At such moments, Jim knew he belonged to no one, even himself.

As for all Catholic boys of the time, there was still some pressure from Margaret and the nuns for him to be a priest. What finally deterred him was not only Thom's more obvious suitability, but an implicit suspicion among Irish men—rarely, if ever, openly expressed—that the priest was not really a man, and even as an altar boy Jim was uneasy in silken surplices.

But it was Thom's childhood decision that seemed to free him. Already in eighth grade, Thom was avoiding the necking parties, appeasing God and Margaret with cluttered devotions and sacristy duties assigned by the nuns. Although Thom was respected as an exceptional student and extraordinary athlete, and two dozen grade school girls considered him irresistible, even his classmates acknowledged his vocation. They were as ashamed to talk dirty in his presence as if Monsignor Doyle himself were listening. He did not neck in the cloakroom or even flirt on the playground, and the parties he attended did not include spin the bottle. When it appeared that Monsignor Doyle might delay his seminary to comfort his parents over Jack's death, it didn't really change anything. Assuredly, Thom would be the priest.

When Bishop Schmidt came from Sheffield to administer confirmation in the parish, Doyle drew his favorite altar boy aside after the ceremony and displayed him to the prelate as if Thom were the child of his own celibacy.

"This one hits like Gehrig and throws like Mickey Cochrane himself. Even got a bit of brain in him. It's a pity he can't sing."

Thom blushed and smiled that shy O'Brien smile.

"God knows we need good priests," said the grinning bishop. Margaret's joy knew no bounds: God had visited His people.

When there were funerals at midmorning, at monsignor's request Thom was exempted from school to serve, and he occasionally assisted on sick calls when the priest attended the old folks at Donner's Rest Home. The nuns at school never objected. Monsignor had called, and Thomas Aloysius Maguire, an obedient, gifted student, would one day be a consecrated priest.

Even though Jim felt no real attraction for the priesthood, Margaret and the Church enlarged his teen-aged struggle to such a point that thoughts of the priesthood remained for a time a kind of oasis from increasingly frequent occasions of sin. One night, Jim, exhausted from scrimmage, was embracing his pillow when Margaret came to check on night prayers.

"You shouldn't lie on your pillow that way. It could be sinful pleasure."

Jim was confused. "It helps me sleep."

"Say your beads for the poor souls in purgatory."

When he protested that he already had, she was ready.

"Twice won't kill you. Jack may need your prayers."

He felt the pressure of God in his stomach, but he was too frightened to hate Him or question his mother. The next day she gave him a confusing Jesuit pamphlet that detailed the categories of "venereal pleasure" and more fully awakened him to the universe of sexual sin. It was Margaret's pamphlet, as well as the conversations in the locker room, that introduced puberty.

Thus began the endless torture of "impure thoughts and desires" and intricate Jesuit rules to decide when "consent" had been given. Soon the idea of going to confession became like a nightmare, and Jim lived in constant fear of death and hell. A billboard showed a touch of summer cleavage and provided enough mortal sins of "thought" and "desire" to engulf a thousand hells. He looked away, then committed a second sin by taking a backward glance. To say nothing of his thoughts for the remainder of the day. It was always impossible to distinguish thoughts from desires, and then to count them for the next confession—two days after each previous one. He kept a blue "Big 5" tablet in his back pocket and tabulated the sins with meticulous accuracy, and he wondered if the priesthood would deliver him from his new agony.

"Bless me, father, I had 114 impure thoughts. Gave full consent and partial consent 97 times."

"How long has it been since your last confession?"

"Three days, father."

"You are scrupulous."

"Is that sinful too?"

The priest was patient. "It's not unusual to have impure thoughts, but you probably didn't consent to them."

The "probably" destroyed him.

"How can I know, father?"

"Did you get an erection?"

"A what?"

The Maguires call it a "nana" so he didn't know what was meant. "I don't think so."

"Then don't worry about it. You're just a normal young man."

His fears became compounded, and he was constantly trying to determine if his penis was getting hard when he was eating breakfast. Even playing football. Confession relieved him for an afternoon or so, then the tortuous cycle began when he saw an African nipple in *Life* magazine at the dentist's office or studied the bulge under Connie Hackett's loose sweater. He wanted to talk to his father, but the defeat of Thomas Dewey and another four years of Roosevelt had brought back the memory of Jack's death and left John Patrick morose and drinking in the leather chair. Only four-year-old Tim was free to entertain him, for even John Patrick couldn't ignore the gentle blue eyes that loved everyone.

Somehow, Jim recovered from the madness of conscience when, during the leisurely week between football and basketball seasons, he finally surrendered to masturbation. Showering athletes who laughed about "jerking off" and persistent visions of Connie Hackett's bare treasures flopping helplessly under her red sweater had kept him in almost constant sexual excitation. It could not have happened if he had not inherited Jack's room and would not have happened if he were not exhausted from practice.

As his pillow was gradually transformed into a suddenly naked Connie, he buried his chest in her softness and began stroking his own erection with a free hand. It was only a matter of moments before he stained Margaret's sheets with the sinful evidence. The intense pleasure seemed incredible, and helplessly he started the cycle again, struggling not to cry out. Only then did the fear and guilt release as he jumped up to wash away the sticky stains from the sheets and his pajamas. He fell to his knees. He knew that his soul would burn in hell until the final Judgment Day when his terrified flesh would rejoin his spirit. Bodiless or in full dress, hell was utter horror, and he feared death that very night. He had to make a perfect act of contrition, since fear of hell was not enough to take away his mortal sin without confession. Only if he were sorry for offending God would the fetid rot of his sin be removed. He recited his devout act of contrition. But how could he be sure that it was not the fear of hell's flame that motivated his sorrow? He shivered in the cold room, knowing that Thom would be disgusted by his weakness, and focused again on his sorrow for hurting God.

He pictured the blood on Jesus's face, the muscle-bound Roman soldiers scowling, Mary weeping. He added phrases to the traditional formula. "God, I'm really sorry I nailed Jesus to the cross." Hell's fire reappeared. No good. He tried again, then got out his rosary and kissed the wounds passionately. "God, I'm awful sorry." Even his guardian angel wasn't convinced. Defeated, he crawled back into the icy sheets. Only confession could really free him. Somehow, he went to sleep and did not die in the night. Which gave him something to thank God for during his morning prayers. Grateful that he could go to confession the next afternoon.

Although he was certainly not Thom, Jim was a devout and serious Catholic. He received communion daily, which required a complete fast without food or water from the previous midnight. It also meant a cold breakfast of egg salad sandwiches and lukewarm milk, which Margaret gratefully packed, with only five minutes to gulp it down between morning mass and school. It meant as well a chance to follow Connie Hackett's almost olive legs up the aisle with his hands folded and his head properly bowed to get the best view. While Thom's eyes were certainly on God.

Jim's spiritual development seemed to him much like football, requiring sacrifice, self-denial, conditioning, routine rituals, and abundant grace. Mysterious and unpredictable "grace."

Grace was everywhere. Although it was a gift from God, it could not be earned. Prayer might bring it, but not for certain. Sacraments did if he put no obstacles in the way. If he sinned, he either didn't have enough grace or he ignored what he had. No one really said that Protestants and Jews couldn't get grace, but Jim doubted seriously that his Dutch neighbors ever did.

It was for him a part of the wonderful esoteric language known only to Catholics—purgatory, limbo, indulgences, gifts of the Holy Ghost, capital sins, and venereal pleasure. And at times, the sacred semantics even produced practical benefits.

He was walking home from school one spring day

when he met a bullying Catholic boy who attended public school, a certain sign of weak faith. He and his friends decided to rough Jim up.

"All dressed up pretty?" The boy shoved Jim.

Since there was no honorable way to back off, Jim prepared to fight. Surrounded by the enemy, he looked at the Catholic boy, who did not appear sympathetic though he probably realized that God disapproved of his public school.

"I want to talk to you," Jim said softly.

"So talk."

"I mean alone." He fought the tears.

They walked a few feet from the circle.

"I just went to confession. I'm in the state of grace."

He looked at Jim through a quiet kind of shock.

"Yeh, so I don't want to fight." He hoped his trembling legs didn't show under the corduroy knickers.

"Yeh." The boy turned to the others. "Let's go, you guys."

"You gonna let him get away?"

"Let's go!" He glanced sheepishly at Jim who walked away casually until they were out of sight.

Jim ran the rest of the way home and mentioned it to no one, afraid that Margaret would have chided him for refusing martyrdom and John Patrick for running from a fight.

During basketball season of his junior year, Jim graduated from fantasy and masturbation. And his innocent childhood religion. After a game and dance, Jim got involved with Connie Hackett. Even as a varsity substitute, he had plenty of prestige, and Connie beamed at his green letter sweater when he finally asked her to dance. The occasional electricity of a pointed breast brushing his chest made him tremble. His hands sweated, and he found it more difficult than usual to talk. Somehow he walked her home. It was a cold night in January and Connie suggested a visit to the shed to sneak a cigarette before she went to bed. Jim, in training, declined; then he succumbed. Their very first kiss seemed "passionate," according to the description in the Jesuit pamphlet. He continued to neck chastely, still on the alert for "passion," until Connie's resistance became the norm. When she backed away momentarily, he feared he had stepped over the vague line that threatened her virginity.

"We mustn't."

"I wasn't. Were you?" This was a move on Jim's part, handing her the moral dilemma.

"Just go easy." She moved a snow shovel out of the way.

He brushed his elbow against her breast. She seemed not to notice. The moral issue was focused rather on the power of his kiss, so he kissed very gently and began massaging her breast as completely as one can with an elbow. He was instantly erect, and he stretched his penis against her thigh.

"That's better," she said, pushing the shovel farther away and kissing devoutly.

He discovered that Catholic girls needed a theological defense to salvage self-respect. Later in the winter Jim moved to even more pleasurable extremes by advancing suitable theological commentaries, especially if he took responsibility for their actions.

Connie first taught him this in the shed the night of a Mardi Gras celebration. It was the first time Jim had tasted wine since Jack had given him a sip from a mass cruet. He kissed her firmly on the lips and pulled her against his groin, noticing that the shed had been neatly rearranged.

"We shouldn't." She moved her foot away from the lawn mower.

His primitive Jesuitical dialogue was ready.

"Don't worry. I'm strong tonight. I went to confession today. My passions are under control." He said it quite seriously. It was the calming idiom.

He felt her body give way, then he began working his hand under her skirt, her panties. She stiffened. "You're going too far!" The language was significant. Not "we." "He" was. It was important that he stay in command.

"There's nothing wrong with touching. That's no sin. It's venereal pleasure that's wrong." He was addressing both their consciences, and he was a Maguire and a good student. With a brother who would be a priest.

"Buneareal pleasure?"

"Well—like—if we took off our clothes and I started and—and we went all the way."

She shuddered, ignoring the lawn mower against her ankle.

"I respect you. I don't want your sin on my conscience." She relaxed and he felt her breasts surrender softly against his letter sweater.

"Let's lie down." His instinct told him he must move quickly after each theological victory—for both their sakes—so he frantically cleared more space in the shed. Connie helped. He began rubbing his fingers up her bare thighs, occasionally fingering the rim of her panties as if by accident. He studied her breathing. On one of his massaging motions he felt the moisture between her legs and noted the freedom with which she kissed. He swiftly slipped his hands under her panties and began playing with startling new softness.

"You shouldn't do that. It's wrong. Oh God, it must be wrong! Don't—you said you wouldn't—!"

Jim could no longer help himself. "Don't consent to it!" he urged. "Just enjoy it." Even at that age his theological subtlety was worthy of an Augustine or an Aquinas, and the innate strength of his casuistry was that, at that moment, he believed all of it.

"It's okay. As long as we don't give in—to venereal pleasure." He took her hand and rubbed it against the bulge of his young penis.

"You shouldn't do that," she said breathlessly, but she now made no effort to take her hand away. She was his disciple. "Isn't it sinful?" The impasse had arrived.

"Not if I don't come." Having exhausted his theology, he had to think of something.

"How will I know?"

"I'll tell you." But he didn't, either time.

That consoled her, and there were no more discussions. A few weeks later, after the Saint Patrick's Day banquet, she put her lips to his penis as spontaneously as a nursing child. He was stunned since she did it without invitation or theological epigrams, and through the following months she was bolder in her explorations than was he; but, of course, they never had intercourse. Such freedom would emerge only after more sophisticated education.

Conscience, however, troubled him most painfully at the end of a long evening of petting—despite glib arguments in the heat of encounter. The next day he was not able to concentrate until he went to confession. Once he came upon the youngest priest, Father Kenelley, practicing his putting in the parish garage. Jim had come to request absolution, and he could not wait until the regular weekend hours. The priest's lean muscled body and the gently disciplined mouth of the newly ordained were an implicit reproach. He tapped an eight footer into the metal hole, pulled a stole from his glove compartment, and wiped away Jim's sins. Then he resumed his putting.

Connie, like most young Catholic girls, was less susceptible to the fear of sexual sin. Her body was more in tune with her psyche, or perhaps she had the simple awareness that she loved him enough to marry him and bear children—eleven if he chose. Thus she had little guilt as long as her virginity was intact. She never knew the embarrassment he did moments after he had come when the logic of passion had vanished. He had shattered all the heartfelt promises made to God, and he was not even certain that Connie confessed their experiences. Her conscience seemed to rest once she had accepted his theological interpretations although there was no way to know her hurt and loneliness when, at his confessor's insistence, he avoided her without explanation for a week or two at a time.

His own admissions were more agonizing. Some priests were more understanding and human than others, but none of them were easy on sexual offenders, especially recidivists. Through locker room conversation he learned which priests were more or less considerate of sexual deviates, and he made every effort to avoid the stringent ones, but in emergencies he had to take whatever priest was available. Father Grimes, an obese man with split seams under the arms of his cassock and small red eyes, was by far the worst of Monsignor Doyle's regular curates.

"Father, I sinned against purity three times."

"What do you mean, you've sinned against purity? How far did you go? Were you by yourself or with someone else?"

"Someone else, father."

"A girl?" He snorted it.

"Yes."

"Single?"

"Yes."

"Did you have intercourse?" Again the snort, almost a snarl.

"No, father." Actually he did not know what it was.

"Well, what did you do?"

"I kissed her passionately."

"Is that all?"

"No, father. I touched her."

"Where? The breasts?"

"Yes."

"Anywhere else?"

"Yes, father."

"Where? Her legs?"

"Yes."

"Under her clothing?"

"Yes."

"How many times–"

Jim was relieved. The priest didn't ask what with.

"Maybe ten, father. Six long touches and four short—I'm not sure."

"Did she touch you?"

Damn! He thought he wouldn't ask.

"Yes, father."

"Did she make you come?"

"No, father, not then."

"You mean later?"

"On my way home—and later in bed."

"Don't you say your rosary in bed when troubled with impure desires?"

"Yes, father, but it doesn't always work." He had broken a pair recently—he had been holding the beads while masturbating. He chose not to mention it, though he was frightened enough to say anything.

"Have you sinned with this girl before?"

"Yes, father."

"You've got to stay away from her. She's an occasion of sin."

That's when he nobly sacrificed Connie for two weeks and felt the brief, intense joy of young idealism.

"I will, father. But what if I see her in school?"

"Avoid any sinful behavior."

When the priest gave absolution, Jim felt a new day of spring. But eventually a glance at the silhouette of Connie's right tit under her sweater destroyed the reform.

It was back to the confessional after another sweating marathon in the shed.

After one of these humiliating sessions with Father Grimes, Jim finally succeeded in terminating once and for all any thoughts of becoming a priest. Father Grimes had squeezed out of him a description of every twitch of a hand under Connie's dress and had reluctantly agreed to give him one more absolution. It was then that Jim asked him quietly, "Do you think I should be a priest, father?"

There was a long pause. The dark velvet curtain reeked its incense and Jim could smell the Lavoris on Father Grimes's breath. "Do you want to be?"

"Not especially, father, but my brother is going to enter the seminary, and my mother and the nuns often suggest it."

There was silence.

Jim didn't want to make it easy for him in his moment of sudden and unaccustomed power. "I can do hard things, father. I would like to do some good with my life."

"There are many ways to do good, my child." Father Grimes's voice was now tender and priestly. "To raise a family is good. Not everyone can be a priest. God alone decides who is worthy! 'Many are called, but few are chosen.' "

"I wonder if God is calling *me*."

Jim heard the deep sigh. "To have one member called from a family is in itself extraordinary. It's rare that God would call two."

Jim was almost jubilant. He had found a champion to fend off the subtleties of Margaret and the nuns. "Thank you, father."

"Go in peace, my child." He had forgotten to give Jim a penance.

Thom would be Margaret's priest. Jim might still be John Patrick's son.

During the year following Jack's death, Jim grew closer to Thom, throwing a football with him in the yard or practicing basketball on a small court they built in the driveway. They purchased the basket out of their own savings and put it up against the garage one Saturday morning with the help of friends from school and a few Hollanders who had grown friendlier. Thom and Jim challenged two-men teams all afternoon in "winner keeps playing" and lost only once when they were finally exhausted. John Patrick and McNulty drank enough beer to consider it a state championship tournament. Even though Jim recognized that Thom was already a better player, he had never been happier. Talented as he was, Thom was not a show-off, and he was loud in his praise of Jim's quick passes and gutsy rebounding. At the end they gulped ice-cold Pepsis until their bellies ached, and they laughed about everything. Especially about John Patrick and McNulty trying to play "horse."

Even family meals were happier for Jim without the power of Jack's dominance. He talked about basketball practice or fistfights in study hall, and he occasionally imitated Monsignor Doyle's pep talks—much to everyone's enjoyment. Especially John Patrick's. Only when John Patrick slumped over the table in some memory of Jack or was lost in a depression did Jim feel the same pain. Knowing he could never replace his brother.

Margaret's religion did not hurt him as much, except he felt that it rudely estranged him from Thom. It was as if all the closeness they shared came to naught. There was no way to talk about Connie or about his desire to make the basketball team, even though Thom told him he was better than either starting guard. Somehow, everything came to Thom without his really trying, and Jim was ashamed to admit his own struggle. Only Sandy knew. Jim was increasingly restless at mass as his own feelings about God and the Catholic Church, always lurking in the shadows, became more conscious. As if some ancient faith, Irish and pagan, older than popes or Saint Patrick, was boiling to emerge.

It was early morning on a chilly Palm Sunday in Kirkwood in the spring of 1945. The war was winding down as 300,000 Axis soldiers were trapped in the Ruhr Valley in the Battle of the Bulge. The Russians moved through Hungary to meet Tito and crush Hitler from the east. Iwo Jima had fallen to the marines, and Tokyo was but 750 miles away.

Jim Maguire was not concerned about the war or the smiling children and stooped old men and women clutching their bits of blessed palm. He did not see the faces in the packed church as they shouted their hosannas to David's son approaching Jerusalem on a jackass. He squirmed on the wooden kneelers and shuffled during the interminable reading of Saint Matthew's story of the passion and death of Jesus. Even as he twisted his piece of palm in discontent, Margaret knelt at attention, ignoring the pain of aching knees and varicosed ankles, to protest the mob's outrageous choice of Barabbas over the gentle, bleeding, silent Jesus. Jim only wondered when it would be over, as he had secretly wondered since birth.

Even as a sixteen year old he could not escape the omnipresent God. As a boy of six or seven in green corduroy knickers, his religion had still been exciting, or at least mysterious. Now he gazed intently at the altar and told God how much he loved Him, aware as he said it that it was probably not enough. God was not easily fooled. He hid behind trees, eavesdropped on whispered conversations with Sandy, demanded painful confidences in confession, threatened hell to those who disobeyed.

Hell was the true Catholic commodity. Even with all their emotional ranting, Baptists had not taught it as well. The Church dug deeper with scriptural briefs and ancient testimonials from Augustine and Gregory and Thomas Aquinas. There was no simple emotional escape such as some dramatic evangelical conversion in reverse. Hell was rooted in the Catholic brain, and even comfortable apostates sometimes awoke in nightmarish terror of its fire. Eternal fire beyond time or measurement, but apparently not beyond the capacity for vengeance of an omnipotent God.

Jack had always been able to laugh at Margaret's God; Thom had seduced Him with cherubic innocence and a pledge of future priesthood. Jim tried, unsuccessfully, to ignore Him.

Finally the long mass was over, but still Margaret and the devout Thom prayed until the early arrivals for the next service began filing in. Margaret's smiling eyes shone on the way home, and they were still beaming as she prepared the splendid Sunday breakfast while Anne read her favorite priest columnists in the *Sunday Visitor*.

Jim gulped his pork chops and eggs, thanked God for his food, then changed from his blue serge suit, still smelling of incense, into khaki slacks, sweat shirt, and blue nylon jacket. He raced out the grade door next to the garage, past the dented garbage cans and weed-covered cistern, to his beloved woods, there to forget Margaret's *Sunday Visitor* and John Patrick's depression and to blot out thoughts of a treacherous Judas and a dying Jesus. But that morning, with Sandy lapping playfully at his heels, even cattails and pussy willows stood like crosses over crusted remnants of a hard Michigan winter. Black muck oozed like blood along the banks of the swollen creek, and a beaver's house interrupted the flat swampland like an empty tomb. Rabbits skittered through the thickets, startled at Sandy's barking approach; nervous wrens trembled at the Crucifixion; and the earth was overrun with water flowing from open wounds in its scourged soil. The Church's somber liturgy had invaded his private druid grove where even Connie and Thom were never admitted.

He rested with a sweating Sandy at the edge of the swamp and reminded the dog, as he had so many times in boyhood, that the water in the marshes was still too deep for exploration. He recalled the spring morning four or five years before when Dave Kinnick had drowned there because he had disobeyed his mother. Jim pillowed his head on Sandy's back and heard the distant sounds of guns in Lemmert's Grove where the hunters, restless for the fall and the pheasant season, leaped from camouflaged blinds to blast the crows from the trees. Sandy growled ominously and Jim stroked his ears and hugged him.

"It's okay, boy; it's okay."

It was too cold to sit still for long. They explored the old peat mine as they had a hundred times before, then Jim threw stones at lily pads while Sandy barked furiously at a teasing muskrat. God was momentarily forgotten. So were Jack's ghost, and Margaret, and John Patrick's critique that Jim was "too damn big to be playing with a dog." He knew his father was probably right, but only the woods and Sandy took the shadows away.

He returned for Margaret's chicken and dumplings, fed Sandy the leftovers, careful to remove the brittle bones, and played catch with Thom in the side yard. Then it was evening services at Saint Raphael's to pray for a speedy end to the war and to stand awkwardly in the parking lot while Monsignor Doyle chatted with Thom and Margaret. Finally they arrived home and settled in front of the radio to hear the last of Fred Allen. Margaret reminded him that he was serving at early mass with Thom during the Easter vacation. He mumbled out of her hearing that he wanted to sleep in.

Then docilely he walked upstairs and, as he passed his old room, saw Thom saying his night prayers. Jim knelt to count the sins of the day and added them to those of the week. Three times he told God how sorry he was for crowning Jesus with thorns, and he asked Mary to help God understand. Then, as Palm Sunday was ending, Margaret glanced into the darkened room and reminded Jim of his prayers. There was no need to remind Thom.

Jim Maguire's perceptions grew in his very isolation although his scope was limited in a home without music (beyond hymns and "The Wearing of the Green") or art (save saccharine saints, Hollywood madonnas, and a sad-eyed Jesus). Saint Raphael's school was not in touch with ancient Irish learning, and there was not a word of Joyce or Yeats or Shaw—even though John Patrick and Jim would have loved them. Margaret did her best, buying *Collier's Encyclopedia, Little Men,* and a complete set of Mark Twain, which would have terrified her had she read beyond *Tom Sawyer*.

Whereas Jack had fought the Church as an unreasonable parent, Thom paid the price of its approval with his life. Only Jim reflected on it and once in his teens even dared to wonder if Margaret really loved her religion or simply loved to hold the priests up in the face of an unmanageable John Patrick. Especially when, after Jack's death, monsignor comforted her regularly.

"Every morning at church, Margaret," Monsignor Doyle would say. "No wonder the children are doing so well." Jim knew that he meant Thom and the devout, meticulous Anne.

"But he's drinking more since Jack's death, monsignor. Maybe I'm doing something wrong."

"Mary herself couldn't do more. Saint Monica prayed for Augustine for twenty years until he became a bishop." Even James Doyle had grown weary of John Patrick's pledges.

"Ah, but he'll never be a bishop. We all think you'd make a fine one though, but we'd die to lose you from the parish."

"I haven't the brains for it." He rubbed his belly. The dark hair was now almost gray and he wheezed from years of smoking cigarettes.

"You preach like an angel. And you care for the sick. I only hope you're around when my time comes." She looked away. "That may not be so long."

Jim felt responsible.

"Get on with you. You'll be saying your beads long after I'm packed in my wooden box." He smiled warmly at Thom and patted his shoulder paternally as if to ordain the boy in his stead.

"Sometimes the bloom on the rose is starving the roots, monsignor. Could I have your blessing?" She knelt.

"Not that you need it." The stubby fingers, stained with nicotine, traced a cross over her head, gently touching her hair. The Holy Spirit descended. "Regards to John Patrick."

She kissed his anointed fingers. John Patrick was not half the man monsignor was. Nor would Jim ever be.

Yet she loved Jim as well as she could, her days consumed in prayer and fear of hell, her freedom lost to duty and devotion to every new little Italian saint from Rome who took care of an aging mother, fed a squirrel, or fought off a pervert. Sin was as omnipresent as God, even though she had not had a sexual thought in years. A dark cloud meant sprinkling the house with holy water, and a sudden breeze under the ironing board moved her to light blessed candles with a superstitious faith the Church would have scorned. The only love she could give was clean clothes, food, and prayers for her family's salvation. And how generously she gave it. What other woman would ever take care of Jim so well?

"Mother, where are my brown shoes?"

"Under your bed."

"Are my corduroys clean?"

"Yes, and mended. I ironed them yesterday."

"Can you sew a button on my coat?"

"The other one needs tightening too." Never a bed unmade or hands too weary to knit colorful scarves and hats. Time to can peaches and make jams and still read Thomas à Kempis's *Imitation of Christ*.

Of course he would pay a price. All she asked was her children's lives, since God and the Church had taken hers.

At times Jim confided in her because there was nowhere else to go. Near the end of his junior year he came home early from a high school party at Mary Maloney's, in celebration of V-E Day. John Patrick and McNulty, still privately celebrating Roosevelt's death with the same enthusiasm as Hitler's defeat, were out drinking in the downtown streets of Kirkwood. Margaret, Thom, and Anne had made a private holy hour with Tim at Saint Raphael's.

Margaret looked up from the dishes when Jim came in. "Back already? I thought they were serving dinner. Leave it to the Maloneys to take the cheap way out." Then she became aware of his silence.

"What happened?"

"They were drinking."

Actually, Mary Maloney had gotten drunk and broken a glass coffee table when she was wrestling with her boyfriend. Although Jim was certainly no prude, as the drinking got wilder and the broken bottles and dishes more violent, he feared John Patrick's wrath. Connie wanted to sneak upstairs to a Maloney bedroom, but Jim ignored her. When finally a senior boy had his shirt ripped off by a passionate and drunk Italian girl, a scared Jim had slipped away just as the police arrived. Terrified that John Patrick would find out, he had deposited Connie at her house without stopping in the shed and had taken a bus home.

Margaret scolded fiercely. "Drinking! My God in heaven! What next? I'm glad you had the good sense to come home. Maloneys never had any faith!"

Suddenly Jim sensed the danger. "Please don't tell daddy!" Sandy whined ominously.

She promised faithfully twice and never mentioned it until three weeks later when report cards revealed a final C-minus in Latin.

John Patrick was angry. "Since when does a Maguire get a C-minus? Maybe you should study this summer and forget about Lake Watseka and that dog."

Without thinking, Margaret blurted, "And the beer parties at Maloney's."

John Patrick demanded the whole story, and a

stuttering Jim was forced to fill in the details. John Patrick slapped him.

Margaret was upset. "He had the courage to tell me."

"He didn't tell me!" Secretly he hoped that Jim was coming out of his shell. He remembered Jack's drunken grin after graduation, and now he worried that he had been too severe.

Later, Margaret was embarrassed. "Your father has a right to know. He's the head of the house." She repeated it twice more.

Jim vowed never to confide in Margaret again, and he did not answer her apology. He knew she had never betrayed Thom.

He also knew she was harder on herself than anyone else, recognizing that, outside of religious life, it was extremely difficult to save her own soul. The nuns were consecrated women, and Margaret was delighted to inconvenience herself for them on the shortest notice. One day she was hanging up clothes when Anne burst into the yard after school.

"Sister needs cookies for the end-of-school party tomorrow."

She put down her clothespins. "Maybe some nice oatmeal or sour cream—"

John Patrick scowled when he arrived home from work. "Tell sister to buy her damn cookies. I donate plenty and you've got enough to do."

"She has no time—with her prayers and all."

"Who the hell says more prayers than you do?" Once he would not have said it, but since Jack, he was more openly rebellious.

Anne delivered the cookies—six dozen, carefully boxed and wrapped in waxed paper. Sister would write a note and Margaret would have her reward. And be forgiven for ignoring the convent.

Peace now meant the ending of another weary day. She violated all the rules of her being, lived by some historic nightmare, and was delighted with the crumbs that were hers. Flowers thrilled her. The sight of peach blossoms and robins stealing sour cherries. A pork loin for dinner, fresh spinach and new potatoes, a cup of tea in the middle of the afternoon. She sang and smiled as she worked, and only when she rested did she ever complain or remind everyone of her sorry lot.

When it came to touching anyone beyond infancy, she was suddenly skittish, her arms lost in the folds of her shapeless rust sweater. She smiled instead in the kitchen and fed them blackberry jam or warm cloverleaf buns.

Like John Patrick, she never displayed her moods to visitors. If a schoolmate was waiting for someone to change clothes or finish a chore, John Patrick always emerged from his melancholy and paid charming attention with playful teasing or outrageous compliments, and Margaret supplied warm cookies and cold milk in a gentle, self-effacing way. Nor were there any expectations of someone not a Maguire. It was enough for Rooney's kid to get Bs or Cs, and Mulaley's boy could bypass college for work in a local paper mill; but not a Maguire. The visitors never suspected. As soon as they disappeared, Margaret went back to her never-ending tasks: "I never get caught up." Or she criticized the recipient of her cookies: "Not one good manner in his whole background." John Patrick slid into the sports page or a crossword puzzle and surrendered once again to his historic depression.

"Your folks are really great."

"Yeh."

"Your dad cracks me up."

"Yeh."

Perhaps James Maguire's self-imposed isolation was a way to salvage some fragile identity from an all-absorbing system of redemption that answered every question before it was asked. Even Connie was only the satisfaction of some disquieting urgency, and she knew nothing of his soul.

At the start of his senior year, there were more positive evidences of a future eruption. A religious retreat troubled him when the priest, a robust Passionist with a booming voice and a fierce crucifix tucked against a rounded belly, described minutely the fires of hell that roasted lascivious hands and charred undisciplined flesh. Since the atomic horror of Hiroshima the previous summer, there was an uneasy feeling that death could descend in an instant. The mushroom nightmare of Japan had not only ended the Asian war, but it had given Catholic preachers a new weapon to help fill the confessionals.

The priest spoke of a high school athlete whose car was hit by a train after he had sinned mortally with a loose young woman the very night of a big game. Another young man had died the same evening—after resisting an identical temptation—and had been admitted to the presence of God: "Well done, good and faithful servant, enter the glory that has been prepared for you since the foundation of the world!"

James Maguire felt his anger rise. If God knew everything, He certainly saw the train coming, or could have warned the young man. Or the guardian angel of childhood could have pulled him from the car before impact. God must have waited for the right moment, caught him in sin, and sent him screaming to eternal torture. It was impossible to love such a God, and for the first time in his life Jim pondered a serious and conscious doubt about his faith. He nourished it for several days, even masturbated once in defiance, and refused to confess his sin or to receive communion for an entire week. Who could survive the petulance and unpredictability of such a vindictive God? And when the priest whispered of God's mercy and Christ's willingness to forgive "seventy times seven times," Jim cursed the contradiction under his breath. Finally he confessed his sins, reluctantly worried about an atomic bomb hitting Kirkwood, but there was a tiny crack in the age-old stone wall of his Irish faith.

Thom's seminary reprieve thrilled Coach Art Doolan, and as soon as Thom began his freshman year, he replaced Jim in Saint Raphael's starting backfield. During the final three games of the season, Jim saw action only when Saint Raphael's had amassed an overwhelming lead, usually owing to Thom's brilliance on the field. Jim humbly endured it until the same humiliation occurred in basketball, and after the Christmas tournaments he exaggerated an injury to his shoulder, complained long after the pain had disappeared that he couldn't lift his arm, and finally emptied his locker.

Fearing that the new leisure might lead to impossible temptations, Margaret reminded Jim that he would have additional household duties, and she was relieved when John Patrick found him a part-time job, clearing ice rinks in winter and planting trees in spring for the city parks department. Jim was thrilled with the outside work and loved the abundant lore of his soft-spoken boss, Ed Thompson, who had spent twenty years as a ranger in Michigan's Upper Peninsula and permitted Sandy to ride in the city truck and romp around the job sites. Jim, who had been troubled with the usual question asked of high school seniors, "What about next year?" was suddenly certain that he wanted to be a forest ranger. It was a way to avoid competition with Thom and to escape the family.

Thompson supplied the details. "They've got a good program at Northern Michigan University. You oughta write them a letter. It's beautiful up there, with rivers you can drink out of and trout that tear the rod right out of your hand."

Jim revealed his dreams to Margaret.

"Is it Catholic?" she asked. Monsignor Doyle would want to know.

"No, but they have a church in Copper City and the priest has classes on campus." He did not mention that he planned to take Sandy and live off-campus.

She was not impressed. "What good would it do you if you lost your faith?"

When he continued to plead, she dismissed the matter. "See what your father says."

He knew what his father would say. Especially during one of his depressions that reduced everyone in the household to whispered communications. Jim outwaited the melancholy and caught his father in an expansive mood after Thom had been written up in the *Kirkwood Gazette* and Harry Truman had taken on Stalin. Even in his father's euphoric state, Jim could scarcely get his breath, and he had to blurt out his request. John Patrick's objections were more mundane.

"That's no job! Trimming trees and posting No Hunting signs and working for the government. That's work for a loafer like Ed Thompson. What the hell does it pay?"

"But I think I'd really like it, dad." It took every bit of Jim's courage to argue, and a final fusillade by John Patrick ended the discussion.

"What the hell does Thompson know about anything? None of his kids ever went to college and his daughter married a Polack! You can go to Loyola or Marquette and get an education. You're bright enough to be a doctor or lawyer. I never had the chance you've got."

It was Monsignor Doyle who convinced John Patrick of the value of Marquette. A younger brother had gone there and become a successful lawyer. Without further discussion, Jim would go to Marquette, and his choices were narrowed to medicine or law, a kind of success John Patrick could understand. When Jim decided on medicine, for no reason except that he preferred it to law, which he knew nothing about, he felt a new respect from his family. His mother and father boasted to everyone of his decision. McNulty started calling him Doc before he was out of high school and even Thom's priesthood and athletic accolades momentarily lost some luster. Soon Jim had convinced himself that he wanted to be a doctor; dreams of snowshoeing out to rescue starving deer were overshadowed by the new prestige of saving lives in highway dramas. He was almost happy.

The move to Lake Watseka the summer after Jim's graduation was postponed until the middle of June. John Patrick requested the delay because of the pressure of work, but Margaret knew that the place was not the same to him without Jack. Only once did he allude to the boy, while they watched the fireworks over the water on the Fourth of July.

"I just wish I could tell him one more time not to blow up the neighborhood."

Margaret's eyes filled with tears and he immediately began to talk of something else.

The delay in the Maguires' move to the lake delighted Connie Hackett. As thrilled as she was with the dream of becoming a doctor's wife, she feared losing Jim to a more sophisticated college girl. She had even approached her father about joining Jim at school in Milwaukee, but on his milkman's salary it was out of the question. She planned to enroll in Morris Business School in September and to work part time as a secretary. It occurred to her to let Jim get her pregnant, but she realized that would mean the end of medical school. Besides, James Maguire, with all of his resistance to the

Catholic ethic, was in no way free enough to actually have intercourse. Connie's scruples were far more pragmatic, especially when her father permitted new freedoms in a darkened living room that made the shed obsolete. James Maguire was a tremendous catch for Connie Hackett in postwar 1946.

The end of the war brought even greater prosperity to the Maguire family, not only because of an expanding economy everywhere, but also because John Patrick had built a tremendous business and Margaret was as parsimonious as when they were first married. John Patrick had to order his wife to get a cleaning lady once a week. They were not rich, but even the relatively high tuition at a Jesuit University was not a serious problem, especially since Monsignor Doyle had recommended that Thom wait another year before entering the seminary.

"Another year won't hurt. Two boys leaving the same year is too much for Margaret after all she's been through. Thom's vocation is solid enough."

John Patrick was delighted, not really because of his radical resistance to Thom's priesthood, which he knew was inevitable, but because Thom's athletic ability was beginning to be the talk of the parish. Even McNulty was aghast at "the boy's unbelievable talent." Jim was tired of hearing about his brother's prowess, and he spent most of the spring—when he wasn't working—wandering the woods, pondering medicine, and plotting to transport Sandy to Marquette. Even Connie resented his relationship with his dog, and John Patrick had given up.

"Christ, he lives with that damn dog."

John Patrick was particularly furious the Sunday they had scheduled the move to Lake Watseka when Jim returned from mass and could not locate Sandy. Margaret had prepared pork chops, potato patties, and fresh raspberry coffee cake.

"Get the trailer loaded. If he's not here by then, we go without him."

Jim raced outside and screamed at the top of his lungs, then honked the horn in the familiar melody the dog had learned to recognize. Then he inquired of the neighbors. Someone had seen Sandy about the time the

Maguires had left for the 8:30 mass. When Jim announced that he wanted to search the woods, John Patrick demanded that he eat his breakfast.

"He's been gone before. Finish your breakfast." John Patrick was still annoyed at rising so early on Sunday and forgoing his ushering at the 10:00 mass.

"He's never been gone on Sunday. He always knows how long we'll be away." Jim was pleading, and Tim, who also loved Sandy, was almost in tears.

"Thom and Anne can help you look after breakfast."

Margaret intervened. "Anne has to help Sister Caritas change the altar linens and Thom has to hear the Latin of some new altar boys."

"For God's sake, they just got home from church! They might as well get a bed down there." He knew it was useless.

Thom wanted to help, but Margaret reminded him of his responsibilities.

Finally John Patrick permitted Jim to leave the table. "Thom and I can load the trailer. Go find your damn dog."

Margaret followed him to the grade door. "It wouldn't hurt to say a few prayers."

Jim wanted to scream at her, but he raced out the side yard and ran the six or seven blocks to the woods at full speed. After an hour of calling Sandy's name, tears began streaming down his face. He knew John Patrick would not delay the trip to the cottage. Soon he began to pray, promising God anything if He would only lead him to Sandy. He continued to call at the top of his lungs, shouting angrily and threatening to leave the dog in the woods. He listened for the familiar bark, but only the shrill cry of distant birds and chattering squirrels interrupted the silence.

Finally he began systematically searching all their favorite haunts: the peat mine, the beaver houses, the secret spring and the soft muck around the little swamp, the climbing trees and the field of wild raspberries, the abandoned apple orchard where Sandy had chased the blue racer, even a cocklebur patch the dog hated.

It was almost four when he found Sandy in Lemmert's Grove. Lying on his back with gunshot wounds on the left side of his chest and head. Killed by a hunter. Already cold and bloated.

Jim fell on him and begged him to come back to life. He screamed at God, promising he would never sin again. Never eat candy or touch Connie, spend a thousand years in the fire of purgatory, even be a priest. But Sandy did not stir and the heavens were silent. Only the muffled sobs of James Maguire could be heard as his arms encircled Sandy's body. He was still there at dusk when Thom and John Patrick finally found him. His father touched him tenderly. "I'm sorry, boy." His eyes were moist with memory. Jim could only sob against his father's chest like a helpless child.

They helped him cover Sandy with leaves, and John Patrick agreed to delay the move to provide Sandy a proper burial the next day. When they entered the back door, Margaret pulled his plate of chicken and mashed potatoes from the oven, and she started to hold out her arms to him. Then she folded them in her rust-colored working sweater and bade him sit down.

"I'm not hungry."

"But you love my baked chicken."

John Patrick rubbed Jim's hair. "Eat something, it's good for you."

"You can get another dog," she said.

He flared. "I don't want another dog."

John Patrick intervened. "Eat."

Later that evening, John Patrick joined them in the family rosary. Jim was still crying.

"Can we pray for Sandy?" Jim asked like a small boy.

Margaret was taken aback. "It's not right. They don't have immortal souls. We can only pray to accept God's will, hard as it is." Anne nodded crisp theological agreement.

Margaret started to say he was too old for such behavior, but John Patrick silenced her with a fierce look. "Indeed we'll pray for him. The Church doesn't know everything."

"But that's sinful, John—"

Thom nodded tentatively.

John Patrick was suddenly angry. "I said we'll pray for him."

The next morning Thom helped Jim dig the shallow grave in a shaded spot in Lemmert's Grove that Sandy loved best of all.

Jim began the final obsequies. "Eternal rest grant unto him, O Lord."

Thom hesitated to reply until he saw anger in his brother's eyes that he had never seen before.

"And let perpetual light shine upon him," Thom said. Knowing it was a most unpriestly compromise.

They searched for stones and Jim arranged them carefully on the grave to spell the name of his closest friend. Perhaps his only one. Then he demanded that Thom never reveal the sacred burial place to anyone.

When Thom shuffled off nervously "to finish packing," Jim continued to sit by the grave for almost an hour, unable to stop the tears and almost powerless to leave the graveside. He could not forget Sandy's gentle, loving face, or the dog's dance of ecstasy every time he greeted Jim from school. Jim's whole boyhood had been shared with Sandy, every fragile hope and secret searing wound.

When Jim finally left, he knew his boyhood was over, and he wondered if anyone else would ever bring him such love and peace.

When he reached the house, everyone was ready to leave for the lake. John Patrick showed no impatience.

"Is Sandy buried?" Tim asked. He stroked Jim's head softly. "Is he in heaven?"

Jim nodded. Then it was silent.

John Patrick spoke very softly. "I understand," he said. "Sandy loved you very much."

II

☙ ☙ ☙

Two Brothers from Kirkwood

Come with Cain and me
East of Eden toward the sea,
In desert lands called Nod
Where murderers live and lovers
Grown weary of Abel and his God.

The mark upon our face is sadness
And horror is the color of our eyes.
We have seen sights too dark for sunlight,
Known pain unweepable by all the waters of
the skies.
We are weary men, too mad for mothers to bear.
Too angry to suck soft breasts of flesh
Lest we bite them to be bathed in blood
And drink the redness, sweet and fresh
For thirst unquenchable in Adam's wells.
We murdered for a father's love—
A trifling price for such a prize.
Now cast from the garden's dullness,
The honest wastes of Nod are paradise
For men who took a brother's life to save their
own . . .

Come with Cain and me
East of Eden toward the sea,
In desert lands called Nod . . .

5

Ora Pro Nobis Peccatoribus

The summer of 1946 at Lake Watseka was quiet. Germany was still scraping away the rubble, and the world was beginning to understand what had really happened to the Jews. Japan was whispering about the extent of the atomic horror as Christian moralists wondered and thanked God for the end of war. Russia was policing its Eastern European spoils with Stalinesque grimness, and America offered the spoils of its new prosperity to rebuild what its B-29s had ripped apart.

Jim, home from his first year at Marquette, trimmed trees for the city parks department and watered the baseball fields where Thom, after assisting the janitor at Saint Raphael's in refinishing desks and waxing school floors, practiced Legion baseball and played his summer league. John Patrick sold more insurance and rushed over to Enslow Field to meet McNulty and cheer Thom's line drives, lamenting a major league prospect who would become a priest.

Occasionally Jim went with them and watched Thom lead the Legion Blues to a division championship. On weekdays after work, Jim usually stopped to see Connie or wandered alone in the woods. At times he rejoined Thom and John Patrick for the thirty-minute ride to the lake, during which he was obliged to relive every one of Thom's base hits. More often he hitchhiked by himself and sat watching the turtles slip into the dark green water until Thom and his father arrived to share the dinner that Margaret kept warm in the oven. In the morning, John Patrick dropped him off at work, and Thom and Margaret took Tim and Anne to daily mass at Saint Raphael's.

Sunday meant morning mass at Our Lady of Watseka

chapel, served by the young Saint Raphael's curate, Father Charles Kenelley, a tall, rangy Irishman with jet black hair combed in a pompadour and gentle blue eyes that softened a hooked nose and a firm jaw. Usually Father Kenelley ate Sunday breakfast with the Maguires before returning to Kirkwood, and Jim always wondered if the priest remembered his confession in the rectory garage. Nothing in Kenelley's manner betrayed Jim's secret. Barely thirty, Kenelley felt right at home, drinking the fresh orange juice Margaret offered and chatting knowledgeably with John Patrick about baseball, insurance, or Truman's refreshing feistiness.

Margaret was in heaven, knowing God had blessed her home as she fried sausage patties and eggs basted and runny the way he liked them. She knew Kenelley's weekly presence was a reward for Thom's approaching seminary. At times, Thom, always his altar boy, was outflanked when the priest received an invitation from a wealthy parishioner or an ebullient convert who ushered dressed in flamboyant sport shirts and pretentiously read the Bible instead of a missal at mass.

Margaret was outraged. "What did he say?"

"He'll come next week."

She was crushed. The following week she reminded Thom several times to invite the priest, and she grumbled at John Patrick who was checking out the sports page and smoking another cigarette.

"We'll be late. Can't the paper wait?"

"For the love of God, Margaret, there's plenty of time!" He tossed the paper aside.

"Thom's serving and he has to help Father Kenelley unpack the mass kit."

"Kenelley's not helpless."

But they arrived a half hour early, secured Kenelley's acceptance of the breakfast invitation, and Margaret's ecstasy was renewed in defeating the Bible-reading convert.

When the summer was over, Jim went back to Marquette in Milwaukee, and the Maguire family life resumed in Kirkwood. John Patrick was lost in business. Monsignor Doyle delayed Thom's seminary again, insisting that his vocation would only be strengthened by the delay. Even John Patrick did not suspect that the pastor wanted Thom for another year to lead Saint Raphael's to championship football and basketball seasons. Art Doolan was all smiles.

Doolan had not seen an athlete like Thom Maguire in twelve years at Saint Raphael's, and he had coached some good ones. Thom had it all—incredible natural ability, an intensity hidden under poise and docility—and the kid could be coached! The opposite of Jack. A dynasty could be built around this one!

And Thom did not let him down. The seminary delay meant an 8–0 record in football and sixteen out of nineteen in basketball. They lost the state finals to Wyandotte by three, 51–48, but the young sophomore scored eighteen points, and sports reporter Jake Moss called it the "most thrilling single performance witnessed by this scribe in a dozen years of covering the hardwoods."

John Patrick read the item a dozen times and McNulty carried the write-up in his wallet like a favorite prayer. Margaret worried that Thom might lose his vocation. A pixieish Madeline Powers stalked him all year, as did a dozen others at Saint Raphael's High, even though they knew he belonged to God. Madeline was the most persistent, lingering in front of the gym after practices, accidentally meeting him at bus stops, dancing with him at the Friday-night postgame celebrations Monsignor Doyle and Father Kenelley encouraged him to attend.

"The priesthood doesn't need any wimps."

Once Madeline brushed a warm breast against his arm and cuddled next to him in the back seat of someone's jalopy on the way to the Hi-De-Ho for hamburgers. When he had wanted to kiss her on a hayride, he retreated to more fervent prayers and watchfulness. The Maguire in his blood had not been totally drained, but he was still the boyeen descended from the fervent Michael O'Brien from Clare and Margaret Anne of Kirkwood. God had called, and Thom dreamed of feeding hungry children and helping old people. There were Hitlers and Mussolinis and Stalins who rose up again and again to destroy God, and an idealistic young Thom Maguire knew it would be over his dead body! Beyond the applause for athletic feats and exceptional marks in school, all of which he accepted humbly, expecting it of himself as a "Maguire," his happiest moments were in the presence of

God. He pledged all of his energy to win the greatest game of all, the salvation of the world.

John Patrick ignored Thom's priesthood and drained every ounce of vicarious athletic glory. Margaret had not seen John Patrick so exuberant since their courtship. Dutchmen talked to him of Thom, and even J. R. Harris seemed impressed when they met in the Victory Cafe. Sundays after mass, there were lingering moments in the parking lot to savor the fulfilled dreams of a lifetime. His arm went around an embarrassed Thom and he tossed a six-year-old Tim in the air with a booming promise: "This will be another Maguire." Tim had none of the old anger, and there were no bristling neighborhood battles with Hollanders. Even in first grade Tim ignored sports and studied distractedly, preparing for his first communion with the same relaxed joy he brought to everything. As delighted with Margaret and John Patrick as he was with himself.

Anne's efforts to ignore her father's blustering and alcoholic bravado gave her increasing zeal to be a more devout Catholic than Margaret. In seventh grade she was confident that she would be a nun. John Patrick would not stand in her way, although it really didn't matter because she had no future on the gridiron, and John Patrick now had eyes for Thom alone.

Jim still paid his token homage to Holy Week and received the sacraments, but Margaret, perceptive and nervous, knew that he no longer said night prayers, and she worried about the stains she saw on the sheets. She said nothing, but she increased her prayers and wondered about Connie Hackett, who had almost emerged as Jim's girl, but still had never been invited to the Maguire residence. It was Mary O'Meara who informed Margaret that she might have a wedding on her hands.

"Wouldn't the blubbery milkman like to have his daughter marry a Maguire?" Mary needled.

Margaret, visibly upset, reported to John Patrick. Only when Jim came home for summer vacation did his father say anything. Briefly and almost cautiously.

"I hope you're not getting too thick with that Hackett girl."

"I'm not." Jim blushed.

"She's not your kind." He wondered if Jim were having sex.

"I know that."

"Just don't embarrass yourself. Medicine takes a long time."

Jim appreciated his father's abrupt candor. Margaret would have lectured for hours. Instead, she avoided the subject and read pertinent articles from the *Sunday Visitor* about the corruption of morals since the war. John Patrick carefully watched Thom's athletic career as the boy led the Legion Maroons to another division title, and even Margaret and Anne attended the finals in Sheffield when Thom hit a double with the bases loaded to win the game; then they all worried together about the outcome of John Patrick's victory celebration. Margaret also worried privately about Anne's furtive glances at boys and doubted that the girl would ever be a nun. In truth, she admitted to herself, it didn't matter that much. It was the priests who said mass and forgave sins. Any average girl could be a nun.

Only when that summer ended did John Patrick grow morose. Thom's priesthood could no longer be delayed. The final Sunday before Labor Day, John Patrick complained of a cold and did not attend mass. Margaret did not argue but offered her communion for his weakness. When Father Kenelley came to the cottage for a last summer breakfast, Thom listened attentively while the priest described his own first year in the seminary.

"You'll probably be home in two weeks. Crying for Margaret's cooking." They had all laughed except John Patrick, but even he knew it could never happen. Jim glanced up from his packing and saw his father's silent pain, but he knew no way to invade John Patrick's prison.

Thom stood at the shore of Lake Watseka like a young apostle at Galilee. He rested under a willow tree for a final look. He watched the camelbacks surface cautiously, then slide up on a decaying log amid the lily pads. They were as solemn and unsmiling as he was. He would never catch another turtle. It was a puberty rite he had met. He leaned against the bark of the willow tree, its branches shielding him from the screaming glare of the dying sun. The tree seemed as ancient as the turtles, whispering with soft sibilants in the breeze that rippled the water. Often he had said his rosary there, begging God to make him less unworthy of the priesthood and fighting a mysterious battle with his own soul. Beneath the serene face and generous idealism there lurked a secret mixture of rootless sadness and fierce responsibility. He knew that his life was not his own, that all the success and applause was only a preparation for the real challenge of the priesthood. He prayed devoutly for strength and wisdom and an end to the never-acknowledged uneasiness that gnawed at his stomach without apparent cause or logic. He knew that only the priesthood could bring him the final peace that had eluded Margaret and John Patrick.

The turtles slipped into the water, soon to begin a long hibernation in some age-old contradiction of nature. Even the willow was silent in deference to the disappearing sun. Black water bugs flitted on the glassy surface and water lilies turned from green to metallic black. Thom knew somehow that the priesthood was more than a desired vocation. It was a hero's burden, a link to an unspoken vengeance he would never have admitted. But vengeance against what? A lost green paradise of rotting black potatoes and ignorant peasants? An America that was still a British colony compounded with a Dutch disrespect of Catholics? A man who drank to forget a dead son, or a woman who bore a son to give him back to God?

The vocation was not really his, or his mother's. It was a sacred draft, the choicest bullock to appease an angry, sometimes peevish God. A chance to rise above the earth in familial closeness with the very Creator. As much perhaps out of fear and revenge as out of love. What did a generation mean? Or a dozen of them? He was the child of a people betrayed by everyone: the land, Cromwell, America, even themselves, but not by their undying faith in God. Catholicism was the only thing that had not been taken away from them, and to be called to be a priest was more than to become a doctor, a lawyer, or a president. It did not matter that John Patrick had lost another son.

Thom was not even really aware of his father's pain. Rather, he focused on his own personal sacrifice. He had seen John Patrick's melancholy before, again and again, and the same despondency that final weekend at Lake Watseka seemed only a characteristic depression that would pass with more work or a Notre Dame victory. It never really occurred to Thom that he had broken his father's heart. The priesthood had been the center of his whole childhood, and John Patrick himself had been thrilled with Monsignor Doyle's attentions and with the breakfast chats at the lake with Father Kenelley. Certainly he was excited by the vocation of his own son.

Jim, busy taking the dock down, knew differently. Like his father, Jim did not really support Thom's vocation. A year at Marquette had made the priesthood seem more remote and unimportant to him. Confessions in Gesu Church were impersonal and safely anonymous, and his attendance at mass was sporadic, without the old guilt and anxiety. Thom's vocation seemed a waste, but Jim would never have admitted it to him. He loved his brother and accepted Thom's lifelong dreams, even as he felt the seminary to be a barrier to a closeness he increasingly wanted. Already Thom seemed to have lost a light-heartedness that had always made his religious fervor less offensive than Margaret's. During the last few weeks, Thom had not laughed as much. Jim had almost said something, then had drawn back. Thom's distant priesthood was already a chasm he couldn't cross.

John Patrick's voice rang out. "Jim! Thom! Get that damn dock down and let's get the hell out of here!"

It was September 1946, a hundred years since the Irish famine.

☘ ☘ ☘

At noon the next day, Margaret and her friend Mary O'Meara delivered Thom and a pudgy Bobbie Foley, also from Kirkwood and barely fourteen, at Saint Robert's Seminary in Grandville. It was a gray stone building trimmed in red brick and hidden from the street by a row of skinny poplars and overgrown lilac bushes.

Once the seminary had been the estate of the lumber heiress, Margo Desarmier, who had married three or four times, slept with gardeners and butlers, held week-end parties and extravagant balls, and bargained with God before her death. A devout Jesuit had brought her viaticum the last thirty days of her life, blotted out past indiscretions, and promised her eternal peace. In gratitude, she had willed twenty acres to the Church and enough money to erect a seminary, requesting piously that it be known as Saint Margaret's. Later, canon lawyers argued that the name was not integral to the sacred behest and was inappropriate for a seminary. They settled on Saint Robert's, to honor the Jesuit, Robert Bellarmine, an Italian archbishop and doctor of the Church who had sparked the Counter-Reformation with his brilliant catechisms and was an authority on church-state relations. In restitution to the lusty Margo, a stained-glass window of Saint Margaret, noble queen of Scotland and ascetic enforcer of Lent in the eleventh century, was placed over the rear confessional of the cathedral in Washtenaw—the diocesan seat—with an appropriate subtitle: *Ora Pro Nobis Peccatoribus. In memoriam:* Margo Desarmier, 1848–1917.

At the seminary, large wooden entrance doors opened onto immaculate terrazzo steps and into the main hallway where there was an imposing statue of Robert Bellarmine. A corridor to the left pointed toward the priests' community recreation room, two faculty apartments, and the rector's suite. To the right the corridor led to junior and senior study halls, a small reading room, and a large toilet. Directly opposite the front door, in the heart of the building, was the simple chapel with rows of oak pews and stained-glass windows recalling the Gospel story of the priesthood. A red-robed Christ stood serenely with apostles and nets, promising to make them *piscatores hominum* ("fishers of men"). A scene of the Last Supper showed Judas poised fiendishly to do his dirty work, and there was another of Christ admonishing a small group: *"Qui amat patrem aut matrem plusquam me, non est me dignus."* "Whoever loves father or mother more than me is not worthy of me." In each picture, Christ wore a golden halo and reflected the joy Thom was feeling.

The newcomers were graciously directed to the third floor by Father Elvin Ward, who had dark, thinning hair, tiny chipmunk teeth, and almost no chin. As if to highlight the chin, he had a dimple that was large enough to make shaving hazardous. He was barely five feet two, and a small potbelly jutted out from the thin frame under the buttoned black cassock. His voice was a surprise, for he had a deep and rasping Italian inflection without the accent. It gave immediate dignity to his dwarfed stature, and a warm, boyish grin made him charming.

"My-a, what a fine-looking group-a! Let me see-a, Thomas Maguire—I imagine you're on the list—Oh yes-a, main dormitory, third floor." He bowed politely to a beaming Margaret and the rapt Mary O'Meara and smiled radiantly. They blushed in gratitude, grateful servants in the Master's house.

They ascended the terrazzo steps to the right of the chapel entrance. Margaret was still beaming and nervously chattering. "He's just lovely—the place is just spotless—" She looked like a bride again, shy and childlike, and she knew Mary O'Meara would convey a complete report to Agnes Dillon and all the women at early mass.

They glanced briefly at the library and classrooms on the second floor, boxlike rooms without decoration save faded prints of saints and a crucifix on the center walls. The library reference rooms had long tables of the same oak with unpadded varnished chairs. There were rows of *Catholic Encyclopedias*, a *Periodical Index to Catholic Literature,* bound copies of *America* and the *Jesuit Missions*. A magazine rack with a Washtenaw diocesan newspaper and current issues of the *Sunday Visitor* and the *Sacred Heart Messenger*. No *Time* or *Newsweek* or *Life*. Even Margaret had permitted the *Saturday Evening Post*.

At each end of the corridor were faculty apartments. A separate area at the left rear housed the infirmary.

They found the third floor and more terrazzo corridors. Opposite the stairs was a faculty apartment with a lacquered yellow sign—Father Terrence Moody—and on a second line—Disciplinarian. To the right were two small dormitories for high school juniors and seniors, and beyond them private double rooms for students in first- and second-year college. The beds were narrow and white, with two-inch pads resting on wire springs. The main dormitory, extending the width of the entire building, was to the left. Thom passed a washroom with four stalls, mirrors, and a dozen small sinks, each with a single cold-water faucet. A brass plug indicated that hot water had been considered but rejected. In the main dormitory there were three long rows of perhaps twenty-five narrow beds each, separated by small gray metal nightstands, and opposite the washroom were a hundred green metal lockers without locks. Theft was punished with expulsion.

The main dormitory was light and airy, with high windows surrounding the room and white cotton bedspreads falling an inch above the same gray terrazzo floors. The walls were chalky white, the ceiling fixtures gray. There were a few cheap prints of Saint Theresa and the curé of Ars, a discolored Saint Joseph with a white lily, and Veronica's veil parched yellow. No desks or chairs or frills, and only ceiling lights on a master switch.

"It's so clean," said Margaret. "Everything is so clean—and such nice-looking boys—all of them!" Mary O'Meara continued to smile and quietly reminded them of the tiny vestments Margaret had made for Thom in first grade. Thom grinned at the recollection.

He had never seen his mother lovelier. Her eyes shone under the soft brown hair, now graying obviously, as if her convent dream had finally come true. There was none of Kate's ancient bitterness, no scars of unacknowledged talents and neglected dreams. After a thousand years the shy girl with crooked teeth was finally recognized—by Monsignor Doyle and the whole parish, by wealthy families who took the pastor hunting and confidently invited priests to dinner. By nuns who never carried loads of wet washing up cellar stairs to hang it on lines until shoulders ached, who never fed a family of seven, three good meals a day. She had said as many prayers as any nun—after sitting up all night with a sick child or enduring a drunken husband, even after burying her oldest boy. But she had lived to see her one son at Saint Robert's Seminary.

Thom loved her more than ever before. He wanted to hold her, who had given so much, truly delighted to bring a smile to her face, as if his life were now fulfilled. He had the same celibate energy as she and the same all-seeing God who added up good deeds and tabulated every weary prayer. Thom had seen her tears when John Patrick mocked her May altars or family rosary, when he drank till early morning and crashed the Oldsmobile into the side of the garage. When he woke the family and swore at her. Once when he had pushed her against the kitchen table. And when Jack, in his helpless, magnetic imitation of his father, destroyed himself.

The seminary was her final assurance that marriage to a chauvinistic and demanding Deity had been the wisest choice. "O dear God, it's so lovely here!" Her nuptials were finally eternally recorded in a white and airy heaven where lilacs filled the air with sweetness and Mary O'Meara witnessed jealously as a chosen maid of honor. And Thom, too, was freed from a little boy's painful sympathy for a mother's ancient agony.

But his vocation was not for her alone. It was the beginning of his own spiritual quest to find an end to some inquietude, some mysterious and private burden of sorrow beyond Saint Raphael's or his parents. Thom had somehow learned to care about the world beyond Irish guilt or private success and maternal expectations; he carried a vague yearning to help those less fortunate than himself. Perhaps it was only an adolescent dream to be loved, or a boy's imagination of heroic adventure and epic involvement. Maybe an O'Brien's own sensitivity to injustice, or the simple hospitality of an Irish hearth extended to bring God's forgiving embrace to an entire world. What did he know of the world? He had heard missionaries preach each October on the Feast of Christ the King about starving babies in Bombay, disease in the slums of Santiago, devil worship and diabolical possession in remote Africa, or the historic invasion of Jesuits into China. Thom would help them. His excitement was that of the young bridegroom in love beyond all words; it was not some passing sensual excitement, but a deep abiding love.

Monsignor Doyle had often spoken of the materialism that destroyed families, the transience of beauty and money and fame. Faith was the big and real game, Saint Paul's Corinthian "race" the test of courage and ultimate worth. To be a priest was the greatest vocation of all, to lead men from lust and greed, fear and anger to the "peace that surpasses all understanding." Only the bravest need apply, and then only when God Himself has called. Everyone knew that Jesus had called Thom Maguire as one of His own disciples, and Thom would not refuse the sacred invitation.

To refuse a vocation was to spurn a gift from the Almighty. It was to choose idleness and self-indulgence and to make salvation almost impossible. A Saint Raphael's boy had left the seminary to join the army and was killed on his way to report for duty. It was presumed he was in hell. Another older theology student had left to raise a family. One of his sons had been born an idiot, a daughter later died while having an abortion, and a son was electrocuted in a rainstorm. It was one of Margaret's most dire stories. To leave the priesthood was an unpardonable sin, but even to turn down a beginning vocation was tantamount to self-destruction. For "What does it profit a man if he gain the whole world and suffer the loss of his immortal soul?"

The seminary also offered immediate benefits. It gave direction to a confused young life as well as affording a sudden respectability, a status beyond athlete or scholar, and it bypassed an adolescent fear of girls. Thom had never admitted to himself that he had been frightened by the strange softness of Madeline Powers's breast against his arm, her gentle caressing of the back of his neck, the hungry merging of sweaty palms, and his own fierce urge to kiss her mouth. And he was embarrassed in the presence of smiling eyes that held a thrilling secret and the feminine poise that exposed his sudden awkwardness.

They had been on a hayride the previous spring.

"Let's get off." Her eyes danced excitedly.

"And do what?"

"Just get off and be alone."

"Everyone's watching."

"What do we care? C'mon." She jumped from the wagon and he followed. Wondering what his classmates thought.

They sat on the grass and she rested her head against his thigh looking at the silent sky of stars. He sat up and leaned against a fallen tree. It was chilly. She rested her back against his chest and then directed his arms around her body. He could feel firm breasts against the inside arms of his sweater, and her butt brushed against his groin. His whole body began to tremble.

"You're cold."

"A little."

"Let's lie down and snuggle." They lay in each other's arms for almost a minute until she cautiously entwined her leg between his. He wanted to kiss her, but he knew he already belonged to God. He felt soft hair against his cheek and smelled her body. She drew him closer but abruptly he pulled away, afraid that he had sinned.

"We'd better go."

"Not yet. It's so beautiful. I think I love you."

It embarrassed him. "Madeline—we'd better go."

Of course he confessed it. "Passionate embracing once and impure thoughts three times—maybe four."

"Did you touch her?"

"Not with my hands."

"Did she touch you?"

"Her breasts brushed my arm and I didn't move away."

"Was it pleasurable?"

"Yes, father." He was almost in tears. "Can I still be a priest?" Father Kenelley was moved by the intense young sincerity.

"Of course. But you must be careful. A vocation can be lost by carelessness and temptation. Say three Our Fathers and three Hail Marys and go in peace."

Thom went in sadness and said his rosary, loving Father Kenelley for his gentle forgiveness. He would be the same kind of priest. Better.

Now he looked around the dormitory's sterile whiteness as Margaret tenderly unpacked his clothes. Already he missed the friendly maple trees that touched his bedroom window at home. Yet he felt excitement amid the pain, as if he had entered a hospital for serious surgery where a mortal sickness would be healed. Here he would find the peace that had eluded him in his too brief adolescent passage from childhood. The wound would finally be healed and an undistracted devotion to pure joy would be his. Never again would he be subject to the torture of a deceitful conscience or an impure heart. "I have a food you know not of—come follow me!"

He followed Margaret down the stairs to the chapel for a brief prayer of thanksgiving. "So lovely here—so peaceful—" Then they went to the basement recreation room for coffee, milk, and homemade sugar cookies. There were two worn Ping-Pong tables with chipped corners, chess and checker sets, and funeral chairs against lacquered beige brick walls. At the far left was the entrance to the rectory and at the opposite end, through a corridor and tiny barbershop, the stage and small gymnasium. Thom eyed the gym appraisingly. A narrow court meant few shots from the corner. He laughed to himself: a minor sacrifice.

He hardly reflected on his new home. It was not really

his to approve. The bishop had assigned him here for the next four years and agreed to pay a fourth of his $800 tuition from diocesan funds. John Patrick would pay the rest. Boys from poorer families paid proportionately less or nothing at all. He was glad his father was not here to ask for coffee half a dozen times, talk too loudly, and treat the faculty priests like old friends from the Knights of Columbus. To ask a hundred questions about the food and the athletic program, drop his cigarette ashes in the corridor, hack and spit out a window. Assuredly he would have asked the rector about liability coverage and if the kitchen nuns had health insurance. Then he would have joked awkwardly with students, smiling that too proud smile.

Margaret was a more proper parent for the seminary. "Such a lovely home—I never expected this."

Then it was time for her to leave. Again her eyes filled: "I'm so proud—so grateful to God." Her mother's heart wanted to say that he was too young to leave home, that the beds were hard and the rooms needed flowers. She wanted to take him back to Kirkwood, and her throat was choked with pain, but faith conquered her heart as it always had. She fought back her tender, always unspoken love for her beautiful boy, and, like an obedient Abraham, sacrificed her child to God.

With a lump in his throat Thom walked back inside and sat quietly in the chapel. A sudden burst of sweet freedom from a heavy burden of waiting. He had made the right choice; now he knelt and buried his head in his arms with the ancient devotion of a Michael O'Brien.

"Dear Jesus, I want to be a good, loving, unselfish priest. The very best kind. Thank you for calling me. Help me with your grace."

He knelt like a knight, staring at the silent tabernacle. Unable to hold back soft silent tears as his mouth trembled like a lonely little boy's. Then, like a Maguire, he stiffened and began to be a priest.

Several hours later, Thom stood outside the refectory door. A bell chimed and there was sudden silence. An older student led the Angelus: *"Et Verbum caro factum est."* Younger voices, back for a second year, knew the words. Thom stood silently, an awkward outsider. Nearby a ruddy-cheeked Bobbie Foley was blushing and sweating like a little boy on his first day at camp. The prayer concluded and the doors swung open. A tall curly-haired priest suggested that they sit anywhere. "Assigned places will be given tomorrow." Again the Latin prayers: *"Benedicte."* A roar went up from the regulars: *"In te sperant,Domine . . ."* It was terrifying.

Thom had never felt so out of place. His high school status and Kirkwood fame vanished in a mouthful of memorized Latin. When they sat to eat, there was a festive mood, nicknames used, and an excited numbering of the summer's mortality rate.

"Duggan quit."

"You're kidding."

"So'd Marve Fedewa and Stan Gorski."

"Washtenaw should walk away with football." Four dioceses fed the seminary: Washtenaw, Sheffield (Thom's diocese), Elliston to the east, and Chippewa in the Upper Peninsula. The other Michigan diocese, Detroit, had its own seminary and held a place of archdiocesan eminence. Athletic competition was fierce in diocesan games, and Washtenaw, with a larger population, was usually the favorite, but the departed students, all superlative athletes, had brought a football title to Elliston the previous year.

"Any new profs?"

"Some Father Duffey. He works in a parish."

"Who left?"

"Tracy had a nervous breakdown."

"Ten years ago." They laughed knowingly and Thom was suddenly hungry for Margaret's mashed potatoes and pot roast with carrots.

The newcomers played with sticky creamed potatoes and thin slices of minced ham, a white bowl full of too-dark green beans with bacon. The homemade wheat bread, despite oleo, was delicious. (Oleo had never graced John Patrick's table: "Tastes like horse piss!") Thom asked for a glass of milk and was told that special arrangements had to be made, so he drank water and munched the bread and ham.

A bell rang and there were more Latin prayers of thanksgiving. The tall man with the tilted head and round shoulders proved to be the rector, Monsignor Raymond Nowicki, and he spoke again.

"We'll meet in the chapel in a half hour. There'll be a warning bell at 6:55. You are to be in place at 7:00.

Fourth-year men, Adams through Grady, will clear the tables and assist the nuns with dishes. Regular assignments will be posted tomorrow."

The roar of voices resumed and students raced to the recreation room or through a basement locker area to a courtyard. Some students began walking around a broad dirt path that circled a pair of three-walled brick handball courts and two cracked tennis courts, then stretched out to encompass baseball diamonds and football fields. At the rear a thick hedge of thornbushes separated the seminary from the neighborhood. Shouting, happy voices recalled last year's events.

Thom made his way through the recreation room, managed to ditch a clinging Bobbie Foley at a chess game, and ended up in a courtyard beneath the chapel. A rangy Germanic-looking farmer with thin blond curly hair smiled shyly. He had the bland awkward look Thom would have avoided in other circumstances. Now he was frantic for any contact.

"I'm Schaeffer, Dennis Schaeffer. Who're you?"

"Oh, hi!—Thom Maguire." He grabbed the bony hand.

"Where ya from?"

"Kirkwood, Sheffield Diocese."

"Play any sports?"

"Some." He was too frightened to say more.

"I pitch. Worked hard at it this summer." He looked muscular and rawboned, but Thom was only impressed by his poise.

"How long you been here?"

"This is my third year." The farmer suddenly seemed godlike.

"Like it?" Thom didn't know what else to ask.

"I wouldn't stay if I didn't." His words spurted out quickly.

"All the Latin seems rough."

"Only at first. You'll catch on. I did and I'm no brain."

Thom was not really relieved.

They talked about raccoon hunting and trout fishing, planting onions and the Detroit Tigers. Hal Newhouser was a hero. And Cleveland's Bob Feller. "He was a farm boy, too."

The bell rang and the chapel filled with warm bodies. Although no uniform was required, the room was a sea of black and brown sweaters, dark blues and gray. Only an uninformed newcomer wore red or green. Another Latin prayer led by the rector in the pulpit. The same smile, almost a weary grimace. But Thom liked him.

His voice, higher than Thom expected, was almost a shrill whine. "Well you're here. Some didn't come back, some won't stay. But you're here and while you're here, there's a job to do. God's work."

There were a few coughs, some shuffling in the pews, and a small boy, wearing a yellow sweater and a brown brush cut, hardly five feet tall, began to cry. An older boy all in black took him out of the chapel. Thom never saw the little fellow again. Monsignor Nowicki was not put off.

"There may even be a few tears. It's not easy here; no one said it was. But you are the chosen ones, sent by your bishop to become other Christs. Some of you are very young, but it is the wisdom of the Church that a boy should be admitted 'in his tenderest years.' Others have been in service and are older. But God has called all of you, and the sound of any bell is His holy voice. When it rings, you move. Every night at this time the 'grand silence' begins, and that means there will be no talking from seven in the evening until breakfast in the morning. No exceptions—ever! It's our most sacred rule! Part of that time is devoted to study and the rest to prayer. Silence will help you to become interior men of reflection.

"The Church has created an ideal program through the centuries to make you men of wisdom and intelligence. Your studies will be demanding, prayers frequent. Nor will we neglect your bodies. *'Mens sana in corpore sano.'* You scholars can translate that for the new men."

A too-loud laugh.

"We have an active sports program, and we like everyone to participate. Everyone!"

Light laughter.

"Whether you choose to or not, two hours every day will be spent outside—winter and spring."

Another low murmur of snickering. They had not forgotten Michigan winters.

"Father Jack Tracy will not be with us this year; a health problem—he can use your prayers—but Father John Duffey will be here to teach English and impart a little culture." The rector smiled broadly, tilting his head even more, and the students laughed loudly.

It grew quiet again, as if they awaited the annual edict. They were not disappointed.

"I've said before that the door swings out here, and no one is obliged to stay. Some are not meant to be here—"

The shrill voice grew louder. His younger brother, also a priest, had run off with a voluptuous high school girl two years after ordination. Thom was not yet aware.

"Better now than later. The priesthood is for men, not for sissies, not for mama's boys, but for strong, courageous men who can take it. No one's holding you here. The front door is never locked. If you can't cut it, get out!"

The chapel was like a tomb. Raymond Nowicki was a powerful man, once a fine athlete, now an ascetic loner, not well liked by the local clergy or even his own faculty, but admired by the bishop. And a fair man who truly loved the boys in his gruff Eastern European way. His final "get out" rang ominously through the chapel. Thirty of the two hundred boys would be gone in two weeks, ten of them by the next morning.

He concluded, "It's been a busy day. You're on your own from now till lights-out at 9:00 sharp. Wake-up bell is 5:40. First we'll say night prayers."

The drone of swift Latin filled the chapel. Thom picked up a book and tried to follow. Hopeless.

"Nunc dimittis, servum tuum Domine, secundum verbum tuum in pace."

Ten minutes later it was over. He was already starved, and he hungered for Margaret's mince pie or leftover pork and gravy. There would be no food till morning.

He left chapel to walk under the clear September sky, hardly appreciating the rare unscheduled time to reflect aimlessly. A strange anxiety took hold of him until he trembled noticeably, then he climbed the steps to the third floor, undressed, slipped on his bathrobe, and entered the washroom to scrub his teeth. A tall, lean newcomer, Gregory Peck handsome, with fine black hair flat on his head, even white teeth, and a chiseled Irish face, stood opposite the stalls against an open window. He smiled not quite shyly and offered Thom some gum.

"I feel like I joined the German army." His voice was deeply resonant. He moved his head back slightly and chuckled. "Where you from?" A mock German accent.

Thom was embarrassed and wanted to keep the grand silence without offending. "I—I don't think we're supposed—"

"Oh shit, I'm sorry—We'll talk tomorrow."

The moment Thom turned to scrub his teeth, he saw a gaunt effeminate-looking priest, brown wavy hair parted in the middle, looking at them through rimless glasses. His voice was crisp, diction impeccable. It was Father Terrence Moody, the disciplinarian.

"Did I hear voices?" The final sibilant roared.

Silence.

"Someone was talking!" Again he held the last syllable until it hummed.

"I was." The black-haired young man in a white terry cloth bathrobe slipped out his gum without a trace of fear or insubordination in his voice.

"Did you miss the rector's conference?"

"No."

"No, *father*."

"Sorry. No, father." He smiled.

"What's so funny?"

He paused and looked at the priest directly as Moody twitched, his gleaming shoes squeaking just slightly.

"It seemed funny—Last night I was playing poker and—"

"What's your name?"

"Collins. Bill Collins. What's yours?" He said it respectfully.

"You're in the seminary, Mr. Collins. Is that clear?"

"Yes, sir—er—father."

Moody swirled crisply out of the room. Collins rescued the gum and chucked it out the window. "Holy shit—I can't believe it—*Achtung!*"

Thom walked down the long silent aisle to bed number forty-seven, slipped on his pajamas, and crawled under the covers. Some were already sleeping. He sat up suddenly, then remembered he had already said night prayers in chapel. Father Terrence Moody was staring narrowly from the exit end of the dormitory. Then he disappeared, and Margaret's son was alone with his thoughts, feeling pure and strong on the narrow seminary cot.

For Thomas Aloysius Maguire, the seminary was only another challenge. Its discipline did not frighten him, its loneliness did not discourage him. It never occurred to him that he really had a choice. There was no pain he could not endure, no self-denial he would not embrace, no matter what he felt, depression or anxiety or black despair. God alone could bring peace and serenity and ultimate happiness. Sadness was but a "dark night of the soul," unhappiness but a heavenly sign that he had not yet surrendered to his God. Margaret knew it well. John Patrick drank it away. Jack had raged against it, and Jim questioned it silently. Only Thom gave in.

He would not merely be another Christ—*alter Christus*—he would be the proud symbol of everything his people had struggled for through famine and persecution and a fever more ravaging than any typhoid. He was proof that the oppression was finally at an end, not merely by England or a Protestant America or an unfeeling Church. But even by God.

In a few minutes Thom fell asleep. He never heard the curfew bell.

Soon the entire long room was in darkness, a few bedsprings squeaking, someone snoring loudly. Tittering. It grew more silent, and a little boy could be heard crying. Then two more.

Thomas Aloysius Maguire slept soundly without tears.

6

"Ad Deum Qui Laetificat"

Thom had no difficulty hearing the morning bell. It rang at 5:40 for a full thirty seconds and jarred every nerve in his body. A few startled newcomers shouted out loud. A prefect's voice mumbled *"Benedicamus Domino"* up and down the aisles. Muffled yawning responses. *"Deo gratias."* There was no conversation.

The washroom was crowded, fifteen sinks and three stalls for ninety men in fifteen minutes. Logistically it couldn't work, but it did. Old-timers had learned to rush to the bathroom at the sound of the bell or to dress first and wash later. Some ignored bladders until they could use the first-floor toilet outside the study hall. Shavers scraped in three minutes of cold water. By the end of the week Bill Collins had taken his shaving kit to the second-floor infirmary where he showered with hot water and dried with seminary towels. It had never occurred to the faculty that any student would dare such audacity. Nor did he tell anyone of his great discovery.

Thom waited for a free sink, cut himself twice with the cold razor, and finished dressing on the way to chapel. His bladder ached. There had been no time to reflect or feel sorry, or to wonder if he was still tired. He hardly made the sign of the cross when morning prayers began. Only half in Latin. Then a fifteen-minute public meditation from the gossamer writings of Père Louis Hemond, who pictured a technicolor Jesus in Gethsemane. The spiritual director, Father Olivier, a kind sallow-skinned Greek scholar, shapeless and fat in his black cassock, mumbled the words in a plaintive, hypnotic monotone. Jesus seemed as tired as he was.

" 'His parched lips made no request of waters he himself had created. His swollen eyes, clotted with the blood from his thorny crown, did not accuse or complain. The homespun robe, over which soldiers would quarrel and shake dice, was matted to his bruised shoulders.' "

Then the meditation became practical.

" 'What have I suffered? I whose sins of self-indulgence and vanity and envy have scourged my gentle Master. How can I complain when no whip has bruised my skin nor thorn has pierced my tender flesh? Dear Jesus, whatever you ask of me today, I will give generously. Without complaint or sullen regret. The world has nothing to offer me. You alone are my hope as I watch and pray with you until the end.' "

Bill Collins was sound asleep, draped over the end of the pew. Bobbie Foley squirmed in place, staring at a stained-glass window of a red-robed Christ next to a grapevine: *Ego sum vitis, vos palmites.* Thom Maguire studied Christ in the garden and promised solemnly never to make him bleed again. Gradually Thom would be taught to focus on his personal failures—to root out pride and vanity and lust. For now he was content to focus on Jesus. Then the daily mass began.

It was the Feast of the Birth of the Blessed Virgin Mary, nine months to the day after her own Immaculate Conception. Beginning with the rector, the priests took weekly turns celebrating the daily community mass at the main altar. Two other faculty members whispered their unbloody sacrifice on smaller side altars, and all students took turns serving. Weekly lists were posted on the bulletin board just as they were for work detail on the grounds and in the refectory. Father Elvin Joseph Ward, the nervous little man with no chin, celebrated briskly at the Virgin's altar, and, on the opposite side, a docile Saint Joseph looked benignly down on Father Terrence Moody. Monsignor Nowicki announced the Gospel: *"Sequentia sancti evangelii secundum Mattheum."* The familiar words made Thom feel more at home, but there was no time to reflect. The mass moved along swiftly. The Gospel was among Scripture's most boring, an attempt to give Jesus a genealogy, illogically tracing the ancestry of Mary's spouse from Abraham to Isaac, down through Boaz and Ruth, Salathiel and Zorobabel, to Jacob, the grandfather of Jesus, "the father of Joseph, the husband of Mary." No one questioned the unused sperm of Joseph. God had become man, and Joseph had never slept with his wife; he was a father without sex or blood descendants. Jacob was grandfather to no one —but Thomas Maguire was not put off by paradoxes. He felt energized to be a part of it all. Collins leaned his arm against the pew as if he wouldn't make it to breakfast.

Everyone received communion. If someone had touched himself during the night—which was most rare —Father Olivier was waiting patiently in a rear confessional. Father Ward, racing through the mass like the Latin scholar he was, finished in time to assist Monsignor Nowicki with the distribution of Hosts. The organ played the soft chords of "Panis Angelicus," and students filed back to their pews with Christ in their own bodies. Thom bowed his head and felt special strength, even though theology decreed there was nothing to feel. He talked privately to his Lord, begging grace, asking pardon for Madeline Powers and help for Margaret Ann to endure John Patrick's drinking. Then the community mass was over.

Thom and the other newcomers were eager for breakfast. They had not counted on the mass of thanksgiving, and no sooner had Monsignor Nowicki departed than Father Olivier appeared to begin again. The pudgy balding head was bent forward by years of reverent obedience. *"Introibo ad altare Dei."* The mass was the greatest act in all of Christendom, and every priest said his own public sacrifice. Two more faculty members appeared at the side altars, offering the same "clean Oblation" as happened at some moment of that day everywhere in the world.

Halfway through the second mass, "the voice of God" rang out, and the old-timers genuflected their way to the refectory. A few prayers were followed by fresh bread and oleo, pasty oatmeal and coffee, and the explosion of happy boys' voices that had been silent for almost fourteen hours.

Each table had its own prefect, a college student who passed the food and got up to cut more bread. On Sunday there was frosted raisin bread and fresh oranges, and it was important to have a fleet-footed prefect who raced up to salvage another loaf of delicious sweetness for his charges. They always had fifteen minutes to eat breakfast before another bell rang that forbade additional munching. Meal prayers were next, and there was just enough time to make beds, find a toilet stall, and catch a breath of fresh air before the mass movement to the study hall. Thirty minutes to cram, then three fifty-minute classes of Greek, Latin, and English from nine till noon. New books were handed out the first day. Five minutes' travel time across the hall to the next class, wild voices until the bell, then perfect silence and an absolute requirement that every student be in place. They all took it for granted without tension, in casual clockwork. At noon the Angelus sounded, and in an instant everyone was motionless, serious and devout in prayer as they had been in studies.

There was another procession to the refectory for the main meal of the day. Barely time for a running leak. More Latin prayers, then the appointed reading of daily saints and martyrs from the Church's twenty centuries of history everywhere in the world. Since the missal only recalled the most outstanding saints, Thom had not been aware that there were twenty or thirty saints honored each day.

The assigned student reader switched from Latin to English above the sound of knives and forks. The food eventually tasted better to Thom, a far cry from Margaret's, but good. Boiled potatoes and floury beef stew, corn and more wheat bread with oleo, a piece of peach cobbler. Then a bell, a few more mumbled Latin prayers, and a procession to the chapel to pray in English. The kitchen detail were exempted and rushed the dishes to the six Dominican nuns who "mothered" the seminary—devoted women, too old or unsuited for teaching, conscious of the dignity of their work. Two young ones, shy and pretty, were teased constantly and responded as though they were popular high school girls.

The English prayers continued in the chapel for ten minutes. "O Sacrament most holy, O Sacrament divine, all praise and all thanksgiving be every moment thine." A moment of silence, then everyone outside for twenty minutes of air. Ex-GIs looked for a secret place to smoke while novices shuffled to find their way around. Soon twenty minutes meant time enough for Ping-Pong or chess, and an extra ten minutes became a delightful bonus.

There were less strenuous classes in the afternoon—

science, religion, history, speech, and music once a week —every forty-five minutes without a break till 3:30.

At the end of the day there was a wild animal roar. Nobody walked. Yelling and laughing up three flights of stairs to the lockers and dormitories, ten minutes to get outside. Clothes were changed under flying bathrobes; only Collins never used one. Then everyone rushed down to smile shyly at the friendlier faculty members returning to their suites. A few were recluses; others, like Ward and Nowicki, loved to circulate amiably but distantly among the boys. Thom loved the camaraderie among the students, a kindness and helpfulness he had never known before. No bitching or provoking, everyone seemingly respected in the world of "other Christs." He soon was racing out the door with new friends to September softball games organized according to age and ability. Almost everyone played football in October and November, basketball or hockey from then till March, and baseball or track in the spring. Handball was played outside all year round. Students were assigned by the Student Work Committee to do everything. No complaints. Get the fields ready, line the base paths and yard markers, flood the skating rink, dig out the high jump pit. *"In corpore sano . . ."*

God's voice screamed again after an hour and a half; pitchers dropped the ball immediately; not a muscle moved recreationally after the bell. Then fifteen minutes to wash up and get to supper, showers only on Saturdays (except for Collins). Rush up the stairs, sixty seconds at the washbasin, clothes changed, boys roaring down the stairs for a quick drink at the water fountain, laughing and nodding to friends. No one pushed or bullied. Christianity in practice. Outside the refectory they assembled to say the evening Angelus. *"Fiat mihi secundum verbum tuum."* More Latin prayers for food. Conversation at the evening meal except during Lent. Cold cuts, potato chips, more wheat bread, and canned plums. Cookies, homemade, one apiece. "Can I have your dessert, Tim?" Tim Hughes never ate dessert. He was a local saint, pale and drawn, with the beatific smile of a distant vision, silent unless spoken to, then intensely attentive and kind.

After supper, a half hour of recreation. Checkers, a chattering walk around the circular gravel path, even a student haircut for a quarter. GIs who smoked finally found the boiler room. No one was permitted on the lawns in front of the building. Tim Hughes and two others always went to chapel, heads bowed or rigidly upright without a flicker of an eye, lost in God. No one forbade them, although to ignore recreation could be an unchristian escape. There had to be balance in God's active service, and seminary rule was the distillation of centuries of monastic wisdom. Another bell, then intense study from half-past seven till nine. The disciplinarian, Father Moody, patrolled the study halls, but there was rarely a need. The students were soundless save for the opening of a desk for another book. Then back to chapel for night prayers. "*Nunc dimittis* . . . ('I am heartily sorry . . .')" Up the terrazzo steps more slowly now, silent, reflecting, three flights to the dim whiteness. Soundless undressing under bathrobes. Twenty minutes to scrub teeth and do it all. Sweaty bodies, flushing toilets, no talking, grand silence. Talk to Jesus. Weary: All for you, sweet Jesus! Coughing, snores, still a few sobs from little boys. Serene and peaceful. Thom's body settled on the thin mattress in ecstatic exhaustion. No king ever enjoyed his bed as much. A nighthawk called, sounding out of place.

The grating bell. Morning already. Leap from bed: "*Deo gratias!*" Rush to the sink. Only second in line today. Too late to change socks. Mortification. God's man. *Alter Christus*. Down the stairs, Latin prayers, the continuing meditation with Père Hemond. Jesus is being scourged today. "Flesh ripped for my sins. . . . What has he done to deserve it? Innocent . . . all for me." Today I will not brag or be proud. Or unkind. Thom was learning the system of meditation. He would be an unselfish saint in no time. Jesus help me! Talk to whomever talks to you. No special friends. Love for even the most unloveable. It is a community. Bobbie Foley or Bill Collins, it doesn't matter.

Meanwhile Thom fought to keep up. Two Latin classes to make up for insufficiencies of Saint Raphael's High, a special schedule prepared by Father Ward who smiled stern encouragement. Beginning Greek and a year's Greek to make up. No history or literature till next semester while he and others—like Collins—who entered late learned the language of Scripture and the Church. The older students were quick and impressive.

"What are the exceptions to *um* in the genitive plural?"

Hands leaped up as Thom grew dizzier.

"Faux, fraus, glis, jus, lis, mas, mus, nix, plus, vis."

"Genitive plural of *jus?*"

"Jurium."

"What about *pater?*"

"Patrum." This was not Saint Raphael's where he got an A in Latin and had never taken a book home.

"Why?"

"Ium—exception rules: *Vates, senex, pater, panis,* with *accipiter* and *canis. Frater, mater, juvenis*—"

Thom was terrified. From *agricola* to this.

"Why *introibo 'ad' altare Dei?*"

"Accusative of motion."

They droned on. More hands raised; shining, smiling, eager faces; alert eyes. "I know." "Ask me!" Pavlov's paradise. No M&Ms, only approval and marks. Checks in a book for every right answer, a smile, a nod. "Fine, Skorski!" "Good work, Lanier." "What's wrong, Higgins?" "You look confused, Maguire!"

Thom would never learn it. Envious of Skorski. Only sixteen and already a genius.

Thom studied Skorski holding forth at supper at an adjoining table. Long lips, greased hair, big nose and shiny forehead and a belching laugh. Nothing in football. He would have been a zero at Saint Raphael's. Skorski praying loudly in chapel: *"Et exultavit spiritus meus in Deo salutare meo."* Confidence. Perfect diction.

"Jesus, help me not to be envious. Teach me humility—in the garden—bleeding, dying—I want to be a priest."

Some would never be. "Leo Schults is gone." Epileptic seizure in the gym, a great athlete. Canon law had decreed: *"Non epileptici . . ."* Eddie O'Toole's left. Swishy little Eddie with the warm smile. Thom had liked him. *"Neque molles . . ."* "What happened to Watson?" "He took food from the table." *"Neque fures."* "George Higgins–"

Thom had especially liked George—kind brown eyes, dusty red hair, slow agrarian speech, from a chicken farm near Draperville in the Michigan thumb area. The pride of a simple uneducated family, he had barely passed his entrant's exam. The saintly curé of Ars, Saint John Vianney, was his hero, a canonized French saint considered too dumb to be a priest who had made it in Napoleonic France. Perseverance, determination, prayer, daily study. Nothing would stop George; he even snuck his Latin book outside during recreation. Serious brown eyes hiding in the bushes. *"Agricolae habent frumentum . . . habent multa ciba."* Eyes moist, mouth slowly forming impossible archaic syllables that meant nothing. Caesar and Cicero and Horace lay in wait while George studied *puer* and *puella* at night in the dimly lighted toilet stalls. He snuck Latin verbs into his missal and glanced at vocabulary during dinner. "Saint John Vianney, help me! *Porta* is door and *portare* is to carry—O God!" God had need of every kind of minister. Vianney was as effective as any Richelieu, a people's padre. ("The weak things of this world God has chosen to confound the strong.") George begged Him, but it wasn't to be. Even prayer wasn't enough. God finally didn't want George Higgins; but neither did Draperville or the aching onions in the soggy muck. So George must have thought. They found his stiff body in the alfalfa field along with a shotgun and an empty shell. And a list of verbs still in his back pocket.

They said the rosary for George Higgins at Saint Robert's Seminary. It was voluntary. Thom organized it and thirty of George's friends came after supper during recreation. The curé d'Ars couldn't make it, but the rosary was in English. George would have liked that. And Monsignor Nowicki stopped Thom in the hall to commend him. Thom had never been happier.

Days raced by and gradually Thomas Maguire caught on. He responded slowly at first, then soon his hand shot up like the others. "*Placere* takes the dative following." A smile. Two correct answers during the same class period and two check marks after his name. Collins never volunteered, but finally even he was challenged. It was a special Latin class for the C boys, those who had completed some high school and were in "combination" classes to make up for weak or nonexistent high school Latin, and pert little Elvin Ward singled him out from the twelve.

"What do you think, Domine Collins?" Ward smiled gregariously.

"About what?" A burst of laughter.

Suddenly Father Ward's missing chin trembled. Beady brown eyes grew fierce and the skinny teeth were bared like those of a cornered rat. "I don't find it funny!" the powerful voice rasped in the sudden deathlike silence.

"About the formation of adverbs."

"It seems logical."

"What seems logical."

"Adverbs! In English you add *ly* to an adjective. In Latin it's just *ter*—as in laugh*ter*."

No one laughed.

"You're quite a comic, aren't you?"

"This place could use a laugh." He said it simply, without anger or arrogance. Thom was sweating.

"I think you're right, Domine Collins." He feigned a warm smile, his upper teeth biting his lower lip. "Suppose you give us one and hand in five hundred Latin adverbs by tomorrow morning's class. Now, Domine Kemmiller, what do you think of Latin adverbs?"

Thom had been accustomed to competition at home and at Saint Raphael's, but never anything like this. Every weekly quiz was a challenge, every assigned paper was red marked carefully and rehashed. The talented were complimented, the average criticized or ignored. Gradually everyone found his scholastic niche. Within three strenuous, totally concentrated months, Thom was considered a "brain." The Maguire competitiveness had nowhere else to go. There were no women to fight for, no beer busts to improve status, no cars to fix or parties to attend. No newspaper or periodical to read, no Jack Benny or Milton Berle, no games to go to, no outside information fed in. So Thom focused on studies with all the celibate energy of a proud young man who had to excel and feared he might be in over his head.

Wednesday and Saturday afternoons were free. Time to fit in league games, catch up on studies, write letters, and worry about grades. Some of the poorer students, and even some of the "brains," studied all afternoon. If Thom, on his way to football, passed an absorbed Stan Skorski, he feared Skorski was getting ahead while he dallied in mediocrity. Sometimes he was troubled during the whole first quarter of the game until he finally forgot about Skorski long enough to win. Then he rushed back, sponged himself hurriedly, and raced to his books.

The effort didn't pay off. His first-quarter marks averaged about 90 whereas the greasy head and thick lips made 96. Thom could hear Skorski's confident voice, strident at prayers, laughing too loudly at recreation, dropping Latin and Greek bon mots and complicated exceptions to grammatical absolutes. Collins didn't seem to mind. He had averaged about 85.

But Thom Maguire made up for his classroom wounds at sports, and in the meager world of seminary competition he was incredible. In touch football, few boys had cleats, and Thom ran circles around boys with tennis shoes, introducing exciting plays for an easy championship the first half of the league season. The Athletic Committee announced that cleats were barred, and teams were more fairly rearranged. Thom was newly loaded with awkward farmers, a pair of girlish linemen, and only a few boys with any talent. Within days he had organized them with growling nicknames and had scheduled practices during the half hour after supper. Again, this time in tennis shoes, he ran away with the senior league title although he was one of only two sixteen year olds in the league. Most players were in college and several were ex-GIs who had promised God the seminary if they got out of Bataan or Corregidor.

As a new and distinguished member of the elite "jock set," Thom began to hold a special place, for he was also a "brain." It was only important not to give the impression that he worked hard. Even the rector, Monsignor Nowicki, himself a former athlete and "brain," was soon particularly fond of Thom and gave the boy his enthusiastic support. Although he had not yet seen Thom play baseball, rumors were flying. A word from Bobbie Foley was enough; just being from Saint Raphael's now gave Bobbie status.

"The Tigers really want him. So do the Cubs." The two teams had played in the World Series a year before.

"Took the Legion title. Batted almost .500."

Thom overheard and prayed for humility, then reinforced his prayer at morning meditation. He learned to make light of sports. Nor was he only posing. Paramount was scholastic improvement and the frustrating quest for sanctity, until he began to live increasingly in his mind. It was a most significant change for a boy who had studied and played spontaneously, as the gifted always seem to do, without stretching or overreaching. Now, sporting events seemed less significant, especially since the slight Skorski played only an awkward game of tennis and was usually content to circle the gravel path with Pliny or Shakespeare. Thom reevaluated his own priorities constantly until Skorski was the target of a gnawing envy and the subject of weekly confessions.

"I was jealous of another ten or twelve times."

"I bragged seven times."

"I was uncharitable to others three times."

"I was even jealous in chapel during prayers."

Father Olivier droned softly of patience and not expecting too much of one's self. His quiet self-effacing wisdom made no impact on Thom who tried to forget Skorski with the same intensity that he rivaled him.

Skorski was undisputed leader of another clique, which was almost as powerful as the "jock set" and more enduring. It was a group of literati and assorted "brains" —some not even outstanding students, but all versant with Aristophanes and Mozart, *Finian's Rainbow* and Robert Penn Warren, liturgical innovations and the poetry of Blake and Yeats. They exchanged views on Eugene O'Neill and John Calvin, attempted conversation in Latin with loud giggles, and were even partially aware of current events. (Thom learned in a letter from John Patrick that Notre Dame and Frank Leahy were national champions, and when Jim wondered why the Church had banned *Forever Amber,* Thom didn't know what he was talking about.) It might have seemed, to an outsider, a kind of homosexual assemblage, although there was no physical sentiment beyond the walks or the lofty discussions on the grass. Athletes were "brutes" or "beasts"; emphasis on sports was "Neanderthal"; and Monsignor Nowicki was fondly named "Bronco Nagurski." It was the only football name they knew. Father Ward gave enough salutary evidence of culture to be admired, but the newly assigned Father Duffey, with thick glasses and a Santa Claus body, who often chatted and giggled with them, was their real hero. Any faculty member who was a jock was the object of their scorn, and it was a great coup to challenge such a prof and win.

Few dared to challenge Elvin Ward, but when Thom proved him wrong about an "ablative of place" in Cicero's *Orations*, there were whispered congratulations. "You've got guts."

Ward had been uncustomarily silent for several minutes, hands folded across his forehead, until he spoke in an unusually subdued voice. "Well-a, yes-a, that seems to be right—Continue with the translation, Domine Maguire—"

Even Collins had taken note. "You stabbed the führer—he'll be out for your ass—"

Actually he seemed to prefer Collins's ass, as did most of the faculty. Collins's strange poise disturbed them. When asked to recite, he slowly rose to his feet without nervousness or the least obsequiousness, and usually he did well. Always adequately. On rare occasions he simply stated, "I didn't have time to prepare this." The class seemed to suck in its anxious breath in unison as Collins stood calm and motionless.

Elvin Ward was furious. "The work too hard, Domine Collins?"

"Not really."

"Then what's wrong?" No one stirred.

"Nothing that I know of."

"Then try writing out the next five pages for tomorrow. Did you have time Domine Schaeffer?"

"Yes, father."

Dennis Schaeffer was yet another type, average jock, slow-footed, and roundly overweight. A medium student who competed with no one, unusually good-natured, never moody or withdrawn, he loved the seminary and everything about it: the food, the silence, the games, the classes, the faculty, the nuns who worked in the kitchen. Even the monthly parades of black suits walking in ranks down the sidewalks of Grandville to visit a parish church or a small museum under supervision of a prefect, forbidden to buy a newspaper or even a candy bar. Dennis rejoiced in everything. He challenged or criticized no one.

The "saints" were more frightening to the faculty. Tim Hughes almost had to be restrained from continued prayer, and his ascetic, pimply face, flushed and thin, didn't flicker during mass or community prayers. He was the last to leave chapel before breakfast, he spent every class break at prayer, and often he made his way quietly to the dark chapel at three or four in the morning. For days at a time he took only a piece of bread and a little water, imitating saints he read about at dinner or in the daily missal. It was not until Thom Maguire had awakened at 4:30 to witness him writhing on the floor two beds away that Tim Hughes was asked to leave.

He was lying on his back without any clothes, his face radiant with some distant joy, eyes not focusing, bony hands held aloft and moving with his swaying body.

"*Rabboni,* master! I am ready! Come to me!" When gurgling sounds came from his throat, Thom thought the boy was dying, and he ran to Father Moody's room. When they returned, Tim Hughes was lying in a puddle of urine while thirty or forty students witnessed his ecstasy. Collins pillowed his head, covered him with a bedspread, then stroked his sweating forehead and rigid arms until he coaxed him back to bed. Father Moody seemed terrified.

"I saw the Lord!" Hughes cried. His light blue eyes focused, but the hysterical smile endured.

Someone giggled, and Collins silenced him with a look. "Get the hell out of here!" Even Terrence Moody stayed rigidly at a safe distance until a doctor led Tim to the infirmary where he ate almost nothing for four days, then was taken home and not seen again. One rumor said he had joined the Trappists in Kentucky, another that he had been committed to an asylum in Traverse City. Collins said he would like to get him laid at once and Skorski said that was crude talk in front of Bobbie Foley. Actually Bobbie Foley had not understood what he meant. No matter. With Tim Hughes's departure, only minor visionaries remained.

Then it was Christmas vacation and Thomas Maguire had two weeks at home.

At home, Thom could not get enough milk, and he gorged himself on Margaret's food. John Patrick was as delighted as his wife. Margaret beamed as he accompanied her to daily mass, carrying his new Latin missal. Monsignor came up to say hello and invite him to a dinner at the rectory. Father Kenelley paid them special attention after evening services, and Margaret prayed for humility. Thom scrimmaged with the varsity, and, although he had not practiced, scored twenty points. Together with Jim and Tim, Thom and John Patrick watched the Christmas tournaments. Saint Raphael's lost in the finals, and Art Doolan grinned sadly. "We coulda used you."

Thom felt proud of his sacrifice and then was angry that he had been proud.

McNulty followed John Patrick out of the gym, growling, "Why don't you bring that kid home for a year or two?"

"Talk to his mother." He said it in a mumble and did not speak all the way home. Then he drank too much with Jim.

Jim seemed older, and Thom found it almost impossible to communicate with him. Jim posed theological questions about the conflict between God's foreknowledge and man's free will. Thom stumbled badly until Margaret insisted that college didn't make Jim "an ordained priest." Then she wondered if the Jesuits were helping him lose his faith.

Jim asked endless questions about the seminary program. Thom felt defensive, showing off his Greek and Latin and attempting to justify the discipline. Grand silence was a difficult assignment to explain.

"What's the point of it if you have to do it?"

"Community life requires some sacrifices."

"So does every other life, but absolute rules don't really teach anyone. That's the Church's problem. No one learns to think."

Jim was not aware that Thom would not study any theology for many years. Actually his own Jesuit education dealt with more topical realities: evolution, existential atheism, the Church's essential involvement in the politics of Europe. Thom was only a boy in prep school, and the wisdom of the Church insisted that foundations be laid, careful foundations such as Caesar's wars and Homer's epic poetry. A second-year philosophy class and another in themes of European history had given Jim a different focus from that of his younger brother.

Jim had instinctively doubted from the beginning. Now, his awareness of more than thirty-five antipopes in the Church's first fifteen hundred years, and of Thomas

Aquinas's belief in a three-stage evolution of the human soul—from vegetable to animal to spiritual—added new and puzzling fuel to his doubts.

Thom was angry and embarrassed that he had no suitable answers, but most of all he felt Jim's disappointment.

"I'm not a priest yet, Jim. It's my first year."

Jim laughed. "I've got so damn many questions. It's like a new world's opening up."

Thom retreated to the company of Margaret and the *Confessions of St. Augustine,* which Father Olivier had recommended. He looked over some Caesar and some passages in Xenophon and read a book called *Dominus Vobiscum* by an Irish priest and another by Canon Sheehan that Monsignor Doyle provided from his private library. When John Patrick favored the Taft-Hartley Act over Truman's veto—"that damn labor will drag us all down the tube"—Thom only nodded in ignorance. Even Notre Dame's national championship had eluded him, and John Patrick wondered what the hell was wrong with letting the boys read the daily paper.

"For God's sake, they're gonna work in the world."

Jim agreed and thought Thom should be able to see a movie while he was home.

"*Miracle on 34th Street* wouldn't hurt anything."

Margaret defended him. "The Church knows what it's doing. If he needed newspapers or movies, they would encourage it. You can waste a lot of time with the paper." She glared at John Patrick, and Thom was spared further abuse. Then she reprimanded Jim for drinking beer.

"It's legal in Milwaukee, mother."

"This is not Milwaukee. And don't get so smart as long as we're still paying for your education."

Thom withdrew to the kitchen and caught up on leftovers. And Margaret prepared every favorite food as if he were returning to prison. Chicken and dumplings, pork roast and gravy, lean spareribs and sauerkraut, homemade bread and savory vegetable soup. Chocolate cake with fudge frosting, Dutch apple pie, and two quarts of milk a day. At meals they were a family again. Jim kidded Thom about being "king seminarian," and they laughed about a chocolate pie Jack had once eaten by himself. Tim asked Thom if he knew the mass by heart, and Jim wondered if there were classes in walking on water. Anne said such talk was sinful, but she laughed when Margaret began to giggle.

Jim learned to avoid serious discussions, recognizing that Thom was struggling with his own uncertainties. In a strange way he was proud of his brother's determination to become a priest, and he told him as much after moving away from John Patrick, who sat in fascination in front of the new television set.

"Is it tough?"

"Not really, but it's hard to catch up on everything." He talked about rigid classes in the minutiae of Latin grammar. Then he grinned. "I'll make it."

Jim smiled. "I have no doubts." He reflected, "I'm having similar problems. Advanced algebra at Saint Raphael's was a joke, and chemistry was five years behind. I didn't really know a proton from a neutron."

Thom smiled. He still didn't know. "It'll be fun when we're finally out of school. I'll baptize the babies you deliver."

"And bury my mistakes." Then they laughed loudly.

It was a warm and special moment for both of them.

Margaret interrupted as Jim was about to talk more honestly. "There's more pie out here." Then it was over.

Thom lost himself in his prayers and the autobiography of Saint Theresa. Jim snuck away to visit Connie Hackett. When he arrived home late from a movie, he passed Thom's room and saw his brother still on his knees. Jim slipped into bed and masturbated without guilt.

The following morning Thom went to the dentist and it was found that he had seven cavities. John Patrick was furious and ordered him to drink milk for the rest of the year. Jim, now the family medical adviser, agreed. Margaret told Anne that to give up milk was a small enough sacrifice, but she did not say it in John Patrick's presence.

It was a happy vacation for them all. Jim still went to his woods, even inviting Tim to come along. They trod carefully across the frozen swamp, lit a fire of cattails and scattered branches, and watched some young Dutchmen playing makeshift hockey on perfect ice.

Anne made visits with her priestly brother and was proud of his missal at mass. She asked about everything and marveled at the morning meditations and the ease with which he recited the Latin Angelus. Devout girl friends gathered around them at evening services or after confessions, and once Thom saw Madeline Powers.

At first he pretended not to notice her. She turned around several times, and finally she gave him a warm smile. He blushed furiously, then nodded brusquely without smiling and wondered if he had done the right thing. Monsignor Nowicki had counseled them before they left.

"This is the test. No movies or parties with girls. Not even in your own home. If your sister is having a party, arrange to leave. The Church gives wise advice to her clerics: *'Nunquam solus cum sola!'* This is a chance to prove your courage, not to look up old girl friends. Your routine is the same. Just some time to see your parents. This vacation is more for them than for you."

Monsignor had said nothing about seeing Madeline Powers in church, but Thom noted that she was in the confessional a long time and her face was flushed when she left. She did not look at him.

When it was time to return to the seminary, John Patrick insisted on driving him. "I want to get a look at the place." He had not visited on the family Sundays in the fall, and, out of Mary O'Meara's hearing, Margaret had apologized to a disappointed Thom and then smothered him with fresh laundry and fried chicken and cake—only permitted on visiting Sundays.

Check-in time after vacation was 6:30. It was an hour's drive even in good weather, but a heavy snowstorm made Margaret begin to be edgy at four o'clock.

"You'd better get started. Do you want me to ride along?"

"No." John Patrick ignored her disappointment and continued to sip more coffee and finish a crossword. When he got up to put on his overcoat it was already 4:50, and she was frantic. "That's a terrible storm!"

"We'll be all right."

"Got everything?"

Thom nodded and took the sandwiches she had wrapped in waxed paper. He invited Jim to ride along but then remembered it was Jim's last night before returning to Marquette.

They set out alone. Always quiet when he was driving,

John Patrick was unusually silent. The roads were slippery and it was almost six o'clock when they reached a halfway point at Plankshaw. Thom knew they would be late, but John Patrick continued to drive cautiously, periodically fumbling for cigarettes. He coughed and spat out the window. Drool froze on the frosted pane. Once the car slipped off the shoulder, slid broadside for fifty feet, and then righted itself.

"Slippery as hell." He muttered it to no one and Thom grunted assent. "Don't let me forget to take care of that milk situation—" He paused. "Do you like the place?"

"I think so. So far."

"Don't be afraid to come home if you don't—Your mother will survive—that's for sure!"

When they pulled into the circle drive it was almost seven o'clock. A few other cars were dismissing passengers with brief good-byes, and John Patrick waited for Thom to get his luggage.

"You don't have to come in, dad. I'll take care of the milk and—we're late." Thom was terrified.

"So what the hell; we're alive! The roads are rough. They know that." He walked casually.

Tiny Father Ward was at the top of the steps. Scowling coldly. John Patrick extended his ungloved hand. "I'm John Maguire, Thom's dad."

The hand was ignored. "You're also thirty minutes late."

John Patrick sputtered briefly but contained himself. "Those roads are pretty icy, father."

"You should have given yourself time: 6:30 means 6:30 here." There was no Italian inflection.

"Well, I apologize." He lit a cigarette.

"I will thank you not to smoke."

Thom had rushed into the study hall to drop his bag, and he returned to see his father red-faced and furious.

"Get right into chapel, Maguire. You're already late, and we'll take care of that later." Thom nodded to his father and disappeared.

"But it was my fault—" John Patrick took another drag on the cigarette, then crushed it under his feet.

Father Ward thought better of reprimanding him further and said coldly, "Will there be anything else?"

"Yes, as a matter of fact. I want the boy to have milk—seven cavities. Why the hell don't they all have milk? Growing boys—" He drew some crumpled bills from his pocket, dropping his keys.

Father Ward waved away the rumpled money. "You'll have to send a letter to the business office." He reacted to John Patrick's indictment. "They do fine without it —fine. In fact—"

John Patrick was furious. "Look, damn it, I want him to have milk starting tomorrow. Send me a bill—"

"We have our regulations. One is that the boy should return after two weeks on time—"

John Patrick grabbed him.

Monsignor Nowicki appeared on the scene and sensed the danger. "What seems to be the trouble?"

"This son-of-a-bitch—goddamn it—he's gonna have milk tomorrow—half hour late in a goddamn snowstorm —I won't take this shit—"

Elvin Ward was quickly dismissed. Monsignor Nowicki continued to talk soothingly with great respect and understanding. He took the money and promised milk in the morning, then he shook hands graciously and led the still flushed John Patrick to the door. He breathed with relief when the door was finally closed and he heard the car drive away.

A moment later, Bill Collins walked in eating a turkey sandwich, nodded briefly to the monsignor, stuffed the sandwich in his coat pocket, and walked serenely into chapel.

From that moment on a petty vendetta began. Elvin Joseph Ward had been humiliated, and he would get even. He sat in his room still trembling. Furious. Humiliated. No one had laid a hand on him since his mother had left his father. Until tonight. He had almost fainted from fear. He could not stop trembling or hating the big, powerful red-faced man who had confronted him. Elvin Ward had won a thousand intellectual battles, even in Rome at the Gregorian University, won them with all the stored frustrations of a man who had never been noticed by the plainest woman, had never been on anyone's team. But tonight, for the first time in his life, he had been really terrified, and he would never forget.

Only a few seminarians were sent to study in Rome, those suited for ecclesiastical preeminence. It was an expensive gamble. Even the bright losers, who returned from Rome to work in anonymous parishes, talked about the experience for the rest of their lives; and the majority, like Elvin Joseph Ward, went to seminaries or chanceries or marriage courts. Raymond Nowicki had never gone, and he felt the slight when Elvin Ward talked of the brilliant theologians at the "Greg" or the side trips to the Forum and Pompeii.

Even though Elvin Ward was classified as vice-rector (or "rector of vice," as the brains said), he felt superior to the Polish rector who was a mediocre student of Latin and spoke no Italian. Bishop Malloy had appointed Ward to head up the ecclesiastical marriage court as *officialis* for the whole of the Washtenaw Diocese. Thus the divorced who looked for a second chance with the pope's blessing had to present their voluminous cases to Elvin Ward. Only a man with Ward's genius and extraordinary work habits could have handled the job in addition to all of his seminary duties. He had worked ably and never asked of any seminarian what he demanded of himself, but in all of the official denials to frustrated loves and lusts in the diocese, in all the painful rejection slips handed to lonely men and women and children seeking parents, no one had ever physically intimidated Elvin Ward—until John Patrick had grabbed him fiercely that day in the main corridor of the seminary and touched some secret chord of vengeance that put him in touch with a lifetime of pain.

What would Elvin Ward have been in John Patrick's world? A sallow-skinned accountant who rushed home to attend his aging mother? A professor of classics at some Catholic college, ridiculed by young women and baited by athletes? An archivist in a dusty library? A government clerk waiting for his raises and retirement? The husband of a woman as ugly as he was?

But Ward had become a priest, protected from all of the normal assaults. Dozens of boys attended his every whim; divorced couples begged his indulgence. He was the well-loved son of a proud and lonely mother, his own loneliness lost in hard work and smiling repartee with students. Or angry attacks. All the rage of a tiny, surly, frightened man sublimated into a scholar's energy —until John Patrick Maguire reached in to unseal some festering abscess. Hitherto the rage had only leaked out in petulance and pettiness; now, as he lay trembling on his bed, forgotten tears erupted, and a fierce, undying anger took possession. Raymond Nowicki and two hundred students would never have believed his face.

Thomas Aloysius Maguire was too many things Elvin Ward was not. Irishly handsome, athletic, as brilliant, a leader of men, and an aspiring saint. It was customary at the end of the semester to hold a convocation at which the local bishop read publicly the marks of every student. A day of great pride for the gifted and one of unspeakable embarrassment for others. Not unlike the financial statement at Saint Raphael's. An episcopal word of praise for the chosen few and a harsh warning for dullards.

Thom heard his name called and stood next to his seat, facing the bishop at the rostrum.

"Religion: 94; Latin II: 95; Latin combination: 95; Greek: 96; Greek combination: 96; history: 95; speech: 92."

Several students turned to observe. Monsignor Nowicki, on the bishop's right, smiled his broad, tight smile and tilted his head. Thom strode to kiss the bishop's red ring and receive his testimonial.

The bishop looked over his glasses. "See if you can't do something about the mark in speech—" The room rocked with laughter, monsignor chuckled, and Thom blushed.

"Thank you, bishop."

"Where are you from?" He put his hand on Thom's shoulder to keep him from moving away.

"From Kirkwood in Sheffield Diocese."

"Ah! One of Bishop Schmidt's boys. Good for you!"

Monsignor Nowicki leaned in. "A fine athlete, too."

"I can tell." The bishop patted Thom's shoulder.

Thom returned with eyes cast down, and Elvin Joseph Ward, at the bishop's left, never smiled.

That was the real beginning. The entire school knew that there was nothing Thom Maguire couldn't do.

Except find peace.

The testimonial convocation further ignited Thom's competitive drive. He had some inkling of it when he resented Skorski's slight advantage in Latin and Greek, and he made a mental note of comparative averages. Skorski was up by a point and a half. He could console himself that Skorski avoided sports and was not particularly popular, but it was small consolation. Scholastic average was the real game, and Thom was not accustomed to being second.

And even as it gnawed, he chastised himself for pride, praying incessantly for relief, and confessed with deep sorrow to a mumbling Father Olivier. But the torture continued. Every recitation was measured against Skorski, every Latin composition. Ninety-four on an original Latin essay; Skorski got ninety-six. Skorski knew the meaning of *frontibus adversis* when no one else did and remembered in a history quiz that Spinoza's father was a lens grinder. It was only a trivial struggle to someone who lived a balanced life, but at Saint Robert's Seminary it was excruciating.

Elvin Joseph Ward added to the agony. Never terribly complimentary to Thom, he had said nothing about the boy's triumph at the convocation, and now in class he spitefully ignored Thom's upraised hand. And, beyond Elvin Ward, Thom also created his own conflicts. He continued to excel, but there was only intermittent and short-lived satisfaction. Every hour of study was full of tension; every morning was the start of another contest that began with how devoutly he made his meditation. Fierce competition settled into all aspects of his life as if some secret insecurity of blood and bone had risen to overtake him.

Even when baseball season came and Thom broke every seminary record, it was never enough. If he was playing, he felt he should be praying, mortifying, growing in holiness. If he prayed, a voice reminded him of Robespierre and Bismarck and the pluperfect subjunctive of *rogare* or the irregular past tense of the Greek verb *orao*. And John Duffey's second-semester English class almost destroyed him.

Father Duffey correctly believed that the seminary education ignored world literature, and he contrived to shame students into wider reading, but he was not aware of the shortage of time.

"You've never read Chaucer? You're joking—"

"Certainly—Dickens and Shakespeare?"

Suddenly, reading became a fierce passion, not because

Thom truly enjoyed it, but because John Duffey had made it competitive.

Skorski discussed the beauty and symbolism of *David Copperfield* and quoted Plutarch. Terry Lanier mentioned the sadness of *Jane Eyre* and wondered if the Brontë sisters hated men. And fourteen-year-old Bobbie Foley was pondering Hilaire Belloc's *Wolsey* and trying to find a copy of *Cranmer*.

Thom's mind was a madhouse. John Duffey didn't know Angelo Bertelli from lasagna, but he knew books. Authors, titles, plots, all came pouring out. So did the agony of a lost youth spent chasing turtles and outfield flies when *Beowulf* waited behind *Wuthering Heights*.

The "brains" adored Father Duffey. Trading *Crime and Punishment* for Sandberg's life of Lincoln, giggling about *Ulysses* in secret, and quoting Cotton Mather and Emerson. The school paper became an exhibition hall, with Father Duffey as adviser and lanky, horn-rimmed Barclay and toothy, arrogant Terry Lanier as literary editors. The sports page, once significant and statistical, was abandoned in favor of essays on the Roman Colosseum and a chatty column that included reports of Skorski's girlish tennis games along with Thom's .475 batting average. With appropriate clever comments that evoked giggles. Faulkner and Graham Greene began to compete with the Blessed Virgin and Notre Dame.

Thom even tried to write, but critiques came back in John Duffey's sprawling hand or, more painfully, in Barclay's neat script. "Baldly prosaic," "lacking in imaginative thrust," "a puerile, preachy approach to an ambivalent subtlety." The only article he ever published was so thoroughly revised that it was more Barclay than Maguire.

Elvin Joseph Ward continued his torment. In the classroom he was stringent in marks and stingy with compliments. He stopped Thom in the corridor and complained that the heels of Thom's shoes were squeaking in chapel, reprimanded him for talking too loud in refectory, and mocked the shy chuckle that postscripted his conversations and exposed his insecurity.

"Can't you just say yes, without the *hnnnn?*"

Almost overnight the smiling pride of Saint Raphael's became a frightened self-conscious boy who lived in the secret reaches of his own thoughts. He seemed to move in a thousand directions. Meditation should be more intense, reading more voracious, study more concentrated, virtue more steadfast and consistent. Nothing was spontaneous or enjoyable.

There really were no advisers for a troubled teen-ager, and most of the faculty stayed to themselves or assisted in local parishes. Thom's only confidant was the portly soft-voiced Greek teacher, Father Olivier.

"One day at a time—you will be what God wants—patience is a priest's best friend—grow daily in God's love." He sounded like one of Margaret's letters.

Thom's life became a growing torment. Even athletic and scholastic success was only a brief assuagement, soon to be followed by the self-imposed demand for perfection of cultural and spiritual enlargement. Prayer was a stilted begging for relief. He began a spiritual diary at the urging of a Franciscan who spoke at a monthly day of recollection—a day apart from sports and classes to hear ascetical conferences and to pray.

"Dear God!" he wrote. *"Help me to hang on. I was not so nervous and depressed today. I tried to speak kindly to Skorski and Barclay. Let me not be too proud to learn from them. Envy is a corroding vice, and I can only be what you want me to be. Without your Holy Spirit I am nothing. I can do all things in Him Who strengthens me! Thank you for helping me in basketball to think of others."*

Increasingly he gazed at the tabernacle, united himself with the crucifix, pleaded with Mary to soften the pain of mounting anxiety he did not understand. Sometimes he spent his evening recreation time at such prayers.

Of course there was no sexual release—or even simple physical contact—to calm his tensions, only sexual disturbances he didn't understand. The dark-eyed nun who ran the groaning commercial dishwasher did not hide her special pleasure when it was his turn in the kitchen, and he looked forward to the innocent contact more than he consciously admitted. Occasionally his hand touched hers as she slid a wooden tray out of the machine to be dried. He positioned himself closest to her every time, planning it casually so no one would notice. The brush of skin was only minutely acknowledged by her momentary flush and the briefest meeting of their eyes. Once she admitted that she had dreamed about him and when he shyly asked what had happened, she blushed coyly and turned away.

It was as intimate as they ever were, and he was only thrilled to be her special friend. He competed feverishly to make her laugh and win her attention until the others were no competition. Only when he glanced at her breast, outlined at the side of her flowing white robes and uplifted by an apron string, did he turn away from temptation. Though he looked again after that and always confessed it, he did not confess his deep affection.

His attraction to a girlish-looking Billy Watson was equally as confusing. It only lasted for a few weeks. Thom liked to gaze at his pretty, always flushed face and the full red lips and delicate skin. Thom made every effort to get his attention and was delighted when he saw Billy watching a Saturday football game. This boy had an almost physical aura that made Thom want to touch a soft pastel arm or stand close enough to inhale some sweetness. It even angered Thom that Billy giggled with the "brains," or chattered happily as he walked around the circular path with Barclay or Lanier. Thom identified his feelings as jealousy and confessed them when he could no longer keep his mind on his studies if Billy walked into the reading room. On a few occasions Billy had brushed against his sweater, and once Thom had touched his arm in conversation, and there was a warm, special pleasure, not unlike what he felt with Madeline Powers, although he never made the connection. But soon, even his feeling for Billy Watson was lost, for the gentle mockery of John Duffey and the continuing hostility of Elvin Ward kindled Thom Maguire's private struggles to excel.

The demanding daily schedule gave Thom no time to catch his breath. Even Saturday showers were scheduled for exactly four minutes.

Monsignor Nowicki made the announcement: "Some of you are taking too much time. Get in and out. Just get yourselves clean, don't indulge your bodies. Saint Paul warned that we must chastise our bodies and bring them into subjection."

There was no discussion. Monsignor Nowicki stationed himself outside the senior shower room, and Elvin Ward surveyed Thom and the giggling juniors. Nowicki had a stopwatch. Bobbie Foley forgot to wash soap from his hair, and someone flooded out one shower. Monsignor sloshed in, cassock tucked into his belt, plunger in hand. The drain was freed and an Out of Order sign attached to one curtain. A plump German boy stayed in a minute too long and was put on report.

Meanwhile Elvin Ward cackled with unaccustomed joy until the smaller boys began to make a joke of it and he grew suddenly angry. All junior showers were to be in silence. A whispering ex-marine with a rose tattoo on his shoulder was sent back to the dorm to wait another week. Nowicki's voice could be heard in the corridor. "All right, ladies, move it!" There was no tight smile, only a master list and the overworked stopwatch. "Look! All of you go in at the same time and I'll give a one-minute warning." Now it was down to a system. Two more bodies were sent back to the dorm and three put on report. Almost two hundred boys had showered in under two hours, with seven operative showers. Congratulations were given at night prayers.

Thom hadn't minded. In fact he hadn't noticed. There were books and conjugations to absorb, prayers to say, and essays to compose. In Latin. Everything but an end to anxiety. Never did he think of leaving. The challenge had begun. God had called him, so had Monsignor Doyle and Margaret Anne and Brian Boru from ancient Ireland. He had never really asked permission of John Patrick.

Thom's face, like Margaret's, gave little indication of inner torment. Elvin Ward's vendetta—the angry tone of voice, the biting comments, the fierce red pencil marks that announced mistakes on papers, the hostile looks in corridors—seemed wasted. He made an infallible effort never to say an endearing word to the bright, handsome sixteen-year-old son of John Patrick Maguire. At the same time, Ward seemed almost to cuddle around a collection of boyishly pretty pets who pleased him. The obvious contrast was most painful.

"How's *Domine Eduarde* this morning—with his eyes barely open and hardly ready for Cicero's attack on Catiline. Well-a, a little-a translation is good for the soul-a."

Then a sullen "*Domine Jacobe* Maguire—"

Thom's translation was flawless.

Not a word of warmth. "Continue, *Domine Edmunde*—"

Even Bill Collins was treated with more courtesy from Elvin Ward, having established himself as a fiercely independent adult. He played none of Duffey's literary games, read what he pleased, studied at his own pace, and listened without comment. He showered whenever he wanted to in the infirmary, never raised his hand for recitation, and ate contraband food his mother packed in a weekly laundry bag. But Collins never provided a suitable reason to be expelled. Besides, he had an older brother who was a priest, and such positive nepotism—common ten centuries before—was still alive.

No one knew how Thomas Aloysius Maguire suffered. He concealed his anxiety behind Irish charm and unfailing humor. He was a great enough athlete to perform superbly in seminary competition while his mind was screaming for release. Occasional explosions of temper were the only subtle hint, and even these were considered normal outbursts in the heat of play, although they had not occurred at St. Raphael's. In class he appeared relaxed and well prepared even though his heart pounded when called to translate and to miss a word was an impossible humiliation. At prayer he was devoutly absorbed in God. At brief recreation periods he was constantly sought after by high level members of the "jock" set and even by "brains," since he was free to wander back and forth between greeks and philistines. Either group would have been shocked to know his survival was tenuous.

Suffering became God's way of purging dross while fragile nuns smiled until their teeth rotted and docile monks lined up for humiliation. Thomas Aloysius Maguire, schooled in the masochistic faith of Margaret Ann, knew that God would deliver him when it suited His provident care. He trusted Isaiah's words: "A bruised reed he will not break and a smoking wick he will not quench." Yet Tim Hughes was a "bruised reed" that had split wide open. And Bernie Meyers was a "smoking wick" that was almost extinguished for good.

Bernie was a brilliant student who avoided any affiliation with the "brains." His only friend was Dick Stockman. They lived in a world of their own, discussing God's creative share in human evolution and the relationship between truth and art. They spent hours circling the gravel path in snow and rain, weighing the medieval reflections of Jacques Maritain and Étienne Gilson. Giggling at metaphysical jokes and clever limericks about abstruse theological concepts:

There's more to a *could* than there is to a *would*,
And neither so much as a *will*,
But you gotta be good,
To be understood,
And God knows everything still!

They had been friends since first-year high school and suddenly Monsignor Nowicki and Elvin Ward found their friendship dangerous. Seminary conferences and retreats had never mentioned homosexuality; instead, they stressed the danger of "particular friendships" and insisted that community life demanded an openness to all. To choose a particular friend meant being unfit for the "all things to all men" dimension of the priesthood. Older students who shared private rooms were forbidden to close doors, and Thom had always considered the rule merely a barrier to smoking and breach of the grand silence. Although Stockman and Meyers did not share a room, they were chatting in Meyers's room one Saturday afternoon with the door closed when Elvin Ward discovered them—both in their bathrobes after completing a four-minute shower.

A faculty meeting was held. No charge of homosexuality was ever made; few in the seminary of the 1940s knew what it was. Stockman and Meyers were told to become a part of the community or to "get out." Stockman, more outgoing, adjusted well; Meyers, a slight, sallow nineteen year old with wispy dark hair and a wide, sad mouth, was crushed. Over the next six weeks he was frequently seen at the fringe of various groups, and since no guidelines had been established, he was afraid to be seen with Stockman at all. Even in classes they were put at opposite sides of the room, and it was common knowledge that they had been "disciplined." At least twice in weekly spiritual conferences, the subject of particular friendships was discussed by Monsignor Nowicki with great passion. No one mentioned Jesus's singular affection for the apostle John.

Meyers began to disintegrate.

At first it was migraines, and he would spend two or three days in the infirmary; later his face broke out and he began gaining weight. His frail frame and face seemed puffy and unbalanced, his eyes glazed and indifferent. When he attempted to recite in class he stuttered awkwardly, and his entire demeanor changed from smiling, gentle sensitivity to isolated monochrome. During recreation periods he often sat alone under an elm tree without moving a muscle. One evening after study hall, his legs wouldn't work. He was taken to the infirmary, and the following day he was committed to a mental hospital, where he stayed for the next two and a half years.

Stockman never mentioned Meyers's name again. He was instructed not to visit him in the hospital. Or to write. A "particular friendship" had been prevented, and even Monsignor Nowicki, a softhearted and caring man, was convinced that God and the priesthood had been served.

Thom had no particular friend, but there was a way about him, and sometimes lonely young men sought him out to bare their souls. He did not want the responsibility of friendship. Friends took him from the awesome pursuit of knowledge, although no one really believed that he had to study hard. If he expressed fears about an exam, he was ridiculed gently. The state of his soul or his secret anxieties were never mentioned, reserved as they were to colloquy with God. Like a man condemned or a prisoner of war, he learned to survive and to find real happiness in fleeting triumphs or in any brief respite from his persistent anxiety. Sometimes in chapel there were moments of great joy, but more often he was deeply depressed, assuming that the enduring cloud was imposed by God for his purification. Even the vengeance of Elvin Joseph Ward was of little consequence, merely a part of some sacred, distorted *weltanschauung* to be transformed in distant redemption. He made an entry in his diary: *"Dear God, help me just to live for today. Whatever you ask of me I will give generously unto the cross. No human success will ever satisfy my heart. Just give me the strength to endure. Already I begin to feel your peace."*

Often, despite apparent camaraderie, the fog would not lift. Bill Collins laughed uproariously at Dennis Schaeffer's "bushwhacked" haircut or arm wrestled during a ten-minute break, accusing Dennis of selling theological secrets to the Methodists. Thom laughed with the rest, but his inner consciousness focused on a Latin quiz or a complex distress. He envied Collins's easy friendship with Dennis and commanded himself to relax and enjoy, but there was no spontaneity in his life.

Every thought was measured and every minute programmed, even his recreation time staggered under the all-seeing gaze of some invisible legislature. The diary read: *"Help me to be a better conversationalist—a priest must attract people. Help me to give others a chance to talk—a priest must listen."* He held each breach under priestly scrutiny; each motive was dissected and submitted to confessional forgiveness. Each day competed with the one before, and the assembled days were weighed by a distant priesthood and a boy's unyielding romantic faith in a God who cared about lilies and sparrows.

No one told him any other way. Except for Elvin Ward's consistent pique, he was considered an ideal seminarian. When the bishop came to read the final public testimonials of that first year, Thom had averaged 96. Only Skorski was higher by half a point, but Skorski hadn't won a league championship for Sheffield Diocese or batted .494. Neither had anyone else in the history of Saint Robert's.

Thom was hardly ready for summer vacation.

In monasteries, community life became family, but for the diocesan seminarian, trained to work in parishes, the three-month vacation was considered a test of character. The life of a diocesan priest provided options beyond any isolated monk's, with freedom to drive his own car, spend money, plan his own vacations. Even to save money. Thus, the summer vacation acquainted a seminarian with the perils of life in the world. He was expected to get a hard job that would instruct without jeopardizing his vocation; he was not to be alone with a woman, not to read modern novels or attend films, not to abuse the power of domestic status, not to miss daily mass or meditation. And because Thom was still deficient in Latin and Greek, Father Ward provided eight weeks' work in irregular Greek verbs and Latin translations to be mailed in every Friday. On time. They would be corrected and returned to be redone. Collins and a dozen or two others could qualify the rule and distinguish its spirit or simply ignore it if it interfered too harshly. Not Thomas Maguire.

A final conference admonished him: "Your adversary,

the devil, goes about as a roaring lion seeking whomever he may devour. And no morsel is as satisfying as an incipient priest. All of hell will stand up and cheer at the loss of a divine vocation!"

The first year was completed.

7

*"Quare Tristis Incedo . . . ?"**

When Thom returned home from the seminary for his first vacation, Jim and John Patrick noticed that some of his self-assurance had been lost, as well as some of his natural enthusiasm for life. Always devout and prematurely serious, Thom had possessed a spontaneous charm that mesmerized even those who resented his talent. Now, in a single year, devouring self-dissection invaded every chamber of his consciousness, leaving him tense and exhausted, in unending combat with an angry Hydra. Jim felt shut out when he suggested a game of horse in the driveway or even hitting a few balls over at Walker School.

Lightheartedness had succumbed to sudden rages and angry tears. John Patrick had sold the cottage at Lake Watseka, and the thick Michigan heat added to Thom's distress. An excited young Timothy interrupted a meditation on Thom's second day home, and his treacherous study of Greek vocabulary was disturbed by Anne's thirteen-year-old friend. He was annoyed by neighborhood dogs barking impatiently at the scorching air, and even rides to early-morning mass with Margaret were tensely wired as she described new neighbors and home additions.

"I'm not used to talking in the morning."

"I'm sorry—just trying to be pleasant."

"I'd rather meditate." He didn't understand wanting to strike her.

"Did you know the McElroys moved to Dayton—ooops! I'm sorry."

He felt remorseful and guilty and struggled to be pleasant. "Looks like Bonner's house was painted." Immediately he resented his charitable effort.

*"Why do I walk in sadness . . . ?" From the Roman Missal.

"I don't like the color." Then she described a new lawn, the advantages of real manure, doctors who cared only about money, and the whole school going to rot and ruin. Tim, now seven, was learning to swear, and Anne had gone boy crazy.

Mass was a rewarding silence, and he struggled to absorb the symbolic mystery of the bloodless sacrifice, to offer himself with bread and wine and be transformed in magic transubstantiation. But distractions pursued relentlessly: Anne's latest girl friend had sprouted plump tits; he remembered a home run over the center field fence during the final game at the seminary; he struggled to ignore a stooped old "saint" whispering her prayers; and he resented Margaret smiling at the nuns. At home he puzzled over a Latin exercise assigned for catch-up work by Father Ward, still hearing Tim's exuberant shouts in the hall and Margaret's hoarse whispers to quiet him.

"Thom is studying the priesthood."

Studying the priesthood—why was she so stupid?

"Can we light candles?" Tim only wanted to help.

Then he was back at mass with a dozen old ladies hanging over the pews and pompous Brian Touhy, a first-year theologian, prematurely mouthing his breviary in the sanctuary.

John Patrick arranged a good job with a customer who owned a sausage factory. It paid more than Jim's work with Ed Thompson in the city parks. Thom shoveled liver into a grinding machine and skinned hot dogs in mixed company amidst embarrassing obscenities. He avoided the redheaded girl with bouncing breasts who loved to seduce the men. ("She gives good head, mate." "That curly red pussy'll give you dimples.")

"We could go to a movie sometime—"

"I—I'm gonna be a priest."

"So I'll be your nun—"

Finally he quit.

Margaret understood, saying, "He could lose his vocation."

John Patrick was furious. "Those people did me a favor—hell, there are women everywhere!" But he found him more work with a customer who did outdoor advertising.

Thom was on the construction crew, digging holes for billboard posts and cementing them in place. Hard sweaty work in the burning sun with tough men, covering the whole Kirkwood area. The physical labor relaxed his tension, but the truck rides were painful.

"Hey! Catch that black ass over there. Christ! Back up, you thoughtless bastard."

"Stay away from them éclairs. My pecker swelled like a balloon after tapping a jungle bunny. Pus coming out my goddamned ears."

"Let's get the kid laid." They actually liked him and would have been more reluctant than he knew to mar his innocence.

"How about old suck-and-fuck Nellie?"

"Shit! That bitch'll chew his nuts off."

He asked for reassignment and worked alone restoring old lumber, pulling out rusted nails, and painting dry, slivered wood. Hot, boring work in an asphalt enclosure. When the construction truck pulled in, the men taunted him, but he stuck it out without complaint. Free from the threats of women and the filthy talk. "Whoever even lusts after a woman in his heart. . . ."

Jim was lusting enough for them both. No longer the pale, wondering teen-ager who had left Kirkwood almost two years before, he was almost twenty now and had completed his sophomore year in premed. He had also come to some important conclusions about the Catholic Church and about James Michael Maguire. His too had been a painful education, not as tense and anxious as Thom's, but far more satisfying.

Marquette was at the peak of its population, although its football teams were rapidly disintegrating. John Patrick was embarrassed in front of McNulty. The Marquette alumni promised an intensive recruiting program "to match academic excellence with national recognition in sports," but Notre Dame had won another national championship, and it looked like none of John Patrick's sons would ever play for Notre Dame. Young Tim seemed to enjoy hopscotch more than football.

Margaret was content that Jim would be protected from the assaults of communism and creeping secularism —the contemporary papal targets—and she was comforted to hear a new Marquette president announce that the college's education was a "fixed star" and "an invariable compass." He spoke with the religious assurance characteristic of a world recovering from the fall of Japan and Germany: "You have witnessed the slow deterioration of our civilization and man's dwindling effort to arrest it. Atomic destruction is upon us, and man is despairing because his finite gods have betrayed him." Hiroshima was the new beast of the apocalypse.

To themselves and to outsiders, the Jesuits were the great Catholic educators, even if their football team was no match for Notre Dame's.

"You are special because you have a long and outstanding tradition."

This could not compute logically, but it gave mediocre marines an impressive swagger and transformed even average Jesuits into creative geniuses. They provided their own public relations and created an extremely viable myth that temporarily seduced Jim to remain in the Church and taught him to distinguish between "Jesuit" and "Catholic." He could dissociate himself from the banalities of Saint Raphael's and the hellfire of high school retreats, and for some months Jim thought logic a Jesuit invention. It was under Jesuit syllogisms that he grew logical enough to know he could make a million dollars, enjoy premarital sex, support Jesuit charities, and still save his soul.

Margaret often insisted that he lost his faith at Marquette. Actually he never lost his faith. The Jesuits only introduced him to a kind of allegiance to ancient intellectual and emotional boundaries that became more absolute and infallible than any pope. Jesuits admitted intellectual problems and, moving beyond them, Jim began to understand that Catholicism, foisted on him like a historic paradox, had transformed his Irish blood into some opposite of itself. Celibacy and virginity scorned manhood; sobriety and restraint insulted madness; hell railed against an innate sense of Gaelic justice; and priests and hierarchs uprooted faith in the currency of poetic wisdom. Although he could not yet clearly verbalize his concerns, a grave assault on his childhood faith had been made. The Jesuits succeeded in making him as anticlerical as any Irishman worth his salt deserved to be, and he began to be something other than John Patrick's second son and Margaret's disappointment. He was beginning to be free, even from the Jesuits.

In his freshman year, he had wondered if he were really suited for the demands of medicine. Saint Raphael's had not equipped him to compete with students from more disciplined and progressive private academies and boarding schools. Crisp classmates from Jesuit High in Milwaukee, graduates of Chicago's Fenwick and Saint Ignatius, and sophisticated students from prep schools in the East understood calculus and organic chemistry and were familiar with authors he had never encountered. It was painful to admit that a near salutatorian at Saint Raphael's was an average student at Marquette, and Jim was grateful for the new anonymity that reduced expectations. With fierce Maguire pride, he redoubled his efforts.

The glib talk was not easy to take at first. Students gathered to boast of girls back home who "really put out," bragging of poontang parties in log cabins, naked beer busts in summer cottages, the umpteen times they had made it with the stacked cheerleader who crowned the Blessed Virgin. Their smooth uninhibited chatter convinced Jim that big cities reeked of sexy girls who would "make out like nymphos." The Marquette girls were called tight-asses; the natives of Milwaukee cretins and dumb krauts or Polacks. Jim was properly intimidated by the sophisticated put-downs and the facile immorality that made Connie Hackett seem naïvely anachronistic.

When his faith and traditional morality gradually surrendered to contemporary standards, it was the Jesuits themselves who were the unwitting agents of his escape. They were more honest and outspoken than any priests he had known. In theology class, an aggressive street-talking ex–air force chaplain questioned the existence of limbo and even qualified the Church's traditional views on purgatory. He liked to shock the students from the lethargy of their parochial faith. Jim was startled to learn that Spanish Catholics were not obliged to observe Friday abstinence, that lending money at interest had once been a serious violation of God's law. He wondered if all morality was but history's desperate conclusion, and he was anxious to talk with Thom.

"Usury gave the Jews a hell of a head start," the Jesuit quipped. "Joe Kennedy managed to catch up."

No one had talked like that at Saint Raphael's. At first it was disturbing to learn that the Holy Family had never journeyed to Egypt to escape Herod's infanticides.

"They would have needed an air-conditioned jeep. It

was only a symbolic journey of returning to ancient Jewish bondage under pharaoh."

Jim's confusion became more acute in a sociology class when a handsome Jesuit with laughing, sensual black eyes talked openly about sex and birth control.

"Did the early Christians use condoms, father–"

Jim was shocked by the prep schooler's question.

"They focused on charity in those days. Not chastity."

The class roared. Jim hardly heard his qualifications delineating Augustine's attitude toward marriage and the gradual understanding of the mechanism of conception in modern times.

It was a class in psychology that permitted Jim to consider sex without thinking of the high school retreat master's warning of hell's eternal fire. The glib young Jesuit professor, who frequently punctuated his lectures with a high-pitched giggle, had earned his doctorate at the University of Chicago. He implied that adolescent tensions required some sexual release.

"Would masturbation be natural, father?"

"Compared to what?"

"Well, I mean, most of us were taught it's sinful."

"And most of you were taught you'd get warts." They roared. "I'm not some Moses trying to free the slaves, nor am I a moral theologian. I'm just saying that no psychologist I know would treat masturbation as deviant behavior."

It was enough for Jim, especially when he heard the psychology professor and the ex–air force chaplain exchanging dirty jokes after a few beers at a fraternity party. He believed the rumor that the chaplain "fucked around." Soon Jim was able to ritualize his masturbation performance with suggestive photos from an art store on Milwaukee Avenue or with memories of Connie. His new sexual freedom was expanded when he confessed a private sexual indulgence that had consumed an entire Friday evening alone in the dorm and the Jesuit confessor counseled him blandly to practice devotion to the Sacred Heart of Jesus. Father Grimes would have suggested eternity in purgatory.

Jim had not advanced beyond Connie Hackett in his contacts with women. Her frequent letters, usually romantic and laced with erotic suggestions, maintained her status as the prime source of his personal fantasies, and a Christmas vacation permitted torrid petting.

Although the Marquette coeds kept him constantly aroused, he was generally too shy to make any contact. Nor was there really any fertile opportunity.

In the days before the pill, college girls were not about to risk pregnancy. Even petting was rare, not merely out of morality, but because it was not convenient without the privacy of a car or a more agrarian campus and temperate climate than Marquette. The local girls, who were the easiest targets, were devoured by upperclassmen, fraternity moguls, and athletes. Jim's peers, in the converted hotels that served as dormitories, had to be satisfied with late-night masturbation and heroic tales about the sexual inebriates back home. Eventually he did sign up, along with his ultrasexed roommate, Mark Nichols, to date girls at Mount Mary College. Mark, a tall, thin blond with a pimplish birthmark below his right ear, had never really necked with a girl, but college had given him new confidence.

They boarded a bus one Saturday night with assorted other freshman students to meet their "ladies of the lottery." The selection was made by height. When he arrived at the Mount, he found that an appropriately proportioned girl had been cataloged for him at the information desk.

"James Maguire, 5 feet 10 inches—here you are, Mr. Maguire, your date is Marsha Denman, 5 feet 5½ inches. Have a seat, she'll be right down."

Jim felt a sudden excitement, and he rehearsed a prefabricated itinerary that might bring an ultimate score. A few beers, close dancing, a premature departure for food and fresh air, then a secluded spot near the river he had discovered in his private wanderings.

Marsha skittered down the aula steps, petite and nervous with medium-length brown hair nicely bobbed, a nondescript face, pug nose, and no visible breasts. Assuredly she was no sensual Connie. He tried to appear calm as she described her entire family, her favorite times in high school, and her complete course of studies before she knew his last name or where he was from. She giggled after every sentence, insisted she didn't drink, and danced stiffly with sweaty hands. It was easy to leave early and to wander to his private spot, but it was impossible to stop her from talking—even when he tried to kiss her and ended up bussing her left nostril. When he touched her thigh, she giggled outrageously. Finally he returned her to the safety of the Mount twenty minutes before curfew. A few others had already returned, claiming unquestioned victory in the "pig pool"—a fifty-cent donation from everyone awarded to the Marquette man with the ugliest girl. Actually, Marsha was a Miss America contestant next to the lanky partner of Mark, who was the unanimous winner. The bus rocked with laughter when the victor said she had peed on a fire hydrant after three beers.

"She thought pizza was a new Polish sausage."

"Her tits looked like peanuts in tissue paper."

"Did she put out?"

"Hell, yes, two belches and a soprano fart."

They roared again, Jim with them, and when he went back to the dorm, he wrote a passionate letter to Connie. And felt sorry for his date. The next day he took a long walk along the shore, then sat for hours and watched the angry waves of the lake.

His virginity probably would have remained intact through college had he not been seduced by a married woman during his sophomore year. She was a thirtyish housewife with an appetite for aggressive sex and the accumulated insecurities of the early married and endlessly pregnant Catholic. Her faith had also crashed in the face of Jesuit therapy and new experiences. When Jim noticed her in the library or the union lounge, classmates suggested, without betraying sources, that a few words in a foreign language turned her on helplessly. He considered it a typical exaggeration, but he studied her more carefully when she audited one of his classes in intermediate French.

Her name was Jean-Marie and she was a short earthy woman wrapped in a tight sweater. He liked her disheveled dark hair and he was excited by the way she held her tongue against her full lips when she paused to think or struggled to enunciate a difficult French sound. She asked to borrow a pen and later admitted it was a ruse to get his attention. They chatted after class about Balzac and *Madame Bovary*, then shared coffee and easier conversation. She was grateful for an end to sugar rationing and wondered about spending sixteen billion American dollars to rebuild Europe. Jim talked of Michigan's Rose Bowl rout of Southern California, and there was a brief parting kiss with enveloping lips and the promise of a home-cooked meal. Actually she hated cooking.

Her attentions released some new confidence as he talked of scholastic difficulties, his brother in the seminary, his dreams of being a forest ranger, his struggles with the Catholic "holy" ethic, and even the story of Sandy. He had never been able to talk openly with anyone before. Her eyes filled with tears. After two more classes, she invited him home when her children were at school. By the second beer, as they sat on the living room floor, she was discussing her marriage as if they were old friends.

"My husband's afraid of birth control, and I've refused to have kids for a number of years. Recently I had my tubes tied, and now he won't touch me." Her directness frightened and excited him.

"Father Madden says rhythm works for most—"

Jim didn't know what to say.

"He doesn't sleep with anyone regularly." Her brashness somehow freed it all.

"So what do you do?" His excitement grew to shivering.

"Get horny."

After another beer they sat closer in conversation.

"Do you like sex?"

He blushed. "Well—yes—but I've never—"

"Does it frighten you?"

"I'm not sure—not really—"

Without a word she led him to the bedroom and began unbuttoning his shirt. He couldn't think. She gently pushed him on the bed, undressed him, and folded his clothes neatly on a chair. Even his blue boxer shorts. Without hurrying. She closed the drapes and began undressing in the dark room. "It hides my stretch marks." Her casual sensuality aroused an animal lust far beyond what he had felt for Connie Hackett.

"Your cock is beautiful. I like the shape."

Connie had never even used such a word, and he almost came. Then her silken, rubbery body, not quite fat, was devouring him in a pillow of sensuality. She began sucking his lips hungrily, then his neck and chest, stomach and legs, as if she had lost all control. Her fingers squeezed and stroked everywhere.

"Do you speak any foreign languages?" She was gasping. He couldn't believe it was true.

"I know some Cicero." He felt deliciously decadent.

"I love Cicero." Her fingers dug into his back.

"Quamdiu Catalina furor iste tuus. . . ."

She directed his hand frantically. Stroking her thick matted hair evoked strenuous muscled passion totally unlike Connie's gentle bleating. He groaned wildly and she pleaded for more Latin.

"That's all I remember. I know some Virgil—"

It was as if he weren't there. Writhing spasms, and then she almost screamed, "Get on top! Hurry, please hurry!"

He struggled, hating his own clumsiness. *"Arma virumque cano, Trojae qui primus ab oris*—O Jesus—uh—*Italiamque fato*—"

"O Christ! That's beautiful!" She grabbed him hungrily and wiggled him inside, then exploded in a wrenching orgasm with frantic screams and moans.

He came, almost as a spectator to her frenzy, came in helpless, panting jerks. She was present again, whispering maternal kindnesses to her child. Then it was over, and a soundless breeze flapped the window shade.

"I'm better at French."

"God, I love French," she moaned.

He began revering the hooded nuns and spartan Jesuits who had forced him to memorize Hugo and La Fontaine. Even Madame de Sévigné was not wasted as he came again while Jean-Marie was whirling on some pleasure planet all her own. Finally he was exhausted. He began to dress, and she was sound asleep before he had left.

She was a good woman, although after a few weeks of secretive, intermittent love, her wild gymnastics put him off. The gentle seduction of Connie was missing, as well as the protective tenderness he felt with her. Yet he was grateful for Jean-Marie's introduction to sex, and the guiltless way she permitted him to walk away. It was not Irish, certainly not Catholic, and not even feminine in the way he had known. Till Jean-Marie, his own sexual appetite had always seemed greedy and beyond control, while Connie was usually on guard until some impossible boundary had been crossed. His initiation contradicted stereotypes and instructed him that sex might be the instrument of his peace. He only had to find the right woman. There was no reason to believe it wasn't Connie Hackett, and he looked forward to the summer when he would share with her what Jean-Marie had taught him.

The very anticipation created some edge of euphoria he had scarcely known in his life, certainly not since Sandy's death. The freedom of young manhood stretched ahead. Even the prep school sophisticates no longer frightened him. James Maguire moved nearer the upper percentiles of his premed class and was invited to enter medical school without completing his final year of college.

Thus it was a more confident young man who tried to make love that summer with Connie Hackett when the rest of her family were attending a Sunday-afternoon parish picnic.

When they were down to near nakedness, panting and fondling in her bedroom, she resisted his most ardent efforts at final seduction. It was not what he had expected.

"Jesus, Connie, you're the one that—"

"I could get pregnant."

"I won't come inside you. I promise."

"Mary Joyce got pregnant with a rubber. Nothing's safe."

Her inflection made it clear that she wanted marriage.

Connie Hackett was not about to lose James Maguire. A year as a secretary at a paper mill together with weekend exposure to Kirkwood's boring singles set had solidly convinced her that Jim was a very special man. Her parents supported her decision enthusiastically. Connie could earn almost as much as her milkman father, and there was no reason for her to risk losing Jim to a Marquette coed, so Connie determined to marry him. Almost unconsciously she plotted.

Pregnancy was an obvious wile, but she feared it would mean an end to medical school. A tighter sexual rein would more effectively accomplish her designs, and, once they were married, she would use whatever means necessary to keep him. Her Catholic conscience only demanded that they have all the children possible once they could afford them. The afternoon of the parish picnic left James Maguire badly frustrated, and on ensuing dates, when he came directly from tree trimming and grass cutting in the city parks, she resisted more than passionate kissing or superficial touching. His increased desires drove him frantic and she became an incredible madonna of irresistible beauty.

Connie was dark Irish and truly sensual, with attractive brown eyes and a full, ripe figure, a trifle too stocky to be beautiful. She had curly hair and a kind of suggestive slouch when she walked, her father's strong nose and swarthy skin, and some mysterious chemistry that made Jim and many others want to touch her. Although she had been a decent student, he never found her conversation particularly interesting, nor was she even a good listener, but the magnetic allure kept Jim coming back. They necked for hours, until his mouth was dry and his groin screamed for relief. Still she held him off, gently pleading for marriage with sad plaints of how lonely life was without him, how much she wanted to spend every night in his bed, even hinting of attentions from rich executives at the paper mill.

One warm night in June she refused to let him massage her breasts. He had taken off his shirt, and she grew angrier when he continued to grab her, trying to laugh her out of her refusal. He had never really seen her matriarchal anger, the very wrath of mother Church, until she accused him of only wanting to use her until he got back to Marquette where there were "plenty of those clever college women." Almost in minutes she was a devout, scrupulous Catholic maiden again, and all the dire warnings of the high school retreat master came cascading back. She was losing her faith; she couldn't hold up her head; she had turned her back on God and feared the loss of her immortal soul. There was no stopping her and her voice grew louder.

When a light went on in her parents' room, Jim grabbed for his polo shirt just as a cursing Mr. Hackett ordered him out of the house. "Goddamn it, some of us have to get up in the morning." After he had stumbled out on the porch and recovered from the embarrassment, Jim knew that Connie Hackett had become an adolescent memory.

Hurt and confused, he arrived home to find John Patrick half asleep watching television and Thom studying Greek verbs at the dining room table. Everyone else was in bed. He muttered a greeting and went to the kitchen for a beer. Then he sat down at the table with Thom.

"Tough stuff?"

"Not too bad. I just have to stick at it." All of Thom's old warmth seemed drained.

"Want to take a break and go for a little walk?"

Thom was torn. "I've still got about eight sentences to do." He wanted to say that he was exhausted and he had early mass with Margaret in the morning and a tiresome day pulling nails out of splintering four-by-eights.

"Might do you good." Jim really needed to talk.

"Honest, Jim, I just can't."

"Hey, I understand." He drifted into the living room feeling totally locked out from Thom. John Patrick had overheard the conversation, and he looked up from watching television.

"How's everything?"

"Not too bad." He suddenly couldn't hold back. "I broke up with Connie."

John Patrick had never acknowledged that Jim went with her. "For good?" His voice was almost tender, sympathetic.

"Yeh, she wants to get married."

"You're a hell of a catch. I don't blame her." He smiled.

Jim felt like crying at the brusque compliment. "I guess I don't always feel that way."

"What d'you mean? You're a Maguire!" He said it loudly, ignoring Thom's grumble at the distraction. "There'll be a hundred women when you're a doctor."

John Patrick smiled in memory of the girls at the Audit Bureau when he first came to Kirkwood. Then he said softly, "I know it hurts." He spoke briefly about an Italian girl after the navy. "Her old man threatened to shoot me." He grinned broadly and whispered so Thom wouldn't hear. "Course, I had her dress damn near off." They laughed together and suddenly Jim knew it wasn't so bad.

He wanted to prolong the moment, but John Patrick had stirred some memories of a wild Irishman's dreams and he was caught up in his own sadness. Jim sipped his beer and went to bed, loving his father. He fell asleep without thinking about Connie.

Thom was still fighting Greek verbs, as stubborn as the graying Irishman in the leather chair who had drifted off to sleep.

It was two days later, on the way to early mass, that Mary O'Meara informed Margaret of Jim's breakup.

"My prayers were answered," Margaret said. "Those Hacketts never had any real background. Her father was a drunk, and that milkman husband was too lazy to get an education. The girl will be as fat as her mother in a few years."

Mary laughed bitterly. "They'd like to get your Jimmy. Can't you hear that old sow with a doctor in the family?"

"I'm glad I didn't try to tell him anything. You can't *tell* a Maguire. He probably would have married her."

"He'll find a nice Catholic girl from Marquette."

Margaret reproached her friend. "There's time enough for marriage. It's not everything. We're making enough sacrifices to keep him in school."

Then they entered the church to beg God's blessing on everyone and to pray for their own doubtful salvation. Margaret reproached herself for the unkind words and wondered if she would ever learn to control her tongue. Even as she begged God's grace, she told Him that no Hackett was good enough for her Jim. And God seemed to understand, as grateful as she was that Thom was lost in his private prayers at her side.

Despite the prayers, John Patrick was concerned about his priestly son. Especially when Thom informed his father that he wouldn't be able to play for the Legion Maroons.

"Why the hell not?" John Patrick had been looking forward to it since Christmas.

"There's just too much to get done." He was afraid to tell his father that it might threaten his vocation. It was his private interpretation of the seminary rule to avoid any occasions of sin. Special sins reserved to seminary students.

"Well, you don't have to work, then. I'd rather have you play baseball. You can quit your damn job. You can't do everything."

"I can't do that either. We're supposed to work."

"Look, damn it, I'm your father. I'm not God, but I'm your father. That means something! Even to God." John Patrick had never been theological before, but he was a salesman, and his own argument impressed him.

"I want you to play baseball. You need it. You might even save a few souls out there if you can still hit." Thom did not return the broad Irish grin. But he decided to play.

Down deep he wanted to, but he told himself he was only bowing to his father's will. Monsignor Nowicki had talked about that as well.

"Don't forget they're still your parents!"

John Patrick had won out, but Thom was still too trapped in himself to see the love and pride in his father's eyes. He would do his "priestly duty."

The Legion Maroons were delighted. Thom showered in four minutes at the shop, pulled a practice uniform from his blue gym bag, and jogged a mile to Enslow field for batting practice. Sweet relief, arms rippling out of the anger of dry lumber and foul mouths.

"Them Jesuits didn't steal your eye, baby." Every priest was a Jesuit to the uninitiated.

Despite mediocre seminary pitching, he had gained power and some concentration. Three consecutive line drives through the infield, then between the outfielders in right center. Two long fouls, a pop-up, then a blast over the right-field fence: 325 feet.

"Jesus Christ! Can that son of a bitch hit!" The new trainer was startled.

"Watch your talk, Eddie. He's in priest school."

"I don't give a shit if he's in prison. That young bastard murders the ball!"

Coach Charlie Dunham was glad to have him back and did not hesitate to tell him. Once a great catcher himself, he was now, at thirty-five, overweight and out of shape, but he was a strong, cunning coach who could motivate young men. And teach them. Two of his graduates had made it to the majors, and he still hoped Thom would be the third. His young wife, Roselle, was almost a comic contrast. Elegant but not beautiful, independently wealthy and usually fashionably dressed, she never missed a game and only rarely a practice. Often preparing elaborate picnics in a wicker basket with china plates and silverware, she nestled on the grass away from an unshaven Charlie in his greasy warm-up jacket and shapeless cap. She smiled easily, and she had a particular affection for Thom, but the flash of a breast under her loose white cotton blouse troubled him.

"It's great seeing you again, Thom. Handsome as ever —but you look more mature."

"Good to see you, too, Roselle." He liked her tanned face and the dark brown eyes. "Good to be home."

"It's difficult, isn't it?" Her voice was soothing.

"Not too bad. I'm learning Greek." He blushed.

"My mother is Greek. They're warm people."

He didn't know what to say, so he smiled and then buckled on the red shin guards. He felt huge behind the chest protector and mask, and he loved the gritty physical power of his position.

It was great to play real baseball again, and for a few moments he forgot himself. Then the diary thoughts returned.

He must be humble, concerned about others, ignore pretty girls who cheered his rifle throws to second. Even between innings he whispered reverences to God to thank Him and to ask pardon for pride or anger. Yet, it did not affect the lightning wrists that could hit to either field, the peripheral vision that helped a well-balanced team win game after game. The crowds grew larger, the celebrations at a nearby drive-in more casual. Charlie Dunham was confident and excited, and Roselle seemed warm and beautiful. To have a "priest" on a team was a real curiosity, and Jake Moss wrote a clever "He's Back" article in the *Gazette*, which pleased John Patrick more than a United States victory in the 1948 Olympics. Thom remained humble, and when Roselle invited him to come home with Charlie after the game, he declined, accepting only a chicken leg from the wicker basket.

First baseman, Warren Reinert, nudged him gently. "That lady likes you, padre—she's too young for Charlie."

Thom went right home, where Margaret's dinner was waiting in the oven, after every game. He played with Timmy for a few minutes and he answered queries from Anne's friend, Mary Ellen, about the seminary. The thrill of the game wore off and he was still a seminarian. Margaret noted Mary Ellen's new breasts, even larger than Anne's, and she told the girls not to wrestle with Thom. He retired to the den to travel a few more parasangs and stadia with Xenophon, trying to ignore Timmy's shrieks and Margaret's whispers.

A note from Father Ward complained of sloppy work and reminded him that the same high standards were expected. Simple mistakes were fiercely underlined in red pencil, and Thom's tension increased. A 76 on an easy Latin translation, a 72 on an exercise in pluperfect Greek verbs; singulars for obvious plurals, datives for ablatives. He was infuriated by his inability to concentrate at home, and he swore angrily, then apologized to an eavesdropping God. He struggled with the meaning of *armis repulsis,* cursed Timmy's shouts, and then focused again. Sounds of giggling came from the kitchen as Jim teased Anne's friend, and suddenly Thom erupted and raced out, shouting almost hysterically.

The frightened girls ran outside, Jim stared in disbelief, and John Patrick dropped his crossword.

"What the hell!"

"Damn it! I just can't concentrate! All the noise—" He burst into tears and clenched his fists in helpless fury.

"Are you gone nuts? Where the hell's the Thom I sent to the seminary?"

John Patrick's anger quieted him, but the tears continued and his voice was a helpless whimper. "I just can't—I—"

His father's voice was more gentle. "I haven't said anything, but there's too damn much work. You were never so touchy before—and afraid of women—"

"I'm okay." He fought for some control. "It's just—" He was suddenly furious at himself for the sinful outburst. "I'm sorry." Jim sensed Thom's embarrassment and went out in the yard to help Margaret water the lawn.

"Sorry, hell—you've gotta get out—see some friends—go to some of those dances at the Hi-Y Club—"

"I'm not allowed to go to dances. Monsignor Nowicki said—"

"I don't give a damn what he said—or what that little asshole dwarf said either. You're my son and you'll damn well go."

Margaret came in from the yard, overheard, and said nothing, but she knew that her priestly son would attend no dances. He belonged to God, and it was her sacred duty to oversee his vocation.

In early August the Latin and Greek assignments were finished, and Thom relaxed a little. A pressure was off and he was learning to live with daily mass and meditation, slivers at work, and John Patrick's disaffection. His father came to all the games and often drank a late-night toast to his lost sons. Jack dead, Jim usually working or in his woods, and Thom caught up in some priestly maze.

The Legion Maroons were in the state finals at Sheffield and Thom was on a torrid hitting streak. Kirkwood met Port Huron on Saturday afternoon for the championship, and John Patrick was already hoarse and hung over from two successive days of celebration with McNulty. Jim drove Tim and Margaret and an assortment of Anne's friends to the game, and Thom and Warren Reinert accompanied Roselle in her green and gold Cadillac.

In the last of the seventh and final inning, Kirkwood was leading 6–4 and Port Huron filled the bases with two outs. It was a tense game, with some doubtful calls in early innings, a fight between Charlie Dunham and the first-base umpire, and a southpaw who had thrown at Thom's head. The stands were filled, there were scouts from colleges and the majors, and a high school band was there from Port Huron. John Patrick was almost out cold and Jim was trying to give him more coffee.

Then a batter hit a looping fly that floated behind second base. Warren Reinert, an outstanding fielder, raced back and snatched it just above the grass and the game was all over. Kirkwood fans began to swarm onto the field when suddenly the first-base umpire signaled that the ball was still in play. Warren had already skyrocketed the ball to the jubilant right fielder, and two runners had routinely crossed the plate when the umpire screamed that the ball had been trapped against the ground. A Port Huron runner had rounded third and was walking despondently to the dugout when he learned of the umpire's decision. He raced back on the field, touched third, and headed for home. Thom had already dropped his glove and was unfastening his knee guards when Charlie Dunham told him to guard the plate. He couldn't believe it.

He took the unexpected throw with his bare hand an instant too late. Port Huron had won 7–6.

Then erupted the greatest brouhaha in the history of Michigan Legion baseball. McNulty coldcocked the first-base umpire while Jim struggled to restrain a newly aroused John Patrick. Fists, bottles, and bats flew, resulting in a dozen bodies groaning and bleeding on the infield. Women screamed. Charlie Dunham broke someone's nose, and Thom was yelling at the top of his lungs when Roselle glided through the mob to his side.

"Charlie told me to take you right to emergency."

"It's okay!" He pulled away angrily, then the tears came flooding from somewhere. She led him tenderly to the Cadillac, and his resistance was gone.

The hand was not broken and, although swollen, it was not terribly painful.

She adjusted the car radio as they drove away. "Hungry?"

"Just so tired—"

"Lean back. I know a place." The sun was still strong, warm and soothing. She drove west toward Kirkwood, headed south toward a nearby lake, and followed a shady gravel lane to a secluded meadow where there were no cottages. She spread a blanket on the grass and poured a glass of chilled burgundy from the wicker basket.

"No, really—I—"

"Please drink it." She said it caressingly, and he breathed her fragrance.

When he finished the wine she slowly took off his sweaty jersey, made a pillow of her jacket, and knelt next to him, massaging his shoulders and chest.

"I'll get the jacket all sweaty and—"

She put two fingers over his lips and continued rubbing his chest and stomach. Then she stooped and kissed his lips. And again. For whatever reason, he did not move, and she took his left hand, slipped it under her blouse, and handed him her breast. He massaged it lovingly for a long instant, then jerked his hand away. She ignored it and continued stroking him.

"Sleep, my darling." And he did, in incredible sunlight.

When he awoke she lay cuddled against him, her bare breasts exposed to the sun. He lay there for a moment, not wanting to leave, then he got up, put on his shirt, and walked to the car. Casually she slipped on her blouse, gathered the picnic things, and joined him. She caressed his arm and fingers all the way back to Kirkwood. Neither of them said a word. When she dropped him at the house, she held his hand, then kissed it for several seconds.

"I know how hard it is—I want to help if I ever can." She looked at his tense young eyes as they struggled with realities that eluded Charlie. His beautiful body and face that denied everything. God! She wanted him. To release all that pain. But she only looked. "I want you to be a beautiful priest."

Margaret wanted to feed him, but she agreed to take him to Saint Raphael's instead. God only knew when John Patrick would arrive, for he had refused Jim's offer to drive him home.

"I like to make visits in the evening. So peaceful—" She sensed Thom's mood and was silent the rest of the way. He got out of the car, walked inside without a word, and lined up near Kenelley's confessional.

Strangely, he was not tormented. In a daze, he knew he had to be cleansed from Roselle, but only his head requested it. He felt a release he had never known before.

It was not a painful confession. Father Kenelley helped. Hardly inquisitive, he sensed Thom's remorse and did not badger. Thom simply told the story as it happened without anxiety or hesitation. He had never done that before, even with Madeline Powers. Inexplicably he almost hoped that Father Kenelley would tell him he couldn't be a priest.

"We're all weak and human. Try to be careful. For your penance, say a decade of your rosary when you can."

That was all. Even the ride home with Margaret didn't trouble him, and he was a gentle foil to her garrulousness. He went to his room, undressed quietly, and soon fell peacefully asleep—remembering Roselle's fragrance and the white breasts against her dark tan.

He did not remember to say his night prayers.

An explosive crash awakened Thom in the dark. Jim appeared and they raced down the stairs to see John Patrick smashing dishes, Margaret cowering near the stove. A pair of white china cups smashed against the wall above the sink. Then a rose-tinted platter with yellow flowers.

"You're so goddamned nice—don't raise your goddamned voice!"

She screamed. "I won't take this! Get out and stay out!"

"You get out—move in with the nuns." He laughed drunkenly. "Doyle will rent you a room—"

His sons' sudden presence startled him and he put down a serving bowl with a sheepish smile. "There's my ballplayer." He reached out his hand and Thom pulled away to his mother's side. She ceased snarling, weeping inconsolably, and he held her close as tears flooded his own eyes. Jim walked gently toward John Patrick as if to listen to him.

He quieted. "What the hell—so I had a few." He hung his head like a little boy.

Jim had lured him from a bar once before. He remembered that John Patrick had put his arms around him, brought him a Coke with a cherry in it, and introduced him to half a dozen drunk Irishmen while Margaret waited in the car with her rosary. And they had all seen him drunk in the leather chair. But never like this raging animal in the kitchen. Jim actually feared the raw power of this man he had always loved and was just beginning to understand.

He gently led his father to bed, removed his shoes, and covered him; then he returned to Margaret and tenderly put his arm around her.

Thom was more upset than she was. "I can't go back to the seminary." It was a way out.

"You must."

"Not if he drinks. I couldn't stand it."

"I'll kick him out. Monsignor Doyle will—"

"He'd break the door down." Then Jim moved her up the stairs into his own bed and spent the night on the living room davenport. Miraculously, Anne and Tim slept through it all.

John Patrick spent the next day in bed. Totally repentant.

"There's coffee made." She snarled it in the door late in the afternoon.

"Thank you, my darling." He searched for his bathrobe, lit a Camel, and walked down to the kitchen, where he fumbled with his toast and spilled his coffee. She didn't help; nor did he ask; and she continued to fix goulash for her family.

Late that night Thom heard them talking. Margaret's voice was firm and loud, his a subdued guttural.

"Now you've driven Thom from the seminary. He's not going back."

"The hell he's not. What's wrong?"

"You're wrong. I should have left you the first time."
"I'll take the pledge."
"That's old news."
"I'll take it for a year."
"A fine father, driving a boy from his calling."

For two or three days she could abuse him and say whatever she wanted. The first couple of mornings he went with her to early mass, read the missal he didn't understand, and joined the family at the rosary. He brought favorite candy, heard Tim's prayers, stopped for lamb chops and city chicken legs, and told her funny stories. Finally she sat on his lap and struggled to get away. Giggling.

Then he took the pledge from Monsignor Doyle, and Thom returned to the seminary.

☘ ☘ ☘

Actually Thom felt a sense of relief at being back, but none of the excitement of greeting a long-absent friend or a familiar favorite place. Monsignor Nowicki's first conference described a seminarian's return in almost erotic terms, whereas Thom only felt freed from confusing pressures and the normal decisions of life. He was finally a bona fide member of his class, having completed the necessary makeup work, even though Elvin Ward was sharply critical of his summer efforts. He was not the frightened neophyte now, but a respected old-timer, and the minutely regulated program allowed him to settle into a benevolent numbness that made weeks seem as days.

He noted the missing faces with the strange self-satisfaction of a stronger and more enduring novice. Of the twenty-two "C" boys who had entered with Thom, only nine remained; another three years would reduce their number to four. The mortality rate itself was a significant motive in his competitive survival. Maguires were not quitters, and Monsignor Nowicki's exhortation on Saint Robert's feast day in September solidified his resolve.

The rector paraphrased Isaiah: "I am Yahweh unrivaled. . . . Does the clay say to its fashioner, 'What are you making?' Does the thing he shaped say, 'You have no skill'? . . . There is no other God."

Only the strong will remain. The door opens out. Better now than later. Nowicki paused to remember his young priest brother who was even then selling Florsheim shoes and enjoying his sensual girl friend somewhere in California.

There was a new faculty member, the recently ordained Father Edward Forgette, director of music. A gentle man with smiling brown eyes and a serene expression, he actually seemed approachable. In general, most faculty played a severe charade. To be honestly themselves might spoil an ancient discipline, so they generally said their masses and disappeared after class to some shadowy silence in their rooms. If Thom passed them in the corridor, they nodded pleasantly but curtly. Father Forgette broke some tradition, cheering loudly at games and recalling stories of the major seminary where priests were finally manufactured. He was a new breed of postwar cleric, and he even made himself available for supportive counseling. Although he lacked experience and was a fragile contrast to the athletic Thom, he was a uniquely appealing reminder of some fraternity between the Roman collar and the docile seminarians who endured a hundred sacrifices to survive.

In the midst of a severe depression, Thom sought his help.

"I want to be a good priest."

"You will. God loves your sincerity very much."

"There's so much to learn, so much to—change." Thom told him about Roselle and the baseball game.

"God was there assisting you all the time." Ed Forgette had never touched a woman's breast.

Thom departed with new understanding and deep gratitude. The kindly priest brushed his knuckles against the intense young face, and Thom restrained himself from tears. The next day his depression returned, but he pulled himself together as he knelt before the crucifix. He focused on a future priesthood when he would forgive and counsel others with the tenderness of Father Forgette.

He had lost intellectual focus during the summer, and it was almost mid-October before the cobwebs disappeared. The silence and the assigned study times without distractions helped, and soon he was again earning the consistently high marks that were his most significant ego strokes. There were also the football games, along with days of inner peace that proved the value of spiritual exercise. At such times, his entries in his spiritual diary were rhapsodic. Boyishly stilted. *"Dear God, I belong to you. All I am or ever hope to be is yours. Let my heart and will be dissolved in yours. Thank you for this undeserved joy, and give me strength to bear any cross you send."*

A three-day retreat interrupted the routine in late September when a brown-robed Franciscan with piercing eyes preached five daily half-hour conferences on spiritual development: prayer, obedience, suffering, humility, charity. And purity. Thom, like most, took careful notes. The seminarians waited with bated pruriency to hear of levites who smeared their celibacy. The talk was as close to pornography as was ever allowed. They heard of the monsignor who died naked in a motel, wrapped around his lifeless organist, suffocated by a defective gas heater. A subdeacon, one vacation from ordination, lost his virginity to a nurse in a French village when he had his appendix out and died a month later of spinal meningitis. Thom pictured Roselle's breasts starched into a crisp uniform, and then the monk's resonant voice interrupted his immoral reverie. His lean monastic hands clutched the rope cincture, symbol of chastity, that belted his rough habit.

"Even Thomas Aquinas wasn't spared. His own brother brought a naked prostitute to his monk's cell to destroy his vocation." The chapel was deathly silent. "Then the aroused Aquinas banished the whore with a burning stick from the fireplace and returned solemnly to his psalms." Even Collins had not fallen asleep.

Thom continued to take careful notes at each conference, then reflect on them during the silent hours that followed. Some students were dismissed. Two freshmen who couldn't stop crying and another who couldn't stop giggling. On the third morning, a tough ex-marine from Sheffield, who had been wounded at Guadalcanal, was caught smoking and immediately expelled, despite two years of makeup Latin at a junior college and a year waiting to be admitted. Thom complained to Father Forgette.

"The priests smoke. I don't understand—"

"I guess it's part of the training." He shrugged helplessly without losing his serene expression. Thom was disappointed, not realizing that a newly ordained priest had no official status among his superiors. Thom promised the crucifix that he would be even more understanding a priest than the kindly Forgette.

Collins complained about the marine's dismissal to Monsignor Nowicki with even less satisfaction.

"Holy Mother Church knows best. It's a long tradition. Augustine said it: 'We love the sinner, but hate the sin.' It's as simple as that."

And it was.

The months moved rapidly as Thom numbly survived each obstacle and found something to look forward to. A basketball game, praise from the bishop at honors convocation, roast beef and mashed potatoes on the rector's feast day in January. A visiting Sunday when Margaret and Mary O'Meara brought Anne and an excited Tim to share German chocolate cake in a second-floor classroom. Or an occasional letter from John Patrick that talked of Notre Dame games and Truman's victory over Tom Dewey, which Thom knew nothing about. It concluded, "Always, your dad," in the sprawling handwriting. At times there was a brief letter from Jim in response to a longer one of Thom's that had detailed seminary life and offered strategems for world conversion. Occasionally Jim suggested an English mass or less pretentious buildings, and Thom countered with rambling paragraphs about ancient Church wisdom and patience.

The priesthood loomed eight years away like some great salvation that made any endurance possible—even joyful. And Thom was beginning to master the seminary challenge and to learn its idiom. His mind grew sharper, his memory was extraordinary, and his interest in sports provided the relaxation he needed. He smiled frequently, was admired by faculty and students, and continued to excel.

A brilliant Thom gleaned from his "classical education" a logician's skills to defend Catholic faith and law. There was hardly room for imagination and fantasies, certainly not for probabilities and real questions. Only for exactitude. Even literature was often a search for God, and history an apologia for the Church.

Nothing was spontaneous. No lying idly on soft grass, warming his face to the sun. No time to stretch lazily in bed; assuredly none to be a silly, carefree, irresponsible boy. But it didn't matter, he was a soldier of Christ. He had never been happier in his life. He mastered Elvin Ward's classes and accepted the plaudits of everyone else. His diary focused more on humility than the courage to endure.

"Dear God, it was another good day. I got a 98 on a Latin Original from Father Ward and 100 on a history quiz. I know it is not my own talent, but You working in me to bring men back to You. I was still a little selfish in passing the basketball, even though I tried harder to be generous."

At such periods of peace and success he was able to reach beyond his own psyche.

"Please watch over my parents and little Tim and Anne, and keep them in Your Love. Especially protect Jim's faith."

☘ ☘ ☘

Jim's faith in himself improved during his junior year at Marquette when he left the dormitory and took a small apartment a few blocks from campus. He had proved to John Patrick that it would be cheaper, and he assured Margaret that he would get more studying done. Actually his academic standing improved without any great effort. Like Thom, he had learned the language of higher education. He dated sporadically. He met a Polish nurse at a Catholic Hospital Guild seminar on therapeutic abortions, and he slept with her the same night in his apartment.

Certainly he was not in love, but she was a pleasant, attractive dark-blonde with a body not unlike Connie's. There was not much to talk about when they were not "making out" once or twice a week, but occasionally they cooked a meal in his tiny kitchenette or listened to his secondhand radio. The one-room apartment was really too small to share for any length of time, and since she still lived at home with six younger brothers and sisters, their options were limited. When she began to fall in love with his quiet charm and gentle witticisms, the only sides of himself he revealed, Jim withdrew.

Increasingly he liked being alone. He did not try to make male friends after his move from campus. He was content to enjoy a beer and an hour's conversation at the

Ardmore, to watch an occasional basketball game, and to work two or three hours a day at the campus bookstore on Milwaukee Avenue. He also managed to borrow books he wanted to read.

Camus fascinated him, as did *Grapes of Wrath* and *Tortilla Flat*. Eugene O'Neill's *Mourning Becomes Electra* absorbed him for days, and at times his whole Irish background became clear, and he began to understand the relationship between John Patrick and Margaret, the separation between their day-to-day life and their most secret feelings. O'Neill's pain and tragedy softened him, and the playwright's bold irreverence seemed to give Jim a new sense of freedom.

He began to dread the thought of going home for the summer, and he explored job possibilities at a golf course in Fond du Lac as well as at a lumber camp in northern Michigan. When he proposed the idea in Kirkwood, John Patrick's sadness and Margaret's mournful reminder that he would soon be gone for good changed his mind. But he gave up the city parks job and took a more lucrative one on construction. In a moment of weakness he called Connie, only to be informed that she was almost engaged. He was able to admit to himself that he missed her, but the construction job, hauling cement in wheelbarrows, and grading driveways, exhausted him, and he was generally content to read and wander in his woods.

He appeased Margaret by going to Sunday mass, and he drank beer with an aging John Patrick, but his presence in the house seemed to make little difference. Anne was now an attractive teen-ager, ready for eighth grade, with breasts already in a bra as large as Margaret's and a shapely butt that John Patrick couldn't resist patting now and then. Her ardor for boys had cooled with the more frightening demands of puberty, and she still spent most of her free time assisting the nuns.

Jim could not really make contact with a happier and more confident Thom. His well-intended questions seemed to frighten his younger brother away. Thom attended morning mass with Margaret and found a suitable job as recreation director at Walker playground. He no longer played baseball, despite requests from an assortment of city league teams, and John Patrick was too weary to argue, rarely strong enough to resist the continuing emasculation by Margaret's God. Though not yet fifty-five, he seemed twenty years older than Margaret, who was nearing her fiftieth birthday. She only admitted to being forty-seven to anyone but Mary O'Meara, and even John Patrick had forgotten.

Tim was Jim's only comfort, an inquisitive eight year old with light red curls, wide blue eyes, and John Patrick's own awkward carriage. Tim still kissed his father goodnight and played tenderly with the graying hair on John Patrick's arms. He liked school and church and Margaret's garden, nuns and priests and stray dogs. He did what he was told, knew exactly what he liked and didn't like, and had none of the Maguire anger. Sports didn't interest him although he was large for his age and exceptionally strong, and religion was but a part of his life—like school and summer vacation. He was overjoyed when Jim invited him to walk in the woods. Usually garrulous and bubbling with excitement, Tim was suddenly silent when Jim shared the story of Sandy's death and revealed to him the secret mausoleum in Lemmert's Grove. Tim promised solemnly never to reveal the site to anyone. It was an exciting trust for a small boy, and their friendship grew when Jim explained all the mysterious holes and strange sounds.

More frequently Jim took his walks alone, enjoying the lifelong familiarities of trees and musty swamps and darting hummingbirds. At home he joined in family meals, occasionally said the rosary at Tim's charming invitation, and cut the grass or repaired the screen doors for Margaret. Curiously, he still felt guilty if he napped on the couch or simply read a book. Margaret's own energies had always demanded that everyone justify his existence by being busy at all times. Even as a college senior Jim stirred uneasily in his chair when Margaret strode industriously into the living room while he was reading.

"Can I help you with something?"

"No, you've worked all day. My work just never seems to get done."

He tried to return to Camus but heard her muttering in the kitchen about a slow drain. He got up, opened the trap and relieved it, then began putting the dishes away.

"You're still the only one around here who can fix anything."

He was no longer moved the same way by her praise.

"Your father just sits in that chair and says nothing.

You don't know what it's like. All these years. At least when you boys were home there was something to live for. He has no interest in anything—and he's drinking again."

Her hair was streaked with gray although her eyes were still those of a startled little girl. She had become more beautiful with age, and only when her face was contorted with anger, as it now was, did she reveal the anguished scars of a life of hard work and meager rewards. But in her garden or humming in the kitchen she was soft and alive. She was alive, too, at mass, and whenever she visited old friends in various nursing homes around the city. Thom accompanied her during his vacations, and even now Jim felt a brief twinge of jealousy at the glow she evidenced around her priestly son. Ecstatic to show him off to the infirm and dying. Jim was never invited.

"We'll take some nice pea soup to Helen. And some warm bread." She moved around the kitchen like a twenty year old.

"Where is she living now?"

"Oakmont Home." Her voice grew bitter. "That daughter of hers lied and said she was taking her for a ride. Some ride! She'll get hers!" Margaret shared the Irish distrust of hospitals.

Thom drove, and Margaret peddled her soup and warm bread amid tubes and disinfectants and the persistent smell of urine.

"Such awful, lonely places. I'd rather be dead." Her eyes grew distant. It was her greatest fear.

"You'll be my housekeeper, mother." He had said it as a boy.

Her eyes shone with a glow reserved for the tabernacle, Monsignor Doyle, and Thom.

Even John Patrick had little to say to Jim although he was proud that Jim had decided to be a doctor and occasionally bragged to McNulty about Jim's outstanding marks. Infrequently they shared a beer or listened to a White Sox game, but even then Margaret reprimanded Jim.

"I wish you wouldn't keep beer in the house with your father the way he is. I guess that's what the Jesuits teach you at Marquette." She was angry that he no longer went to daily mass or evening services.

Jim did not answer her, but opened the beer and disappeared to the darkness of the back porch. She got to him, even as he knew it was all ridiculous. He had done everything but become a priest and Margaret was still as dissatisfied as ever. Thom and the minutely devout Anne were not enough. At times he wanted to scream, but more often he felt guilty about not being able to make her happy. It had not yet occurred to him that her unhappiness was her own, that even his priesthood would not have relieved her radical distress. It did not matter that he would graduate near the head of his class, that he labored strenuously in the summer and part time in Milwaukee, that he went to mass and lived a decent life. She was still not satisfied, and Jim was not yet able to understand that she was more a wounded victim of herself than he was.

One evening he sat up late with John Patrick. Margaret had gone to bed in anger at their drinking.

"I hope you like studying medicine," John Patrick said. "You don't talk about it much. Maybe I interfered."

It was a rare admission, and Jim felt a burst of love.

"There's not much to talk about yet. I like it. Marquette has been good for me."

"They're not much in football." He laughed hoarsely.

"To tell you the truth, neither am I."

John Patrick laughed loudly again as the beer took hold.

"That's not everything. You've been a good boy."

Then he drifted off to sleep, and Jim felt strange tears in his eyes, wishing he could talk to Thom, who was lost in private meditation.

It was part of Thom's summer job to organize softball teams to compete in the Kirkwood Recreational League. Theoretically, no child was denied a chance to play, but fierce rivalries had emerged, and everyone played to win. Thom was no exception.

His mornings were free for mass and breakfast with Margaret and for reading. Tim, who was already slowly learning his mass Latin, was instructed not to disturb him. Thom began reading *Crime and Punishment* with his accustomed intensity, gradually getting lost in Raskolnikov's frightful isolation, feeling as if he himself might be on the verge of some inexplicable madness. Jim would have been delighted to share his own confusions, but Thom could never have admitted his fears lest he reinforce Jim's weakening faith.

Thom's afternoons at the playground were generally boring. Quarrels over teeter-totters; peewee games with neighboring schools; mothers wondering when their child would get to play. Thom built a miniature golf course with rock bridges, staged a track meet, and designed an obstacle course that occupied his charges for hours at a time. One of the mothers considered him the best director Walker playground ever had, and several times she invited him for a beer after hours, but he declined gently. His resistance fascinated her and she hinted at wild dreams and tried to entice him, but nothing worked.

When Jim wandered down after work to watch a ball game, he accepted her invitation and did not arrive home till well after midnight.

He mentioned her to Thom one day as they walked home together. "That Sally Harrison is an attractive package." He was testing, wondering whether he could talk to Thom about sex.

"Who? Oh—Donald's mother. Yeh—She seems really nice."

Jim felt the rebuke. "I enjoy talking with her. She's been to Europe and is really well read."

Thom did not comment and the wall between them seemed higher.

After that, Jim wandered more frequently in his mysterious woods and saw Sally surreptitiously from time to time.

Margaret didn't understand him. "No one ever calls him. It wouldn't hurt him to go to early mass some mornings. I wonder about those Jesuits—"

"He works hard, mother."

"Don't we all!" The bitterness settled in her throat and Thom wanted to scream. Or strike out at her. He quickly regained his composure; then he remembered Raskolnikov and was again afraid.

In September, Margaret drove Thom back to the seminary with Mary O'Meara and Bobbie Foley, who was taller now and pudgier. He had a nasal confidence when he talked, and he giggled a lot. Bobbie had become a tentative "brain" in third-year high, and Thom found it difficult to be around him, even at Monsignor Doyle's annual dinners for seminarians.

Margaret and Mary had their cookies and milk at the wooden tables in the basement and then helped Thom unpack his clothes, exclaiming as usual about how clean it all was. They made a visit to the chapel with shining eyes and then drove off. Thom was relieved to escape the turmoil of Kirkwood.

He had become a handsome young man in the black suit, white shirt, and tie that was the prescribed uniform for a student in his final years at the minor seminary. The blond hair had hardly darkened, and he had the same full lips and dark blue eyes under dark eyebrows. He was barely over six feet with the muscled body of the athlete, and he would have been pretty were it not for the strong Maguire nose and chin and a crooked smile that seemed seductive only if you didn't know him. With new confidence born of mastering Saint Robert's Seminary, he smiled easily and frequently.

It was difficult, even for Thom, to distinguish the years spent in the minor seminary: There was no graduation until after second-year college, and the classes were only more classics, a smattering of physics and chemistry, math and biology, a strong course in Genung's English composition, and a controlled history that highlighted the Church. The main emphasis was on more sophisticated Latin and Greek.

For Thom, it now all came easy. He had edged Skorski, and he was no longer interested in writing literary challenges to John Ruskin. He simply wanted to be the best priest possible.

The seminary was now a more comfortable community for him, and, by the time he was in college, he was really at ease nowhere else. Even friendly conversation at wakes, or with former classmates who chatted after Sunday mass, unnerved him. The seminary had become his whole life, with its own particular language and common interests, its limited questions and narrow culture. He needed to be special—Margaret's unique son—and only in the seminary did he feel that way. The spiritual conferences of Father Olivier and Monsignor Nowicki, in addition to retreats and days of recollection, reinforced his sense of superiority and transformed his anger and resentment into solid virtue and personal asceticism.

There were few privileges in the final years, except a tiny, private room shared with Collins, who continued to hear his own distant drummer. Collins ate in bed, read Zane Grey and *Moby Dick* by the light of a flashlight, and never used a bathrobe. Actually he didn't own one, or even a missal. Since they were only in their rooms to sleep or to change their clothes, they were scarcely roommates at all.

Thom went through alternate periods of depression and elation at his distantly approaching priesthood. The routine was the same: lights out, five-minute showers (a concession), organized walks to selected sites. The walks were embarrassingly conspicuous, and since neighbors stared at ambulances and marching seminarians with the same expression, Thom no longer went along. Collins did, to sneak off and replenish his supply of candy bars and oatmeal cookies.

Summers at home, as trying as they were, gave some identity to the passing years. Each job was more safely isolating from worldly temptation. Digging Catholic graves, repairing the gabled rectory roof (Father Grimes had been given a parish in Steelmont and Father Kenelley was sent for canonical studies to Washington), resodding the football field, painting the house for John Patrick. And rescuing him from the Shamrock or the Knights of Columbus when Jim was not around to assist Margaret. He visited the sick with his mother, giggled with the nuns at Saint Raphael's during their evening recreation, and shared meals now and then with Monsignor Doyle and two silent new assistants.

"When's your graduation, Thom?"

"The fifth of June. Not much to see."

"I'll try to make it. How's the old batting eye?"

"Not bad—.575 this year." Doyle beamed. Thom would be one hell of a priest!

Finally graduation. There was a full-scale war going on in Korea, and General Douglas MacArthur was relieved of all power by President Truman. John Patrick was furious. "If it's war, goddamn it, it's war." In June 1951, Thom was not really concerned.

Marks were announced by the Washtenaw bishop in another solemn gathering. Thom edged Skorski by two percentage points. Everyone knew he would go to Rome. Or at least Washington. Thom said it didn't matter and he meant it. Collins wanted him to set up a wine import business, and even a relaxed Skorski joked about spaghetti for breakfast.

Monsignor Nowicki gathered the twelve graduates, the residue of eighty candidates, in his room and spoke seriously of the need for priests and of his pride in their achievements. He likened them to modern apostles who would divert the world from destruction.

"All our ancient moral values are questioned: marriage, sex, prayer. Atheism is already rampant in Sartre's France, and communism is struggling to take over Europe. Our own America reeks with immorality. We've given you the tools for the next two years of philosophy and the four years of theology after that. There's nothing more we can do—"

His blue eyes were moist, and Thom realized his own affection for this simple, dedicated man.

Even Elvin Ward was uncustomarily charming and served fruit punch on his cluttered desk. Stacks of marriage cases lined the walls next to sinister lexicons and canonical studies. He cooed over his student pets, congratulated Skorski and Barclay with special mention, and kidded Terry Lanier about a misread exam question. Almost as an afterthought, he mentioned Thom.

"Domine Maguire, you, too, have done well."

Done well! He had led the class with the highest scholastic record since the school's founding. He was president of the student body, and he excelled in every sport. Thom felt the hurt and looked away. Collins winked at him and continued munching a handful of cookies.

"You bake a mean cookie, pater."

Everyone roared.

The night before graduation there was a banquet, at which graduate appointments in philosophy were announced after a dinner of roast turkey and mounds of mashed potatoes. Real butter, milk, and vanilla ice cream with chocolate sauce. Monsignor stood up after his coffee, enjoying the excitement of the pending announcements. Skillfully he prolonged the foreplay.

"This has been an unusual class—superb athletes like

Maguire," the students cheered Thom wildly, "and great philosophers like—" he paused just long enough, "well, like Collins." The students howled for several minutes. Then it grew silent.

"Three of this year's class will have to learn Italian, one will probably run for Congress." The students buzzed curiously, and even Elvin Ward was smiling. "The other eight will only travel as far as Cincinnati and Detroit, but they'll probably live longer." The students laughed nervously. Skorski giggled, Thom's face was flushed, and Collins continued eating extra dessert.

"Mr. George Kulich will study philosophy at Catholic University in Washington." He was barely a B student but the best that Elliston Diocese had that year. A loud cheer went up.

The moment of great excitement had arrived, and monsignor continued to tease them. "Let's see, where's that list? I must have left it on my desk. No—here it is." The students groaned and were suddenly silent. Skorski was biting his nails and grinning tightly, and Thom stared quietly at the floor and asked God to make him humble.

Then the rector's voice broke the silence. "Two men from Oak Rapids will study in Rome. Mr. Skorski and Mr. Barclay."

Skorski beamed, and tears of joy trickled down his cheeks. Barclay was stunned, and he let out a great roar of astonishment. The students loved it, and a prolonged cheer went up for the surprised underdog. Father John Duffey waved from the faculty table. Those sitting near the honored graduates shook the hands of the budding bishops.

Then the room quieted and Thom continued to look at the floor with genuine embarrassment. "And from the diocese of Sheffield—" Everyone stared at Thom. "Bishop Schmidt is sending Terrence Lanier." There was a long moment of shocked silence. Then some applause and finally a loud cheer of approval. Terry Lanier had never even considered the idea. He was an only child, and his parents had already planned to move to Cincinnati. He remained pale and speechless. So did Father Forgette at the faculty table, who had voted for Thom—and thought that everyone else had. Elvin Ward smiled.

Thom felt the blood rise in his forehead; his face was

red and hot, and he fought back tears. The rector's voice droned the other appointments and Thom hardly heard his name. "Maguire to Cincinnati." It was an unexpected and unprecedented put-down. The whole assembly was puzzled, and Thom heard the startled remarks as he made his solitary way to the chapel. His legs were trembling. Control was gone. His hands tingled as if the blood had drained out, and his throat was painfully dry. He lost power to concentrate on anything. Again he flashed on Raskolnikov and feared he was losing his mind. As Father Forgette approached to say something, Thom moved away. He knelt before the silent tabernacle and let the tears come. Skorski and Barclay knelt at the rear to whisper humble words of thanksgiving, then rushed out to join the excitement. Thom Maguire was too sad and confused to whisper a prayer. He just looked at the crucifix and managed to say, "Thy will be done."

The baccalaureate mass was a token finale. Diplomas were handed out after the ceremony. Monsignor Doyle couldn't make it. Nor could John Patrick. Margaret and Mary O'Meara sat proudly with Tim and Anne behind a row of nuns. When a student's name was called he approached the bishop at the communion rail, then genuflected to the tabernacle and kissed the episcopal ring. The bishop shook hands and handed him the parchment testimonial written in difficult Latin. Thom was hardly aware of anything until Bill Collins approached the altar. He kissed the ring for his diploma, turned, and began to walk down the aisle. Then he stripped off his coat, revealing a large red-lettered sign affixed to the back of his white shirt. It read "Kiss my ass" in Latin. With a broad arrow instructing the ignorant.

He continued to walk down the aisle and out the door. In the fall he would enroll in law school.

☘ ☘ ☘

Jim's graduation was as inconsequential. He had already completed a year of medical school, and he hardly listened to the sermon in Gesu Church—until the eloquent Jesuit preacher irritated him with a familiar Catholic arrogance Jim thought he had left behind in childhood.

He was told that Chartres and Notre Dame had survived the Great War, that Hitler's atheism had been beaten to its feet, and that even the Russians would look west for their salvation. The Lady of Fatima had won, God had spared his own, and the corpses rotting in Normandy were only a bitter symbol of a decayed world without faith or hope. Marquette graduates had somehow triumphed with God, the new hope of a solid reconstruction beyond the Marshall Plan and the North Atlantic Treaty. It was as if atomic war had been God's lesson to His enemies.

Jim wondered why the preacher was not able to work in the corpses of dead Jews in a Catholic Bavaria, the masses offered for Mussolini, or the two thousand tons of bombs on Berlin. It was not really important whose blood was shed. It only mattered that God had won. Nor did the priest mention that Truman had approved the development of the hydrogen bomb. He only knew that God would come out on top.

When the preacher bowed to the archbishop and returned to the sacristy, the congregation rose to announce their communal faith. James Maguire rose with them, then slid from the pew and walked out on Milwaukee Avenue to the river. The water rushed murkily under the bridge as if it had some important place to go. James Maguire had earned his college degree. A long, long way from Tipperary.

The summer after his graduation, Jim spent eight weeks working in the woods of northern Michigan. Although he had completed a year of medical school without difficulty, he thought more than once about not returning. John Patrick's pride, more than anything else, finally dissuaded him.

Margaret wrote, worried about his attendance at mass. Although he did not go, Jim replied reassuringly about the beautiful chapel in the woods and the great sermons on nature preached by an aging Franciscan. He was still afraid to confront her with his own indifference to the Church. Margaret also reported that Connie Hackett was rumored to be seeing a divorced man.

He watched a forest ranger band a fawn, wondering if he wanted to be a doctor, and Kirkwood and Connie Hackett seemed a long time ago.

The following year, while working as an extern at Milwaukee General, Jim met Judy Greene. She was hard not to notice. She had an incredible body in the Jewish tradition of *zaftig* sensuality, light brown hair exaggerating dark brown eyes, and a gentle diffidence that made her laugh shyly at the least provocation. Having been frequently pursued by doctors and medical students alike, she had grown uncharacteristically cautious after a series of unfortunate experiences. Jim's apparent sincerity and his increasing confidence—born of successful studies and personal growth—were dramatically appealing to her.

Jim had grown more handsome with maturity. He had the Maguire face with a strong nose and chin, and he was a shade over five foot nine, with brown unruly hair and deep-set eyes of some innocence. An almost pale complexion that seemed vulnerable and ascetic. Most of all, his manner set him apart. A quiet confidence that refused to push or demand attention. Even from Judy.

Judy was as bright as she was beautiful, and for the first time in his life Jim related to a woman who was his equal. Even where she surpassed him, she had none of the WASP arrogance he was used to. Her own religious background was far from orthodox, and her parents, sensitive and openly expressive of love, had not endowed her with sexual guilts or bias against Christianity. She was her own person in the best sense, without self-conscious protestation, and her parents trusted her and supported her decisions, especially her choice of nursing as a profession.

At first they had only talked, about O'Neill and Korea and socialized medicine. He told her about John Patrick and Margaret, about Jack's death and Sandy. And Judy listened as no one he had ever met. She talked about growing up Jewish in Chicago and the guilt of dealing with the pogroms of Europe.

They also laughed, as he had not laughed in a very long time, and they could not stop talking—about dreams and disappointments, about Fulton Sheen's *Peace of Soul* and Humphrey Bogart's *African Queen*. She taught him Yiddish insults and she learned to say *Dominus vobiscum* like any Jesuit. It was a full three weeks before they had sex, and for the first time in his life Jim made total, deep, warm, uninhibited love with a woman. When it was over Judy could not stop laughing—the most relaxed, musical laugh he had ever heard. When she finally stopped, she screamed joyfully.

"My God, you crazy Irishman, never in my life! I wanna be a Catholic!"

Then they made love again, softly and tenderly, as if they could never stop touching. James Michael Maguire, namesake of Monsignor Doyle, was in unbelievable love with a Jewish girl. The most beautiful person he had ever known. And she with him.

When Jim visited her parents in Chicago one weekend, they were delighted with him. The serenity of the family communication and the unpretentious enjoyment of life's good things were almost rapturous to him. He had never known such harmony existed, and he wanted to marry Judy immediately. There was no reason for them to wait. If John Patrick would continue to help him with tuition for two more years, Judy's salary and his part-time work would be more than ample income for the simple cohabitation they craved. It was after meeting Judy's parents, near the end of school in May, that Jim wrote the letter home. And, two weeks after Thom arrived from his seminary graduation, Jim and Judy drove to Kirkwood in her father's Buick. Jim could hardly wait.

Thom greeted them at the door and Judy felt immediately welcome. John Patrick rose from his leather chair, gave an approving look, and charmed her with a fervent hug and a beaming smile.

"Welcome to our home." He was immaculate in his gray suit and burgundy tie, and he had not been drinking.

"Nice to know the lad has some taste." Judy was not accustomed to his kind of blustering directness and she blushed shyly. Jim felt some urge to protect her and briefly wished that John Patrick were another kind of man. Especially when he inhaled his Camel noisily, went into a prolonged coughing spell, then spat unceremoniously out the front door. Judy took it all in stride. Margaret waited in the kitchen and Jim led Judy to meet her.

Suddenly Margaret was like an awkward six year old who could neither look at Judy nor say anything at all except a whispered, "Nice to meet you." Fortunately John Patrick took over, noted that the Detroit Tigers had won five in a row, and bragged that Thom could have earned a major league contract. Even Thom was hard pressed to talk about anything, and Jim felt compelled to rescue Judy by taking her on a tour of Kirkwood. Jim's unexpressed feeling of embarrassment seemed to elude her, and as they drove through the city she only commented how nice looking and down to earth his parents were. Thom particularly caught her attention, and Jim felt a burst of jealousy that did not go away until he walked with her through his familiar woods and they made gentle love in a sheltered meadow where only he and Sandy had been before.

Margaret's chicken dinner was magnificent, and she relaxed as she settled into her familiar role. Only the need to apologize for a flawless meal betrayed her insecurity.

Judy was ecstatic. "The biscuits are incredible. The whole meal is."

"They're not as fluffy as I like—maybe I left them in just a little too long. Are the potatoes sticky?" A clean flowered apron protected her violet dress, and Jim noted that her graying hair had a new permanent.

"Not at all. They're perfect."

Judy seemed the most comfortable of anyone. John Patrick only looked up occasionally to remark too loudly with his mouth full. Jim knew he had been drinking. Teen-aged Anne was overwhelmed at Judy's ripe beauty and seemed enchanted, as did a babbling Tim, who continued to charm with natural innocence. Thom was strangely silent, only opening up when Judy asked about the seminary.

"Is it hard?"

"Not really." He grinned. "I've completed the roughest part." He went on to explain the course of studies, how the years were divided, and he gave a brief explanation of the routine.

Margaret interrupted. "You're not Catholic then?"

Jim was furious and fought for control. "I told you that. mother." He couldn't believe it was happening.

"I must have forgotten. So much to remember these days."

"No. Actually, I'm not much of anything. My parents are Jewish, but we were never active in any institutional sense."

She went on to explain her interest in Catholicism, but her words were lost on a startled Margaret who excused herself and went to the kitchen, commenting inanely as she departed, "The Bernsteins are Jewish."

"Oh." Only then did Judy glance at Jim, wondering if she had said the wrong thing and knowing immediately that she had.

John Patrick did not lose his poise. Actually he was delighted with her, and he rubbed her hair and caressed her shoulders at any opportunity, once patting her gently on a very well-rounded butt. He found it almost impossible to restrain himself.

Tim broke an awkward silence. "Do Jews believe in God?"

They all laughed in sudden relief, and Thom made a joke of it while Margaret disappeared again into the kitchen.

"They sleep and eat and even throw snowballs."

Thom found it hard not to stare at the softness of her brown sweater. At one point he felt a strong urge to embrace her, then banished the temptation with almost visible self-disgust. Margaret reappeared, offered more food, and then began clearing the plates. Judy jumped up to help and gently pushed Thom back in his chair.

"There's a maid today. I'll spoil you a little." Then she assisted Anne in bringing in the pie.

After dinner Jim informed his parents that he had to drive back to Chicago.

"Mr. Green needs the car tomorrow." Actually Judy's father had planned a trip to Denver with his wife.

"We can rearrange things—"

"There's no need, mother. It's not a hard drive and I'm wide awake." Thom and John Patrick were as disappointed as Anne and Tim. Only Jim and Margaret were relieved, and Margaret wondered where they would spend the night.

She prodded gently. "Will you drive to Chicago?"

"Yeh. We'll stay there tonight and I'll take the train to Milwaukee on Sunday." He knew she wanted more information, but he'd be damned if he'd give it.

Nor did the subject of marriage ever come up. When he kissed Margaret good-bye in the kitchen, she was noncommittal.

"A lovely girl—good manners and not afraid to do a little work." But Jim saw the pained look in her eyes.

John Patrick was sipping a bourbon, and he continued his boisterous teasing. Thom smiled politely. He had almost forgotten she was Jewish.

They were hardly out the door, after another of John Patrick's all-devouring hugs, when Margaret suddenly found her voice.

"Marriage," she said. "The idea! Scrimping and saving to send him to school—that's the thanks you get for a Jesuit education. And Jewish on top of that! God help us and save us! What's the world coming to? I suppose there aren't any Catholic girls around. Love, indeed!" She spat the words.

The following Tuesday Jim received a curt letter from John Patrick, shaped only in part by Margaret's endless tirade. He felt Jim was old enough to know his own mind, and there was nothing anyone could do to change that. He reminded him gently that he owed something to his mother, but the real ultimatum was in the final paragraph.

> I'll have to ask you to choose between marriage and medicine. There is no hurry. You can continue to date the girl, but marriage is two years away if I am to pay your tuition. I can understand your love. She is a beautiful young woman, but you'll have to sacrifice to be a doctor.
>
> Love, your Dad

Although Margaret had agreed to let John Patrick handle the matter, her own letter arrived two days later and was a profound expression of heartbreak. She recounted her own sacrifices, the trials with John Patrick's drinking, Jack's death, her own aborted childhood, the sacrifices made in Jim's behalf, her dreams of him marrying a nice Catholic girl, and how grateful the family should be to have Thom studying for the priesthood.

> Marriage is hard enough, God knows, when you're united to someone of your own faith. But when your backgrounds are entirely different, especially someone Jewish, it's almost impossible. Your father couldn't believe you'd actually bring a Jewish girl home to meet your own parents after all we've done. Please come to your senses and have some appreciation of all that's been done for you and the opportunities you have.

She signed it "brokenheartedly."

Actually John Patrick had made no comment about Judy's Jewishness except to McNulty. After several bourbons.

"You shoulda seen the ass on her. And tits—"

"I hear they fuck like minks."

"I wouldn't mind a shot at that one before he cashes her in."

"You can't trust them though; they have no morals. He'd have to chain her up."

"She was talking about becoming Catholic."

"I don't think it's allowed."

"I think it is, but I doubt it would last. Isn't there a curse on them or such like?"

"As far as I know, but Bernstein's a good man. He doesn't seem Jewish. Hell, John, he'll find a nice Catholic girl."

Even Thom wrote, adding his semipriestly opinion, although he was more sensitive then either of his parents. At least he seemed to have some understanding of his brother's pain. He noted how well suited they seemed, how painful it must be to sacrifice someone as beautiful as Judy to pursue a medical vocation. He even shared some of his own disappointment about not being sent to Rome. Just when Jim began to feel good about the letter, Thom sermonized about God's ways not being man's and promised that "something greater was in store, something planned by God Who writes straight with crooked lines." He concluded with "sincerely yours in Christ," and there was no mention of Judy's Jewishness. Nor her brown sweater.

Jim was furious and planned impulsively to abandon medicine. After a weekend of rehashing, Judy refused to be responsible for such a decision and decided to back off from the relationship. It was desperately painful for both of them, and although they continued to see each other they gradually recognized that something had changed. They became cautious and analytic, and the postponement of marriage had dulled an edge. Even sex was not what it had been, and Jim felt trapped by some persistent aching that would not release. Soon an oppressive melancholy was as constant a companion as the euphoric love had been. He hated his own indecisiveness.

Finally, they walked away from each other because they didn't know what else to do, and Judy moved to Chicago.

Jim was several weeks recovering despite renewed efforts to plunge into his medical studies and lose himself in books. Reading was distasteful. He hated his culture for its unfeeling devotion to duty, and he hated the arrogant bias that made Catholics place themselves above anyone else. Most of all he hated himself for being trapped in childhood guilt and for not being strong enough to walk away. It was a deep, enduring hate that somehow dulled his pain.

Six months later Judy was married to a Catholic intern and she moved to Pennsylvania. For a few days the wound was reopened and Jim permitted himself to hate Margaret as the real depository of all that troubled him. It was a brief anger that disappeared when he fantasized his mother's face and remembered all she had done for him.

Jim worked almost all summer at the hospital in Milwaukee, emptying bedpans and taking temperatures, and for several weeks he did not date at all. Occasional sex only made him feel lonely and guilty. Judy's gentle humor was hard to forget and her relaxed, nurturing sensuality continued to haunt him. He had no desire to return to Kirkwood, and, when he did, he spent almost no time at home.

At a wedding reception he reluctantly attended in early September, he saw Connie Hackett again. And danced with her. A revealing red linen dress complimented the dark flashing eyes and velvet skin. After two glasses of punch, Jim was excited.

She had finally given up the idea of marriage to a divorced man who had for two years tried unsuccessfully to have his first marriage declared null in the Catholic Church. She could not disguise her delight in seeing Jim, and she agreed to go out drinking with him after the reception. They made love in the back seat of John Patrick's new Oldsmobile, and it was the most happiness Jim had known since Judy. A warm, familiar body that he knew loved him.

He returned to Marquette and they began corresponding. Mary O'Meara reported the rekindling of "the Hackett fires" to Margaret.

Margaret surprised her. "He could do worse. At least she's a decent Catholic."

Mary quickly recovered. "Indeed! I've seen her receiving the sacraments lately."

Margaret whispered a prayer of thanksgiving. Jim was

over the Jew and dating a Catholic, and John Patrick had not been drunk since the Fourth of July. Thom was already in the major seminary at Cincinnnati. Humbled by the painful rebuff he had experienced, but unshaken in his priestly resolve.

And finally powerless to resist a great explosion.

8

Of Bruised Reeds and Smoking Flax

That same fall of 1951, Elvin Ward was hurriedly unpacking from a trip to Buffalo with his mother when Monsignor Nowicki entered his open door. The students were due back the following day. The monsignor's broad forehead was creased, and his tight smile had vanished.

"I'm still bothered about young Maguire." It had troubled him all summer.

"Oh—?" Ward nonchalantly continued unpacking. The Italian inflection was gone. "How so?"

"Bishop Schmidt quizzed me—I really was at a loss." Nowicki loved Thom.

Ward put down a pair of black socks. "In my judgment, he's arrogant—in some ways dangerous."

Nowicki was unmoved. "I never really noticed." He could not forget the look on Thom's face when Terry Lanier's name had been announced for the assignment to Rome. Not sadness or even shock, but an almost insane rage that had immediately disappeared.

Ward's voice rose noticeably, again without the Italian flare. "If you don't value my opinion, there's—"

"No, no, it isn't that, I'm just—bothered!"

Nowicki never mentioned it again, but he did not forget Thom's look. Nor did he know that Elvin Ward had also seen it—the same flash of madness he had seen in John Patrick's eyes in the corridor at the end of a Christmas holiday.

Bishop Henry Schmidt was confirming at Saint Raphael's the same September, and Monsignor Doyle cornered him in the plush rectory. He moved cautiously, for the bishop was often belligerent when he was drinking.

"I thought you'd send young Maguire to Rome."

"I delegate my decisions." He slurred badly. "They tell me he's—headstrong."

"He led his class." Doyle had felt a deep personal hurt and considered it a sign from the bishop.

"That's not everything. Attitude counts, too."

It was a subtle rebuke. The bishop gestured and splashed scotch on his red cassock. He was ordinarily a gentle, compassionate man.

"What the hell's wrong with his attitude?" Doyle was speaking for himself.

"The faculty's a better judge." He drained a third drink and directed Doyle to fill his glass. "Apparently he's got a temper." He said it with rising impatience.

Doyle laughed wheezingly. "You're not exactly Saint Francis." He fumbled with the ice bucket.

"We'll see, we'll see." It was a signal he'd talked enough and he signaled Doyle to pour.

Twenty minutes later he passed out, and Father Grimes helped Doyle deposit him in the guest bedroom. Fully dressed in red robes. No one was shocked.

Thomas Aloysius Maguire took the night train from Kirkwood to Cincinnati in search of perfection. John Patrick, encouraged by Monsignor Doyle, had also anticipated Thom being sent to Rome and he blamed the ugly weasel, Elvin Ward. Doyle had consoled him that Rome was a miserable place to live. "The heat murders you." Margaret said it was enough to be a priest, and she resigned herself again to God's will. Secretly, she was disappointed, and Thom felt it. To have a priestly son was solid assurance of heaven, but a bishop was sacred vengeance for a lifetime of slights. Thom had soothed Elvin Ward's revenge with all the spiritual strength he had. Bleeding with Christ in Gethsemane and dying on a private Golgotha; joining the nameless procession of silent, uncomplaining heroes who humbled themselves to accomplish God's designs. A thousand times he had whispered to the large yellowing crucifix at Saint Raphael's that he only wanted to be a priest, and now he was certain that God had used Elvin Ward as a necessary instrument to teach him humility.

But as he convinced his lips, the deepest corners of his being disagreed and nourished some private life of survival. Elvin Ward, like Hollanders and Yankees and Cromwell, had displaced some naïve Irish faith in truth and justice. An innocence, though far from lost, had been dangerously uprooted in his soul, and this wound would begin to challenge even his strong religious faith.

Whatever the boy was who left Kirkwood to become a priest, he was sincere and innocent. Vain, perhaps, refusing to be ordinary or second best, with a yearning for recognition that predated his own consciousness, but ready to deny himself food or sleep, soft clothes or worldly riches, ready to abandon success and approval and the very love of a woman—all for God. He would have given his life had it been asked. With the right understanding, he could have led crusades or challenged presidents, fed a million poor or died on a cross as resignedly as any Christ. But beyond that simple faith was an Irish heart that would never endure disrespect. Even from God.

Cincinnati rests on seven hills, but, unlike Rome, Saint John's Seminary was hardly a factory for bishops or princes of the Church. Set in a quiet suburb, the bland prisonlike stone structure was the major seminary for several dioceses from Oklahoma to western Pennsylvania. Although Thom was assigned there for two years of philosophy, it was possible to complete the final four years of theology there as well. Some three hundred philosophers and theologians shared the facilities in common pursuit of the priesthood. Only deacons, a year from ordination, had special privileges.

To Thom, it was like emerging from an austere boarding school. Although the black cassock and Roman collar were requisite attire, smoking was permitted during recreation, a student canteen offered Cokes and snacks, and food was well cooked and plentiful. The whole mood was more casual. Little attention was paid to grades, and even the grand silence was scarcely enforced. Only first-year students had roommates, and all but the most scrupulous students smoked in their rooms or congregated in the johns long after the ten o'clock curfew. Occasionally a faculty member intervened with a tender, often humorous, reprimand, but most of them had additional parish duties or other outside interests and were rarely visible except during classes.

It was a new arena in which to battle for attention.

Athletic abilities helped, although games were hardly serious, and numerous students chose to ignore them or played only for diversion. There was none of the minor seminary passion for an outlet; however, Thom's extraordinary ability gained some attention.

Joe Beahan noticed. Beahan was a Sheffield deacon, a tall, thin sandy-haired man with thick glasses and a trace of effeminacy in his inflection and stride. Joe was rumored to have an outstanding mind, though poor health prevented his going to Rome.

"You're quite the athlete."

Thom grinned modestly.

Beahan's frequent companion, Freddie Weber, also a deacon from Sheffield by way of Baltimore, laughed. "The rugged type."

Freddie laughed easily. A roly-poly little man with a cherubic face, wavy light brown hair, and nervous eyes, he had switched dioceses after his parents' divorce to avoid a possible scandal. He was considered bright as well as very ambitious, and he often discussed the politics of Sheffield.

"Heinrich would be proud." It was his name for Bishop Schmidt. "He admires jocks!"

Thom was embarrassed, and he continued to smile sheepishly. No one had talked like that at Saint Robert's.

Jim O'Brien, another Sheffield deacon, noticed too, and Thom was particularly proud of this attention. He admired the lean dark-haired O'Brien, who respected the kind of priest Thom aspired to be. O'Brien was also outstanding in sports and serious about saving souls. He seemed hardly interested in diocesan politics, but he was a solid student with excellent preaching skills and a warm, humorous way, and his whole face shone when he smiled.

"You beat that baseball real good, lad."

"Sometimes."

"You must be a hell of a golfer."

"I've only fooled around—when I caddied." Thom and Jim had tried caddying one summer, until John Patrick decided it was demeaning.

"Maybe we'll get a chance to play. You're from Kirkwood?"

"Yes."

"Lake Watseka's a good course."

"That's where I caddied."

Thom liked his casual way although he felt uncomfortable in conversation. It never occurred to him that a deacon such as Jim O'Brien had any of his own problems. Thom only knew he would be an incredible priest—the kind that even John Patrick could like.

For the most part the deacons, the theologians in their final year before ordination, lived among themselves, practicing mass rubrics, gathering material for sermon files, teaching religion classes at neighboring high schools, and trying to learn all the canons and casuistry that professors had promised to "cover next year."

Thom was absorbed in his own new world of higher learning, and to be exposed to the random discussions of older students was suddenly terrifying.

"I'm with Duns Scotus. Otherwise there's no human freedom."

"Then Aquinas must be a heretic."

"What the hell's *premotio physica?*"

"That's not what Plato said."

"Is it *gratia efficax* or not?"

"What about Canon 209?"

His mind reeled with theories of Adam's sin, the free will of Christ and the kind of tears he shed, Josue's wars and Jericho's walls, Gilgamesh epics and the dimensions of the ark of the covenant. Jews in limbo and the licit use of perforated condoms. Thom was almost immediately off kilter. Listing badly.

There was no center to all the information. He asked questions and didn't understand the answers, or he didn't know enough to ask questions. Christ was really born in 7 B.C., the three wise men didn't actually pursue a star, and the bloody waters of a plagued Egypt were only infested with red insects. Freddie Weber giggled about it; Jim O'Brien pondered it and could still talk about Ben Hogan. Thomas Maguire could only promise to study harder, beg God for strength, and slowly come apart at the seams.

The daily philosophy was torturous. It was not really philosophy at all. Hume and Kant were covered in a day and a half of history with a brief glance at Voltaire. Spinoza was a Jewish pantheist and Nietzsche a disgruntled madman; John Stuart Mill was bypassed while Adam Smith was mentioned a few minutes before the bell. Only Thomas Aquinas, who baptized Aristotle, was taken seriously. Ponderously. Each definition of his was memorized in cathechism reborn.

Since everyone at Saint John's was expected to believe that all important truth had been revealed by God, scholastic philosophy was really only a preparation for theology. Aristotle's *Physics* could only clarify the sacraments, and his natural ethics were but a repetition of Catholic law. Birth control was wrong because the pope had so decided, and human reason stood shyly aside to whisper assent. Plato's caves were really Vatican archives, and Kant's categorical imperative an obvious fallacy. There was nothing to search or explore, only material to memorize accurately for exams.

"What is time?"

"Numerus motus secundum prius et posterius."

"What is the principle of learning?"

"Quidquid recipitur secundum modum recipientis recipitur."

"How do we know there is a God from reason?"

"Motion, causality, perfection—"

"How do we know man has a soul and will live forever?"

"Reasoning is a spiritual power and hence incorruptible."

In such narrow boundaries, Thom did well at first. The Latin words gave an aura of unreality to each new concept until he thought he understood it, then he memorized it carefully and added it to his block of truth. Marks were announced privately only if requested—unless a student were doing poorly. At the midsemester he averaged 96. And felt miserable. All the joy and success of the last two years at Saint Robert's had vanished.

Gradually and almost imperceptibly he discovered he was only going through plastic motions to get back to his impossible studies. Baseball games, meals, conversations, even prayers—it didn't matter. It was all the same. Constant anxiety took possession until he could only focus on all there was yet to learn. He raced to his room after a ball game and pored over a ten-page digest of Berkeley's idealism. To refute it. Then rambling notes on Tetzel's indulgences and Cesare Borgia, a sermon of John Chrysostom a theologian had recommended, and an hour with Joyce's *Portrait of the Artist*. Then back to Thomistic metaphysics and a brief chapel meditation begging the

Holy Spirit for enlightenment. When he finally stopped for dinner, he realized that he couldn't remember what he had read.

A table mate interrupted him. "Have you read Thomas Merton's books?"

"No, not yet."

"I'll give them to you when I get through."

"I'm reading Gilson."

"What's he say?"

"It's a kind of history of being. You know—"

"Yeh. I'll have to read it."

His explosion had nothing to do with faith or reason. And everything to do with an exhausting desire to succeed. Suddenly there were no boundaries to protect an insatiable thirst for all truth—at once. He was hardly aware of people, and even conversations gradually reverberated in a giant echo chamber as if soul and voice had separated. He felt compelled to splatter Bertrand Russell against the wall, then to assassinate Voltaire and rebut the sullen Camus. How would he ever preach or hear intelligent confessions or bring his brother Jim back to faith? It did not matter that he had six more years; he had to absorb lectures and master libraries and listen to every voice—except his own. After every meal or class he ran back to his room to pore over more books. He never finished anything; the dry, colorless books never enticed him. He only forced his way through—to learn it all.

Nor was there anyone to talk to. Freddie Weber giggled about "Heinrich's" alcoholism, and Joe Beahan was learning Spanish on records. Most of his classmates had been in minor seminaries together and were well established in laughing cliques. Thom found it more difficult to be sociable, but he was embarrassed to admit defeat to the admired Jim O'Brien.

Or to Margaret.

His breakdown was hardly dramatic. It began with the ticking of his roommate's clock during an evening study session. They had a good-sized comfortable room with twin beds, two dressers and footlockers, and a small sink with hot and cold water. Large windows looked out on an attractive campus. He stuffed the offending clock in a dresser drawer, under heavy sweaters, but he could still hear it. Then a deep gouge on his oak desk distracted his eye while he tried to read. He covered the spot with his book and found himself glancing at one page while struggling to focus on the other. He began to panic and felt a tingling in his legs and arms and a rush of fear in his groin. He dragged himself to fierce concentration, fighting the dilating words, and trying to bore deeper inside his own mind.

Life is lived at many levels, and who can say which is profound or superficial? Margaret had surrendered her every desire to the fearful God who traded consolation, and John Patrick lived as helplessly with some unexorcised sadness. Now their son, victim of both the demanding God and the historic sadness, lost his tenuous contact with their reality and entered a private, inescapable hell.

There was no relief. Soon it was all torture as he fought for sanity, as if he demanded a total vision of truth in a burning bush or a remote Sinai. There was no time for routine study, so he pushed his mind far beyond patient reflection and imagination. Distractions disappeared in a vortex of concentration, pages flashed by in instant clarity. He could not stop. Faster and faster he absorbed, without awareness of time. His eyes did not blink, voices were distant or nonexistent. The room and desk and ticking clock disappeared, and his very flesh was lost in the hunger of an insatiable mind.

One afternoon in November he felt no fatigue, only a detached euphoria, and the tingling in his hands and feet and groin forced him to read faster and faster. He grew giddy, his tense, constricted body surrendered to his mind in fearful detachment. Soul and body finally separated. He would master all of philosophy in a single sitting, absorb theology as well. No more painful assimilation of disconnected truths. An all-encompassing unity feared to rest lest the dizzying vision disappear. He careened over paragraphs and caromed over pages, laughing at the simplicity of wisdom and the ease of enlightenment. Perfect understanding. Illumination.

Soon there was no control, and he raced to keep up with whirling concepts like a man driving brakeless down the side of a mountain, flashing around hairpin turns and plummeting down the steeper inclines without choice or conscious fear.

A bell rang and he looked up, unaware of day or night,

life or disembodiment. Beyond all ability to slow the torrent of rushing thoughts or to separate his identity from a devouring mind, he sensed something was wrong when he stood up. His whole body breathed in rhythm with the convulsions of his cortex, in total, helpless, echoing pulsation. He tried to halt his brain, to shake himself back to lesser reality, to retreat from some fearful depth of inner focus, but there was no escape.

He walked stiffly out into the hall as if his dervish mind would race off in separate orbit around some other universe. Or beyond. Suddenly terrified, he needed help. He saw a familiar face and spoke as a helpless child.

"Help me!" It came out softly, as if he must maintain control.

"What's wrong?" Thom looked too normal to create panic.

"I think I'm cracking up or something." It was difficult to speak.

"You seem okay."

He wanted to scream. "It's—like my mind is whirling—" Suddenly the terror emerged. "O Jesus, Jesus, help me—" The words came out robotized.

The student led him to the infirmary: his walking legs increased his terror and his detached hands began to tremble and sweat. He tried to lie down, but acute anxiety compelled him to keep moving as his mind refused to comply.

"O Jesus, Jesus, knock me out—do something—I can't stand it."

They made a phone call and led him to the car and drove to Providence Hospital. The reception desk asked interminable questions.

"You don't remember your social security number?"

"It's in my wallet. O Christ—is this necessary? I'm dying—"

"You'll be okay. What is your mother's maiden name—father's middle initial?"

"Help me! Help me—my mind won't stop." The humiliation was unbearable.

"Date of birth? Who's your family doctor—group plan?"

Finally he was given a room and his own stiff fingers undressed him, each motion an unbearable agony. His tired mind gave direction; then the resident doctor appeared.

"Please—please, just knock me out—I'm so frightened."

"Did you move your bowels today?"

"Yes—I don't know—Jesus help me!" It was as if he stood outside giving lazy orders to hand or tongue. "I'll be okay if you just put me to sleep."

He pleaded, begged to lose consciousness, to end the hellish nightmare of indescribable fear. There was no relief as long as his mind tumbled uncontrollably like a giant projector gone awry, spooling film all over an antiseptic floor. The doctor remained calm. Thom wanted John Patrick to be there to push the doctor aside.

"Has this occurred before?"

"Jesus, no—never. It's like I hypnotized myself, or—" Then the anxiety enveloped him and he whimpered pathetically, "Put me out—please put me out."

A nurse rubbed his arm with alcohol and a stunned white coat finally gave him a shot, and fifteen minutes later another one. A moment of numb peace, then the increased horror that he was losing his mind in a never-ending gyration. Even the shots took no immediate effect. He begged God's release, pleaded to die or be dissolved, again asked John Patrick to come, promised God anything to be restored.

He woke up late the next morning, testing cautiously; he uttered a deep prayer of gratitude and peeked out under some embarrassed haze when the doctor looked in.

"You gave us a scare."

"Me too—what happened?"

"I'm not sure." He had checked Thom's seminary history, and this, as well as his ruggedly healthy appearance, made a breakdown seem unlikely. "Maybe a kind of self-induced hypnotic state with mild hysteria. And fatigue—I'm not sure."

"Can I leave?"

"You should spend the day here—perhaps overnight."

"I'll be all right. I know it's okay now." He had to get back to his studies and see if his mind had been impaired.

"Well, you get some sleep and we'll see—"

They released him after dinner in time for night prayers, and back at the seminary he was assigned a private room recently vacated by a departing theologian. Then he began covering his tracks and dispelling rumors.

"A kind of self-hypnosis. Really strange—"

"I've heard about it."

"I never had. I must have studied too hard when I was tired."

"Hardly necessary, with your brains." They laughed.

The horror was over, he had learned almost nothing, and an important warning had been disregarded.

For a few days he relaxed and studied gently, still fighting every kind of distraction and frightened that the madness would reoccur. As he settled back to seminary routine, he believed his own story, perfected in the retelling, and his tense struggle metastasized.

Noises continued to drive him almost to tears. A food spot on the front of his cassock, the clanking of a water pipe, or birds chattering outside his window. It was a continuing agony. He refused to give in, fought harder to concentrate, and only sleep finally rescued him.

The compulsion was easier to deal with in private, although equally as painful. He cleared his desk of debris, removed spots from the floor, covered marred varnish with unlined index cards, covered plaster cracks with clean cardboard, then struggled to ignore the cardboard. There was always another and another obsessive harassment. His body grew rigid; he forced his scattered attention to converge, bound his mind in chains. Nothing stopped the divided focus. Finally he visited the spiritual director, a gently smiling rural man who listened soothingly. The entire experience eluded his simplicity.

"I've read that green is a relaxing color. Maybe paint your room—"

Later, Thom explained himself to the seminary doctor who supplied a dozen quarter-grain phenobarbital. He looked at Thom over bushy black eyebrows.

"You'll make it. It's a tough program, but these may help—"

No one recommended a psychiatrist's alien, unchristian art, so Thom prayed and studied and somehow survived the two years at Saint John's waging an uninterrupted private war. From morning till night there did not seem to be one minute of unselfconscious attention. But he did not know what else to do or where to go. He forced himself to ignore each new symptom of distress until more energy went into dispelling distractions than into prayer or philosophy. Baseball was an occasional diversion with its own set of maddening distractions—a dandelion or a blowing leaf—but the agony never let up from the moment he woke and tried to pray until he fell exhausted into bed. When he talked to someone, a flake of dandruff on a black shoulder demanded his attention even as he struggled to ignore it. It was impossible to do anything—even eat a meal—without the constant compulsion to divide himself in anxious parts. Unbelievably, he appeared relaxed and brilliant. He graduated at the head of his class, led a haphazard baseball league, and met the assorted fears head on. Refusing to give in or quit. There was nothing else he knew to do.

He would not go to Rome for theology despite his achievements; the next four years would be spent in a new provincial seminary (Pius XII) on isolated acreage in southwestern Michigan. Carrying with him a bachelor's degree in liberal arts and a tortured psyche. It did not matter. He had somehow survived—no matter the price—and the priesthood was but four years away.

Perhaps survival only requires some important focus, something to accomplish and look forward to—however minute. Suicide may be the silent center of a tornado when there is nothing left to do or even feel. Thomas Aloysius Maguire survived not only the strange obsession that reduced life to an orbiting cerebrum, but also a new and disappointing assignment to a final four years of theology at Pius XII Seminary outside Steelmont.

The letter of appointment arrived in Kirkwood at the end of June 1953 when Dwight Eisenhower was promising an end to the Korean War and Joe McCarthy was readying his fusillades against Communist espionage in America. John Patrick voted for Ike because he didn't know "what the hell that walleyed bastard Stevenson's talking about." Thom and Margaret were more concerned about Bobbie Foley's assignment to Rome. Bobbie was still the flabby, docile seminarian but now he had a new, unbecoming arrogance.

A newly ordained Freddie Weber was Bishop Schmidt's cherubic secretary, and Joe Beahan, pale and thin with thick glasses and thinning blond hair, was named assistant chancellor. Charlie Kenelley, who had never studied in Rome, returned from Catholic University in Washington to serve as chancellor and was appointed as a papal chamberlain, a lesser-ranked monsignor.

Jim O'Brien was sent to Kirkwood's Saint Raphael's to replace a young Polish priest who upset Monsignor Doyle. A graying John Patrick was delighted with Thom's glowing descriptions of the new assistant, and Margaret appreciated the name O'Brien.

❧ ❧ ❧

Jim settled into medicine for his final two years, externing in Milwaukee County General, where exciting realities replaced the cadaver named Mort. It was an optimistic time in medical history, with expanded uses of sulfa and DDT to wipe out typhus, with "questionable" antihistamines, miraculous antibiotics, the new streptomycin, and exciting transplants and surgical techniques developed during World War II. Penicillin, which Jim's favorite professor called the most significant advance in sexual freedom since Adam discovered Eve, had become a household word; apparently it would cure anything except mortal sin. The Church still claimed the only effective healing of that.

The Church was not really significant to James Maguire. Even a Jesuit medical school only paid token homage. A slow-talking sleepy hospital chaplain taught a course in ethics from yellowed notes, attacking abortion as genocide and birth control as an apocalyptic sign of the end of civilization. He told the aspiring doctors how to baptize in emergencies and attacked the old dilemma about saving the mother or the baby.

"It's a doctor's job to save any life, not to make moral judgments about which life is more important. The mother might have additional children to take care of, well and good, but the baby might grow up to be Cardinal Spellman."

Ethics was not Jim's best class, and he never asked a question, even when the chaplain summarized the Church's hostility toward psychiatry, replete with clever attacks on Freud by Monsignor Sheen.

Jim had read Freud, finding in him a doctrinaire arrogance. For a young man just liberating himself from a dogmatic Church, Freud merely seemed to be a replacement of Catholic certitude. Jim was more partial to the works of "heretics" who saw the psyche in a context of the entire social environment, not as a collection of anal and oedipal scars. John Patrick, although increasingly proud of his son, was not impressed with Jim's interest in psychiatry.

"That's not being a doctor, just a damn fool who's sicker than his patients."

When McNulty insisted that "only Jews do that," John Patrick asserted that a Maguire could do any damn thing he wanted. McNulty knew he was in over his head and mumbled apologetically, "If the Jews do it, there's probably a lot of money in it." Jim never brought up psychiatry in Kirkwood again. Even to Connie.

His relationship with Connie Hackett had grown until they were almost engaged. She complained bitterly in his final two years about the little time they had together, but in a sense, it kept their relationship alive. They still shared nothing intellectually, and weeks went by when he was unable to be with her. Then they would have a brief two-day sexual explosion that took him away from dying children and the complexities of patient history and diagnostic medicine. Only rarely did she permit intercourse, usually when her period was imminent. Then she confessed her sin and told Jim that they had "to behave." He convinced her that there was no need to confess anything else since they were in love, and she accepted his Jesuit training as Gospel. The training, of course, was neither Jesuit nor Gospel, and Jim had not been to confession in almost three years.

The sexual excitement kept Jim around, even though he felt brief spasms of shame when she showed her lack of education among his friends at the hospital. She insisted on telling long stories about her brothers and sisters or her co-workers at the paper mill, but no one wondered what Jim saw in her. Her sensuality explained that, and even John Patrick enjoyed embracing her. Margaret appreciated the fact that Connie received communion every Sunday and occasionally met herself and Anne, now an attractive cheerleader, at evening devotions. Even Mary O'Meara agreed that Connie was a lovely young woman and rarely made derogatory comments about her milkman father.

Jim was only remotely concerned about Connie's religious devotion. Although he kidded her about her rounded, wide hips as "a great obstetrical risk," he knew that she would instinctively be a fine mother to the children he wanted to have, especially when he watched her patience and gentle good humor around the demands of five younger brothers and sisters. And aside from the sexual pleasure she gave him, they often had fun. She danced sinuously at the Lake Watseka Palladium and at Emil's Roadhouse near Milwaukee County General, and her simplicity was a refreshing relief from the tedious review of all the various medical subspecialties in his third- and fourth-year clinical work at Milwaukee County General.

Jim's focus was now hospital medicine. He gave his very first spinal tap to a child with meningitis, nervously sewed stitches in the arm of a six-year-old boy who reminded him of a younger Tim. It was exciting to wear the official white coat, to have unsuspecting emergency patients call him doctor, to feel his own stethoscope bounce proudly on his chest. He was exuberant—and always horny when he retreated to Connie. There was neither time nor inclination to compare her with other women. Jim was a "doctor," and dreams of being a forest ranger and rescuing snow-trapped deer paled before the reality of bloody emergency rooms and dramatic births. He delivered his first baby with the skilled eye-hand coordination that had fixed Margaret's appliances and now impressed a second-year resident.

He completed his national boards in the spring of his senior year, and Connie took the train to meet him on a warm night in March 1953. After drinking and dancing until the bar closed, they made congratulatory love all night in a room at the Holiday Inn. The following morning at breakfast, as she chatted nonstop about the new house that friends of hers had bought and the nervy flirt at work who had finally lost her job, Jim wanted her to get back on the train so he could return to the hospital. Then he reproached himself and took her to a favorite cove on Lake Michigan, north of Milwaukee near Whitefish Bay. When she finally quieted down in his arms, he knew why he loved her innocent Irish simplicity and the warm, sensuous body. He talked of his own desire to have children, heightened by his memory of delightful walks in the woods with Tim and thoughts of the helpless little hands in pediatrics. He confessed that he would probably specialize in children. John Patrick's displeasure over psychiatry and the excitement of "real medicine" had changed his mind. Besides, he had discovered that children took to him, often insisting that he do the painful I.V.s.

His dreams of a specialty, however, were threatened when Connie announced that she was two and a half months pregnant. It was two days after Jim had been accepted at Detroit Receiving Hospital for his internship.

"Jesus, Connie, why didn't you tell me sooner?"

"I didn't know."

"But it was right after your period!"

"Well, it might have been longer than I realized. I don't always keep track when you're gone so much." She was on the verge of tears.

"Christ, don't worry about it. We'll just get married. That's all there is to it."

But that wasn't all.

John Patrick was angry. "A doctor should have more sense. Well, you'll just have to get married."

"I know that. It just moves things up a little." He didn't mention the shattered dreams of a residency in pediatrics.

Margaret secretly blamed it all on Connie and later called her a "little slut" to Mary O'Meara, who was bound to solemn secrecy. Now she only worried that a scandal would be avoided and that the banns of marriage would be properly announced in Saint Raphael's. It was no surprise to anyone, and Margaret said a prayer of gratitude that Connie and Jim would be in Detroit by the time she started showing.

"We don't have to tell anybody the exact birth date. It's no one's business."

"People don't count the weeks, mother," said a concerned Thom.

"That's all you know. Indeed, they count!" It was a rare rebuke to her priestly son, and she recalled three or four "premature" births that were talked about all over the parish.

Jim was warmed by his younger brother's support. It was a rare moment of intimacy during Thom's two years in Cincinnati and Jim's final years of medical school. To Jim, Thom had only seemed preoccupied and set apart. He was not aware that, even as they talked, Thom was struggling to focus on the problem of Connie's pregnancy while the same painful obsessions—John Patrick's smoldering cigarette, a speck of egg on Margaret's apron, Tim's shout in the backyard—tortured him beyond words. His compulsive self-focus had become a way of life as he struggled to placidly ignore all irritants. His body was tense and screaming every second as he continued to wage war with a conflict he didn't understand. Desperately, he wanted to ask Jim's help, but he feared the admission of failure and the effect it would have on Jim's faith.

Jim smiled at Thom as the family meeting broke up.

"I'm sorry you can't perform the ceremony, padre."

"I'd really like that." He could not stop focusing on a bit of toast on Jim's lower lip.

They were married the first Saturday of July. Thom and twelve-year-old Tim, still a clumsy, exuberant Maguire anomaly with sandy curls and innocent blue eyes, served at the mass. It delighted Tim, who only forgot to ring the bell once, while Thom was too tortured with his own afflicting preoccupations to appreciate the beautiful bride. Which Connie was—radiant and flushed with nervousness; proud of the new esteem she felt as Dr. Maguire's wife.

Jim slipped a ring on his bride's soft perspiring finger and he loved her little girl's unsophisticated joy. Margaret wondered if Mary O'Meara had told anyone.

Then the summer was over. John Patrick continued to drink silently in his brown leather recliner. Jim and Connie were already in Detroit where Jim would begin his internship; Anne entered Mount Saint Mary's, a nearby Catholic girls' college, and Thom was leaving for Pius XII. Only the bubbling Tim remained at home, a lovable and almost perfect son.

"It all goes so fast." Margaret lamented the disappearance of her children.

John Patrick did not reply as the shadows crept into the living room. Tim had gone to bed. The fruit trees and Margaret's beautiful garden were almost in darkness as she stared out the window, near tears. Kneeling alone in the parlor, she said her silent rosary, her Hail Marys only interrupted by the tinkling of ice in John Patrick's glass and the sound of him lighting another cigarette.

She finished her prayers and walked into the living room. "Don't stay up all night."

He grunted gently as she kissed him on the cheek and went alone into the bedroom. Tomorrow it would be better.

☙ ☙ ☙

Pius XII Seminary was only three years old, a joint financial venture of the five Michigan bishops, located where Sheffield and Elliston dioceses bordered on Detroit. Steelmont, the nearest major city, was in Bishop Schmidt's domain although the seminary itself was within the archdiocese of Detroit. The land had been donated to Cardinal Foley by the Ford family and was part of the original tract of Henry Ford's grandfather, John, an immigrant Cork farmer who lost his wife to the fever and migrated westward from Canada through the Great Lakes. The sprawling twelve-million-dollar Spanish-style estate—with airy corridors of terra-cotta tile, frescoed ceilings, arching windows, and marble walls—housed two hundred Michigan theology students in modern classrooms and comfortable private rooms that had individual baths. Raymond Nowicki and Elvin Ward, members of the episcopal planning commission, had protested the luxury of built-in desks, indirect lighting, innerspring beds, and separate showers, but it was a new age, and Pius XII was an architect's model for an expanding Church whose strength had never been more widespread nor its finances as sound.

The French-founded Mauricians who ran the seminary were devoted, disciplined men who had dedicated their lives to priestly formation, and they numbered seven cardinals and over a hundred bishops in their alumni. Bernard Fox, the rector, was a wiry, athletic man of fifty, with close-cropped gray hair and a wide thin-lipped mouth. He wore rimless glasses and spoke in a surprisingly soft voice with a gravelly baritone resonance. The weak voice, rasping from such an expansive mouth, demanded attention. Students readily heeded the easily angered Fox, and even the faculty priests feared his feisty loyalty to ancient Maurician principles.

Thomas Maguire was his kind of seminarian, and he called on Thom frequently in a moral theology class. Fox still played an occasional baseball game, and Thom listened attentively to his wordy description of Ty Cobb's batting style. He also devoured the spiritual development lectures that Bernard Fox gave each evening in the prayer hall beneath the elaborate neo-Byzantine chapel. Fox offered a spiritual milieu that suited Thom—masculine, ascetic, disciplined, and uncomplaining. God was an all-seeing coach of a championship team, a tough general who led His infantry into Calvary's ambush and emerged victorious.

Fox often dramatized his lectures. "What do you tell Christ when you're faced with temptation?" He peered over his glasses, his shoulders arched into his neck. "Maybe it's a beautiful woman or a life of self-indulgence."

His voice changed and he became a whining effeminate with drooping shoulders and flabby mouth. "Would you take it easy on me, Lord? I'm not very strong." He held the pose for several seconds.

A few students smiled nervously, but there was not a sound.

Then the shoulders snapped back, the head went up, and the arms reached squarely heavenward. His voice was suddenly powerful, almost a discordant scream. "That's what Augustine said—'Make me pure, but not now.' " He spat out the words. "Well it didn't take Augustine long to discover that 'our heart is restless until it rests in thee.' " The voice grew gentle, almost benignly paternal. "And at the end of a devoted life, he still reproached himself, 'Too late have I loved thee.' "

The silence was tense and exciting, and Thom felt Fox's words in his own shoulders and chest. A bicep spirituality that denied weakness. He flashed on the sensual Roselle and banished any thoughts of her bare breasts, feeling like Thomas Aquinas in his monastic cell, knowing he would never sin again. God's grace was suddenly an uncomplicated calisthenic, and sanctity a marathon race that eliminated weaklings. Margaret had known it all along.

The total emotional explosion did not reoccur, although the contagious obsessions persisted. Gradually he accepted them as a congenital deformity and, illuminated by Bernard Fox's homilies, he understood that God was only testing him for combat. The conquest of a single symptom was grateful proof that healing would occur at God's suitable pleasure. It did not matter that three more symptoms took its place. The serious, organized horarium of prayer and study, not unlike that at Saint Robert's, gave only a modicum of leisure, and there was little of the intellectual ambience that had tortured him at Saint John's in Cincinnati. He was back in boot camp where grand silence was minutely observed, boundaries rigidly established, and classes consistently unchallenging.

Actually Thom could have completed four years of theology in half the time since his honed memory and facility with Latin reduced garrulous textbooks to catechetical simplicity. He felt smugly secure within the well-defined intellectual boundaries, and despite the persistent tension of his strange affliction, he found time to tutor his classmate, Mike Fogarty, a cigar-chewing ex-marine from Sheffield, eight years his senior, who knew no Latin. The stocky Fogarty had a good mind and only needed to hear the translation while he took copious notes. Chet Golas, another Sheffield classmate, was a separate story. A handsome athlete who had spoken Polish until confirmation, Golas was mystified by theological concepts that Thom struggled to simplify for him. Thom delighted in Golas's sincere adoration, even as he was tortured by his own inability to ignore flakes of dandruff on the shoulder of Chet's cassock.

In Maurician seminaries, each student was expected to select a spiritual adviser among the faculty, and Jack Durrell, a gentle intellectual, was a popular choice. Since he had exceeded his quota of penitents, only a special favor admitted Thom to his enthusiastic flock. He was always available for emergency sessions or confession, but his customary ministrations were one weekly confession—face-to-face in his room—and a quarterly private conference on spiritual growth. A shy man of about thirty-five with sad eyes and assorted moles on his balding head, he centered his supportive spiritual direction around biblical parables. Thom looked forward to the conferences.

"Isaiah compares suffering to a primitive smelting crucible whereby dross is purged away by heat. Similarly, all of our sufferings purify our soul until God can see His own image there."

Thom continued to hide his secret affliction, and his

confessions were as boringly routine as any nun's: "I was distracted at morning prayers three times. Impatient during study seven or eight times. I talked after grand silence."

What could Durrell advise? He drifted into Christ's devotion to a Father's will and recommended greater trust in Mary, who interceded for more wine at Cana's wedding feast. It was the preplanned nosegay, and Thom accepted a "three Hail Mary" penance with gratitude.

Jack Durrell knew he was shepherding a fledgling saint.

Had not Thom been absorbed by his never-ending conflicts, it would have been a totally idyllic world—routine, isolated, benignly childlike, and usually without pressure. Not a grunt of lust or a simple fistfight, no word of Europe's reconstruction or the mutilations in Southeast Asia; only a sports page tacked to a bulletin board—with distasteful ads removed—heralding Bobbie Layne or Al Kaline or thunderous Gordie Howe. An occasional *Going My Way* or *Song of Bernadette,* a visiting missionary, or a provincial banquet when Bishop Schmidt paid annual homage. Even vacations in Kirkwood were too long, and Thom waited impatiently to return to the programmed solace.

There were occasional evenings in Kirkwood when Thom joined the nuns in their cloistered recreation room, and they giggled outrageously at every shred of Thom's humor. A young Sister Marietta matched him joke for joke, her dark eyes flashing coquettish excitement and her face flushed to new warmth. She was a fine organist with a rich alto voice. Students loved her, and even the older nuns, disciplined to more discreet repartee, considered her an attractive source of new vocations.

"David Maher brought a garter snake to class."

"So what'd you do?" Thom asked.

"Reenacted Eden." The room throbbed with giggles.

"I suppose you were an award-winning Eve." They howled again.

"Drop by someday. We could use a more convincing Adam." There were tears of laughter, then they ate fresh brownies with cold milk, and after a brief prayer in the convent chapel, Mother Mary Louise thanked him at the door.

"Do come again soon. It's good to laugh." Her handsome motionless face smiled cautiously. He was a new kind of cleric she wondered about—like Father O'Brien—and she also wondered if Sister Marietta had been too forward and subtly sexual in the Garden of Eden discourse. She planned to discuss it privately, but the young nun anticipated her concern in the chapter of faults, a public admission of guilt.

"I was too forward with Mr. Maguire and sought too much attention, ignoring the needs of others. I ask your forgiveness. And God's."

Mother Mary Louise was partially relieved, and Sister Marietta was more restrained when Thom came again. But she thought about him at mass.

During Christmas vacation of his first year of theology, Thom was named godfather to Jim's first child. After Monsignor Doyle baptized another John Patrick—he rarely baptized now except the offspring of prominent parishioners—the Maguires gathered for dinner at John Patrick's table. Even Margaret had forgotten the premature birth, and John Patrick had to be warned not to crush his first grandchild with an abundance of love.

John Patrick was in rare form, proud of Jim's internship at Detroit Receiving Hospital and almost equally proud of Thom's approaching priesthood. As if the long years of laboring at an abrasive, demanding business and living with a rigid marriage had finally been worthwhile. The Maguire children had proved their mettle beyond the transient boundaries of high school football and Saint Raphael's parish. Certainly beyond the Hollanders of Kirkwood.

"You're still not going to specialize?" John Patrick had grown more sophisticated about the medical milieu.

"Not now, dad. With a family on the way I've got to make some money. If I have to go in the service, I may. Otherwise I'll just wait until we can afford it."

Even Thom paid new attention. "Where will you practice?"

"In Kirkwood. Doc McGregor wants me to come in with him. He has a hell of a practice, and he just can't handle it anymore. These Catholics do have big families."

Thom resented Jim's softly cynical laugh and wondered about his brother's faith. Margaret was too delighted with little Johnny to take her eyes away, until she almost burned the gravy.

John Patrick discussed business arrangements, questioned the partnership percentage with Doc McGregor, and recommended some cautious investments.

"I'd like to pay you back some of the tuition you laid out." Jim had a new awareness of money on an intern's three-hundred-dollar monthly salary, and he appreciated his father's continuous help.

"That wasn't a loan—it was an investment." He beamed proudly and recommended Seabord Surety Stock, a safe insurance investment with decent dividends.

"That'll be a while yet. We want to get a house and—" They were living in a tiny Detroit apartment.

"Don't try to do it all at once. You can kill yourself, you know," said Margaret. Already she resented Connie's complaints about the baby's crying and their cramped quarters in Detroit.

(She had remarked to Mary O'Meara, "What'd she come from? That little box on Elm Street. Now she has to have a house." "Well, she's the doctor's wife!" Mary had said mockingly. "Indeed.")

Jim resented his mother's intrusion. "Getting a house is not doing it all at once, mother. For Christ's sake, I'm twenty-six years old."

"I don't know anything," she said. "Times are different. Your father and I had a four-room rented house with two children and a Depression to worry about." There were tears in her eyes, and Jim felt sudden guilt.

"I didn't mean—"

"No, it's all right, I'm only your mother. What do I know?" She could not bring herself to look at Connie, and she moved to the kitchen to warm some mince pie.

Connie followed her. "Let me help, mom."

"You watch the baby, dear. It'll only take a minute. I want you to enjoy yourself today. I know how much care a new baby is." She didn't want to be called *mom.*

Connie was relieved and returned to the dining room.

Later Margaret would report to Mary O'Meara, "Now it's mom this and mom that. Until it comes to doing the dishes. I'm the old workhorse who can do for everyone. She's the lady."

"Indeed," said Mary. "She'll be as fat as her mother soon. Has the doctor's wife hired a maid yet?"

"No need. I suppose I'll be the baby-sitter. Well, I've got news for her."

She added it all to the litany of her distress over John Patrick's drinking and Jack's death. Another thorn in a thickening crown. Thank God she had Thom.

John Patrick ignored her complaints, delighted with his busty new daughter-in-law and a grandson who bore his name.

Jim was happy with his beginning family, and even the postponed specialty had not really saddened him. The internship was an exciting one in a high-crime neighborhood of Detroit. Shootings and stabbings among poor blacks, frozen winos and infected children, emergency births and a waiting room full of groaning people who were incredibly patient as Jim rushed around to help them. No one distinguished between residents and interns. The white coat meant health and pills and sewed-up arms.

Jim rotated from medicine and surgery to obstetrics and pediatrics, ENT and urology, minimal psychiatry—usually dealing only with acute psychotics and hopeless alcoholics—and the free-for-all in the emergency room. Although he liked the children most of all, the majority black and poor, his most exciting accomplishment involved a birth where the head appeared to be restrained by shoulder dystocia, a kind of locking of the baby in the uterus. He had recently observed the difficult procedure of rotating the shoulders to shorten the diameter of delivery, and now the resident could not be located and Jim had to act. He broke the baby's clavicle and made a healthy delivery, then worried terribly that he should not have resorted to the emergency measure. The resident finally appeared and was delighted with Jim's resourcefulness. James Maguire would be a good doctor.

His father was delighted when "Dr. Jim" and Connie returned to Kirkwood. Jim was ready to get on with his life, and Doc McGregor's practice was an active one. Almost sixty-five, the kindly McGregor had grown up with his patients, and the waiting room looked much like one of Margaret's rest homes. These were people who trusted no one else, and at first Jim was hard pressed to win their confidence. Sick people, he discovered, especially old and neglected ones, liked attention and compassion over anything else. He prescribed for arthritis and edema and hypertension, but most often for loneliness and anxiety.

"Seventy-five percent of all patients only need a good word or a little encouragement. Twenty percent will live damn near no matter what you do. Four percent will die unless you're God. All that newfangled medicine is only for the one percent. It's humbling." McGregor chuckled and stroked his chin.

He was a deeply religious man, and Jim, now attending mass again with Connie and the baby, often saw the white-haired head and stiff back kneeling devoutly, rapt in prayer. He was quietly opposed to birth control—"It'll put us out of business"—and had never aborted more than a tubal pregnancy in his life. A third generation was bringing him their deliveries, eschewing the more expensive specialists. Doc McGregor rarely consulted anyone and had learned by trial and some errors, painful ones, his own obstetrical skills. "It's all in the hand and the eye—you've got that naturally. It's God's gift."

There were inoculations, well-baby care, sore throats and bee stings, broken arms, and minor surgery. It was a concerned family medicine that made house calls and treated patients with compassion. James Maguire was never happier. He had a warm, sensual wife, a fat, happy baby, and an exciting practice that made his daily work a recreation.

☘ ☘ ☘

In late February of Thom's third year of theology, John Patrick had the accident. The rector called Thom from Sunday afternoon vespers as melodic Gregorian cadences rose and fell like mountain rivers. It was Thom's favorite devotion, and, during it, even his obsessive and dividing distractions usually tortured him only mildly.

"Dixit Dominus Domino meo: Sede a dextris meis,

"Donec ponam inimicos tuos scabellum pedum tuorum."

Fox slid up the aisle during the majestic Magnificat and motioned for Thom to follow him out.

They walked down the marble corridor to the rector's office suite. "I have some bad news. Your father is dying!"

It had no meaning. Jack had died, the reckless, crazy

daredevil Thom loved, but his father couldn't die. An angry, often drunken, unknown man, he was some anchor that couldn't die. They were just beginning to be friends again.

"Your sister called. An auto accident—slid off the road and hit a tree—bad shape."

Thom, in tears, called the hospital expecting an intensive care nurse. "Yes—he's in 405. I'll refer you." He heard the ring.

"Hello—hello. Damn it, I said hello—" It was unmistakably John Patrick.

"Dad—is that you—?"

"Hell, yes, it's me—who'd you expect, Saint Peter?"

Margaret took the phone. "He's all doped up—but the doctor said he's going to make it." She whispered in the phone. "He was drinking—Dr. Jim is going to talk to him."

"Of course I'm going to make it!" The voice thundered in the background.

"Do you need me there?"

"You'll be home for Easter in a few weeks. I can handle it." Assuredly. It was only another tragedy. God had visited His people.

Bernard Fox offered him time off, but Thom considered it unnecessary.

John Patrick almost died the same night and was anointed by Father O'Brien, but by the next afternoon the crisis had passed. He began flirting with nurses—in spite of two broken legs, some fractured ribs, and assorted cuts and bruises. Dangerous internal bleeding had stopped, and Margaret attributed his recovery to the grace of Extreme Unction. John Patrick agreed with McNulty that it was a "history of expensive whiskey."

Thom was approaching the subdiaconate, the first major step toward priestly ordination. He had already been tonsured and had earned the four minor orders of porter, lector, exorcist, and acolyte—each a dramatization of future powers wrapped in ancient history. Subdeaconship was far more important, however, and imposed a solemn promise of lifelong celibacy and the reading of the daily breviary—an hour-long recitation of psalms and hymns, Scripture readings and selections from Church fathers. The book was to be read *attente et devote,* under pain of mortal sin.

Thom had new doubts and worries about proper motivation, and he began to find classes repetitive and predictable. There was no music beyond Gregorian chant, no real art or literature or political awareness. Classroom discussions generally dealt with sterile and insoluble conflicts of another day. Interesting discrepancies between traditional faith and archaeological discoveries in the Dead Sea Scrolls; the true nature of Noah's flood and Lot's saline wife; and the creation myths and evolution had already been dissected ad nauseam. Increasingly, it hurt to admit that all of Catholic theology was less graduate learning than simple grade school catechism in loftier terms. Without freedom or surprises, assuredly without discovery.

Easter vacation offered some diversion. John Patrick had to be carried to and from the toilet. He had aged markedly in six weeks, and he wondered nervously about his business. Margaret attended to his gruff orders and rationed liquor—with surprisingly few protests. Thom watched a TV ball game with him, then Milton Berle, "What's My Line?" and a fight from Chicago. John Patrick was delighted by the companionship.

"I'll take the nigger."

On Easter Sunday he loved the attention his wheelchair drew at the seven o'clock mass. Doyle shook hands with him at the communion rail, ushers nodded, and Mulaley, the aging undertaker, smiled benignly. McNulty wheeled him to the parking lot.

"Mulaley had you in his bank account already."

"It'll take more than an oak tree."

"Good you had a wee drop to soften the blow."

"You know I never touch the stuff. I'm a God-fearing man." John Patrick looked stooped and gray.

Margaret prolonged her thanksgiving to meet monsignor in the vestibule.

"How's the old man?" Doyle was nearing sixty himself.

"Like a bear in a beehive. Anne gets home on weekends—"

Anne was in her third year of college. A beautiful dark-haired girl with fine round breasts and her mother's ability to defend them, she had considered entering the convent but decided that she passionately wanted children. She was an all-A student in liberal arts—which John

Patrick called a waste of time—waiting to earn her "Mrs." degree. She was not fond of her father, but she assisted Margaret without complaint.

Doyle accompanied Margaret to the parking lot. He admired Thom's breviary, rubbed a smiling Tim's curly hair, and assisted with the transfer of John Patrick from the wheelchair to the front seat.

"He may never want the casts off."

"You're wrong, monsignor. It's her that likes me shackled."

They laughed easily and Doyle invited Thom to dinner the next night. Margaret was in heaven.

When Thom returned to Pius XII after Easter, his tension had increased. He suffered a three-day headache that ran from the back of his neck up over the top of his head until the skull surface was painful to touch. He feared an unknown meningitis or brain tumor. Aspirin hardly helped, and he could barely focus his attention in class. There were two dismissals of unsuitable candidates. The first was a pale, effeminate sacristan who had twice been detected masturbating in the woods. A handsome, athletic ex-GI had also been asked to leave. Consistently late for morning prayers, he had been caught at the rear door of his residence hall at two in the morning with grass stains and lipstick on his cream sport shirt.

Thom's blinding headache persisted, irritated by the frequent obsessions, until he consulted a neighboring physician who prescribed codeine. "It's just pressure—you've got to relax." It didn't help. He continued to lose interest in things, even baseball, and he found it impossible to concentrate on *latae sententiae* excommunications and Ezekiel's visions. After two days of fitful sleep and tortured, disconnected dreams, he knew he had to approach Bernard Fox. He knocked on the dark oak door like a tiny, terrified boy. Fox's firm jaw smiled broadly. Then his face softened with priestly concern when he noted Thom's sad eyes and trembling lips.

"What's wrong, boy?" Fox looked aghast, as if his own certitude was shaken.

Everything came pouring out—tearful, stuttering, despairing.

Fox interrupted quickly. "It's just exhaustion, boy, nothing to worry about!" Thom was chalk white, and

Fox worried about another breakdown. There had been two that month, but it couldn't happen to the stalwart pride of Sheffield, Thom Maguire. Fox reassured himself that it was Thom's concern about his family and offered Thom and himself an out.

"Take some time. You won't lose but a month or so of class—"

Even as Thom's heart leaped with relief, he heard himself protesting. "But I'll miss the subdeaconate!" Already he wondered if he had admitted too much weakness.

"You can catch up in the fall." Fox smiled thinly through his disappointment. "You'll be saying the breviary for a long time."

Thom packed his bags without a word to anyone, and Jack Durrell drove him to the train station early the following morning. Father Fox announced crisply in prayer hall that Thom was needed at home and would return in the fall.

"I doubt he'll miss the month of classes." The students laughed loudly. Especially Chet Golas.

Margaret didn't even smile when he showed up at the front door.

"My God in heaven! What's wrong?" Her expression was deathly.

"I've had terrible headaches—"

"Now it's you. O dear God!" Her world was finally shattered.

"I think I'm going back in the fall."

Her features were distorted. "It's not sex, is it?" she snarled, not waiting for an answer. The words had slipped out in her sudden anger and she immediately softened and looked away.

He was stunned.

"You'd better tell your father. He's still not up—the life of Riley."

John Patrick heard the disturbance and reached for his walker. He struggled and cursed, then sat back exhausted on the bed when Thom entered the room. He had aged even more, as if some shadow had fallen across his image. It hurt to look at him.

"What the hell's wrong?" His mouth dropped open and there was a fiber of drool between his lips.

"I've had these headaches—so they gave me an early vacation."

"You're going back?"

Thom had not expected his concern. "In the fall."

He was barely relieved. "It would be the end of your mother."

No one asked how he felt.

Surprisingly, it crushed Thom to know that John Patrick had lost some energy to resist, and it was terribly painful to hear him admit anxieties to Margaret later that evening.

"I don't know if it's worth it. I lost the Jordan account."

"There will be others." She spoke soothingly.

"What the hell does that mean? That's one of my best accounts." He had no ambition even to get drunk.

"With that smile of yours you'll get more."

"It's not the same." He looked so much older. "It's just not the same—"

"I've been praying—Saint Anne will help."

Once he would have roared at her. Now he spoke softly. "I've been praying too."

"God takes care of His own."

"I hope so. I can't seem to do it myself anymore." His face was drawn around the mouth, and Thom noticed folds of wrinkled skin at his neck.

"Are you cold, John Patrick?"

"Not really."

"I'll turn up the heat. You look tired."

"I'm only thinking."

"I'll get you a pillow."

He seemed finally not strong enough to resist her power. He had withstood as long as he could, but she had simply outwaited him. Thom could not understand his own disappointment. Somehow he resented that her God had won, that John Patrick would follow her to mass and recite his night prayers with increasing fervor. She made more coffee, ironed more shirts, guarded his health, and hid his whiskey.

And herself secretly mourned the end of some war.

The migraines diminished. Thom went to mass with Margaret and read his breviary with her watchful approval. He smiled at Mary O'Meara and Agnes Dillon without answering unasked questions, and Margaret explained that he had come home to help her with John Patrick. They took soup to Anne Conway and said the rosary with a carefree Tim and a solemn John Patrick. And they watched television while Margaret stared at Thom's profile and wept silently enough for everyone to hear. After two weeks, he wondered if he would go back. But what else could he do?

Almost twenty-five, he seemed to himself too old to begin anything, and there was no one to advise him. He played golf with Jim O'Brien, ate pot roast with Monsignor Doyle, and made a clandestine appointment with an academic counselor at Kirkwood College, a private liberal arts school with a strong graduate program.

"I doubt we'd accept your theology. No accreditation. Even your B.A. in philosophy might need refurbishing."

"I think Saint John's in Cincinnati is accredited." He knew it probably wasn't.

"We can investigate. What program would you consider?"

"Maybe psychology."

"That could mean four years—if we accept your credits." The smugness was unbearably demeaning, and the odor of anti-Catholicism stirred old hatreds. A breath of ancient O'Brien emerged.

"I'll try Loyola or Marquette."

"That might be more suitable."

The next day he was deeply depressed, and the symptoms of distress continued to haunt him. He remembered Margaret's older brother Vinnie who after his first wife's death had moved from Chicago across the lake to the small-town simplicity of Sauganash, Michigan. He had given up a successful construction business to make cabinets and remodel kitchens in the resort community. Jim had frequently assisted him for a week or two during his vacations from Marquette; and Thom, with Margaret's reluctant permission and John Patrick's approval, decided to spend some time there. He arrived the same evening and was greeted by Vinnie's second wife.

"This is a surprise!" Mary smiled invitingly. She was twenty years younger than Vinnie, and she waddled out to drag him from his workshop. Four fat-faced children, a second family ranging from seven to fourteen, giggled nervously. They scattered when a sturdy, ruddy-faced Vinnie appeared, still holding a square.

"This calls for a beer. Holy Mother Church himself!" He slapped Thom on the shoulder, opened two beers, and strode out onto the screened-in porch.

"How's the old batting eye, kid?"

"A little out of shape."

"Can you stick around?"

"Why not?"

"Great! Jesus, great! I've missed old Jimbo. I hear he picked himself up a bride and a kid." Margaret's letters kept everyone informed. "I know he had a hard time getting over that sexy little Jewish girl."

Mary shuddered and said nothing.

Thom wandered the beach for a few days, slept on the porch, and endured Mary's overcooked food.

Vinnie apologized laughingly. "These Irish girls cook like mess sergeants. Shoulda married that cute little German."

Thom began helping Vinnie with cabinets, fastening hinges, sanding and staining, gluing the fragile veneer. He had not been so content in years, and his anxieties disappeared for hours at a time.

"You're not bad, padre," Vinnie told him. "Well, I guess it's only right—your boss got his start this way."

They drank more beer, installed a neighborhood sink, and rewired a kitchen. "In the sticks you gotta do it all." Vinnie was delighted with the camaraderie. He hardly seemed like Margaret's brother.

After a month, Thom grew restless.

"Why don't you wander around town? I know you've got different plans, but Jimbo used to have a hell of a time. Like ole Father Tim used to say, 'I can't buy the stuff, but I can damn well shop.' A hell of a guy—"

Mary had never favored Father Tim. "Don't push, Vinnie; let him do what he wants."

He wanted to wander. And he did. To the Dock Tavern and the Crooked Gull, where laughing young singles danced long enough to find a night's romance on white sand or in the back seat of an old Chevy. He felt stiffly out of place, but he managed to sit down and order a beer. Friendly coeds approached with ample gambits for open-ended excitement, and his shy refusals to dance only intrigued them. The fourth night, Sharon Murray, a Chicago lab technician who was stubbornly insistent, finally lured him to a side table away from the loud music.

"If you don't dance, we can talk." He liked her slow manner of speech that rolled the words around her lips.

"I just never have—sports and all—"

"So what are you studying? Phys ed?"

He laughed uncomfortably. "Actually I'm in graduate psychology at Marquette." The lie came easily and his memory of Jim's conversations about Milwaukee supplied adequate details.

"A Catholic. That's a relief! Most of these savages are latter-day hedonists." She softened. "I went to Loyola."

They finished a second beer and she gently persuaded him to try a slow dance. "Just hold me and shuffle a bit. Is that so hard?"

"The shuffling's not." He was pleased with his sense of humor and did not remember that his compulsions were gone.

"You bastard!" She giggled and snuggled against him while he danced in awkward circles. Then he began to relax, and he felt a firm breast against his bicep. He was instantly hard. They bought another beer and drove to a place where flowing white dunes were framed by birch trees and soft grass; then they lay on the grass at the dune's edge and burrowed their toes into the warm sand. It was a perfect balmy night, with pale yellow moonlight shimmering across the dark emerald water. They held hands and talked about childhood's favorite places. He told the truth about everything except his approaching priesthood; he even discussed Saint Robert's Seminary in Grandville and lied that he had dropped out after graduation. Once he wanted to tell it all, but he was too lost in his own fantasy of graduate psychology and new freedom. His distress melted away, and late in the evening she leaned over to kiss him softly on the mouth.

"God, I like you," she said.

Silently he returned a real kiss for the first time. Then again and again, until he didn't think he could stop. Thinking of nothing except a new desire he couldn't believe. Until his groin ached and his lips were swollen. He took her home and kissed her again for a long time with increasing need, then he talked nervously while she lay silently nestled in his arms. Thom was ravenous to explore her body, but he felt afraid and awkward. Sharon couldn't believe him.

After that he worked a few hours for Vinnie each day and spent the evenings with Sharon. Even an afternoon. Explaining that "guys from the seminary" had a place ten miles down the beach for swimming and volleyball and poker. Mary never suspected, and if Vinnie knew he was considerately silent.

"Just what you need. Get them books out of your lungs. Father Tim used to—"

Thom phoned Margaret once a week.

"Is dad okay?"

"I can take care of him. I've done it all my life—" Then she probed. "Are you saying your breviary?"

"Yes." She had not asked about daily mass, but another lie would not have been difficult.

"Do you plan to stay all summer? We'd like to see you before you go back. So would your brother Jim. The baby's a year and a half old already."

"I'm not sure I'm going back." It was the first time he dared say it aloud.

She flooded the phone with her sobbing. Then a little girl's tears. "I just can't take any more—I just can't." Her voice trailed off in a pitiful, agonized whine.

He pounded his fist against the stuccoed wall, and blood dropped down his knuckle.

Sharon's vacation ended the next weekend, and they spent a final evening together in the dunes. "Back to the Bastille. I'll need your address."

"I'll be in a new place this year. I'll send it when I'm settled."

"I'll really miss you. Will you come down?"

"Of course."

"I can come up, too—if I'm invited. I have a girl friend there." She added it quickly. Sharon Murray was in love.

They kissed for more than an hour, legs entwined in the soft grass, her moistening warmth pressed against his thigh. Finally she said, "I love you, Thom Maguire."

"I love you too." They kissed again with tongues and lips devouring. When her hand reached down and stroked his swollen slacks he stood up—not quite abruptly. "Wow—I'm dizzy. And losing control."

"Have you ever—you know—?" She said it shyly.

"No."

"I think I want to—I love you. God, I love you!"

"I can't handle it. Not now—" His voice trailed off.

She loved him even more.

When he returned, Margaret could not look at him. Her eyes were glazed and red, her voice hoarse and weakened from grief. John Patrick limped around trying to be friendly.

"How's Vinnie doing?"

"Good. Really good."

"You got quite a tan."

Thom accompanied her to mass where she avoided an inquisitive Mary O'Meara and Agnes Dillon. She was appalled that he did not receive communion.

He answered the unasked question. "Sometimes it's good not to go—it prevents routine."

She was not satisfied, and he knew it.

There were no scheduled confessions for four days, so he would have to go privately. Monsignor Doyle was out of the question, and he couldn't face Jim O'Brien, but there was a visiting Franciscan covering for the vacationing hospital chaplain. Thom took the car keys.

"I'll be back shortly."

"Where are you going?" She had lost some trust.

"Just to do some thinking—"

"You've had the summer to think."

He drove to the hospital and waited for the chaplain to complete his rounds. Thom approached nervously in the corridor outside his suite.

"I'd like to confess, father."

"Sure thing." He was a thin, bouncy young man with simple humor. He unraveled the purple stole and draped it around his neck. "Fastest stole in the West."

Thom made no mention of the seminary. Moral theology had taught it was unnecessary to do so for valid absolution until he was in major orders.

"I necked passionately six or seven times and french kissed."

"With the same girl?"

"Yes."

"Are you planning to marry her?"

"No, father, it was just a—kind of summer romance."

"Do you feel you used her?" The humor disappeared.

"Not really—I mean—it was mutual."

"Did you consent to sinful pleasure?"

"I don't think so—I'm not sure."

"Did you touch her impurely?"

"No—I didn't." Thom enjoyed the new freedom of being a layman dealing with sexual sin, making the priest struggle.

"Did she touch you?"

"Once—but I moved away."

This was not usual, and the young priest was impressed. A quick "five Our Fathers and five Hail Marys," then unhesitant absolution. This was a fine young Catholic.

"Thank you, father."

"Thank you." It was a rare confession. He refolded his stole.

Three nights later the young Franciscan was introduced to Thom at Monsignor Doyle's dinner table.

"Father Bede, have you met Thom Maguire? He'll be ordained in June."

The priest paled briefly. "No—no—I haven't." He stared at Thom. "A subdeacon?"

"Not till fall." He almost whispered it.

"I see." He looked nervously at Thom's hands. "Nice to meet you."

Thom left immediately after dinner, and when he got home he leafed through his breviary in the kitchen.

Margaret noticed and whispered a prayer of thanksgiving to Saint Jude. She reminded Thom that Jim wanted to see him.

The visit to his brother's was uncomfortable. Connie showed off their new living room drapes, and Jim wondered if the Church would ever change its stand on birth control. Thom worried about a new cynicism in his brother's tone.

"The pope should have a few kids—"

He also noted that Jim frequently interrupted Connie's chattering as if he weren't listening. Then he began thinking about Sharon and left soon after.

He returned to the seminary. There was no real choice. He had written a long letter to Sharon, telling her the truth and asking her forgiveness. Someday he would like to see her again, as a friend. He mailed it before Margaret noticed, then quickly put together a sermon that was required to be submitted to Father Fox upon checking in. It was to be delivered without alteration in the refectory at a designated date. Thom had been assigned the topic, "Therapeutic Abortion: Legalized Murder." He developed a dramatic sequence about two teen-aged mothers in similar unmarried distress. One aborted under parental pressure; the other felt a tiny heartbeat and resisted her angry father's urging to have an abortion. The child grew to be a doctor who saved his mother's life on the operating table. Margaret typed it, corrected misspellings, and deemed it absolutely beautiful.

John Patrick wondered who put the son through medical school.

9

Priest Forever

After one miscarriage, Connie and Jim finally had their second child. It was shortly before Johnny's third birthday, on a cold February morning in 1956. James Thomas Maguire was small and wiry, like his father, with the darker hair and complexion of a Hackett. John Patrick was still rejoicing over Eisenhower's reelection, blacks were boycotting buses in Montgomery, Alabama, and John Foster Dulles was struggling nervously with the agony of a continuing "cold war" with the Russians. Sputnik I was waiting in the wings. Jim, waiting for Connie to deliver, read Eugene O'Neill's *Long Day's Journey into Night*. It was the only nonprofessional reading he'd done in months, and it sent him into a deep depression. He felt vaguely that all his noble dreams had been frustrated by his own fears.

Of course, he was a successful doctor in Kirkwood; he was the brightest light in the professional life of old Doc McGregor, delivering babies, assuaging arthritis, and making more money than he had dreamed possible. But when Connie's delivery slowed him down long enough to reflect, he realized he was not happy.

When a woman asked for a diaphragm, out of deference to Doc McGregor he referred her to someone else. When birth control pills were finally available, he denied them to a simple Italian woman who had four kids after four years of marriage. Teaching her about rhythm was like trying to depend on the Kirkwood buses, and eternal salvation seemed to depend on a regular menstrual cycle. She begged him for the new pill.

"I can't prescribe it, Angelina."

"But why, Dr. Jim? Is it against the law?"

"Well, Doc McGregor is an old-time Catholic."

"Aren't we all?"

He couldn't forget the twenty-four-year-old face that looked thirty-five, and it was hard to continue to blame Doc McGregor. He himself had done nothing except make snide remarks to Margaret and teasingly question Thom.

His life with Connie settled into a suburban routine. They bought a house—a mile from John Patrick and Margaret—in a new subdivision of popular ranch styles with three floor plans and four color schemes to choose from. Connie learned to make martinis and drink French wine, and she was caught up in the exciting new world of being a doctor's wife. She gave luncheons for her admiring classmates or secretaries from the paper mill, attended medical auxiliary book reviews and card parties, and spent hours with a fawning decorator who agreed with her bizarre, uncultivated tastes in order to sell her whatever she wanted. After only three years of marriage, Jim was too busy to care. What conversation there was between them centered on imitation oriental rugs and cute new outfits for the kids. Jim even had a leather chair, a green one, where he sipped bourbon and read the paper to recover from an exhausting day. Connie went to evening services with Margaret and prayed for his salvation. But, unlike Margaret, Connie was still exciting in bed, even though almost imperceptibly oral sex had become rare, then obsolete. He never asked her why.

Johnny was the center of his life. As well built as a young Thom, with the same blond hair and blue eyes and ingratiating smile, almost since weaning, Johnny was his daddy's boy, and they wrestled and played football for hours at a time. Jim took him on Sunday house calls or left him in the care of a nurse when he had to check a hospital case. He couldn't wait until the boy was old enough to spy on rabbits and startle frogs in the silent swamp.

At Jimmy's baptism, where Tim and Connie's sister were the godparents, Jim was still reflecting on his newfound melancholy. John Patrick stood stooped and finally docile at reverent attention while Margaret's eyes glowed with private satisfaction that gave Connie credit for little except childbearing. The milkman and his wife were delighted to be admitted to the fringe of Saint Raphael's nobility. Only Johnny made any sense—he left the musty old baptistry and walked outside to watch the end of a Michigan winter. Unimpressed by baptismal water and the Holy Spirit. Little Jimmy was equally as honest. He cried in protest of the cold oily water on his innocent head.

Anne, now twenty-two and engaged to a devoutly Catholic doctor, smiled thinly. "The devil doesn't leave easily."

Jim wondered why he wanted to slap her confident mouth. He also wondered why he wanted to run away with Johnny. Or cry with Jimmy.

☙ ☙ ☙

At Pius XII Seminary, Thom was also at the point of tears.

His ordination for the subdiaconate was postponed. Bishop Schmidt was concerned about Thom's latest instability. Bernard Fox was advised to delay the ceremony after a review of Elvin Ward's evaluation and a medical report from Saint John's. Thom was angry and humiliated, and he balked at Father Fox's explanation. "What's wrong? I'm ready—I've had all summer."

"My hands are tied. The bishop wants you to wait." Fox lowered his voice confidentially. "He's funny that way." Then he smiled broadly. "There's no law against saying the breviary."

Four days later, there was a letter from Sharon Murray. Thom was relieved that the pink envelope had not been opened, since censorship was a faculty right that had terminated more than one duplicitous vocation. He stuffed it under his cassock, walked quickly to his room, and locked the door. His heart was pounding and the memory of her soft warmth on the beach came flooding back. He ripped the letter open and lay on the unmade bed. The first line dissolved his erection.

"How could you? God, how could you?"

She told of the excitement of eight days on cloud nine, of racing from work to the mailbox every evening. Girl friends had laughed jealously and demanded a picture of the "blond god." Then his letter! And more pain than an entire lifetime. She hated him, wanted to break his mouth and rip his hair. She had remained home from work to cry for three days, until finally she could write.

The letter grew cold and cryptic. She never wanted to see him again, doubted he would be a good priest, wished him every success in finding whatever he was looking for. There was no complimentary close. A postscript requested that he never contact her again. It was a letter Margaret could have written, and, as Thom lay motionless on the bed, he felt strangely as if she had.

He recovered in the chapel and begged God's pardon for his carnal weakness. Sharon had only been the devil's attempt to lure another priest who could destroy Satan's hold in the world. "A wolf in sheep's clothing" as foretold by Christ. Thom gave up all desserts for a month to strengthen his resolve. No Sharon Murray could seduce Thom from his God. Ever again.

Although a delayed subdiaconate was disappointing, only the postponed breviary obligation obviously distinguished Thom from his classmates. But with their ordination to the diaconate in September—and the right to distribute communion and preach in a nearby prison—Thom felt left out and angry. Even so, the deacon year was especially gratifying since the faculty treated the young men as priests and classroom theory was directly related to parish work. Dolls were baptized and anointed with oil of the sick; makeshift altars were set up to practice the complicated mass. Thom and Mike Fogarty were partners, critiquing every motion of hand or head or tone of voice—all of them governed by serious ancient rubrics. The mass, a memorial of Christ's death and resurrection, permitted no intrusion of personality—whether in Rome or Kirkwood or deepest Africa.

The refectory sermon was another highlight. Each day at the noon meal a fourth-year man delivered his assigned sermon. The faculty scribbled their critiques between spoonfuls of soup. The tension was severe. Most preachers did not sleep the night before. Memories failed, voices squeaked, cassocks were often soaked with sweat; and the same evening in prayer hall Bernard Fox prefaced his spiritual lectures with the faculty appraisals on delivery and content. The preacher was never mentioned by name, but occasionally a repeat performance was ordered.

Fogarty had done well on "Guardian Angels" although he relied too heavily on superstitious medieval traditions. Chet Golas was praised for his straightforward sincerity in handling "Hell," but he had showed signs of nervousness. Actually, he had wet his bed the night before and vomited his breakfast. Bill Kincaid, a brilliant orator from Detroit, was accused of breakneck, pell-mell speed and commanded to repeat the same sermon.

Thom had a strong speaking voice, and he eloquently challenged a noisy stew with the "Abortion" sermon Margaret had typed. At first the noise and motion of silverware triggered his mad compulsions, but with intense effort he ignored them, and it was quiet during the part when the young doctor saved his own mother's life in open-heart surgery. Whispered congratulations followed Thom back to his table, and later at recreation Golas reported that Bernard Fox had not touched his favorite rhubarb pie. It was a good omen. "You freaked him out, Tommie boy!"

Thom silently agreed, awaiting the critique with some anxiety.

That evening, Bernard Fox said the introductory prayer and cleared his throat. "Today we had a sermon on abortion. The speaker had a strong, pleasant voice, intelligent inflection, and a forthright delivery. It is agreed that he can become an extraordinary preacher."

Thom bowed his eyes to Fogarty's wink. Chet Golas was beaming.

"As far as theological content goes—," he paused and looked querulously over his glasses, "there wasn't any!" He was suddenly furious. "It was a vacuous, emotional, *ad hominem* appeal—totally devoid of substance."

Then he embarked on a scathing tirade of the dangers of sloppy, sentimental, unscriptural rhetoric and warned that such arguments could become two-edged swords.

"What if the mother had died?" His voice was shrill. "There wasn't a hint of the intrinsic value of life itself!" His fist on the desk punctuated *life itself*.

Thom knew the rector was right, but it did not soften the blow. He wanted another chance, but even that was denied him.

"The sermon was particularly upsetting because the speaker has been given an extraordinary gift."

He tossed Thom's paper aside, graded it "barely acceptable," and announced the showing of *Boy's Town*, with Spencer Tracy, for Friday night.

Thom walked from night prayers to his room, locked

the door, and lay down on his bed, angry and hurt. Then he offered God his pain as another sacrifice to unite him with Jesus on the cross. The humiliation would only make him a better priest.

There was a quiet knock, interrupting grand silence. Fogarty's hoarse voice whispered his name, but he didn't respond. God had already provided sufficient comfort, and there was no emergency to break a rule.

Monsignor Doyle had expected Thom to assist with the distribution of communion at Christmas masses at Saint Raphael's, and, unaware of the postponed diaconate, prematurely announced it in the parish bulletin. Mary O'Meara was thrilled.

"To receive Our Lord from Thom's own hand—"

Margaret smiled humbly. She planned a face-saving trip to Chicago. "It may be pa's last Christmas."

Later, word of the postponement leaked from Agnes Dillon's nephew in first-year theology, but Mary O'Meara said nothing. John Patrick endured the icy trip to Chicago and Margaret avoided the embarrassment, delighted that Thom was reading his breviary. On the return trip she offered him her engagement ring for the base of his chalice, a two-carat diamond John Patrick had given her three months after their first dance.

"Mother—I can't—"

"What better place!"

"But it's your engagement ring!"

"I still have my wedding band."

John Patrick lit a Camel and ordered Thom to watch the road.

After semester exams the deacons began serious preparation for the priesthood, ordering appropriate invitations to a first solemn mass, memorial holy cards, graduation photos, and menus for the banquet. Selecting a preacher for the first mass, deciding on a master of ceremonies, and designing representative chalices. Each chalice was uniquely fashioned from silver or gold, adorned with ivory or precious stones, and often inscribed with a favorite scriptural quotation. Most came from European craftsmen and were usually buried with their owner: clasped forever in cold consecrated hands.

Since Thom had not yet received notice of his major

orders, he worried about ordering a chalice. The skilled workmanship usually demanded at least three months and the deadline for ordering was hardly three weeks away. He had already sketched a design when he approached Father Fox in his office.

"No word yet." Father Fox smiled warmly. "Any day now."

Thom was angry. "Am I being punished?"

"Certainly not." He answered too quickly. "Bishop Schmidt is just—well—indecisive. I'll call him early next week."

By Wednesday, Thom was still uninformed. He approached Father Fox again.

"The bishop said he would let me know."

"Will I be ordained in June?"

"Of course—of course. There's no question—"

"There is to me, father." His voice rose, his face was flushed. "I feel I'm being punished."

"That's not true, Thom." Fox's voice was unsteady.

Thom looked directly at him. "I want to know by Friday, father—" There was a hint of some madness in his eyes, but Fox did not look to see it.

"I'll try—I—"

"Or I'm leaving—I won't live under some damn cloud." Thom couldn't believe he said it.

Bernard Fox had never experienced the Maguire rage. It frightened him, and he spoke quietly. "You're making too much of this."

"I have to know." He left abruptly and went to the chapel.

Father Fox sat motionless at his desk. Drumming his fingers.

On Friday, Thom learned he would receive the subdiaconate on Saint Patrick's Day and the diaconate the day following.

Fox smiled warmly. "He knows you're Irish."

Thom nodded quiet thanks and apologized for his anger, then he ordered his chalice from Schwartzmann's in Germany and sent Margaret's diamond under separate cover.

A calisthenic was almost over. He would be a priest.

Ordination to subdiaconate and diaconate were almost anticlimactic to new and dramatic preoccupations with sex. The study of sexuality was traditionally postponed until the final months before ordination, and then the young deacons were set swimming in the arcana of Latin semen and damp vaginas. Detailed diagrams of secret folds, oral bestialities and sinful diaphragms, unruptured hymens and sacrilegious seductions by sick priests. Every possible abuse was explored. Classes were a litany of pornography, and Thom fearfully fought for control. He had visions of Roselle's pink clitoris and of Sharon Murray massaging and sucking on white sand dunes. Even Sister Marietta from Saint Raphael's went mad in his illusions as she slipped off her sweating veils in a lusting choir loft.

After a month of it, one night he lay on his bed trying to induce sleep. Wet pubic mouths dripped like a torturing faucet. He had never masturbated in his life. Not a drop of semen or a single wet dream. Even necking with Sharon had only created a tingling yearning in his groin for unknown satisfaction, for which he begged forgiveness a hundred times.

This was different. His penis stood straight, demanding touch. He asked God's grace, and a torrent of dripping lips whispered madness. A leering priest absolved some private Lolita in papal excommunications; swirling cassocks seduced married nipples. He rolled over in agony and flushed his swollen penis against his stomach. Roselle appeared. He moved. A rush of sensation to his groin. His stomach froze on the verge of some consent. He had given in. Only partially. Hold on! He pressed against the mattress. "God, help!" Sweat dripped deeper into the sheet. Again he tightened in rigid suspension. His whole body tensed refusal. But it was too late. He felt it coming like an avalanche.

"O God, God—I don't want to consent—I—" Still it came roaring out of history. He felt his penis lurch spasms of fluid against his sweat. Again and again, twitching in denial even as it spurted pleasure. Then it was over. He felt his penis withdraw in wilted rubbery repentance.

He had sinned mortally. For the first time in his life. Two months before ordination.

Father Jack Durrell spoke soothingly. "God understands—you tried to resist."

"I think I wanted it—conning myself—" Maybe he hadn't given in.

"You struggled. That's what counts!" Aquinas in his cell and Noah in his tent. Father Jack touched his shoulder. "Go in peace!" Thom was crying.

It happened twice more. The same war and the same gentle forgiveness. "You will be a good priest."

In all the seminary years, Jack Durrell was his warmest priestly friend. And Thom hardly knew him.

A final week's retreat preceded ordination. Interrupted by last-minute invitations and signed photos to friends: *"Hang in, Bill, it's worth it!" "If you could only hit a baseball—" "Fraternally yours in Christ."* When there was nothing else to say.

A tall gray-haired Jesuit warned solemnly, "People will fuss over you and prepare your favorite foods. And flimsy women will fall in love with the plainest of you."

They were being missioned like doves to a greedy, self-centered, lusting world. Only a man of prayer could persevere. Then came the horror stories and tales of *cherchez-la-femme* apostasy.

"Father Tim was my classmate. Brilliant!" (All Jesuits seemed to be.) "Handsome, zealous, devout. Soon he was too busy to pray. Time for everyone but God—souls to save, confessions to hear, classes to prepare."

It was a kind of heresy the pope had called "Americanism," where activity replaced prayer. There was a dramatic pause, an oblique glance at the lopsided face of a gothic stained-glass Good Shepherd. "Father Tim is pumping gas in Dallas—separated from the woman who lured him away—a lonely, desperate, pathetic man. But still a priest!"

The chapel was silent and the Jesuit's bushy gray eyebrows focused for several seconds on clear, young eyes. "Two weeks ago he phoned me about coming back." He deftly broke the spell. "I think I'll go to Dallas and get some gas."

They grinned. Chet Golas laughed aloud.

Thom's chalice arrived in a black leather case lined with violet satin. A traditional tulip cup with a hexagonal base dramatized Margaret's diamond, and the inscription read *Domine, Non Sum Dignus,* "Lord, I am not worthy!"

Elvin Ward would have agreed.

Bishop Schmidt had misgivings. "You know Thom Maguire?"

Freddie Weber, grown even plumper, was cautious. Working all this time as Schmidt's secretary, Weber had learned the bishop's pendulum moods, and now Freddie's nervous brown eyes darted for a place to rest. "Not well. A fine athlete—and bright." He had already listed him as a possible rival—which would have startled Thom.

"His attitude?"

"I can't say. He seems—"

"Yes?"

"No, I really don't know."

"I'll have a talk with him."

And he did. Twenty minutes before the Saturday ordination. After a few encouraging words with the five candidates, he called Thom aside. The bishop's kind eyes stared from under the golden miter while his stubby fingers brushed back the luxurious cape.

"Are you ready for ordination?"

Thom stood in the cinctured white alb that touched the top of the shined black shoes. He flushed. "Yes, bishop." More humble than he felt. He tried not to focus on a thread hanging from the gold miter.

"I'm concerned." Freddie Weber stood a few feet away, absorbed in the silver crosier. "It's not too late—" The small, stocky German bishop looked comical in the tall hat.

It didn't seem real. Monsignor Doyle waited in regalia to assist as chaplain; Margaret in a tailored rose suit fought tears of joy; Connie had little Jimmy; and Jim sat with Johnny clinging to his daddy's hand. A feebler John Patrick in his favorite gray pinstripe hunched wearily over the pew, and Tim, in high school now, struggled to light a stubborn candle.

"I'm ready," Thom said. A touch of surliness as distractions disappeared.

"You've had doubts—" The violet ring swept the air in stubby elegance and the soft brown eyes were sympathetic.

"Not since September." He wanted to scream about the delayed subdiaconate.

Finally a warm smile, revealing dark nicotine stains on Schmidt's lower teeth. "As long as you're certain—" The apostolic successor struggled with theology. "Morally certain, that is—" He liked Maguire's strong gaze.

Thom returned to the group. Chet Golas, handsome in the white alb, grinned. "He's got plans for you, Tommie baby."

The red-faced Fogarty snarled from a tough Irish mouth, "What'd he offer you? Freddie's job?"

"He wanted to know if Fogarty can sing."

They all laughed nervously.

The organ boomed *"Ecce Sacerdos Magnus,"* and the Sheffield Cathedral choir harmonized welcome to its high priest, who was flanked by an elfin Freddie Weber and an owl-eyed Joe Beahan. The local priests poured into the front pews and then came the nuns dressed in browns and whites, blues and blacks. A subdued Sister Marietta glanced shyly at Thom's processional candle flickering on his blond profile. The tight-jawed, buxom Anne stood crisply smiling at her gangling fiancé and hummed along with the choir. John Patrick knelt humbly for the bishop's passing blessing and smiled proudly at a grinning, red-faced McNulty. Jim seemed miles away. Margaret was finally the bride she had never really been, a consecrated nun taking vows in some divine rite of incest. She was never more beautiful.

They were all there. Scattered proudly and joyfully through the Immaculate Conception Cathedral to honor a special young man they had known since his boyhood. Mary O'Meara with the orchid corsage to match Margaret's. Uncle Vinnie in his too-warm blue serge suit whispering to Johnny Muller. Coach Charlie Dunham, recently moved to Sheffield for a job with General Motors, looking naked without his grimy cap. A tanned Roselle, awed by the strange ceremonial beauty.

The five young deacons lay prostrate on the sanctuary floor for the Litany of the Saints. The bishop fell to his knees at the faldstool, and faithful worshipers crashed down in devout imitation. Cantors invoked Saints Cosmas and Damien, Dominic and Francis, even Gervase and Protase, to pray for the prone levites. And begged deliverance.

"Ab omni peccato."

"Ab insidiis diaboli . . . A spiritu fornicationis . . . Ut hos electos benedicere, sanctificare, et consecrare digneris."

Then the profound silence of eternal ordination as the young men approached their bishop and felt his thick hands firmly on their heads like the descending Spirit. All the priests filed by to do the same. Jim O'Brien's golf grip and Monsignor Doyle's stiff joints, a fleeting Father Grimes and an officious Freddie Weber, the soft palms of Joe Beahan and the strong hands of his new chancellor boss, Monsignor Kenelley, looking older and wiser than his forty-five years. A few moments later came the solemn words immortalizing their priestly pact with God:

"Da quaesumus, omnipotens Deus . . ."

The people had found them worthy of ordination. The priestly stole was yoked crosslike around their shoulders, a chasuble of love slid over bowed heads, and the melodic *"Veni, Creator"* echoed among the Romanesque arches. Thom's heart was pounding with joy and the fear of entrance into the holy of holies. Obsessions were gone, and he felt strong and pure in his priestly vestments. Ready to bring the whole world to God.

Accende lumen sensibus,
Infunde amorem cordibus,
Infirma nostri corporis,
Virtute firmans perpeti.

The bishop dipped his thumb in holy oil, anointed their hands from thumb to index finger in the form of a Greek cross, and presented the chalice and Host to be touched symbolically by priestly fingers. They were ready to concelebrate the mass. Like an intense young lover, Thom whispered fearfully and passionately his first words of solemn consecration.

"Hoc est enim corpus meum."

Margaret held her breath and Monsignor Doyle bowed his head. Mary O'Meara wept and Sister Marietta flushed with new joy. Only Jim Maguire was unmoved and reflective as he smoothed Johnny's hair.

The bishop waited quietly on his throne and again placed his hands on the young heads, conferring the awesome sacramental powers of forgiving sin—even adultery and brutal murder, thieving and whoring, and indignities not yet conceived. Then a gentle Bishop Schmidt wrapped Thom's hands carefully in his own and asked, "Do you promise obedience to me and my successors?"

"*Promitto,* 'I promise'!" With all the firm confidence of generous youth.

Margaret's son, Thomas Aloysius Maguire, was a priest forever!

Thom's first solemn mass was celebrated at Saint Raphael's the next day at noon. Monsignor Doyle was archpriest and the virile Jim O'Brien was deacon. Mike Fogarty, who had delayed his own celebration a week, acted as subdeacon.

It was twenty-eight years since Father James Michael Doyle had come to Kirkwood to help improve things at Saint Raphael's parish.

It was a fitting Pentecost Sunday with fiery tongues of Spirit descending on Coach Art Doolan and on J. R. Harris, who was thin with cancer. Even Lois Bonner was there, the chubby child who had mocked the Maguires long ago, now blondely attractive and newly converted to Catholicism, and Bronk Davenport, still a plumber's assistant. Old Mr. Bernstein sat ecumenically bareheaded with a somber Mulaley, and Art Rooney's lips twitched. All the faces from the past emerged from wrinkled shadows to pay homage to Margaret's son and to receive his blessing. Anne and her doctor passed out liturgical leaflets with the mass of the day in Latin and English. Margaret wished she and "the gink" would mind their own business.

Thom sang a beautiful tenor chant to distant cherubim and seraphim, and Margaret could not restrain her tears, remembering a baby's hands she had patty-caked, tiny childhood vestments she had sewn, and a bruised knee soothed under a fallen tree hut. Jim solemnly received communion from his brother while Thom wondered if the practice of medicine had destroyed Jim's faith. John Patrick looked stronger than he had in months and hardly wondered if a baseball contract would not have made him happier.

Jack Durrell had driven from Pius XII Seminary to preach the sermon for his favored penitent. From a trembling Moses and a stuttering Jeremiah, he traced the priesthood to Jesus and Paul and Thomas Aloysius Maguire, then talked briefly of his own aging mother and Margaret's unparalleled joy.

"To be the mother of a priest is to taste Mary's own bliss, to foreshadow the secret rewards of paradise—only God and a priest's mother can understand."

After the mass, Margaret was the very first to receive a second blessing. Tears streaming down her cheeks brought tears to Thom's own eyes.

"May the blessing of Almighty God, Father, Son, and Holy Spirit, descend upon you and remain with you forever. Amen."

She kissed Thom's anointed fingers with all the denied passion of a lifetime. Monsignor Doyle, worn but still resplendent in his red cassock, embraced her warmly. She wept again. The nuns lined up to pay homage to a privilege they could never know.

Jim, still pale and thin, studied his brother and despised the waste. Then he reflected on their childhood and wished they had become close friends. Now it seemed impossible. The laughing, innocent, affectionate Thom was gone. Now there was a priest Jim hardly knew. He felt it was a sad day.

On Monday, Thom offered a mass for Jack and revived ancient wounds in his father's soul. Margaret cried some more, and at breakfast Jim opened a tense discussion about the Church's position on birth control.

On Tuesday, Thom celebrated an early mass for the nuns and Margaret, and he joshed with Sister Marietta. Then in the afternoon he played golf with Father Jim O'Brien and they talked of a trip to Fort Lauderdale. Margaret fixed chicken and dumplings and said Thom should get more rest. Jim asked Father O'Brien if Catholic morality was spawned with an incomplete understanding of human physiology and of the possible problems of overpopulation. O'Brien was appalled at Jim's questions and muttered something about the Jesuits. Thom tried to squelch Jim with clever comments about Malthus and the outspoken Margaret Sanger, but Jim refused to be put off.

"The Church has changed its views before," he said.

"Not on matters of divine law. Contraception is no Friday observance or Lenten rule. This is as unchanging as papal infallibility and the permanence of Catholic marriage. Even the Jesuits can't change that," Thom said sarcastically.

"I'm not so sure," said Jim. "Even you could be wrong."

Thom blushed furiously.

Connie grinned. "Jim's just getting tired of the kids."

Margaret quickly made coffee, and Jim shared a final beer with his father.

"How's the practice?"

"Okay."

"You may be right about birth control. McNulty agrees with you."

It had never dawned on Jim that John Patrick ever discussed such matters. There was a long, intimate silence; then his father laughed. "I see your cowlick's finally under control." It was their private joke, and he smoothed Jim's hair playfully.

Jim knew he loved John Patrick.

He only wished he could say it.

On the following Thursday, assignments came special delivery. Mike Fogarty went to Saint Stan's in Steelmont, a Polish parish consisting mainly of automobile assemblymen and their overworked wives. Chet Golas, who was sent to Oneida Saint Mary's, offered to teach him the language. Fogarty accepted, promising Chet a subscription to *Farmer's Almanac.*

Thom was sent as an assistant to Father Joe Quinn, *pro tempore* administrator of Immaculate Conception Cathedral in Sheffield.

The decision about Thom's placement had been difficult for Bishop Henry Schmidt. He had consulted with his chancellor, Charlie Kenelley, newly elevated to the status of monsignor, and with Joe Beahan and Freddie Weber. Only Weber had really been reluctant.

"He's had a lot of success. Maybe some seasoning—"

Kenelley laughed. "Spoken like a true fascist! Who's afraid of a little spirit?"

Freddie flushed. "Who's talking about spirit? It's arrogance we're talking about—" He paused before he continued, "and emotional problems."

"For Christ's sake, Freddie! That's inconsequential. I've known this kid for years. He's great!"

Kenelley despised Freddie Weber, not out of petty jealousy, but out of a deep historic loyalty to the Church. Still a tall well-built man with bushy graying hair, Kenelley's now reddish complexion screamed of too much alcohol, a problem he had struggled with for the last two years. He had never wanted to be a chancellor, let alone a monsignor, and he longed to return to parish work where he had labored as a genuine shepherd much beloved by his flock. Bishop Schmidt had wisely recognized Kenelley's honesty and balance and had requested his assistance in running the diocese of Sheffield. Although truly upset by the bishop's request, Kenelley, in simple, unquestioning faith, assented immediately. When he had been made a monsignor, he was only embarrassed.

Freddie Weber was no match for him.

Bishop Schmidt reflected softly, "He looks you in the eyes."

Charlie Kenelley's judgment was enough. Freddie was outnumbered, and he concealed his ambitious resentment. "I have no serious objections—"

Nor did the friendly, myopic Beahan.

Father Joe Quinn, who was not consulted, welcomed his new assistant. Too young to be cathedral rector at thirty-five, Quinn had been promoted as temporary administrator after Monsignor Hallinan's sudden death. The parish was generally delighted by the former curate's relaxed, human manner, and only a few of the old guard mourned the loss of the mordant leadership of their deceased pastor. Quinn had already been in charge for over a year when Thom arrived, and an indecisive Bishop Schmidt still could not settle on Hallinan's replacement. Monsignor Kenelley, who lived at Immaculate Conception's sprawling brick Victorian rectory while directing the chancery office, assured Bishop Schmidt of Quinn's ability.

"It's smoother than when the old bastard was alive," Kenelley reported, and it was true. The food was better, the booze free, and the new easy camaraderie appealed to him.

The bishop, although theoretically director of the cathedral, lived in a private house near the Sheffield Country Club with Freddie Weber and Beahan and two elderly nun servants. His office was in the chancery, where he kept businessman's hours, and he only visited the cathedral rectory occasionally to drink and chat with Kenelley. Far into the morning. Thom's first awareness was overwhelming. He returned from a novena sermon to find Bishop Schmidt weaving helplessly on Drambuie.

"Well—sit down here and join us." Kenelley offered a drink, then remembered he had administered Thom and his classmates a five-year pledge against hard liquor.

"How about a cold beer?"

Thom agreed.

Kenelley held his liquor honorably.

"Where's Father Quinn—he should be here to host." The bishop's words came out badly, his anger vastly disproportionate and totally uncharacteristic of his normally mild and compassionate behavior.

"He had a sick call." Thom said it quietly. He respected the bishop deeply.

The bishop grew suddenly devout. "You can't do enough for the sick. Father Joe's to be commended." His words were slurred, and Thom wondered if he had removed his upper plate.

The bishop coughed emphysematously, and Freddie Weber looked away and grimaced painfully while Kenelley brought the bishop a glass of water.

Weber, who usually drank sparingly, sipped a glass of scotch. "So how's it going?" His cherubic smile warmed Thom.

"Good, Freddie!" It was still hard to call an older priest by his first name. "There's lots to learn!"

"I understand you learn fast. Quinn says you're quite a preacher."

Thom blushed. "He's a kind man!"

And he was, zealous and fun-loving, with no clerical jealousies. Thom had preached a sermon on the Good Shepherd searching for a lost lamb in a covert, and half the congregation had been in tears. Quinn had called him "another Sheen."

Even the first assistant, Dave Beauchamp, and Charlie Kenelley enjoyed hearing "the wild young Irishman" let out all the stops, as Kenelley said. The chancellor ignored the dozing bishop for a minute and added to Thom's reputation. "You were great tonight, Thom."

Thom blushed but knew he had been great. He had compared Mary's Assumption into heaven to every man's struggle with "an impossible flesh that has its own logic." Then he had insisted that no sin was too evil for forgiveness, and that God was willing to forgive "seven times seventy times." His intense Irish eloquence filled the Church.

"We are all weak and human, God knows that. He made us. None of us, even priests, are above temptation." (He remembered Sharon and exploded with new passion.) "Why have a confessional if we are all perfect? 'If your sins be as scarlet, they shall be white as snow!' And God chose men to be instruments of forgiveness to other men. How terrifying it would be to meet the Almighty in thunder and lightning. How easy it is to meet another man whom Christ has appointed to forgive. A man as sinful and frail as you are. A man who also has to make his own confession!"

Thom recalled the silent impact until the bishop dropped his glass and passed into a stupor. Freddie Weber motioned Thom to assist and he took the bishop's arm nervously.

The bishop looked over rimless glasses. "Are you keeping the faith, father?" Thom saw drool on the slack jaw.

Freddie assisted him into the black Oldsmobile and drove away.

A sober Bishop Schmidt was a minutely kind shepherd, and a gifted businessman. As a young bishop, he had founded Sheffield Diocese before World War II as an offshoot of a burgeoning Detroit and a mixture of medium-sized industrial cities and farming towns. The majority Irish at first resented the ineloquent, stodgy German, but the German farmers in Frederick and Tuckerville were delighted.

Thom truly liked Bishop Schmidt, who warmly singled him out at clerical gatherings for special attention (Mike Fogarty and Chet Golas, and even Jim O'Brien, were consistently ignored).

"There's young Thom. How are you, father?" a broad smile and a stubby hand on his shoulder.

"Fine, bishop. I liked your talk." He said it without embellishment.

"Not as polished as yours, I hear." The offhand humility was a product of an hour of daily meditation and not mere courtesy.

Thom grinned, then looked down. "But probably more effective."

The bishop was pleased. Past problems had been erased. He was not a vengeful man, and even his caution flowed from a sincere and deep appreciation of the sacred priesthood. To censure one of his priests caused him great physical pain. He was the devoted, concerned father that every bishop aspired to be.

Thom's relationship with Freddie Weber, who was now a growing power, was soon far less deferential.

"Here's the handsome young athlete who wows the novenas!" Freddie's increasing cynicism set the tone.

Thom was not cautious in his response to Weber's barbs. "How's the bishop's chubby errand boy?" A crowd of priests laughed.

Weber turned quickly pink and hid his anger. "The bishop's bartender, you mean?" More laughter. But it was commonly known that Freddie did little to impede the bishop's drinking, and Monsignor Doyle thought he encouraged it.

He was partially right. Freddie Weber needed Bishop Schmidt, unsober and indecisive, for his own designs. It was only gradually that Thom understood the politics of ecclesiastical power. Meanwhile, he was content to grow in admiration for his bishop and trade witticisms with Weber. It was a mistake.

Rectory life in Sheffield was shared with a gentle, easy-going Father Joe Quinn, Monsignor Kenelley, and Thom's dearest friend, the first assistant, Dave Beauchamp. Although Quinn's age, Beauchamp had spent time in the marines and was only four years ordained. A square, powerful man with thinning black hair, his gentle, cultured warmth appealed to Thom. Like Joe Quinn, Dave Beauchamp took great pleasure in Thom's passionate Irish abilities and devout prayer life, and he was always available to encourage Thom in unfamiliar territory. They discussed hospital techniques, classroom and convert procedures, conduct at funeral parlors, and all the varied practicalities not covered at the seminary. Dave laughed proudly to Quinn that Thom would convert the whole damned city.

Although not one to search out unassigned duties, Beauchamp performed skillfully and was well liked by the parishioners.

It was an extraordinary combination. The cathedral faithful boasted of the most mellow leadership in the world. Quinn, an understanding pastor; the softly charming Dave Beauchamp; and Thom Maguire, the handsome, energetic newly ordained priest who had all the generous enthusiasm of a dozen apostles. In the warmth of the people's praise and affection, together with a marvelously happy "home life," the anxious affliction that had troubled Thom since Cincinnati almost disappeared. Only in moments of stress did the compulsions return—but never again with the same fury and pain.

The cathedral priests enjoyed food and were frequently invited to parishioners' homes. They rarely accepted, since it was time-consuming and hard on the waistline, but each of them cultivated a particular family where he felt especially at home. Joe Quinn was a frequent visitor at Helen Lubiato's, a fifty-year-old widow with two attractive daughters and a married son. One laughing-eyed daughter, Flora, was working on a doctorate in chemistry, and the twenty-nine-year-old Angela, still unmarried after a broken engagement, owned an exclusive dress shop. In the fall, one Saturday night after confessions, Joe invited Thom to meet his special friends.

"He's a handsome one, Father Joe!"

Thom blushed at Helen's directness.

Joe laughed with Angela at some snapshots, talked quietly as they sat on the sofa, then walked with her to the kitchen to assist with her mother's antipasto. He touched the back of her hair and she kissed him lightly on the cheek.

"God, I've missed you!"

Thom overheard and was embarrassed.

"I'll have more time now that I have a new assistant. He's good."

"I can tell." She laughed mockingly. "I hope he's safe with my sister."

The meal was superb, and Thom enjoyed Helen's mothering and Flora's dark-eyed attention. He felt painfully shy despite the comfortable atmosphere. Helen excused herself after cleaning the kitchen and bringing Joe up to date on her second grandchild.

"There's zabaglione left," she said. Then she disappeared upstairs.

Thom checkmated his laughing new friend in mediocre chess, listened to a *Music Man* album, and relaxed long enough to talk about baseball and finally, Sharon. Discreetly. Then he wished he had said nothing.

Joe and Angela talked softly on the sofa until Joe handed Thom his car keys and excused himself.

"Dave's got the early masses, so you can sleep late. Angie will drop me off later—"

They disappeared into a basement recreation room where Thom heard soft music and muffled conversation. Flora adjusted the lamp until her face was dark and beautiful in the dim light.

"I'm glad you came. I'd noticed you in church weeks ago." She brushed Thom's arm gently.

"I wish I could stay longer. The breviary—"

"Say it here. Joe does."

He resented the familiarity. "No, thanks—but it's been a great evening." Suddenly nervous, he lit one of her cigarettes.

As he snapped on his collar to leave, he could still hear soft voices from the basement and an occasional laugh. Flora walked him to the car and held both his hands warmly.

"Make this your home, father."

"I will." The cigarette made him dizzy, but he was proud of his strength and he stopped in the church to pour out his grateful heart to the shadowed tabernacle. The priesthood was far more than he had ever anticipated.

When he entered the back door of the rectory, Monsignor Kenelley was sleeping in front of a warm bourbon and a Saturday night television horror. He walked quietly up the winding staircase, and he heard classical music and voices coming from Dave Beauchamp's room. Dave answered his knock dressed in white jockey shorts and a T-shirt that displayed rippling weight lifter's muscles. Dennis Tracy, a tall, personable priest from the neighboring Resurrection parish was there, still in his confessional cassock thrown loosely open. The two had been best friends since first-year philosophy and preferred their own company to clerical gatherings. Each year their vacation together was exotic and well planned.

"Hey, Thom!" The broad smile. "How was Mama Lubiato?"

"Great."

"Those daughters aren't bad either." He smacked his lips playfully.

Dennis laughed at his friend's performance. "I love to save beautiful souls."

Dave returned the laugh and directed Thom to a cane chair next to Dennis, adjusted the stereo, and withdrew another crystal wineglass from a teak chest.

"How about some sherry to subdue Beethoven?"

The room was like a Buddhist temple—with bamboo curtains, silk tapestries, and oriental rugs. Dave spent hours there, lost in a wide assortment of classical composers of whom Thom knew nothing.

"No—really, Dave, thanks. The breviary awaits."

"Is Joe downstairs?"

"No—I drove his car."

Dave sensed Thom's embarrassment. "Angie will probably drop him off." He looked directly at Thom. "It's a good friendship for Joe. It really is!" Dennis nodded agreement, and Dave's warm smile perdured to reassure the sensitive young priest who was just learning how life really was.

In his own room, Thom undressed and stretched out naked on the sheets, then sat up restlessly and settled at his desk to outline a sermon on the Pharisee and the publican. It was an hour later when he saw Angela's blue Mercury slide into the rectory parking lot. She kissed Joe Quinn lightly on the cheek and drove away. He smiled, tucked his breviary under his arm, and unlocked the side door of the cathedral.

Thom was asleep when he came out.

Father Quinn introduced weekday confessions during the eight o'clock mass for high school students and stray adults. Younger penitents, who treated confession as a birthday party, were restricted to assigned times on Friday afternoons. Or on Thursdays before the first Friday of the month.

One typical morning late in the spring, Thom said the 6:30 mass for the nuns and the devout laity, like Margaret, who began their day with the Church's official prayer.

The mass continued to thrill Thom with its beautiful Gregorian power and spiritual energy.

After breakfast, still munching raisin toast, he walked across the parking lot from the rectory into the side door of the cathedral. The eight o'clock mass had already begun and the *Kyrie de Angelis* shouted through the nave in young fervor. A dozen teen-agers were assembled outside his confessional.

"Bless me, father—" The voice was low, and Thom pressed his ear close to the whispering screen. It was a male adolescent.

"I masturbated about twelve times, looked at girls improperly about twenty times, and had dirty thoughts a hundred times." He paused. The worst was over. "I also cheated on exams and missed my morning prayers—and let's see—there was something else—oh, yeh, father, I ate a hamburger on Friday but I forgot."

Thom ignored the hamburger. "Have you prayed for grace?" Why did he feel personally wounded?

"Yes, father, and I'm going to communion—"

"Do you date?" Twelve masturbations in a week.

"Well—I'm afraid of girls. Actually—they don't dig me too much."

He had to hurry. Communion time was the deadline, and Joe was already singing the Gospel.

Thom gave the boy his ten Our Fathers and ten Hail Marys, presuming mortal guilt, and heard the mumbled act of contrition.

"Thank ya, father." It was always as one word.

He closed the wooden slide and opened another on his right, wishing he had said something meaningful to the pimply-faced masturbator, struggling painfully with the thin line between kindness and softness in forgiving.

A girl's voice, liquid and frightened, said, "It's been two and a half weeks. I've been very bad and I think I'll need help." Boys never asked this indulgence.

Another time consumer as he struggled for patience. "Don't be afraid. God is forgiving." He heard the Credo intoned as the mass rushed along.

"Well, there's this boy I know and we've been dating quite a bit and he's not Catholic, but he's really a good person, and well—we started necking and—well—petting, and one thing led to another and I let him go all the way." It was the longest sentence in the world.

"Did this happen more than once?"

"About four times, father." She was lying.

"No more?"

"Well, I guess it was five." She knew damn well. He felt an angry sense of failure for her weak will, and he prayed for patience.

"Are you going to marry this boy?" Christ, she's only sixteen!

"We hope to, someday. He's just starting college—"

"You'll have to break up." Thom felt the pain in his own heart.

"But, father, I really love him." Thom heard the Offertory prayers. "I just can't break up." She was ready to cry.

He struggled. "It's not love, it's only lust." He weakened. "If this happens again, I can't absolve you."

"Oh thank you, father. It won't—I promise it won't." She was delighted with the mercy of the young priest. Firm enough to diminish guilt and gentle enough not to embarrass her or refuse absolution. Thom did it well.

"Say your rosary as soon as possible." His voice was kind.

The Preface came smoothly to an end, and a thousand knees bowed to the *Dominus Deus Sabbaoth.*

A friendly voice: "Bless me, father. It's Martha."

Thank God! Martha was a very special girl he taught in freshman religion class who, with a unique honesty, chose to identify herself. Thom had recommended it.

"I was inconsiderate of my mother a few times, careless about schoolwork, gave bad example to classmates, and I listened to a dirty joke and laughed." Two separate sins. "I think that's all."

Thom relaxed. Martha gave new meaning to his priesthood, and he rewarded her with tailored spiritual direction. He felt warm and loving—God's priest.

"Keep up the good work—patience is difficult, but Jesus lived with his parents until he was thirty." There was no time to elaborate, even for his special Martha. "When I give absolution, God floods your soul with Christ."

Her breasts tingled. "Thank you, father." He was beautiful.

Thom left the confessional hurriedly to assist with communion.

Of course, Martha came too, her round sincerity and

pink tongue wetly waiting for the Host. And the special brush of his fingers against her lip in occult symbol of his affection.

Finally he replaced the ciborium through silk tabernacle skirts, genuflected with Joe Quinn, and disappeared into the sacristy. Carl Kovack waited, an awkward, pathetic sociopath.

"I missed confession, father. Same old problem, father. Three masturbations yesterday." It sounded like a sales report as Carl smiled sadly.

What could he say? Carl had come fifty, no a hundred times and Thom had made every suggestion in print. He continued to be kind and patient.

"Hang in, Carl." The flush of absolution. A giant vacuum.

"Thanks a million, padre." Carl had no other friend.

Without masturbation and Father Maguire, there would have been no one.

Thom enjoyed the power of consolation. Celibacy was certainly no problem in an eighteen-hour day of religion classes and marriage instructions, private prayers and hospital work, converts and athletic programs, school dances and novenas, old folks' homes and unwed mothers. He gave his money to poor Mexican families and begging bums and turned no one away. Alcoholics and released convicts, scout troops and psychotics, broken homes, migrants, desperate homosexuals, and slum landlords. The cathedral rectory was a giant waiting room for the sick and oppressed of the world, and Thom became another healing Christ in Galilee.

Matt Kelly had given up booze to recapture his wife and two little girls. Thom helped move them into a cheap one-bedroom apartment that had no electricity turned on. When a candle revealed roaches biting the baby girl in her crib, Thom called the landlord.

"Christ, it's almost midnight."

"I don't give a damn. I want you over here or I'll call the mayor."

He found them another apartment and two men to move them in. At two in the morning. The ruffled landlord was distressed.

"This one's more money." His fat face was sweating.

"I'll take care of that." He was now earning about three hundred dollars a month with salary and mass stipends.

Thomas Aloysius Maguire, like Christ in the Temple, was not to be trifled with.

He fought with the farmers who oppressed the wetbacks, demanding clean latrines and better pay, and with Martha's help he organized hedge schools for their children. He remembered names, he laughed easily, and the Mexicans adored him even more when he learned enough Spanish to hear their confessions, revalidate their marriages, and attend their fiestas in the parish hall. His zeal for Christ, and his enthusiasm and energy were boundless.

The second year he took over the Immaculate Conception High School athletic program, begged money for new uniforms, and assisted the coach with a newly organized baseball team. The basketball team, which had never won a district title, won their Catholic league and lost in the state semifinals by only three points.

Soon the biweekly convert classes were swarming with new applicants. Word got around that a dynamic young priest, handsome as a movie star, was the toast of Immaculate Conception. The congenial Dave Beauchamp alternated classes with Thom and added to the excitement, but it was the intense and affable Thom they really loved. Wives, who had brought their non-Catholic husbands to stuffy or arrogant ecclesiastics in other parishes, tried again. Adult baptisms multiplied, and Bishop Schmidt, humble and grateful to God, conducted a special confirmation class for seventy-five new converts, extolling the dedication of the cathedral priests.

After the ceremony, he called Thom aside. "You've done a great job." He was beaming with fatherly pride.

"Thank you, bishop."

"Your work with converts is an inspiration to the whole diocese."

Thom noticed a strange look in Freddie Weber's eyes as Freddie officiously reminded the bishop of another appointment.

If Thom had a shortcoming, it was in the confessional. Since his seminary morality was deeply entrenched, he was still too devout to attract real strays. Penitents who appreciated his easy personality in conversation were sometimes startled inside the wooden box when he became a gentle but firm spokesman for God.

A whispering voice. "It's Ruth Abbot, father. I think Joe is going to leave me."

He remembered seeing the attractive woman at a basketball game. Sharing her popcorn and telling stories about the Maguire family table and happy arguments.

"Five kids are all he can handle. He told me to get my tubes tied."

"Have you tried rhythm? There's a Doctor Marshall—" Thom was sincere and compassionate.

She laughed bitterly. "I've taken my temperature everywhere but in my eye. I've got three kids in diapers—if Joe touches me, I flinch."

He had heard it a hundred times before, but there were no magic words. "Temporary abstinence" slipped out softly and hesitantly.

She grew feistier. "The whole world can't be wrong—I'm losing my faith."

"God's testing it." He was pleading with her even as he feared her slipping away.

"Then I flunked. I'm not losing Joe—"

She left without absolution. Thom was truly crushed and could hardly force himself to hear another confession or hold back tears of frustration.

Engaged couples came, looking for a way to finish college without marriage. But Thom's hands were tied, and the celibate Church hung on. Homosexuals came, promising a monk's morality to satisfy God, then they weakened, and there was nowhere else to go. Lusting teen-agers had no chance at all. Thom was forever benign and patient, fatherly, but what did it matter if the executioner smiled?

It had become a Church to save the already saved and only a few foresaw the coming revolution. Monsignor Kenelley did after a few drinks, at Forty Hours. He challenged Freddie Weber and the assembled priests as they munched Joe Quinn's hors d'oeuvres. He called the bishop's crosier the "stiffest prick in Christendom." Freddie Weber, flushed with scotch, grew unwontedly angry.

"Your oversimplifications are in damn poor taste, Charlie."

"That's the difference between us, Freddie. I'm not going anywhere, so I can be the asshole I am. You have big plans—"

The room was hushed. Freddie's growing power with the bishop had become a reality to be reckoned with, but Kenelley was not put off, and he laughed outrageously at the chubby secretary's discomfiture.

"Soon there'll be nothing but quivering old ladies, young fanatics, and flabby bishops—" He sipped his bourbon and slipped off his cassock.

"There is a Holy Spirit guiding the Church." It was a rare theological defense, and even Freddie recognized his own weakness.

Kenelley laughed again. "Put the farmers in charge—they understand that Jesus probably whacked off as a boy—"

Even Joe Beahan groaned. "For Christ's sake, Charlie, that's disgusting—there are young priests here!"

"I hope to hell they're listening."

☘ ☘ ☘

Dr. Jim Maguire would have agreed. Connie was pregnant again, and in the spring of 1958, Thom's second year as a priest, Jim attempted further discussions with him about birth control. Thom was outraged when Jim suggested that Connie had become a "baby machine." And wondered why, in the Irish way, he was harder on his brother than on any parishioner.

"God's been good to you. You're not poor. You forget where you came from and how many sacrifices were made. You of all people can afford the children God wants you to have."

He had taken the words out of Margaret's mouth. John Patrick, silent and noncommittal, was rooting for Jim.

Jim raised his voice. "Look, Thom, for God's sake, it's not a question of finances. Every kid takes time and energy. So do four pregnancies. Do you know how long it's been since I've had a conversation with Connie? I don't have a wife anymore; I have a nursemaid who's scared to death of sex." Johnny was just past four and Jimmy had recently enjoyed his first birthday party.

"There's such a thing as discipline and self-control." Thom tried to soften his priestly voice.

"I know all about that. I also work just as hard as you do. And don't throw your celibacy at me! You chose it, I didn't."

No one talked like that to a priest, and Margaret wanted to intervene, but a strange look from John Patrick made her decide otherwise.

Thom felt his anger rising and wondered why Jim had that effect on him. Their discussions had always been academic, but now there was a bitter personal reproach that cut deeply. He knew he was losing any hold on his brother and some control over himself. He fought to soften his resistance.

"Jim, you either have faith or you don't. I face the same conflict in counseling couples as you do in your practice. But I'm not God, I just try to do what the Church asks." He was almost pleading, but Jim remained pale and direct and spoke in a quieter voice.

"I don't think faith was ever meant to be replaced by stupidity, and I don't understand this rigid, unfeeling God. What you're telling me is the same thing I've heard since childhood. 'Take it on faith!' I can't anymore."

Margaret groaned, made a remark about the Jesuits, and left the room to find her rosary. Thom struggled to remain kind even as Jim hated his fatherly tone.

"That's a decision you'll have to make, Jim. Faith is tough, I know, but it's also a gift from God that can be destroyed by pride and self-pity."

No One's son felt all alone, conscious only of a sympathetic look in his father's eyes as Margaret fed her grandchildren and asked him to carve the pork roast.

When Christine Ann was born late that same year, Jim knew that a private battle had begun between himself and his Catholic culture. As Doc McGregor was now spending only a few hours a week treating aged arthritics and the high blood pressure of lifelong friends, Dr. James Maguire began prescribing birth control pills to anyone who requested them. He also attended mass only when five-year-old Johnny asked him to. As Connie was lost among two babies still in diapers, and paralyzed with fear of another pregnancy, Jim lost himself in his practice and the occasional joy of his oldest son, finally old enough to walk in the woods and visit Sandy's grave. It was a happy time.

Johnny was ecstatic with every spider and scampering rodent. Father and son wrestled on soft marsh grass and took their shoes off in the cold waters of a tiny brook, building a dam, then a whole mud city with its own private lake where children could swim without their parents. Jim interpreted the chattering of squirrels.

"What did he say, daddy?"

"He says he loves you very much."

Johnny had to be dragged away after a picnic of peanut butter sandwiches, milk kept cool in the brook, wild cherries they found, and Margaret's oatmeal cookies.

They would arrive home to confusion. Connie's parents and a couple of her younger brothers or sisters were frequently there for Sunday dinner. The milkman drank and fell asleep, and Connie and her mother talked about potty training or someone's scandalous divorce. Jim usually escaped to the basement recreation room to sip a beer and read the *Kirkwood Gazette* or Eugene O'Neill. Or to tell Johnny stories about green-eyed men with purple skin and long yellow fingernails.

Connie was usually asleep when he retired. She got up religiously to nurse a crying Chrissie, and when she returned to bed, Jim cuddled her gently, answered her questions kindly and respectfully, and then withdrew into a private world where only his patients and Johnny were ever admitted.

☘ ☘ ☘

Thom came home to celebrate Anne's marriage to her sallow obstetrician. Their engagement had been solemnized the year before at the Virgin Mary's altar in Saint Raphael's; it was a guarantee that not one of Richard Francis Dorgan's obstetrical fingers would touch a pink nipple before marriage—and only chastely after it.

Dorgan was a devout, outspoken Catholic with large teeth that were almost frightening when he drew back his lips in a tight smile to make a point. He was critical of Jim's untrained obstetrical efforts, but he mentioned his concerns only to Anne, and once (at the engagement party) to Margaret. In a single rasping reply, Margaret reminded him that Doc McGregor was around before God had even thought about Dick Dorgan. Anne had blushed angrily but said nothing, and Dorgan never mentioned Jim's practice to Margaret again. The day of the wedding, Jim himself refused to discuss even an appendectomy with the pompous neophyte, but talked politely about Floyd Patterson's fast hands and Truman's bitter attack of President Eisenhower's recession. John Patrick totally ignored everyone whenever Dorgan was in the house. Thom had few political opinions, always aware that his years in the seminary had obscured the events of a whole decade. Even in his priesthood he never had the time, or the interest, to read a paper.

On his monthly visits home, Thom consistently avoided Jim and Connie in favor of the Dorgans. He expounded about the need for unquestioning faith, while Margaret complained to Tim that Anne was too devout to fix a meal or help with the dishes. While the Dorgans and Thom talked, Tim cleaned up the kitchen with his mother and made her laugh.

Margaret wondered aloud to John Patrick why Thom had bothered coming home at all if he only talked to the "Holy Rollers." John Patrick said nothing. Usually Thom had little to say to his father beyond warm formalities, and only once had Thom really done him a priestly favor when he agreed to bless the imbecile daughter of an old Jewish customer. It was a unique request, and Thom, hardly aware that John Patrick only considered it a courtesy to his longtime friend and a way of keeping his business, was eager to comply.

Thom also came home when Tim graduated from Saint Raphael's in June 1959, surprisingly near the top of his class and was already accepted at Notre Dame. A letter of recommendation from Bill Collins, Thom's former roommate and a Notre Dame law alumnus, had helped. Much to John Patrick's unspoken disappointment, Tim, six foot two and rawboned, was hardly interested in athletics.

Thom was fond of Tim, who had no apparent religious conflicts. It was as if he had been raised by different parents. He endured Margaret's laments without obvious guilt and amused John Patrick with tales of weekend canoe trips and brook trout simmering on sassafras skewers. At seventeen, he loved his parents and had hardly discovered girls except for obligatory proms and occasional parties. He seemed to have no enemies, taking people as he found them, and he usually related to Thom without any mention of religion. As if he were not a priest. As Thom gathered up his breviary to leave, Tim grinned.

"Let me know if any cute cheerleaders need me."

"You can count on it," Thom said. "Notre Dame men are at a premium."

John Patrick beamed proudly at finally having a son under the golden dome. Even if he wasn't a football player.

Margaret was only relieved that she had succeeded in keeping Tim from the Jesuits.

When Thom returned to Sheffield after Tim's graduation, there was a message that Roselle had called.

"I hope I didn't wake the kids," he said when he called back. They had adopted a boy and a girl after Roselle was pronounced sterile. Charlie had brooded for months until the first adoption.

"No, actually I was just listening to music—"

"So what's happening?"

"I want to take instructions to be a Catholic."

He was delighted. "There's a class in two weeks—What does Charlie think?"

"I didn't ask—but he likes you."

He was excited enough to extend his private visit to the tabernacle for almost an hour before he went to share the cake Margaret had given him with Dave Beauchamp and Mozart.

"Roselle's a great lady," Thom said.

Dave grinned. "I've noticed." He enjoyed Thom's blush. "Seriously, I'm delighted." He laughed again. "Now you won't be having dinner with those damn Protestants."

Dave was a different kind of priest from Thom, with French and Italian blood that knew how to compromise and make concessions to human weakness. He did not have Thom's charismatic charm, but he was deeply loved by those who got to know him. His faith was never a distortion of humanness, nor did he have any need for modern theological arguments that upset entrenched Roman ethics. He simply forgave anyone who came to him without question, then lost himself in a Verdi opera or a cheese soufflé.

Thom lingered for a second glass of good dry port after he and Dave had finished the cake. He wanted to tell

Joe Quinn about Roselle's call, but he hadn't seen Joe's car in the rectory garage.

"Is Joe around?"

"I think he had dinner at the Lubiatos'. Well—anyway, Angela called this afternoon."

"I'll tell him tomorrow."

But there was no tomorrow. Joe Quinn was killed when his Thunderbird overturned on a freeway access road. Angela was thrown clear, suffering a broken shoulder and multiple bruises. The call came at 2:30 in the morning, and Dave sped forty miles to identify the body and make arrangements to transfer it to Sheffield. Kenelley called a friend at the *Chronicle* to subdue the story.

"Christ, father, I don't know what I can do. I'll try—"

He had it reduced to an "unidentified passenger," but the six o'clock TV news had more information. Bishop Schmidt called a morning meeting to prepare for the public scandal, and Freddie Weber suggested a private funeral in the Quinn family home near Colfax. Beahan agreed.

"Are you out of your mind?" Kenelley was livid. "What the hell has the man done? He's a great priest—"

"At two in the morning with a young woman in a Thunderbird?" Weber held his ground. "We have some obligation to the people."

"Christ, the people loved him. They'll think the best. What the hell do we care about evil minds?"

"Was he drinking?" Bishop Schmidt probed gently, in need of more facts.

"Apparently they had wine for dinner." Weber was grim-faced and the cherubic innocence had vanished.

"Damn it! So what! She's a family friend. Since when can't priests have friends?"

"It's the circumstances; we've got to—"

"Christ, bishop, no one knows the circumstances! Only God Himself! The only scandal would be to bury him as an outcast."

Bishop Schmidt agreed.

Freddie Weber was not convinced.

Arnie the janitor said it was the largest funeral in his memory. The Masonic Temple sent extra chairs, and the Crystal Cafe supplied coffee during a two-day public wake. The cathedral bell tolled solemnly and hundreds of people paid their respects. The Knights of Columbus were on duty for thirty-six hours, and the local department store draped its ancient stones in black crepe. The state police paid formal honor.

Kids came and left flowers, Martha arranged for hourly high school rosaries, nurses wept in their blue capes, assorted nuns whispered "eternal rest." Joe Quinn's family was there through the night: a thin, gray-haired father; a wispy, staring mother; and two younger brothers with their sobbing wives. Only glancing up occasionally to acknowledge the sympathetic touch of a nun or a friend. Clusters gathered through the night in front of the church and remained till the morning of the funeral.

"He can't be dead." It was the leader of the Legion of Mary.

Someone else embraced her. "Now, Mae, it's God's will. I was slicing potatoes and dropped the whole pan—"

"He never knew—right through the windshield."

"Who was the woman?"

"A family friend—known her for years."

A pale Bishop Schmidt, truly grief stricken, called Weber aside to review a few rubrics. Bloodshot eyes were the only trace of last night's private drunk. He bowed his head for the miter, extended his hand for the crosier, and leaned wearily against the vestment case while Freddie directed the assembled attendants.

The entourage circled the rear of the cathedral and entered the front door to the sound of somber bells tolling. Hundreds were gathered on the sidewalks and spilling out to the street. The mayor and four assemblymen sat in front of the clergy on the left, monsignors knelt in sanctuary, and the fourth-degree Knights of Columbus clasped their swords. Hundreds of eyes were shedding tears, reluctant to let a good shepherd go, certain that there were not many left.

The mournful requiem groaned throughout the nave and through loudspeakers out to the people assembled at the curbs. With a final *"Requiescat in pace,"* Monsignor Kenelley ascended the pulpit, adjusted an unfamiliar red cape, slipped on his dark-rimmed glasses, and made a few announcements about transportation to the cemetery and a meal for the visiting priests. Mass offerings could be made in the vestibule. He greeted the bishop and dignitaries as the huge church grew silent.

Kenelley expressed his sympathy to the parents and their family and recalled the Christlike quality of Joe's work, his concern for anyone who needed him. His eyes were moist when he brought the brief eulogy to a conclusion.

"I perhaps knew Joe better than anyone else. I loved him, and I'll miss him more than I can say. He helped me have hope in a Church that can be unfeeling and cold. He had his faults, but they were as human as he was. At times he wanted to give up, but he knew the people needed their shepherd. So he hung on.

"I thought about this sermon and Joe Quinn for two days. There's a lot I'd like to say that the confessional seal forbids. I also know the circumstances of his death. Better than anyone."

The church grew suddenly hushed and Freddie Weber looked at Bishop Schmidt. The bishop's eyes were closed.

"I suppose there are rumors. It doesn't matter. The people who count know that he was a good priest. They need no assurance. I only wish I could have been a better friend—for reasons that will always be locked in my own heart. I advised him the best I could. I only pray to God I was right. But there's one thing I'm sure of, Holy Spirit or no Holy Spirit. The Joe Quinns will save the Church. Not the theologians or canon lawyers, not even the pope or the bishops. Only human priests who love their flock.

"I feel sorry for Jack and Marie Quinn and their family. I feel sorry for myself for losing my best friend. But most of all I feel sorry for the Catholic people of this city. You lost one hell of a priest, and you'd better pray to God for more like him.

"That's all she wrote."

He ended with Joe's favorite expression.

There was an intense silence at the faldstool, then a shuffling as Freddie Weber assisted Bishop Schmidt to his feet. Schmidt walked up to the pulpit with his crosier and spoke for fifteen minutes, and the people listened politely to expressions of gratitude and grief, of the dangers to faith and the shortage of vocations. He ended with a plea for eternal rest and perpetual light.

He did everything but mention Joe.

The people thronged to the cemetery where they walked and wept and waited long after the final prayers had droned away. Until the coffin was lowered and the flowers were hauled off to the hospital. Until the priests filed back to ham and scalloped potatoes at the gymnasium and Freddie Weber removed the bishop's cape and lit his cigarette.

Only Dave Beauchamp and Charlie Kenelley stopped to embrace a beautiful dark-haired woman with a cast on her right shoulder. She was weeping inconsolably. Dave kissed her gently and walked away. Charlie waited until the cemetery custodian threw on the first shovelful of dirt. Then he led her off.

"God, I loved him, Charlie." Angela's eyes were swollen.

"I know, I know. He loved you, too."

He also knew that Joe had wanted to leave and marry her, but had stayed for the people.

And died without ever making love.

10

Mea Culpa, Mea Maxima Culpa

It is hard to imagine a more prestigious period in the modern Catholic Church than the fall of 1960. Pope John XXIII, smiling servant of all men, succeeded the ascetic autocracy of Pius XII and announced a new council to open windows in the repressive Italian curia. John F. Kennedy, charismatic Catholic, gave new excitement after the flabby Eisenhower years, and American Catholics were certain the Messianic era had arrived.

Few Catholic laymen knew how repressive the Church had become in the twentieth century. New thought was innately suspicious. Any attempt to understand Christ's death and resurrection as symbols of man's own personal experience—rather than historical fact—was rejected as "modernism." Any effort to relate the Bible to science created bitter controversy. Too-liberal Catholic professors were relieved of their posts, the works of Teilhard de Chardin were banned, and the objective truth of all Catholic dogma was reiterated. Including the sin of Adam and Eve.

Thus, as the world opened its heart to Pope John, most Catholic bishops and canonists clung angrily to the past, scorning change and resisting any influence that might bring the Church into the modern world. When John exuberantly announced Vatican II and asked the assembled cardinals for comments, he was met with cold silence. However, he remained undaunted. He refused ancient titles, walked and shook hands, and admitted to enjoying an occasional cigarette. The whole world loved him—except the conservative bishops and entrenched curia.

Even among the priests, he was a symbol of division. To Charlie Kenelley and Dave Beauchamp and Thom

Maguire, he was the greatest hope for a human Church since their own ordination. For the gentle Bishop Schmidt, he was a pastoral pope who was concerned about his flock. To Joe Beahan and Freddie Weber and Bobbie Foley, he was a rude joke and a dramatic embarrassment to everything that had kept the Church alive through twenty centuries. It didn't matter what the people thought. People were impulsive and emotional and seduced by anyone who gave bread to the poor. It didn't matter that John Patrick Maguire loved him almost as much as Margaret did, that Anne and Jim finally agreed on something "Catholic," that Tim, who never thought about religion, loved him almost as a close friend.

In a few months, Pope John had transformed the Catholic Church and brought more attention to it than Pope Pius XII had done in twenty years. There was finally hope for the millions of excommunicated Catholics who had divorced or married outside their Church. Hope for the poor and lonely, the sinners and oppressed nuns, hope even for the Communists who became real people again with eyes and hearts. As stubby arms and fat fingers and a warm smile of the peasant pope reached out in love of the whole world. Not to mention warding off a religious revolution that canonists mocked as they remained complacent with Christ's promise of protection.

To succeed the beloved Joe Quinn, Monsignor Herschel Schaeffer was appointed rector of Immaculate Conception Cathedral. Freddie Weber and Joe Beahan were sent off to earn Roman doctorates in canon law, and the newly ordained Bobbie Foley returned home from Rome to Kirkwood to celebrate his first solemn mass and then was assigned to Sheffield to take Freddie Weber's place as secretary to Bishop Schmidt.

Thom was angry to learn that Elvin Ward was made a full monsignor and appointed as rector of Saint Robert's Seminary. Father Stan Skorski, Thom's competition at Saint Robert's, was named as Ward's assistant. Thom celebrated his third anniversary as a priest, sharing cake, champagne, and Chopin with Dave Beauchamp and Dennis Tracy in Dave's room.

Late on the same evening, Thom gathered with a few priests in the rectory living room. He noted that Bobbie

Foley had changed. The obese cheeks, filled with clever Italian syllogisms, remained immobile, and he was almost haughty. Thom found it hard to take seriously the thin-pitched voice that called cardinals by nickname and re-told Vatican gossip. Like most aspiring hierarchs, he was a closet conservative, and, like most "Romans," a cautious, cynical pseudo-aristocrat with an acquired rolling of his r's.

"Bea's more Protestant than Catholic." Cardinal Bea, an extraordinary Scripture scholar and liberal, was head of the Secretariat for Christian Unity, and most Protestant scholars loved him. As did Pope John.

"He cares about people—not archaic nonsense!" Thom said, furious at Bobbie's new glibness.

"We'll see. The spaghetti man will probably resign in two years." It was his nickname for the new pope.

"The 'spaghetti man' gives the whole world some hope!"

Bobbie laughed cynically. "If the people run the Church, we don't need a pope. Fortunately, *Roma locuta, causa finita* still endures." The Italian accent grated.

Monsignor Kenelley finally looked up from his scotch. "Bobbie, you are so full of shit your hair could grow strawberries! Another wise-ass remark and I'll break your goddamned skull."

Bobbie's fat jowls turned scarlet to his hairline. No one talked like that in Rome.

Herschel Schaeffer, the new rector of Immaculate Conception, was a squat, bald German, known as a liberal host to visiting priests and a fanatical antagonist to whomever came late for Sunday mass. Although he had never built a single church or school, he had remodeled more ecclesiastical edifices than any man alive. His specialty was sealing off doors and opening new ones. A stickler for legalities of priestly decorum, he said his breviary at the appointed hours and always appeared in appropriate clerical dress.

He never gave convert instructions or taught in school, he avoided weddings and funerals unless protocol required, and he despised people who brought personal problems to the rectory. A few confessions, an occasional hospital visit, the daily mass and breviary—and the weekly collection—concluded his apostolate. Yet he was a warm, friendly man who encouraged Thom and even Dave Beauchamp not to work so hard.

"Say your prayers and don't socialize with the laity. That's what makes a good priest—" He slapped his pot-belly, sipped his scotch, and cackled delight at his private philosophy.

"These hard workers burn out—then they begin to avoid priestly gatherings."

"Priestly gatherings" meant weekly confirmation dinners throughout the diocese, banquets concluding forty hours devotion—when the Eucharist was publicly worshiped for three days annually in every parish—and parties honoring anniversaries or new assignments. There was something, somewhere, every week, and most priests attended nearby affairs or even traveled as much as fifty miles for a close friend. Herschel Schaeffer covered the diocese and often stayed somewhere overnight to recover from an inoffensive drunk. He loved the company of laughing, drinking, poker-playing priests as much as Dave Beauchamp avoided it. The camaraderie was extraordinary, and generous, affable pastors vied to create the tastiest dinners, but few matched the productions of Herschel Schaeffer, and priests simply passing through Sheffield frequently dropped in for spectacular meals.

"Priests are always welcome!" He would drop everything to play triple-bogey golf (free at the Sheffield Country Club); and he offered a private room for the week and an expansive liquor cabinet.

It troubled him that Beauchamp spent so much time alone, listening to music, or with Dennis Tracy.

Occasionally he gossiped to Thom. "He's too much of a loner—and that friendship with Tracy—dangerous! Dangerous!" He hesitated to confront Dave directly or spell out why the exclusivity was dangerous. The genial Beauchamp was too solid a priest to warrant criticism, but he just didn't spend enough time at gatherings.

Herschel's real enemies were the latecomers to Sunday mass.

At first he upbraided them during his sermons or stared as they slipped into an empty pew, but gradually, his distaste became an obsession.

"It's an act of discourtesy to Christ." He then ordered those standing in the rear to move forward before he would continue.

"It's not only impolite—it's sinful!" His struggle for theological justification exaggerated. "It can be a mortal sin—bad intention—! Why come at all?"

Some few agreed to stop coming. Pope John had given new freedom against old arrogance. But streams of latecomers, often convention visitors, continued to challenge his paranoia. He screamed from the altar. "It's outrageous—mortally sinful!" His bad theology grew worse. "A sacrilege!"

At times he ordered people to leave, and some red-faced laymen never returned.

At a Saturday night dinner he announced a new policy: "Tomorrow we lock all doors as soon as mass begins. No latecomers!"

Thom flashed, "Sometimes there's an excuse!"

"Nope, nope!" He snorted it. "They get to work on time!"

"But the traffic—"

"A half hour is plenty of time. If some make it, they all can!"

Dave munched his Waldorf salad without looking up.

After pecan pie, monsignor sought a cigar and cognac.

Beauchamp wiped his mouth. "No one locks my masses." He laughed and raised his eyebrows playfully.

"Well—argue!" Thom said to Dave, feeling alone.

Dave grinned. "He's nuts! There's nothing to argue."

The excitement erupted at ten o'clock mass. Herschel bounced into the sanctuary, genuflected briskly, and ascended to arrange the starched corporal. Then he turned and ordered the ushers to lock all the doors. Triumphantly, he proceeded without interruption. In the middle of the sermon, a distinguished-looking gray-haired man entered from an unlocked sacristy door and sat confidently in front of the bifocaled pastor. Herschel Schaeffer abandoned Christ to the bickering Pharisees and turned on the intruder.

"No latecomers! Get out!" His face was martyr red, and his fist pounded the pulpit.

The tall stranger did not stir.

"Did you hear me?" he screamed.

"Of course I heard you." The voice was calm and resonant.

"Then leave!"

"I have no intention of leaving. I came to attend mass."

"Then why don't you come on time?" Thom heard the shouts from a sacristy prie-dieu and covered his face in his arms.

"That's my business. Mine and God's!"

It worked. Monsignor Schaeffer strode angrily back to the altar. Defeated.

It was the final confrontation. The gray-haired challenger was an eminent surgeon from Detroit who had left a cardiac consultation to attend mass. A formal complaint to Bishop Schmidt the next day aborted Herschel's campaign when he received a stern reprimand scrawled across the physician's letter: "Enough of this!"

The following day Herschel sealed up a door between the dining room and the study. And invited two neighboring pastors for filet mignon. With giant mushroom caps.

The priests of Sheffield gradually began to understand that the sincere, hardworking, and devout Thomas Maguire was somehow special, and they treated him with deference beyond his years. Even Bobbie Foley grew cautious. It was important for anyone who wanted an "ecclesiastical plum"—an outstanding parish or diocesan office—to attach themselves to potential success and not risk future turmoil. Some few, like Charlie Kenelley and Dave Beauchamp, ignored politics, but even aging monsignors feared a new administration "that knew not Joseph." Freddie Weber and Joe Beahan were gaining influence over the gentle Bishop Schmidt, and more than one prominent pastor was assigned to spend his declining years instructing farmers, or surviving enforced retirement.

Thom had outgrown his resentment toward Elvin Ward and his delayed subdiaconate. Even the Cincinnati breakdown left only minor scars that occasionally disturbed him. He had become a confident young priest of extraordinary promise. For Thom's fourth anniversary in June 1961, Dave Beauchamp prepared a special midnight platter.

Martha, still Thom's favorite penitent, gift wrapped an expensive blue sweater and a carton of cigarettes.

He chided her. "That's too much money!"

"It's from graduation. I got too much—"

She had flowered considerably in the four years he had known her. Still the same shy smile and quick wit; the serious, almost too-intense religiousness; and an attractive figure usually hidden under oversized sweaters. Her short hair was the same color as his. And, without trying or really understanding it, they had become best friends.

At first he had been attracted by her dark brown eyes absorbed in a freshman religion class and her gentle confessions. They had brief conversations in school corridors and at dances he chaperoned, or quiet confidences at football games. Once, during her sophomore year, he had driven her home from a sock hop after everyone had raced off for hamburgers. Even Bill Doyle—Martha's fondest admirer—had finally left them lingering in the shadowed parking lot. Thom unlocked the church to whisper their rosary at the dark communion rail. With the tabernacle lamp flickering, he felt the glow of her body next to his. He held her hand as they prayed, and he experienced an excitement he had never felt before. Then they drove home without a word until he parked in the trees near her house and slipped off his collar. They talked for an hour as spontaneously as lifetime friends, and he shared himself as he never had with anyone. Without thinking.

It was a beginning. When high school students noticed or were jealous, their tremendous respect for a priest made them know that nothing was amiss. When an outspoken senior made a remark about the "priest's lady," Thom became more cautious. He approached Dave Beauchamp.

"There's nothing wrong—but use prudence! Some might misunderstand." The warm smile was a total absolution.

Joe Quinn's death had frightened Thom as much as the loyalty of parishioners had helped him. Martha admitted that many of her tears at Quinn's funeral stemmed from fears that their own friendship might end.

"I don't think I could stand it."

"We'll do what God wants."

He touched her hand gently, and her soft childlike lips kissed his consecrated fingers. For a long time.

They grew bolder, going on lazy picnics in sun-filled meadows and dark drives in the country after dances or games. He left priestly gatherings to meet her outside the library or to whisper in the trees after her date. She was the closest and best friend he had ever had. It was not the confused, experimental passion he had with Sharon Murray. Martha was his first love, and a few minutes under softly sparkling stars nourished his priestly work.

They knew the restrictions of the Church and accepted them with improbable faith. They would never tarnish a consecrated commitment beyond time and earth. They embraced softly, occasionally kissed gently like frightened children, and let entwined fingers say what was better left unsaid. She was a tender Héloïse with the wisdom of innocence and he an unselfish Abélard who anointed the sick and urged recalcitrants back to God. And their very love, with its sincere beauty and untainted purity, was the test of his confessional demands and eloquent pulpit.

He preached to her. Her eyes never left his face. She knew each crevice, anticipated every inflection, studied each Christlike word from his mouth. He was her priest and she his inspiration. He told her with moist eyes of the lonely convalescent stench of urine and decay, of dying old women with no one to notify. He spoke of the battered children of angry alcoholic parents; bruised wives who crawled to the rectory door at night; ex-cons who couldn't get jobs. And he told her how much he wanted to be another Christ in his daily duties and prolonged prayers late at night before the tabernacle.

And they laughed. God they laughed! At silly gifts, and second helpings of her mother's lemon cake, and Herschel's latest excavation. He left funny poems in her missal and phoned at arranged times to tease about the day. They went separately to bed, convinced that there was no relationship in all the world as pure and unselfish as theirs.

Martha's mother realized their affection and hushed her husband's occasional suspicions. He liked Thom as well—the handsome, athletic, enthusiastic son he never had who came unannounced for dinner and spent the evening playing with the other children or watching TV. And glancing lovingly at Martha.

It was difficult for Thom to leave her for a single day to visit Margaret and the increasingly silent John Patrick. He paid them token respect, munched on pork loin and homemade bread, then drove back, talking aloud to Martha. He passed her house to see the light from her room signaling love. And kissed her in chaste fantasy on his pillow as he fell asleep. Dreaming of the day when she could work full time as his housekeeper and they would never be apart.

He knew he could cross some lusting threshold, undress her petite form, kiss and touch until she trembled unyielding invitation. Her trusting eyes would not have intervened. He could make a gentle afternoon of sunshine love without a single protest. She belonged to him. Adored him. He was everything her culture and education had taught her to love. He was her conscience, and she would have surrendered to him if he had said a word. But he never said it. That would have ended it, and he could not have endured. Martha was the strength of his young priesthood.

In the summer after her graduation in 1961, she waited expectantly at a Fourth of July party in the parish hall. She was no prude by Catholic standards, dancing the slow ballads as warmly as anyone, but it was understood that she didn't "make out." She even told Thom in confession of more than one boy who grew excited.

"I felt him get big."

He was embarrassed. And jealous. "You didn't purposely enjoy it?"

"It scared me." She paused. "Maybe I enjoy knowing I can do that to a boy."

"But it doesn't excite you?"

"I don't think so. Maybe I'm a little curious—"

Thom hadn't appeared at the dance by half-past ten, and Bill Doyle asked her to dance a second time. She had dated him regularly during her sophomore year until he had tried to touch her breast. The next morning Thom suggested she drop him for a time.

She liked Bill, and now let him pull her close. She began to ask him about college.

"Let's just dance."

Thom came in, looking tired, and she tensed noticeably. Then the song ended and she made her way to the crowd surrounding him—wallflowers dying to talk to someone and Carl Kovack lurking for confession.

"Wouldn't monsignor let you out?" Her friends giggled to him.

"The bishop needed advice."

She whispered, "I've got the car. Meet you by the country club?"

He nodded. A few athletes drifted up, and Bill Doyle stayed close to Martha, acknowledging Thom.

"How's it going, padre?" He liked Thom but he resented

his relationship with Martha, even though he could never have verbalized it.

"Want to go to Kewpee's for a hamburger?" Martha asked.

"I'll buy," said Bill, not meaning it.

"Not tonight—still got breviary."

Martha saw him to the door. "You look tired—and lonely." She wanted to kiss his face.

"I'm okay. See you then—"

Bill approached her attentively. "He's really great!"

"He is."

She parked her father's car in the country club lot and slipped through the darkness into Thom's car. They drove to their special spot east of the city and parked among the trees. He slid a blanket out of the trunk, and they watched the fireworks explode across the sky from the pavilion; then they stretched out on the ground, her head on his shoulder as he tenderly caressed her fingers. For a long time they said nothing: a seventeen-year-old girl and a thirty-year-old priest.

Often he called her the sister he never had, while he was the brother she wanted. He had revealed his loneliness, the difficulties with Herschel, his dreams to bring all to Christ. She shared his love for the poor and helpless, told him of the boredom of adolescent friendships and the sacredness of moments with him. Now, for whatever reason, he drew her closer than he ever had before, waiting for her resistance. She had heard him tell in class of all the penalties inflicted on those who sullied the purity of a priest, but she loved him and cuddled at his touch. Then he looked into her eyes, and she saw his tears.

"You're not my sister, Marty. I love you!"

He kissed her. Washed her with his lips, and she responded with all the passion of a woman schooled in love. He rubbed his hand over her breasts and she did not protest or move away. No words except her name. He could not get close enough, and his heavy breathing was matched by her unexpected animal sighs. Until a distant voice startled him to pull away and immediately he felt the horror of his sin.

She looked at him plaintively, as if she didn't understand. "It wasn't wrong. I love you!"

He couldn't reply, knowing he was responsible for her sin as well.

They sat there silently until it grew very late and she had to be home. She straightened her clothes and brushed her short hair. Her skirt was wrinkled, her lips swollen, and her face beautifully flushed.

When she got home, her parents were still watching TV. "You're late tonight," her mother said without looking up. Her father was absorbed in the movie.

She went directly to the kitchen.

"There's fruit salad."

"I'll just have milk."

She said good night from the stairs and went to bed, then got up, said her night prayers, and told God how much she loved Thom.

Thom could not return home immediately. He lay on the country club grass looking at God's stars and begging forgiveness. Sorrow did not satisfy his guilt. He feared the scar he had given to innocent faith, promised God never again, and hated himself for still wanting to hold her. He must go to confession. He gathered the blanket and made his way to the rectory and the soft classical guitar music coming from Dave Beauchamp's room.

"What the hell's wrong, Thom?" He saw the child's tears.

"O God, Dave!"

Dave embraced him warmly, holding his friend against his strong, protective chest. "Hey, it can't be that bad—"

They knelt together. Dave in a blue silk robe with a gold dragon threatening anyone who might hurt his repenant friend.

"For your penance say three Hail Marys and forget it. You're just another man!"

Then he smiled his broad grin, held Thom briefly in his arms, and ruffled his head like a favorite younger brother.

"A glass of sherry is also part of your penance."

Thom nodded appreciatively. "Can I still see her?"

"Hell, yes! Why not?" Again the smile absolved everything. The soft guitars were still playing.

Martha found him in the confessional during the eight o'clock mass.

"Thom! It's me." She hadn't called him father. "It's

been about a week and all I have to tell is—last night. I guess maybe it was wrong. I don't know—" There was no anxiety or guilt.

"Did you think it was wrong?"

"I didn't think. It just happened."

He feared the absolution. Stiff canonical penalties followed the absolution of a sexual accomplice. Immediate excommunication. But only if she were guilty of mortal sin.

"Did you consent?"

"I just loved you. Nothing else."

It was a painful decision. He hesitated for a few moments, decided it was "partial consent," and absolved her.

"We can't get carried away." He couldn't give her up. He had fantasized over and over their growing old together in God's service.

"We won't." Then she moved closer to the screen. "Thom?"

"Yes?"

"I love you."

He wondered if it had even been said in a confessional before. "If we really love each other, we can be strong." He had said it before, and she loved the challenge.

"Did you have to go to confession?"

"Yes. To Dave."

"Was he mad at you?"

"He just said to be careful."

"We will." She got up to leave. "I really love you!"

Then the strange voices of repentant sinners whispered, and he was kinder and more understanding than ever before. The old lady told of "motions of the flesh"; a troubled boy had tried intercourse without success: "I couldn't get it. Too tight—but I woulda."

"I know it's hard. Just a few kisses and then good night. God will help."

The startled sinner had expected more. "Thank you, father. Thank you very much."

The following Sunday he spoke of the Trinity in terms of love, looking frequently at Marty.

"When a man loves a woman, it is almost as if he discovered her with his own mind. Otherwise how would he know her? She is the perfect word he has been waiting to speak. And when love flourishes they conceive a child that is the perfect reflection of their love—the bond that really unites them. It is the spirit that flows from their love."

She wanted to belong to Thom, never to be separated from him. She also knew she wanted his baby.

And believed that, somehow, God would make it possible.

Throughout the summer, their relationship conformed to the strictest codes of Catholic morality. Their chastity was now his sole responsibility since she would love any way he asked. He brought up the idea of her entering the convent, but her innate sense of freedom found the idea too oppressive. She had crossed a boundary beyond gospels or pamphlet morality, certainly beyond that of a seventeen-year-old Catholic virgin. She was his woman, definitely not a nun, and her very posture and bearing—even her facial messages—expressed new and total surrender. A hidden sexuality emerged that frightened him. On a humid afternoon picnic she stripped to her panties without warning and plunged into a backwater pool of the Algonquin River, then she lay naked in the sun, not even stirring when a canoe passed within fifty yards.

It was not easy for him to maintain control, but he knew that mortal sin would terminate their relationship, and he was not strong enough without her. On his annual summer retreat—three days at Assisi in the Pines outside of Sheffield, led by an ascetic Franciscan—he realized that he had already dangerously ignored priestly decorum and had not avoided proximate occasions of sin. Beauchamp's warm support and an elasticity of conscience regarding Marty—that vaguely looked to Pope John—had enabled him to elude dire warnings.

"The Church's injunction still holds: '*Nunquam solus cum sola*—never alone with a woman.' St. Jerome said it as well as anyone: 'Man is paper, woman is fire, and the devil is a strong wind.' Those who make light of sinful circumstances are no longer with us."

So Thom pictured a life of pure service with a smiling Martha as his devoted housekeeper.

Apart from interludes with Marty—which only gave the appearance of evil—he was a priest beyond reproach. Although gradually conscious of an ambition fueled by his success, as well as by the bishop's accolades, he still enjoyed the daily challenge of the priesthood. Attractive aspirants in convert class might momentarily distract him, but he protected himself with a veneer of kindly distance. Even Roselle, who glowed in his presence, maintained the appropriate restraint his aura required. At the dinner celebrating her baptism, she treated Thom only as her favorite priest; although, after Charlie had left for the Oldsmobile assembly line, she admitted there was trouble in her marriage.

"When Charlie's not working nights at the plant, he's out drinking." He had lost his coaching assignment.

"The kids—"

"They adore him, but he hardly knows they're alive. Maybe it was a mistake—"

Charlie agreed to private conferences once a week in Thom's rectory office. Thom spent a half hour with each of them alone, then another half hour together. Mostly he lectured, for he had no therapeutic skills of improving communication or exploring feelings. He prepared sermonettes on patience and humility and Christian marriage, hoping that Charlie would take instructions. Roselle often called the following day.

"I think it helps Charlie."

"How about you?"

"I love hearing you."

While Marty prepared to leave for Dominican College, outside Detroit, Thom took two weeks' vacation to go golfing in Florida with Mike Fogarty and Jim O'Brien, and he usually managed to forget her, except at night. A wealthy parishioner's winter home in Fort Lauderdale —a gathering place for Sheffield clergy—provided plush comfort as well as cutting down on expenses; although with Herschel Schaeffer's frequent generosities his monthly salary now averaged five hundred dollars. They slept late, read breviary to the waves, and played eighteen holes after elaborate brunches at the country club. A competitive match in the low 80s risked a dollar a hole with carry-overs, and after the game they had a few drinks before showering. Mike—who had taken the same five-year pledge that Thom had and never kept it, even when he was with Charlie Kenelley who administered it—delighted in Thom's virginal drink.

"We'll have you drinking scotch like O'Brien."

"I hope he can hold it better," the angular O'Brien said with a grin.

On more than one occasion O'Brien had fallen asleep after dinner before the poker game began, and Mike and Thom sometimes slipped away for a nightcap at one of the singles bars along the beach. Thom admitted over a second Drambuie that he felt somewhat guilty about ignoring daily mass. Even on Sunday, they merely attended the parish church in golf attire.

"It's good to break the routine."

Thom glanced at a stunning young woman whose breasts jiggled invitingly.

Mike grinned. "Not that routine."

Thom blushed and talked about lowering his hand position on iron shots and Mike described Sam Snead's intentional fade of a tee shot.

As they got up to leave, the young woman was expertly dancing the cha-cha with a muscular man in a white Palm Beach suit. His profile emerged as they headed out to the parking lot, but neither of them recognized Father Chet Golas.

Martha went off to college after an exchange of promises that separation would only deepen their love. Thom plunged into his work and waited impatiently for each of her letters, devouring her words of love and responding with his own eloquent and romantic brushstrokes on the life he fantasized with her. Occasionally they had long, frustrating telephone conversations which only helped until his recurring loneliness pushed him into more work. Resenting her excitement with college and the new friends who had taken some edge off her loneliness, he spent more time at prayer and meditation, still feeling shame at the Florida dissipation, and he resolved to be more generous in every phase of his priesthood. He labored among the Mexicans (giving away most of his money), organized baby-sitting on Sundays in the grade school, and prepared even more outstanding sermons. When he missed Marty's eyes in the high school religion classes, he increased his efforts to make Catholicism an exciting way of life—even for the lethargic masturbators. Even as his chest ached to hold her and feel his tension dissolve.

It was the middle of November when Marty wrote him

casually—after three weeks of awful silence—that she was dating a second-year dental student, Lawrence Cullen. He reminded her of Thom, and they had gone to a Detroit Lions game, attended a "great" fraternity dance, and were excitedly planning to ski "up north" after Christmas. Only at the end of the letter did she talk briefly of her everlasting love for Thom, and she said nothing at all about missing him.

He was crushed. He fantasized the young dentist cuddling her under a football blanket, fondling breasts and kissing; then he dropped the letter in his desk drawer and entered the silent cathedral to shed angry tears. Cursing her fickleness and despising the weakness that could not stand a few months' separation. He would never again risk his priesthood, and he felt his pain was suitable punishment for his disloyalty. He resolved not to write to her, but after a few weeks of renewed prayers and serious conversation with Dave Beauchamp, he still felt the emptiness of Martha's desertion. Every reminder of her was a sharp physical pain, and he buried himself in work, sought new converts, and applied for Pauline and Petrine privileges to dissolve marriages. He fiercely closed down Shady Oak convalescent home with a dramatic assist from the mayor and appropriate publicity that pleased Bishop Schmidt. To celebrate, Herschel Schaeffer had his housekeeper, Mrs. Grimes, prepare a special leg of lamb dinner. Dave Beauchamp called Thom "the giant-killer," and Chet Golas phoned enthusiastic congratulations and announced he had applied for chaplaincy in the navy.

"The boys need some leadership—you're my ideal!" Chet told him.

"Great, Chet! Great!" But even Thom's words of support sounded hollow to him, and the feeling of emptiness returned after each priestly triumph. Martha had left a void that needed to be filled.

Early in December, Thom hurried to meet a member of the Mexican Club in the sacristy at half-past three. It was almost four when he returned from the hospital. The previous year they had honored the Señora of Guadalupe in the gym, and with Thom's recent encouragement the club had requested a rear alcove in the cathedral to erect a permanent shrine on the December feast day. The janitor had remembered a Mexican madonna statue in the sacristy storeroom, and Herschel agreed reluctantly to let Thom make arrangements for the inauguration.

"These damn Mexicans are still Indians."

"They seem devout—and kind."

"I always wonder what's behind those big grins of theirs."

"A lot of pain—and faith."

"A lot of panhandling too. Every time I've been to Mexico, some damn grubby kid wants to sell you Chiclets or dust your car. It doesn't cost anything to be clean."

But he changed directions, outraged when Thom told him that hundreds of the wetbacks in Sheffield had become Baptists and Jehovah's Witnesses.

"Why they've always been Catholic—fought Calles and Obregon and all those filthy Commies."

He agreed on the alcove near the guest confessional and suggested a few racks of red and blue vigil lights. He mentioned charging a dollar a light, then changed his mind.

"Maybe fifty cents is enough. They only cost us eighteen dollars a hundred. I'd rather make a quarter than have them pay nothing. Give 'em a bargain—Yeh, fix it up nice!" He smiled warmly at his own sudden charity.

Thom stopped in the rectory to tell Mrs. Grimes he would miss her Friday night omelet, then hurried to the sacristy and found a woman there, waiting patiently. Still out of breath, he apologized sincerely and directed her to the workroom.

He opened the door, fumbled for the switch, and found that the bulb was out. He pulled the door open wide to let in light from the sacristy, and they saw the dark outlines of forgotten angels and Christmas animals. He would need a candle to find the Mexican madonna. As he slid out the door, his arm brushed against her breast, and he shuddered, then was embarrassed. He finally glanced at her for the first time. Her low blouse displayed extensive cleavage and she grinned, showing attractive white teeth. He moved back into the dusty storeroom, placing the candle on a worktable near the door. Finally they located the colorful statue, almost four feet high, and dragged it gently toward the light. As he cleared the door, he could feel her hip against his thigh.

He stood next to her in the corridor outside. "There it is! Like it?"

"Oh! *Nuestra Senora muy bonita!* Very beautiful, *padre.*" She stopped to caress the statue and her blouse fell open.

He was powerless to look away. Her thigh brushed carelessly against his as she continued extolling the statue. He was paralyzed. She touched his arm or shoulder spontaneously whenever she spoke, now as excited as he was.

"You are nice to do this," she said.

No one had taken this much interest in the Mexicans before. Even Joe Quinn had only supplied essential services and attended their special feasts to enjoy his favorite tacos. As much as they had loved Joe, Thom was now their saint. He smiled tensely at her compliment.

As he tried to move the statue onto a small dolly, she bent down to assist, brushing against him firmly. Nervously, he pulled a small dais from the workroom and balanced it against the statue, then pulled the dolly through the dark sanctuary, past the communion rail, and down the center aisle to the rear alcove. All the time she assisted, leaning forward to maintain the precarious balance of the sacred statue, and displaying outrageous breasts. He tried to look away.

They set up the statue, brought red and blue lights from the vestibule, and posted them on either side of the sinister alcove. The display was simple and attractive, and the Mexican woman sighed with delight. Touching his arm warmly. He returned to the sacristy to show her where she could find vases for fresh flowers. Still terribly excited. He had never experienced this kind of animal intensity.

He knew that she had seen the vases and that a return trip on his part was unnecessary, but she docilely followed. Understanding all of it and as frightened as he was. He walked part way into the dark sacristy and pointed.

"These are for your use." It was hard to breathe.

Again she pulled in close and her leg fell against his. He felt her breast massage his arm, and without resistance he turned to face her. Now there were no words, no feigned sophistication that could rescue him, for he did not want to be rescued. The Easter candle tottered, and he moved his shoulder.

"You like being padre?" She was still asking his permission, and his silence was all the consent she needed.

He could not answer or move. She put her arms around his waist, then circled her body next to his groin. Sweat appeared on his forehead.

"You very pretty, padre. Very young."

He could have moved away, Instead, he felt his back brush the candelabra as she pulled her body tighter against his. His face was hot and he still could not speak when she continued to rotate slowly and gently. He felt the sweat move to his cheeks and lips, and the pain of Martha's rejection was finally gone. Encouraged, the woman drew her arms behind his neck and pulled his mouth to hers in a single motion. Tongue and teeth and lips deep into the garden of some sensuous serpent that writhed and swallowed with soft groans. He could not pull away. She led his fingers under her blouse to caress her breasts and held them in circling massage until his whole body grew rigid.

The candelabra fell, shattering the plaster wing of an archangel and crushing a wise man.

Thomas Aloysius Maguire came. Fighting to resist the explosion under his cassock, groaning his regrets to God in harmony with the spasms. She cried out in delight as he whimpered helplessly. Then it was over, and he felt the sweaty weight of her body against his. He tried to move.

"Momentito, padre, momentito!" She kissed his dry mouth as he waited in listless disgust. Finally he left her with the broken archangel's wing and the splintered myrrh of the wise man. Among staring sheep.

He felt sick when he entered the back door of the rectory and heard the pastor talking with Mrs. Grimes over after-dinner coffee. He snuck up the stairs and fell on his bed. Then he began to sob like a little boy.

"God, O God!"

It was the first time in his life he knew he had committed a mortal sin. Thirty years old and four and a half years into his priesthood.

"Eli, Eli, lama sabacthani? (My God, my God, why have you forsaken me?)"

He continued to sob for more than an hour. He had failed the test of a dozen years' discipline. The retreat masters had been right: Women were seductive, and powerless to resist a priest. Only his own prayerful vigilance could prevent sin. Now it was too late. He brushed his eyes, his anointed fingers still smelling of musk, and then he rose to wash away the stain of his disgrace. There was no excuse, no gentle Jack Durrell to soften his guilt or the comforting chest of a smiling Dave Beauchamp to assuage consent. He had denied God, and now he stood as some naked Adam with the scarred forehead of a sullen Cain. Without hope. Like the blinded, naïve Sampson, all the past struggles had come exploding down on his head.

He had survived adolescent passion and the loneliness of seminary years, survived Sharon and Roselle and the sexual assaults of moral theology during his final year. And the temptations of his priesthood. High school and college girls who adored him; fresh young bodies just emerged from sleep; cheering young breasts at football games, devout ones at the communion rail, perfumed ones at dances. The adoring housewives who hated their husbands; and the beautiful Marty he still loved. He knew he could never face her innocent eyes again.

Perhaps his very celibacy had all been a fraud, a coward's rejection of sex. His strength a pharisaic scorn, the people's open affection only egotistical protection. He had loved to discuss his celibacy when he lectured on vocations, to tell stories of the lonely people who needed the Christlike love too valuable to be shared with a special spouse. Even as he had talked, he had enjoyed the misty-eyed girls who looked at him so passionately.

"A priest's or nun's love is beyond sex. This is not to discredit but to describe a deeper love. Sex individualizes and narrows. This, too, is part of God's plan. But He has chosen servants to offer unselfish love without sexual involvement. To share the secrets of a thousand without belonging to anyone, to be brother to the young, a son to the elderly, a friend to anyone who needs. Then even the loneliest will not lack a love. This is the 'why' of celibacy; prayer and faith is the 'how.' "

Flattering eyes had sustained the glow of his oratory; romantic eyes, ready for any sacrifice to rescue confusing adolescence, were like a comforting embrace.

His work had made the celibate struggle less difficult. His day never ended. The phone's ring announced another and another suppliant reaching for his hand, the doorbell meant a scarred traveler looking for God. Father Thom always had the time, the young celibate energy, the neophyte zeal. He was soldier in battle, hero in a sea of reaching hands. Celibacy had been no problem at all. Until a musky peasant's breasts had brushed his arm and the motion of her hips had stirred his groin.

Not some silken Roselle, or Sharon on spotless sands. Or a devout Marty, sublimating her love to God.

But a dark, sweating peasant whose devouring breasts, voracious hips, and musty animal smell had destroyed his will. My God, that smell! It had sucked him into her mouth and exploded his writhing cassock against her legs.

And he never knew her name.

An anonymous mother of all the living.

He lay on the bed defeated. Semen stained his black pants. He stood up and looked at his tearstained face in the mirror. He washed the matted hair on his sticky legs and still smelled her musky odor. Then he moved down the stairs, passing Monsignor Schaeffer, who was in search of a cigar.

"Did you eat anything?"

"I got tied up in church."

"Mrs. Grimes will fix an egg sandwich."

"No, really, I'll catch a bite after rosary."

He walked into the church and saw the lonely women who had nowhere else to go, the nuns lost in private prayers, and an altar boy struggling with a candle.

In the rear alcove an old Mexican man was already lighting a candle to his Lady of Guadalupe.

For fifty cents.

Feeling unworthy of his calling, he finished the novena prayers to a Sorrowful Mother and replaced the Blessed Sacrament. It was as if a dream had ended. Then he slipped out of the silk cope, abbreviated his patter with the altar boys, and knelt at the sacristy prie-dieu, peering at the gold crucifix. Wondering about confession to the pale hospital chaplain or the new Franciscan at Holy Cross. Suddenly it didn't matter. He had to be rid of the sticky, humiliating sin.

Ascending the rectory stairs, he heard Dennis Tracy's belching laugh in Dave's room, and he knocked cautiously.

"Hey, Thom!"

"How's it going, Dennis? Can I see you a minute, Dave?" It was not an unusual request, and Dave followed him downstairs to his office wondering if Herschel had locked the Mexicans out of the gym or if Charlie Kenelley had totaled his car.

"I want to confess."

"For sure!" Thom knelt in front of the desk. Dave blessed him.

"I committed an impure act with a woman—a Mexican lady from the club. It happened in the sacristy—and—I came." It seemed there should have been more.

Dave asked no questions and spoke softly with his hand on Thom's shoulder. "Sometimes it's tough. You're only a man like anyone else. Do the best you can. God understands His children. Say six Our Fathers and six Hail Marys."

It was a barely mortal penance. Dave got up and smiled quickly as if nothing had happened. Thom never knew he could love anyone as much.

He returned to the darkened cathedral to say his penance and then he knelt for two hours at rigid attention. Begging God's forgiveness and promising a daily schedule of prayer and mortification. He would quit smoking, rise at five for prolonged meditation, read Scripture an hour every day, and deny himself favorite desserts. He would have climbed Everest if God had asked, or shimmied up the cathedral campanile.

He concluded his prayers feeling stronger and went to bolt the front doors. There was a movement in the shadows near the fated statue. He smelled the musky odor before she emerged from the darkness to kneel and kiss his hand.

"I very sorry, padre."

He touched the black hair gently. "It's okay. I'm sorry, too." He blessed her.

The dark eyes looked innocently into his and he knew her breasts were still visible under the white blouse. He looked away. She squeezed his hand, kissed his fingers warmly, and made her way from the church. He bolted the doors behind her. As he moved up the aisle toward the flickering tabernacle lamp, the smell of musk enveloped him again. Helplessly, he still wanted her breasts.

He clenched his fists and knelt rigidly on the marble floor that surrounded the red carpet in the sanctuary, then lay prostrate there until midnight.

A few weeks later, after a convert class, Thom noted some unfamiliar sadness in Dave Beauchamp's face when Dave returned from a novena service.

"How many at novena?"

"The usual. A dozen teeth clackers and thirty hopeful virgins."

Thom grinned. "We gotta get more men. That's what they are praying for!" It was their standard joke, and Dave laughed halfheartedly.

"Something bugging you, Dave?"

"Dennis has been reassigned to Danville." It was about two hundred miles away and an unusual assignment in December. Dave looked as though he had been crying.

"What the hell for?"

"Who knows? I think it was Herschel's idea, and the bishop must have agreed."

"You can still get together?"

"We're supposed to make new friends—" After six years together in the seminary, they had been close neighbors for almost eight years.

It was the first time Thom had ever seen a droop in those muscular shoulders. His heart ached for the man—this good friend who made no request for understanding.

Dave grew more despondent after Christmas and spent longer hours alone in his room listening to music, seeming only to light up on days when he planned to meet Dennis at some rendezvous. Thom sometimes succeeded in cheering him with exaggerated parish gossip, and occasionally Thom heard snatches of phone calls from Dennis, sharing daily trivia or comparing new record albums and exciting vacation plans. Thom made more frequent visits to Dave's room, and their friendship, always instinctive, moved beyond trivia. Thom learned something of music, of Dave's love of serenity and eastern thought about God, and Dave delighted in Thom's warm Irish humor and his outrageous stories about Jack and John Patrick. Finally Dave talked about Dennis.

"I never had a brother. It's like we're closer than that. We each know what the other one is thinking."

"I never had that—even with a brother." Thom admitted that he had not really seen Jim in the two years since he had baptized Jim's third baby and heard him tell John Patrick privately that there would be no more kids. John Patrick had quoted McNulty: "The pope should be obliged to sleep with hot dago pussy and silence a bawling baby on alternate nights—then he might know his head from his ass!"

Beauchamp actually laughed aloud. "I'm sorry, Thom, but it is funny!" Realizing he had silenced his friend, Dave grew more understanding. "It really hurts you, doesn't it?"

Thom admitted his concern about Jim's kids and the possibility of a divorce that would kill Margaret. Jim and Connie were barely getting along and even the children were old enough to be distressed. "There's no talking to him. He knows it all."

Dave mused quietly, hesitating to tell Thom what he really thought because he knew his friend wasn't ready to hear it. Dave never intruded on anyone.

"What about the others?"

"Anne's already got two kids, but we're not really close." He hesitated. "We share a lot of ideas about Cana conferences and Catholic morality, but it seems to be just talk. Tim's a good kid, a junior at Notre Dame, but I don't know him that well because I was gone when he was growing up."

"I guess I'm luckier than I know. I really miss Dennis!" He smiled radiantly. "We're going to the Bahamas in July, and I can't wait!"

Thom saw Marty over Christmas and was briefly introduced to her young dentist, Larry Cullen. Thom resented the way she clung. Not to mention the brief kiss for her "first love" as they went laughing out the door. He drove home to watch television with Margaret and John Patrick, learning that old Mulaley had died and Ed Bertelson had married outside the Church. Margaret complained of Thom's infrequent visits, and John Patrick asked him about money and fell asleep after rump roast and gravy.

Short-tempered since Marty's new love, Thom had been increasingly tense. Some edge was off his priesthood. Even Charlie Kenelley suggested a few days' vacation when Thom snapped at an altar boy over a garbled Latin phrase.

"For Chrissakes, Thom, the little guy's scared shitless!" Charlie put his arm around Thom and admitted to his own weariness from time to time.

"It's only natural—and I never worked like you do!"

"Maybe I do need some time—"

There was so much to do. Dave had lost a lot of his vital energy, and Herschel was content to putter around between priesthood and travel. News of Thom's generosity had circulated throughout the environs of Sheffield, and wounded excommunicants, rebuffed by "brick-and-mortar" pastors or lazy timeservers, sought him out to resolve their tangled cases. He baptized over a hundred converts in a single year. The national average was less than two per priest, and no parish in the diocese had more than twenty-five. Again the bishop had a private confirmation and publicly extolled Father Thomas Maguire's dedication.

Thom drove to Detroit with Mike Fogarty, stopping in Steelmont to have lunch with Jack Durrell at Pius XII Seminary.

"I hear great things." Durrell was now totally bald, and his face was puffy and more obviously sad.

Even Bernard Fox was impressed with Thom's work and hinted at Bishop Schmidt's "great plans" for him.

Mike and Thom went bowling, had dinner at the London Chop House, and stayed overnight at the Park Sheraton Hotel. It was welcome relaxation. Thom finally confided his occasional tensions to Mike.

"You take it too seriously," Mike told him. "Three or four years and you'll have your own parish in some little resort town with a few families and weekend help. You can run your own show and give good service. And have a damn good income." It was true. A Sheffield pastor in a medium-sized parish could accumulate a comfortable estate. With mass and baptismal stipends, wedding and funeral offerings, and the entire Easter and Christmas collections—plus a liberal use of the petty cash that was Sunday collection money not in envelopes—he could probably put aside about a thousand dollars a month, often tax-free. There were also clerical discounts, private gifts from parishioners, and great real estate tips from brokers who took no fee.

"Maybe I'll try service, like Chet. He loves Pensacola."

"Schmidt would never let you go. You're not Chet Golas." Four years in the air force had enlightened the bull-like Mike. "That's a goddamned kindergarten."

Mike had found satisfaction. He was a good, hard-working priest who took extraordinary care of the old and sick and was apparently untroubled by sexual temptations. Free of Thom's kind of ambition, he dreamed of a small parish with plenty of time for golf, and quiet conversations sipping scotch by his own fire. Until he retired with a house on Lake Michigan and enough money in mutual funds to last till Judgment Day.

Thom's new personal weakness succeeded in making him a more considerate and far less rigid confessor, and the lines at his confessional grew longer as frightened recidivists discovered his reluctance to rebuke. Masturbators were gently asked to try harder; engaged couples were encouraged toward more frequent prayers; and even scrupulous old maids were allowed to talk out their fears.

On a humid night in June 1962, a week after Dave and a visiting Dennis joyfully and ceremoniously honored Thom's fifth anniversary and their own eighth, he sat in confession and patiently heard whispered admissions of birth control use, petting in back seats, forgotten Fridays, and missed morning prayers. A familiar voice broke the monotony.

"Thom, it's me, Marty."

She had not written since Easter, and a friendly phone call inviting him to a spring festival had left him depressed.

"Hi Marty! Good to hear your voice." All his suppressed feelings came back. He had still not lost hope that they would finally be together.

"It's been about two weeks, and I've got a problem."

He felt his hands shaking. "So tell me—" More gently than he felt.

"Well, Larry and I went—well—like all the way. Three or four times." He knew it was four. She wasn't through.

"And he, well—like—put his mouth down there—three or four times, too. Maybe more."

He was almost panting and he felt a chill through his body. He couldn't speak, and he felt as though giant arms were crushing his chest and choking out all his breath.

"And Thom, I did it to him—quite a bit—like it didn't seem wrong, but I guess it must be."

"It's wrong." He struggled with the words, gave her a whispered rosary for penance, and heard the intense act of contrition. He wanted to hurt her.

"Thank you, Thom."

"God bless you." He couldn't bring himself to say her name.

He closed the screen and sat motionless. Like a rejected lover. As if his whole being had been mocked.

Marty had been the pride of his young priesthood. Now she was as weak and impure as all the rest, as distant and unreachable as his brother Jim. Thomas Aloysius Maguire knew he had failed them both.

11

Aggiornamento

A man's life does not crumble suddenly, but usually disintegrates as a result of impulsive and destructive decisions made during times of great stress. On such occasions he refuses or is unable to look closely at what he is doing, and he seduces himself into believing that his conflicts will dissipate according to his own fantasies. Thus, Jim Maguire had married Connie Hackett because she was comfortable and available, even though they had never communicated at any satisfactory level for Jim.

Connie had no need for deep communication; and, despite a lack of intellectual interests or a capacity for self-understanding, she was a good mother, and for the right man she could have been a resourceful and satisfying wife. Unfortunately, she truly believed she loved Jim, and she used what abilities she had to win his love. Only sex really worked. She was as conscious as he was of her own shortcomings, and her efforts to make an impression at medical auxiliary meetings, to wear fashionable clothes, or to decorate the house were far more her desire to please him than to gratify any youthful vanity of her own. Only when she knew she had failed him did she turn back to her religion for survival.

Her native sensuality, her solid common sense, and her gentle humor never fully emerged, and artificiality became her way of life. She had no real affection for the Church and probably had less faith than he did. But for whatever reasons—a lack of self-esteem or an aborted education—she had no proper tools with which to become herself. There were times at the wives' auxiliary meetings—during petty arguments over a theme for a spring dance or the proper menu for a luncheon—when she wanted to scream and become once again a north-side Irish girl who liked "sloppy Joes" at picnics and was content entertaining her children while the men played half-drunken softball. Instead, she simulated interest, bore Jim's children, and was delighted when she pleased him in bed.

When he lost interest in her body, she knew she had lost him, and instinctively she gathered her children around her and chose the only institution outside the family that could protect her: the Church. She would have practiced birth control if he had approached her, as he did in high school, with soft words and loving touches, but he had lost respect, and if she was nothing else she was an Irish girl who would do anything she felt necessary to survive.

Thus the conflict, simmering since Chrissie's birth, really erupted over Johnny's first communion, when Jim refused to receive the sacrament with his son. The nuns had primed the children to bring their parents, especially the strays, to the sacred table. Even John Patrick, his legs still stiff from the automobile accident years before, had agreed to hobble up to the communion rail to please his oldest grandson and namesake. But Jim, not wanting Johnny to be as lost as he was, and hoping that his own most precious son would reflect all he himself had learned about life, resisted the boy's pleas as well as the subtle strategies of Connie and Margaret. He talked to his son with a directness that characterized their relationship.

"I love you very much, Johnny, but I don't believe in going to communion anymore. I find God and Jesus in my work helping people and in my walks with you in the woods. We can still be the best of friends even if we believe different things. Holy communion doesn't help me, but I want you to go if that's what you want."

Johnny seemed to understand. "I thought everybody had to go, daddy. I didn't really know I could make up my own mind. Grandma said—"

"Grandma goes every day, and it helps her, but grandpa only goes once in a while. They're just different people, but they love each other."

The boy was silent for a long time. Finally he looked at his father, the blond hair highlighted by the sun and the innocent blue eyes reminding Jim of a young Thom, and he said simply, "I like your kind of communion too, daddy. It's pretty and quiet." Then they walked through a green meadow and cuddled quietly in the warm sun of a crisp April day. Jim told him about the death of leaves and the new buds of spring and likened it all to Good Friday and Easter Sunday. Johnny was spellbound.

Margaret and Connie, however, managed to break the spell. Not a week later Johnny approached his father. "But you might go to hell, daddy."

"No. God knows that I'm a good daddy and that I love you very much. He won't punish me."

"But sister said—"

It was useless, Jim was powerless to compromise in a battle he couldn't bear to lose. Finally, he demanded that Johnny go to the public school. He was not about to give his beautiful son to Margaret and the nuns.

Connie threatened to leave him, and Margaret, wondering where she had failed, confronted him.

"Have you lost your mind?"

"Maybe I've found it. He's my son, mother."

"Don't you talk that way to me. He's God's son first, and besides, you wouldn't be a doctor if your father and I hadn't sacrificed everything we had. Sold the cottage at the lake and denied ourselves clothes and vacations. Now you're so high-and-mighty that God takes a backseat." She was wild-eyed and crying, but Jim no longer felt the same guilt at her tears and bitter protests.

It was Johnny himself who sobbed that he wouldn't make the move to the public school. Margaret and his mother had frightened him with the horror of hell's fire for all eternity. Margaret remembered her own childhood fantasy taught by other nuns: "If a drop of water falls on a rock as big as the world, when the world is worn away, eternity will have just begun. And hell's fire will still be burning." Johnny could never take such a chance.

Jim finally gave in after Johnny had nightmares and sobbed convulsively for three successive nights.

At about the same time, his partnership with Doc McGregor came to an abrupt and dramatic ending.

The old doctor had liked him and had paid little attention to what Jim did in the office. Although he had been prescribing birth control pills to harried young housewives, word had not reached Dr. McGregor until—at Anne and her mother's insistence—Anne's husband, Dick Dorgan, still a sallow and intensely Catholic obstetrician, made a private appointment to report Jim's behavior. It seemed a sensible way to bring Jim back to his childhood faith. No one realized that Dr. McGregor, grown mildly senile and scrupulously concerned about his own salvation, would immediately terminate the partnership. After an objective appraisal by an outside accounting firm, he bought Jim out and awarded most of the young mothers to Dick Dorgan.

Anne reassured Margaret. "Jim was never trained in obstetrics anyway. Dick's a specialist."

Margaret was not convinced that the awkward, officious Dorgan could hold a candle to her son, but she consoled herself that God had not been mocked. Even as she despised Anne's arrogance.

John Patrick exploded with an anger that had been dormant for years. "Why the hell can't that candy-assed son of a bitch mind his own goddamned business! Jim knows what he's doing! He's the one who made the money McGregor bought him out with!"

Only when Jim reassured him that it was a good financial deal and that he preferred to work by himself was John Patrick gradually calmed, but he refused to allow Anne or her "mealymouthed asshole" in the house.

Jim refused to speak to his mother or his sister.

He had taken to sleeping in the guest room of the sprawling white colonial he had bought the year before.

The stocky Johnny remained estranged and tense, and five-year-old Jimmy seemed distant and possessed of some secret life, just as his father had been. Even Chrissie, freckled and lively at four, sensed the tension and usually refused to sit on his lap anymore. Once she called him a "bad daddy" after a loud argument with Connie, and, pale and near tears, Jim had slapped Chrissie's bottom, then left to visit Sandy's grave in the woods. With Connie shouting after him to find some young nurse to tell him how great he was. Madness and anger and bruised feelings settled over the home of Dr. James Maguire.

Connie discovered lipstick on his beige jacket and first names with phone numbers on bits of paper in his coat pockets. It was the ultimate humiliation for her. He made no effort to lie. Connie had grown distasteful to him. Her body, which once had excited him even when her bland ignorance and dullness irritated him to silent screaming, now seemed bloated and waffled with midde-aged decay. She was thirty-four.

Medicine, too, had lost its luster even before he broke with Doc McGregor. Although he had never made the really big money made by the specialists, his large family practice had earned more than even Connie's insecurity could spend. As long as he devoted the sixty or seventy hours a week that it required. He was considered a compassionate, informed healer by his patients, and he truly was, but he lost interest in tonsils and earaches and Catholic mothers with too many children. He experienced a distress he had not felt since his first year at Marquette.

Margaret arranged for a meeting with Thom. Jim consistently appeared on Sunday evenings to appease John Patrick's growing hypochondriasis and stayed to chat about Notre Dame or the Green Bay Packers. Saint Raphael's team had lost some significance. It was a different age.

"All these damn kids have cars now, and girl friends by the time they're in eighth grade. They lost to the Polacks last year by three touchdowns. Doyle oughta convert some of these niggers on the north side. Those boys can play ball." He laughed the same outrageous laugh of twenty years ago.

Thom appeared in the midst of a rehash of Jack's touchdown on the kickoff, and the house suddenly tensed. The two brothers had not really communicated since shortly after Chrissie's birth and Thom's ordination.

"How's the practice going?" Thom spoke with brisk interest.

"Not bad. Like starting over." Jim did not look at him.

There was no easy way to introduce religion. After a few minutes of pointless pleasantries, Thom attacked with priestly courage.

"I understand you're giving out the pill." He didn't know what else to say.

"I give out a lot of pills."

John Patrick laughed.

"Damn it, Jim, you know what I mean."

"No, I don't. Why don't you tell me, father."

"The Church still forbids birth control, you know?"

"Does it now? Well, do me a favor. Tell the Church to stick it up its ass!" Jim got up and walked out, reminding John Patrick to take his new prescription every four hours.

Margaret trembled as the door slammed, and she wondered if Thom had been too abrupt.

Thom flushed angrily, and John Patrick tried not to smile.

Increasingly Jim spent weekends away from home, at first blaming seminars or conventions, finally without explanation. He drove to Chicago or Detroit, got a motel, searched the bars or resort areas for a never-forgotten Judy, and settled for occasional half-intoxicated sex with a nondescript partner who made him forget for an evening or even a weekend, finally loathing her as the empty source of new loneliness. It didn't take long for him to realize that the Judys were not waiting in bars or smoky dance halls for lonely, overworked, unhappily married doctors who had three kids and the monstrous expenses of a guilt-ridden upper-middle-class masquerade.

James Maguire had lost his spontaneity to a mountain of responsibilities gathered without wisdom or honest appetite. And his innocence had been surrendered almost imperceptibly. Connie had been paid off to leave him alone.

He began to spend his free time wandering the woods of his childhood, startling frogs and noting the changing seasons, still the same lonely boy. Now No One's father or husband or brother. Certainly No One's son.

And desperately missing Sandy.

Johnny changed dramatically in the year after his first communion. He was still a talented athlete in third-grade football and playground baseball, but a new religious devotion made him every bit as conscious of God as a young Thom had been. Johnny served mass frequently without forgetting a bell or missing a hand cue from the priest. Occasionally, Monsignor Doyle, now a rambling, forgetful preacher and kindly old man, called him Thom by mistake, and the nuns were certain he would be another Maguire priest. Especially when Thom, at Margaret's insistence, visited Johnny's class and then drove him home from school to give encouragement to Connie. Thom always disappeared before Jim returned from work, but he had become a favorite uncle to the three children.

Little Jimmy was still remote, involved in a private struggle he never mentioned, and content to do what was asked of him or to lose himself in collecting stamps or matchbooks or preserving butterflies he chloroformed with laundry bleach under Margaret's supervision. The freckled, pig-tailed Chrissie was irrepressible and outgoing, and she was the only child who still paid any attention to her father. When he came home late and missed meals, which he usually did, she loved making him an awkward sandwich or pouring his coffee. Usually Connie interrupted and found homework for her to do or family prayers to say (enthusiastically led by Johnny). Chrissie returned to play with the hair on her father's arms or to read him a story until Connie directed her to bath and bed. Then there was only silence.

John Patrick, who was surprisingly insightful, had become Jim's single friend and confidant.

"Doyle must be a lonely old man with no children."

"It doesn't seem right somehow."

"Kids teach you more than any catechism," said John Patrick. "They give you something to live for, too." He reflected quietly. "It never turns out the way you think." Then he turned away from Jim into some painful memory.

John Patrick came to life when they watched football games on his new color TV. He groaned when Patterson lost to Sonny Liston after two minutes of the first round.

"My God, that big nigger can fight!"

They worried about Vietnam and gave Kennedy every possible break in any difficult decision to fight U. S. Steel or preserve the sovereignty of Berlin. Margaret never joined their conversations, nor did John Patrick ever lecture Jim about his coldness toward her. Jim was polite and appreciative of her cake and coffee, but he never talked about his family or his practice except with John Patrick.

John Patrick's relationship with Margaret had mellowed into a quiet routine. She fixed his meals and evening coffee and said her own night prayers. She attended morning mass, usually picking up Johnny, who loved to go with her, then she fixed John Patrick's toast and coffee—to which he had added prune juice and an assortment of pills prescribed by Jim. Most of them mere placebos.

John Patrick turned over the legwork in his business to two assistants. He felt like an important man again when he entered the office each morning. Although he had grown forgetful and was often confused about rates, no one dared confront him, for in an instant his rage could explode. He was still a charming, smiling Irish salesman who took the important accounts himself, but he had slipped badly. His face was thinner: the proud mouth drooped with false teeth he despised and twitched frequently to be rid of. The once curly red hair was now thin and gray, and he walked slowly, stiff and bent forward. At times, the powerful voice could not muster the timbre that had threatened umpires and bellowed in ticket lines. Assuredly he was too tired to battle with Margaret's God, and he became more devout when they were alone. Agreeing sometimes to say the rosary, then slipping into his old melancholy.

Thom's visits made little change in his daily rituals. A warm greeting and handshake and a brief question or two about Thom's health and priestly work. But only when Jim arrived did John Patrick really become alive.

When Jim returned home from visiting his father, the kids would be in bed and Connie talking to her mother on the phone. Or there would be a note that said the garbage disposal didn't work. Jim read or mixed a drink and went silently to the guest room. He had not touched Connie in four years, and for the last year had not even had a weekend affair.

Of course he fantasized leaving, starting over in California or Florida, but he wouldn't consider it until the kids were older and Johnny had come to his senses. He knew Johnny would ultimately be his when puberty set in. Meanwhile, he bided his time, enjoyed John Patrick and the serenity of the woods, and was even occasionally interested in his practice. Home, however, was a lonely place where only Chrissie gave him any pleasure. He sat alone in his leather chair, the same pale, silent man he had been in boyhood. Wondering if anyone ever really changed.

☙ ☙ ☙

Thom was facing serious conflicts that were only gradually becoming clear amidst the excitement of Pope John and the liturgical changes. Although sacraments were now administered in English, rules on the Eucharistic and Lenten fast had been simplified, and there was more lay participation in the administration of the Church, Thom was disenchanted. There was an incongruous tradition in the Catholic Church of the mid-twentieth century. The majority of bishops—controlled by the Roman curia—were expertly trained in canon law rather than in scriptural theology or pastoral arts, and this phenomenon had more to do with the Church's strength and weakness than anything else. Pope John knew this as well as anyone and offered a pastoral ideal, hoping to win support by example rather than by the kind of arrogant encyclicals issued by his predecessors.

It was a rare bishop who ever came out of a busy confessional or an office full of converts or unhappy spouses. Rather, bishops were chancery officials—as absorbed in finances, legalities, and ecclesiastical politics as they were ignorant of the lives of real people and their problems. Thus, ancient attitudes toward birth control, sexual mores, and divorce could remain intransigent while Friday abstinence and liturgical irrelevancies were reformed. Only a great revolution—threatening finances or the flow of vocations—could really disturb the thinking of the entrenched and often angry legalists.

And there was certainly no threat of revolution in June 1961 when Joe Beahan and Freddie Weber returned triumphantly to Sheffield as *magna cum laude* doctors of canon law. Pope John's "fresh air" council had already been two years in preparation. Journalistic rumors from Rome foretold an approaching showdown between impatient pastors and smug legalists who understood the Church—as did *Time* magazine—as the world's richest and most successful corporation. Yet Pope John, almost by himself, a brilliant historian and warmhearted shepherd, still offered hope to a docile laity and to the frustrated younger clergy.

To honor the newly trained apostles, Bishop Schmidt held an impressive banquet for civic officials, priests, and prominent laymen of the diocese at the Empire Room of the Sheffield Hilton Hotel. A facile dignity marked the after-dinner remarks given by the celebrated scholars—

Weber and Beahan—who had learned not only the minutiae and breadth of ecclesiastical law, but the political refinements of the ancient curia—the pope's cabinet—that really governed the Church. Bobbie Foley sat at the speakers' table and exchanged giggling Roman anecdotes with Joe Beahan. Charlie Kenelley poured scotch from a private silver flask while Freddie Weber, flushed with Valpolicella, bragged of a dinner with the apostolic delegate and a party at the Palazzo Calonna in Rome, casually dropping the names of a subsecretary of the Holy Office who gave him fisherman cuff links and the powerful Cardinal Ruggini of the Sacred Consistory who had arranged an audience with Pope John. Freddie had obviously studied more than canon law.

Following Beahan and Weber's return, there were no significant changes in the diocesan politics. Both men were appointed vice-chancellors under Charlie Kenelley, and they took up residence with Bishop Schmidt and Bobbie Foley in the episcopal mansion near the Sheffield Country Club. Freddie outfitted his suite with Florentine antiques, classical Italian carpets, large marble replicas of *David* and *Moses,* and an impressive bronze of *Adonis.* Beahan's suite was equally exotic, with colorful medieval tapestries, as well as a fine collection of rare French wines. Which he served ceremoniously (on Bishop Schmidt's absence) to visiting "Romans" and an assortment of young priests who were fascinated by tales of the forthcoming Vatican Council. Among them was Thom Maguire, suddenly feeling upstaged by the gregarious canon lawyers who were versant with European art and the idiosyncrasies of cardinals.

At first it was exciting for Thom to be invited to the bishop's mansion—as if he were still in contention for ecclesiastical preferment, despite the new pretenders to the throne. Yet it was difficult to adapt to gossipy chatter about farting archbishops and missionary cardinals who ate with their hands. Dave Beauchamp, always a caustic critic of the charade and an infrequent guest, wanted to leave when Beahan played Bach's Mass in B minor and Freddie giggled about Lutheran music "carrying ecumenism too far."

"Let's get the hell out of this pansy patch," Dave said.

Thom hesitated, wanting some strange approval, then agreed and left with Dave.

Frequently the "Romans" held court at the cathedral rectory after Saturday night confessions, enjoying expensive wines and liqueurs that Herschel Schaeffer had been educated to provide.

Gradually, there were quarrels, especially when the bishop stayed home and the three "musketurds"—as Charlie Kenelley named them—stayed till after midnight. Thom asked about Vatican II which would open the following year.

"Nothing's going to change," said Freddie. "The majority of the bishops are as stupid as Fritz." It was his new name for Schmidt.

Bobbie Foley agreed. "A college of bishops would be denied accreditation anywhere but in Rome!"

Beahan smiled. "That's good, Bobbie, very good!"

Thom extended the conversation. "What about practical matters like birth control and divorce?" He had been deeply troubled by a growing number of angry couples who found him an understanding confessor. And he was worried about Jim.

"Let them eat hot cross buns!"

"You're hot tonight, Bobbie!"

Even Herschel grinned and poured more wine, retelling a stale story about the confessor who recommended orange juice as an antifertility pill: "Before sex or after, father?" "Instead of!" Herschel cackled happily.

Kenelley finally looked up. "Thom, your problem is that you still believe in God. These prissy bastards think that a degree in canon law makes them dago nobility." He looked at Weber. "Wasn't your old man a car salesman who deserted your mother?"

Freddie turned pale.

Beahan interrupted. "That's unfair, Charlie!"

"Unfair, my ass. To hear you talk, you'd think your old man wasn't a hardware clerk. Or was it chicken shit?"

Charlie picked up his breviary and scotch and walked out. It was a full minute before Herschel offered more anisette. The three musketurds declined quietly and headed for home.

The next afternoon an exuberant Dave Beauchamp and Dennis Tracy headed for the Bahamas.

Thom went to visit Margaret and John Patrick and to baptize Anne's new baby. He heard as glowing a report about Jim from John Patrick as Margaret's was dismal, and he read Tim's excited letters from a logging camp in northern Michigan. Father Jim O'Brien came to dinner to discuss the new regime, and then came the same self-conscious lingering good-byes that were easier to handle if he became a little boy returning to the seminary.

"Don't forget your breviary!" It was Margaret's way of telling him to remain a priest.

He adjusted his collar, picked up his cake, and thanked his father for the cigarettes. It was his little act of love. He paused at the front door to kiss Margaret on the cheek. Her eyes grew moist, and he noticed that she was pudgier than he had remembered. John Patrick followed him slowly to the car while Margaret remained waving in the doorway. Mary watching Jesus make his way back to Calvary. She called after him. "If you think of it, give Dan Siler a call. He can't get over Muriel's death—and he thinks so much of you!" Thom nodded assent.

"Have you got enough money?" his father asked.

"Collections are good, dad!"

John Patrick grinned impishly. "Don't drive too fast. Watch that lead foot of yours." Another of their ritualistic exchanges.

John Patrick looked older than Thom had ever seen him, twenty years older than his wife, and Thom felt as if his life had somehow robbed them both of their strength. Watching them standing together waving from the porch always brought the same pressure of tears behind his eyes.

He drove past Marty's house when he arrived in Sheffield. All the lights were out.

The following week he read Dave's delighted postcard from the Bahamas and heard Mrs. Grimes exclaim, "He must be having some time!"

Thom was still imagining Dave snorkeling in crystal waters when a phone call from Freddie Weber asked him to report to the chancery at two the following afternoon. His heart skipped. It was probably his autumn appointment to Rome or to Catholic University in Washington. Finally.

"Hello, Father Maguire, I'm Don. The bishop and Father Weber will see you now." He opened the door of a conference room with crisp grace. Freddie Weber and

Joe Beahan and Bobbie Foley were lined up around Bishop Schmidt at a long oak table. A yellow legal pad rested in front of Bobbie, and Freddie directed Thom to sit down.

Thom was suddenly nervous.

"Father, this is a formal hearing at which you are requested to testify *sub secreto* and, of course, under oath." Freddie administered a formal declaration and explained the difference between external and internal forums of testimony. After requesting Thom's name, age, and address, he asked, "Father Maguire, how long have you known Father David Beauchamp?"

Thom was aghast. What the hell is this? he thought.

"Well—about five years."

Freddie explored the frequency of contact and reminded him that confessional information was outside the scope of the hearing. He then asked a series of questions about Dave's friendship with Dennis Tracy.

"Does Father Tracy stay all night on occasion?"

"No! Why? What are you suggesting?" He suddenly understood, and his face burned.

The bishop intervened. "You're absolutely certain of that, Father Maguire?" He said it kindly, and his sad eyes looked as if the whole ordeal were torturing him.

"Morally certain, bishop." He flared. "Dave Beauchamp is a great priest!" He looked directly into the bishop's gentle eyes and pleaded for pastoral understanding.

Joe Beahan raised his hands. "Please, Father Maguire, just try to respond to the questions. This is not pleasant for any of us." Beahan looked detached and dignified behind his thick horn-rimmed glasses. Thom noted that he must have gained twenty pounds.

Bobbie Foley continued to write. When they completed their questions, a second inquiry began about Charlie Kenelley's drinking. Thom could not believe it was actually happening.

"Have you ever seen Father Kenelley drink when about to conduct mass or religious services?"

When Thom hesitated, the bishop gently probed with the same pained look. "It's all right, father. He's only human, like all of us."

"Well, once when he'd had a few drinks, Herschel—er, Monsignor Schaeffer—asked him to take novena."

"What about in the morning?"

Thom had once found Charlie on the rectory steps on his way to early mass for the nuns. It was impossible to rouse him, and Joe Quinn had later dragged him up to bed.

Thom looked up squarely and fiercely at Freddie Weber. "I don't think he ever drinks in the morning."

"How often would you say he is intoxicated?"

He wanted to scream, but he said softly, "Never often enough to hurt anyone."

"We're not asking for judgments, father. Just facts!"

"I can't answer. He probably drinks more than he should at times. But so do a lot of people." The bishop squirmed minutely, toying with his pectoral cross and twisting his ring in a private agony he seemed powerless to resolve.

"Thank you, father. We remind you of the secrecy of this hearing."

Thom walked out the door, and a victimized Herschel—who really did not want to hurt anyone—was there in the lobby, smoking a cigar. He nodded warmly as Don's too pretty face politely dismissed Thom.

"Thank you for coming, father."

Thom wondered what had happened to the gray-haired woman who had been chancery receptionist for fourteen years.

Two weeks later, a tanned Dave Beauchamp greeted Thom warmly.

"God, I missed you, guy—but not this place. You should taste the fruit down there! You gotta go! Dennis wants to be a missionary in Nassau."

Three days later Dave was called to the chancery. Joe Beahan explained "serious moral misgivings" about his relationship with Dennis Tracy, saying that their separation had been a warning that was ignored and that now Beauchamp and Tracy were considered "contumacious" under the definition of Canon 2242. Further contact of any kind would result in a *latae sententiae* censure. He was to pack without a word to anyone and report immediately to the Trappist Monastery in Gethsemani, Kentucky. Suspended from all priestly powers until further notice. He was not informed of Dennis's destination.

The following afternoon, a sober-faced Charlie Kenelley was stripped of his chancellorship and sent to a Carmelite

Convalescent Center, in the Arizona desert, for alcoholic priests. He made no defence. The same secrecy was invoked.

Two weeks later it was announced in the *Sheffield Journal* that Freddie Weber had been appointed chancellor of the diocese and Joe Beahan its vicar-general. They would be invested as monsignors, with the rank of domestic prelate, the following month. Donations for their expensive vestments and an offering to the pope would be accepted at the cathedral rectory.

A strange *aggiornamento* had come to Sheffield—and it had only just begun. Thom's heart ached painfully with the loss of his best friend, and without Charlie Kenelley he felt defenseless against the new onslaught.

Changes of assignment, usually made after ordinations in June, were delayed until the middle of August 1962.

Jim O'Brien got his first parish in Daltonville, twelve miles outside of Kirkwood; Mike Fogarty was sent as assistant to Jensen, midway between Sheffield and Kirkwood; Thom Maguire was moved fifty miles away to Christ the King parish in Steelmont. An upsetting appointment. And the Mexican work was turned over to the Catholic social service agency.

It was difficult to assess why Bishop Schmidt acceded to the unmanly coup, since he had been raised and trained in a chauvinist Church that rewarded strong, decisive men like the Doyles and Kenelleys and Jim O'Briens. It may well have been the insecurity generated by Vatican II or the glib self-assurance of Weber and Beahan. Schmidt had lived for almost twenty-five years in the obscurity of Sheffield Diocese, and his own ambitions of an archbishopric in Detroit or Cleveland, never really strong, were long since dead. It was also possible that he had simply given up to the subtle ravages of alcohol. Thom had hardly seen him sober since Freddie and Joe returned from Rome.

Yet in some profound way Thom loved his bishop, not simply for the approval he had given, but rather for his gentle concern for the poor and lonely. His pastoral letters and public statements, not to mention the programs he had financed, demonstrated a sincere effort to heal and to feed the hungry, and even his brooding insobrieties seemed more a temporary balm for a wearying apostolate than an escape from personal pain. He was a good shepherd who would have died for his flock. He approached Thom after a solemn mass honoring Mary's Assumption into heaven. It was August 15. His gentle eyes were concerned.

"I hope you'll be happy with Monsignor Rabidoux in Steelmont." Thom knew Rabidoux's reputation as a firm disciplinarian of unruly young priests. He was nicknamed the "priest breaker," and Thom was actually offended by the assignment.

"Haven't I pleased you?" Thom asked him almost suppliantly.

"Of course, father, of course!" The bishop's voice was suddenly choked, and his hands trembled terribly. "You have always been an outstanding priest, an example to your old bishop." Then he touched Thom's shoulder. "Monsignor Weber will talk to you."

It was a cold, officious Freddie Weber in full dress who confronted him. Crisply.

"You've done outstanding work—but there have been dangerous outbursts and—" he looked away "—a series of letters and phone calls to a young woman at Dominican College."

Thom turned the color of Freddie's cassock. "It was only a friendship. She's engaged—"

"We're not punishing you, father, it's merely that you need seasoning for your great abilities." He glanced down at a manila folder and leafed slowly. "Your seminary was, well—unusual, and we still see evidence of the same conflicts."

A short letter from Jack Durrell after a province meeting of the Michigan bishops—to recommend episcopal candidates—had warned him, but he had resented the advice.

> Subdue your beautiful Irish honesty if you want to make the best use of your extraordinary talents. Msgr. Weber, especially, can be dangerous. Bishop Schmidt is extremely fond of you and we reinforced his admiration, but Weber's misgivings can prove your undoing.

He had crushed the letter firmly into the wastebasket, certain that his Church was not a politburo. God was still in charge. Mike Fogarty had fervently reaffirmed his reflections—and laughed for five minutes when Thom served Freddie lard for provolone at one of the Saturday night gatherings.

Now, as Thom looked sullenly at Monsignor Weber, there was nothing to laugh about.

"A couple of years with Monsignor Rabidoux can be of great help. We hope you will accept this assignment in the spirit of Christ." The words were ill suited to his lips and he seemed embarrassed uttering them.

"I guess I have no choice."

"Not really." He smiled softly. "But you can choose to make the experience profitable—"

It was the first time Thom Maguire actually realized that war had been declared.

When the smoke of reassignments and exile had cleared, the dozen or so parishes within twenty miles of Sheffield revealed a curious roster of priests. A confident new breed lacking the traditional virilities. The celibacy that had once survived by excess of maleness had now capitulated to neutered gentility. With tatted surplices and decorative albs and garrulous dreams of liturgical reforms, they gathered effusively around Joe Beahan and Freddie Weber with fastidious tastes in food and expensive assortments of tailored silks and pointed Italian shoes. The gentle disciple John, who leaned on Jesus's breast, had replaced the sweating, swearing, brawling Peter as paradigm of the apostles, and a new Church was emerging. Full of guitars, folk hymns, and inverted altars; stuffed with vernacular phrases and love shibboleths that grew clichéd a thousand times faster than mellifluous Latin. Most of all, it was becoming a Church bereft of mystery, as if some ineffable God had been transformed into a prissy castrated theology. The God of Exodus was a fierce desert chieftain, and the God of Rome wore a full white beard. Even Christ had upended the tables of tax gatherers and challenged Herod and Pilate to silence. And bore a staggering cross no woman alive could have budged.

Nor could the smiling fops who took charge of Sheffield Diocese, reforming its catechetics with catchwords, decorating its liturgy, and covering the wounds of a crucified Christ with silk vestments. They chattered of the "people of God," scorned the rosary and novenas, and ignored the real wounds of the mothers with too many children and the frustrated, silent men. Especially the men. Overwhelmed for centuries by ecclesiastical arrogance, they had lost their voice, and now they were smothered by an effeminate distraction that still forbade the appearance of a God who understood their ancient pain.

The dream of Pope John had become a nightmare characterized by an indecisive, confused assemblage that set aside old people in an attempt to seduce youth who would only be briefly amused. The only kind of men who could have successfully led the Church into the modern world were removed from power. And in Sheffield, Michigan, the people shook hands during the kiss of peace at Sunday mass and blushed at the meaningless new ceremonies that began to take away the identity of a childhood Church they loved passionately despite its faults.

Thus a small diocese in midwest America became a poignant symbol of a great Church's mortality. No one seemed worried.

Two days after Thom arrived at Christ the King parish in Steelmont, Elvin Ward was announced as auxiliary bishop of Washtenaw Diocese to assist an aging Bishop Malloy. Thom's classmate, Stanley Skorski, was made monsignor, with the rank of papal chamberlain, six days after his thirty-second birthday, and he was installed as rector of Saint Robert's Seminary in Grandville.

Thom was deeply depressed, and he spent two hours in the presence of the Blessed Sacrament. Begging his God for humility and peace.

And somehow finding it.

Thom's new pastor, Monsignor Rabidoux, was dean of Steelmont and founder of the vital Christ the King parish. He was a wiry man with gray hair, dark penetrating eyes, and a prominent French nose. A devoted priest for thirty-five years, he had worked hard, gaining the respect of his parishioners and even the love of those who needed him at times of crisis. A series of difficult assistants, who usually stayed for a year or two of disciplined direction, had developed his reputation as a reformer of troubled priests, but it had in no way hindered the growth of a loyal and expanding congregation.

The rectory was located in a residential area some

three blocks from the church, and Thom was shown to a small, neat room. He would share a bathroom with the pastor and his seventy-year-old aunt who served as his housekeeper, Marie Tremont, now Rabidoux's only family.

"It's modest, father, but we're not in business to live in our rooms." His previous assistant built model trains as well as his own toy mountains and bridges. Marie had skinned her leg more than once until the pastor had instructed the bizarre priest to make his own bed, and Thom was expected to continue that tradition. Rabidoux outlined the time for meals and asserted gently that he expected Thom to be home by ten o'clock except on days off. The dark eyes frowned. "I like to start with a clean slate, father, and form my own opinions. If I have any complaints, I'll make them known, and I hope you will return the courtesy." A warm smile relieved some of the tension.

"It's a small house, but Marie keeps to herself pretty much and is as neat as a pin. She likes to watch a little TV with us in the evenings, and I hope you won't mind." It was a canonical violation that had become common.

"Not at all, monsignor."

"You'd probably like to unpack."

He did. And wondered if Monsignor Rabidoux would ever call him Thom.

The people at Christ the King were thrilled with the new assistant, who preached beautifully, sang melodiously the ancient Gregorian chant, and took time to learn their names. His religion classes were an exciting contrast to those of his predecessor, and the high school coach was delighted to have an athletic director who could accurately throw a football fifty yards. Midway in November, convert classes began to swell, a stream of marriage cases came to Thom's church office, and the enrollment at the parish high school increased noticeably. Occasionally, Thom did not make it home by ten.

"You're working late." Monsignor Rabidoux admired Thom's zeal and wondered if the young priest could stem the increasing leakage from mass attendance.

"Lots to do."

Like most Catholic pastors over fifty, Maurice Rabidoux was content to manage parish finances and visit a few favored sick. Unlike Herschel Schaeffer, he had built two churches and was already raising money for a splendid Romanesque building to replace a Christ the King parish hall, which could then be converted into classrooms and a gym. He was obsessively worried by a serious decrease in contributions.

Once he confronted Thom after Thom arrived home late from a high school dance.

"Far too late, father."

Marie nodded agreement.

"I get to know the kids outside of class."

"You can waste a lot of time with the young."

Again Marie agreed. "They'll wear you out," she said, and she retold a story of an ungrateful student who had borrowed a car from one of the assistant priests and wrecked "the distributor or something."

Thom was furious that Rabidoux saw more merit in watching TV and listening to Marie's monologues, but he ignored the rebuke and fixed a peanut butter sandwich, then cleaned up the kitchen carefully, as he had been instructed.

Meals were unimaginative and starchy.

"If there's anything special you want—"

"No, it's fine." He complimented a mediocre meat loaf.

Contrary to plenary council regulations, they ate all their meals together—like mother and father and thirty-two-year-old son. Adolescent son.

"She's part of the family—"

Marie inhibited or interrupted shoptalk with brusque ex cathedra statements on everything from going steady ("they should be working") to convert classes ("the catechism's enough if they mean business"). But she grew deeply fond of Thom who charmed her with inexpensive gifts and had unruffled patience for her lengthy stories. An occasional note of gratitude from Margaret "for taking care of my son" beatified the relationship.

As Thom's popularity grew, high school and college girls found excuses to drop in. Monsignor Rabidoux warned discreetly of feminine wiles and usually made tasteless and uncharacteristic comments about menstrual odors and anal fixations.

His favorite shady jokes were gross tales of women peeing their pants or suddenly flowing during weddings, or of the encumbrances of senile sex and leaking prostates.

Yet he himself was delighted by any feminine attention—almost like a shy teen-ager—and he never indulged his tasteless humor in Marie's presence.

By the spring of Thom's first year, Maurice Rabidoux was almost convinced that Weber's letter of warning to him about Thom had been an exaggeration. He had never trusted the slick Freddie, but a lifetime of unquestioning obedience responded to any ecclesiastical authority as to God. His first real suspicion of Thom emerged when two short-skirted secretaries came for evening appointments four or five times within a month. When he quizzed, Thom commented briefly about Catholic graduates needing to meet other Catholics in suitable social settings. They were planning a Catholic Alumni Club that would embrace the whole county, offering entertainment and adult education for young working people not eligible for the Catholic Newman clubs at colleges. One evening the pastor heard high-pitched giggling behind the closed door and pictured bare, shapely legs.

He burst in without knocking. The girls shrieked from their couch, and Thom almost capsized in his swivel desk chair.

"You girls get out of here and stop trying to get father!" They stared in disbelief, and Thom was pale and speechless.

"Did you hear me? Get out!"

They gathered up purses and folders, adjusted short skirts several times, and left.

He turned to Thom almost meekly. "These women are out to get you, father. Sniffing your cassock. I don't want them hanging around. And leave your door open! It's safer!" He started to tell the story of a blackmailed priest, then thought better of it when Thom looked away. He departed quickly.

A young couple arrived for pre-Cana instructions. For an hour Thom lectured on creative married love, patient understanding, and the positive side of occasional sexual abstinence. The young woman's eyes were misty when he talked of a man loving his wife as his own body, "even as Christ loved his Church. And died for it."

When the couple left, Thom walked the dark neighborhood for almost an hour, returning to the rectory just before eleven. Marie had retired to her bath and Maurice Rabidoux looked up warmly from a "shoot-'em-up" show.

"Sit down, father."

Thom slipped off his coat without responding.

"Marie left a piece of apple pie."

Thom ignored the pie and sat on the uncomfortable couch, slouching his legs toward the TV.

"I want to tell you something, monsignor."

Monsignor quickly turned off the TV. "If it's about those women, you can't be too—"

"It's about you and me!" The deliberate tone and flashing eyes silenced the wiry Frenchman.

"I don't know what kind of report you got about me, and I really don't give a damn! I just want you to know that I'm a thirty-two-year-old man, and that I will never again—I repeat, never again—be treated like a seminarian!"

Maurice Rabidoux trembled slightly as he spoke softly. "I'm very pleased with your work. Like I've said—"

"I'm not through yet!" The blue eyes flashed angrily and the firm jaw was thrust out.

"And if you ever break in on me like that again, you can look for another assistant!" He grabbed his coat and collar and strode up to his room.

No one had ever spoken like that to Maurice Rabidoux. And the strange thing was that it pleased him.

Charlie Kenelley was dried out in the desert and sent as pastor to Hamlin, a countrified village not far from Jensen, where Mike Fogarty was. Charlie's eighty-year-old mother lived in as a surprisingly spry housekeeper, unaware that he had been anywhere but on diocesan assignment, although she was delighted that he had ceased drinking.

Dave Beauchamp sent Thom a tragic letter from California, where he had been reassigned. He was still shocked by the whole incident.

> I can't imagine why it happened. If General Motors had done this, I'd have legal recourse. The very thought of anything with Dennis would be repulsive if it weren't so ridiculous. Two years from having my own parish and I'm at the bottom of the list under a cloud. If I'd gotten someone pregnant I'd probably get a Laetare medal.

He had not lost his sense of humor.

I'm afraid to shake hands with the janitor, so I do my work and wear out Verdi's Requiem. God I miss you!

All Thom knew of Dennis was that he was working somewhere in Georgia. Beauchamp's absence was a permanent ache for Thom. Something irreplaceable had left his priesthood. He wrote a newsy letter about the coup and Elvin Ward's bishopric, promising to assassinate Herschel and the three musketurds on Good Friday. He promised a prolonged visit soon, mentioning Chet Golas as a possible friend at Alameda Naval Air Station.

Gradually he waded into the problems of Christ the King parish until the name of Father Maguire became a household word, as it had in Sheffield. He bought a small cot for the room off his office, took over a lavatory, and began sleeping in the parish hall, working as late as he wanted. The unfamiliar faces brought new energy. Maurice Rabidoux never questioned him again, and Thom served the people eighteen hours a day without complaint, occasionally driving to Kirkwood to visit his parents or eating dinner in Sheffield with Charlie and Roselle. Sometimes he visited the devoutly pastoral Mike Fogarty or the hardworking Jim O'Brien, usually at Charlie Kenelley's rectory, where they complained of the new regime and played midnight poker.

Marie admitted to Monsignor Rabidoux, "Father Maguire's the best you ever had."

"No comparison."

She also knew that Rabidoux loved Thom but could never say it.

"He's almost like a son," she said. "Or sunshine."

In the fall, a proud Bishop Schmidt made his way to Rome to attend the Second Vatican Council. Freddie Weber and Joe Beahan acted as his *periti* and Bobbie Foley as secretary and errand boy. The two new monsignors renewed acquaintances with smiling classmates with modest stories of success. Bishop Schmidt's two previous *ad limina* visits to bring diocesan reports to Pope Pius XII had been almost anonymous, since a shy bishop from an obscure diocese generally received little attention, but now, in the company of his gregarious *periti*, he lunched with Archbishop Verentini, assistant to Cardinal Ottaviani of the awesome Holy Office, and bragged of his diocesan growth to Cardinal Ruggini of the Sacred Consistory. He did not admit to an alarming loss of the faithful in the past two years.

A tall, almost femininely beautiful undersecretary to the cardinal, Monsignor Teddy Dorrow, originally from Boston, attended the bishop's every wish. Hardly thirty-five, Teddy had been in Rome since his ordination, serving in various curial appointments, and it was rumored that the powerful Ruggini was grooming him as successor. As doctoral students, Weber, Beahan, and Dorrow had become inseparable friends, and it was Dorrow who introduced them to the lavish parties of the Italian nobility that were frequented by power ecclesiastics. They covered art galleries, concerts, theater, and outdoor operas, and they dined in the most elegant of Rome's restaurants. Teddy's expensive habits were handsomely funded by a wealthy couple who were intimate friends of the historic Calonnas. It was rumored by his many enemies and joked about by as many friends that both husband and wife were secretly in love with Teddy. It was a very Italian joke which Bobbie Foley pretended to appreciate. Teddy only smiled seraphically.

He was consistently gracious to Bishop Schmidt, supplying an air-conditioned Fiat and more suitable accommodations, arranging trips to catacombs, basilicas, and Michelangelo's Florence, and organizing exciting dinners with Vatican officials, American hierarchs, or theologians Bishop Schmidt had only read about. When a favorite scotch was hard to locate, Teddy sent a complimentary case to his room, and a dozen times he assisted Bobbie Foley in carrying a stumbling, grateful bishop to bed. He often called in the morning from his office to inquire about Schmidt's condition, now and then making an appointment for the bishop with his own masseur.

Bishop Schmidt could not really consume much alcohol, and his recovery periods were rapid. Two scotches and dinner wine were enough to slur his speech, slip out his lower plate, and convince strangers that he had been nipping all afternoon. The drinking made it impossible for anyone to recognize his real charity and wise pastoral insights, and even though he instructed Bobbie Foley to see that he received no wine, Teddy's frequent toasts were usually irresistible.

The bishop often ate quiet meals in his room with Bobbie Foley or in the hotel dining room with friendly American bishops who were as confused as he was by the unfamiliar theology and Latin. Long council sessions and interminable position papers were exhausting, but he read them carefully to attempt some comprehension of the new directions.

As much as he was thrilled by the attention paid him, he was glad to leave for New York at the end of November with Bobbie Foley and a disappointed Freddie Weber, who wanted to remain with Teddy and Joe Beahan to visit Paris. Despite Teddy's pleas, the bishop remained adamant.

"I need my chancellor to help translate these directives into action and to prepare a pastoral letter." He was deadly serious about transmitting Pope John's desires to his own hungry flock.

Joe and Teddy traveled alone.

The bishop's pastoral letter at Christmas was truly beautiful. A hopeful message for a suffering and confused laity in a rapidly changing world. Begging them not to be disturbed by unsettling changes; telling of Pope John's loving concern and of hundreds of bishops of every color mingling at the first council session, debating as had never been possible before in Christendom. Even Protestant observers had not been ignored, and the pope had stretched out his arms to visiting Jews: "I am Joseph, your brother!"

The letter was read at all the masses on Christmas Day. On January sixth, the Feast of the Epiphany honored the Magi at Bethlehem and the tribute of an entire world to the Infant King—as if to celebrate Vatican II.

> The kings of Tharsis and the Isles shall offer gifts;
> The kings of Arabia and Saba shall bring tribute;
> All the kings shall pay homage; all nations shall serve him!

An excited Bishop Schmidt delivered a loving homily at Immaculate Conception Cathedral and confided to Herschel Schaeffer that he had not had a drink since he returned from Rome.

On the afternoon of the same day, Schmidt was

removed from office. By order of the Holy See through the apostolic delegate in Washington, D.C.

Freddie Weber was named as apostolic administrator until the appointment of a new bishop.

To the laity it was only a sudden and unexpected retirement, unusual for a sixty-seven-year-old bishop who, despite a drinking problem they were largely unaware of, was still in good health. And seemingly exhilarated by Pope John's council. In his letter of resignation he sadly cited the need for younger leadership amidst the strain of council debates and new ecumenical challenges, and he expressed his hope that God was satisfied with his unworthy stewardship.

Then he proceeded to stay drunk in his room for three days.

Charlie Kenelley offered him a private house near the rectory in Hamlin and promised that his mother would look after them both. The bishop warmly declined and took up residence with the Charity nuns at their hospital in Kirkwood, the only other genuine offer he had received. He was no longer a bishop, but a broken old man. At a farewell dinner at the Sheffield Hilton, Freddie Weber was master of ceremonies, and Joe Beahan gave a statistical history of his Christlike work—"thirty-two schools, twenty-one convents, forty-nine churches"—then presented him with a ten-thousand-dollar purse and a new Cadillac. Also a spiritual bouquet from the children of his diocese. Margaret sent a nice letter and enclosed John Patrick's check for a hundred bucks. A sober bishop rose to thank the priests for their loyalty.

"The priesthood can be a lonely life, but to be a bishop is to stand all alone. Even without intimates."

He glanced at Freddie and Joe flanking him and then directed his eyes to the assembled priests.

"I never really wanted to be a bishop. It came as a surprise and was a heavy burden I have endured. Now that it's over there's really no place to go where I wouldn't be in the way. The hospital in Kirkwood seems the least complicated. Please forgive my faults. Good-bye and God bless you."

His eyes were moist, and Charlie Kenelley and thirty more were crying. So was Thom Maguire, wondering what he could have done. And what the Sheffield Diocese would become.

Freddie Weber announced a reception in the cathedral rectory where almost half of the two hundred priests returned to sip Herschel's liqueurs. The dispossessed bishop sipped scotch slowly, chatting softly with Charlie Kenelley, and as he got up to leave, he noticed Thom. "Keep the faith, father." His eyes were moist with deep affection and sadness.

"I will, bishop." He struggled with words as he knelt to kiss the ring for the last time. "You were a good bishop —and I've loved you."

The same evening Thom drove to Hamlin at Charlie Kenelley's invitation. Mike Fogarty and Jim O'Brien were already there. Charlie, sipping only ginger ale, offered Thom a glass of scotch.

Jim O'Brien was angry. "We're living in the diocese of pussyville."

Mike Fogarty agreed. "Bunch of goddamned queers running things!" Thom joined the bitter protest until Charlie Kenelley put down his glass and lit a cigarette.

"Not queers, Mike. Give queers some credit! These sons of bitches are capons! Goddamned eunuchs that don't really give a shit about anyone. That's the danger. I don't know what's happened to the Church."

They grew silent until O'Brien spoke. "Maybe everybody's wrong! We drink too much; they giggle about new surplices. Nobody faces the real problems. This isn't what Pope John meant. It's like he's been made a fool of!"

Kenelley sucked the ice in his glass and spat it out. "Gentlemen, council or no council, I think the Church is in for some dark days!"

There was nothing else to say. Fogarty's round Irish face was flushed. "Deal 'em," he said softly.

And they played poker until after midnight.

Holy Week services in Immaculate Conception Cathedral were relaxed and unfamiliar with Freddie Weber in charge. Attendance was off, and few knew what was happening. All the certainties of so many years were gone. Thom was called from Steelmont to serve as an acolyte. A solemn Epistle chant with thrilling cadences, followed by a never-used Gospel melody for the first-class feasts, echoed through the cathedral. The sanctuary was flowing with knee-length surplices, and a dozen young clerics removed their Gucci sandals at the episcopal throne as a sober Freddie Weber washed their feet. Later the ceremony was dramatized in the sanctuary by fine actors in ancient symbol of Christ kneeling humbly before Peter. Thom watched sadly.

The novelties were not without a certain beauty, but the historic Catholic Church, in Sheffield as everywhere, had become a flock without a shepherd. The Church had been sacred and predictable. Whatever its faults, and they were many, the Church was never merely a medium for imaginative clerics to find creative outlet for their religious fancies. The crucifixion and death of Jesus, whatever their redemptive significance, were as old and familiar as the Gospels themselves, and loyal Catholics who had built the churches and even the seminaries had been taught from infancy that the Church could not change because it was Christ.

Thom knew they had flocked to Latin masses they didn't understand, recited creeds too complex to fathom, and smothered any doubts against their holy faith, not because they were stupid or only afraid, but because the Church had given them a strength and an identity they could not do without. When Fridays disappeared and Lent passed away, they were puzzled. When English appeared in the mass, they were startled, even willing to be pleased. But when the ancient ceremonies that had tested their patience and measured their faith were changed to suit personal tastes, they were outraged. It was an offense against the courage and discipline that made them Catholic. Thus, a cathedral that two years before had played to standing room only, now had plenty of seats. The Tre Ore, dramatizing the seven last words of Christ, was cancelled. The all-night adoration on Holy Thursday was curtailed at midnight. Wrinkled old faces, and some not so wrinkled, wondered if it were a sign of the end.

After the altars were elegantly stripped, in symbol of Christ's death, the Eucharist was removed to a newly decorated repository of flowing oriental silks and bronze lamps that replaced the traditional candelabra. Created uniquely by Bobbie Foley and three seminarians from Pius XII Seminary.

On Good Friday there was an artistic driftwood cross

and a dramatic reading of the Passion with priests and major seminarians acting out the parts. The cathedral was one-third empty. It was agreed that Freddie was a superb Christ, but a young deacon from Jensen's Holy Angels was an absolutely incredible Pilate. The *Venite, adoremus* at the adoration of the cross was done in five-part harmony, a big improvement on the cathedral choir, and for the first time in memory the purple veil slipped easily from the cross. Yet a number of parishioners were upset when the crucified Christ emerged in priestly vestments (which Freddie Weber explained as an act of faith in the resurrection), and at least twenty-five people walked out.

No one asked the vanishing parishioners what they thought.

At the end of April, Freddie Weber's term as apostolic administrator was abruptly abbreviated by an astounding announcement: Elvin Ward was appointed bishop of Sheffield, with Joe Beahan as his auxiliary. Freddie went into brief seclusion at the diocesan retreat house, then emerged to run the diocese until the bishops were consecrated.

Mike Fogarty paid off a diocesan pool in which Joe Beahan was five to two and Elvin Ward eight to one. Freddie Weber had been even money.

Thom Maguire did not know whether to laugh or cry. He called Mike Fogarty.

"What the hell difference does it make? Just keep your nose clean and get a little place of your own with a decent income."

Thom wasn't sure. Fogarty had never faced the anger of Elvin Ward. Bill Collins read the news in his law office in Washtenaw and sent Thom a telegram:

IF YOU PLAN A COUP DON'T LEAVE ME OUT.
SNOW WHITE AND SEVEN DWARFS FOR POPE!

John Patrick heard the news from Margaret, who read it in the *Kirkwood Gazette*, and he remembered a young ball player who left for the seminary the year of Jack's death. Then he asked Margaret for a drink.

Pope John XXIII died on June 3, 1963. Never had a pope's death caused such grief. All Thom's hopes for another kind of Church, already dimmed by the coup in Sheffield, were now dead also.

❧ ❧ ❧

A week later, when Jim stopped by to visit John Patrick, Margaret nodded coldly and stepped aside as he walked toward his father's chair, then she followed him cautiously across the living room. Jim, exhausted by his work, had not seen his father for almost three weeks, and he was startled by the change in John Patrick's appearance. Margaret had never mentioned two serious attacks of emphysema and a severe kidney infection, and Jim realized that John Patrick was in far worse shape than anyone knew. He had watched his father's gradual surrender to Margaret's greater strength and the increased religiosity that had marked the last two years—his too-devout recitation of the family rosary and his willingness to drive with Margaret frequently to daily mass—yet Jim was not prepared for this sudden, frightening transformation. John Patrick's eyes were glassy, his breathing labored, and he refused to shave. No matter how sick, he had always been immaculately clean.

"Why the hell didn't you tell me?" he asked Margaret. "He should be in the hospital. Right now!"

"I wasn't sure anyone cared. I know you've all got your own lives. Besides, you can't tell your father anything."

Jim hated her martyrdom. "Well, for God's sake, I could have taken him."

"There's no need to swear," she said. "He's ready to do God's will."

John Patrick's eyes were watery and his figure was small and bent in the familiar recliner. Only his hands were the same, soft and shapely, and Jim noticed the rosary beads where an ashtray had once been. John Patrick grinned broadly as if to tease him about his cowlick or his clumsy walk. In his mid-sixties, he looked eighty-five.

"It's about time you got home," he whispered hoarsely. "Do you need money?" Confused, he thought Jim was returning from Marquette. He laughed quietly, the same proud laugh. His eyes were distant as he struggled with some memory, then took charge of himself with unlikely discipline.

He pointed smugly to the cowboy boots that Jim had bought him for his last birthday to wear around the place in the country he had always dreamed of. Now they hung pathetically on skinny legs. He smiled again. "I can still kick a few asses." The feeble rasping voice cut Jim almost in half.

At Jim's command, Margaret quickly brought his medicine and adjusted the rosary. John Patrick started to protest but thought better of it and shifted to a more alert position in his chair as Jim, suddenly a concerned doctor, attended him.

The medicine and Jim's visit seemed to revive him. He became more talkative and his eyes regained a spark Jim had always associated with his anger. In the present again, he asked briefly about Jim's marriage, out of Margaret's hearing, and told him to stand his ground.

"You've been a good son. I'm proud of you."

Later in the evening, John Patrick drifted into some hallucinatory reverie, again thinking Jim was still in college and would return to Marquette.

"Not much of a football team." He glanced at Jim as if he hadn't seen him. "Are you leaving tomorrow?"

Jim stroked his arm. "Yes, dad."

"I want to tell you something." He stared at Jim, wide-eyed and childlike, his eyes bluer than his second son had ever remembered. His mouth remained slightly open when he paused. He had never been so direct. The hoarseness was gone. "Life's a pile of shit," he said.

Margaret crossed herself. "John!"

"She knows it, too. Just a circle leading nowhere."

"There's a better world, John Patrick." She spoke as to a naughty child, but he ignored her.

He was suddenly furious; his body looked lean and younger as the senile stoop disappeared and he sat up straight.

"How the hell do you know?" He shouted it, coughed momentarily, then regained his voice. "And if whoever runs this world has anything to do with the next—he can fuck himself."

Jim had never heard him use the word in Margaret's presence. He almost smiled, but the rattling cough erupted to frighten him.

Margaret was pale with disbelief. "John—"

"Don't *John* me! Why the hell—it's John this and John

that—monsignor said and sister wants! Putting up with this bullshit! All these years!"

"I hear you, dad."

"Don't side with him!" Margaret was on the verge of the desperate tears Jim remembered from childhood.

"Hell no," John Patrick continued. "We all sided with the Church. Not a damn picture in the house that doesn't smell of it! God! I was so weak."

Jim held his arm. "You weren't weak, you were trapped!" Jim said it softly to calm him. "You did the best you could."

Margaret began whining. "God knows I did my best. All that I've had to put up with all these years. I never thought—"

"Goddamn it, Margaret! Shut up! I'm tired of hearing you! I never pleased you. Only the goddamned priests. They knew everything!"

Margaret was finally silent, and his fury, silenced for years, frightened away her tears. She was cowering.

Jim feared an attack and he continued to talk calmly. "You were a good father. You tried—"

"Like hell—I knew all the time! I even let her down—she was a good woman when I married her. I just wasn't a man!"

He leaned back in the recliner breathing hoarsely. Then he looked up at her. "I want a drink."

"You need—"

"No priest! I want a drink. Grand Dad, straight!"

She hesitated.

"Get it!"

Margaret moved quickly at his command as she hadn't in years.

"More, woman! I want a real drink!"

He took the glass firmly in his hand, then swallowed it slowly with obvious pleasure. He chuckled softly, clicked his boots together feebly, and looked at them both with a new smile.

"I feel better." He moved forward in his chair as if to make a speech, gesturing with his drink. Then he gurgled softly, gave a startled look, and dropped the glass, slowly. As if he were reluctant to let go.

He died before the priest arrived. Monsignor Doyle was at a confirmation dinner with the bishop. The flustered new assistant arrived fifteen minutes after Jim tenderly closed his father's eyes and turned gently, almost professionally, to Margaret. "He's dead, mother!" John Patrick was still in the recliner with the cowboy boots arching awkwardly on his cold legs. Margaret could not move.

The nervous young priest gave his first conditional Extreme Unction in English, a translation of the ancient Latin words of forgiveness over each sense, absolving eyes and ears and frozen lips. Then, with stiff dignity, Mulaley's son came and took the corpse. Margaret sat with her faithless son on the couch across from the same chair in which they heard her husband's final protest. Not yet weeping, she offered coffee for the priest, who declined politely.

"He lost his mind at the end. God can't hold him accountable—"

"I'm sure He won't." Jim put his arms around her.

"I tried to be a good wife." Then the tears came.

"You were a good wife—for a very long time." He was glad he understood her helplessness. There was no reason for bitterness.

"It doesn't seem so long." The tears flowed freely. She seemed small and frightened like a child and pleased that Jim was friendly again. His coldness to her hurt more than she could ever have admitted.

Jim stayed with her that night and the next day until she was calm, and her friends delivered the consolation Irish women excel at. Father Thom traded assignments with a classmate and was able to be near home for two weeks. He still treated Jim with cool formality and asked nothing personal. The evening before the funeral, Jim sat for an hour or so in his father's recliner, consoling a brokenhearted McNulty who was crying helplessly.

"There's not much left." The old fighter was hunched over. He looked up and grinned. "God, he loved them boots—"

Jim nodded.

"And he loved you."

Jim nodded again and felt the tears.

He helped McNulty into a cab and returned to the recliner. His father's medicine had fallen behind the cushion. He reached for it and felt the pages of a magazine wedged there. He pulled it out carefully. It was a well-worn copy of *Nymphomania California,* and it fell open in Jim's hands to a picture of three big-breasted women sucking and fucking an ecstatic man.

He tucked it under his coat. Not exactly sure why it made him feel so relieved.

He got in his car, drove toward the edge of the woods, and parked at Walker School. It was still barely light. By the time he reached Sandy's grave, the moon was offering an ethereal light that turned Lemmert's Grove into a shimmering grotto. The stones on the grave were still in careful order as he rested against the familiar mound of soft grass and gazed at the summer stars. It was warm, but a cool breeze rustled through the darkly glistening oak leaves. Jim's tears flowed freely again, and they were tears that longed to be words of respect and affection for a man he truly had loved.

John Patrick had been trapped until the very end, and his final drink and toast were a legacy to Jim. He realized now that his father had never escaped from the rattle of death. Vicarious hope in his children had momentarily freed him, thus he had loved Jack best of all. Jack dared to do what John Patrick only dreamed of silently—beat against the very bars of Kirkwood and Saint Raphael's, demanding release with such ferocity that he had no choice but to tease death.

Thom had been his father's rising hope until Margaret seduced him to her priesthood. Only in childhood and early adolescence had he evoked that proud smile Jim could never forget. Thom's priesthood was a deep disappointment, and John Patrick's final refusal of a priest was an angry rebuke of Margaret's victory. Jim was his last hope, the only real Maguire left, the pale and silent one his father never really understood. Until the very end. Then his death shouted that Jim must live his own life as John Patrick Maguire had never done.

Jim watched the moon slip behind a smoky cloud and felt that somehow he had surpassed his father, no matter the lonely and circuitous route. He had become more than just his father's child, which few children ever do. Children shout, "Look, daddy, look! Watch me!" but now there was nobody watching Jim. His own wife and even his children had learned to live without him. Thom had given up on him; Margaret paid token respect to a memory; and

Anne and her devout husband didn't speak to him. Tim, gentle and friendly, was hardly a Maguire.

Jim's life was his own, without a moment owed to anyone or an hour committed to the past. No more statues or angels to appease, no apologies to make or guilty prayers to a whining God. John Patrick was his final tie with childhood, and John Patrick was dead. Now his oldest son was finally beginning to come alive.

He walked back to the car and drove home. The house was dark. On the kitchen table there was a note from Connie about fixing the toilet in the children's bathroom.

Elvin Ward, the new bishop of Sheffield, celebrated John Patrick's funeral mass, an irony that Jim and Thom noted. There was also a sympathetic word to Margaret and a gentle handshake that thrilled her beyond expression. Stanley Skorski appeared in full monsignorial dress and talked as if Thom were an older altar boy. Margaret was delighted by the honor and the five hundred people at the funeral, a hundred of them priests and nuns.

Jim wondered aloud to Thom if John Patrick were turning in his grave, and Thom was disturbed at Jim's levity.

"It's kind of tragic really." Thom was still remembering Stan Skorski's greasy arrogance.

"Our whole family is." He had already quarreled briefly with Anne that morning about cremation and Catholic education.

"How's that?" Thom asked him.

"Christ! Jack's dead and so's the old man. Margaret's lost in some God, Anne's a bitch, and I'm a reprobate. Even you seem miserable."

Suddenly Thom wanted to share himself with Jim, but he was still afraid.

Jim made a final, more gentle, attempt. "Thom, we haven't been close for a long time, maybe never. I didn't make it easy, I know, but I really admired you and can even admit I was very jealous at times. And hurt. You were the chosen son, and I always felt I had to prove something."

Thom was caught off guard. "I didn't mean to—"

"I'm not jealous anymore. A little confused, maybe, but not jealous." He looked directly at his brother and his eyes were moist. "I want to be your friend—I really miss you and care about you. What's happened to us?"

Thom fidgeted nervously. He missed Dave Beauchamp terribly, and he wanted to tell Jim about everything that hurt him. His insides churned, but he only stuttered painfully, "It's just that your lack of respect for the Church—it's like your life makes a mockery of all that I am!"

"Christ, can't we disagree and still be friends?"

"Jim, I pray for you every day. I worry about you and Connie and the kids. I know that doesn't impress you, but it's—"

"It does impress me, but I want more. I want friendship!"

Thom was teetering, but he reminded himself that he was first and always a priest. "I guess I don't respect you somehow—" He saw the flash of pain in Jim's eyes.

Then Margaret interrupted them and there was nothing more to say. Jim wandered off without cake and coffee, and Thom prepared to leave. He glanced around the kitchen and remembered doing dishes with his brother, trying to break a previous night's record. He remembered them begging Margaret to let them play football until dark, or pleading for a chance to catch just one more turtle. And he remembered his father as well, not as a withered man, but as a gruff, proud Irishman.

Thom began to feel a sadness he had never let himself feel over the sudden disappearance of his own childhood when he entered the seminary. He remembered a little boy he had forgotten, quick to anger and quicker to forgive, smiling and breathing excitement, on the verge of laughter and tears at any moment, eager to rush from bed each morning and hating to end a day. John Patrick coming home from work and honking his familiar horn to gather his boys in his powerful arms and wrestle them all the way into the house. The hoarse shouts from the bleachers and the excited postmortems with McNulty; the warm summer water fights at Lake Watseka; the awkward hands cutting the roast. The lonely man brooding in some private agony that Thom could rescue him from with a single victory.

For Thom, John Patrick had died a long time ago. When a vibrant boy had surrendered his life to God only to return from the seminary as a tense shadow of himself. Even the priesthood, with its first fervor and excitement, had never restored the enthusiasm of that loving boy. He was as dead as his father was now, and the loss had broken John Patrick's heart. But as Thom left for Steelmont with Margaret's cookies and her tearful admonitions to come home again soon, it was his own heart and personal disappointments he was worried about.

Jim's gentle words had struck a painful blow. Thom's shoulders ached from some pressure, his stomach was rigid, and he regretted that he had turned from Jim so abruptly. Monsignor Nowicki's favorite quotation from Saint Augustine came ringing back: "Hate the sin, but love the sinner!" Thom felt like a sham. Parishioners saw only the collar and the celibacy; Jim had seen it all.

What had he become? He saw his own hungry ambition, his smoldering resentment, the pain and humiliation of constant rejection by Weber and Beahan and Elvin Ward. His Church was being destroyed before his very eyes, the new leaders in Sheffield unconcerned with the real pain of lonely sinners and death and broken hearts. Thom had not fought back, content to resign himself to the cruciform will of God.

Or was he only afraid?

He had planned to spend the night in Jensen with Mike Fogarty and return to Steelmont the following afternoon, and when he learned that Mike had driven to Detroit with Jim O'Brien, Thom was even more depressed. He drove away and his mind continued to race with memories of a childhood that seemed a century ago. Then he thought of Skorski in red and Elvin Ward in miter, and he had to stop by the side of the road to throw up. The disconnected thoughts continued to distress him in waves of sadness, and he knew he needed to talk to someone. When he reached Sheffield it was almost nine and he wished desperately that Dave Beauchamp were still at the cathedral. Impulsively, he stopped at a pay phone to call Charlie and Roselle. Charlie expressed sympathy at his father's death and apologized that they had confused the day. Then he demanded that Thom stop by for a drink. His voice seemed far away.

Roselle greeted him warmly, seeming concerned over his pallor. He stripped to his T-shirt and black pants and felt better after two of Charlie's scotches. Roselle admitted that she missed his sermons since he had moved to Steelmont, and Charlie talked about a chance to work with freshmen batters at the junior college. He began to reminisce about Thom's power at the plate.

"It woulda been nice if you'd had a shot at the majors. Shit, you coulda made 'em." His eyes glowed. "Your old man woulda loved that!" The memory hurt Thom again, and he remembered Jim's wounded eyes and his own words to Jim: *I don't respect you.*

It helped to know that Roselle admired his priesthood, and her very presence relaxed him. The soft voice, the gentle inquiries about his father's death. When Charlie left for the night shift at 10:30, Thom still looked pale and distressed, and Charlie instructed Roselle to make a pot of coffee.

"These damn Irish can't hold their liquor. I know!"

Roselle served coffee and warm blueberry muffins; then when Thom asked for another drink, she blended some grasshoppers.

"I'll be okay. I could drive all night."

She sat near him on the couch without saying a word. Finally, he released the abundance of pain he had held back for so long. Tears flooded from the lost boy, John Patrick's son, and she held his hand and caressed his arm as he sobbed. When he was finally quiet, she leaned over and kissed him gently on the lips. He returned her kiss more deeply, clinging to her like a frightened child. Helpless. Soon they were devouring each other's mouths on the lamb's wool rug in front of the couch. They kissed and stroked for a long time, tasting the sweetness of surrender. Then they embraced. Two hungry spirits and lonely bodies. He fumbled gently until she was finally naked in his arms. Then slowly she undressed him, continuing to kiss and caress him until they were both naked, without shame. She lay back and guided him inside her, and only then did they gasp in a moaning frenzy of long-awaited love. And then, with joyful, speechless tears, they began again. As if they could never stop. He loved her and tasted her from eyes and ears to thighs and toes without instruction. Then lay back until he fell exhaustedly asleep.

At six she wakened him and they made love again as if they had never stopped. They shared coffee and toast and kissed again and again until they were dissolved once more in final, now familiar, love. He dressed and drove back toward Steelmont, knowing that there had been no sin, only a rewarding gift of God.

Roselle had wanted Thom since they had been together in a sun-filled meadow almost fifteen years before. She knew what kind of lover he would be although she had never tried to seduce or even hoped to ignite him. He had belonged to God.

She had watched him labor in the parish, refusing no outstretched hand, never impatient, always concerned. The kids and Charlie loved his Christlike beauty as much as she did. She knew the cost in the sadness of his eyes in repose, in the gentle smile that never really erupted, in the never-ending work that forbade him time to be anything but a priest. That night, she knew it was time to release the man. Fearing, even as she leaned to kiss him, that her impulsive love might drive him away forever. In an instant of exchange she knew it was right, holy even, and there was not the least shadow of guilt in her heart. She had loved a whole man, whose heart and soul were as beautiful as his body. It had not been sex at all, but the religious experience she had longed for all her life. Her body continued to glow as if Thom had never left. She wondered what kind of passion she had released in this tormented man. And what would become of his priesthood.

☘ ☘ ☘

That same night, Jim slept in his car in the circular driveway of the stately colonial house he once hoped might save his marriage. Connie had bolted the door from inside when he returned from the Shamrock Lounge where he and McNulty had drunk toasts to John Patrick, then to each other. Connie ignored the pleading of the doorbell and forbade the children to admit their father. Only Chrissie had cried and worried about daddy "catching a bad cold."

"Let him sleep with me, mommy—"

Jim considered breaking a window, then worried about frightening the children, so he settled with a drunken grin into the back seat of his Buick.

The next morning Connie permitted him inside, and

nine-year-old Johnny glowered at him. Connie threatened to talk to Monsignor Doyle. Her parents had advised that she throw him out.

"The children and I don't want to see you."

She silenced a protesting Chrissie, and Jimmy disappeared out the side door. Johnny stood by to protect his mother.

"We'll talk about it tonight. Doyle doesn't run this house, and I don't need any advice from your parents. And we'll talk without the kids."

"I want you out of here. I don't want you giving your bad example to the children, drinking and carousing and neglecting your family. I'd rather see you dead!"

Again she silenced Chrissie's weeping protest.

Jim changed his clothes and shaved and left the house.

Connie, hurt and frustrated not to prolong the fight, screamed angrily out the door, "You'll turn out just like your father!"

He turned suddenly and walked back toward the door. She had never seen his face as angry. He raised his hand and pointed his index finger in a gently rocking movement, then spoke very slowly and softly.

"I never want you to say one bad word about my father. Ever again! Is that clear?"

Connie was terrified. "Yes," she whispered.

"I want you to know I loved him. Really loved him!"

Connie stood staring, as if she had just met a stranger.

12

In Desert Lands Called Nod

When Thom arrived in Steelmont, the eight o'clock mass was just over, and departing parishioners nodded to him devoutly. He went immediately to his room in the parish hall, checked his mail without interest, then fell asleep again, reliving Roselle's softness. It was almost six o'clock in the evening when Monsignor Rabidoux knocked gently on his door.

"How about some dinner?"

He drove to the rectory and picked at Marie's casserole as words floated across the room.

The guilt was slow in coming, and it took the shape of a labyrinth of pain and longing. A lifetime's spiritual search had finally been silenced in a more tangible mysticism not described in seminary ascetics. She had become eucharist enough, prayer and meditation and ancient sacrifice on a hill outside the city's gates where lonely criminals were transformed. Blood and water, milk and honey flowing all at once through parched crevices of anticipation and desiccated joints of Ezekiel's desert bones. Her very weakness and wet surrender had become his unassailable strength, and his mind, nourished on dark religious mysteries and Draconic laws, finally drew back far enough for his blinded eyes to see. Finally to see!

"You're not hungry." Marie poured coffee. "It's hard to lose your father."

She recounted her own father's lingering death and burial, then served banana cake. He still tasted Roselle. In wordless transcendence.

He leafed through the evening paper while Monsignor Rabidoux talked about marble for a sanctuary floor and acoustical tile in the nave. He commented approval and excused himself to finish some breviary.

Only in the sanctuary did the torment of conscience begin. Slowly at first, mingled with memories of moist touching and sweating bodies lost in love. A dull emptiness that grew progressively more disquieting as the tabernacle fell into focus and a traditional crucifix stared sadly back. Then the virginal Joseph and a serene Mary, too pure and sincere to ignore. He gazed at the crucifix and tried to state his sorrow. Calmly, without drama. Perhaps he was not really repentant. He recalled Bernard Fox gesturing from a silent prayer hall. Whining!

"You don't have to weep! Sorrow's an act of will!"

He was lost momentarily in the memory of Fox's gravelly mouthings, then he came to and planned confession. Slowly reciting an act of contrition and trying without success to forget the mergings of legs and arms and mouths. He checked his watch. It was after ten, and the hospital chaplain would be ready for bed.

He got in his car and headed for Saint Charles on the east side, trying to imagine confession to the obese, introverted pastor, Ed Grimes, whom he remembered from childhood. It was humiliating and impossible. He pulled into a gas station and turned around. Suddenly he remembered Ziggy Denko, pastor of Our Lady of Czestochowa, the scarred black madonna of Warsaw.

Ziggy was a short, fat Croatian, slow-witted and eternally sleepy. Thom did not care what he thought. If he remembered. He drove quickly to the rectory and parked in front. There was a light in the front room as he approached and rang the bell. A shrewish housekeeper answered. It had been rumored more than once that she shared Ziggy's bed, but no one really cared. Ziggy bothered no one.

"Is Father Denko in?"

"Was he expecting you?" It was never asked of a priest.

"No, I just wanted—"

"Come in." She nodded toward the living room. "He's probably asleep in front of the TV." She sighed. "As usual."

Ziggy was slouched in a chair, dressed in wrinkled black slacks and a dirty T-shirt. His cassock was draped over the ottoman and the evening paper was scattered on the floor. A couple of beer bottles, one half full, rested next to an ashtray spilling cigar and cigarette butts. A small statue of the Sacred Heart and a breviary opened to Vespers were on a crusty lamp table along with part of a rye bread sandwich. Ziggy was snoring, his glasses drooping below puffy eyes.

Thom approached apprehensively. He didn't know Ziggy well.

"Father—can I talk to you?"

He did not stir.

Thom shook him gently.

"A-a what's up?" He looked carefully around. "Oh—Maguire—what's up?" His slick greased-down hair stood up in back and a red sleep mark rimmed his right eye.

"Will you hear my confession?"

"Sure, what time is it? I musta fallen asleep." He looked at his breviary. "Good you woke me up. I got book to say. Lemme get my stole. Let's see—where the hell is it?" He bellowed, "Mary, where's my stole? Damn woman, always picking it up."

She appeared at the door. "Did you call?"

"Christ, where's my stole. Maguire wants confession."

"It's in your office. I'll get it." Thom was embarrassed. She returned the stole with its frayed linen collar.

"Where's my surplice?" Thom was nervous. There was no need of a surplice but Ziggy was of the old school. Mary did not reappear.

"The hell with it. C'mon in the office. We'll be alone." Ziggy led the way, wheezing as he went. Books were scattered on the desk and three or four packages of cigars were stacked against the parish seal. The air in the room was stale with smoke, and a dim light from a ceiling fixture gave things an eerie pallor. Ziggy struggled with a prie-dieu that was lodged between the file cabinet and a huge safe; then he dusted it off, and Thom knelt.

"Wait a minute." Ziggy got up and closed the door. Thom noticed his fly was open under the loose cassock. He grunted, and Thom began.

"Bless me, father, I have sinned. I had intercourse with a married woman."

"How many times?"

"I'm not sure. One whole evening—and in the morning."

"Been seeing her regularly?"

"No, this was the only time."

"Can she blow the whistle?"

"Pardon, father."

"Can she get you in trouble?"

"Oh, no father."

"That's good. Anything else?"

"I missed my breviary that day."

"Okay, say six and six and make a good act of contrition."

Ziggy began the words of absolution. "*Dominus noster Jesus Christus . . . ego te absolvo a peccatis tuis . . .*" The words were muffled, but it did not matter. Thom said the words of sorrow slowly and sincerely.

"I firmly resolve with the help of your grace—"

"Go in peace and God bless you."

"Thank you, father, thank you so much!"

"Got time for a beer?"

"Not tonight."

"Drop by for a bite to eat."

"Thanks again, father."

"Any time. Don't bother calling."

☙ ☙ ☙

In the fall, Bishops Elvin Ward and Joseph Beahan left for the second session of Vatican II. They went without Freddie Weber, who deeply resented being left as chancellor in charge of the diocese. Bobbie Foley also remained to assist him. A vindicated Mary Douglas had returned to replace the handsome male receptionist.

It was a more subdued Bishop Beahan who greeted the newly consecrated Teddy Dorrow at the Café Milano in Rome. A luncheon with Cardinal Ruggini, former law professor of Elvin Ward's, was brief and cordial. It was Ruggini's influence that had swayed the selection of Beahan and Ward from the list of candidates for the bishopric recommended by the Michigan Provincial Conference. Despite Dorrow's protest, Ruggini had questioned the ability of either Beahan or Weber to manage a diocese, and when he spotted Elvin Ward's name and remembered a bright, disciplined little man with exceptional language skills and deep Roman loyalties, the discussion ended.

Teddy had written Weber a consoling letter promising that Ruggini would soon retire and hinting that the future would offer more than an auxiliary post in Sheffield. Weber wrote back expressing his gratitude and secretly wondering what had happened on the trip to Paris. Despite his expression of warm affection, he felt betrayed.

The Second Vatican Council proved exciting with the powerful Holy Office challenged by Cardinals Bea and Suenens. Cardinal Ottaviani bristled back, and the debates grew explosive. Liberals were questioning papal power, and conservatives were cursing the aggressive laymen. An African bishop pleaded for married deacons, and a salty Italian cardinal insisted that it would destroy celibacy entirely. Pope Paul struggled—without John's charisma or courage—but the Italian curia would not roll over and die, and they condemned the theologians who were "subverting the bishops." Archbishop Pericle Felici, secretary general of the council, attacked a German bishop, trying to wrench petitions from his hands, and there was another uproar.

But on Friday, November 22, 1963, the council was brutally interrupted, and partisan considerations were laid aside in united grief. John F. Kennedy had been assassinated.

Bishop Ward and Bishop Beahan spent the weekend watching TV, only emerging from their rooms to eat and offer mass and prayers for their deceased president. On Sunday there was an urgent call for Joe Beahan from Charlie Kenelley. At first Beahan thought Kenelley might be drunk, then he remembered the ginger ale at his consecration banquet, and he took the call, complaining about the connection. A few minutes later he returned, ashen-faced, to his room, and the following morning he left for New York.

Freddie Weber had been picked up on a morals charge in Sheffield's city park.

Freddie had been caught in a wooded area of the park with Don, the beautiful male secretary from the chancery. A plainclothesman ferreting rumors of marijuana had stumbled on them and booked them without formality. Freddie, weeping and distraught, was without identification, and he called Charlie Kenelley immediately, a singularly wise decision. Charlie swung into Catholic action and had the incident wiped from the blotter. The event of Kennedy's death kept it from the media, and District Attorney Philip Scott Hallinan, a fiercely loyal Catholic and ex-colonel in the air force, demanded that the bishop be informed immediately. A furiously cursing Charlie Kenelley couldn't talk him out of it. His Irish layman's image of the Church was that it was a crusading army.

"The general has to know!"

"You'll ruin the son of a bitch!"

"He ruined himself. I'm only keeping it quiet for the sake of the Church. The bishop has to know!"

"You're a rigid, unfeeling bastard!" How could he explain bishops to a stupid layman? With Irish allegiance?

"I have my principles too!"

One of them was to inform the arresting officer that if he ever breathed a word to anyone he'd be collecting total disability the rest of his life.

By the time Bishop Beahan arrived in Sheffield, Charlie Kenelley had things completely in hand. Even though he had no respect for Weber as a man, his deep reverence for the sacred priesthood took over. Even Freddie was "another Christ," and at Kenelley's advice, Freddie faked a heart seizure. Kenelley sent his mother to visit her sister and rushed Freddie to the rectory in Hamlin.

Even Bobbie Foley never knew.

When Elvin Ward returned from Rome in December, he demanded that Weber receive psychiatric help.

Which Charlie Kenelley resisted. "I'm all the psychiatrist he needs."

"This is a serious problem, monsignor!"

"Too damn serious for a shrink, bishop. Freddie's never had a real friend. Let me just try for a few weeks—" Knowing that Freddie Weber would soon be forgotten.

Which he was.

So was Thom Maguire.

Freddie Weber's heart attack created mixed feelings in the diocese. Enemies were relieved, whereas former sycophants studied the public psyche of Elvin Ward and watched Joe Beahan, in new orange-rimmed glasses with tinted lenses, grow subdued. No longer hosting the bishop's mansion. The new diocesan motif seemed to be a serious implementation of Vatican II: a more intelligible liturgy, improved catechetics, an active lay participation, and smaller parishes. All influenced by Elvin Ward's grammatical approach to leadership, as if life were a cautious translation from the Latin or Greek.

"We could be assigned to our own parishes within a year." Mike Fogarty liked to talk of small parishes. He expected his own pulpit and his own trout stream, carefully calculating seniority with elaborate charts and graphs, mortality rates and potential retirements. And he established a hundred-dollar pool with appropriate odds. Thom listened respectfully.

"That quick?"

"If McConnel finally dies and Doyle retires—"

Thom was not as delighted. Some needed recognition had not come, and prospects of his own pastorate only provided more of what he already had. As it was, Maurice Rabidoux had turned over most of the management of Christ the King to immerse himself in architectural sketches, air-conditioned confessionals, and stained-glass windows that would bear the donor's name for ten thousand dollars. Privately, Rabidoux was already a wealthy man from his keen investments in the stock market.

"The rose window will go for twenty—no, thirty-five."

Thom nodded distractedly, wondering where he stood with his chinless ordinary and worrying about the fact that what happened in Steelmont made little difference in Sheffield. Freddie Weber had admitted as much over wine one night.

"You might just as well be in Siberia!"

Thom missed the private congratulations and subtle promises of Bishop Schmidt and the warm pastoral leadership. Elvin Ward did not know he was alive and seemed only interested in slavish, unimaginative obedience to Vatican II directives.

Parochial demands, however, gave little time for self-pitying reveries, since Vatican II had roused the discontented Catholics to greater hope, and confessions and office conferences were less docile. He recognized the weekly voice of a General Motors vice-president, Frank McInerny, a dark haired, handsome Irishman with five young children and a beautiful, sexy wife. The confession seldom varied.

". . . and incomplete intercourse three times."

"Was it mutual masturbation?"

"You could say that! We call it 'love'!" He struggled for control. "It doesn't make sense, father . . ."

Thom recommended prayer and separate beds and

McInerny accepted penance and absolution without further resistance.

Two more prominent ushers and a half dozen unfamiliar voices made similar confessions and stronger protests. Curiously, most of the wives of the sexually repentant husbands confessed only impatience and missed prayers, and only one was as honest and angry as her husband. The next week in his office, a soft spoken, attractive blonde, exuding unaffected warm love, approached Thom anxiously. She reminded him of Roselle. Divorced from a brief Catholic marriage to a sadistic alcoholic at nineteen, she had been married outside the church to a gentle, hardworking second husband—long enough to have four beautiful children.

"Is there any hope, father? Andy and I die every time another one makes first communion—and we sit there . . ." There was no hostility.

"I don't know, Jo. Theologians are reconsidering the true nature of marriage but that's a long way from canon law."

"But God understands. I know he does." Her tears upset him.

"It'll work out somehow."

"Is it wrong to pray for my ex to die?"

"Not if you accept God's will."

She dried her tears and left, thanking him profusely—for nothing. He hated himself for his benign impotence.

Thom's visits to Margaret were more frequent after John Patrick's death, and Rabidoux, advised by Marie, often encouraged him to spend the night and return the following day. Thom indulged his mother's loneliness, visiting sick friends with her, delivering her homemade bread to a sometimes senile Monsignor Doyle, and taking the nuns shopping. Sister Marietta, after ten years a tradition at Saint Raphael's, was Margaret's favorite. Most nuns were blithely inconsiderate, and Margaret reserved her most bitter salvos for Thom's ears.

"That Sister Anita—a lazy lump—calling at the last minute." She mimicked a saccharine whine. " 'You're so good to us—could you bring the umbrella around—whatever would we do without you?' No wonder she's got such a rump on her!"

Sister Marietta had changed. Now thirty, she was softly beautiful with a strain of sadness in her eyes. The convent had subdued the lively wit after a hundred encounters, but a fierce independence concealed by that humor had refused to die. Thom missed her musical laugh, but he was grateful that her strength had not surrendered totally, as often happened. They talked honestly as equals.

"I don't like the English in the mass much," she told him.

"I guess it helps some people to understand."

"Words have never been my best communication," she said almost coyly. "They can get in the way." Thom remembered that she still directed the choir.

"I know what you mean," he said, and he thought of Roselle. Staying away from her had been difficult, especially when he drove through Sheffield each time he visited Margaret.

Usually Margaret remonstrated. "Last time you slept here."

In the morning, when he wanted to sleep in, she would waken him for their private mass at Saint Raphael's. It was her proudest moment. "You'll be a long time dead," she would say. "And I won't be around forever."

He sometimes gave in to his guilt, but usually he left the same night, preferring to spend the night with Fogarty or O'Brien, or occasionally at a motel, just to be alone, even to watch television. After several months, he called Roselle.

"Please stop by—just for a few minutes."

He did, promising himself that what had happened would never happen again. And sincerely believing it until he kissed her. Then there was no stopping. More aggressively undressing her, slowly, sacredly, slipping off the silky wrappings of a ciborium, probing the cool, rustling skirts of the tabernacle. Kissing and touching until she begged and wept, then merging easily into her dark fragrance, caressing her breasts, burying his face in the long brown hair that now fell about her waist.

When they were together, he loved without any guilt. The total devouring of body and spirit left no energy for remorse, and an all-absorbing present obliterated any past.

The guilt came later, and it bordered on despair, even though Ziggy never rebuked him.

Months went by, and Thom kept slipping back into Roselle's arms with the helplessness of an alcoholic.

Drinking her to the dregs. Then confession and remorse and a sincere promise never to see her again under any pretense. He feared he had destroyed her faith, ruined her marriage. She saw an end to the relationship and only wanted to enjoy him as long as it was possible.

He despised his weakness, increased his already overtaxed ministry, and gave up cigarettes and desserts for a month. Weeks passed between encounters, and he never consciously called her with the explicit intention of breaking his celibate promise. His vocation, despite all the rebuffs he had received as well as the confusion of a rapidly changing Church, was the one solid hope he clung to. He only longed to be with her, and at the first touch—as if in passing weeks he had really forgotten—he was helplessly dissolved. Her very odor had become his passion and the taste of her mouth and moisture drugged him beyond control. Occasionally the sound of her voice on the phone so excited him that he playfully instructed her to unlock the door and wait asleep in bed. Never really believing at the moment that he was offending God. He approached the room as if she belonged to him and no one shared her bed, then wakened her with mouth and hands to make lingering, wordless, exhausting love. She was his sacred madonna whom he loved with gentle reverence and unrestrained passion.

Never did she make demands, not because she feared driving him away, but because intuitively she understood the subtle rhythms of his need. She was content to be his whenever he was there and she did not complain when he stayed away. Never calling or planning or interrupting his life, never asking anything except to return his intermittent love. Although she loved her new Catholic faith, he was her most religious experience. Their union never lost its edge because he never called until his body and soul were unable to survive without her. And she kept their love a secret. Only once a sleepwalking child startled them, then docilely followed Roselle back to bed.

Part of his work during his second year in Steelmont was as Newman chaplain to Catholic students at a branch of the University of Michigan. It was challenging work that received only token attention from his predecessors. Typically, he plunged in, organizing dances and weekend retreats, ski trips and special services during Lent or Advent that were tailored to their needs. Convenient, gentle confessions made him a hero, and he began almost to swagger across campus, conscious only of his own good looks and grateful that he was not like an ordinary parish priest. Even non-Catholics sought his counsel, and engaged couples flocked to instructions to avoid a more traditional assault at their own parishes. His classes in Scripture and theology were well attended, especially by young women who lingered after class. After a brilliant lecture on the evolution of God in the Bible he was approached by a Catholic faculty member.

"You could get accreditation for your course. Call it Christian theology."

When he approached the academic dean, there was initial reluctance, although he admired Thom's unusual rapport. But the restored Maguire confidence took over despite the dean's objection.

"It would be hard for you to be objective," the dean said.

"Of course! But you're the one who stated that committed Communists should teach communism—otherwise it's empty theory."

Joe McCarthy was gone, and academic freedom won out. Thom was offered a two-credit course in religious studies as an instructor with modest salary. Monsignor Rabidoux was ecstatic.

"Marvelous! There's no telling what—"

Bishop Ward gave curt approval and warned sharply of a need for loyalty to "solid faith and morals." Even Ward's lack of enthusiasm did not dampen Thom's ardor for the new apostolate. By spring term, classes were overflowing, and admissions were cut off. The class was a refreshing change from stiff academics, and "Father Mac" had a reputation as an open-minded priest and an easy marker. Everywhere on campus students waved and introduced Protestant friends to a "really cool priest." Thom worked hard, explained the origins of all four Gospels from Mark's brief history, then showed that John's narrative was the first to introduce the water of baptism and the bread of the Eucharist as extensions of Christ in time.

"Each Gospel is different because each was written for a different audience. Matthew proved to the Jews that Christ fulfilled their Old Testament prophecies. Luke showed the Romans that Jesus was a miracle worker. John wrote to establish Christianity to a later generation. Mark simply told the story, like a reporter."

He talked of creation myths in other literature, of the rise of religious orders among hermits who were protesting the corruption of Roman civilization; he even admitted the crimes of the Borgia popes. The course was more exciting when he moved into such practical matters as the morality of war, the responsibilities of newspapers, and especially sex.

"Hey, I don't make the rules." He paused just long enough. "You guys think you got it rough?" They roared at the handsome celibate.

Then his face flashed serious and he was passionately eloquent. "Sex is more than orgasm. You might not believe it, but sex without love is like last week's macaroni. *Playboy*'s no answer. The saints, Peter and Magdalen, were probably the hottest potential pair in Jerusalem."

Thom Maguire was unbelievable, and a hundred coeds knew they were in love. And Thom knew it. He smoked in class, mocked academics, challenged scientists, attacked Bertrand Russell. He did not talk like the priests back home, and Catholics roared silent approval. Even Protestants and Jews had new notions of what priests were like.

John Conlin, a devoutly Catholic professor of philosophy, raised his hand one afternoon in class. Notre Dame educated, father of seven kids, and a daily communicant, he often sat in Thom's classes, smiling occasionally or gently pondering. Thom acknowledged his upraised hand.

"It might be interesting to arrange a broader discussion of these topics—sex, birth control, divorce, abortion, all the hot potatoes—in a more open forum. A kind of debate. I'd be glad to play a mediocre devil's advocate."

The students cheered approval.

Thom hesitated. "I might need permission from the bishop for anything that public—"

"Nothing as formal as that! Just dramatic dialogue."

Thom agreed.

Conlin hung around after class, waiting patiently for admiring coeds to disperse. He was a tall man with wavy light brown hair, a strong face, and a kind of academic sway to his back. He folded his arms, rocking while he talked, and shocks of the unruly hair fell over his eyes when he moved his head for emphasis.

"Let's start with birth control. It's hot enough to be exciting and remote enough to discourage public confession."

"That makes sense."

John suggested a format. They could each take ten or fifteen minutes to set the stage, confront one another for half an hour, and open up the floor for questions. Then coffee and doughnuts and a ten o'clock good-night.

A group of five or six hundred sprawled casually on the floor of the student union lounge for the first session, and the speakers were introduced by a polite Newman Club president. Thom hadn't realized that John Conlin had studied for six years with the Redemptorists, two of the years in Rome. The debate began innocently with Thom explaining the Church's position on birth control and describing new British research on rhythm. The students liked his handsome intensity, and his charm helped them overlook any unpleasant conclusions he made, or any vague non sequiturs. He was eloquent and interesting.

John Conlin spent little time on pleasantries and immediately went for the jugular with professional experience. If procreation were the primary purpose of sex, and loving pleasure was subordinated to conception, how justify menopausal sex? Or twilight marriages? Or even rhythm. A brief aside about "Vatican roulette" brought much laughter.

Thom asserted that the act of rhythm in no way positively interfered with conception.

Conlin attacked. "That's ridiculous! A pill or diaphragm becomes sinful, while scientifically arranged abstinence during fertile periods—totally contraceptive in nature—is beautiful and virtuous. What's natural about that? Thus the Church supports mental contraception!"

The auditorium grew silent and Thom Maguire knew he was in more than a sandlot ball game. It was no time to quote Pius XI or Saint Augustine.

Conlin continued. "The same Church considers the intent to abort, an abortion; the intent to kill, murder. Yet a contraceptive intent is sanctifying. That, I submit, is celibate-inspired balderdash!"

Students cheered wildly at the brawl, and Thom attempted to focus on what makes an action good or bad.

Not merely the intention but what is done. The "object" of the action. There was no applause at his dry philosophizing, and Conlin moved for the kill.

"But, father, why focus on separate acts? That's not real! What about the totality of the marriage? Under Rome's program a couple who has nine kids and practices birth control is damned! Another couple who can't stand one another and abstains is blessed." He paused for the climax. "One fight doesn't make a divorce and contraceptive acts don't make for a contraceptive marriage. Except in Rome!"

Again they cheered wildly, and Thom Maguire, armed with Aristotle and vague Scriptures, went down to resounding defeat. He had not anticipated Conlin's Irish eloquence. The comforting words of a few coeds who thought he had won didn't help.

The following two sessions on abortion and divorce were even more painful. The meetings were moved to a second-floor auditorium to accommodate fifteen hundred people, many of them faculty.

Conlin knew more about current theology than Thom, quoting contemporary Europeans who identified sacramental marriage only as committed love and questioned the presence of a "human" fetus until after the third month. Even Thomas Aquinas had talked of vegetable and animal souls. Conlin focused on marriage.

"Rome has its priorities misconstrued when legal consent in front of the proper minister creates an invincible sacrament. Even if the spouses hate or cheat or never have children. Even if the husband turns gay! As long as they had one intercourse—"

Groans from the audience as Thom's response was stumbling and inadequate.

When they ended the series on premarital sex, Conlin's summation was devastating. "In the eyes of Rome, casual intercourse between drunken strangers is probably less sinful than the loving sex of a couple who have been engaged for five years. Thus Rome pushes children into marriage to legalize sex, and in the process interrupts careers and damns immature couples to bitter resentment and failure."

His final words rang ominously in Thom's ears.

"The celibate Church—which cares so much about love and children—turns love into legalities and children into victims of guilt-ridden, angry, ill-prepared parents who end up with children they don't want and spouses they can't stand. Doomed for life in the name of God!"

The real problem was that, deep in his heart, Thomas Aloysius Maguire agreed. And hated John Conlin's devastating arguments for making him aware.

Word of the debate reached Elvin Ward when press coverage was given the final two sessions. A stern letter warned Thom that he was not an *ex officio* spokesman for the Catholic Church.

> . . . that right is reserved to ordinaries (bishops) in their own dioceses or the pope anywhere in the world. Only if you were delegated—which you were not—can you engage in such debates! Please refer to Canon 1325, section 3.

He was ordered never to act in such a "reckless, foolhardy, and immature manner" or he would face "serious ecclesiastical penalties."

Margaret Ann Maguire's son was crushed, and some ancient, unspeakable wrath—long dead—began to stir as never before.

That same June 1966, on the ninth anniversary of Thom's priesthood, moon-faced Mike Fogarty was given a small parish at Squirrel Lake, and he paid off odds of five to one. There was a trout stream in his backyard and a golf course hardly a five iron away. Bobbie Foley was officially made chancellor of the Sheffield Diocese and elevated to the monsignorate with the rank of domestic prelate; and Terry Lanier, who had been sent to Rome instead of Thom, succeeded the pudgy Foley as Bishop Ward's secretary. Stanley Skorski, a four-to-one shot in Fogarty's pool, was made auxiliary bishop of Chippewa in Michigan's Upper Peninsula. There were no odds covering Thomas Maguire's new appointment: "Vicarius cooperator-assistant" to Ziggy Denko, who had been slowed down by gallstones. It was an unmistakable slap from Elvin Ward.

Thom sat silently in Monsignor Rabidoux's office.

"I sent only the best reports to Bishop Ward—What can I do?"

After a two-hour conference with Charlie Kenelley and a bottle of scotch with Jim O'Brien and Mike Fogarty,

Thom determined to accept the assignment as God's will.

"Piss on the weasel!" John Patrick's nickname had endured. "Do it for God!"

Three days later a phone call from Chancellor Foley informed him that he had been relieved as chaplain of the Newman Club. When Monsignor Rabidoux suggested a few days off, he drove toward Sheffield to contact Roselle, then changed his mind. Suddenly he wanted to be with his brother Jim whom he had not seen since John Patrick's death three years before. He knew that Jim had moved from the colonial house months ago, and when the strange impulse grew stronger than his pride, he pulled into a roadside bar and called his brother collect. After an embarrassing pause, Jim agreed to accept the charges.

"I need to spend some time with you." Thom's voice was almost pleading. "Have you got any time?"

"I've got all kinds of time," Jim said. "But I don't need a sermon." He laughed gently.

Thom flushed. "No sermons. I'm really hurting."

"Welcome to the club. Maybe we can be brothers again."

"I'm sorry to bother you. I know you've got your own problems."

"Christ, you sound like Margaret. I'll see you when you get here." He gave directions to his Kirkwood apartment.

Thom was not aware that Jim's whole life had changed. After John Patrick's death, Jim had wanted to run away and begin again. He had even gathered enough money for Connie and the kids and taken in a young partner he had known from Marquette to whom he could sell the business as an annuity for his family. He wanted to be free to live the life he had abandoned with Judy.

It was the children who changed his mind, especially Johnny, who had become Margaret's little twelve-year-old saint. He could not simply leave and permit the Church to steal his son. John Patrick would have died in vain and Jim's whole life would have become a failure. As futile as John Patrick's.

So for a time he plunged back into his homelife. Although he no longer went to church or said the family rosary, he outfitted the basement recreation room with Ping-Pong and pool tables; he helped serve at family meals, carved the roast, and attended school plays; and he helped Chrissie with reading and assisted with Jimmy's arithmetic. He never demanded that Johnny come any closer than he wanted to.

Johnny resisted. He attended early mass with Margaret and his mother, served at most funerals, and assisted the nuns with beginning altar boys and Holy Week decorations. Jim went to his baseball and football games, applauded his marks in school, and showed no pique at Johnny's continuing disappointment with his father's lack of religious faith. He picnicked with Chrissie and sometimes Jimmy in the woods, took them on his infrequent house calls, and barbecued hamburgers with them in the backyard. Even Connie gradually trusted him and, at the end of the first year, at Margaret's urging, she talked of having another child.

She purchased a sheer pink lounging robe to compliment her new diet and attractive new pixie haircut, and one night she lounged next to Jim on the couch.

"You look handsome tonight."

"You're not bad yourself." He grinned and sniffed an unfamiliar perfume. "I think I'm being seduced."

"It didn't used to be so hard." She giggled, reminding him of their courtship, and Jim was aroused. He reached over and stroked her full breasts, and Connie wriggled and groaned softly.

"O God, that feels good."

He undressed her and began sucking her breasts until she pleaded for him. He pulled off shoes and pants, more excited than he had been in years, and she screamed with pleasure when he entered. She continued to writhe wildly until he felt himself coming, sooner than he wanted, tremendously excited by the long absence. He thrust a few more times and then abruptly withdrew to come against her thigh. Connie was dissolved in angry tears.

"You dirty son of a bitch! Goddamn you! You know I want a baby." And she slipped on her robe and sobbed her way to the bedroom.

Jim sat naked on the couch, fantasizing his freedom in a few more years. When Johnny was rescued and the others were older.

Truthfully, Connie did not want another child. She wanted Jim and focused on pregnancy instead. After her thirty-seventh birthday, she grew despondent. Stretch marks and waffled thighs disgusted her, and she was certain that Jim was making love to his buxom office nurse who swiveled her hips and never stopped grinning. Connie hated her almost as much as she began to hate Jim.

Christmas night of that year was the final blow. Connie's mother and Margaret conspired to put a gift under the tree for the "next baby." A rubber duck that Jim had played with as a child. Jim ignored the rude joke and continued helping Johnny break in a new baseball glove. Connie read Margaret's note and burst into uncontrollable tears. The merriment stopped immediately and Jim assured the children that their mother was exhausted from all the excitement of a big family dinner. Connie continued to cry as they kissed her good night, and Johnny hesitated to leave.

"It's okay, Johnny. Mother and daddy need to talk."

The boy put his arms around his mother again and reluctantly went to bed, on the verge of tears himself.

Connie Hackett had endured enough. She began to strike at Jim and accuse him of every infidelity. Then she demanded that he move out of the house.

"That won't solve anything, Connie. I don't want any more kids. That's no crime."

"That's what marriage is for," she pleaded. She had been humiliated long enough.

"It's for us too," he said. "We have our own needs."

"We'll have years after the kids are raised. You just don't have any faith!"

"It's not my lack of faith that's destroying us, Connie. It's the Church."

She didn't hear a word he said, and during the following week of vacation, the house of James Maguire was silent and tense. Jimmy was paler than ever, and he disappeared whenever Jim came in the door. Even Chrissie was subdued and afraid to jump into his lap. But, worst of all, Johnny watched his father with an anger Jim had only seen in Margaret's eyes when John Patrick was drinking.

It crushed him, and the following week he moved out of the house. At first he took a furnished apartment in a new singles complex near Kirkwood College and visited the children once or twice a week. Only Chrissie spoke to him, against Connie's orders. Soon he stopped coming. His apartment seemed sterile and ridiculous in the mélange of pool parties and Friday night open houses. He longed for a simplicity he had not known since college, and he found a neat three-room apartment on the east side of downtown Kirkwood, a colorful area that had been increasingly neglected as Kirkwood moved west. It reminded him of Marquette. Workmen's bars and small noisy cafes, used-clothing stores and pawnshops, an old hardware store and a New Salvation Church for winos and repentant or hungry transients. His own apartment, in a small hotel, was a simple bedroom and sitting room and tiny kitchen. Worn gray rugs and beige furniture. The bathroom was painted green and had a decent shower, and the manager promised a small mirror to replace the one that had been stolen.

He loved it. His neighbors were an assortment of down-to-earth characters who suited his new freedom. Foreigners and muttering old ladies, waitresses, mysterious salesmen, a porno movie operator, parents without children to help them, a retired sailor and two ex-cons, and a smiling black man who claimed to have fought Jack Dempsey. No one asked for any more information than Jim wanted to give. He wore jeans and sweat shirts, khaki pants and sweaters, and soon he was known as Irish Jimbo in 303. No one could have imagined he was a doctor, even when he brought free prescription drugs to half his neighbors. They believed he had a "connection" and were delighted with the gifts. Almost as delighted as Jim was to be there.

Only Tim ever visited him, considering it a "cool pad." Now twenty-five and living with a girl an hour's drive from Kirkwood, Tim had long hair, still light red and curly, and dressed not unlike Jim in brown cord pants and combat boots. Margaret seemed to accept his life, though she pretended to ignore his brown-eyed girl friend with the "dirty hair." Jim, on the other hand, was considered mad. Only Chrissie ever asked about him and was informed that he was "sick." He continued to be mentioned briefly in the family rosary. Anne and Dick Dorgan and their five children refused to do even that.

Although there was a mild stir among Jim's patients, he seemed more devoted than ever. With little financial pressure aside from supporting his family, he never badgered for bills or even sent a bill beyond what he collected from insurance money. For Mexicans or blacks who didn't have insurance, he asked only token payments. His Marquette partner, if he was disappointed, never said anything.

Jim was a happy man and a good doctor, and only the absence of his children caused him real pain. At times he couldn't stand it, and he drove to the house, only to talk briefly with Chrissie and to leave feeling worse than before. Johnny was as devout as ever and guarded his mother ominously. Finally Jim stopped going, and he sent a weekly check, increasing it whenever Connie complained. She continued to attend auxiliary meetings and was considered a noble martyr by Margaret, her parents, and those of Saint Raphael's guild who knew about her "situation."

Thom heard about Jim from Margaret and Connie over and over again, and his decision to visit his brother was an admission of his own desperation in a confused Church and a priesthood that was frustrated at every turn. He would have turned to Dave Beauchamp, but Dave's letter from California sounded increasingly despondent. Without Dave's friendship, there was only Jim.

Thom slipped off his collar and found Room 303. The sight startled him.

Jim was sipping a beer. There were scattered books and newspapers, medical reports, and the remnants of a half-eaten hamburger and stiff french fries.

Thom grinned to break the tension. "You keep a nice house."

Jim grunted and directed him to the couch, which slumped as Thom sat down. He handed Thom a cold beer from a small refrigerator and offered a soup bowl as a makeshift ashtray.

"I've got scotch somewhere if you want it."

"No, this is great." Thom felt uncomfortable. Jim seemed to have slipped badly, and Thom forgot about his own problems.

"What's happened? I don't understand."

Jim laughed. "I'm John the Baptist." Thom didn't laugh, and Jim reflected seriously, "I don't know what's happened. I'm just living the way I want to. I've got everything I need." He paused and looked away. "Except the kids."

"Is your marriage over?" Thom struggled with the words.

"It's been over for years. Connie just didn't want me around anymore. I don't even blame her. We're different people. If it weren't for the kids, I'd go somewhere and begin again."

"You don't just walk out on a marriage, Jim."

"Damn it, don't lay your thing on me! I don't want lectures. I'm doing what I want to do and I know what I'm doing. Exactly what I'm doing." He talked more softly. "I'm not going to lose my kids. Someone's got to give them the chance that none of us ever got."

Thom was defensive. "We had a good life."

"How can you believe that? I'm not blaming anyone, but we were as trapped as mother and dad."

"I don't really feel trapped. I feel hurt and confused."

Jim was quiet again. "I know the hurt."

"Would counseling help?"

"There's nothing to counsel. Our marriage was over from the beginning. We never had a chance."

"Have you given up the Church?" Thom could not ignore his priestly responsibilities.

"The Church gave up on me a long time ago. Sometimes I wish I had a Church I could believe in. It's easier when you have something simple. The Church never taught us to grow up. It wants to hang on forever!" Jim looked away and spoke softly. "It helped when I was angry about it. Now even that's gone. I'm pretty much reduced to James Maguire—and that's frightening as hell!"

Thom struggled to comprehend. "But nothing makes sense without God."

"For me, Thom, God is an escape I can't use anymore. I never really could. I look at the tragic people around this place and wonder what keeps them alive. They just don't ask anything of life or expect much more. The struggle to survive seems to be enough. It's not for me. I have to wonder what it all means. Maybe it means nothing!"

Thom felt helpless. "Doesn't the Church mean anything?" He fought his own fear.

"Hell, I gave up on it before my first communion, really. It just wouldn't leave my guts. Like cancer. I've been miserable for years. Now I think the Catholic Church is finally gone and I'm fighting to find a way to live. To start from the beginning."

"But your kids—?"

"Jesus, what about my kids? The Church stole them, and I'm fighting to get them back. Johnny's like a frightened little monk. How the hell did I ever let it happen?"

Thom wanted to explode at him, but struggled not to drive him farther away.

"Shit, if I gave birth control pills on Monday, Margaret and Doyle knew about it on Tuesday." He looked at Thom. "I guess I considered you part of the trap. You've been Margaret's living proof that I'm an irresponsible bastard."

Thom felt the hurt deeply, but it was softened by an almost desperate look in Jim's eyes that he had never seen before.

"Margaret did the best she could," said Thom.

"Please don't be so damn forgiving. Christ, don't you have any more passion? You look at me like a goddamned priest!"

"Damn it, Jim, I am a priest! What the hell do you want from me?"

"I want some blood, some guts, something, damn it! It's nothing to be a priest wrapped in that collar. I need a person! A brother! Everything I ever wanted in my life the fucking Church took away! Losing Judy almost killed me. I've never known that kind of love—before or since—until the kids. Now, they're gone! Chrissie is the only one who ever says anything: 'Daddy, are you gonna stop being naughty and come home?' Jesus!"

Thom wanted to tell Jim everything about Marty and Roselle, the excitement and ensuing guilt, and his own struggle to be a priest. But he couldn't risk it. He had to be an example, even to his brother. He talked instead about the debates with John Conlin, his own embarrassment and doubts, and when Jim did not seem impressed, he fought for some attention and mentioned his deep affection for a particular woman.

"It's a start. She's obviously no Margaret!"

Thom felt the sting of Jim's words. "I feel put down."

"I want you to, damn it! You're talking about shit the rest of us did in high school. Why don't you take a chance? See if she's a good piece of ass! Then maybe you'll come to terms with your priesthood!"

Thom finally flared. "You angry son of a bitch!"

Jim laughed. "I wish I could be angry. I was. Furious! My whole life was ruined by guys like you and Doyle. You're all gutless! Why don't you stand up in the pulpit and tell people that God gives them the chance to get it together. Tell them they can marry anyone they love; they can start over if they make an honest mistake! Have the kids they can handle and sleep together without being terrified of another pregnancy. You bet I was angry. You stole my kids. You know, my anger kept me alive—now I gotta find something else."

Thom could no longer hold back, and he blurted, "I *was* with a woman! Do you understand?"

"So big deal! Who gives a damn?"

"I'm not proud of what I've done."

"Why the hell not? You did it. A piece of ass for a lonely celibate becomes an existential struggle? That's bullshit!"

Thom was furious now. "It wasn't just a piece of ass! It was beautiful and painful and a lot of things. To me it was a sacred relationship that changed my whole life. Maybe that's why I'm here."

"Hey, Thom, I'm talking about love and kids and your own son hating you. Your daughter crying her eyes out. Gut realities. Not just stray pussy. You might hate that broad if you spent three straight days with her. Maybe she'd lock up her box except once a month because she was scared to death of another baby. Or maybe she'd bore the hell out of you. You make a goddamned affair sound like the Immaculate Conception. Maybe some of us are confused and hurting enough to need someone for an hour. Maybe that's all you need. But for Christ's sake, join the human race! We're dying in guilt and bullshit! Connie's dying, I'm dying, the kids are dying! Who the hell is your God?"

"I don't make the rules, Jim. I'm not God." Still he held back.

"Like hell! You damn well made the rules for every scared kid that listened. You made the rules for Connie and my kids—"

Finally, Jim was exhausted, and he looked away, his eyes moist.

It was a long time before Thom could speak.

"Jim, I'm as confused as you are. That's why I came tonight. It's all happening so fast."

"It's a long battle, Thom, and you've only just begun. I guess I'm glad it's begun, but I have a feeling that you wanted to get somewhere, to be a bishop or maybe a cardinal. Would that have done it for you? What if you took Ward's place? Who really needs another bishop, or a priest for that matter? Priests are just professionals; we need good people."

"But the Church will change, I know it will—" He wished he hadn't mentioned his own sin.

"Christ, Thom, you really don't understand. It's not the Church, it's us—it's the way we were formed and branded with one eye on death. It's being Irish. Death is all there is! The Church gets its power from death. What's the Church without the idea of hell?" He sat down and said softly, "They did some kind of job!"

Thom was silent for a very long time. "What's the answer?"

"You're the priest." Then he started over. "I didn't mean that. We're in this together. I feel closer to you now than I've ever felt."

Thom feared he had been too lenient, and he struggled for some reaffirmation.

"I think the priesthood is important. People need it!"

"Only because it's there. You know, when you think about it, it's all so damn serious. We don't laugh very much; we never did."

"What's there to laugh at?"

"Everything—you, me, God, Margaret, life—death. Especially death! It's all so damn funny."

"It doesn't seem funny."

"That's the problem! But it is. Beady-eyed, sweating Father Grimes, that dwarf bishop, you and me afraid to talk, Monsignor Doyle, your friend Beauchamp sent to Siberia for nothing—"

"Was Judy funny—or dad's death?"

Jim slowly began to construct his thoughts.

"Not funny the same way—but I was so serious about my relationship with Judy—and about pleasing John Patrick. Maybe *funny*'s not the word. Maybe all I'm asking is why is it so serious? We had to create laughs. They never just came. How much time did John Patrick spend really laughing. Or you? Or me?"

Thom was more moved than he could admit.

"Maybe you're right; maybe death is the only fear." He paused. "I don't think I'm afraid to die—"

"Hell no! You've got a whole insurance program to keep you from thinking about it: angels, resurrections, final judgments, Christ, purgatory, all the bases are covered."

"But that's what faith is! I believe all that because it's

real to me. It's always been real." He fought to control himself, reminding himself that he was still a priest.

"Not to me! Living the way you have to and dying without knowing what's next—that's faith! That's really faith!"

"It sounds selfish. Your whole life sounds selfish."

"Of course it does. We never learned to trust ourselves. Jack had to get killed to fight it all."

Thom tried to let the words soak in. He had to answer, but his head reeled from the exhausting combat.

Jim sensed his weariness. "You take the bedroom. I'll sleep here on the couch."

Thom protested.

"No, really, I usually do anyway. It's an old friend."

When Thom awoke in the morning there was a note from Jim that he had left to make a few calls and would be free late in the afternoon. Thom straightened the apartment, then decided to visit Connie and the kids. He knew Jim didn't want him to, but it was for his own understanding. When he knocked at the door, a cleaning lady informed him that Connie was visiting her parents for the day, so he drove over to find Connie Hackett in her original setting.

The small frame house was in a much older section of Kirkwood. In Thom's childhood it had been the neighborhood of the outspoken Irish who had only been controlled by the fierce leadership of young Monsignor Doyle. Mrs. Hackett let him in enthusiastically. He could hear the children bickering in another room. On top of the TV he noted a picture of himself, a black-suited seminarian standing between a softly smiling Jim and a radiant Connie at their wedding, and suddenly he felt sad, and sadder still when a washed-out Connie greeted him quietly. Mrs. Hackett told them there was coffee on the stove and whisked the children out the back door to the school playground. Connie only began speaking when she heard the door slam shut.

"O, Father Thom, I'm so glad you came! I was hoping you would."

"I really just heard about it. I knew you had some problems, but I didn't think—" He remembered Jim's room.

"It's been coming for a long time. I just can't talk to

him. I thought it would be better after we were in the new house, so beautiful and all, with a big kitchen and a nice yard for the kids. We even got a piano for Chrissie."

She couldn't stop talking, as if no one had listened to her for months. Thom encouraged her tenderly. It was comfortable to be treated as a priest and he felt some strength return. She had gained weight but was still attractive. He had always liked her thin legs and full breasts and the dark eyes that flashed excitedly under the dark Irish hair. She seemed the same except for an overpowering sadness and a new puffiness in her face. Her voice grew softer when she began talking about sex, as if she were in the confessional, describing the struggles with birth control, the fierce fights over contraception, then finally the cold isolation of separate rooms. She began sobbing helplessly.

"It's like he doesn't even see me—doesn't touch me—never—like, well like I'm dirty or something. O God, God!" The tiny living room with its neat, cheap furniture and holy pictures scattered around the walls throbbed with her hurt. All the dreams of young Connie Hackett from the north side becoming a doctor's wife, bearing the baby of the man she had loved since grade school, and furnishing a house like no Hackett had ever owned had been reduced to an impossible embarrassment.

There was nothing for Thom to say. All Connie's catechism faith in God came pouring out, her refusal to break His law or risk her soul's salvation and that of the children. She was ready to make sacrifices, never to know love or sex again, to wither and die in the name of justice and truth, to raise her family and even support herself. She was ready to do it all, until her body was as frayed as her mother's curtains and her soul as barren as the worn brown rug, because Thom had taught her, he and a thousand like him, to love Christ above all else, no matter the personal cost. "What does it profit a man . . . ?" She still had her faith, and it was enough.

But now Father Thomas Aloysius Maguire could not find the words to console her. Or even himself. There was nothing to say. So he let her talk and weep and make promises to God.

He stayed to have a late lunch, played with the children, and encouraged Johnny in his vocation. He promised to visit the school, and to visit them again soon. Then he offered his blessing. No one mentioned Jim until Thom was opening the front door and a young Christine, with her mother's dark eyes and the Maguire freckles and red hair, kissed him softly and asked, "Will my daddy stop being bad pretty soon?"

She caught him unaware. He wanted to explain that her daddy was not really bad, but he didn't know how. She waited patiently for Father Thom's answer.

"I'm not sure, honey, I'm really not sure. But I know he misses you and loves you very much."

"I love him too," she said softly, as if she were afraid her mother might hear. He stooped to kiss her again and closed the door behind him.

Thom drove around for a long time before his pain went away. He felt that Jim was deluding himself and making excuses for his irresponsible behavior. Thom hated himself for revealing his own indiscretions and for not fighting back, fearing to lose priestly decorum. He knew better. A priest had to stand above the people, to be strong enough to provide them with hope, not merely human enough to offer understanding. Otherwise the whole world would do what it damn well pleased! God must not be mocked!

Margaret's son decided he was ready to do battle with No One's child.

Jim was cooking hamburgers on a hot plate when Thom returned.

"I hope you like garlic—pour yourself a scotch unless you want beer. How do you like your burger?"

"Medium. And scotch's fine." He tried to remain cool.

"I was never good with hot plates." He stabbed the meat with a fork. "Maybe five more minutes." He completed tossing a salad with bits of salami and artichoke hearts and grated cheddar, then divided it in soup bowls.

"Very professional," Thom said softly.

"Connie used to say my salads should be eaten with a club—in case anything moves." He handed Thom a bowl and fork.

"What about Connie?" Thom's tone was accusatory.

Jim was immediately defensive. "You tell me! You apparently have made up your mind."

"You're damn right I've made up my mind. There must be a way to resolve this thing."

"Sure there is, hell yes! Just set up my leather recliner, hide my whiskey, and start saying the family rosary! You should know the way. You lived with it till you ran away to the seminary and found your easy God."

His words touched some open wound, and instinctively, without an instant's reflection, Thom struck him in the face. Jim made no effort to protect himself or to wipe the blood from his cut lip.

"Thank you, father. I'll go right over and get Connie and the kids." He turned away and began wiping his lip with a paper towel.

Thom was beside himself and began crying almost hysterically.

"Jim, Jim, I'm sorry. I really am—I didn't mean it—honest to God I didn't." He had never struck anyone in his life. The feeling of his fist against his brother's mouth had sickened him. He feared he was losing his mind as well as his faith.

"No big deal. I've been hit before. Eat your salad."

Jim fixed himself another drink and offered one to his brother.

"I'm so sorry—" Thom had lost the edge of his anger.

"Let's have a drink and forget it. We just won't talk about it anymore." He offered his hand and Thom embraced him warmly.

"I guess it was just seeing Connie and the kids."

"You went over there?"

"I just came from there. It—well it hurt."

Jim paused for a long time and then looked directly at his brother. "Thom, I think we got somewhere last night, and I don't want it ever to be like it used to be. I want to keep talking straight—like you're my brother."

"I want it that way, too."

"I don't ask you to admire me or even like me, although I want that. But I'm not going to be another John Patrick. No matter what! I can't. I just want you to know that I'm going to do what I have to do, regardless of what it is or how much it hurts."

"I understand." He said it softly.

They finished the hamburger almost in silence. Jim poured another drink and Thom declined.

"I need a little more to release something," Jim said, and he laughed. "Like Margaret's claws."

Thom lit a cigarette and poured more coffee. "You've really got a thing about her."

"So have you, you just don't know it yet. Who the hell wouldn't have—she's the strongest of all of us!"

"Are you still blaming her?"

"Hell no! It's my struggle now. You're the one who's still tied to Margaret. Your whole priesthood's your gift to her."

Thom flared. "Damn you! My priesthood is my sacrifice to God. I fought long and hard for it, harder than you'll ever know!" He thought of his breakdown at Cincinnati.

"Sacrifice? What sacrifice? You've got a nice comfortable framework, plenty of dough, everybody fawning over you, and undemanding pussy whenever you want it. Hell, your only sacrifice is a result of your own ambition. That dwarf bishop shit on you!"

Jim's words hit hard. Thom didn't back away. "That's the past! That's over! I just want to serve people who need me. Damn it, Jim, I hear your pain, I've heard tons of it in the last few years. And it tears me apart. You can call it anything you want, you can make up any reason you like for my faith. I don't give a damn. I want to be another Christ, and I don't give a shit what you think of it!" Thom was almost breathless.

"I think I'd like that. There's a place for Christ, just not for that easy God of the Church with all the priests and pat answers. My God understands!"

"Well, I'm glad He does. Does He also let you ignore your kids because you're too damn selfish to love your wife? Hell no, you're an intellectual. You make God whatever you want Him to be. Why don't you face it? Your God is Jim Maguire."

"What the fuck do you know about kids and wives? You never loved a kid in your life—or a woman for that matter! And keep your goddamned collar away from Johnny! Do you understand? He doesn't need your damned priesthood and your phony Church."

"You don't own Johnny, you arrogant son of a bitch! That's his decision!" Thom lost all control, pleading for his own vocation.

"Fuck decision! You never made one in your life. Margaret made them; now the Church makes them. It's all the same damn thing! Margaret, Mother Mary, Mother Church! You guilt-ridden son of a bitch, why don't you break free?"

"And spend my life experimenting with other people's lives like you? How many more people will you destroy, Jim?"

"Destroy? You should talk about destruction!" His voice was suddenly softer. "You don't really understand, do you?"

"I know I've sinned, Jim, and I know I've betrayed my priesthood. But I still don't approve of what you've done. You can't run from your responsibilities."

Jim laughed through his flowing tears, then turned toward the picture of his kids and the neon flickering through the rusted screen of his only window.

"Go in peace, Father Maguire, your conscience is clear! I'm on my own! I'm not a Catholic anymore! Only a Maguire. I finally received the only sacrament the Church isn't mature enough to offer. It's called graduation."

13

Easy God

Thom's energy was rekindled. Jim's very faithlessness was curiously the inspiration Thom needed to plunge back into his priesthood. Jim's life was proof enough of the futility of self-indulgence, and Thom determined to be a total priest.

After he left Jim, he spent the night in a Sheffield motel, untempted to call Roselle until the morning. He asked her to meet him for breakfast.

"Will it be okay? I mean—will anyone see us?"

"It'll be okay." There was a new firmness in his voice that frightened her.

He waited in a booth, then ordered coffee and smoked another cigarette. She finally slid into the booth next to him, gently stroking his thigh. He didn't stiffen or turn away; but it was as if she had not touched him. She ordered coffee.

He had never been more handsome, and she wanted to tell him, but she hesitated, speaking tentatively.

"I've missed you." She said it softly, without judgment. "How is your brother?"

"Okay." His tone told her that he hadn't called out of casual loneliness.

She shivered faintly while he fumbled for words. "Is something wrong?" she said.

"I'm wrong!" he said angrily. Then he talked about Jim and about his own self-pitying ambition and his childish deference to the bishop.

She brushed his face with her fingertips.

"I've got to put the pieces together—and I'm confused about us," he said. She had anticipated it, but she could not hide the pain. "I mean—I love you, Roselle, I really do—especially the way you've never pushed or prodded, or wanted more than I could give." He felt guilty.

"You don't want to see me anymore?"

"Of course I do." He struggled to be honest, reflecting on Jim's words and wondering if he had ever been able to tell the truth. "It's just that—well, I can't see you now, not now. I just can't! Our love can't go anywhere—" It was more difficult than he expected.

"Where does it have to go?" she asked without a trace of bitterness.

"Jesus, Roselle, help me! I mean—I don't know what the hell's wrong! I'm so damn confused and hurt—and guilty, so goddamned guilty! I keep feeling I owe you something—"

"You don't," she said. "If I never see you again, you've given me something more beautiful than I've dreamed of for a lot of years." She touched his hand. "And I treasure my faith. It's right, you know?"

"I even wonder about that."

"You take it more seriously somehow. I thought it was your priesthood; now I think it's just you." She smiled. "Maybe your teachers weren't as understanding as mine. But you are so intense, so beautifully intense—it's hard on you."

"Jim and I talked about that—about everything being so damn serious, so significant!" He squeezed his cigarette.

She laughed. "Even when you talk about it, you're intense. Almost like your God never lets up. Mine's more understanding."

He began to relax, and they ordered omelets and she teased him about the wrinkles in his forehead.

"Even love can be too serious," she said. "Sometimes we were so playful together—like children without a past or a future." She grinned. "My little Marcie never knows what day it is or whether the next meal will be lunch or dinner. Day and night, that's all there is, rain, snow, sun." She laughed beautifully.

"You're good for me," he said. "Sometimes I wish we had weeks just to roam beaches and sip wine."

"You're on the verge of something," she said. "Something very important. I can understand your needing to walk alone until—well, until you know." She smiled over her coffee. "That must have been some meeting with your brother!"

"It was." Then they were silent and he felt a strange, unfamiliar pride. It was as though a door had opened in his chest that would never close again. He was a man talking to a beautiful woman friend, not an adolescent insatiably sucking a soft round breast.

That afternoon he drove to the retreat house outside Sheffield. He made a general confession to a gentle monk of all the sins of his priesthood, and, to strengthen his new resolve, he made a private holy hour in the tiny chapel. In the evening he drove to Hamlin to visit Charlie Kenelley. Freddie Weber answered the door in his red cassock, explaining that Charlie was expected back from the hospital within the hour. He invited Thom to watch TV with him.

It was a game show, and the audience began to shout advice. Freddie pleaded for an excited couple, chewing the ends of his fingers. The frantic couple answered three questions in a row and won an electric dishwasher and a Ford sedan, and Freddie screamed with delight.

"That's a great show! The next one's a quiz show on music—"

"You look good, Freddie." He had gained weight and the once-small paunch had expanded around his hips and rear end. His face was fatter, and flabby folds under his chin made him look older.

"I feel good—just have to take it easy."

"I thought maybe the chancery would send some cases—"

"I never hear from them."

He struggled with eight bars of a Glen Miller favorite. "Oh, what is that?" He squirmed and munched his nails.

" 'Little Brown Jug,' " Thom volunteered.

"You'd be great at this!" He smiled in admiration. Thom would have won over two hundred dollars with "Atchison, Topeka, and the Santa Fe," "Juanita," and "In an Old Dutch Garden," when Charlie Kenelley returned, greeting Thom warmly.

"Let him finish, let him finish! He's sensational!"

Thom missed on "Amapola" and retired with Charlie to an office.

He briefed Charlie on the visit to his brother and his new insights about his own priesthood.

Kenelley had no magic words of support, and he talked briefly about his own survival. He had lost some fire with the confusing changes.

"I don't know what to tell you, Tommy, you're a fine

man and a hell of a priest. They can only hurt you if you let 'em."

"What's going to happen to the Church, Charlie?"

He sipped his Pepsi. "I suppose whatever happens to us. How's Dave Beauchamp?"

Thom mentioned a letter that sounded sad and defeated. "I guess his pastor's a tyrant from the old sod."

"He took enough shit for ten men. He's about as queer as I am! It's so damn ironic," he mumbled softly.

"How's Freddie doing?"

He laughed. "He's good to my mother, says his mass, and enjoys TV."

"Is the scar healing?" Charlie had kept the secret intact.

"I doubt it ever will. Then there's the anxiety—"

Thom nodded sympathetically. "It was good of you."

He waved the compliment away with a wrinkled hand. "There but for the grace of God— You know, I still can't take a drink."

Thom accepted a bourbon and they sat on the back porch enjoying the cool breeze whispering through a grove of willows. A flock of blackbirds gathered in a lonely oak tree to watch the last embers of twilight.

"I never thought it would turn out this way," said Kenelley softly.

"Are you happy here?"

"I really don't know if that matters. It's as good a place as anywhere. My mother's happy, and Freddie is —that counts for something. I still miss the hell out of Joe Quinn."

Finally he got up to leave, and Charlie touched his shoulder. "Do what you have to do, Tommy. It goes faster than you think—"

They watched the moon sneak behind thin clouds, casting an eerie light on silent blackbirds now snuggled in their own wings, as night finally descended to extinguish the last bent rays of a vagabond sun. And the day accepted the exchange as uncomplainingly as Charlie Kenelley.

Freddie looked up from an Alan Ladd movie. "You should get on that music show—you can, you know?"

"Maybe I will, Freddie."

Marty was married in August that year, and Thom sent her and Larry a subscription to the *National Catholic Reporter* and a warm note pledging his prayers for a happy, fruitful union and promising mass on the nuptial day. Marty seemed a very long time ago.

There was a note from Connie.

> He's drinking more, I understand, and neglecting his practice, but your mother and I have not given up on our prayers. We say the family rosary every night and ask God to straighten him out. We also pray for you and long for the day when Johnny will be a priest. Monsignor Doyle says he reminds him of you, and your mother and I thought how beautiful it would be if he would one day be your assistant.

She concluded with "Love and prayers" and wanted him to know that she would be glad to be his housekeeper when Margaret was too feeble to handle the job.

His visit to Jim had apparently had no effect. Ironically, the painful meeting had forced Thom to look deeper into his own soul and emerge a better priest. But he still wondered if he should have acknowledged his sin.

It was during the late summer of 1966 that Thom became aware of the impossible struggle of black Americans, and his priesthood found the focus it needed. Like most midwestern Catholics, he understood bigotry as a residue of Southern slavery that was not possible in Steelmont. He considered blacks as easygoing and content, believing the Detroit race riots more a result of the sultry climate and the crowded living conditions than a symbol of ideological warfare. His expanded education began one day when a young black college graduate rang the rectory doorbell. Since Ziggy was struggling to repair a power lawn mower, Thom invited the man to his office. In almost too elegant rhetoric, the black man talked of discrimination at General Motors. It was difficult to dismiss him as paranoiac. He simply told his story, listed his qualifications, and noted calmly that six white men had been promoted ahead of him. None of whom was his equal. Thom offered to investigate, not truly out of concern for racial justice, but simply out of a growing boredom.

The following day, Thom contacted a parishioner from Christ the King who was a plant supervisor. He was referred to Drake Gifford, plant manager, and, fortuitously, a recent convert to the Catholic Church. Thom accepted coffee and a brief tour of the plant, then explained his problem.

Gifford betrayed mild pique. "The Church can get involved where it doesn't belong, father—"

"Racial justice is part of Christ's Gospel, too, Mr. Gifford—"

"Please call me Drake." He rang for a secretary to bring more coffee along with the file of the complaining black man; then he skimmed through the file.

"Hmm. Graduated from Michigan State in engineering—good student—couple years of track. Let's see—married, two kids, cooperative, yes, father, he seems to be a good man."

He put down the folder, removed his tortoiseshell glasses, and tilted his head just slightly, almost benignly.

"It doesn't always work the way you want it, father. Sometimes uneducated people resent black supervisors. I grant you that Simpkins is a good man, but I can't make over a whole society. He's also a black man—"

Thom's sudden anger had as much to do with Jim and Elvin Ward as it did with an abused black, and he interrupted fiercely, "What the hell does Christianity mean to you, Mr. Gifford? We're not supposed to accept the world and apologize for it. We're supposed to change it!"

Drake Gifford's smile faded quickly. "Look, father, religion's great. It's done a lot for Arlene and the kids, and even I enjoy a good sermon, but I'm running a business, and I run it the best way I know how. This isn't a Sunday school."

"Apparently not, Mr. Gifford, it's a plantation! Well, I won't rest here. Either Billie Simpkins gets what he deserves, or I'll be on your ass."

The benign smile reappeared. "Look, father, I respect your concern. After all, you're a priest—"

"I'm also a mean son of a bitch, Mr. Gifford, and I'll go after your job or anyone else's if Simpkins isn't moved ahead." It felt good to be alive again. "And as a Catholic priest, I'll tell you one more thing. Don't go near the communion rail until you meet your moral responsibilities!"

Drake Gifford had met his match.

The following Monday he promoted Billie Simpkins and wrote a fierce letter to Bishop Elvin Ward about his personal contributions to the Church and "Father Maguire's immature rantings about things he doesn't understand."

Billie Simpkins told everyone he knew about "one hell of a priest" and began taking instructions from Father Thom Maguire.

By the fall, Thom had nine blacks in his instruction class and another thirty who had returned to the Church, and he had applied for a dozen scholarships for blacks at Steelmont's new Catholic Central. The diocesan superintendent of schools, Monsignor Leo Rademacher, called to warn Thom that he was moving too fast.

"We've got half a million dollars of unpaid pledges, Thom, and we don't want the laity thinking Catholic Central's going to be a racial powder keg."

"Twelve among eight hundred is hardly a powder keg."

"Depends what kind they are. A few radicals could—"

The scholarships were granted, a few pledges were withdrawn with hostile letters, and Bishop Elvin Ward received complaints from Don Bennett, the diocesan architect.

"Recognizing, as I do, our mutual commitment to Christian principles, I also realize that a lot of good people resent catering to black demands. Few Negroes are ready for our more difficult curriculum, and we could be obliged to lower our education standards."

Maurice Rabidoux, as dean, was asked to caution Thom.

"You haven't been in Steelmont that long, father. There's a lot of tension under the surface that could erupt."

"Twelve blacks?"

"One family can destroy property values. I'm only suggesting prudence—"

Thom ignored the wrist slap and began taking a door-to-door census of the black families within the boundaries of Our Lady of Czestochowa parish. He was provided an education that life in Kirkwood and the seminary had not offered. Poverty, oppression, police harassment, job discrimination, excessive rents, and frightful living conditions, but most disturbing of all, a resigned kind of hopelessness. At first the blacks were suspicious of his concern. Although they sustained a traditional respect for Christ, there was also a long history of being exploited by churches and unscrupulous ministers. When Thom challenged landlords and probation officers, provided bail for a young man falsely accused of auto theft, and confronted welfare workers who used humiliating gestapo techniques, his status in the black community grew. So did the publicity—good and bad.

He was appointed to the mayor's committee on racial justice, consulted by adult education experiments, and interviewed by the *Steelmont Journal* on the subject of slum landlords and ghetto crime. With the infallible assurance of a new convert, he made sweeping condemnations and outlined ambitious reforms. His Irish eloquence provided an abundance of inflammatory quotes which delighted the newspaper. Parishioners complained that he was turning the parish into a political platform, and two members of a lay trustee group—both of them generous contributors—resigned. Ziggy Denko, although somewhat intimidated, proved to be an honest, uncomplicated Christian, and he supported Thom in a suddenly exciting crusade, even attending a few meetings and drinking less beer.

A decaying priesthood came roaring back to life. A sleepy Saint Vincent de Paul Society was revitalized with clothing drives and canned goods collections; the Czestochowa ladies auxiliary, with an influx of younger members, held raffles and bake sales to provide furniture and more scholarships; and increasing numbers of college students and young professionals were lured back from urban parishes.

As his Christlike work became his most important prayer, Thom began to neglect his breviary. Only for a time did it trouble him, then he was able to ignore it for an entire week, and finally to leave it on his bookshelf as the pointless ritual of another culture. Nor did he confess his neglect. Or confess at all—even when, after months of rent strikes and job-opportunity meetings that exhausted him, he avoided priestly gatherings out of preference for contact with people who treated him simply as another man and not as a priest. He began by having a bowl of chili or a late-night taco at a cheap cafe, dressed in a sweater or a suede jacket without his collar. Then, sometimes after an explosive meeting or a tedious seminar, he started making solitary visits to out-of-the-way low-class bars. It became a ritual in itself, and it seemed to relax him.

He would slip his collar into the glove compartment and pull a gold golfing sweater from the trunk, then circle the fringes of Steelmont's east side in search of the right atmosphere. Most often it would be a bar with a jukebox and small dance floor, dark and secluded, where the clientele consisted of tattooed factory workers and plain, uneducated women who waitressed at dingy cafes or packed spark plugs and custom gas caps.

Usually he sipped a beer or two at the bar, posing as a high school baseball coach or a traveling salesman. He enjoyed the instant camaraderie of men and women who seemed content with the inevitability of their lives or else were too secretly fragile to deal with their own dissatisfactions. He felt incredibly free. There were no moral dilemmas or psychological interpretations of behavior or attitudes, no need to impress or to be an example. A person was what he said he was until he proved otherwise, and if a woman didn't want to "get laid" it was because she felt misused or feared pregnancy. It had nothing to do with God.

The dance floor was a mélange of grinding bodies that barely moved their feet, and on the fourth or fifth visit to one such place, after a third beer, Thom asked a sepia-skinned nurse's aide to dance. Without a word they moved to the dance floor and immediately were locked legs over warm thighs in a squeezing embrace. His right hand fondled an incredible ass as her fingers played with the back of his hair, and he rolled her full breasts around his chest and arm, feeling her snuggle against his erect prick. Not a single sentence was spoken. Then they walked back to their seats, smiled gently, and moved off into their private worlds until someone else asked her to dance and she began again.

Thom chose not to pursue anyone beyond the dance floor, and frequently he only sipped beer and observed, strangely refreshed by the earthy, often loud environment. As exciting as it was unlikely and forbidden for Margaret's sheltered son.

Nor did he confess his sinful indulgences, as if his work among persecuted blacks and his dalliance with unsophisticated lust had freed him from some middle-class Catholic conscience. He didn't feel even slightly guilty when he exchanged jacket for Roman collar and slipped past a snoring Ziggy at 3:00 A.M. In the morning he rose —like an O'Brien—to say the seven o'clock mass and to battle the oppressors. Challenging petty bureaucrats, as well as the conscience of the Church itself.

At an area meeting of the American Civil Liberties Union, Thom encountered his seminary roommate, Bill Collins, bearded and fiercely outspoken but with the same droll and boyish sense of humor. After a tense meeting about cruel and arbitrary slum clearance, they drifted out for a beer and laughed for almost an hour about Saint Robert's Seminary and Elvin Ward. Thom learned that Monsignor Nowicki was a reasonably popular pastor of a Croatian congregation, and he admitted his own resentments about the Sheffield Diocese. Collins understood.

"It's no different in Washtenaw. Bishop Malloy's senile, and the new auxiliary thinks sex was discovered by Margaret Sanger to expose the virgin birth." He threw back his head and laughed.

Thom wondered about Collins's connection with the Church.

"I don't go much. Actually it bores me, but I still feel I'm a Catholic who's rejected some narrow-minded God."

Thom grinned. "My brother calls Him the easy God. Just keep His rules and you're home free."

Collins agreed quickly. "You never have to worry about justice for blacks or a more complex morality than approved sex and mass on Sundays."

"How'd you get involved in the racial justice scene?"

"I married a black girl in South America, and we've had three 'nigger' kids. It doesn't take a hell of a lot more."

Thom breathed surprise. "You don't fool around!"

Collins smiled quietly and shook hands. "Call me sometime."

The city of Steelmont condemned twenty-eight houses on the east side and made plans to replace them with cheap apartment buildings despite the fact that the residents had paid exorbitant rents for as long as ten years and made what improvements they could afford. Including well-loved vegetable gardens and a small community playground created with secondhand equipment and volunteer labor. Thom alerted a reporter who was looking for recognition, assisted him with interviews, and stumbled on the perfect lead quote from a small boy: "Hey, Father Thom, this ain't no slum. It's mah neighborhood."

Thom approached Jack Hughes, a banker from Christ the King parish whose American Federal Savings Bank was involved in financing the project.

"Why not refinance the houses for the residents and let them become owners?" He knew that Jack, despite his job, was a concerned liberal.

"I doubt there's enough credit down there, and besides, father, there's big money involved in this."

"What if Ziggy and I cosigned in the name of the parish?"

"All your property's a corporation solely in the bishop's name." He sucked his pipe reflectively. "There might be a chance if the bishop got behind it."

Thom called Harold Eberlee for advice. "You're getting in over your head, father. The bishop's already disturbed by your involvement. He'd go crazy!" Thom sensed Eberlee's own resistance and called Bill Collins.

"Hell of an idea!"

"What if it comes from you?"

"I think you're probably right. Grumpy was never too fond of you."

Collins drafted a letter to Bishop Elvin Ward and briefly outlined the problem and a Christian solution to it, suggesting that it might become a "Catholic model for the entire country." He also made passing reference to the advantage his seminary Latin classes had given him in his chosen profession, hoping Elvin had forgotten graduation day. An appointment was arranged, and four dark-suited, bearded young attorneys and accountants invaded Elvin Ward's mahogany and royal red office. Ward greeted Collins without a flicker of a smile, then listened attentively to their proposal.

"It's a noble proposal, gentlemen, but not our function. We are not in the financing business."

Collins attacked. "I think it's more properly called housing the homeless." It was an unfortunate thrust, but it probably made little difference.

Ward bristled. "Is there anything else, gentlemen?" A comma pause. "Then I bid you good day!"

He sent a brief official warning to Father Maguire not to involve himself in "dramatic confrontations that have precious little to do with your limited jurisdiction." Thom was reminded of the "unfortunate debates" at the university and asked to devote himself to the spiritual welfare of his assigned parish.

Thom did not back off. A few days before Christmas, he outlined "Operation Cosign" for the *Steelmont Journal,* appealed to wealthy Christians who "feel some responsibility to persecuted blacks," and arranged a reception in the parish hall where possible cosigners could meet the families who needed help. Attractive black children stood in front of a Christmas crib and told about "fun in the neighborhood," and the most articulate parents explained their hopes and Christmas dreams. Magnificent press coverage was given by the wire services, and Operation Cosign became a national story. More than forty volunteers approached a delighted Jack Hughes to cosign mortgages that included ample money for home improvements and new appliances at less cost per month than the original rents, and the city fathers promised to consider acreage for a municipal park in the area. Hundreds of letters came to Our Lady of Czestochowa's rectory offering help and requesting Thom to establish similar programs in other cities.

And dozens more came to Bishop Elvin Ward demanding that "the Church stay out of politics." He called his auxiliary, the owl-eyed Joe Beahan, to his office and arranged a meeting after the holy season.

Thom arrived at Margaret's on Christmas afternoon. She was delighted with a new liturgical missal he brought, even though she would continue to use the old one. She hardly seemed older, and Thom sensed a new serenity, as if she had slipped behind a silver shadow where no one could hurt her anymore. Even Jim's apostasy had been relegated to God's own time. As they drove to Anne's she briefed Thom on her assorted complaints.

"I can't talk about anything at Anne's. She's such a holier-than-thou Catholic, and that big goof she's married to thinks he's the pope."

Dick Dorgan, misunderstanding Margaret's loyalties, had made the mistake of condemning Jim in her presence.

Dorgan could "damn well look after his own life," she had told Mary O'Meara. "His kids could stand a few manners."

Even Connie, a tentative ally in Margaret's battle to win Jim back to God, did not escape her indictment.

"Leave it to the ones who never had anything to spend the money. You should see her in the supermarket, never looks at a price—and the kids' clothes are scattered all over the house. If she'd spent a little less and fixed a decent meal, maybe Jim wouldn't be running all over creation. God knows he worked hard enough—we all did—little enough thanks you get."

The grandchildren were to be pitied, and she would do her best to keep them close to God. Her love for the children was pure and generous, although she thought Anne's children were "too fresh, like that father of theirs." Jim's children, especially young Johnny, were very dear to her. Actually Thom agreed with her assessment of the children and her evaluation of Dick Dorgan. Margaret, for all her faults, had an uncanny sense about people. Even her assessment of Connie was far from inaccurate—though Margaret never mentioned sex.

At Anne's, they were lost in dolls and trains and a first red bike. "Don't forget to thank grandma and Father Thom."

"Thom, watch me, watch me!"

A rigid Anne corrected, "Father Thom, Patrick!"

After too much turkey and some tears over a fire engine's demise, the five children were dispatched, and Thom settled down in the living room with Anne and her husband. Margaret, after joining in the rosary and a fierce round of militaristic prayers of the Legion of Mary, insisted on cleaning up the kitchen and bathing the little children.

Anne extolled the English in the mass as well as the new participation in priestly work. She looked forward to the day when Dick, and even she herself, might distribute communion.

"They're doing it in some places in Europe, already," Thom said, recalling a remark of Bobbie Foley's.

"Not with papal approval," Dick asserted loyally. "They're jumping the gun!" He was the first lay reader selected at Saint Raphael's, and he had joined Anne in conducting Cana conferences throughout the Sheffield Diocese to wage war against birth control and therapeutic abortion.

"It's not therapeutic at all," Dick said agitatedly to some distant enemy. "It's simple murder!"

He described mangled fetuses and crunching craniotomies, preaching in his weak, unresonant Irish tenor too rapidly to be believed. His face looked flabbier. He worked hard at a busy practice that was composed of devout Catholics who followed his temperature charts in rhythmic faith.

Anne echoed a younger Margaret. "Abstinence never hurt anyone. The whole world's so damned self-indulgent." She was still thinking of Jim.

Dorgan nodded too much assent. "Abstinence's not that tough—we've done it."

Anne's matronly breasts swelled to silence him and she changed the subject abruptly to bring Thom up to date on Tim, who was still at the lumber camp.

"You should write a strong letter. He says he can't get to mass up there in the woods. Dick thinks he's sleeping with that girl friend of his."

Dorgan's thin staccato supported her: "Immature—takes no responsibility—probably lives with her."

"Notre Dame's half Protestant," Anne said. "If you say anything, Tim just grins like it's one big joke!"

Thom listened impatiently as they attacked Jim—out of Margaret's hearing.

"Lives in that run-down hotel—Dick thinks he has cheap women there—neglecting his practice—drinking all over town. Wanders around the woods like he's twelve. All he needs is a dog!" she scoffed.

Dick nodded. "I didn't want his practice. He knows my stand. Doc McGregor did what he had to." He had never recovered from the guilt of reporting Jim, even though it was at Anne's insistence.

"And the doctor's wife is such a martyr! Now she's even got mother hoodwinked." Anne's rasp was more biting than Margaret's had ever been.

"Where are the kids? I thought they'd drop by here."

"I didn't invite them," Anne said. "She never had time for us with her new Buick and her country club friends. She's getting hers."

"For God's sake, Anne!"

"Fine language for a priest. You sound like your brother."

"Connie's been through a lot—and so have the kids!"

"She's got plenty of money. Your brother took anything that could pay. Besides, her parents are alive and they do for her. I've got five children. Did you forget?"

There was no talking to her. She fixed more coffee and began extolling Bishop Ward and Monsignor Foley.

"They stand for something!"

Thom almost mentioned Operation Cosign, but he already knew that Anne considered his labors a disobedient act.

Margaret finished cleaning the kitchen and was as eager to leave as Thom. The Dorgans knelt for Thom's blessing.

Margaret settled into the car. "There's no need of a pope with the two of them around." She had overheard it all and couldn't wait to share it with Mary O'Meara.

The house was ablaze with lights when Connie greeted Margaret and Thom, who were loaded with more presents. Mrs. Hackett heated tea and flat mince pie, then apologized for her husband who snored loudly in Jim's easy chair. No one made any move to wake him.

Connie's face revealed a new firmness around the mouth. "I'm better now," she said.

Thom felt the shame at his brother's irresponsibility, but he was sad when the children ripped open their presents and never mentioned Jim.

"He didn't even send a present," whispered Connie.

"Can you imagine?" asked Mrs. Hackett.

They spoke out of Margaret's hearing.

Thom could think of nothing to say, and Margaret only smiled at the children. Eager to tell Mary O'Meara about the pie.

Mrs. Hackett continued. "The whole world's going crazy, father. I'm glad I won't be here to see it. Even the Church is changing." She sighed heavily.

Margaret was relieved when they finally left. "What does she know about the Church? That shiftless son of hers never even went to a Catholic school—and that slob of a husband in Jim's chair."

Thom saw her into the house. There were a few soft

lights around the Christmas crib on the mantel and a small tree blinked sadly.

"Can you stay tonight?" She already knew.

"No, I've got the early mass." Seeing the lonely figure lost in the large house, Thom felt like crying.

Margaret made no protest.

"It's strange," she said, "how much I miss your father."

"I know."

She looked gray and sad, but still barely wrinkled. Her child's blue eyes misted, but she recovered quickly.

"I put mince pie and turkey sandwiches in the back seat. Stop along the way and have coffee."

He held her gently and kissed her on the cheek.

"I failed somewhere," she said. Her eyes filled with tears again.

"You didn't fail, mother—"

"Maybe you could reach your brother. It's so sad, the kids and all." Then she was caught in some memory. "He was a good boy. He always fixed my stove—"

"He'll come around."

"I'm not so sure," she said. "I dreamed of mice twice last week. It's not a good sign."

"Mother! You sound like a pagan."

"I did the best I could," she said.

She stood at the door and waved sadly as he drove off.

Then she knelt before the crib and said her rosary for her pale Jim.

She turned out the Christmas lights, brought the three wise men a few inches closer to the crib, and smiled at them like a small child.

"It won't be long," she told them, "and you'll see the Christ child!"

☘ ☘ ☘

In January, Bishop Ward assembled Auxiliary Bishop Beahan and Monsignor Foley to discuss the contumacy of Thomas Maguire.

The bald, lanky auxiliary counseled patience. "He may have gotten the attention he needed. There may be no further incidents, bishop," Beahan said.

Bobbie Foley's puffy jowls wiggled a nasal agreement. "We could come down hard the next time with a threat of suspension."

Ward snarled unbecomingly. "He's always been stubborn and hard to reach. Arrogant! Any further outbursts, and we'll act decisively." The regal plural did not include Beahan and Foley.

In February, there was another explosion. A careful plan to erect a federally funded vocational school on parish property was submitted by Ziggy Denko. It was promptly turned down by the diocesan building commission at Elvin Ward's recommendation. Ziggy was heartbroken, but Thom took another tack. He scoured the area looking for a building and enlisted the aid of sympathetic parishioners and assorted candidates without asking anyone's permission. It felt good to be his own person. Finally, a banker called him about a suitable building that needed a tenant who had some imagination and good credit. It was a real bargain, and, with the banker's help, Thom qualified.

It was a solid old concrete factory with adequate floor space and a good-sized parking lot, and Thom leased it and began remodeling with federal funds. At the groundbreaking ceremony, his picture appeared in the *Journal* with Ziggy Denko and Billie Simpkins, and the following day the story and picture were carried in Sheffield. When Thom returned home that night, there was a special-delivery letter from the chancery office. He was to appear the following afternoon—Ash Wednesday—to meet with Bishop Ward.

And he was ready! Eager and excited! As ten years of priesthood pounded wildly in his brain, he sat up late and carefully outlined everything he wanted to say. Freddie Weber and Herschel Schaeffer; a slurring Bishop Schmidt and Maurice Rabidoux; the snarling, demeaning Italian inflection of the diminutive Elvin Ward. It would all come out, every last angry scream, as he practiced his raging eloquence and pounded his fist on the littered desk. He only wished Jim could be present for the confrontation. He realized that he missed his brother and promised himself to visit Jim right after Easter. It would be a different Thomas Maguire.

For more than two hours he rehearsed the agonizing humiliations until his brain was raw and an entire yellow legal pad had been covered with angry indictments. Then each page was ripped off, crumpled fiercely, and thrown into an overflowing basket. He was ready for Cromwell and Elizabeth and every arrogant Yankee who starved his forebears and robbed them of their ancient dignity. Ready without whiskey or melancholy songs or beguiling charm that concealed pain and manipulated fat-faced landlords and thin-lipped tycoons. His boiling blood and thick Irish chest were prepared for the whole British Commonwealth and WASP America. Assuredly he was prepared for a dimple-chinned dwarf called the Most Reverend Elvin Ward.

He slept fitfully, said a distracted seven o'clock mass, refused a scowling Mary's bacon and eggs, and paced nervously in his office, devouring cigarettes. To strengthen his resolve, he recalled his last conversation with Jim. This time he had nothing to lose. Finally it was one o'clock, and he drove to Sheffield like a crusader in final battle with the Moslems over Jerusalem. In his arsenal was every drop of rage from each O'Brien and O'Dwyer and Maguire who ever lived. It was 2:15 when Terry Lanier acknowledged his presence in the chancery and informed him that he was fifteen minutes early.

"I just wanted to be here on time." He saw Lanier flinch momentarily at some new power he felt coming from Thom. A buzzer rang and Lanier picked up the phone. He nodded timidly to Thom, led him to the entrance to Ward's office, then nodded again. Thom walked in without a trace of nervousness, his face almost as flushed as the carpet. Then he turned pale.

Bobbie Foley sat behind the bishop's desk in full monsignorial red. Almost comically out of place, he cleared his throat and nodded crisply. His hands trembled as he gathered his notes, his voice thin and faltering.

"Bishop Ward asked me to—"

"I want to see him, monsignor." The fierceness startled Bobbie as he tried to catch his breath.

"That won't be necessary, or possible. He instructed me to tell you that any—," he glanced officiously at his notes, "any further involvement in racial strife or any dramatic, irresponsible confrontations that are not your personal concern will result in your suspension *ex informata conscientia* by your ordinary. Depriving you of all rights and privileges. . . ."

The bland nasal monotone rang in Thom's ears. There was nothing he could do, nothing to say to the obese jowls that parroted Elvin Ward's continuing vengeance. Thom was on the verge of explosion, but there was no one to hear him except the flabby Bobbie Foley, still reciting what the censure entailed.

Then came a tense silence.

"That about does it, eh Bobbie!" The words were like bullets.

"Yes, that's all of it." His tone was gentle and inoffensive, as if he wanted to prevent an argument. There was not a shred of the Roman arrogance.

"Well done, Bobbie, very well read. See you around!" He moved toward the door. The room was electric. Elvin Ward had calculated his insult well.

"The best way to reach Maguire is not to pay any attention to him. He's an attention seeker."

It had worked. At the door Thom moved back toward Bobbie Foley, then extended his hand. The sudden motion frightened the pudgy monsignor, and he cowered and backed away.

"There's nothing to be afraid of, Bobbie." Thom pumped his hand vigorously. Then he strode out the door, ignoring Terry Lanier's acknowledgment.

Bobbie Foley was still trembling at the episcopal desk. Sweat rolled down his face as he disappeared into Elvin Ward's private bathroom.

14

Holy Week, Spring, and Resurrection

When a man has learned since weaning that life is played for heaven and hell, and when he truly believes it, he is as marked as Cain ever was. Even when he turns from childhood faith, life becomes forever serious—the pursuit of money as tense as the hoarding of grace; the search for love as preoccupying as the desire for heaven; and Calvary itself merely changes location. And in the futile search for the master plan to peace, sex must be as ecstatic as it once was sinful.

James Maguire, apostate, was as scarred as any priest. It had never been enough simply to live, and now family and ambition had become as pointless as heaven and hell.

No culture is perfect, despite its claims. It is only a history of survival, and freedom simply means the capacity to discriminate between the good and the bad of that survival. To abandon an entire culture is to be left with nothing, not even one's self. Not to understand this is to ignore origins, to fight a lonely battle that never can be won, to spend one's life alone. As No One's son. Like James Maguire.

Jim's dramatic move to the hotel was considered final proof that he had gone mad. After his last confrontation with Thom, he grew a beard, dressed even more casually, and spent fewer hours at his office. His new partner hardly complained, since putting up with Jim's eccentricities seemed a small price to pay for the generous partnership. Connie and the children were well provided for, and their devout Catholic faith, together with almost universal sympathy, continued to sustain them. Connie was especially grateful that Jim no longer bothered them.

On the first day of spring, in 1967, Jim finished a few calls at the hospital and stopped for a midmorning breakfast on the outskirts of town. He studied the waitress. Pale marble skin, long black hair, and an open face, she was Irish, there was no need to ask. He might have loved the paleness of skin too long absent from the sea, or caressed the hunched posture that hid her breasts. A younger Connie. He could have stripped off her cotton dress, rubbed his hands over her smooth thighs, snapped the gold cross from around her slender neck as he fondled and sucked until she screamed Jesus's name in purest joy. As unaware as he himself that history was her sadness, the bitter centuries her pain, and the induced lust only a chance to regain what rightfully was hers.

He paid his bill and serenely made his way back to his hotel. The lobby was as quiet as death. A gentle old man shuffled papers behind a desk, an old lady knitted in a worn chair, and two men mumbled in Polish and smoked cheap cigars. Jim walked up to his room feeling strangely at home among the poor and forgotten. He was comfortable. There was an end to some lifelong pressure and never-ending competition. There was no need to call anyone to disturb his peace.

He finished a cup of coffee, took a pill to quiet a headache, and went out to wander through Kirkwood's east side. The weather was still cool in late March, so he sat in a disheveled cafe and studied a fat lady in a green print dress eating voraciously with her skinny husband, even as she talked of dieting rather than dying.

Death was everywhere, but it no longer frightened Jim. Waiting behind heaven and hell, waiting behind redemption and sorrow for sin, waiting behind Connie and the kids. On the streets, death was not hidden. No Church camouflage or affluent disguise. No mystic interpretations.

A young waitress in a spotted yellow uniform served him coffee. Her rural sensuality attracted him. Only when she asked "anything else?" did he discover that she had no teeth, and he stared at a grease blister on her right thumb while she scribbled a check. When Jim dared to look up and ask for cream, there were no questions in her soft blue eyes.

A trucker settled near Jim and greeted her warmly. "What's happening?"

"I've been in Detroit, Dave. Had my teeth pulled." She

rubbed a finger over bare gums. "The dentist won't make new ones till I give him three hundred dollars, so I'm working double shifts."

"You'll be some kind of lady with them new teeth."

Jim wondered about her husband.

It didn't matter. There was a frontier strength in her jaw, a quiet joy in her eyes as she moved skillfully from counter to tables, smiling coyly at Dave. Jim could have helped her out, but what sense would money have made? She was working to buy new teeth and that was enough to keep her mind off of loneliness and death. She asked nothing of life, expected less, and could live for a promise of teeth, grateful, as she told Dave, "that the aching is gone," ready to face Jim and the itinerant laborers with a mouth like a baby squid. Competing with no one.

Jim smiled at her beauty, not understanding his own reaction. Once the raw gums would have obsessed him. He would have been obliged to pursue her with an outburst of middle-class pity. He would have wanted her to have teeth that he might be free from pain—to blot some ancient Catholic tragedy from the landscape. But she had found a greater reason to survive than most. With nothing. He felt a new joy pounding at his temples.

Once he had created his own pain. Even his children had finally turned away because in some strange Irish masochism he demanded it. He paused to remember their faces and felt briefly the pressure of tears, especially for Johnny. Jim now relished the freedom of standing outside of life and looking in, and the unfamiliar focus seemed to make his senses more acute. And everywhere he walked he saw the procession of pain with new understanding.

Later that evening he walked joyfully into a bar where a drunk Mexican was singing the songs that had given meaning to his childhood. A louder man with a black patch on his eye was talking to a fat barfly who was dressed in faded orange pants. Jim saw the tattoo wiggle on the man's arm as he scratched the woman's thigh. A wino with tape on his glasses bought drinks for everyone, while a skinny whore offered to suck him off for ten dollars.

When he declined, she shouted, "Okay, cheap muthafucka!"

Jim laughed.

When he turned, everyone had gone. The bar was like an abandoned church, deserted by even the most tawdry gods.

He left to wander among the dying. Even the sight of the children no longer upset him. He had seen his own children, once fresh and loving, warm and curious, sensitive to pain of man or animal, already begin to surrender. Soon it would be too late to salvage them from God and success and the rattle of death.

He made his way through the lobby of his hotel, and two old ladies who were sitting there knitting smiled sweetly at him. Life was no longer serious. It was finally a game. In his room, he glanced out the window at the last patches of melting snow. The ground was already muddy, and winter had become as odorless as life.

Soon there would be cherry blossoms and wild roses in the woods, the mildew of rain and celery muck and decaying leaves. The pungent manure of the hedgerows and the sweet smell of the pines surrounding Lemmert's Grove. Frogs and turtles would surface stealthily near giant water lilies, and April rains would warm the cold earth.

Already penitents were making their way to Lenten services at Saint Raphael's, and children were gaining plenary indulgences to rescue souls from purgatory's fire. The nuns were pressing purple hoods to cloak the statues and ordering palm fronds for the procession, and his own Johnny would be serving mass. And, while sinners were mumbling their wrinkled confessions, kites would fly over fresh green hills, and boys and girls would fall in love near Lake Watseka. Flowers would rise everywhere; ladies would buy feathered hats for Easter—winter's pall would have proved an illusion. And James Maguire would be among the first to welcome spring!

☘ ☘ ☘

At the end of the same winter, Father Thomas Maguire had finally found his priesthood although Margaret worried about his forgotten breviary and Anne criticized his problems with Bishop Ward.

"Pride goes before the fall." Dick Dorgan had nodded appropriately.

Jim's departure from reality troubled Thom, who took it as a personal affront, more than anyone, and his fierce intolerance of his brother's plight was the only clear evidence of an imperfect conversion. Thom had opened his soul to Jim, humiliated himself as never before to anyone, and still his brother had slipped away like an embittered sheep. Thom Maguire did not like to lose.

Yet, despite Jim, he had new energies. His struggle for the dispossessed blacks was reason enough to be a priest. He was ready to be a martyr for the people, as strong and unafraid as any Margaret.

On Palm Sunday, his picture appeared again in the *Sheffield Chronicle*. He had led a march on city hall to demand the release of property for a promised park and low-cost housing in east Steelmont. It was unmistakably Thomas Maguire, singing "We Shall Overcome," his mouth wide open and his Irish eyes laughing wildly.

At the breakfast table, Elvin Ward turned pale, then red, and he left the table to summon Joe Beahan and Bobbie Foley. God would not be mocked!

On Monday of Holy Week, Thom received a message from Sister Marietta announcing that she was registered at the Thunderbird Motel on Drake Highway and that she wondered if she could take him to dinner before she returned to Kirkwood on Wednesday. He surmised an educational conference and checked his calendar. As he prepared to call her, the doorbell rang. A special-delivery letter from the chancery. To Reverend Thomas A. Maguire.

He was to appear in the bishop's office at ten o'clock the Monday after Easter, the first business day after Holy Week. The letter was uncustomarily signed by Elvin Joseph Ward, "Sincerely your servant in Christ." He knew a confrontation was imminent, and he was not in the least afraid. In fact, he was jubilant.

He glanced at the previous week's letter from Dave Beauchamp in San Diego. Dave complained of sickness, which was not like him, and Thom promised himself a trip to California to visit Dave and Chet Golas. The trip might come sooner than he anticipated. He laughed. "Like next week."

He dialed the Thunderbird Motel and heard Sister Marietta's familiar voice.

"You sound in a good mood," she said. "What's funny?"

"Everything."

"I need your help."

"You've got it." It was great to be a priest.

Thomas Maguire was fulfilled! Even Jim would have been proud.

❧ ❧ ❧

But Jim had little time for pride. Lost in boyhood memories, he drove to the edge of the woods, walked across the playground, and followed the familiar path toward the swamp. A final spring snow was falling, softly protesting the victory of the approaching spring. Jim walked along the stream and felt the snowflakes melting on his cheeks. The ice was beginning to break, and black rivulets of water flowed bravely along and swallowed the hissing snow. The air was almost balmy, and the woods were silent. A few oak leaves, dried and yellow, still clung to the branches of a small tree, stubborn survivors of a long Michigan winter. He gently took a leaf in his hand as he watched the silhouette of the day merge into twilight.

Spring was about to erupt—his special time, a silent promise of survival, stronger than depression or a lost family or a scarred religious faith. An end to the dismal grayness of the Michigan landscape. Soon the black-eyed Susans would grow up along the edges of the dusty roads, there would be buttercups and violets wandering across the fields; and the goldenrod would wait patiently until the summer's sun was fiercest to release its yellow dust into the burning air. Then he would be finally free of the winter that had lasted all his life

Shadows moved across the swamp, a nighthawk warned of an end to twilight, and darkness began to settle in. The snow stopped falling. He followed the familiar path up the long hill to the playground and found his car. There had been no time to visit Sandy's grave in Lemmert's Grove, but he would come again soon. When it was spring.

As he drove away, he felt the most profound sense of peace he had known in years. Only the thought of

Johnny's serious face still troubled him. He decided to stop at the house on his way home.

When his car chugged to a stop in the driveway, Jim could see Chrissie at the piano framed in the picture window. Jimmy answered his ring, startled at his father's beard, then admitted him and disappeared. Connie and a protective Johnny came in from the kitchen, and Chrissie stopped playing the piano. Jim smiled warmly at the confusion.

"I just stopped by to say hello. Is everything okay?" The room was tense. Even Chrissie was at a loss for words after the yearlong absence.

"We're fine," Connie said crisply.

No one else said a word.

"I'm okay, too. Really fine." His smile lit up the room, and Chrissie grinned back.

"I like your beard, daddy." Connie's look silenced her.

"Thank you, darling. You look very pretty, too." She blushed happily. He knew it was time to leave, and he moved toward the door. Connie followed at a safe distance.

"Johnny has some dental expenses."

Jim nodded approval. He opened the door.

Connie was not through, as a sober-faced Johnny, tall and strong, stood by. "It might interest you to know that he's been accepted at Saint Robert's Seminary. He'll leave in September."

It was like a sharp pain in Jim's heart. Then the pain disappeared and he walked to his car and drove away.

The worst had happened. He had lost Johnny to Margaret's God. Now it was suddenly easier. There was nothing more to fear or to be angry at. He was all alone, stripped of Church and family and even children. There was only James Maguire. He returned to the edge of the woods and watched the moon revive all the old memories in soft, luminous shadows. Then No One's son —or father—fell asleep, and he awoke shivering to see the promise of a splendid sunrise over the silent pines.

The same week, on Holy Thursday in Kirkwood, when Lent's purple gave way to the Last Supper, a bearded James Maguire sat joyfully at the back of Saint Raphael's Church. A detached critic reviewing the spectacle. He grinned, thinking, Well cast. Should enjoy a long run. Ending's a real shocker!

Monsignor Doyle, stooped and graying, bent to wash an assistant's immaculate feet, and then the high altar was stripped of its garments. Judas snuck from the banquet to collect his silver fee. Hardly an evil traitor—only a depression child like Jim, looking for a return on his investments.

He saw the familiar intensity on the repentant faces of the congregation. Jim was a boy again, but without the restrictions and fears of childhood. Freed from competition with Thom, from the guilt of Margaret and Connie and her children, from John Patrick's wordless despair. Freed even from the whispers of a few parishioners who recognized him under his beard.

Kirkwood and Saint Raphael's were no different from the world. The competition there was as keen as in New York. J. R. Harris's son, now a Catholic, owned his own lumber company and talked more slowly than the president of General Motors. He knew the first names and birthdays of all of his employees, yet his ambition was as fierce, his greed as obvious and dishonest as the greatest of moguls. Ed O'Toole looked like a small-town lawyer in a ragged turtleneck sweater, but he understood contingencies and didn't hesitate to take forty percent of the Ryans' settlement when Tommy was maimed by the beer truck outside of the Shamrock Lounge. Ryan himself manipulated the city council with his zoning changes as well as any broker in the country. And Doc McGregor knew how to cheat on insurance claims.

There might be fewer dirty books in Kirkwood Drugs, but the aftermath of a cocktail party at the Kirkwood Country Club could match the most extravagant fantasy. A barber had managed to kill his ex-wife last year; the retarded Kelly girl had been raped; the American National Bank had been successfully robbed twice.

On Friday afternoon, Christ was dying between two thieves, and faithful mourners assembled, reluctant to weep for themselves. The tabernacle was empty and the banks were closed, the money, like Jesus, waiting in a secret vault. Good Friday! James Maguire walked the silent streets of Kirkwood's east side. He hoped Christ was not dying for him. He knew at last there was only one's own death, not to be put off by epic interpretations. He smiled. Christ should have died anonymous.

It was misting, still chilly as evening approached and Judas haggled with the high priests. How much for a man's blood? Not much on the streets. Jim felt surrounded by death, but there was nothing left to fear. The bishop was running barefoot, and Jesus finally smiled. Even at Judas!

On Holy Saturday, Jim was jubilant with his new freedom. The day of Saturn, ancient god of farmers and struggling Irish peasants who gave him life. God of happiness and consort of the fruitful Ops who mothered Jupiter. A god no longer, now only a lifeless planet, as barren as earth.

Jim sold his car and distributed the money on the streets. Only the bums would take it. The final fifty dollars went to a red-eyed man with bushy black eyebrows, a huge Irish nose, and an outdated brown suit neatly patched in three or four places.

"Christ Almighty! Thank ya—thankya! What the hell's going on? Christ Almighty!"

"It's spring!"

"You're damn right it is!"

Jim walked the three miles to Lemmert's Grove and Sandy's grave. Happier than he had ever been in his life. To celebrate the spring.

Early on Sunday morning, while Christ still waited in the tomb to surprise his friends after a brief weekend, Margaret sent Tim to Jim's apartment to invite him to breakfast and see if he would make his Easter duty.

Tim entered to the smell of cabbage. The lobby was a menagerie of used people. A lady with dyed red hair newly rinsed to honor the Resurrection. A black-eyed bearded man with half a nose chatted in Croatian with a fat scar-faced black who smoked cigars and spat periodically into a plastic bag on his lap. Not understanding a word. A wrinkled old woman in a rainbow velvet hat waited for her son to take her to church, fearing he would be late. Tim searched for his brother and felt the pain of the city, hoping Christ would arise again and again if He could erase it.

Finally the clerk directed him to Room 303. Tim knocked, but there was no answer. The clerk agreed to let him in. Irish Jimbo in 303—with no family and a few clothes in a dark closet—was gone. The soiled chair, the worn rug, and the green painted walls were silent.

Behold he is risen! He is not here!

Tim returned to report the empty tomb to Margaret.

Jim had already risen in the cool darkness of Lemmert's Grove to celebrate his own Easter. He studied the woods as a dreaming child with sleep marks on his face, and he rearranged the stones on Sandy's grave. Where had Saturn gone? He disappeared before Jim had a chance to say good-bye, just as Sandy had. Perhaps it was better. Jim never liked farewells.

As he opened the small white box, the sun appeared, soft and promising. It was Easter! Christ's brief sleep was interrupted, and Mary Magdalen mistook him for the gardener. Peter and the apostles snuck from hiding. So did the divorced Catholics and lapsed sinners. Alleluia! Alleluia!

Jim rested on Sandy's grave to bid good-bye to Easter and welcome to spring! Alleluia!

☘ ☘ ☘

Thom's own Holy Week was almost as joyful. At a corner booth in the lounge of the Thunderbird Motel, the veils of Sister Marietta had been replaced by a trim burgundy skirt worn stylishly above the knees and a matching jacket. Her short hair was hidden by a shoulder-length brunette wig, and Father Thom Maguire had replaced his collar with the gold sweater.

"I can't get used to you."

She blushed. "Is it that bad?"

"It's not bad at all, it's great!" She was a trifle heavier then he had realized. Large brown eyes and an oval face with prominent cheekbones and full lips. She looked twenty-five.

"Hair makes all the difference."

"My own's much nicer—if it ever grows." She laughed like an embarrassed teen-ager at a first prom.

She explained her leave of absence. She had requested a year to teach music as a civilian in a Catholic high school in Denver. She was to begin immediately after Easter, replacing a sick nun. It was a painful decision.

"At first I wanted your permission."

"Why mine?"

"You were important to me." She blushed again. "You still are." She talked freely of her youthful crush, of her efforts to hide it, and finally of a mature affection.

"I hope we can remain friends."

"I may be in California." He laughed. "I think Elvin Ward is going to clip my wings."

"Over the black thing?"

"Hmm? I suppose. But really over me."

"What will you do?"

"I'm not sure yet. It really doesn't seem to matter."

"I've wondered about marriage," she said, "and children."

He was startled. "You're moving faster than I am."

"And I've made up my mind to experience a man." She reached for her wine as soon as she said it.

Her honesty unnerved him.

"Just don't move too fast." It was meaningless advice to fill an awkward space, and he ordered more wine.

"You look better," she said.

"Something's resolved—I'm not certain what."

She reached for his hand. "Will you do me a favor and dance with me?"

He couldn't keep up with her transitions. Nor had he noticed the combo playing softly at the far end of the bar. He glanced around to see if he recognized anyone.

"Marietta, I haven't danced since—well, really since tenth grade."

"It doesn't matter."

He followed her to the dance floor, grateful for a slow, middle-aged beat, but not expecting her to lean snugly against his legs.

By the third dance he was struggling with disturbing fantasies. In all of his bizarre permissions of the last few years, he had never imagined a nun. It was a lewd joke that prurient and ignorant Protestants told. Or Jews wondered about. Priests always dismissed it simply: "ashes and holy water don't mix."

Sister Marietta continued to press a sensuous body against his, and suddenly he wanted her.

"Let's go to my room," she whispered huskily.

He paid the bill and followed her through the parking lot, around the rear of the building to a middle room on the ground floor. She fumbled with the key, slipped open the door, and closed the drapes. Only when she lit a tiny candle on the dresser, blue and virginal, did he realize her planned seduction. He watched her pull off her jacket and blouse to display the paleness of splendid soft breasts. When she slipped off her wig, she looked like an innocent boy, with dark brown hair that barely covered her temples. He felt her softness splash against his sweater and her lips devour his mouth. Almost too hungry and awkward to be exciting. Gently he moved her back to the bed, slipped off his sweater and shirt, and held her against his chest.

"Easy, easy, it's okay."

She lay next to him still kissing in frantic thirst, and she pulled his hand down to stroke her panties. He felt only thick wet hair and heard her moan softly like a feverish child. She pulled at his pants, unbuttoned and reached into his shorts, too roughly, gasping surprise when she touched his erection; but there was no time for Thom to feel anything except strange detached physical excitement. She pulled him on top of her and fumbled with his pants. He helped her. She continued the mad kissing as he felt himself hard against the coarse matted wetness. Searching for entrance.

Suddenly she burst into tears. "O God, I can't, I can't —what am I doing? O Thom, I'm sorry!"

He held her gently, almost relieved. "Hey, sister, it's okay, it's okay." He lost his erection and slid the pants more comfortably around his waist, still feeling her soft breasts like the gentle strokes of a frightened little girl.

"I just wanted to know—I'm so sorry—"

"It doesn't matter. I'm your friend. So's God, so's everybody." He didn't know what to say, and he held her sobbing in his arms for an hour.

"I wanted it to be you," she said finally.

"I know—but we're not ready. It will happen when it's supposed to."

She begged him to spend the night holding her. And he did, until she fell asleep. He left a note on the dresser.

> I never realized you were so beautiful. Whatever happens, I'm your friend. Thank you for wanting me. And give 'em hell in Denver—

He kissed her gently and drove back home to find Ziggy reading *Soul on Ice*.

"This is really something!"

"I know."

Then they shared a beer and went to bed.

At the Holy Thursday ceremonies, under the approving eyes of the black madonna, Ziggy Denko stooped, in imitation of Christ at the Last Supper, to wash the sweating feet of six blacks and six whites. There were tears in many eyes. And the daily confessions were double the previous year. Word had gotten around that Christ lived again at Our Lady of Czestochowa. The frightened, long-rejected sinners came in droves.

Theology didn't matter anymore, only Christ and His tangible beatitudes of comfort and compassion for the silent adulteries and hidden lusts, the angry children and wounded parents, the lonely masturbators and hungry lovers. Father Thom Maguire forgave sins in the name of a new and not so easy God. Jim had made his mark on the Catholic Church.

"It doesn't matter what you've done. Tell God what you'd like to do! He's heard enough regrets and guilts." Thom did not want their lists of sins, their secret touches and feeble reforms. They would learn of sex when it was time, not by demeaning descriptions and torturous confessions. Even as he himself was learning.

"God understands. You are His child. Learn to forgive yourself! If you have lusted, I have lusted too. If you have fallen, I am as weak and lonely as you. 'Who will throw the first stone?' 'Seventy times seven times—go in peace!' God bless you!"

"I practiced birth control ten times."

"Did you love your wife and children?"

"I masturbated twenty times."

"Do you have a friend?"

"I committed adultery seven times."

"Are you in love?"

They swarmed to him like sheep without a shepherd.

"The bruised reed he will not break, the smoking flax he will not quench."

They came in fear and trembling, in shame and humiliation, and they left in love and peace and smiling joy. They came not to Rome but to Cana and the Lake of

Gennesaret, not to Clare and Tipperary but to Galilee and the district of the Ten Cities.

They came to the black, smiling madonna of Czestochowa and to Father Thomas Maguire. Who could forgive everyone but his brother Jim. Or himself.

At dinner on Holy Saturday, Thom and Ziggy celebrated the end of Lent with roast lamb and dressing and a fine bottle of chablis.

"I never saw such lines." Ziggy Denko was alive again, and he knew for the first time in a dozen years why he had become a priest.

"Tell me about it!" Thom laughed, then looked directly at his renewed, childlike pastor. "I'm going to take some time off."

"I figured you'd want to. I have a Franciscan lined up." He looked warmly at Thom. "Take the time you need." He reached into his cassock and pulled out a thousand dollars. Thom objected. Ziggy was already dividing baptismal fees and funeral and marriage stipends with him, and Thom had accumulated a decent savings.

"I want you to have it. Part of the Easter collection."

Then they sat silently, comfortable. When they moved back toward the confessionals, Thom turned to his pastor.

"You're a hell of a man!"

"Thanks," said Ziggy. "So are you."

Thom stood in the pulpit at a final Easter mass facing a sea of black and white faces he had learned to love. Some intensity had vanished, yet he was unafraid to speak the truth he understood.

"I may be leaving the parish for a while. I'm not sure how long. My superiors are not pleased. But it doesn't matter. Something has happened here that has made a lot of us very happy. Others are afraid of the changes, but there's probably nothing anyone can do to stop them.

"I think the Catholicism we knew as children is dead. Even the Vatican Council did not really know what to do. There may be a new Easter in store, when God will not speak in rigid laws and harsh commandments through infallible popes. We may have to decide for ourselves about sex and marriage, birth control and divorce, race and brotherly love. We may have to grow up.

"To be a priest is only to be a friend, as weak and struggling as anyone else. I am just as sinful as you are. I sense some of you are shocked. Priests don't talk like this. They stand above, consecrated and alone. I can't live that way anymore. I never really could. I only endured it because I was afraid to be myself.

"It seems like my first Easter. A real resurrection from some musty, stifling, rigid, ancient grave. I wanted to share it with you. And wish you a happy Easter as well."

There was hardly a dry eye in church when he returned to the altar to finish the mass. After thanksgiving prayers he shook black and white hands with unashamed tears.

Feeling the thrilling ecstasy of an exuberant priesthood, he returned to the rectory to have Easter breakfast with Ziggy. His forthcoming meeting with Bishop Elvin Ward seemed of no consequence.

After baptizing three infants and two adults, Thom returned to his office and at three o'clock took a phone call from Tim.

That morning, his brother Jim had committed suicide on Sandy's grave in Lemmert's Grove.

15

A Silent Country Graveyard

Few Irish Catholics in Saint Raphael's parish had ever committed suicide. Jack Murphy did when his left side was paralyzed by a stroke. His right hand had still been strong enough to stick a gun in his mouth. Jim was only seven at the time, but he had heard the whispered conversations.

"Will he be buried from the church?" It had been Margaret's great concern. "I heard the children begged monsignor."

"He'll write to Rome and they'll reply after the worms set in." John Patrick played poker with Murphy and drank at his tavern when his insurance came up for renewal.

"Man has no right," she had said quietly.

There was no service. Everyone knew Jack Murphy was in hell, except Glenna and the kids. They never went to church again.

Virginia Harrigan put a gun to the breast a divorced man had kissed. She had waited four years for a dispensation, too long for the divorced man, who married her roommate. Virginia had been twenty-seven, with a pale face and long brown hair, and she died while the newlyweds were on their honeymoon. And Terrence Byrnes was only sixteen when he hung himself in the basement. He had gone to confession almost daily, revealing frequent masturbation. And possible homosexual feelings. No one really knew, but there was no requiem.

Father Stanley died when Jim was at Marquette. He had taught chemistry. The paper said it was an embolism, but everyone knew that Dr. Seamus Coyle, a loyal alumnus, had made the report. It was carbon monoxide in the priory garage. A Jesuit said the mass and students sang it, and he was buried in priestly vestments with a chalice in his hand.

Michael O'Brien, great-great-grandfather of James Maguire, had died by his own hand in Clare by the river Fergus. But only Jimmy Hallinan knew it, and he had told no one.

The Irish usually preferred the slower death of secret rage and alcohol. Ambitious children and infallible priests; brooding melancholy and broken dreams; that "domestic giant named despair." All they asked was a final anointing and burial from the Church. Proof of some victory. Over death.

Jim Maguire had decided to meet death head on. Tim found his body on Sandy's grave. He was not quite dead. Margaret had felt a premonition after Mary O'Meara had recognized Jim watching Johnny serve at mass on Holy Thursday.

"He looked like Jesus," Mary said, "with a full beard and a gentle smile on his face." Margaret was hardly comforted.

On Good Friday she felt a sharp pain in her heart at the very hour when Jesus died. It almost doubled her over, and it disappeared as mysteriously as it came. When she returned home from her Tre Ore, a shadow fell across her face without any apparent explanation, and the same night she dreamed of field mice frolicking in a deserted room. Easter Sunday was the most portentous of all. There was a strange black bird in the cherry tree when she returned from the first mass on Easter—"neither a starling nor a crow"—and it simply stared at her boldly without flying away at her approach. It was then that she wakened a visiting Tim to go and find his brother. He tried to reassure her, to no avail.

"Something's amiss. I know it."

Jim was smiling softly when Tim found him, and barely able to breathe from the excess of morphine that finally killed him. He made a single panting request which Tim had not revealed to Margaret.

"My ashes—here—Sandy—" he smiled again.

A few minutes later he was dead, and Mulaley's son was called to remove the body.

"He lost his mind like his father," Margaret said.

"He was smiling at the end, mother."

"That's little consolation. May God have mercy on him."

Mulaley called Monsignor Doyle to reveal the circumstances of the death, and Doyle, deeply troubled, called the bishop for a decision about Christian burial. The bishop made no immediate ruling.

"Perhaps a private ceremony—we'll see." The Maguires were a constant concern to him.

James Maguire would have told him not to bother his head.

Bishop Elvin Ward traditionally ate Easter dinner with Herschel Schaeffer at five o'clock. It was a festive occasion after a solemn pontifical mass at noon announced the spectacular beginning of the Easter season. Thom decided to stop in Sheffield on his way to Kirkwood to postpone his Monday meeting with Ward and to receive permission to bury his brother from the church. When he arrived at the rectory, he entered through the back door and glanced in the dining room. Mrs. Grimes was just serving hot fudge sundaes.

A jovial Elvin Ward protested, "Oh, that's too much!"

"Lent's over, bishop. Just eat what you want." She tittered.

Herschel laughed loudly and slapped his leg. "You can't say no to her. That's why I've got this." As he rubbed his belly, he caught a glimpse of Thom and immediately left the table and approached him in the corridor.

"I'm very sorry, Thom. So terribly sorry—"

"Thank you, monsignor." Thom's eyes were red and swollen. "I'd like to see the bishop when he's through."

Herschel ushered Thom into his office, brought him a cup of coffee, and walked back to the dining room to confer with the bishop. Thom could hear the festive mood resume.

"There's always a place here for priests," Herschel said jovially. "Even for bishops."

Finally they finished, and Thom moved from the office into the corridor. Monsignor Bobbie Foley nodded sympathetically as he gathered the bishop's vestment bag and handed it to a prim Terry Lanier, then arranged the miter and crosier cases near the door. Mrs. Grimes appeared to say good-bye, accepted congratulations for her cooking, and disappeared into the kitchen. Ward nodded to Thom, offered brief sympathies, and directed him to the business office without closing the door. He had no intention of sitting down. He glanced at his watch as Herschel and his two attendants shuffled nervously in the outer corridor. Thom could hear the ushers counting money in an adjacent room.

"Perhaps we could go into monsignor's office."

"I've had a long, exhausting day, father. We can postpone your appointment till later in the week. Will Thursday or Friday give you time enough?"

"I'd like to talk about the funeral."

Bishop Ward spoke patronizingly. "There's really nothing to talk about, father. You know the law. It was apparently a willful act." He avoided Thom's eyes. "I'm very sorry."

"We don't even know that he intended to die, bishop. He was despondent—I know that—with his wife and kids—"

"He was a doctor, father; he knew the effect of the drug. I know how hard this is, but it was a premeditated act. He had made hospital rounds earlier in the week and was perfectly rational. If there were any moral doubt, I would—"

Thom was humiliated by the public discussion.

"Lord, bishop. My brother's dead! Is it too much to ask for a little privacy?"

Elvin Ward had never learned to sense physical danger. Like a stubborn child, he held his ground. Thom couldn't believe it.

"Father Maguire, you don't seem to understand." His rasping voice struggled for control. "There is nothing more to say. There's nothing anyone can do! I'm very sorry." He turned to move away and started to nod to Bobbie Foley.

With a single motion, Thom grabbed Elvin Ward's red cassock with both hands, scrunching it up under his neck, and carried him into Herschel's office. Then threw him into the red leather desk chair.

"Goddamn it! I want your attention!" He slammed the door and bolted it.

Ward was suddenly terrified. Something like this had

only happened once before in his life—in a corridor of Saint Robert's Seminary. A very long time ago. His hands were trembling.

"Look here, Maguire, this is utter madness!" He started to move toward the door.

Thom grabbed him and threw him back in the chair. "You're goddamned right it's madness! And if you open your mouth again I'll break your jaw!" There was a crazed look in his eyes beyond anything Elvin Ward had ever imagined.

It was fortunate that Elvin Ward did not move. Thomas Maguire had waited a dozen generations for this moment.

"I won't keep you long!" Thom regained some control. Elvin Ward trembled visibly, and for several minutes Thom studied him as he never really had: the tiny pale face, the missing chin and chipmunk teeth, the small soft hands shaking helplessly, and the little potbelly pulsing under the red cassock.

Elvin Ward was too terrified to move.

"You pitiful son of a bitch!"

Then Thom slipped off his coat and folded it neatly on the desk, moving slowly as if he were unvesting after mass. Then he unbuttoned the back of his Roman collar, undid the snap at the waist, and slid out of the elastic arm straps. Still moving in some ritual tease. Readjusting the collar of his sport shirt, he moved toward Elvin Ward, who flinched visibly as Thom brought his collar and black dickey around Ward's skinny neck and pigeon chest. He was close enough to hear the hoarse uneven breathing and feel the heaving of the little body.

He continued to move deliberately, pulling his collar around the scrawny neck and snapping it in place, lifting Ward's arms through the elastic straps, and finally fixing the black vest around his pudgy waist. There was no sound except the panting of Bishop Elvin Joseph Ward, successor of the apostles and most reverend ordinary of the diocese of Sheffield.

Then Thom unbolted the door, angrily telling Ward not to move, and walked out into the corridor. Glowering fiercely, he picked up the boxed crosier and miter case and returned to the office. Herschel and Bobbie Foley turned pale, their lips twitching. Neither moved. Inside the office Thom bolted the door.

Elvin Ward did not stir. Thom slid the miter out of its silk shrine and slipped it on his own head, adjusting the linen tails. It stood as comically on his large Irish head as the loose collar around Ward's neck. Then he stooped carefully to unpack the crosier, reassembled it, and stood with the shepherd's staff in his hand—as majestic as any archbishop—and began a mock episcopal blessing, with a heavy Roman accent like Ward's.

"Benedictio Dei omnipotentis . . ." In solemn Gregorian chant he invoked Father, Son, and Holy Spirit on his bishop.

"Now I'm bishop, you son of a bitch! How do you like it?"

Ward continued to whimper.

"All the shit—all these years—you followed me like a goddamned plague! Well I'm through, do you hear? I'm through!" He was shouting.

He reached up and tore the miter off his head, threw it on the desk, and slammed the crosier to the floor. Then he ripped his collar from Ward's neck. "And shove this up your consecrated ass!"

Thom grabbed his coat and strode past a terrified Herschel Schaeffer and Bobbie Foley, remembering only Jim. Then he broke into the convulsive tears of a very little boy.

Elvin Ward sat in Herschel's chair, Thom's collar resting on his chest like an angry pall. He could not move.

His ministers helped him to his car and took him home to bed. He was unable to keep his scheduled Monday appointment with Thomas Aloysius Maguire.

Thom drove to Mulaley's to read the coroner's report and view his brother's body. He touched Jim's hair, stroking it gently, and then he drove home to Margaret. He had instructed Mulaley to delay arrangements.

Margaret sat on the couch with Connie on one side and Mary O'Meara on the other. There were no tears. Margaret stood up as he approached her and hugged him warmly. Moisture appeared in her eyes.

"It must have been God's will—on Easter and everything. It's all so unbelievable—Monsignor Doyle called—it was good of him—he hasn't been at all well—there can be a rosary but no mass." Then there were brief tears. Connie still sat solemn faced, almost relieved, as if an impossible nightmare had finally passed.

"I don't want the children involved," she said. "It's bad enough—in the papers and everything."

Thom made no response, declined an offer of food from Mary O'Meara, and walked with Tim to Lemmert's Grove. Tim mentioned Jim's final muffled communication.

"I can't be sure—"

Thom went to Sandy's grave and sat there for almost an hour, tears trickling down his cheeks. Not a word was said. He got up to leave.

"We'll do it," he said softly.

Without protest, Connie signed a release that empowered Thom to determine his brother's disposition. Connie refused to be involved.

"Man has no right," she said.

"Man has every right," said Thom.

He drove to Mulaley's with Tim.

"It's not allowed."

"I understand."

He had the body moved to Everdale's, and the cremation was scheduled the same afternoon. He picked up the urn the next morning and walked with Tim to Lemmert's Grove. Mary O'Meara and Margaret went to mass. Connie worked in the garden, and the children had been ordered to clean the garage. Dick and Anne, who had reported the cremation to Bishop Ward, said nothing.

Thom held his brother's ashes over Sandy's grave. Tim bowed his head reverently and wept. Thom was crying so hard he was unable to say a word as he sprinkled his older brother's remains in the gentle wind.

The pines rustled softly. A squirrel was chattering in a neighboring oak tree, and a pheasant stirred in the high grass. The last remnants of snow had disappeared, and the water in the creek was running free. At the edge of a slope not twenty yards from Sandy's grave, a lilac bush was barely beginning to bud.

And No One's son was finally free.

A telegram from Bishop Ward suspended Thomas Aloysius Maguire from all priestly duties, effective immediately, and he was to report to the chancery office the following morning.

Margaret stared nervously as he read.

"Is it bad news?" she asked. She was already reaching for her rosary.

"No, it's good news, mother. The bishop wants me to take some time off."

"You do look tired," she said. "Will you stay home?"

"I'll go to California."

"That's so far," she said softly. Finally convinced she would never be his housekeeper.

He shredded the telegram and tossed it into the fireplace. The oldest surviving son of Margaret and John Patrick Maguire.

"How long will you be gone?"

"I'm not sure."

She repaired his coat, washed a few socks, and prepared the center-cut pork chops she knew he liked, along with fresh spinach.

"I could have fixed a nice roast."

She asked about his morning mass the next day.

"I'll be leaving at dawn."

She said nothing for several minutes, her face wrenched with sadness. Then her whole body caved in, finally looking all her years. Two dead sons, a buried husband, and now her priest. Her heart ached with the greatest pain of her life.

"I'll live with the nuns," she said. Then she prayed her rosary all night, unable to sleep, and rose at dawn to feed her birds and fix a final breakfast for her favorite son.

Thom fought not to give in to all-possessing guilt. He held her close and let her tears come, then kissed her and walked to his car.

☘ ☘ ☘

Thom drove across the plains, still uncertain of his future, taking delight in the flowing streams and the blossoms of spring. A tremendous burden had been lifted. There was no need to decide anything. For the first time in years he felt no pressure of time. He drifted through Iowa, spent a night in the Rockies west of Denver and another in Salt Lake. Impulsively he decided to visit Chet Golas, now a chaplain in Alameda, then to travel south to San Diego and visit Dave Beauchamp.

After some difficulty, he located Chet Golas at the

naval base and they drove to a steak house in Oakland. Chet's blond good looks were exaggerated by his uniform as he slipped off his gold cross and talked enthusiastically about an approaching promotion and an assignment in Europe. He also drank far more exuberantly than Thom. Straight Bombay gin.

"I'll be retired at fifty."

"Then what?"

"A little parish in the sticks—with a good income and a cottage at some beautiful Michigan lake. I want the whole damn lake, baby!"

Thom brought him up to date on Mike Fogarty and Dave Beauchamp, Elvin Ward and Bobbie Foley.

"The little fat creep's a monsignor? Jesus Christ!"

"That fat little creep may be your next bishop."

Then he talked about Jim's death, his own revived priesthood, and Ward's vindictive suspension.

"Jesus, Tommy, you gotta cool it! You got too damn much talent to waste!"

It was good to laugh about old times. After a third drink and a toast to Bernard Fox, Thom admitted his discouragement.

"I thought you'd be sent to Rome—with your brains and leadership abilities."

"I guess it wasn't to be."

After a steak and a bottle of Châteauneuf-du-Pape—"in honor of Pope John"—Chet grew more personal. Then, unceremoniously, he unloaded. "I've been living with a lady for almost four years—that's really why I went in service."

Thom's expression did not convey his shock. He sipped amaretto as Chet talked of a vacation in Fort Lauderdale and of meeting a young woman who was vacationing there from Chicago. Three days later he knew he was in love, and, after having told her he owned a car dealership in Toledo, he admitted his priesthood.

Julie MacDowell, a Catholic graduate of Rosary College and a trained legal secretary, was crushed. She returned to Chicago with no intention of ever seeing Father Chester Golas again. He wrote a moving letter of his total love for her and his deep devotion to his priesthood—suggesting chaplaincy as a way out. She resisted all such eloquent letters for three months, then finally joined him in Pensacola, where she rented an apartment several miles from the base and found work with a legal firm nearby.

It was a neurotic existence until they learned to handle the exigencies of a double life. Avoiding office parties and even close friendships with other secretaries, carefully contriving stories about a fiancé who came on weekends or flew her to Atlanta, even using a post-office box and making only vague references to her general neighborhood. His priestly privileges made it easier to simulate responsibilities, whereas her very personality and beauty attracted curiosity. She subdued her warm spontaneity with a new, quiet reserve. Old boyfriends stopped looking, parents ceased asking about marriage, and Julie devoted herself to the isolating, solitary love of an exciting man she adored. Always on guard, even on weekend trips or Bermuda vacations or on isolated beaches in the Caribbean. At times the intrigue was romantic and exciting, at other times it was maddeningly restrictive. More than once, it had been terrifying. An enlisted man who had been to painful confession the day before sat in an adjoining booth at the Hilton. They feigned illness and snuck out. Another chaplain, a devout Methodist with his smiling wife, greeted Chet in a theater lobby while Julie powdered her nose. Upon her return she saw the problem and drifted into the crowd, then left with him to try another movie. Finally giving up to go home to television and bed.

There were long nights when duty kept him away, weekend retreats when he couldn't leave, paranoid suspicions when he felt obliged to ignore her for days at a time. Sneaking from the BOQ to crawl into her bed at midnight. From Pensacola to San Diego, from San Francisco to Alameda—changing jobs and apartments, perfecting stories and resisting advances, lying to parents and friends, lying to doctors and landlords, even lying to each other when their love became too painful or even sterile—screaming for other people and outside nourishment. Afraid to admit their life to anyone, even to less cautious chaplains whom they knew were living similar charades. Once she left him for a month, tried dating, and even sleeping in another man's bed, only to race out in the middle of the night and run weeping back to Chet. They dreamed of the future, when she would wait for him at a secret lake cottage while he shepherded a small parish. Always hiding, always watching, always afraid in a totally implausible love.

Why did he stay in the priesthood? As the restaurant emptied, he admitted his dilemma.

"I love the priesthood! These kids need me, damn it, they really do! I just can't leave them!" It was difficult to know if he was trying to convince Thom or himself.

It was after eleven when they drove through the tunnel and entered the nondescript plastic luxury of a Bay apartment in Alameda. They parked cautiously, surveyed the lot for possible informers or associates, and avoided the elevator. Julie MacDowell was momentarily startled.

"It's okay. Thom knows it all."

Tears came to her eyes. "You'll have to excuse me, Thom, you're our first houseguest—ever!"

She served fresh coffee and homemade brownies, then made chicken sandwiches Thom nibbled at and an avocado salad he couldn't touch.

"Tomorrow I'll cook a real meal."

She sparkled warm exuberance, and they sat talking until after two. Thom agreed to spend the night in the guest room, with flowered sheets, towels of every size, and a final cup of cocoa on the night table.

Thom slipped exhaustedly into bed, forgot his night prayers, and soon fell asleep. He awoke to the sound of Julie's barely muffled orgasm across the hall. Then again, louder, as if in an explosive celebration of her first guest in four years.

There were tears in Julie's eyes when he left.

"You'll come back?"

"Of course, I never ate like this at home."

He embraced Chet warmly at the base and slid into his car, headed for San Diego. "Hang in, Tommy baby, it's worth it!"

Thom drifted along the coastal route to southern California, exploring the Seventeen Mile Drive and pausing to marvel at Big Sur. At thirty-five, the thought of starting again was terrifying. He knew nothing but the work he had been trained for since early adolescence, and even his educational degrees, provincial and unaccredited, were practically useless. With all his language skills, he was not qualified to teach even in the most nondescript junior high school. Everything he owned in the world—his clothes, a two-year-old Pontiac, a few books, and perhaps three thousand dollars in traveler's checks—hardly constituted a comfortable stake for a man who had never been on his own.

Nor was he really free of the priesthood. It was not like changing jobs or even leaving an unfortunate marriage. It was a soul's responsibility assumed in childhood; every fiber of his energy had been directed to fulfill a divine commitment. Jim's final words and sudden suicide had shocked him to discover some new freedom, but even that was only the beginning recognition of a God beyond laws and traditions and Elvin Ward.

His Roman collar had gained him instant respect, not to mention clerical discounts at every level, and now he became acutely sensitive to new unkindness and slights he had never experienced. Waitresses were surly and impatient, strangers rude and suspicious; but more than anything else, it was painful to be ignored. When he ran out of gas near San Luis Obispo, he was upset because the attendant demanded a ten-dollar deposit for a gas can and did not volunteer to drive him the two miles to his car. A hundred motorists ignored him when he tried to hitchhike, and the California Highway Patrol ordered him off a freeway ramp. Father Thomas Maguire was not accustomed to such humiliations.

Nor was there anyone to talk to. He had not really learned the art of casual conversation, for people had always catered to him. Now his confidence was gone, and he was painfully shy around women. At a chic singles bar in Santa Barbara he exchanged a few remarks with an attractive brunette, but he soon lost her to the sophisticated attentions of a smooth salesman who bought her a drink and invited her to dance.

Dancing was out of the question until he had two or three drinks. Even then, unless it was a slow beat he could fake with a twenty-year-old high school box step, he was terrified. He selected a woman who was suitably overweight and unattractive, and he made a weak request, certain she would refuse. She was delighted at having such a handsome partner, and she pushed her way to the crowded dance floor. The melody was mercifully slow and he moved stiffly and awkwardly in safe squares, hoping she wouldn't notice his naïveté. Suddenly the tempo changed in mid-song, and assorted dancers broke into a jitterbug and did their own thing. His beefy consort chose her own version of the "monkey," and his eyes began to blur, his hands to sweat.

"C'mon, cutie, loosen up!" She said it good-naturedly.

He was crushed, desperately anxious and self-conscious until the music wound down. Then he stumbled back to his place at the bar and remained a frightened spectator for the rest of the evening, filled with self-loathing and near despair, totally disproportionate to what had happened. Hating the men who danced with reckless rhythm that left their partners breathless with excitement.

He would have to return to the priesthood. There was no real choice. At parish dances or high school sock hops he had been the poised and handsome priest who circulated deftly among the admiring crowd. At a nondescript bar in Santa Barbara, as common and unthreatening to anyone else as a ball game, he was a terrified adolescent sweating his way through a first date.

It was a relief to arrive in San Diego and hear Dave Beauchamp's voice on the phone. "My God, Thom! I can't believe it. You're here!" He gave directions to the Holy Angels rectory. "You're in for a shock when you meet the pastor, Reverend Malachy Martin O'Shea. You've got to stay for dinner!"

The pastor was a mild shock compared with Dave's appearance. He had lost fifty pounds, and Thom couldn't hide his feelings.

"I don't look so good, eh! Well, I'm not." The grin was the same, but the dark sparkling eyes were sadder than Thom could ever have imagined them.

"It's cancer," he said matter-of-factly. "It doesn't look so good." He smiled again. "The treatment's taking what little hair I have left. Any more radiation and Bishop Schmidt will be vindicated about my sexual preferences."

He laughed loudly.

"And if you think Herschel Schaeffer was tough, you ought to work for this FBI." It was the clerical expression for the foreign-born Irish, whose countrified arrogance insulted the American clergy. Prevalent in dioceses that lacked sufficient native vocations, these men saw themselves as dedicated missionaries to a pagan America. Beauchamp mimicked his pastor expertly: " 'No one had to teach my own dear 'mither' about sex—and she had twelve healthy children—four holy nuns and three consecrated priests.' You wouldn't believe his sermons on the pill. He spells it with six *l*'s to rhyme with hell."

Thom had still not recovered from Dave's appearance when Dave announced it was time for dinner.

"Ah, we mustn't be late, father. Five o'clock sharp at Malachy's table. No excuses accepted. Here's your chance for a little exposure to the nineteenth-century Church."

Malachy O'Shea was immediately put off that Thom was not wearing his collar, and he offered to provide an altar for daily mass. Margaret would have liked him.

"I presume you modern priests still offer the Holy Sacrifice on vacation?" The lilt of sarcasm irritated Thom.

"I presume."

Beauchamp smiled secretively, delighted by the presence of his beloved ally.

"I understand you're quite a preacher."

"Dave's kind to say so."

"How do you handle birth control, father? Do you think the holy father has made it clear enough?" There was no avoiding him.

Thom toyed with his lamb chops.

O'Shea continued to bore in with all the grace of his peasant rudeness.

"You seem unhappy with things in America, Father O'Shea." Thom wanted to say something about Cadillacs beating the hell out of oxcarts and mutton soup, but he held his tongue.

"Not in the least, father, I'm here to serve my God. It's all a matter of having the courage of your convictions." It was one of Margaret's expressions. "Of course, now we have meat on Fridays and no Eucharistic fast—it might upset a few stomachs."

Thom wanted to slap the fat red cheeks and the mocking wet lips that were spouting bits of half-digested lamb.

"How do you stand it?" he asked Dave later on.

"That was nothing," he laughed. Then he grew serious. "I guess I haven't stood it very well."

Thom could see the skeletal outlines of his forehead and temples.

"Is the treatment helping at all?"

"It really doesn't matter, Thom. I have nothing to live for. Sometimes I think I created my own cancer—"

"Do you still believe?" Thom asked for himself.

"In God? Yes, I do. In the Church?" He looked away, listening to Rimski-Korsakov for almost a minute before he answered. "I really think the Church is dead, Thom." He paused. "And I know I am."

"Jesus, Dave—" Thom's eyes filled.

"I'm resigned to it," Dave said. "The only thing is—" Tears flooded his eyes and he couldn't speak for a moment. "Except for Dennis and my music, there wasn't much to life."

"Have you heard from Dennis?" Thom wanted to hold him.

"I know he's still in Georgia—but I haven't seen him." He paused and the tears came again. "I really don't want him to see me like this. I couldn't take it—"

"God, Dave, I wish there were something—"

"You were such a good friend," Dave said. "I can't tell you how much you meant." He smiled through misting eyes. "You were something—full of energy and life, ready to take on the world! Joe Quinn and I used to laugh our asses off—there wouldn't be a sinner left in Sheffield."

He chuckled the same familiar way, coughed hoarsely again, then looked at Thom.

"Don't let them destroy you, Thom! No matter what! It means more than I can say."

"It's hard to start over."

"Not as hard as dying."

Thom reached out and drew the frail body of his closest priestly friend next to him, remembering the gentle forgiveness he had received on the broad chest of this man. Dave began sobbing, and Thom continued to hold him until the tears flowed on his shirt. Then Dave composed himself and drew back bravely, only able to smile the warm smile as he nodded good-bye.

Two weeks later, when Thom called, Dave Beauchamp was dead.

Malachy Martin O'Shea, not recognizing Thom's voice, informed him that Father Beauchamp was buried Wednesday and that Father John McDermott, the new assistant, was taking his calls.

Thom hung up the phone and let the tears come.

At that moment he knew he could never be a Catholic priest again. Dave was dead in exile without obsequies or mourning friends. No Elvin Ward or Freddie Weber could ever explain this tragedy. Nor could God. Thom was ready for Jim's final sacrament.

Graduation.

III

☙ ☙ ☙

Beyond Kirkwood

I have lost my easy God, the one whose name
I knew since childhood.
I knew his temper, his sullen outrage, his
ritual forgiveness.
I knew the strength of his arm, the sound
of his insistent voice.
His beard bristling, his lips full and red
with moisture at the moustache;
His eyes clear and piercing, too blue
to understand all;
His face too unwrinkled to feel my child's pain.

I never told him how he frightened me,
How he followed me as a child
When I played with friends or begged
for candy on Halloween . . .
He the mysterious took all mystery away,
corroded my imagination,
Controlled the stars, and would not let
them speak for themselves.

Now he haunts me seldom; some fierce
umbilical is broken.
I live with my own fragile hopes and
sudden rising despair . . .
I walk alone, but not so terrified as when
he held my hand . . .

16

The New Priesthood

Thom's decision to leave the priesthood was at first only exhilarating, but the demands of a new kind of survival gradually emerged. Late in the summer of 1968 he took a furnished studio in a small singles complex in San Diego where there was an attractive pool and a clubhouse. The male occupants of Sleepy Hollow were mostly navy pilots, a strange breed who tanned themselves between flights, sipped endless beer, and ruminated about their next wild bash or how much they drank at the last one. They paid little attention to Thom.

The women—secretaries and nurses, teachers and interior decorators, pseudosophisticates in the self-conscious milieu of chic noninvolvement—were almost as aloof. Although they seemed friendly enough, even offering beer or recommending a movie or a new novel, Thom remained a tense outsider.

Flesh was everywhere, oily and teasing and exotically tanned. Hands languorously applied balms to long, voluptuous legs; sun-bleached hair splashed over shoulders, sensuous bodies drifted on inflated mats in pouty repose. A starving Thom lusted in a hundred directions, wanting to taste it all but powerless to find the elusive entrance to a new idiom.

His blond good looks, restricted by the vanishing securities of his priesthood, were not enough. He hadn't abandoned his vocation just to become another resident of Sleepy Hollow.

Most people would have been curious about his priesthood, but he made no reference to it, content to have "taught a little and coached some" or "worked on construction in Michigan," and such a bleak biography hardly warranted continued interest from the people of the mysterious West Coast port of new beginnings.

In Thom's state of mind, finding work was as frightening as a shy child's first day in a new school. Even his summer employment during his seminary years had been arranged by John Patrick or Monsignor Doyle. He was too guilty just to make money or find some exciting employment. He still needed a vocation, and he applied for a job as editor of a psychological newsletter. His paltry résumé did not warrant more response than a form letter, which destroyed him. The reply from the *San Diego Union* was even more painful: "You just don't qualify."

His dreams became less ambitious, and after five more rejections by creative possibilities, he was accepted on a trial basis as a welfare caseworker. His job was to assist a battle-scarred and much feared supervisor, Mrs. Vivian Moore, a cynical social worker in her early fifties who was drowning in red tape. It was humiliating work for the man who had organized Operation Cosign in Steelmont, but after ten frustrating weeks of searching he was ready to accept anything.

The job orientation was wordy and superfluous, his suggestions were ignored, and his reports were returned to be redone according to the "more suitable method experience has found satisfactory." There were four hours of paper work for every hour he spent in east San Diego's dingy slums. Illegal spouses hid from "the welfare cat," and babies were passed from house to house to fatten allowances. A cunning Vivian Moore, with her schoolmarm's thin smile, would not be jived. Thom was to sneak back at night or make a second stealthy visit the same day. To lurk, connive, suspect, confront, insult, and threaten. All for $450 a month before deductions.

Whatever he was, Thomas Aloysius Maguire was not a quitter. He had made his decision, and he had even informed Margaret of his intentions to continue his leave of absence until he could find some "direction and peace of mind in a most confusing Church." Although Margaret agreed in a return letter that the Church was undergoing dark days, she did not appreciate his decision to "abandon a sinking ship."

God has called you. It is the most noble vocation in the world and is not to be put aside because of personal concerns. You well know what I have suffered . . .

She recited the entire litany of pain, not the least of which was that she had given up her own home to spend the rest of her life in a Catholic institution. She hoped and prayed that God would bring Thom back to his senses before it was too late, and she signed the letter "Broken-heartedly, your mother."

Her letter upset him, but not enough to return to the priesthood and the impossible world of Elvin Ward. Actually he felt some relief that Margaret was settled in the home with the Sisters of Charity.

Vivian Moore continued to lecture him about his decisions as if he were less than a college boy. She reminded him that the welfare department was not a charitable organization like the Church, and when he approached a neighborhood banker about helping a black family purchase their own home, she was livid.

"No wonder you can't keep up with your cases. I'm putting you on notice. Any more pious nonsense and you're through!" Her eyes darted from side to side.

"I don't consider it pious nonsense! Mrs. Washington could buy that house if Willie finds a job after school."

"Willie's not the only one who will need a job!" She cackled at her own sharp humor.

She increased his case load and reminded him to put a dime in the plastic cup for each cup of coffee he drank. She also complained bitterly about his gas mileage, and she returned three reports from migrant blacks who had not remembered previous addresses in Georgia. She would not feed them or their "illegitimate little apes." Thom Maguire had never been treated as a disposable employee, and when she denied him a customary raise after three months, he confronted her.

"You're on probation, Mr. Maguire. You don't take direction very well."

He wanted to slap the tense cheeks. "I'm sorry—I need the money." It was an impossible admission. His savings, now less than two thousand dollars, had become a preoccupation. He had never thought about money before.

"That's not my problem. This is a business. You may not know about such things with your monastery mentality, but perhaps you'll be a little more careful in dispensing public funds."

A soft-spoken obese young woman named Laura, also a caseworker, invited Thom to her house for a drink one

Friday after work. He was still nervous around women, and it never occurred to him that Laura was as lonely as he was. They shared a scotch and he used her toilet, glancing at himself in the mirror. He still liked his face, but the sadness in his cheeks troubled him. Laura saw only a vulnerable, sensitive man. Men as handsome and gifted as Thom Maguire never looked at her fat thighs and full face. Only her tits, sometimes, on the San Diego beaches where she showed as much as she dared. Thom was different. He made her feel like a person. They shared another drink, and Laura sensed he would not make a move, so she took the initiative, with hungry hands and fingers and warm lips, slipping off her glasses, then her clothes, and rolling passionately and silently with this magnificent man in wet, blubbery sex.

He knew he had made a mistake, but he dared not tell her lest he hurt her feelings. He said he had reports to finish, and she let him go, afraid to challenge or oppose and lose him. Only later at work did she wonder, while he remained politely distant and racked with private guilt, that he had used her. He was unable to admit to himself or Laura that the encounter had simply meant an hour of forgetfulness from unbearable pain.

There were other Lauras during the months he struggled at his job in the welfare department. Always the same pattern of sincerity. In his adolescent naïveté and the rising excitement of alcohol, there was the frenzied intercourse he mistook for love, then the overwhelming embarrassment and depression. His disgust with himself left him more wounded than before, and the former priest, nearing forty and hardly appearing thirty, stumbled through the puberty rites he had escaped at fifteen.

When he did not involve his emotions, he seemed mature and worldly, seductive and desirable. The afternoon he met Dick Clawson at a welfare barbecue, he was smiling and outgoing, hiding from Laura and sipping rum colas. He was alive and confident as his eyes flashed and his Irish hands gestured vibrantly in an exciting conversation about modern and ancient Greek. A cluster of caseworkers were fascinated. The whole discussion was initiated over an innocent reference to a vacation in the Greek Islands. Thom suddenly launched into a treatise on Eastern European cultural invasions by the barbarians and the subsequent influence on Romance languages. He was actually startled to recognize facets of his own education that amazed his hearers—Greek and Roman mythology, Gregorian chants, biblical poetry, sex worship in ancient mystery religions and medieval guilds. Trivial facts that were common knowledge among priests, such as the breviary and the significance of sacramental rituals, were fascinating, brilliant lore to simple college graduates. Thom was thrilled to discover how much his disciplined education had taught him, and his confidence increased.

Dick Clawson, tall and trim, with styled black hair and the confidence of a leading man, was the director of a counseling clinic in La Jolla, a charming, posh community a few miles north of San Diego. He provided expensive encounter groups and private therapy for the searching rich who had lost touch with their "real feelings." Humanistic psychology was in sudden vogue, and a shrewd Clawson was making big money in an expanding practice. Always looking for new counselors, he made a mental note of the charming and brilliant ex-priest.

It was almost three months later, late in the fall of 1969, that Clawson called Vivian Moore's recalcitrant caseworker. Thom did not recognize the name at first, but he was impressed with the resonant baritone voice. They agreed on a midafternoon meeting when Thom knew he could escape Vivian Moore by going out on "home visitations" and still return at 5:30 to prove his alibi.

Dick Clawson took Thom on a tour of his clinic, which consisted of an entire floor of a new Spanish-styled stucco building. There were plush carpets and exotic rheostated lights, colorful Danish modern furniture, and expensive impressionist oils. The group rooms were exotically sensual, with the same plush carpet in soft shades of brown and beige, pillows of orange and chocolate, and floor-level coffee tables of redwood burl. A thousand light-years from the ponderous oak desks and scratched green file cabinets of Vivian Moore. Dick offered home-ground coffee in hand-molded mugs and talked of Thom's opportunities with the Human Potential Institute.

"You could immediately qualify for a marriage and family counseling license. California is one of the few states that licenses to protect against quacks, and your priesthood would be sufficient credential."

Thom was amazed to know that his priesthood qualified him for anything. "Is there an examination?"

"Not presently, though there's talk of it. I'll send you a form."
Thom struggled to hide his excitement. "Whether we get together or not, it won't hurt to have the license."
Clawson had no intention of losing this one. Each successful counselor added substantially to his own income and gave the growing institute greater prestige. "Shall we talk salary?"
Thom's heart beat faster, but his Catholic culture inhibited. "I guess I want to make certain that I really am doing something important." He was suddenly nervous and embarrassed. "It's a hang-up of mine."
Clawson protested. "I like that kind of concern." His handsome face grew intense and compassionate. "People are dying because they can't communicate. Feelings are tearing their lives apart instead of freeing them to be—to become what God wanted! Don't let the luxurious surroundings fool you. Our institute may be the beginning of an entirely revolutionary liberation of the human spirit!"
Thom was deeply moved by Clawson's zeal. "It may be just what I've been looking for. I need something I can really believe in, not just a comfortable way to make a living."
"Thom, your religious background will help. We get dozens of tragic marriages each month where the couples have given up on the Church and are looking for some spiritual relief from the angry God syndrome—depression, anxiety, guilt, sometimes despair—and have nowhere else to go."
Thom was tempted to talk about Jim's suicide, but he feared some reflection on himself. He was, however, immediately conscious that the Human Potential Institute was exactly what Jim had been talking about. It offered a real "graduation"; maybe it could have saved his brother's life.
"I'm afraid my background makes me a little directive and preachy, but I can learn."
Clawson smiled his warm Hollywood grin. "I have no doubts." He went on to explain. "I worked with the Rogers group at Western Behavioral and am much impressed with the accepting nondirective atmosphere that characterized the group. Of course, we've developed our own insights, but the analysts and behaviorists are convinced that we're

superficial upstarts and heretics." He smiled. "It's not unlike the Church."

Thom appreciated the analogy. He was only vaguely familiar with the new psychology.

"We'll put you in a few groups with myself and other more experienced counselors and psychologists and tape a few of your private interviews for professional feedback. You'll learn it all in no time." Then he clinched the deal with the skill of a refined salesman. "We'll start you at a thousand a month, but you'll be at fifteen hundred as soon as your private hours pick up." Again the beatific smile that hovered somewhere between Jesus and Elmer Gantry. "And that, my friend, won't be long!"

Thom tried to remain cool, explaining that he would inform Clawson as soon as he had been licensed and had notified the welfare department. After a handshake and a "Welcome aboard!" he drove to a deserted Pacific beach and let out a prolonged howl of joy. Margaret's son had arrived!

The license came within two weeks after he submitted proof of ordination from Monsignor Charlie Kenelley and a transcript of credits from Father Jack Durrell. Thom had written to both of them explaining that he needed documentation to begin graduate work. He had also lied about his hope of returning as a better priest. Jack Durrell mentioned turmoil in the Church and the declining vocations to the seminary, but he said nothing about his own alcoholism that had required brief hospitalization. Charlie wrote of Joe Beahan's new status as archbishop secretary of the Sacred Congregation of Sacraments in Rome. Bishop Bobbie Foley was the new auxiliary in Sheffield. Kenelley did not mention that Freddie Weber had been institutionalized in a hospital for disturbed priests and nuns near Baltimore.

Thom's final meeting with Vivian Moore almost made the year with the welfare department worthwhile. During his last two weeks on the job he granted even the most questionable requests for public moneys, delayed or purposely abbreviated his reports, and refused to pay for his office coffee. When he put an extravagant lunch on his expense account, she was furious, her taut cheeks purple, her drawn lips ghostly white.

"You're not entitled to executive lunches!"

Thom grinned. "It was my birthday and I thought—"

"You're not paid to think!" she screamed. "Just get your goddamned reports in on time!"

"Please, Vivian, your language. There's no need to lose control!" He reached in his pocket and offered her money. "Have a lunch on me, and don't tell anyone."

The following week, under the expert tutelage of Dick Clawson, Ph.D., Thomas Maguire began a new priesthood to rid the upper middle class of buried emotional distress.

It proved exciting work, coleading groups with Clawson himself whose studied, relaxed approach under heavy emotional attack impressed Thom tremendously. An angry stockbroker, recently separated from a "schizy" wife who had been "acting out" in a two-year affair with his best friend, erupted at Dick's probing.

"Goddamn it, Clawson, you encouraged her. How the hell would you feel if I fucked your old lady tonight?"

Clawson sucked on his pipe with Academy Award calm. "I think it's more important to understand how you'd feel, Ed. I know I would feel hurt." Thom marveled over the fact that there was not a tremor of fear in Clawson's voice.

The stockbroker was suddenly silent. Thom, gradually more confident after six weeks of assisting the masterful Clawson and imitating his technique, probed gently. "Tell us how you feel."

"You seem more human," he said to Thom. "Goddamned Clawson just sucks his pipe like a mama's tit and looks wise." These were sophisticated clients, often expatriates from analysis, who knew how to fight.

Clawson continued to smoke his pipe without reacting, and Thom attempted to "focus" the man's feelings. "Maybe Dick reminds you of the man who fucked your wife." Thom had already learned to make use of the four-letter words that Clawson called "feeling-laden." It worked. The stockbroker was furious.

"He's the same kind of cocky pipe-smoking motherfucker! I'd like to punch that shitty goddamned smile off his face—"

Violence beyond simple words was not permitted although occasionally clients lost control and were asked to seek psychiatric help. "We work with the healthy neurotics," Clawson had said.

Thom took charge of the stockbroker. "Punching Dick would accomplish nothing. Why don't you imagine that Dick is your wife's friend and tell him off?" It was a touch of psychodrama beyond Carl Rogers.

After the group session, Clawson congratulated Thom. "You're a natural at this. Another month or so and I'll let you try a group on your own."

Thom was euphoric. "I just love it. It's what I was really meant to do. God, people need this so much!"

So did Thom Maguire.

The charisma that attracted converts in Sheffield was just as effective in bringing clients to the institute, and by February 1971, Thom was coleader of seven groups and handled twenty-five private clients. Dick Clawson was delighted.

The Human Potential Institute ran like a fine machine. The therapists were never involved in economics, and approximately fifty percent of what they earned covered the rent, office help, and operating expenses, in addition to Clawson's personal investment profit. The rest became salary and subsidiary benefits, and at the end of every year Dick Clawson declared generous dividends. Thom Maguire could never have approached the same kind of money in any private practice. Not only did Clawson's name attract widespread attention, since he lectured charmingly to myriad local college audiences and service groups, but the health insurance coverage of most clients would not recognize a simple licensed counselor such as Thom. Clawson, as a clinical psychologist, signed the insurance claims that provided relatively free psychological help for the generally affluent clients, and when a policy demanded psychiatric supervision, a friendly neighboring psychiatrist was paid generously for a signature.

A long bout with the Asian flu was the first warning that fifty hours a week of other people's problems left Thom exhausted. He was nearing forty, and he had lost considerable physical conditioning which, he realized, had made him a target for the virulent disease. He smoked and drank too much and worked impossible hours on too little sleep. Repentant, he evoked the same fierceness he brought to every endeavor. He quit smoking and drinking immediately and began working out daily in a health club. He moved from Sleepy Hollow to a more elaborate two-bedroom beach apartment in La Jolla Shores, which meant far less travel time on the San Diego freeways and an easy opportunity to run on the beach. As his appetite returned, he was careful to eat more fresh fruits and vegetables and to avoid rich foods.

Finally, in the summer of 1971, he was well. His life had settled into a comfortable routine, but he felt a vague dissatisfaction he didn't understand. Until he met Jennie.

His first encounter with her was dramatic, although the setting was banal San Diego. It was an early evening cocktail party (devoutly, Thom sipped ginger ale) attended by business people and attractive young women. After circling the room and nodding recognition to a few vaguely familiar faces, Thom had almost decided to leave.

Then he saw her. She seemed to have a gentle humor and a touch of some remembered pain, but above and beyond anything she was a madonna of incredible softness and sexuality. She was glib and flippant, perhaps her only protection from the assortment of grinning men who circled her and leered at her, yet when she directed her attention to an individual she was flatteringly attentive. It was the first in a series of contradictions Thom would experience.

She hardly took notice of her own body, as if she had owned its exuding succulence for an eternity, and her very indifference excited Thom even more. His body seemed to vibrate some compulsion to touch her. Instead, he simply stood and shyly stared like a schoolboy, not unlike the rest of her drooling admirers. However, only the most persistent of them hung around, for she was almost too much woman. While most young women in the room stood in safe clusters of three or four, she stood by herself. Thom could think of nothing but tearing off her clothes and devouring her.

Finally he forced himself to stand near enough to nod a greeting. She smiled, her lips parted slightly, her eyes newly alive. Her hair was long and dark wheat, her cheekbones almost Indian, her mouth moist and barely sad when she was not smiling. Only her forehead seemed controlled and conservative, as if she would have been naked without it.

She knew that Thom was intrigued. Her eyes teased. "You're a new face!" Her voice was low and the words rolled out slowly.

He could barely breathe. "I would like your phone number." He knew she saw his nervousness, and he expected her to ignore his request.

"A fast mover." She grinned coyly. "I'm in the book," she teased. "Aren't you going to write it down?" She spelled her name.

He couldn't take his eyes off her breasts, which screamed to be free from her white cotton blouse. His face was warm and he felt sweat roll down his forehead. I'll remember it."

She looked back as he moved away—as if they had just started a lusting adventure. He was still trembling when he left and he pulled over to a deserted beach and masturbated frantically.

He called her immediately, and their first date was an uncomfortable dinner and distracted conversation he could barely endure in the face of her simmering appeal. Though already thirty-five, she appeared ten years younger. Finally he took her home. She did not invite him in, but kissed him with wet lips and rolled her magnificent breasts against his chest. Then she pulled back when he became too insistent.

Jennie was not a naïve newcomer. She had known hundreds of men and enjoyed many of them until she grew restless and bored. Or they did. She was not the kind of woman a man married. She was almost a pornographic fantasy made real, but to a starved celibate she became a consuming love. Even Jennie knew that this shy, handsome blond was different as she revived dead dreams and moved with the caution of a lifetime. The past year had been her most frightening. Brief sordid affairs and increasing need of alcohol, warnings at work, a blackout, and at times an insatiable appetite for sex. But Thom was a man she could love, and she sensed that his desire for her could be molded into a lasting relationship.

As she became Thom's new religion, the institute paled for him.

He was like a frantic teen-ager lost in new excitement, giggling wildly over her fake Mexican accent as they sipped margaritas and ate enchiladas. She talked of cheerleading tryouts, her first kiss in a sandpile, summer Bible school in the Adirondacks when she necked all night with two boys under a chapel porch. He became obsessed with her. Her shoulders and arms, gently perfumed; her very skin tormented him as much as the breasts that always hung teasingly under open white cotton blouses. Her narrow sinuous shoulders made her breasts seem startling and exaggerated, almond-shaped mounds of pleasure that he was desperate to suck and fondle. After half an hour of talk, his groin ached, his legs trembled with a mingling of pain and yearning he had never known, until he thought he would go mad. Then she left him at the door of her apartment, laughing at his final kisses, his groans to spend the night, kissing him again and promising that she would know when it was right. Even admitting that she thought she already loved him.

When he returned to his own apartment he made a mound of pillows on the soft rug, turned on the stereo, and was lost in sexual fantasies of Jennie.

Uncontrolled ecstasy enveloped his long-ignored flesh. Masturbation in her honor obsessed him for hours. Morning and night. He saw her body writhing in the seminary chapel; he caressed her nakedness under a silk surplice or sibilant nun's robes. He could barely distinguish between waking and sleeping as thoughts of Jennie became like a floating drug that only increased his sexual hunger. He sucked her thighs and devoured her at high mass, undressed and fondled her in the confessional until he was exhausted. For the very first time he was acutely aware that sex, distorted and denied, had been lurking in the background his whole life.

One night, Jennie admitted that she had sometimes made love with a man the first night she met him.

"But you're different. I love you; I did when I first saw you."

"Jesus, Jennie, I love you, too, but I'm going nuts."

She finally submitted the following night, and his body erupted with a ravenous hunger, as if he had never known even the odor of sex before. It was more than stored hormones or frozen brain lobes bound by the shadow of confession or the fires of hell. It was a treasured gift of the deviate God, a final fusion of body and spirit that time had almost destroyed.

Before Jennie, Thom still thought he wanted to survive for a higher reality of service and fulfillment. From the moment of that explosive merging, Jennie became his high priestess, and he knew that his body entwined with hers would be his salvation.

Among all the men she had known, there had never been anyone like Thom Maguire. The strong body and handsome face that was almost beautiful when his eyes pleaded for her undying love. He would never leave her; he would take care of her even when she was no longer beautiful.

Already she had noticed a beginning crow's foot near her right eye and had labored every morning to conceal it. A few gray hairs, a minuscule sagging of her breasts, the weariness of a dental technician's job that led too quickly to old age without security. She wanted him desperately, to get even with all the men who had used her; to prove something to her parents in Youngstown, Ohio, who no longer wrote; and, more than anything, to prove to herself that she had not destroyed herself. No matter what it took, she would marry him and love him more than any other woman ever could. She focused all the anger and hurt of a lifetime on the seduction of Thomas Aloysius Maguire. Not unlike Margaret.

For the two weeks after the first sexual explosion, they never saw anyone except each other. They never did anything except kiss and embrace, massage, knead, caress, and make devouring love. They ate something somewhere, laughed and sipped wine, then returned to her apartment to share the marijuana she taught him to smoke. After an initial coughing spell and a long night of giggling, a shared joint opened the doors of a sexuality he never conceived of. They tasted and flowed and groaned, entered and left every orifice and cranny of each other's body. She was as lost in him as he was in her, ingesting every patch of skin and hair, sucking toes and fingers, nose and eyelashes with only the sound of mouths and lips and tongues and the startled animal cries of every new pleasure. Thom was not a forty-year-old man, but a raging high school senior who came again and again in defiance of every physical possibility of a man his age.

They lived and breathed sex for days. Still drugged from her, he finally went to the institute, feigned his way through groups and private hours, interpreted his tests and drank his coffee, then returned to her without ever having interrupted his sexual obsession.

To Jennie, nothing was wrong or forbidden, embarrassing or sordid if it gave pleasure to Thom Maguire.

Sex now absorbed the energy of every prayer before a lonely tabernacle, every seminary pain scratched into a boy's diary, the courage to ignore a nervous breakdown. Even Jennie had never before seen a drive that matched her own neurotic need to lose herself in a lifelong orgasm.

She was his only morality. He loved her with the same dedication that he had given to Christ and Mary. She was his new madonna, tangible and irresistible; and his penis was his vocation.

Every part of her excited him. Her texture, her musty fragrance, the motion of her hips and pouting butt, the delicate fingers that stroked and pinched and plucked expertly in a thousand directions. Her smile alone could reduce him. Just to see her undressing, wiggling herself naked, aroused his addictive desire. Even her underwear rubbed across his face dissolved him. They made love everywhere. He played with her breasts and labia, damp and gurgling, in dark steak houses. She never wore panties, only flimsy shifts that made her body always available. She loved to be stroked continually, and when her own passion mounted she was helpless to keep her hands off of him. Without his restraint she would have sucked him under restaurant tables or made love in public parks. As it was, she took wild and crazy chances. Masturbating him against her bare thigh while eating dinner at an Italian restaurant, unzipping him and taking out his penis while they danced at a dark bar in Ocean Beach, later rubbing his cock against her clitoris until she came in muffled, wrenching orgasm.

Even when Jennie was only mildly responsive, he questioned her pruriently about a world he had never really thought about.

"But what was it like, with the black woman I mean?"

"It was gentle and nice, different than with a man; not better or worse, just different." She described the warm feeling of sucking a woman.

Then he begged her to tell him again.

Although it was hard for him to leave Jennie's body in

the morning, his hours gradually picked up at the institute and his group skills improved enormously. Clawson was impressed with his new buoyancy.

"I've never seen such a change in anyone. You're a great ad for this place."

Time spent with other couples in an increasing summer social life were confusing. He would have preferred to keep her to himself, but she loved parties and gatherings as much as she loved him. He liked intellectual discussions and dinner with two or three couples, but Jennie wanted to display her new man to the world. She nodded proudly at familiar faces who had scorned her. She was already a young bride, smiling and touching, drinking and laughing, clinging to Thom's arm.

When she arrived at a party her sensuality glowed from beginning to end—flirting safely, embracing and driving other men to the same wild distraction Thom had first known. Of course he was jealous, far more than ever in his life. Under the influence of drugs or even alcohol he was mildly paranoid. He watched her touch a man's shoulder and counted the seconds. Yet all the while he knew she loved him. Brushing breasts was only a way to keep her new man properly insecure. She had used it before, although most men had finally seen through her destructive games and quickly disappeared. But they hadn't been anything like the intense, unworldly ex-priest who had fought desperately to win every contest he ever entered.

As men stopped to gaze at flashes of bouncing almond breasts or the dark whisper of pubic hair peeking under a mini-dress, she kept them at a safe distance. However, as alcohol took greater effect, she became more expressive.

She kissed a man lightly as they danced, then drew her groin teasingly against his, and once she even pulled her dress down briefly when she caught a young doctor staring at her breasts. Thom struggled not to react. He had protested once and she had grown suddenly bitter.

"If you don't like it, find yourself another roommate!"

He apologized, not daring to lose her, and soon she was warm and purring while she opened his fly to devour him as they drove home. There was no real way for Thom to fight with her, and she knew it.

Jennie had no capacity for evaluating people apart

from their reaction to her. If people paid attention, they were "nice" or "really great" or "super." If not, they were "snooty" or "weird" or never mentioned at all. Thom knew she was incredibly fragile, and he tried to protect her.

Jennie had come to California to be the maid of honor for a friend from Ohio, and she had stayed on because the people seemed "nice" and there were enough parties and excitement. In a short time she felt a painful lack of sophistication in herself. She remained essentially a shy girl from the Midwest who leaned on social drinking to survive the new pressures, and she developed enough skill to make assorted bons mots and cute malapropisms, disguising her anxieties and pleasing the men who pursued her. More than anything, she wanted marriage, and she fell in love with a young navy pilot who was everything she had ever dreamed of. His death in a crash, while training for Vietnam, almost destroyed her. An attempted suicide was barely aborted in the emergency room of Sharp Hospital, and during almost two years of grief she developed a serious drinking problem and had sex with anyone she chose. Soon her sexual drive was as addictive as her drinking, and she moved from wild weekend affairs to two- or three-month relationships that usually ended in violent arguments over her seductive exhibitions. The dream of marriage and a houseful of children, though almost extinct, never really died, but as she approached thirty there were only married men or divorced fathers who had no intentions of trying again amidst the luster of liberated San Diego.

Before Thom, she lived with one of the dentists she had worked for, a six-month relationship of sex, drugs, sailing, and occasional weekends drinking and fucking in Las Vegas or Palm Springs. She loved him in her way, but lost him to a professional designer they had entertained innumerable times, with whom Jennie herself had twice had sex. Again she drank away the pain and contented herself with brief sexual explosions. She adapted to whatever man she was with. If he liked golf, she liked it. If baseball, she learned a few batting averages and enough names. Sometimes she shared an apartment, and her roommates usually ended up thinking of her quarters as a guest room, but she always came home in the morning to feed her cat, Stockings, and water her coleus.

She was bright and perceptive, with an assortment of domestic and creative talents. She was a gourmet cook, she designed and sewed many of her own clothes, and she was an outstanding skier and archer, but despite her abilities, to Thom she was only his extraordinary sexual partner who listened to him talk about his ambitions and anxieties while revealing none of her own. She rarely talked about herself except to recount inane stories, never to explore a feeling or reveal a disappointment. Even when she admitted to aborting the dentist's baby, she said it offhandedly.

Thom was not really sure she understood anything he said although she laughed at his comic monologues. After an evening joint or a drink, he questioned the meaning of existence, sexual differences between females, capitalism, football, doctors' fees, rape, styles of dress, and the advantages of large families. All the while those incredible sensual eyes looked at him like an admiring eight year old listening to the wise man next door. Until they were in bed. Then her magical simmering body made everything right.

By the third month of their relationship, in late August, he was glad to have a night or two a week away from her, not merely to rest from the exhausting sexual marathon he was powerless to control, but some rising restlessness in him required periods of silence and freedom from her chattering pressure and the cloud of drugs. Thom Maguire had never lived with anyone, and long periods alone had been his source of emotional recovery. He also was beginning to need someone to talk to who did more than listen. Occasionally after an institute group he shared a drink with a woman at his own level of intellect, and it was refreshing to experience some platonic feedback. He didn't miss Jennie, but after a night alone his body ached for her. Often, as soon as she walked into his apartment, he undressed her and began devouring her without restraint. Then an hour later he was struck with the same restlessness and, as she offered him cocaine, he asked her to recite the sexual narrative about the black girl in the dress shop.

Jennie began talking of marriage. When Thom hesitated, she seemed to withdraw, wondering if he really loved her, suggesting fiercely that he might have merely used her for his own sexual release.

It troubled him deeply, and for the first time in their relationship, he felt guilty. He began to reproach himself with dormant Irish Catholic advice. He owed her marriage for the happiness she had given him. At forty, he should know what he wanted. What was he afraid of? He knew he was terrified to lose her. Jennie was certainly more than sex, and he mocked his own selfish needs for deeper communication and understanding. Then he began feeling sorry for her until he was lost in their passion. Still, he resisted marriage, and Jennie began to torment him.

On a Labor Day weekend they spent in Mazatlán, she danced with an attractive Latino recreation director at one of the beach hotels. With Thom's tense permission, she later invited him to their room for more drinks. Thom went out for cigarettes, almost purposely to torture himself, and when he returned a half hour later he found them half naked and kissing passionately on the bed. Thom fought for control, and the terrified young man ran out the door.

Jennie looked up drunkenly. "You shouldn't go away like that."

Suddenly it didn't feel so bad. His chest and stomach quieted momentarily, and he felt stronger. She was a helpless child.

"It's okay if you want him," Thom said. The pain reappeared in his chest and he felt tears of rage.

"I want you. He doesn't interest me."

"But you danced with him all evening."

"He's a good dancer; you never really had a chance to learn." He was crushed by the inconsequential truth. The pain came back full force until she pulled him down on the bed.

But by the next afternoon he was bored as she chattered with a suburban housewife from Chicago about lasagna recipes and homemade Christmas decorations. The woman's husband droned on about a series of fishing trips to Bermuda, and Jennie insisted that they have dinner together. Thom did not know how to protest. He smoked a private joint, then watched the waiter stare at Jennie's inviting breasts all evening.

They visited an elderly couple who had invested in the institute, and they were sharing a quiet barbecue when a neighbor dropped in to borrow something. Jennie took an immediate interest in the man, so he settled down to spend the rest of the evening. Thom noted his broad shoulders and glib confidence, and the jealous rage began rumbling helplessly. He wanted to kill the man, and Jennie, but he remained almost motionless in his chair. He rationalized elaborately and then made himself as cynical and unattractive as the circumstances permitted. Slowly he gained control and finally excused himself, politely asking the smooth seducer if he would be kind enough to drive Jennie home when she was ready. No one except Jennie realized that Thom was in the least distressed.

In the car he screamed and cursed himself for ever getting involved with her. He drove around aimlessly and shed angry tears, then went home to drink and smoke until he heard the car door two hours later. He fantasized that she had gone to the man's apartment, or that he had driven her along the ocean and fucked her in his car. Even at that moment Thom knew the bastard was fondling breasts and wet pussy as he seduced her in the parking lot. When she came into the bedroom, Thom feigned sleep. She undressed quietly, not out of guilt, he was certain, but in genuine concern that he get enough sleep. She crawled into bed and snuggled against him, kissing and nibbling his nipples and arm.

In the morning he decided to marry her.

She was determined to have a church wedding. It was a girlhood dream to walk up the long aisle in gentle rhythm with an organ playing and a thousand eyes upon her. An elaborate sheer dress was a brief obsession. She consulted friends, scanned magazines, contacted designers. For a week it was all she talked of, but after modeling a number of traditional gowns, she suddenly became practical and settled on an expensive, clinging Pucci she could wear to parties. When he offered to fly her parents to the wedding, she wrote them but received no response. There was no reason for him to notify anyone in Michigan. Margaret had written only to tell him of Bobbie Foley's consecration—"all you could see was his little fat face wrapped in red"—and to complain about changes in the

Church—"it might as well be Protestant." There was a brief mention of her hope that Thom would come to his senses, "like the little boy I once knew," and one paragraph about Johnny's success in the seminary.

They arranged for a chapel in Carmel in October 1971. Jennie selected three bridesmaids and, as a little flower girl, the daughter of the Filipino janitor at her office. Dick Clawson was best man, and other counselors made appropriate ushers. The dentist Jennie had lived with agreed to give her away. It was her day. Thom denied her nothing. Red carnations and favored daisies were everywhere but in the shrimp cocktail. Gounod's "Ave Maria" and the "Tennessee Waltz" were sung by a former hatcheck girl from the Hacienda. More than a hundred people came to the buffet in Monterey, and Jennie kissed all of them at least twice. By late afternoon she almost passed out. Thom tenderly put her to bed in a honeymoon cottage by the sea and told her a dozen times that she was the most beautiful bride in the whole world.

Before she fell asleep she looked up drunkenly. "I never dreamed it would be so perfect."

She was crying. So was Thom.

Knowing he had made a mistake.

After the wedding, Jennie drank very little for several weeks, and although their life together was less traumatic than it had ever been, Thom was even more convinced that he had rushed foolishly into marriage. Jennie was not aware of his distress. She delighted in using her married name, she shopped and cooked with great energy, and she adorned their beach-front high rise with plants, shells and driftwood, gold and orange candles, glass sea gulls, and homemade God's-eyes. She rejoiced to quit work and almost daily she recalled the "beautiful wedding" and the glut of gifts they received. Thom spent more time with her and they made daily love, sometimes even meeting at home for a passionate lunch of wine and cheese and more sex. Jennie continued to live so completely in the present that the past was insignificant and the future only an afternoon away. She might talk of a train ride to Pittsburgh or her father's love for chop suey, but nothing of past lovers or previous conditions. She was all his, as certain of her happiness as he was that he wanted to run away.

Two months after their wedding, a problem arose at the institute.

Clawson, serious and unsmiling, called Thom into his office.

"We've been reported to Sacramento for a licensing violation. They say you posed as a psychologist."

Thom was outraged. "Who says?"

"Apparently the Burdick boy. They owe us five hundred dollars and we've been trying to get them to pay for four months. When we threatened court action, the father retaliated."

"I never told Burdick I was a psychologist. I didn't tell him anything."

"Did he call you doctor?" Clawson was skeptical, and Thom felt rising Irish anger.

"Hell, no; he called me Thom. Besides, my counseling certificate's in plain sight."

"It's obvious he's just pissed. He said we taught the kids to have sex as often as they could. Apparently Sacramento is checking with our clients."

"They can't do that, for God's sake!"

"They're doing it!" Clawson bit at his pipe.

"But the kid's homosexual—or thinks he is. We sure as hell never recommended that."

Young Burdick had been picked up by the police for soliciting sailors in downtown San Diego. His father, a rugged retired fireman, had been crushed by the public shame, and he blamed the institute. When Clawson's accountant had badgered him for the bill, he became fiercely vindictive and wrote to Sacramento—which already wondered about new psychological trends—and his gratuitous charges precipitated a wholesale investigation.

"That son of a bitch has no right." Thom was outraged. "We've got to fight this thing right down to the wire. It's goddamned totalitarianism." It was also a reminder of tactics used by Elvin Ward and Freddie Weber.

Clawson was more balanced. "They'll just slap our wrist. We could destroy everything by fighting back. That scumbag would be bound to uncover some revenge-minded former client. Look at all the people who have been threatened by what we do."

"But for God's sake, Dick, we've been accused! Now we operate under a cloud. I can't do that."

"I suppose we take that chance. But I still think we're better off proceeding as usual. Sacramento only licenses us—those stupid bastards don't know what the hell modern psychology's all about." He sucked his pipe. "They're the very hypocrisy we're fighting."

"Then let's fight!"

"Prudence is the better part of valor, Thom. Don't lose your perspective."

That was the end of it. But Thom lost some important respect for Clawson, and the warm Hollywood smile never gave him the same relief. No Maguire had ever backed off from a fight.

The crisis passed when Thom finally admitted to himself that Dick Clawson was only another frightened businessman with a product to sell. Not unlike General Motors or the Catholic Church. It had been Thom's own need to create a holy allegiance that precipitated his despondency. Therapy at the institute was simply another religion which gave people the courage to survive. "Honesty" was its credo, "touching" its communion, and "feeling" its sacramental grace. There was even a hierarchy—with Dick Clawson as bishop and the latest theorist—Rogers, Maslow, Skinner—as candidates for pope. Health insurance became the guarantee of a kind of tax-exempt status. And, like religion, therapy had to pay tribute to the system that supported it—in Washington or Sacramento.

Thom continued as a therapist, but what was once a holy vocation became a job. Jennie was his greater concern, and as his faith in every absolute diminished, she sensed the change in their marriage.

When their sexual communication continued to cool, Jennie drank more and began to push him away. She foresaw the end and refused to be abandoned. If he failed to compliment a meal or refused to go to a party, it precipitated a snarling quarrel. Still, guilt inhibited him from leaving her. He also feared he would be thrust back to his easy God, or that all the future passions of his life could not recreate ten minutes of Jennie.

Jennie's anxieties became more dramatic. Thom was not able to discuss his unhappiness, and, to a superficial observer, the conduct of their marriage was scarcely different, but he felt almost torn in half, wanting to make his marriage work and knowing that he had to run away to save his own life. Jennie, like Margaret, tried to hang on to him, but, unlike Margaret, she tried just as hard to push him away—knowing that no one had ever loved her for very long and believing that no one really could.

Sex had been Jennie's unique gift, and in desperation she focused on nothing else, seducing him at every moment. She knew their exploding chemistry had diminished, but she was as afraid as he was to admit it. She bought a vibrator, masturbated herself rhythmically to soft music on the candlelit living room floor in some exotic fertility rite, then laughed wildly when he was stirred. The state of his penis had become the measure of her worth. When he came, she was briefly at peace.

The institute began to drain him as much as Jennie did, and he decided to take a leave of absence from his job and concentrate on his relationship with Jennie. Without drugs or excessive alcohol. He had to make it work. He had married her, and he could not walk away from his commitment. The decision immediately calmed him and the mental torment of his struggle seemed to vanish. He felt the first real peace in weeks, and Jennie was delighted by the prospect of an exciting vacation.

They rented a motor home equipped with enough luxury for a long trip through Mexico and South America. He ignored going-away parties planned in their honor, and they left unceremoniously on a June morning in 1972—almost a year to the day since he had met her—driving leisurely down the coast, through Tijuana, and east across the bleak desert until they came to the tranquil, mysterious Sea of Cortez.

They found a lovely spot along the shore. Sweeping sand dunes, clear green water, pelicans, and bulky fishing boats drifting by in the distance. Across the bay was a village of thatched roofs and rotting wooden piers and an old windjammer with orange and red sails. They had a freezer full of food, skin-diving gear, books and magazines for lazy hours in the sun under the protective umbrella, and no drugs of any kind. They lost track of time, played like children in the water, and sipped coffee in the cool mornings. They waded nude when tropic heat scorched the air, then made love in the afternoon in air-conditioned comfort. Late at night they cooked elaborate meals over a hibachi, sipped wine, and watched the moon shimmering on the gently lapping water. But Thom began to feel the same restless boredom, wanted to scream out, and tried to lose himself in books and magazines or private explorations on the beach.

They had seen no one, but it is impossible in Mexico to hide from persistent Indian peddlers—dark-skinned and soft-spoken, shuffling slowly along the sand with blankets, grass mats, and plaster madonnas—and Thom almost welcomed the intrusion. Their vehicle had been spotted from the village. Two young men selling turtle oil and conch shells surprised them when they were sitting in the nude in the late afternoon sun. Jennie did not cover herself until she saw the men grow self-conscious and then she draped herself loosely in a beach towel.

Thom slipped on his shorts, chatted with them briefly, then put them off when Jennie began her seduction. "*Nada. No gracia,*" he said.

They lingered.

Jennie remained intrigued and tried the Spanish he had patiently taught her. "*Momentito, yo quero* seashells."

They grinned, showing perfect white teeth.

They stayed to drink tequila and offered the leaf they chewed. She grew drunker, and they were aroused by glimpses of her breast and a flash of pubic hair under the towel. Then the towel slipped to her waist and Thom suggested that they go. His wife and he would eat dinner. But she invited them, coyly readjusting the towel. He knew it was hopeless, so he continued to drink. On the advice of a client at the institute, he had bought a .32 automatic as protection against rumored bandidos in Baja, and for several minutes he fantasized murdering all three of them.

It was an evening made sinister and beautiful by the moon, dark against the sky. It was a kind of twilight zone of warm fragrance, snatches of clouds tinged with black streaks; and hazily a half-drunk Thom saw Jennie throw off her towel and run toward the water. The two Mexicans followed, dropping their clothes, and he could see their brown bodies in startling contrast to her whiteness. They splashed and frolicked while Jennie moved against them laughing like a child. They all waved to him. He heard Jennie call out, "It's beautiful! Darling—come on!"

Thom was certain the tall one was fucking her. He walked into the motor home and slowly unpacked the gun. He had never fired one, and it felt heavy and awkward in his hand. He was drunk with tequila and remembered pain. The barrel of the automatic flashed sharply as he headed for the beach, hearing her moan. The sand was deep and still warm from the day as he plowed clumsily toward the water.

He could shoot her.

Then, one by one, he could shoot them. He released the safety.

Then he heard the Mexicans scream with fear and saw Jennie stumble out of the water. They scrambled away, first diving under the water and then running frantically down the beach.

He shot twice! Once up at heaven! Then down at hell!

She did not seem embarrassed or frightened. He shot viciously again at the sky to empty the chamber.

Then he dropped the gun.

She was in water up to her ankles facing him. There was no sound.

Disjointedly she walked toward him, playing in the water with her foot as she moved through the foam. Thom looked down at the automatic stuck in the sand and heard the cry of a gull. Thick, eerie clouds now encircled the moon. Farther down the beach water splashed against the black rocks.

The pain was finally gone.

When she reached him, he wrapped her in the soft blue beach towel she had dropped on the sand. She always seemed helpless when her hair was wet, her face smaller somehow. He dried her like a child, sat her down, wiped the sand from her feet, and slid on her sandals.

"Where did they go?"

"Away."

"Did you hit them?"

"They're okay."

"Are you mad at me? You are."

"No, I'm not mad." Thom paused. "You better rest. We'll drive home tomorrow."

"Can I have another drink?"

"If you want." He poured her tequila and lemonade.

"God, I'm thirsty."

She began pawing his shorts. "I want to suck your cock. Hurry. I want your dick in my mouth!" It had always worked before.

"Not now. You go to bed. I'll wake you later."

In minutes she was in a deep sleep. He lit a cigarette and sat next to her, stroking her damp hair. He kissed her gently on the forehead.

The divorce was difficult, but not as painful as Thom had feared. He told her the next morning as they drove back.

She looked at him. "I knew it wouldn't last. I don't know how you put up with me as long as you did." Then she paused. "It was nice—to have loved you."

Thom couldn't hold back the tears. "Jennie—"

She held his hand next to her face for a long time as they drove back across the border to San Diego and north along the ocean. Then she kissed it gently.

"I'll always love you," she said quietly.

A light rain echoed softly on the roof of the camper.

"Tell me once more that I was a beautiful bride." It was the only request she made.

17

Storming the Palace

San Diego had never been real for Thom. Like Jennie, it was a transition, a mirage of instant salvation and immediate love, too readily available without obvious anger or healthy passion. There seemed to be no city, only a chain of beaches connected by sterile freeways. It was time to leave and begin again—a kind of geographic therapy even the pipe-smoking Clawson might approve for someone other than his favorite counselor.

Thom broke his lease, sold or gave away his furniture, and numbly drove his Porsche, stuffed with clothes, a few paintings, and a TV and stereo, up the coast to San Francisco.

He leased a sunny Victorian apartment at the middle-class edge of the upper Mission District and attempted to settle into a new life. There was little of the informal ambience of San Diego, and people did not seek him out as they had in La Jolla, so he was obliged to find some framework for his life. His brain was still raw, his anger naked and intense. He needed something that would absorb him immediately, and, if possible, something that would make physical demands on him. He was weary of thinking; his mind, stretched beyond endurance, protested further abuse. He needed to work with his hands; and his body, aroused from sleep by Jennie and his long-buried anger, demanded attention.

While driving around San Francisco he found a decrepit Victorian house on Dolores Street which he considered remodeling. He had enjoyed the summer spent with his Uncle Vinnie, and, although he had few illusions about his manual talents, he felt comfortable in knowing what had to be done. He had seen an article in the *San Francisco Chronicle* describing the profits that could be made by amateurs, and on his forty-first birthday, in October 1972, he bought the Dolores Street house.

He sold the Porsche and bought a yellow Ford pickup truck that gave him an immediate feeling of masculine involvement. He opened an account at the Bank of America and outlined his new construction program to a square-shouldered manager who was not impressed until the Maguire charm, hiding a smoldering contempt, had him talking about football.

"You were an athlete?" Thom said.

The manager slid off his glasses, slipped them across the mahogany desk, and settled back with trim athletic modesty. "Oh, I gained a few. But I had a line! Pitts was little all-American; Dyke and Seaman were all-conference two years; Hammy Eggers never got the credit, but what a ballplayer!"

They talked for more than an hour and ended up having lunch together.

"Let us know when you're ready for a construction loan. We're all on the same ball team!"

Bullshit! Thom thought as he smiled agreement.

Thom was exuberant. He was already a "contractor," forgetting that he had never really done any actual construction work except for one bookshelf and the refinishing of a table for Margaret. The summer with Vinnie had been magnified in some romantic memory. But, despite mild misgivings, Thom had the determination of his anger, and nothing seemed too difficult. Even when the job proved gargantuan.

For the first several weeks he tasted plaster dust in his soup, and in his dreams. He cut his hands on wire, got splinters from hundred-year-old redwood boards, wasted poorly cut Sheetrock, and consistently misread stud measurements. He never seemed to have the right tools no matter how much he spent, and he was forever running out of material. When the winter rains came, he had not anticipated the leaking roof and plugged drains. Finally he advertised for a nonunion handyman and carpenter. The first applicant was a spaced-out hippie who knew less than Thom; the second, a stubborn German, tore down the wrong wall and was physically thrown off the job. On the third try he hired an Irishman, Dan Crotty, whose entire family had been in construction. Dan had lost out to a serious drinking problem. Now, over sixty, tough and wiry and generally soft-spoken, he had been out of work for six months. He honestly admitted all of it, and Thom considered him another mutilated victim of an overbearing wife and Church.

"Let's see what we can get together."

Dan taught Thom to cut Sheetrock and lower ceilings and widen windows, to refinish hardwood floors and install copper to replace rusted iron pipes. Thom even learned to lay bricks and tile and to do simple sandblasting.

Dan hired help when they needed it and taught Thom to save money by paying skilled specialists for difficult tasks. Thus he became acquainted with the talents of plumbers, electricians, sheet metal and furnace men, tapers and roofers, masons and cabinetmakers. E.J., Dan's easygoing and talented nephew, who was about Thom's age, joined the team, and in three months they renovated the house.

Thom began to make different friends and to appreciate the élan of craftsmen and laborers who shared the skills he once considered insignificant. They were people he had never associated with. Occasionally they went to Forty-Niner football games and bragged of fucking women. They hated hippies, niggers and Jews, and, especially, "fat-assed" WASP big shots of all shapes and sizes. They knew government was crooked and they despised politicians, but, paradoxically, they accepted a kind of conservatism to protect the very status that indentured them to bankers. They supported Nixon for a second term. Thom himself did not bother to vote, and he considered Watergate only what he expected.

When the house was completed, he sold it within two weeks and turned a profit of fifteen thousand dollars. Even E.J. was impressed. Thom now knew workmen from every trade, so the remodeling business seemed a simple and certain way to instant wealth. He cajoled Dan to work for him, and he became the sole owner of Victoriana, Inc. With credibility at the Bank of America he despised, he arranged for more financing and promptly bought two other three-story Victorians in an improving mission neighborhood.

The buildings were only a few doors apart on Sanchez Street, so he began on both at once—his first mistake. Neither of them seemed to get completed. He was under new pressure from the bank, and Dan was still a periodic alcoholic who, during moments of crisis, disappeared from the job. Finally, Thom reluctantly let him go and attempted to supervise himself, but he was not as competent as he had thought. It was one thing to interpret bids with Dan's help; it was quite another to deal with subcontractors without him. Costs slid ten to twenty percent higher, and he tried to remodel rooms he should have torn down to bare studs. He left an electrical system intact, then decided later that he wanted more outlets. Permits were delayed, a plumbing leak ruined a hardwood floor and a pair of exotic French doors. Every day created a hundred decisions he had not been aware of before.

He would have abandoned the project before he finished except for his burning resolve to succeed, and luckily one of the houses sold before it was completed. When he finally sold the second house, he might have abandoned the whole idea of Victoriana, Inc., had not E.J. come forward.

Edward Joseph Crotty was an outstanding craftsman and experienced contractor who had been raised in the building trade. He lacked business flair as well as imagination, and he had none of Thom's natural instincts for "fat" properties, but he had the same Irish anger. E.J. was dark Irish, with black wavy hair and blue eyes that smiled easily; a thick, broad-shouldered, muscular body with a beer paunch, a fighter's chin, and a sensuous, melancholic mouth. He was a traditional man with modest ambitions, and in the summer of 1973, over drinks in the Pony Lounge after a Giants' doubleheader, he and Thom entered a partnership.

From that moment on Thom called him E.J., although his wife, Rose, and his longtime friends called him Eddie. They joked about the prestigious name, but within a month he bought an E.J. Crotty plaque for his desk and listed himself the same way on their joint checking account.

Thom furnished a private office next to E.J.'s office, redecorated the whole place, and managed to fire an inept secretary after two weeks. He interviewed a number of gumchewers before he found Millicent Mayer who, although only twenty-four, had worked summers with a construction firm during college, knew the business well, and had excellent office and accounting skills.

E.J. and Thom were an ideal team. Thom eagerly

brought in projects, and E.J. "built the jobs" with abundant new energy. Millie organized every detail, made skillful use of her great rapport with subcontractors, and dreamed of one day being a part owner of the business. Success seemed as inevitable as it was important to all of them.

After work, Thom delighted in meeting E.J. at the Pony Lounge, and over drinks and ribs they finished the day and outlined the next. And flirted and plotted and bragged about clever new "steals." After three drinks one night, Thom revealed his priesthood.

E.J. laughed outrageously at the impossible joke, then realized that Thom was serious.

"Jesus fucking Christ! Incredible! I didn't think you could get out."

"I didn't ask." He had not intended to mention it in San Francisco.

E.J. was overjoyed, as if his own past bitterness and growing indifference to Catholicism was justified.

"For Christ's sake, don't tell my fucking wife!"

For that moment on he trusted Thom totally. And even amid the wild camaraderie of a Lake Tahoe weekend or an all-night Irish bull session, he treated Thom with a subtle reverence a Catholic instinctively reserves for a priest.

Thom had not really dated in the year and a half since San Diego, fearing to give any woman the power to destroy him—as he felt Jennie had with sex, or Margaret with guilt. He met Roxanne Whitcomb at a buffet hosted by a Hillsboro architect. Thom felt like a noted athlete in the softly elegant context; his body was lean and hard from months of physical work.

"You'll score tonight, baby." E.J. envied Thom's bachelor status regularly. "There's pussy all over this place."

Thom was more impressed by the WASP gentility. In his childhood it had seemed the ultimate respectability, and he felt moisture on his palms.

E.J. was not impressed. "We might as well get shitfaced! All this polite crap! Don't nobody sing or start a fight?"

"You could use a little culture, E.J." He noted Roxanne's pastel sophistication. "We're in the presence of class."

E.J. wanted to leave. "She looks like a fucking blue blood. She wants a prince, not a wild mick, padre."

Roxanne continued to intrigue him. Striking dark brown eyes and soft caramel hair, with the cared-for complexion and assured air of the consummate WASP, she compensated for a cold elegance with warm textures and a friendly manner that was condescendingly calm. In Kirkwood, she would have ignored a Maguire. Now, a third glance told Thom she found him attractive, and he was suddenly challenged. He moved closer and waited until she made the first contact. When he told a seminary joke with a French punch line, he knew it was a ploy she wouldn't resist.

"Oh, *vous parlez français, n'est-ce pas?* Did you study in Paris?" She said it as if Paris were as close as Sausalito.

"I studied under a fat old nun from Quebec."

"Tell the nun her accent was perfect."

"That might be difficult. She was ninety when she taught me."

"Where are you from?" It was not an idle cocktail party question. She was genuinely interested and looked directly into his eyes.

"Back East." He couldn't bring himself to admit to Michigan, so he used the California euphemism for anywhere beyond Arizona.

"What sort of work do you do? No—let me guess! You design lingerie."

"No, actually, I model it."

She blushed, then threw her head back and laughed deliciously. Thom noted her perfect teeth.

They glided to a private porch, and Roxanne continued the banter: "Are you available for benefit luncheons?"

Then she grinned gently, announcing that the game was over. "What do you really do?"

"I'm a contractor." He loved the masculine ring and felt his shoulders stretch in the trim blue suit.

Again she teased. "Do you do any remodeling? There's this porch of ours—" She laughed again, ordered them each another drink, and settled next to him. Far more comfortable than he was.

Actually he felt as if he had won a battle. There was an almost obscene exhilaration in being her equal as he munched cold lobster and sipped perfectly chilled champagne. He felt this was no place to drink bourbon although he didn't know that Roxanne, at twenty-five, had known enough swaybacked WASP men who crewed at Princeton and sucked meerschaums with sexual restraint. Thom felt too awkward to make any move beyond conversation, but he also felt no urgency to take her to bed.

He learned that she was the Whitcomb family rebel who had flunked out of Bryn Mawr, dated a black in her senior year at San Francisco State, and driven her father, Charles Whitcomb III, to a state where there was a barely civil truce between them. Her rebellion had only been a ruse for his attention, and when it failed she settled down to playing tennis and casual boredom. Thom aroused new passions in her. He was a wild Lancelot blown from some strange Irish sea, a handsome, musky slave whose apparent strength and serious blue eyes enticed her.

While E.J. drank too much and grumbled about the taste of caviar, Thom and Roxanne covered Eastern religions, the war in Vietnam, Kennedy's impact, Nixon, and Watergate. She admitted to a degree in English, and Thom talked of philosophy studies with the Jesuits in Chicago. Only when she talked of travels to Europe and the Middle East did he feel outclassed.

"Are you working now?"

"I'm recovering from Europe and school." She laughed, then was serious. "I have a friend, Daphne, an interior designer. I work with her a bit and occasionally organize charity events. Muscular dystrophy, hearts, cancer, whatever's wrong with the world. It's a family tradition."

"We drink," he said.

She laughed her musical laugh and Thom wanted to kiss her.

E.J. approached and said he was ready to leave. Thom, embarrassed by his friend's flushed face, introduced him briefly then turned to Roxanne.

"I hope I see you again." He hated his own shyness and wanted to make something definite.

"I would like that." She said it softly without taking any initiative.

Thom still could not find the words, and he got up awkwardly, feeling dizzy from the champagne.

"I'll call you." It hadn't occurred to him that Charles

Whitcomb was unlisted. Before she replied, he nodded and walked off with E.J., chattering to cover his embarrassment. The yellow truck seemed out of place in the parking lot. So did E.J. munching a handful of shrimp.

E.J. laughed. "She probably fucks with her drawers on."

"You got no class, E.J." They both laughed loudly, and Thom drove to the Pony Lounge for bourbon and ribs. A second Jack Daniel's relaxed him. He knew he wanted to see Roxanne Whitcomb again, but he said nothing to his friend. He also knew he was far more comfortable with E.J. in the Pony Lounge, and soon they were making excited plans about more Victorians.

E.J. was Thom's first real friend since he had left the priesthood. A devoted family man with a simple, honest wife and four kids who were the center of his life, E.J. was the brother Jim could have been, and they worked together as an unbeatable team. When E.J. stammered in front of a banker, Thom charmed him. If Thom grew impatient with subcontractors and venal officials, E.J. won their respect and obtained their cooperation. In the first year of their partnership, Victoriana showed a fifty-thousand-dollar profit after their thirty-five thousand in salaries. A booming real estate market promised even more.

Early on, there was childlike excitement in transforming the sturdy old Victorians into comfortable contemporary showplaces. Thom's increasingly bold ideas thrilled E.J., and E.J.'s natural talent gave substance to Thom's boldness. Nothing was a problem. They expanded narrow bedrooms and restored stained glass, opened roofs for courtyards and garden patios, built sunken tubs or circular stairways where closets had been. They dug out basements for recreation rooms, and once they even opened a living room ceiling all the way to the attic to create a twenty-five-foot A-frame effect.

"Hell—nothing to it," said E.J.

The old Victorians were well built, but the redwood and walnut had layers of paint. Beautiful paneling might be hidden behind plaster, bathrooms were puritanical, kitchens impractical. Closets and alcoves were wasted; wiring was inadequate or dangerous, plumbing archaic; and gas jets and marble fireplaces had been carelessly sealed. But the renovated houses were worth every painful effort.

Most of them were sixty to a hundred years old, and to remodel them was to unravel a history of the discipline and sentiment of another era. With the ghosts and secrets of an entire century.

Victoriana, Inc., made the houses comfortable without destroying innate power. They introduced light and color, dishwashers and garbage disposals, spacious closets and dramatic tiled baths. Kitchens were a specialty, with handmade oak cabinets, ceramic tile floors, and barbecue grills built into uncovered chimneys.

They each looked forward to the start of a new day. E.J. was always there at 6:30, and Millie and Thom arrived at seven.

"How about a cup of coffee to clear the head? Then let's go look at that place on Valencia Street."

"Christ, E.J., it won't disappear."

"This one is unbelievable!" No one could say *unbelievable* like E.J. It took a full two minutes to pronounce.

"What are they asking?"

"You won't give a shit. It'll take four units."

"Zoned R-2?"

"O'Brien's the inspector. He loves me."

"He also can be an asshole. What are they asking?"

"Unbelievable! Thirty-two five."

"Jesus! Who owns it—rats?"

Although San Franciscans were learning to appreciate Victorians, there were still innumerable bargains.

Usually they worked late, not only out of a fierce ambition for profit, but because they loved what they did. When they rescued a spiral oak staircase or restored mahogany paneling in a dining room, they sat on the floor and stared, sharing a six-pack an admiring Millie brought on her way home. When she left, they talked about the past. Football games, teen-age dances with priests chaperoning the sexy girls, childhood fears of mortal sin. Thom's rejected priesthood seemed to free E.J.

"Christ, one time I asked the priest to hear my confession at half time," E.J. told him.

Thom laughed loudly. "Don't tell me you were one of those creeps, E.J.?"

"No shit! We were getting the piss kicked out of us, and I was sure God was punishing me for whacking off."

They laughed until the sunset darkened the rescued

wood to splendor, then made their way to the Pony Lounge to celebrate the warmest friendship either of them had known in years.

E.J. was a barely believing Catholic who sent his children to parochial schools and received the sacraments on first Fridays, Christmas, and Easter. Or a first communion. Raised in the city, he visited his parents regularly, then continued on to grandparents and Rose's family. They had been childhood sweethearts who married while he was on leave from the army, and she was already a mother when he returned from Korea. Eddie, the oldest boy, was in his first year of prelaw at the University of San Francisco. Mary, a high school senior, with Rose's plain face and crooked teeth, was a little mother type to her twelve-year-old sister, Regina. The youngest son, Danny, fourteen, was a good student and an outstanding athlete, and E.J. favored him, as well as the seductive Regina. Thom usually spent Sunday evenings with E.J.'s family.

When Thom began seeing Roxanne Whitcomb, he began to neglect his Sunday visits. E.J. was puzzled.

"You're out of your league, baby. That prima-fucking-donna don't give head unless your cock's been soaking in caviar."

Thom met her again a month later at a decorator's open house on Nob Hill. She had planned to call him that very day, but she didn't mention it. Nor did he admit that he had tried to phone three different Whitcombs on the Peninsula. Roxanne touched his jacket. It excited him.

Again he felt uncomfortable and hated his shyness. She seemed like a poised contemporary, and it was hard to believe she was only three or four years out of college. He wanted to be alone with her but didn't know how to ask. The champagne punch was an appropriate lead.

"I could use a real drink. It's been a tough day."

"My mother told me never to drink with an Irishman."

Roxanne was not really the cool WASP of Thom's insecure imagination. Behind the cautious veneer, she was hungry for his attention. A busy, successful Charles Whitcomb had ignored her as a child, then sent her, at the first sign of inconvenience, to boarding school. Her mother was a pale invalid of considerable wealth who spent most of the day in bed. Roxanne had been given far more than she had ever wanted, until clothes and trips and sports cars meant nothing. Her parents only asked not to be involved.

There were no apparent conflicts in her life except of her own making. Success was in her blood, and America belonged to her father and his friends. Although she had a talent for interior design, there was no real incentive to pursue. When she dropped out of college, there was no dramatic scene, but simply an oily suggestion that she enroll somewhere else. If she worked as a secretary or a waitress, it was only to get a kind of sociological experience, never to prove her worth or make a living. That had been handled at her birth.

Thus her attraction for a strong self-made man who loved his work and projected an intense animal sensuality. Her flimsy barrier of cool cleverness only kept her fears and loneliness a secret.

The Pony Lounge was crowded when Thom arrived with Roxanne. She was delighted by the ride in his yellow truck, even though it briefly embarrassed him, and she was thrilled with his favorite hangout.

Waitresses smiled, and the owner escorted them to Thom's favorite booth and took their drink orders personally.

"The ribs, Mr. Maguire?" the waitress inquired.

Roxanne agreed.

"And mashed potatoes instead of french fries?"

Thom blushed like a small boy and Roxanne was delighted. Characteristically, she put him at ease.

"Mashed potatoes it is."

After three bourbons to her daiquiri and a complimentary liqueur, Thom was totally relaxed, and he talked of his dreams for Victoriana.

"The idea's great," she said. "You could move in a dozen different directions."

He talked of the beauty of restored redwood and of E.J.'s ability.

"You're a perfect team." She played with his fingers, then gently stroked his knee as he continued to describe a rescued old house on Army Street.

Then he took her home with him.

"It looks just like you." She explored the six-room flat. A suede couch and brown leather chairs, an antique oak refectory table he had picked up from one of Victoriana's houses, and a solid walnut coffee table a subcontractor had found in Marin. The kitchen floor was thick terra-cotta tile, and there were scattered glasses, a few empty cans of E.J.'s favorite Olympia beer, and the remains of a steak sandwich on the counter.

"All that's missing is a moose head." She laughed excitedly. Then kissed him warmly.

Without a word he led her into the living room, eased her onto the couch, and began kissing and undressing her. With enough bourbon, he was ready. She had been ready since the first night.

He kissed her and slipped off his shirt. She ran her fingers over his muscular arms, then kissed him hungrily.

He continued undressing her and began sucking her exposed breast. Roxanne's whole body trembled as she lost all composure, and when she was finally naked, he picked her up and carried her into the bedroom, barely noting the sculpted ivory thighs and shapely butt. Her breasts were small, round and firm with long attractive nipples, and there was appealing thick brown hair between her legs where he instantly buried his face and began sucking her like an animal. Roxanne Whitcomb went crazy. So did Thom Maguire.

She groaned with pleasure, then whined like a child and begged him to rest. He sucked the long nipples and stroked the marble thighs, inserted fingers and tongue, then drove his penis, enormously swollen, again and again into her whole history. They became equals as he emptied every ounce of fluid from some vaginal ecstasy she had only read about. Still he was not through, mounting and thrusting, kneading and stroking until she was again as excited as he and sucked hungrily until he exploded in her mouth, crying out like a startled animal.

Then it was as silent as a gentle turf fire in a winter cabin. She stared with wide, frightened eyes in disbelief. She could only whisper hoarsely as she still tasted him.

He couldn't speak. Whimpering, she knelt before him and began gently kissing his legs, then again began licking and sucking his penis.

Until she slept all night like a rag doll in his arms.

Thom Maguire was ecstatic. Already a successful businessman, now he was in love. A man-child with a new elegant toy.

They spent hours conversing in small French cafes or quaint bars along the bay in Marin. They laughed about the bigotry of Kirkwood and about Grandma Whitcomb entertaining Roxanne's black friend from San Francisco State. She continued to love the Pony Lounge, watched a Forty Niner football game, and cooked corned beef and cabbage with boiled potatoes. Thom talked of John Patrick's business, Jack's accident, baseball games with the Legion Maroons, and the rigidity of a seminary prep school. He never mentioned Jim's death or his own priesthood.

And Roxanne introduced him to a new world of the San Francisco symphony, occasional opera, plush affairs for charity, and a night of Wagner.

"Did you like it?" She knew he had been bored.

He grinned. "Like a German funeral."

Again the musical laugh as she began undressing him.

At a Christmas party at the Whitcombs, he chatted briefly with her older sister, recently divorced and childless, who traveled between San Francisco and Paris, dabbling at art.

"Do you like Monet?"

Thom feigned an understanding of Renoir and Modigliani, talked noncommittally about music, and was able to keep her attention briefly with a few remarks about the history of Gregorian chant.

Her brother, Charles IV, a law student at Harvard and his father's only pride, rebuilt Thom's confidence after a discussion of professional football and a promise of a future tennis game.

Roxanne's father, absorbed in grain brokering and importing, stayed politely detached. Once he inquired about Thom's business, then barely listened when Thom answered. Even a lie about bidding on a high-rise office building in San Mateo did not impress the elder Whitcomb who excused himself to answer a phone call in the midst of Thom's explanation.

Mrs. Whitcomb, a plump, fiftyish woman from old money, smiled politely. She also seemed unmoved by Thom's good looks and shy Irish charm, and Roxanne finally rescued him with an offer of a private swim in the indoor pool.

"I appreciate your going through this, darling. Aren't they impossible?"

"I like them," he lied.

"I don't." That was all. It was her way of dismissing the pain, and it made it impossible for him to really know her.

Then she floated in his arms like a little girl and begged him to make love to her in the pool.

"For Chrissakes, Roxanne, not here." She laughed impishly and swam away. Later they returned to his apartment, talked about Victoriana's new acquisition and her plans to join Daphne in business, and went to bed. The tension of the evening had disappeared.

Roxanne brought order into his life. Thom had never liked living alone—without the attentions of a Margaret or a housekeeper—and Roxanne was thrilled to be of service to someone who needed her. She was also thrilled when he encouraged her to help in the redecorating of remodeled Victorians.

Although Millie resented Roxanne's presence around the office, E.J. was delighted. Proud of Thom's ability to attract a Whitcomb. She was the right woman for their continued success.

"She's got class, baby! Them bankers look at you a little different when that Whitcomb lady's on your arm."

Thom knew E.J. was right. At a Wells Fargo Bank open house, Thom observed whispers when he walked in the room with Roxanne. The new manager never left their side. Roxanne was not conscious of any special attention, and Thom did not let on when she complimented him.

"That banker likes you."

"And I like you." She blushed beautifully as he covertly rubbed her thigh.

Occasionally she made brief mention of her loneliness and told him how much she loved him, but she did not say that her whole life had changed, that she was interested in things again—in a beginning sculpture class and a design seminar she attended with Daphne, in a new job selecting drapes and carpets and contemporary furniture for a plush office building in Redwood City. And that she truly felt needed for the first time in her life.

Unlike her father, who never discussed business at home, Thom talked over every decision with her and wondered about new expansions.

"I don't want to take on more than we can handle. E.J. has limits, and he loves to spend time with his family."

"It's hard to set limits," she said. "A business has to grow." She looked at him lovingly. "I'm so proud of what you accomplished! No one handed it to you. You can become whatever you want."

Then she kissed him and freshened his drink; they watched a late movie on TV and she fell asleep in his arms.

He reminisced. Roxanne was the relief he needed after Jennie. A bright, attentive equal who understood his ambitions. Without mad jealousy or debilitating sex. She was more: she was the perfect wife for the president of Victoriana, Inc.

They were married in September 1974 at Grace Episcopal Cathedral by a celebrated canon who was a longtime friend of the Whitcomb family. Roxanne took care of everything, even making a few changes in the menu to suit his Irish tastes.

E.J. was best man, despite a mild protest from Rose about the ecclesiastical violation—which was no longer enforced in new ecumenical times.

The details of the wedding were described in the Chronicle, and the event did nothing to undermine the prestige of Victoriana, Inc. The soloist had sung at the Met, twice, and Roxanne's parents presented them with an heirloom dining room set. The reception was held at the Hillsboro Country Club with French maids serving crab and lobster—and mashed potatoes and gravy from a giant standing rib roast, served with fresh spinach. E.J. got outrageously drunk and his wife Rose spilled her drink on one of the bridesmaids. Millie told E.J. the whole wedding was too impersonal, but when Thom came over and told her she looked gorgeous, she began to relax and enjoy the celebration.

The newlyweds decided against a honeymoon.

Thom teased her: "You've been everywhere! I've got work to do. You can get the house in order and start learning to cook!"

Although Roxanne would have preferred an apartment on Nob Hill or a sprawling house on the Peninsula, she was delighted to move into Thom's apartment.

"Old houses are like old people," he said. "They've got character." Roxanne did not disagree.

Thom's marriage to Roxanne gave him the same sense of importance as his business. He bought a blue Lincoln Continental and a new wardrobe. Millie located some bargain lots on an expanding Peninsula, as San Franciscans continued to run from crime in the city, and Victoriana extended itself to construct small apartment units. Soon there was little time to sit and admire coved ceilings or rescued wood. E.J. rushed around to inspect three separate teams of framers, roofers, plumbers, electricians, and finished carpenters, and Thom bought acreage for a subdivision and wrestled with zoning restrictions and paper work. Without Millie, they would have been buried. She put in the same long hours, accepted new assignments without complaint, and worked so systematically and coolly that it was impossible not to take her for granted. She never complained, still hoping that her contributions would be recognized by an offer of future ownership in Victoriana, Inc.

Roxanne continued to blossom. There was hardly time for tennis or idle lunches at the Hillsboro Country Club. Or the Pony Lounge. With Daphne she decorated Victoriana's new apartments, and she was hired to furnish the offices of a Bank of America in San Bruno.

Like any excited young bride, she learned to prepare Thom's favorite dishes, and she packed sandwiches on days he would be too busy to go out or prepared a picnic and met him on the job. Once she even tried to make a raspberry pie like Margaret's.

Thom only heard from Margaret on Christmas and his birthday, when she reminded him of his childhood faith and talked of Johnny's progress in the seminary. Johnny had completed Saint Robert's and was studying philosophy in Cincinnati. "Just like you, although Connie expected him to be sent to Rome . . ." It all seemed like a bad dream. Hopes of going to Rome were a long time ago.

The growing business demands took their toll, but Roxanne made his homelife a paradise. Always freshly bathed, her hair soft and fragrant, her skin perfect, she waited with his chilled drink, the evening *Examiner,* and the ability to listen to the details of his days. Or to respect his silence. With three and then four crews working in the city and down the Peninsula, evenings with E.J. at the Pony Lounge became a rare treat. It was difficult to find skilled foremen who could run an entire job, and E.J. was furious. He had missed Danny's first football game.

"Fucking sons of bitches call themselves carpenters. Shit, they don't know framing from plumbing! Every bastard who picks up a hammer thinks he's Saint Joseph."

"There's gotta be good men, E.J.! You can't run all over hell."

"Well I'll be damned if I can find 'em. These are good times, padre; every decent motherfucker is going in for himself. Every patch of land big enough for a shithouse is pouring a foundation."

"We won't be doing this forever!"

E.J. didn't grin. "That's what we said six months ago. How the hell much money do we need? I liked it better in the old days—"

Thom was as weary. A stop-work order interrupted a whole day. When a retired schoolteacher complained about a new window that stared into her bedroom, Thom ignored her as a "stupid old bitch." A month later she dragged Victoriana to a Board of Permit Appeals hearing, and although they won, it cost five thousand dollars in legal fees and another day in court waiting to be heard. Any neurotic in the area could drag them into court, and Victoriana was constantly involved in expensive litigation. When litigation eased off, there were tax investigations, new rates on workmen's comp, and fire doors required in four apartments. Even with a raise, Millie grumbled about twelve-hour days.

Roxanne was more understanding, although she too missed the leisurely evenings of their courtship and looked forward to having a house on the Peninsula and greater freedom to entertain. She helped organize his day, drove around with him to search for new properties, even wondered if E.J. were not unsuited for their expanding business.

Thom defended his friend. "Without him, there never would have been a Victoriana, darling."

"I doubt that," she said warmly. Then she kissed him softly on the cheek and massaged him with oil before he fell asleep.

At the end of their second year in business, E.J. confronted Thom.

"We're just too damn busy. I don't get home till nine or ten o'clock, and even then my phone's ringing, and at seven in the morning it starts all over again. Rose is starting to complain, and I never have time to talk to the kids. I've seen Danny play three times all year."

Thom again reassured him, and they drove to Milo's for draft beer and pizza. Then they explored Farmer's Market for an hour, sampling seedless grapes and munching fresh walnuts, and soon E.J. was his smiling self.

"Like the old days! Did you hear the one about the priest who found a jackass in his front yard?"

He laughed his belching Irish laugh, knowing instinctively that life was to be lived and not thought about. "Hey, Thom baby, we never had it so good! Two little micks right up there with the best of 'em. Incredible!"

The following night they watched Danny throw a touchdown pass to lead Saint Ignatius to a last-quarter victory, then they ate a late supper of Rose's cold chicken.

"It's like old times," a beaming Rose said to Roxanne. "Thom used to come over every Sunday night."

Roxanne smiled. Then she glanced at Thom and signaled with her eyes that it was time to leave. Rose saw the glance and her feelings were hurt.

"What's the hurry?" E.J. asked.

"I need a little time with my man," Roxanne purred.

E.J. grinned. "You can't fight that!"

Back at the apartment, Roxanne tried vainly to arouse Thom.

"I guess I'm exhausted, darling. Or maybe too much booze—"

"It doesn't matter. We'll take a trip soon."

It was the second time that month, and Thom was worried.

Business pressures increased over the next few months and assuredly there was no time for any vacation. Roxanne didn't complain. She busied herself with decorating and enrolled in a pottery course with Kelly Osbourne, a longtime Whitcomb friend and a member of the Peninsula aristocracy. After six classes, "Os" pronounced her "smashing!" It was the favorite compliment of the lanky, balding artist.

"You should have your own kiln."

"In a Victorian apartment?"

"Move back to the Peninsula." His sprawling family estate was only a mile from the Whitcombs.

"Thom likes the city."

"So change his mind." He grinned over his red moustache, and Roxanne plotted to have her own kiln. She admitted to Daphne—after smoking marijuana—that she was bored. For the first time since she had met Thom.

"You need kids."

"Maybe you're right. We really haven't discussed it."

When she brought the idea up to Thom that night in bed, he fell asleep with a mumbled "We'll see." He complained in the morning that he was still tired, then the phone rang and he rushed to the office without having his coffee.

Ironically, Thom began to adopt Roxanne's culture. During a rare evening at the San Francisco Symphony, she missed his customary humorous critique; and at a tedious *King Lear,* with five perfect endings, he was content to philosophize with Daphne and her stockbroker friend about Shakespeare's vision of women. He even agreed to a midnight supper of smoked salmon when Roxanne knew he wanted a hot roast beef sandwich with mashed potatoes and extra gravy.

Imperceptibly he upgraded his speech. His once refreshing opinions became educated critiques worthy of the Jesuits he claimed to be his college mentors. He became acutely conscious of style and of personal hygiene, and he started having weekly manicures and took to wearing lounging robes and monogrammed silk pajamas. He even began purchasing dark English-cut suits from Charles Whitcomb's tailor. The changes were entirely his own and he dressed with almost obscene pride. He developed a new emotional control that pleased him enormously, resenting the crude outburst when he persuaded E.J. to visit the family tailor.

"No fucking way! Three hundred bucks for a piece of shit? I'll take Robert Hall."

Rare dinners with Rose and E.J. were tense and ritualistic, and Thom suddenly felt critical of Rose's appearance.

She had gained weight and her hair seemed forever in disarray. Her down-to-earth remarks, once amusing, now wearied him. At Thom's suggestion, Roxanne invited Os and Daphne one evening to relax things. Os was charming on grass and too much wine, and Rose enjoyed him immensely. Thom was restless and bored.

"Tell me about your children, Rose." Os's eyes twinkled.

"I'd trade 'em all for a two-week vacation."

"I don't know how you do it," Daphne said.

"Just bounce with the punches," E.J. added.

"I punch instead," said a scowling Rose.

"Smashing!" Os giggled and Roxanne laughed loudly. Thom didn't even smile. There was an awkward silence.

Thom took E.J. into the den to discuss a new project and he was relieved when they all finally left.

"You look terribly tired, darling." Roxanne stroked him gently.

"There's so damn much to do." For the first time, he wondered about E.J.

"Business is like that," she said gently. "It will all come together soon." She was suddenly excited. "Let's take a long trip—to Hawaii or the Caribbean."

"Jesus, Roxanne, not now—maybe after the first of the year."

Almost without knowing it, they had drifted apart. It was hard to assess fault, or to know whether they were still in love. Curiously, Roxanne would have stood by him had he admitted to her that his strength was as limited as hers, that his fears were only buried in his drive to succeed. She would have understood as well as anyone, and his honesty would have freed her from a burden of restraint and cleverness as ancient as his. He never really knew who she was. She was the symbol of his success, a poised and attentive hostess, and after the first few months he was caught up in his own myopic battles with unseen enemies against whom no success would ever be enough. He could not see Roxanne as a sensitive, lonely child who wondered why even her husband chose to ignore her for his work.

So she continued naïvely to want her Peninsula estate. He wanted an even greater success than Charles Whitcomb, who had never uttered a personal word to Thom since his marriage.

As Roxanne spent more time with Daphne and Os, sipping wine and smoking grass, Thom struggled to keep up with the growing corporation. Even E.J. was powerless to rescue them with his humor and balance. Amid the tension of multiplying problems the original excitement was lost, and gradually creative remodeling took second place to quick profit. From time to time, Thom felt that Millie was disappointed with the evolvement, but she said nothing. She was the one who first saw the wisdom of keeping choice units for rental to strengthen cash flow and relieve the tax burden. Millie's vision had made them rich. She was a Victoriana fixture—bright, loyal, and never unprepared. Her only fault seemed to be her disastrous coffee.

Once a good-looking man came to pick her up while she and Thom were working on a complicated estimate.

"I'll finish it in the morning," she said.

"No, forget it, it doesn't matter!" He hated his own pouting.

The next day the man appeared again to take her to lunch.

"What the hell is this—homecoming? I want that McMillan estimate!"

"It's on your desk." She said it gently, without reproof.

He apologized. "You have two hours."

They both laughed, and she was back in forty minutes. He never saw the man again.

When they attempted new construction in late 1975, Millie learned to modify zoning restrictions without arousing the people in the neighborhoods; she interested real estate writers on the *Chronicle* in "par-Victorian apartment units" that were built for quick resale; and she entertained younger bankers at lunch without getting involved. Consequently they were able to borrow more money than their buildings actually cost by submitting inflated bids and "adjusting" financial statements at the banker's advice.

But even Millie found it hard to hold Victoriana together when E.J. refused to work more than fifty hours a week.

"Damn it. All a guy's got are his kids. We got more money than we can spend, and nothing's fun anymore."

Thom couldn't hear him. Although his marriage was falling apart and his best friend refused to cooperate, he was consumed with the success of Victoriana. Nothing else mattered. He began to have headaches, his facial muscles felt tight, his stomach and shoulders ached, and even without eating he gained weight. The increased net worth and fourteen-hour days merged into long grayness. He had not had sex with Roxanne for weeks.

E.J. continued to complain. Roxanne spent more time playing tennis and following Os and Daphne to weekend pottery seminars or design institutes. Only Millie worked the same long hours as Thom without the least complaint. But she worried about Thom's nervousness and silently criticized Roxanne for abandoning her husband to his own private frustrations. Roxanne never suggested that he slow down the operation.

The week that E.J. and Rose returned from Christmas vacation in Hawaii, tanned and refreshed, Victoriana made an ambitious new move that was initiated by Roxanne. In her persistent search for Peninsula property, she and Os discovered that the Van Deusen estate in Atherton was for sale, over forty acres of forested land with its own rolling hills, a redwood grove, and a year-round stream. A sprawling thirty-room main house with hardwood floors, tile wainscoting, turrets, and terra-cotta patios. There was also a huge solarium, a carriage house, a ten-room guest cottage, a large private pool, and wooded glens and grottoes, all surrounded by a stone wall. Van Deusen, a newspaper pioneer, had been dead for some years, and his wife had finally given up the estate.

On Roxanne's lead, Millie did the homework and produced approximate figures. Thom was cautious about the enormity of the risk.

"What will it take, a million?"

"I think two. Five hundred thousand down should do it, and the rest can be financed. A nephew is apparently pushing the widow."

E.J. was terrified. "Jesus Christ, man! We'll be up to our ass in problems. It's bad enough now. Count me out!"

When Thom was put off by E.J.'s reluctance, Roxanne suddenly became a fighting Whitcomb. Her chin went up, the ivory complexion flushed pink, and the brown eyes were stone cold. She was not about to lose her Peninsula dream.

"E.J.'s become a liability." She said it with an Anglo-Saxon coolness that sent chills down Thom's back.

"For God's sake, Roxanne. He's my closest friend!"

"My father fired two of his best friends. Business is no backgammon game."

The mention of her father crushed him, and two years before he would have roared. Now he said nothing, and the next day he approached E.J.

"Christ, E.J., it's the chance of a lifetime. Don't worry about it." Thom himself was terrified but tingling with excitement at a final success.

After lunch, when E.J. came in mildly drunk and angry, Thom quickly arranged for E.J. to take a private business trip to Las Vegas. Then he focused on selling some San Bruno apartments for the down payment. Millie worked twelve hours a day, but the deal could never have been closed without Roxanne. She offered a block of General Motors stock to reassure a nervous banker, and she interested an exclusive girls' school in considering the Van Deusen property as a relocation spot.

Thom was at the point of accepting any help, but he warned, "This is a business deal, not a place for us to live."

"There's plenty of space for us and the business deal, too." Roxanne took total charge.

Finally the coup was ready to be consummated. Victoriana, Inc., was the envy of every broker and contractor on the Peninsula, especially when Ogilvie Academy agreed to purchase the main house, solarium, and twenty-two acres in an all-cash deal. When Thom was able to peddle six acres to a Palo Alto physician, Victoriana stood to make almost a half million dollars. It was perfect.

Until E.J. refused to sign the agreement.

Thom couldn't believe it. "My God, E.J., it can't miss. You've got to sign!"

"I don't gotta do nothing, baby! I've had enough! Now your old lady's taking over our company." The sincere eyes flashed straight at Thom. "I love you, baby. You're my best friend! But look at what's happened to us. Shit, we haven't laughed together for months. For Christ sakes, we got more money than we can spend. When the fuck are you gonna start living?"

Thom didn't hear him. "You don't have to do a damn thing! The work's all done. All we need is your signature!"

"Well, you ain't getting it, baby. Not as long as I'm your partner!" The jaw was set, the rugged chin ready to take on the world. Thom knew there was nothing he could say.

Roxanne was furious. "You should have dumped him a year ago. He's just a carpenter! There are thousands of those! You're an executive."

Thom had never seen her rage. It was not an Irish explosion, but a cold, determined edict. In clipped syllables. Thom was frightened. He protested weakly.

"My God, Roxanne, this isn't the last deal in the world. If E.J. doesn't want to go with it, it's his right—"

"This is the perfect chance to be rid of him. And you know it." When Thom still hesitated, Roxanne took another tack.

"Darling, Victoriana is first and foremost a great idea. It was your idea! You made it what it is! I understand your beautiful loyalties and I love you for it, but E.J. will be better off. He's not built for this kind of pressure. You can take it! And with the Van Deusen deal, Victoriana will have arrived!" She was pleading. Then she laughed softly. "Besides, it'll blow daddy's mind!"

"It seems so cruel somehow—it's like a divorce."

"Sometimes a divorce isn't cruel, Thom. E.J. will have all the money he needs." She paused for her final coup. "It could be the kindest thing you've ever done."

He nodded sadly. "You may be right."

Then she took him to bed.

Thom procrastinated for two more days. Finally he broke the news to E.J. after Millie left the office.

"Take whatever you goddamned please! I don't give a damn!"

"I don't want to take anything, E.J. We'll have the auditors decide. Then we can divide the company. You can take the construction end and most of the cash and I'll take the real estate division with certain properties. Millie will get the books together and—"

E.J. didn't want to hear more. His strong face was flushed, his eyes moist as he looked away.

"Ain't no sense getting upset," he said quietly. "You've been a good friend, padre. Do it any way you want!"

The trade looked fair. But construction was on a tighter trend, which was not yet reflected in the books, and a portion of the receivables were uncollectable without suit.

There was no way the books could demonstrate that, or a sudden narrowing of the market with increased competition. Even as real estate prices continued to escalate wildly.

Millie knew all of this. She supervised the accounting firm, and within three weeks, before escrow had closed on the Van Deusen deal, the agreement was signed and notarized. E.J. had some fat property, nearly a quarter of a million in cash, and a construction company he had started with: E.J. Crotty and Son.

Almost five years of friendship and a lucrative partnership had ended. But Thom was too weary and depressed to reminisce. He was relieved that Millie would remain with him.

E.J. grinned bravely. "I can't stand her damn coffee anyway."

Millie was too choked up to say anything.

She rented them three rooms in a renovated glass office building on Union Street, a prestige address for Victoriana, Inc. They were now mainly a property management and investment company, where Millie collected the rents and supervised resident managers. Even in the limited remodeling work, Thom had only to find the building, make the deal, and secure the financing. Millie had learned to handle the subcontractors' bids and inspect the progress when he was not available.

One depressing Monday morning, when Thom was missing E.J. terribly, Millie made a request she had thought about for months.

"I like the new responsibilities," she said, "but I should be compensated. I know this is a bad time, but I need a decent car and a credit card for expenses. I also should get a substantial raise since we can afford it." She said it quickly, as if it were difficult, knowing she had lost all chance at part ownership.

She got everything she asked for, and he got the increased freedom and diminished guilt. She was soon able to handle the loans and offer suggestions about when properties might be traded. She took bankers to lunch and she decided to get her real estate license. Her independence began to frighten Thom, for soon he did little but sign checks.

Occasionally Thom saw E.J. at the Pony Lounge. E.J.

acknowledged the business Millie sent his way and announced that Danny had received a scholarship at Santa Clara.

"It ain't Notre Dame, but it's a damn good school!"

Thom wanted to tell E.J. how much he missed him, but there never seemed to be the right moment. A new sadness in E.J.'s eyes cut Thom to the core.

Once Rose called Thom at the office. "I wish you could do something. He really misses you. Your name comes up every day. He's drinking more than he ever did and he spends too much time at the Elks. I don't want to say anything, but I thought—" Then she begged him not to tell E.J. she had called.

Roxanne was jubilant with her Peninsula home. The Maguires now owned the guesthouse and pool, the carriage house and stables, and eleven acres. With frontage on the stream.

"Daphne and I have already planned a garden court beyond the pool and a covered walk. Os is designing a kiln, and we can add two wings to the guesthouse—"

"That's a lot of money, Roxanne." He said it almost boyishly, knowing he was no match for her.

"You don't want to die with it like Van Deusen. Can you imagine what we can do with the carriage house? You'll have your own Walden when you get home!"

Thom was relieved that Roxanne finally had her estate. The story of the sale appeared in both the *Chronicle* and the *Examiner,* and Roxanne responded to his gift with a few weeks of gently loving attention and two patient attempts to arouse him. Then she was lost in her beloved project with more enthusiasm than he had seen since they were first married. Too excited to worry about having children.

When they had the open house on their third wedding anniversary in the fall of 1977, it was worth the anxiety and expense to watch the faces of friends and competitors surveying the Maguire estate. Even Charles Whitcomb III seemed impressed.

Three days later, E.J. appeared in Thom's office for the first time since the breakup, and Millie and Thom were delighted. They sipped coffee, and as he looked at E.J. Thom felt a sharp pain in his side and knew he had made a mistake. He didn't know what to say.

E.J. grinned. "What the hell do you look so glum about? You got rid of me."

"I miss the hell out of you, E.J.!"

He wanted to say they could start over again. Find an old Victorian and go to work. Then share a six-pack and drive to Milo's for pizza. Or drink and brag at the Pony Lounge. The words froze on his lips.

E.J. shifted nervously. "We had some good old times." He looked at Thom like an admiring little boy. "You were the first one to ever call me E.J." Then the unforgettable grin.

Thom felt the same sharp pain in his side, yet he could only mumble unconvincingly, "We had some great times."

"Incredible! Shit, we turned this town out!" He paused and suddenly looked all of his fifty years.

"Well, that's something, ain't it, padre?"

"Yeh, that's something, E.J." Thom wanted to scream his regrets but there was only thick silence.

E.J. turned to leave. "Good to see you guys. I think your coffee's getting better, Millie-Nillie!"

They walked him to the door. He stopped, grabbed Thom's shoulder, and punched him gently on the arm.

"We had some times! Incredible, baby, incredible!"

The following Friday, E.J. and one of his employees fell off a third-floor porch they were remodeling in Sausalito. E.J. broke his neck. He died at one o'clock the next morning.

Thom was called in the middle of the night and he drove over to the house. A priest was there and Danny and the two girls and a few stunned relatives. Rose was talking in a disconnected stream.

"My poor dead baby!" She threw her arms around Thom. "O my dear God, he loved you. More than anybody. Dear God, what are we going to do?"

He tried to hold her and let her cry. Finally a doctor arrived and gave her something to make her sleep.

Thom drove to the Union Street office, stripped to his shorts, and lit a marijuana cigarette. After making a cup of tea, he walked into the empty conference room, put his head down on the table, and began to cry.

He heard the doorbell ringing. It rang again. He came to. It was five o'clock and Millie was standing outside.

"I didn't want to barge in. I was afraid you'd be too upset." Tears were streaming down her face.

"God, Millie!" He pulled her against his chest, then she led him back to the leather couch in his office, covered him with an afghan, and found some soft music on the radio. He thought he was melting, and he struggled to be conscious, to focus on Millie or the music. He couldn't stop trembling and he pulled the colorful afghan around his shoulders. He wanted Millie to talk, but she said nothing, and he was powerless to ask. He could feel the tears pouring down his cheeks and the sobs convulsing his whole body. He would never stop crying. Then he heard her voice from a great distance.

"You'll be all right now."

He clung to her like a small child who had lost his way.

Then he thought she kissed him.

Finally the phone rang. It was Roxanne. She was very sorry. Could she do anything?

"Do anything? Jesus! What do you want to do? E.J.'s dead! My best friend is dead! I killed him!"

He hung up the phone. Then fell into Millie's arms.

"Jesus, Millie, I killed him!"

Then he passed out.

18

An Irish Wake

Rose called him two or three times a day. Would Thom select the pallbearers? Could he arrange for a traditional requiem mass? The pastor, Monsignor Dunnigan, was a noted liturgist and refused to say a Latin Mass even for E.J. Rose had heard of an aging hospital chaplain of the old school who might oblige. Would Thom arrange it all and smooth things over so Monsignor would preach? Millie took care of it. Thom was numb.

Although he said nothing, he was deeply hurt when Roxanne complained of a sciatic nerve and declined going to the funeral. Especially when Os appeared the same morning to heat the kiln.

Thom arrived early for the service, but the altar boys were already receiving hoarsely whispered instructions from the chaplain in the sanctuary. One of the nuns was rushing frantically to accommodate him. Father Emil Zasski had a large wart above his right eyebrow which moved upward when he asked a question. His slight Eastern European accent was exaggerated by a beautiful, deep voice.

The church soon filled with contractors, city inspectors, bowling teams and lodge brothers, hordes of relatives, and the assorted friends gathered in three generations of life in the same city. Since E.J. had been good to the Church, both in liberal donations and uncompensated construction work, there were five pews of surpliced clergymen mumbling their *Miserere mei, Deus* and fifty or sixty nuns in statuesque prayer flanking the extravagant bronze coffin.

Thom was lost in a world he had barely thought of in years. Saint John's was a beautiful church, basilicalike with Gothic arches and a Romanesque nave. Thom looked up at the familiar fat cherubs holding the gilt-edged banner. *Gloria in excelsis Deo.*

He remembered. God, he remembered and thought of all the prayers to all the saints, and wondered how many children Anne had and if Margaret was even now praying for his return.

The old priest came down the aisle to meet E.J.'s coffin, directing the altar boys, "Get up ahead! Not you, blondie, you hold the cope!" The boy looked like a young Thom. "I gotta sprinkle the holy water." He sprinkled in his hand at first to test the stream, then on E.J. more generously, and he bellowed out the haunting *Subvenite.* The choir was made up of a few old nuns and the retired church members who remembered the Latin responses and commissioned E.J. to Abraham's bosom. Father Zasski moved up the aisle eyeing the Knights of Columbus, then roared the ancient words and supplemented the singing of the choir as they continued to ask God's mercy. Thom sang softly to himself, surprised that he still remembered the thrilling Gregorian rhythms. The Dies Irae with its vivid description of the fearful Judgment Day seemed almost a warning to the modern priests who scorned celibacy. Zasski chimed in loudly. The ancient cadence of the gospel promising life to Lazarus thrilled Thom as it always had.

A surprising number of people moved forward to receive communion. Father Zasski had not expected this, but he shrugged and opened the tabernacle while two men in cassock and surplice approached the altar to assist him. He looked at them. "One of you is enough. I ain't crippled." One of the men moved to his side awkwardly, omitting a genuflection and causing Zasski to ask, "You a priest?"

"No, father. I'm one of the lay readers."

"Den don't touch anything! Laymen around the altar only in emergencies!" A startled Thom wanted to cheer his last stand. Zasski turned to Monsignor Dunnigan who was waiting in full regalia in the sanctuary to deliver the sermon. "Father, give me a hand here!"

Monsignor Dunnigan looked coolly at Zasski. "Mr. Davison is quite capable of assisting with communion."

"But he's no priest. What's the emergency?"

"An emergency is not required."

"That ain't what the pope says."

The monsignor made no move.

"I'll do de thing myself." He grabbed the remaining ciborium in his chubby hand with an iron grip—ready to die for the Holy Grail.

Thom was exhilarated by Zasski's crusade and almost unconsciously he walked up the aisle, proudly, to receive the Host from Zasski's hands. The cardboard taste orbited him back to Saint Raphael's, and he only wanted E.J. to be alive to challenge the Dutchmen on Maple Street and annihilate them in two-man basketball in the Maguire driveway. With John Patrick and McNulty getting blissfully drunk.

The sermon reminded them that they were part of the risen Christ and that God's ways were not always man's. In the name of the parish, Monsignor Dunnigan expressed condolences to Rose and the family, then he moved back to his place in the sanctuary and Zasski marched to the coffin to "sprinkle" E.J. for the last time. The smoke of the incense rose toward the cherubs on the ceiling: One was smiling as E.J. was sent to the heaven for laughing angry men with broken hearts.

When Thom arrived home, Os was there, showing Roxanne pictures of Etruscan pottery. They were lying on the living room carpet smoking grass and sipping muscatel. They sat up like guilty children and Roxanne poured her husband a glass of Wild Turkey.

Os got up to leave. "There's no need to run off—" Roxanne gently touched his shoulder. "Stay and have a bite with us."

"No really—you have things to discuss."

She reassured Os by pouring more wine, and then she addressed Thom's brooding. "E.J. had nothing before you—"

"He was my friend, Roxanne. I'd like you to remember that. I owe him a lot." He struggled not to order Os from the house. "He's also dead!" Roxanne was embarrassed by his loud attack.

"Well, have some masses said! Isn't that what Rose wants? To pray him into heaven?" She passed the joint to Os.

Os had no awareness that Thom had ever been a Catholic, and he playfully assisted Roxanne in relaxing the mood. The grass and wine had dulled his perception.

"Mother Mary will appear in a fire engine."

Roxanne laughed. "No, no! The pope will issue an indulgence. Isn't that how it's done?"

Thom's sudden explosion cut their laughter short.

"Look, goddamn it, that's enough! I don't want you to open your goddamned mouth about my Church unless you know what the fuck you're talking about. Is that clear?"

Os could only nod helplessly. Roxanne trembled. Thom was not through venting his stored anger on all his ancient enemies.

"Mocking the faith of simple people! Goddamn it, their faith makes as much sense as your fucking vases! Giggling your way through life on grass and someone else's money. I was raised around arrogant assholes like you!"

Roxanne had begun to recover. "Really, Thom, there's no need to begin true confession time. You can—"

He slapped her. Os groaned but did not stir. The queen WASP no longer found Thom's Irish anger amusing. She discovered it was real—bone deep and out of control. He was suddenly a brawling Irish maniac.

"Now sit there, goddamn it, until I tell you to move!" He poured himself more whiskey.

"I want to make a toast to E.J." No one moved. "I said a toast! Raise your fucking glasses to my Catholic friend!" He was shouting. "Wait a minute, your glass is empty! Let the butler take care of that little number!"

He sloshed the wine in Os's glass, spilling it over the sides. "Christ Jesus, pardon me! We Maguires were never very well-bred. Stupid, ignorant, superstitious fucking Irish Catholics! We always drank wine out of the bottle." He began laughing.

They raised their glasses obediently as a grandfather clock chimed somewhere.

"To the best friend I ever had. To the best friend any man could ever want! E.J., you crazy son of a bitch, I love you! We turned this town out, baby! Incredible! Incredible!" He savored E.J.'s favorite word. "Two fucking little micks came out of nowhere, man! Right up there sucking champagne with Roxanne and Os. Now that's class! Hey Mr. Crotty, I mean class! Like fucking pilgrims, E.J. baby. Now that's got to get you a few days out of purgatory." He laughed. "There oughta be a plenary indulgence for associating with fucking cultured turds." The words were hardly slurred as he poured a fifth drink and refilled his guests' glasses. Then he grinned broadly.

"We micks can hold our fucking booze, can't we, Os?

Your fucking aye, we can!" He slapped him on the back, then noticed that he and Roxanne had set their glasses on the coffee table.

"Jesus, what kind of a host am I at my best friend's wake when the toast ain't even finished yet—no way!" Again he filled their glasses, then tossed the empty bottle against a marble bust of Thomas Jefferson.

The maid rushed in from the kitchen to examine the splintered glass.

"Later, later, we're having a delayed Irish wake. Bring more wine, sirrah!" She scurried out for another bottle. "Os needs another drink. Grab your glasses everybody! That's better! Now let's hear it: To E.J. Crotty, one hell of a man!"

A trembling Os made the toast bravely. "To E.J.—er —Crotty—one hell of a man!"

"Smashing," said Thom, "really smashing!" He turned to Roxanne. "Now you, bitch!"

On the verge of tears, she repeated it.

He pried open a new bottle of wine. The cork fell in and he poured around it. "Christ, it's hot in here." He ripped off his jacket, then tore the monogrammed silk shirt to shreds and stripped to his shorts. "C'mon, Os, get comfortable, buddy!"

Os slipped off his shirt.

"Shit, Os, get down, baby. Right down to those old shorts! E.J. wouldn't have it any other way."

Os stood pale in his black bikini briefs. Thom poured more wine.

"Os, you old bastard you—you been holding out on me." He slapped him on the buttocks. Thom began unbuttoning Roxanne's blouse.

"C'mon, bitch, we're all family. Just one of the guys!" She tensely slipped out of her blouse and then her jeans, then she giggled almost hysterically as she and Os began pointing at each other and dribbling more wine. Thom pinched her butt; Os hesitantly did likewise.

"Smashing," said Thom. "Really smashing." Then he raised his arms as if he were silencing an unruly mob.

"Now we're gonna sing, by God, sing for old E.J. who loved a good song." And they did: all of John Patrick's favorites. The maid brought more wine at Thom's command and rushed out in new embarrassment.

"Sing, you motherfuckers! Sing for E.J.!"

Thom never saw Roxanne again.

The next morning there was a note on the kitchen table. Properly in an envelope so the maid would not be privy to their life. She would be at her parents' house and would like a divorce. Nothing more.

The divorce was in no way painful. He agreed to give Roxanne the house, and the attorneys arranged a suitable payment for his half of the equity. Spread over ten years for tax benefits. She wanted no part of his business, nor did he want anything they had accumulated. He moved to a furnished apartment south of the city near the ocean.

Os and Daphne came to live with Roxanne. Her parents were never really sure what had happened.

Nor was Thom Maguire.

In the ensuing weeks, during a busy autumn season, the business would have collapsed without Millie. She told people that Thom was out of town or examining property; she even signed his name on checks to transfer funds. On the rare occasions when he saw her, he said nothing. Nor did she. At times he hated her and the guilt her placid support could produce in him. He wanted to shake her so she would curse at him, but Millie did her job as efficiently and respectfully as ever.

He was more alone than he had ever permitted himself to be, and he struggled to live with the raw rage of a lifetime. After Jennie, there had been the company of the pain of missing her. Now, there was no one to blame and no one to want. Jennie was gone, Margaret a doting stranger, and Roxanne was spinning her soupy vases with the clay-fingered Os. Thom tried to think of a reason to live—or die. There was none.

He developed severe headaches that did not respond to aspirin or even codeine. He blamed them on heavy financial pressure, most of it of his own making, but the less he worked, the greater his energy loss. There were times when he would have drowned save for Millie, not simply because she continued to run his business, but because she treated him with the same respect she always had. Only rarely did she become personal.

Two weeks before Christmas, she stopped him as he came into the office late in the afternoon.

"There's something to sign."

"What?"

"Your former wife, Jennie, is converting to Catholicism."

"What?"

She spoke softly. "It's an affidavit stating that you were not married in the Catholic Church and that there was no secret revalidation."

"Christ, I can't believe it."

"The young priest wanted to interview you, but I told him it was impossible. It's all filled out; you just sign and I'll have it notarized."

He needed a drink, and he invited Millie to go with him to the Pony Lounge.

She hesitated. "There's an eviction notice and two—"

"Jesus Christ, Millie, forget it. Can't you ever let up?"

She blushed. "Easier than you know."

She might have been right. What did he know? She was like Victoriana, an old friend. No, she was a fixture in his life.

Although he had been considerate with gifts and time off, their personal contacts had been rare. In business he confided in her absolutely and talked out every conceivable problem, but beyond this, there had only been lunches or late working hours.

Millie had made an exciting job a kind of sexless marriage and had merged her best energies with the business. She belonged to Victoriana, and her innate loyalties left little room for competition. It might have been difficult to have kept her working there so long had she possessed dramatic sexuality, but hers was an inner warmth that emerged less perceptibly. Only during rare moments did Thom become aware of how deeply fond of her he was.

The Pony Lounge was overflowing with Christmas spirit, and Thom avoided the bar to find an empty booth in a far corner. He ordered a double bourbon and Millie a vodka gimlet.

"You miss Jennie?" Her directness startled him.

"Not really. I guess on top of everything else—well, it was a shock." He didn't really want to talk about Jennie.

She sensed it and was silent. Then she looked at him. "I think I understand you more than you realize," she said.

"That's good to hear. I'm glad somebody does."

"I want you to know that I'm more than your secretary. I'm your friend." Then she changed the subject to talk of sailing on the bay, a weekend trip up the delta in a houseboat, backpacking and skiing in the Sierras, and a horse she had owned in San Mateo. She never mentioned men.

He was startled by the conversation. "I had no idea you were—well—so involved." They ordered a third drink and he began to be conscious of Millie's fragrance. He felt ashamed, and he distracted himself.

"I don't know what the hell's wrong, Millie. I never should have married Roxanne."

"Maybe we do what we have to—" Her directness and calm continued to unnerve him. Millie had become a woman over three drinks in the Pony Lounge. He grew even more uneasy, and he wanted her to leave. She sensed it.

"I'll see you tomorrow," she said.

"You don't have to leave."

"Yes, I do."

He was relieved that she was gone, but he missed her as soon as the waitress came to bring another drink. It was difficult to assess his new pain. If Jennie had been a celibate's sexual binge, Roxanne was the symbol of an Irish peasant's arrival. But, despite all the suffering and success, he was aware that nothing had really changed since his boyhood. He was still enveloped by the same mysterious sadness that had troubled him on the shore of Lake Watseka the night before he left for the seminary. He was still not in charge of his life.

He felt a rising anger toward all women, hating their power over him. The tall, thin waitress reappeared to offer another drink. Long bony legs and thin lips that struggled to hide an extreme overbite. He fantasized seducing her, and the reverie calmed him. He studied her until she blushed. There was a pale strawberry coloring to her skin, a mole on her right cheek, straight mousy hair that bounced when she walked. Such a woman he could own. No sensuous Jennie or antiseptic Roxanne; assuredly not a domineering Margaret. She was one of the unfashionable and unwanted, ignored in high school and considered unfit for college, relegated to simple jobs, moving from city to city when she had been ignored or abused long enough in one place. She talked too much or too little, wore clothes badly, and had assorted rashes and blemishes. Such a woman he could enslave.

He had learned that women were natively more physical. When their passion was unleashed, they were ready to wallow in arms and legs and vibrators, to kiss until their lips were raw. Although one man was unquestionably preferable, ten could not have dissipated their lust. His own passion was less honest. He had fucked percentage points, sucked figures until they swelled and lubricated, jacked off without regard for sex or age, assaulted any aperture where an advantage would fit, ripping and tearing any flesh in the way.

The fantasy of the waitress continued to calm him as he imagined rubbing his hand freely on a skinny thigh, and her mouth down on his cock.

You shouldn't—But he did. As much as he wanted. He was in total control, and her grateful eyes were in love as she warmly asked him about next time.

He withdrew from his musings and looked around. The lounge was crowded and a few couples were dancing. As he ordered another bourbon, he caught the eye of a woman, smiled, turned back to his drink, then impulsively forced himself up from the booth and walked over to the bar.

"I noticed you." He was still excited from his fantasy.

"I noticed you," she said without embarrassment. "You seem—sad."

"Isn't everybody?"

"I'm not. At least, not tonight." She rambled on about her day. She was a psychologist at Stanford. She joined him in the booth and munched hot ribs while he continued to drink.

He followed her back to Telegraph Hill in his own car. She pointed to a place where he could park and pulled into a parking area that served a whole building.

"I love this place." Telegraph Hill was resplendent in the evening light.

They walked up the back stairs over wearspots in the patterned carpet. Her place was sparsely furnished with an abundance of plants and wall hangings.

"Would you like herbal tea? Oops, I only have red wine."

"I'd prefer wine."

"Get comfortable." She poured herself a glass as well. Thom took off his tie and coat and fell against some colorful pillows piled near one wall.

She handed him the wine and put away her things. "You smoke?" She sat down next to him, kicked off her shoes, and lit a newly rolled joint. He didn't want it.

He wanted her, but he didn't make any kind of move. She was too open, almost transparent. She closed her eyes and listened to the music and drew on the joint. He touched her hand and then began to caress it softly.

"You seem very tired," she said. "I'm glad you came home with me. A bar's no place to be when you're tired —or lonely."

He put an arm around her and kissed her awkwardly, then leaned over again. Her lips were warm and soft. She was not unresponsive, and he began fondling her breasts.

She pulled back. "I feel kind of like a stranger who's been invited to watch you," she said gently.

"It would be good."

"I'm sure, but I'd like to be part of it."

He continued to touch her and began removing her blouse.

"Please!" Again she said it gently.

He stopped for a moment and looked at her. Her forehead was wrinkled. Thom was rolling more and more into desire for her. "I—"

"You need someone. Anyone, but not really me. You're here by yourself. I think you have been for a very long time."

"You're still at the clinic!" He sat up abruptly.

"Don't be angry. Let me hold you for a while."

"I'm okay." He spoke firmly. "Don't bother." Thom picked up his tie and slipped on his shoes.

"I wish you wouldn't go—I don't even know your name."

"Neither do I."

He returned to his apartment, still angry, struggling to understand the hostility toward women that had finally surfaced. What did he really know of women? For thirty-five years he had hidden from them. Now he knew that love was a woman's morality, her protection against hell or economic death even as the priesthood and Victoriana had been his. Each gender had its own survival technique, but women's were less symbolic.

The reflection quieted him and he realized he was not ready for women. He needed to be away from them. They were an infection he could not tolerate. Soon he fell asleep with new celibate determination, and in the morning he fixed himself toast and eggs for the first time in weeks. Some buoyancy had returned; he wanted another Victorian in the Mission District with a view of the bay.

Millie was able to locate one on Guerrero Street near Twenty-fourth. He loved this area of San Francisco. Alive, genuine, Bohemian. Bakeries, bookstores, and small restaurants. He could begin again.

His new house had a solid kind of elegance, and he enjoyed doing some minor remodeling himself. Millie brought towels and sheets, blankets, place mats, a hundred household items he had forgotten were necessary. And in the process of frequent shopping, they began to spend more time together. It occurred without the drama of dating that would have intimidated him. Somehow Millie was not a woman. She was his friend.

He was actually shy and unprepared for her in other than secretarial garb. He had never seen her hair worn up before, not tightly drawn or forbiddingly fashionable, but in loosely piled strands of soft mahogany. She was his equal without contrived feminine charm, and soon they were going out every evening, and their conversation moved beyond business and E.J. He talked of his family, of Jennie and Roxanne, and finally, one night after too much wine, of his own priesthood. Her response startled him.

"I knew of your priesthood. A remark E.J. made years ago—and the priest who investigated your marriage to Jennie. It all seemed logical."

"What do you mean?" He felt defensive.

She lowered her voice as the couple at the adjoining table got up to leave.

"A Maguire like you should have at least five kids." She smiled totally.

"Why didn't you say anything?"

"It was your secret." She spoke softly. "You must have been a very good priest."

"I don't want to talk about it."

But he did. For hours that night and over long dinners the whole following week until he had released it all.

Millie said little, absorbing every nuance of an unbelievable life. When there was nothing more, her silence disturbed him, and he spoke without wanting to.

"From priest to corrupt executive, twice divorced. Margaret should be very proud."

They sipped their wine for several minutes. Finally, she spoke almost in a whisper.

"I'm proud of you."

"Proud of what, Millie? A brother I let down, a partner I helped kill. Hell, I couldn't even face Margaret. I'm a goddamned coward and you know it!"

"I wish you could be a coward. You'll kill yourself trying to be strong and brave. It takes a lot of courage to be human."

"I let a lot of people down," he said quietly.

"And they let you down. Maybe everybody lets everybody down—"

"I should never have been a priest."

"I don't believe that, Thom. That's who you were. You still are in some strange way. I've known you for a long time and watched your struggle. You want far more than Victoriana. I wish you were coward enough to be proud of your priesthood. It's part of you, it always will be."

"No way, Millie, no fucking way!" He got up to leave, and she followed silently.

After that they became close friends, at times with a playfulness that Thom hadn't experienced in years. One evening they went to a French restaurant of some reputation, and Thom was not wearing a tie. The maître d', looking like a triumphant Doberman at the Maginot Line, waved them back and said loudly, "This is a formal dining room, sir; don't you have a tie?"

"Not a single one." The awaiting San Francisco crowd caught Thom's mood. "It's delightful to be without a tie."

The Doberman simply stared. "Perhaps we could supply you?"

"I couldn't bear it." The sophisticated crowd loved it. "It has taken me years to be rid of ties."

"Then you cannot dine here, sir."

"Then, sir, I shall not. Obviously we shall starve!"

They walked out like giddy schoolchildren, and that evening they made love for the first time.

She was not the near virgin he had expected, but a mature, relaxed woman. Her flawless complexion had a soft rose tint, her lips became full and sensual while she undressed, and her body surprised him.

"I've loved you very much," she said without drama.

She did not thrash wildly or explode in violent, twitching orgasms, nor did he feel any pressure to prove wide experience or evoke some extraordinary arousal. There was no signal to mount her, no screaming demand to take possession, no wild, exhausting thrusts to get her off. He did not really know whether she had entered him or he had entered her. He only knew the warm serenity of love without anger or expectation or seduction. Then she moaned softly like the wind on Lake Watseka, and he felt his whole body surrender to the warm water and sunshine of a lost childhood.

Only in the morning, as they lay softly and silently holding hands, did he reflect that Millie was more than substitute mother or daytime wife. She was the crossing of a dangerous boundary—a person. She was direct and independent, a modern woman, and he was a very ancient man who somehow feared such honesty and unassuming strength. She was only Millie, and she simply asked that he be Thom Maguire.

Of course there were conflicts for him in the new, frightening relationship. At the end of January, when she purchased a small apartment property on her own, he expressed a growing fear of her independence.

"Does this mean you need another raise?"

"Not at all, it's a property I found, and I'd like you to advise me, but I want to buy it on my own for the security—and the experience."

He agreed to help, then mentioned sarcastically that she could only get the loan at the Bank of America—with Victoriana's help.

He was disappointed that she didn't flare.

"The B of A turned me down. I went to Wells and got a 9½ percent loan." It was not a bargain rate.

She bought her apartment, and, in pouting response, he set up a small company independent of Victoriana in which he alone could write checks. Then he purchased a twenty-unit building from Victoriana at lowest market value by arranging a bogus offer from a friendly broker and outbidding him. Thom refinanced the whole package at 9 percent in a childish response to Millie's integrity.

When he was finally able to laugh and admit his paranoia, she confessed she had enjoyed the competition. Suddenly she grew angry.

"My father was so damn weak. God, I hate weak men! I like your strength," she said quietly. "And the strength you gave me."

He was startled. "Maybe you're the strong one, Millie."

She looked at him. "I could never have gone through what you have. I'd be dead by now."

Her words moved him. It had never occurred to him that his struggle had been anything but recurring failure.

"You don't have to prove anything to me, Thom. I love you." Then she felt his fear and laughed. "That doesn't mean anything except I love you. I'm your friend."

She began to spend more time at his house, and Thom marveled that she did not bind him with guilt. He discovered that love could survive between a man and a woman without unspoken and unresolved strife. He never had to entertain her, since she usually seemed to have something to do. When new household duties became too much, owing to increased responsibilities at Victoriana, she simply hired help; if Thom promised to fix a closet doorknob or a leaky faucet and it went undone, she located a handyman; and when they argued, the fights were brief and to the point, not guilt-producing tragedies. It was unusual for a Maguire to see facets of his own character with a woman who gave him no reason to rage or run away. And Millie never felt the need to play some falsely feminine role or to deny her own abilities lest she threaten him. She loved to make his strong coffee, freshen his drink, or cook his favorite foods, without fearing some loss of sovereignty. Nor did she expect him to sacrifice his personal freedom.

Even sex was without serious problem. Frequently, her appetite was stronger than his, but he was for the first time able to discuss the pressure without escaping to angry impotence. With his help she learned to take responsibility for her own needs without draining him with artificial seductions. Or talking their sexual love to death.

Even when he needed time apart, so did she, content to spend two or three evenings a week at her own apartment, going skiing on a weekend when he preferred to do some reading or resolve some conflicts on a meditative trip to Big Sur. She knew he was struggling with a lack of interest in Victoriana, but she never intruded on his privacy unless he asked.

Yet even their love did not overcome his increasing distress over unmistakable signs of middle-age. Gray hairs appeared on his chest and a few in his groin, his neck bulged when he turned his head, and a casual photo revealed how much his hair had receded on one side. Although he was a reasonably wealthy man, Victoriana no longer pleased him. He needed a vocation that produced something besides money and responsibilities.

He jogged briefly, watched his weight, even began to play tennis. A stiff knee, a hint of arthritis, a lower back pain—for a week he ignored it, but then he felt a new despondency. And for the first time in his life he lied about his age. He wondered if he were too old for Millie, if she would leave him for a younger man. A new depression, deep and painful, attacked his confidence. He wondered why she loved him, wondered if he would ever be more than a frightened adolescent still reacting to Margaret and her Church.

He attended the thirty-fifth wedding anniversary of Millie's parents, and the day proved strangely traumatic.

He sipped mediocre bourbon under tissue paper cupids, and each time he tried to slip away, a relative pinned him—"You must be Millie's boss!"—and he was launched again into family origins and fluctuating real estate. Millie knew it was dreadful for him. Finally, as Thom reached the door, her father appeared.

"It was considerate of you to come."

"I've enjoyed it. Millie means a lot to me."

"I'll agree to that. You know—she was first in her class at State College. She could run her own business."

"She runs mine."

He wouldn't let up. "I'll say. She's never had time to get married!"

"There's still time."

"She's thirty." His chin was trembling. He blurted awkwardly, "She's our only child."

"She's a very beautiful young woman. She'll find the right man."

"There's not much time," he said. His eyes moistened. "Life goes by very fast."

The blunt encounter continued to trouble him, reactivating dormant guilts.

He decided he had to marry her.

She was the best woman he had ever known. She had devoted her life to his business and made no demands. A man could not want a better wife, and even though the thought of marriage frightened him, he attacked his own reluctance mercilessly.

The impulsive decision removed some pressure.

On a Sunday morning at the end of March, he got up early while Millie still slept. He gazed at her as she stirred and then fell back to sleep. His beautiful Millie.

It was she who had flowed with his moods, understood his anger and his buried priesthood. She had managed Victoriana because she loved him. Yet she had never talked of marriage, fearing to destroy some tenuous, fragile freedom. Again he reassured himself that he wanted to marry her. It was logical. To bring the order into his life that she had brought to Victoriana, to rescue him from the confusion of searching for a new vocation. Or to save him from the embarrassment of further sexual encounters.

Thom felt a rising panic, then abruptly banished it and decided that he was no good alone. Marriage would be a final ratification, the roots he needed. Finally, Millie awoke and showered, and matter-of-factly he told her of his decision.

He was stunned when she hesitated.

"Marriage could ruin it. You just don't seem ready—"

He thought it a feminine ploy and hardly took her seriously.

"I've decided," he said quietly. "I want to marry you."

"Thom, you still have something to do," she said softly. "I don't want you to trap yourself again."

Her resistance challenged him. "I love you."

"I love you, Thom. But marriage—now—we'll know when it's right. Thom, I really believe you're still struggling with something, running from something. Before Roxanne, I would have jumped at marriage, but now I know you're not over the past. I'm happy being your lover and your friend, happier than I've ever been. Please don't make me say no!"

Thom was crushed. He couldn't believe she had rejected him. He turned away, fighting boyhood tears he didn't understand.

"You might as well leave," he said quietly.

"Thom, I don't want to. I want to stay with you. I don't need marriage; I just need you."

"Please go!" Even as he said it he knew he wanted her to stay, but he didn't know how to admit it. Or to understand the sadness that engulfed him.

Millie gathered up a few clothes and packed silently. When she opened the door to leave, Thom was convinced that she meant what she said. He fought the tears at his cheeks, then erupted in anger.

"Get the hell out of my life! I don't need another woman to save me!"

Then a weeping Millie was gone, and Margaret's son was finally all alone.

19

A Coward for Them All

Thom Maguire landed at Detroit Metro Airport and drove west through Ann Arbor and then to Sheffield. There was nowhere else to go. He was tired of running. Running from home to the seminary, running from Jim and the priesthood, running from Jennie and E.J., from Victoriana and Roxanne. Now running from Millie. But most of all running always from himself. No wonder he was exhausted. No wonder he had no roots. Now he would come back to his beginnings—to confront it all and start again.

The familiar landscape evoked the memories he had tried to silence for ten years. It was late when he reached the Jack Tarr Hotel in Sheffield, but at half-past nine the next morning, he called the chancery office and requested an appointment with Bishop Elvin Ward.

The voice hesitated. "It's not customarily done. Can't you go to your parish priest?"

"I am a priest—Father Thomas Maguire." He was startled by his own words. "I have a personal matter to discuss with the bishop."

The controlled young baritone was ruffled. "Oh, I see, father—this is Mark McCarthy. I was in grade school when you said your first mass at Saint Raphael's. You probably don't remember me—" He laughed warmly and his inflection was now conversational. "You were one of my heroes in the seminary, with Operation Cosign and all."

He left the phone to establish an appointment, and his voice was formal again when he returned.

"It will have to be a couple of weeks, father—"

"I won't be here that long. Only this week. It's important that I see him." He was surprised at his own calm and wondered about the new tone in the young priest's voice.

"It will have to be Saturday afternoon at two. It's Holy Week, and the bishop is usually off all week."

Thom had forgotten. "Tell him I am most appreciative," said Thom. It was like a dream. The fear and anger flooded back. The grinning boy waiting for Monsignor Doyle's pat on the head. Margaret's dutiful son. The seminary and priesthood years erupted like a procession of accusing faces. Freddie Weber and Joe Beahan, Skorski and Bobbie Foley, Herschel Schaeffer. And especially Elvin Ward. The hated Elvin Ward.

With two days to wait, he headed toward Kirkwood and Margaret's rest home. To find release from a womb that had imprisoned him all his life.

The stone building of the Charity Convalescent Home looked smaller and more barren than he remembered; the naked oaks and maples were only beginning to bud. A circular drive flowed silently around the peaceful building to a parking area near the main entrance. Neat signs instructed delivery trucks and salesmen to enter in the rear. He rang the bell and heard it echo inside. A smiling old portress, her eyes cast down, her hands lost in flowing black sleeves, led him down a glossy corridor and up a flight of terrazzo steps to a small room adjacent to the chapel.

She pointed to an open door. He was suddenly nervous, at a loss for words like a small, shy boy. There was nothing to be afraid of. He would say it all, tell her of the endless struggles and the elusive peace, finally admit his dishonesty and reject her angry God. Hoping she was not too senile to understand how much she had hurt him.

He walked into the darkened room and saw a shadowy form kneeling at prayer before a wooden crucifix. Gradually she emerged in the flickering light of a small candle and he was certain that his eyes deceived him. He looked again and thought he would faint.

The startled nun touched his arm, whispered concern, and then moved back in surprise.

"You didn't know?"

The kneeling Margaret was dressed in the black habit of a Sister of Charity. He lurched back, but Margaret remained motionless and unaware of any presence save her God.

As Thom moved back toward the corridor, his gentle guide smiled seraphically.

"Bishop Ward made it possible—a rare dispensation. She gave all her earthly possessions to God. She is so radiantly happy—such a beautiful soul. We all enjoy her so!" She paused as if to comfort him. "Your mother is a saint."

"What's her religious name?" he asked incredulously.

"Sister Mary John Patrick—after her late husband, I believe."

It was the final blow. His guide hesitated to leave.

"It's all right," Thom said softly. "I'll wait until she finishes her prayers."

She smiled the beatific smile. "You may be waiting for a long time."

She led him to a small cafeteria where he had coffee and institutional stew. He smoked two cigarettes and chatted with a janitor about the Detroit Lions' need of a quarterback. At 1:30 he ascended the terrazzo steps and knocked on the closed door of Margaret's cell. His heart was pounding.

"Just a minute please."

Her voice moved him almost to tears, and a thousand images went through his mind. He saw her smiling in the kitchen, serving homemade bread and raspberry jam after school. Chattering joyfully on the way to early mass and humming in the yard as she hung up two dozen fresh T-shirts.

"Come in if you're good-looking." He had forgotten the expression she had used in his childhood, and his eyes filled with a boy's tears.

It was still Margaret Ann; at eighty, her face was hardly wrinkled under the white cap framed in a thin black veil. The same strong hands rested in the lap of the black habit.

"My God in heaven!"

Her eyes filled with tears as he leaned over and kissed her on the cheek. She trembled. The silence was awkward for both of them. When Thom was finally able to speak, his anger was gone.

"You look beautiful in your habit."

She turned away shyly. It was the same Margaret, the blue eyes as innocent and childlike as ever. Her lips trembled not to sob and her hands twitched just slightly as she struggled not to reach out and hold her favorite boy. Every childhood memory came flooding back; his first communion suit and the tiny biretta she had made, the May altars and the curious boy who loved the baby Jesus in his crib.

"The young ones don't wear the habit anymore—you can't tell them from college girls hardly. Of course some of the older ones try to be fashionable when they don't even know how to dress. Too much makeup and all. I don't know anything. I don't know where it will all lead—" She was rambling nervously and she knew it.

Finally she regained some composure and looked at him.

"You've left the priesthood? You didn't write—"

"I was afraid to write," he said quietly. "I didn't want to hurt you." Thom felt as if he had never talked to her before.

"It hurts more not knowing." Her eyes were sad again and the tears began to well up. "You're not coming back?"

"No, mother, I don't want to be a priest anymore."

"It's not something you just walk away from." She had never been a coward.

"I know you feel bad, mother, and I didn't leave to hurt you. I did it to be honest."

"Are you married?" The words came out hard.

"No, not now." He wanted to leave it there, but something wouldn't let him. "I was—twice—but I'm divorced."

She looked away. "It's hard to find an old-fashioned girl nowadays—certainly not in California. Even your brother Jim didn't—" Her eyes misted again and he told her about Millie.

"Is she Catholic?"

"No."

"Maybe it doesn't make any difference anymore. People are people," she said. "Good and bad."

He couldn't believe his ears. "Are you happy, mother?"

"Most of the time," she said. "I have my faith. But I miss all the confusion and the excitement of you children growing up—and your father." She turned toward the small window. "Sometimes I wish I had it to do all over again. I think I pushed you all too hard." Again tears. "I did the best I knew how."

Thom was crying. "I love you, mother. I really do. You

did so much for us." He bent to kiss her, holding her hands in his, and felt her give in to him. Ever so slightly.

"You were a good boy," she said. "It broke my heart when Mary O'Meara and I took you to that seminary. You were so young and all—"

"I never knew. I thought you wanted it."

"I did," she said. "Or I thought God did. I had no right to question Him. But I cried all the way home—you were such a little boy."

Thom could not stop the tears.

"I love you, mother."

"I love you too, Tommy." She looked up hesitantly. "Will you write to me sometimes–"

"Of course."

He kissed her again on the lips. He had never remembered doing it since he was a small boy.

She looked at him through her tears. "Maybe you could stop and see Jim's kids. Johnny is home from theology."

"I will, mother." It was hard to leave her. "How's Anne?" he asked, knowing it would stop her tears. She did not disappoint him. The old rasp of sarcasm that once had angered him now became as beautiful as she was.

"Oh, that one. She's a charismatic. She'll be starting her own church soon." She giggled at the thought of it. "She's speaking in tongues now, she and the big goof!"

He was relieved beyond all words.

"Do you need anything?"

"Not a thing," she said. "I have my flowers and the chapel."

Then she looked as if she were hiding a secret from John Patrick, and she whispered, "The food's nothing to write home about here. Once in a while Tim brings me a nice pie—lemon or chocolate."

He kissed her again. "I'll write you soon! God, you're beautiful!" She turned away shyly. Then he was gone.

He drove to the bakery, ordered a dozen lemon meringue pies, then drove back and handed the boxes to the delighted portress. "Have a party on Sister Mary John Patrick!"

"God love you! She's such a beautiful soul!"

"I know."

Then he drove off, laughing and crying at the same time.

He called Connie to see if he could spend the night at her house, and when he arrived, Anne and Dick were there as well. A drab Connie reintroduced him to Anne's seven children and her own three. She had not remarried, and she looked thin-lipped and matronly, still overweight. Thom knew she resented his lost priesthood and feared a bad example to her children.

"Tim has two now," she said. "He finally got married."

"How's he doing?"

"He never stops smiling. Still a forest ranger!" She didn't say he never went to church. Tim was from a different family.

A wide-eyed Anne and a grinning Dick Dorgan chattered of their new Pentecostal spirit of love and faith beyond the Church. Their faces radiated hysterical joy. They had left Saint Raphael's after a fight with the pastor, who objected to Dick's private outbursts of glossolaly—the apostolic gift of speaking in tongues—during the sermon. Even Anne had shouted "Praise the all-giving God" during a Gospel reading, and sung "Lift Jesus Ever Higher" in the middle of a benediction service. A senile Monsignor Doyle had almost dropped the monstrance and had ordered an usher to remove her. There was no mention of Thom's former priesthood. It did not seem important as they proselytized for a new religion beyond sects and bishops.

"The Holy Spirit has been so good to us!" Dick was almost bald, and his elongated yellow teeth seemed to jump out in excitement.

"All praise to God!" said Anne.

"All praise!" said Dick and two of their preschool children monochromatically. Everyone else looked embarrassed. Finally they left, still praising, and Thom was relieved when an exhausted Connie made him coffee, mentioned a guest room and clean towels, and left him with Johnny who was only a few months from his subdiaconate. They exchanged pleasantries, and then the handsome young theologian looked directly at his uncle. He had Thom's blue eyes and blond hair and the same Irish mouth and sad look in repose.

Thom knew that Johnny had been commissioned to talk to him.

"Anne's something else!" he said, breaking the silence. "I thought we might be in for an earthquake."

Johnny looked embarrassed. "There's lots of Pentecostals around these days. Grandma says they're holier than the Church. I like that." He hesitated nervously. "Are you ever coming back to the priesthood?"

"No, I'm not. I already told your grandma. I think I've graduated from the Church."

"Then you're not Catholic?" He struggled to be understanding.

"I'm still Catholic." He grinned. "And Irish."

Johnny was suddenly intense. "It's not possible to be Catholic if you don't worship with the family of God! That's what the Church is all about—to join Christ in the praise of the father through the Holy Spirit."

It was a new semantics, bland and intellectual, without any of the fire of the old. "Christ, Johnny, that sounds dull! And it's bullshit to say the Church is a family. Those are just nice words."

"Was the Last Supper bullshit?" Johnny asked. "It was a family meal to worship the Father through the Spirit!"

Thom saw a flash of Jim and was heartened. "Was it now? That's what John's Gospel said seventy-five years later. The Last Supper was twelve apostles who spent every day for three years with a Christ they knew and loved. It was the night before his death and they didn't want him to die. You're damned right it was a family meal! It was their last living contact with a best friend!" He recalled his final cup of coffee with E.J. "You make it sound like a liturgical service that had been rehearsed the day before! It was a meal that tore their guts out!"

Johnny was not accustomed to this kind of discussion. All his seminary friends had accepted the Church as a worshiping community, and the whole focus of his preparation had been the new liturgy.

"It was a hell of a lot more than a meal," Johnny answered angrily. "It was a memorial banquet that would last forever!" Now he looked even more like a Maguire. "If you don't worship with the family, you're not a Catholic!"

"That family of yours sounds more and more like a seminary classroom! You can tell the Catholic people anything you want, Johnny, and most will probably smile back—but they won't really agree. They don't come to church to satisfy your Holy Spirit, they come because they're lonely and afraid and they need someone to listen to them. Because they don't know what the hell else to do."

Johnny's face was flushed, and he seemed on the verge of tears. "But people didn't know how to worship in the old days; they were only worried about heaven and hell. There was no joy in the community, nothing but mortal sins and indulgences and all that crap. It's a new Church now!"

"It sure as hell is, Johnny, and it's dying."

Johnny struggled. "But people have to be led and directed. The Church isn't a democracy that takes votes. People need the Church. They're lost without it!"

"I don't think I am, Johnny. Maybe some people are. But I'm still Catholic, and your new family of worship won't tell me I'm not!" Even as he spoke, he was amazed at his own words. Suddenly he knew he had changed. He was no longer the frightened priest who ran away from Elvin Ward. He had a new faith that continued to surprise him. "Maybe I can trust people more than you do. I think Christ did. He was concerned whether people ate or not, not whether they wiped their ass on the sabbath or pissed toward Jerusalem. The Jews thought they were chosen by God, and you think you've got a corner on the Spirit. My God, buddy, you can't lose."

Johnny grew suddenly silent. "Is that how I sound?"

Thom was moved by his honesty. "To me it is."

"That's not what I believe, it's just that—well—Sunday's the only time we have with the people. We want them to be a family of love."

"But you can't fake it, Johnny, or demand love. You've got to make the people really be the Church!"

There was a long pause before Johnny spoke. "Do you think there's a place for priests, Uncle Thom?" He was almost whispering.

"Yes, I do, I really do. Not for me anymore, but I think the Church would be a real power for good if there were some connection between what priests are saying and what people are feeling."

Johnny was moved. "That's the kind of priest I want to be."

"Then that's the kind of priest you will be, Johnny."

Thom felt at peace. Proud of himself and his priesthood. He had not really left the Church. The Church had left him. He felt a strength he had never known in his life.

It was a more nervous Thomas Maguire, son of Margaret and John Patrick, who walked from his car outside the chancery to the large oak door. Father Mark McCarthy, the bishop's secretary, revealed surprise and then a hesitant kind of admiration.

"The bishop will see you in a few minutes—er—father—"

"It's okay to call me Thom."

He blushed. "Thom—"

A buzzer rang at McCarthy's desk. Then he led Thom to the door and opened it. The red carpet was the same, and the walnut desk had been newly refinished as had the matching credenza. The room seemed smaller than Thom remembered, and Elvin Ward looked much older and more subdued, the thinning hair now gray, his face fuller, his neck showing the first signs of old age. Thom had expected the same feisty, thin face and crimson cassock, but Ward was dressed in the black suit of a parish priest. Only a bishop's cross and a touch of red under his collar revealed his authority. He looked up from his desk, then glanced nervously at his watch.

"I'm very sorry to invade your free afternoon, bishop."

Ward breathed relief, sensing a new gentleness, and mumbled a brief forgiveness. Thom's heart was still pounding like that of a young seminarian, but his words were spoken as a man.

"I came to apologize, bishop, for the way I left the priesthood. The only way I could have left then was to explode. I was really afraid." He felt calm and strong. "I've grown to understand that you did what you had to do."

The tiny bishop seemed helpless and shy, almost impotent behind the large desk, and Thom could not believe all his years of anger and anxiety.

"There are new permissions now—," Ward said nervously. He seemed to have lost all his energy, and Thom felt sad.

"I'm aware of that, bishop," said Thom. "I came to be released from my priesthood according to the Church's requirements." He had not intended to make any such request, but he suddenly understood that his Catholicism stretched far beyond Evlin Ward—to Michelangelo and Vincent de Paul, to Augustine and Thomas More and the late Pope John; beyond Sheffield, to Carthage and Rome, Armagh and Jerusalem.

Bishop Ward explained the papers briefly, and Thom gave his address in San Francisco.

"I've been married twice, bishop, and divorced."

"That can be covered," said Elvin Ward without alarm.

Thom settled back and lit a cigarette. The bishop stirred uneasily.

"How is the Church these days, bishop?"

Ward was unprepared for the question.

"Well—it's difficult—we've lost a lot of priests and nuns—and people."

"What do you think it is?"

"Troubled times," he said too quickly, then paused. "I'm not really sure. What do you think?"

Elvin Ward had never asked him before, but fifteen years since Vatican II had altered something.

"I'm not really sure what the Church is, bishop." He spoke slowly. "I know what it was. It all got lost somehow despite a lot of passion and sincerity. We really cared. I don't know if it's the same now." Thom continued more quietly. "Maybe the Church was only meant to be a place where lonely people could find love and understanding. Or where poor and wounded people could find battlers for justice. We felt different in the old days; there was a war to be won! A naïve war, lost in a lot of legalism that really hurt people, but we believed. We really believed! Damn it, I still do!" He surprised himself.

"What is faith?" asked Ward.

"I know it's not intellectual. Maybe it's just believing that life means something—and doing something that seems worthwhile!" He paused. "I guess that's all I ever wanted to do."

There was nothing more to say. Elvin Ward, who once would have exploded about a misplaced comma, had no more guts for anything.

Thom looked at him one final time. "I think the Church needs a new war, bishop!" He was only sad that Elvin Ward had lost his spark. "A real one!"

As he got up to leave, he made a final request. "I'd like to reimburse you for my education, bishop."

"That's hardly necessary." Ward shuffled uncomfortably.

"It's really important to me. Would you please accept it?"

"Well, yes, of course—," he said quietly.

Thom wrote him a check for ten thousand dollars. Then he smiled expansively. "I feel better. And you'll be proud to know I remember the third-declension nouns that take *um* in the genitive plural."

Elvin Ward smiled like a little boy. John Patrick would not have recognized him.

"That's more comforting to an old man than you know." He paused. "You might like to know we adopted Operation Cosign two years after you left."

Thom smiled. "That's more comforting to a middle-aged former priest than you know."

They exchanged grins.

The bishop politely excused himself to prepare for the Easter vigil service. The secretary had already left, and Thom let himself out. When he reached the rented Ford, he was laughing, not at Bishop Elvin Ward, but at himself.

He had time before his plane to San Francisco, and he decided impulsively to attend the Easter vigil. He was only a block from the cathedral. Once a traditional European imitation with a crucifixion scene behind the altar, it was now a cold, empty white auditorium with a marble banquet table and the Bible displayed prominently on a gold stand. Thom felt despondent until the church began to fill with people. Not nearly as many as before, and only the gray heads and stiff shuffling bodies entered with a remembered reverence. Younger families smiled and waved, chatted and embraced too easily—like a therapy class—ignoring genuflections and private prayers of preparation. It was a friendly church now, a passionless fellowship of too much love—Congregational or Episcopal, it no longer mattered. Ecumenically empty. Only when Bishop Ward appeared and clergy filled the sanctuary did it briefly seem the same. The church darkened, a new Easter fire and the traditional paschal candle were lit. Torches appeared throughout the shadowy congregation, and the joy of Christ's triumph over death exploded in song as the people prepared to renew the promises of a baptism that had made them Catholic. Without the anxieties of adolescence and the confusions of his priesthood, Thom Maguire began to feel some connection with his own history.

He remembered Margaret and John Patrick, Monsignor Doyle and Saint Raphael's, and a little blond boy who wanted to do a noble thing for God and to take away people's pain. Jack waged a wild war; Jim died alone with the understanding that struggled against twenty centuries of history. Anne was addicted to each new promise of salvation; and Tim, free to band his ducks and love his children, had somehow escaped it: he was a different son raised by different parents at the beginning of a new age. Thom's priesthood had marked the end of an old one.

In the light of Thom's new understanding and forgiveness, he saw that the old kind of faith had been more exciting than he had imagined. Enough, in other times, for men who wondered if they could survive oppression and famine and the nightmarish voyage across a fierce ocean to a hostile land. And enough for a child who came to the crib and smelled incense and wondered if Jesus whispered behind the tabernacle, who watched Christ die in thunder and rise in rolling rocks. Almost enough for a lonely Margaret, but finally not enough for a brooding John Patrick and his three oldest sons.

Although the threat of hell seemed as mythical and impossible as modern liturgies seemed unripe and anemic, Thom saw that there was a Catholicism, and even a priesthood, beyond modern anxieties and ancient hostilities.

Certainly beyond narrow popes and rigid, unfeeling laws. Thom was a Catholic and always would be, but there was no Church to go back to. Perhaps it was just as well. He could not turn around; he could only feel some ancient connection and know that it had been an exciting struggle from then until now. He slid from his pew, genuflected devoutly to his childhood and to the Church he had loved, and then left. No one followed or begged him to stay.

He boarded the plane and made his way westward to San Francisco. Still an O'Brien from Clare and a Maguire from Kirkwood. Freer than he had ever been in his life.

Grateful for the Irish wit born of poverty and turf fire camaraderie, for the Irish strength and courage learned in tiny mud huts and in battles with the English and an unrelenting sea, for the quick Irish anger evolved from undying resistance to injustice; and grateful for the eloquence and imagination that looked beyond slavery to preserve the land and the freedom of a people.

Proud to be Catholic as well. Beyond purgatories and popes and immaculate conceptions, beyond bias and bitterness, certainly beyond grinning civilities, hysterical alleluias, worshiping communities, and arrogant authorities. Grateful that he had known Charlie Kenelley and Ziggy Denko, Jim O'Brien and Mike Fogarty; grateful that there was a Catholicism that cared about the sick, that fought for the workingman, that protected children, sanctified marriage, built universities, and protected artists. And battled to make of man more than a greedy, destructive savage on the earth.

The excesses, Irish and Catholic, were no more than most. Their wars and persecutions no more bitter and misguided, their superstitions and arrogance no more destructive. Their love as feeble and well intentioned, their forgiveness as fragile. And Thomas Aloysius Maguire was their child. With their roots as his rite of passage to manhood and their noblest dreams as his destiny, Thom was, most of all, grateful to be alive.

When he arrived at his house, it was nearing midnight, on the anniversary of the eve of Jim's death, and he glanced over the beauty of San Francisco as thousands of flickering lights promised some new and final hope. He poured himself an Easter drink and prayerfully toasted his past.

In the morning he called Millie who excitedly invited him for Easter brunch.

"You almost glow!" she cried when she saw him.

He embraced her warmly. "I just can't tell you how different I feel."

"You don't have to; your face says it all."

After a second cup of coffee, he spoke quietly into her eyes.

"I'm leaving Victoriana for a while."

"Will you stay in San Francisco?"

"I think so. For a while at least. My plans are vague." He grinned at her. "There's something else. I want you to accept a partnership in the business."

Her mouth dropped. "Really, Thom, that's too much—"

"It's already decided," he said. "Just draw up the papers."

Her eyes filled.

"And there's one more thing, a very important thing."

She looked almost frightened. "Yes?"

"I want to be your friend."

"Always!" she said.

Then he kissed her softly and got up to leave.

"What will you do?" she asked.

"I'm not sure. Maybe travel and savor my freedom, then find something to do that excites me and seems worthwhile." He laughed. "I'll probably start an Irish Catholic war! Then get married and have those five kids you mentioned!"

He promised to call the following week to make final arrangements, and then he drove to the beach to celebrate his own Easter. He was glad it was deserted. The sky was clear and blue, the sun warm, as the gulls and the majestic pelicans searched for fish.

There was no one to be angry at anymore—not even himself.

He felt alive, ready to pursue a childhood dream without feeling unique or set apart. He was only a man among men, another struggling human trying to live honestly and decently on the earth. Without the assurances of heaven or the anxieties of hell, without a role to play or an expectation to meet, without a Church or a creed he could easily put into words. Finally one person, connected with childhood, as proud of his past as he was excited about his future. As free as he needed to be without despising his own weakness; only as wise as he was without needing to know every answer.

Grateful to be the coward for them all!

ABOUT THE AUTHOR

JAMES KAVANAUGH, one of seven sons of an Irish-American family, grew up in Kalamazoo, Michigan. He was one of two brothers to be ordained a priest. He left the Catholic priesthood in 1967 after writing an explosive, bestselling book, *A Modern Priest Looks At His Outdated Church.* This was followed in 1968 by *The Birth of God,* a challenging look at contemporary religious myths which Alan Watts called "prophetic and courageous." Kavanaugh began publishing his poetry in 1970, beginning with the now classic *There Are Men Too Gentle To Live Among Wolves,* followed by *Will You Be My Friend* (1971), *Faces In the City* (1973), *The Crooked Angel, America* (1975), *Sunshine Days and Foggy Nights* (1976), *Winter Has Lasted Too Long* (1977), and *Walk Easy on the Earth* (1979).

James Kavanaugh holds a Ph.D. in religious philosophy from Catholic University in Washington, D.C. (1966) and is a licensed clinical psychologist in the state of California (1971). He has co-authored a musical reveiw with Darrel Fetty of Los Angeles, called *Street Music,* has written lyrics for Burt Bacharach's album *Futures,* and has recorded *There Are Men Too Gentle To Live Among Wolves* with an original score by Elmer Bernstein.

An avid outdoorsman and a "decaying athlete," Kavanaugh makes his home in Nevada City, California, a small gold mining town in the Sierras where the ghosts of Mark Twain and Bret Harte still linger. He lectures at colleges throughout the country, reads his poetry, and continues to wander in search of "whatever there is to find." *A Coward For Them All* is his first novel.